# CHILDREN OF SOLO

## Steam and Stars Book One

### Andrew D.H. Moore

WORLD SYSTEM BOOKS

To LeAnna Dawn
for her unwavering love and support

"The seed of Solo quickens with the blood of Azure and Ferinox, as void and ichor combine. When Basalt's maw yawns wide, when twin sanctity becomes betrayal, and creation is obscured, when the blue aster blossoms, the Mother calls her children home."

Celestial Codex IV.3.1-2

# PROLOGUE

P allantier did not often leave the moon Xys. Their moon, given to them by their mother, the goddess Solo. Yet today they had to travel.

The God of Creation stepped through one of Xys's gaiagates into the tall grass on a low hillock several hundred yards north of the Crucible. They dabbed at the pink blood on their arm with a handkerchief. They had to use aetherial magic to create gates, and that required life force. To spare other lives they used their own.

The cut was already healing, but it would leave a scar. Aether wounds always left scars. Because they seldom visited the moon Saba, they took a moment to orient themself. The ringed gas giant Solo, the symbol of their mother's power over the World System, filled the western sky as it began to set. Dawn was an hour distant. They watched as young Adison Faide approached the massive karst outcropping of the Crucible for her test. Though she stood half a kilometer away, the sharp metal tang of the child's first moon blood reached their nostrils. She hesitated on the threshold. The lithe androgyne settled in to wait.

Lord Daniel Faide, patriarch of House Azure, accompanied his daughter to the margins, where the grasses of the valley gave way to the stone pavement of the Crucible. The dawn breeze ruffled the child's blue hair and the dewy grass dampened her shift so it clung to her legs. Her hair mimicked the color of Pallantier's skin, and they smiled as they remembered Selene the Sojourner. It had been their union those distant centuries ago that had given rise to House Azure. Though Pallantier would never bring themself to regret those years of illicit love between a god and a traveler from another World System, the price they had paid, the price they continued to pay, was steep. It was what brought them here today. For the safety of all, Adison Faide had to fail the Crucible.

The child cried and clung to her father's arms, begging him not to force her into the test. Pallantier watched unmoved as acrid smoke curled from fissures and cracks in the rock. A shadow fell across the mouth of the central cave as the Keepers of the Crucible emerged from its depths with measured steps. They were the demigods Droth the Minotaur and Kelek the Serpent, the children of the Kratoi, Aner and Bella. Steam rose from Droth's nostrils and he leaned heavily on his great labrys. Kelek flicked her tongue and venom dripped from curved fangs. Pallantier did not trust demigods. They were not immediate descendants of Solo, but the Crucible must be guarded and these creatures suited the task.

House Azure was one of three bloodlines the Celestial Codex had warned them about, bloodlines capable of wielding the power of Avernus, a power granted them by Pallantier's philandering. The second had been House Killeen, but they were wiped out by the destruction of Acadia. The third was House Ferinox. But there was no such house. In Old Draconic, ferinox meant bringer of night. Pallantier and Djinnar had spent centuries trying to discover to whom this referred and so far they had been unsuccessful. Adison Faide held the most potential of any of the descendants of House Azure in ten generations. This reality forced them to travel to this hillock.

Pallantier looked toward the horizon. Their brother was supposed to accompany them, but they had not heard from their twin in a fortnight. When they last spoke Djinnar was planning to travel to Seniphet's great forest, the Bosque, to interview a mystic of the Greenspear line. Rumor said she practiced miracles of the kind once associated with Avernus. Pallantier dismissed the reports. There was no mention of any Greenspears in the Celestial Codex. Still, the gods could not afford to take risks. The moon seals had to remain closed. If they were compromised, as they had been at the fall of Acadia, the gods themselves would be in danger. It was during that last crisis, seven millennia ago, that the false Sojourner Kade had overthrown Corendar, Solo's mate. Kade had risen to become the God of Chaos, though he was no child of Solo's.

The thrum of blended magic pulled Pallantier's attention back to the scene below. Adison Faide had crossed the Crucible's threshold. She wept as Droth took one arm and Kelek the other. They dragged her toward the smoking chasm. The Keepers did not respond to the dormant power in the child's veins. If they had sensed it, they never would have allowed her to cross the threshold. Drums rumbled from deep within the caverns. Pallantier felt an unusual pang of guilt. No human child should be forced to face the horrors buried deep in the Crucible.

The God of Creation had altered the myths of House Azure's founding, removing themselves from the story. The bloodline did not know of the opportunities their divine heritage could provide. Most children of their line did not possess the affinity, but Adison Faide did. Pallantier would have to destroy the child, though this was antithetical to their nature. That was why Djinnar was supposed to join them here. Together, the twin gods of creation and destruction could undo the knot of celestial power that clung to the child. Pallantier could see the auburn threads of power whirling around her. They needed to act. If she descended into the Crucible, they would have to go in after her, a risk they did not want to take.

Pallantier closed their eyes and extended their power toward young Faide. Her father was no mage so he could not perceive the spiraling quartet of colors that drifted over the rustling grass toward his daughter. The Keepers would know, but seldom did a demigod defy one of their superiors. Eyes closed, Pallantier felt their power encompass the child. She fought him without knowing what she was doing. The god felt the nascent tendrils of celestial power beating against their web. They heard her cry out and gasp for breath, but they could not finish the ritual, could not sever the bond between the girl and her power without—

"Brother," Djinnar's voice interrupted Pallantier. They opened their eyes and their power receded from the child.

"You're late. The child is about to enter the Crucible. Help me complete the ritual."

"I have had an interesting journey," Djinnar said. Pallantier split their focus between Adison and their brother. Their brother wore a wide conical traveling hat, the dried cap of a butterwhip mushroom. It looked ridiculous.

"Tell me about it when we have finished here and returned to Xys. Time grows short."

Their brother would not make eye contact and Pallantier grew suspicious.

The twins were identical in every way, the same height, the same build, the same star-filled eyes, the same silver armor over smooth skin. Their skin shone as if polished and neither pore nor follicle marred its glassy surface. Their only differences were in sex and color. Pallantier's skin was blue, Djinnar's was midnight black.

"There's been a change of plan, sibling," Djinnar said.

A woman stepped from the shadows that whirled and twisted around the death god. She wore a formal dress of black and red and a porcelain mask obscured her face. In one hand she held a length of verdigris copper chain.

"Who is this?" Pallantier demanded, but their eyes fixed on the chain. It connected a pair of golden manacles. They recognized the runes engraved upon it as celestial, granting the power to bind.

"I found House Ferinox. Are you not pleased?"

Pallantier took a step backward. "What treachery is this?"

Djinnar grabbed his sibling's arm. "I have learned some alarming truths and I am afraid it changes everything." The God of Destruction tightened his grip. Pallantier struggled against him, but the woman was quick. She snapped one manacle over their wrist. Djinnar forced Pallantier's hands together and the other cuff snicked shut. The woman chuckled.

Pallantier shivered. "Why are you doing this?"

Djinnar looked toward the Crucible. "Certain sacrifices must be made. For the good of the World System, you understand." With that, the God of Destruction opened a gaiagate and ushered his sibling into the darkness.

An earthquake rocked the moon of Xys, and though it was at first imperceptible to the inhabitants, the moon's orbit around Solo began to decay.

Adison Faide descended into the Crucible.

# CHAPTER ONE

# ADI CRESTONE

## MOON OF TYRE, MILLSDAY, 27TH OF HEBE

Freedom was one stolen yacht away, and pirate Adi Crestone had stolen many yachts. She crouched behind the gantry, sword drawn, and waited for the signal from Captain Torrance. Thunder cracked in the distance, threatening rain. The sheltered waters of the harbor remained calm despite the rising wind. Her men waited, their makeshift armor creaking. If today's heist came off as planned, Adi's debts would be paid, the Blood Queen would unlock the iron collar on Adi's neck, and she and Lucas could be a family again.

The towering stone city of Thail rose along the flanks of Mount Baldwin. Adi could see the spires of the Academy of Engineering where her son was a student. She could not visit him there without endangering him or dredging up her own failings. In the early glow of dawn, the city stirred as it prepared for the day's business. Airships flew between aeroports, steam carriages chuffed down the paved streets, and the stellarium array near the peak of the mountain glowed a cerulean blue as its nets harvested the night's remaining astral dust. The humid air surrounding the docks carried the tang of sea salt and engine lubricant. Thail simmered in the orange light cast by the vast flank of the ringed gas giant, Solo, the Mother Goddess of the World System.

Torrance and his crew were here at the behest of Sasha Riven, the Blood Queen, to steal the Thalian pleasure yacht *Sidereal*, owned by High Chancellor Simon Vanguard. Adi alone knew of the artifact, a rare star key, hidden somewhere on the nobleman's ship. The magical device could open gates, enabling travel between the moons of the World System. Anyone controlling it could wield tremendous political power. When Adi presented the artifact to Riven, the Blood Queen would release her from indenture. Torrance and his crew did not know the Blood Queen's true purpose in stealing this yacht. Adi had kept that secret and never asked why. She did not care. The secrecy and sorcery of it was of no concern to her. The iron collar of indenture hung heavy on her neck, the skin beneath the coarse metal red and inflamed.

Adi motioned her contingent of Torrance's crew toward the entrance of the maintenance dock. Their informant, a stocky, disgruntled Grym stevedore, four feet tall with a chunk missing from one pointed ear, had let them know the *Sidereal* was dry-docked for routine engine maintenance. She adjusted the angle of her tricorn and crept along the pier. Her men followed. They assumed positions on either side of the rear door.

"Hope the capt'n moves quick, we're too exposed here," a scarred man said.

Adi placed two fingers against her lips for silence. *Phoebe's light, the last thing I need is for the stevedores to hear us.*

The man grumbled but said nothing further.

Adi reached for the reassuring coolness of her dragonstone pendant. The unpolished hunk of jade in its silver setting allowed her to pull in astral dust and excrete the refined form, stellarium, to influence the world around her. The feel of the familiar ridges and facets on its rugged surface calmed her nerves. Adi's wildling astral magic was little use in battle, but it provided an excellent accompaniment to all things mechanical.

*If it works,* she thought. Her lack of formal training made her a wildling, and wildling magic was notorious for going awry at inopportune moments.

Two soft bird calls punctuated the morning air.

"Let's go," Adi whispered, easing the door open. She and her men erupted into the maintenance dock while Torrance and his half of the crew charged through the main entrance. Two mechanics, drowsy at the end of their shift, jumped up, startled.

"Wright, Morgan," Adi said, "bind the mechanics and tuck 'em in the office there. Vista, follow me to the engine room. I want eyes on the situation down there. The rest of you prepare the cannon. If we have to shoot our way out of here, I want to be ready."

"Aye, aye."

Vista, the massive gray Ankhim with tattoos that rippled across his bare torso, hastened up the gangplank. Torrance's men grabbed the huge wooden mallets used to strike the pilings from beneath the hull.

"Crestone," Torrance called up at her, "be ready for the drop."

Adi nodded and followed Vista below.

She let out an appreciative whistle when she joined the engineer. The dull thud of hammers on pylons reverberated through the hull.

"That's an Ainsley 457," Adi said. "I thought those engines were still prototypes."

"They are. Pays to be high chancellor to the emperor."

Adi took in the engine array. The *Sidereal* had three modes of power: wind, a stern bank of four steam-powered rotors, and stellarium engines. With a combination of astral dust and a mage to channel it, the Ainsley 457 could fly across the water.

"So, the boiler's under us?" Adi asked, eyeing the intricate plumbing that connected the engine to its steam source.

Vista nodded and tapped one of the gauges. "And it's empty."

"Djinnar's blood," Adi swore.

"Probably didn't want the weight in dry dock."

"There's a water tower on the pier. Have the men get some coal down here. We'll need steam and wind, first, to take advantage of those astral engines." In these tense moments she missed Rehka and the camaraderie of their old crew on the *Snowcrest*.

*A fine pirate crew they were*, Adi remembered. *Until Rehka's betrayal.*

"Aye, aye," Vista said. He headed up to relay her orders. Adi checked her pocket watch. They had a half hour before their rendezvous with the hydrogate to return to Xys.

*Better hurry,* she thought.

Adi made her way topside. Two crewmen were already shoveling coal from the hopper into wheeled carts. Torrance stood on the pier. Another pair of hammer blows thudded against the pylons. The ship groaned and tilted forward into the water. Adi grabbed ahold of the closest rigging.

"Ship's away," Torrance called.

"Ship's away," Adi repeated.

Everyone on deck found something to hold onto as the *Sidereal* pitched forward. Its prow crashed into the water below. The boat rolled and pitched as it slid down the ramp and into the bay. Adi winced at the crunch of wood as the keel scraped along the shallow ramp.

*With my luck we'll be taking on water before we leave the dock.*

Once the ship settled, Adi disembarked.

Torrance greeted her by asking, "Engine report?"

"It's an Ainsely 457."

His eyes widened in appreciation.

"Boiler's dry."

"Blood of the Nine," Torrance swore, the beads in his gray beard jangling.

The captain was in his mid-fifties, a quarter-century older than Adi, and was on retainer with the Blood Queen. Torrance had grumbled and sworn at Adi's intrusion into his crew, but her competence at sea soon allayed his reservations. Adi admired him as well. His crew was efficient and capable, if prone to the normal piratical excesses of gambling, whores, and alcohol.

The sun brightened the eastern sky. A handful of mechanics and stevedores moved about the far end of the pier while they chatted and finished their morning coffee.

*I'd kill for coffee right now,* Adi thought. She had not eaten anything that morning, as was her custom before an engagement that might include a battle. Torrance hoped they could get the *Sidereal* away without drawing attention, but Adi was less optimistic. Stealing from the high chancellor felt scandalous, even for a seasoned pirate. If they managed it, she worried about the powerful man's capacity for retribution.

Adi sauntered across the pier toward the water tower. A pipe extended from the bottom of the tower's curving belly. A long, heavy canvas hose lay coiled in a neat circle on the pier. Adi hefted the hose nozzle and strained against the weight of it as she dragged it to the yacht. Usually, two or three men would manipulate the hose together, but a decade of sailing had strengthened her. Adi wiped sweat from her brow and knocked on the back door of the dry dock.

Wright came out to help Adi with the hose. Once they had wrangled it to the port side coupling, Adi went back across the pier and turned on the water. She was cranking the valve when a voice behind her said, "Hail Solo."

Adi had not heard the approaching footsteps over the squeal of the handwheel. She turned to face the newcomer. A stevedore blew on a mug of coffee and smiled at her.

"You with the *Sidereal* crew?" he asked. "I didn't realize she was finished."

"I am, and she is." Adi said, aware of the scimitar hanging from her belt. Swords were not standard issue for crews of luxury sailing yachts.

"Quartermaster won't be here for another hour yet," the stevedore went on. "You'll have to sign out with him. And pay for the water, of course."

"The *Sidereal* is High Chancellor Vanguard's ship. Wake the quartermaster if you must, but I'm under orders to put the ship under sail with all speed."

The stevedore hesitated but held firm. "We received no such orders."

"Maybe you'd like to take it up with the high chancellor?"

The stevedore blanched and stuttered.

Wright poked his head out of the building. Adi tried to wave him back, but the stevedore turned. Wright wore two bandoliers, one with knives and one with bullets for a breech-loader. His weapons said "pirate" to anyone accustomed to working on the water.

"What's going on here?" the stevedore demanded. "Who is that?"

Adi did not hesitate. In one smooth motion, she drew her sword and hit him hard on the back of the head with the hilt. He dropped like a sack of sand, his coffee splashing across the boards. Adi glanced down the pier. No one had noticed. There was a rumble of thunder in the distance.

*No one is going to ruin this for me,* Adi thought, *I will be free of the Blood Queen.*

Adi sat the man against the supports for the water tower. She turned off the flow and trotted back to the ship to uncouple the hose. *Hope that's enough to reach the gate.*

"We need to go," Adi said to the captain when she returned to the *Sidereal*'s deck. "A worker at the water tower is onto us. I bought us time."

"How did he know?" Torrance asked.

Adi gestured toward the well-armed pirates swarming over the deck. "We don't exactly blend in."

Torrance laughed. "I suppose we don't." He raised his voice, and it took on a tone of command. "All right, gentlemen, step lively. Get us outta here before that storm hits."

Crewmen scrambled up the rigging toward the mainstays to loose the canvas. Adi checked in with the gun crews. The yacht had only one deck gun on a horizontal pivot and two twelve pounders to both port and starboard. If they were chased by anything larger than a schooner, their shot would just bounce off the pursuer's hull. Adi laid a hand on each cannon, her dragonstone aglow. Astral dust flowed through her and was refined by her body and the stone until the stellarium chamber of each cannon was full.

"Guns are primed, Crestone, but we've only got twenty shot."

"That'll have to do," Adi said. "If it comes to it, hold your fire until you're guaranteed a hit. Aim for the rigging."

Morgan saluted. "Aye, aye."

A siren whined near the water tower, and Adi knew they'd been discovered.

"Cast off!" Torrance shouted.

Adi hurried to the engine room. Crewmen were frantically shoveling coal into the firebox. The heat in the small room was rising, but it would be another ten minutes before it would be hot enough to drive the screws.

"We're still building pressure in the boiler," Vista said. Adi checked the gauges, pleased to see the needle creeping upward.

Another crewman appeared in the doorway. "Crestone, capt'n wants you at the helm."

"On my way."

As first mate steering and navigation often fell to her. The ship had sweeps on the gun deck, but they could not row this close to the maintenance dock. Instead, the crew used the long oars as poles to lever the ship out of the berth. Adi found Torrance at the helm.

"You didn't bind and gag the guy?" Torrance asked.

"I was in a hurry."

Torrance let out a string of profanity. Adi didn't fret as the captain swore often and for any reason.

"Take the helm," he ordered. "I'll take charge of the defense."

The yacht floated out of the maintenance dock and into the bay. Men on the pier shouted and waved their arms. Adi ignored them. There was little her crew could do until the steam engines were hot. She tacked to starboard and a whoop of delight rippled through the crew as the wind filled the sails and the *Sidereal* picked up speed.

Torrance ordered the sweeps stowed, while Adi checked the gauges on the pilot's station. They were mirrors of the ones below in the engine room. The boiler was heating faster than she'd expected.

*It must be lined. Score one for the Ainsley.*

"Chief," Wright came and stood beside Adi. "Have a look." He handed her a telescoping spyglass and pointed toward Isla Justicia near the center of the bay. "What is that?"

It took Adi a moment to find the offending shape. It resolved into a ship on the leeward side of the isle. A big ship. An echoing boom rolled out from the city wall behind them.

"That's a signal cannon," Adi said. "They're alerting the authorities on the island."

*The shipyard was too quiet, the theft too easy.*

At that moment, the screws spun to life and the prow of the *Sidereal* pitched upward. They were soon skimming across the bay at incredible speed. Adi held onto her tricorn hat with one hand and the wheel with the other. The wheel was incredibly smooth, the tiller ropes worked with almost no friction.

"What a ship." Adi exclaimed. *Time to engage the astral engines. Surely, they can't catch us then.*

"Wright, what's the time?"

Wright checked his watch. "The gate will be in position in twenty minutes."

"Perfect."

Then Adi witnessed an explosion of white canvas as the ship behind Isla Justicia un-furled its sails and saw the rod and serpent of the royal house stitched into the main topsail. The ship picked up speed and the prow emerged from behind the scrubby landmass. Blue stellarium emissions emanated from the stern of the vessel.

"Nine bloody gods," Adi said. *They must have a dozen mages to power the engines to move a ship that large.*

"That's a *Dreadnought*-class sail-stellarium hybrid," Wright said from beside her. He put the spyglass against his eye. "HMS *Dragonhammer*."

"The Imperial Navy?" *They were expecting us*, Adi realized, then hollered over the thunder's rumble, "Captain Torrance!"

The wind was picking up. Torrance had seen the ship and was shouting orders to the gun crews. The *Dragonhammer* would try to cut them off. Adi needed to shoot the gap between two small barrier isles to the southwest. The *Dragonhammer* was slower than the *Sidereal,* but the dreadnought was already in the middle of the bay. It did not have to outrun them, it only had to intercept them before they reached cover.

Cannons boomed and smoke erupted from the gunports of the distant ship. Half a dozen cannonballs crashed into the water ten yards off the port bow.

"Should we return fire?" Wright asked.

"Dreadnoughts have reinforced hulls," Adi said. "Even our augmented shot will never penetrate it."

The *Sidereal* raced forward under the thrust of the turbines. The storm winds blew toward shore so Adi had to tack the ship to keep the wind from working against them. Captain Torrance raced around the deck, encouraging the men, and helping the riggers adjust their lines. Another fusillade erupted from the *Dragonhammer*. The cannoneers had found their range. One shot tore through the rigging of the *Sidereal*'s foremast. Rope and tackle spun through the air. A man screamed when a wooden pulley crashed into him, throwing him off the deck into the water.

"Man overboard!" Wright shouted.

"Take the helm," Adi shouted. "I can't steer and channel at the same time."

Wright grasped the felloes with stubby fingers. He was a Grym and the top of the helm was even with the top of his head. Adi turned toward the navigation controls where a polished quartzite focus gleamed. Most mages could not channel enough astral dust on their own to move a ship, and Adi was no exception. The ship's focus augmented her abilities, allowed her to wield enough power to add thrust to the already thrumming engines. She shut her eyes against the mayhem and opened herself to the magic. Astral dust flowed through her until it was refined into stellarium and boosted by the ship's focus. The *Sidereal* picked up speed.

Adi felt the wind stiffen. She opened her eyes and saw the gap widening between the *Sidereal* and the *Dragonhammer*. She whooped in delight as their pursuer's cannonballs fell short and splashed harmlessly in the *Sidereal*'s glittering wake. Then Adi felt it, the familiar tickle behind her eyes that signaled her wildling abilities were about to fail and become erratic. She poured every ounce of power she could into the focus, but it was not enough. The *Sidereal* lurched and shed speed. Adi and Wright were tossed into the helm in a tangle of limbs. She felt her gatemarker slide from its belt holster and *thunk* onto the stern. She reached for it, but the rocking of the ship sent the interlunar navigation device sliding toward the railing. She watched in horror as her tool for locating their escape plunged into the bay.

"Phoebe, Goddess of Light, protect us," she whispered, then ducked instinctively as the whine of cannonballs grew louder. The *Dragonhammer* was finding its range once more. The anti-tamper mechanism caused the focus to retract into the bowels of the navigation panel, cutting her off from trying again.

Adi watched another cannonball sweep low across the deck, shattering the port railing and careening off the central mast collar before colliding with Captain Torrance. Despite the ricochet, the cannonball's momentum tore through the unsuspecting captain like a rag doll. Adi saw shock on Lucius Torrance's face as the ball sheared him in two, spraying blood across the fore deck. His torso disappeared over the starboard side.

# Chapter Two

# ADI CRESTONE

## Moon of Tyre, Millsday, 27th of Hebe

"Captain" Adi Crestone had no time to celebrate her battlefield promotion before the full weight of responsibility crashed down hard upon her shoulders.

"Capt'n Crestone!" Vista, the Ankhim engineer, shouted. Vista's lips moved noiselessly as Adi struggled to focus. Her ears rang and the wind snatched the rest of his words. She tasted salt and felt blood on her face. She wiped her eyes and the hulking Ankhim stepped closer.

Another cannonball ripped through the mizzenmast and the *Sidereal*'s lateen sails crumpled. Adi ducked against the shower of wooden wreckage. A splinter struck her right cheek. The pain anchored her attention and she bent toward the engineer, leaning in to catch his words.

"Captain!" the engineer shouted again. "We took a hit at the waterline! There's water in the port engine room."

The ship shuddered and groaned as the remnants of the mizzenmast crashed to the deck and Adi fell into the man. The *Sidereal* floundered, losing speed.

"Take two men and try to patch the leak." She grabbed the two nearest sailors and thrust them at him. "You two! Grab a pitch barrel and go with him." They leapt to obey, but a swell hit the ship side-on and it rolled hard. The engineer and sailors collided, broke apart, and bolted for the hatch.

She hoped there was a gatemarker in the *Sidereal*'s navigation controls. By some miracle, the pilot's station was intact. She surveyed the navigation panel beside the helm, but there was no gatemarker.

*When did everything go so wrong?* Adi wondered. *The Augur's weather forecast was wrong, that stevedore shouldn't have been there, the Imperial battleship coming out of nowhere, and now Torrance is dead.*

Adi needed to find the artifact, a star key. With it she could navigate the hydrogate, even create one if she could hold onto her magic long enough. If she couldn't locate the artifact she would have to locate the original gate by memory. It was supposed to be beyond the last set of barrier islands. Adi gripped the wheel and leaned into it, fighting to counteract the portside tilt. The *Sidereal* responded to her helm, but it wallowed.

*There's more water down there than I thought.*

A thunderclap echoed over the pitching deck. The storm was upon them. The wind that filled the remaining sails lashed them with hot summer rain. Blood, rain, and lightning obscured her vision. Another volley of cannonballs swept the deck. Adi flinched but maintained her grip.

*At least they can't bring all sixty guns to bear at once. Thank the Nine Gods for that.*

The looming bow of the HMS *Dragonhammer* towered above them as swivel guns locked onto the *Sidereal*. She prayed the *Dragonhammer*'s crew would only incapacitate the *Sidereal*, not sink High Chancellor Vanguard's pleasure yacht and risk his ire, but she didn't want to test this theory.

She longed to return fire. What the *Sidereal* lacked in teeth she made up for in speed. She slid the acceleration lever all the way forward. They would be limited without the stellarium engines, but the ship was light and fast even without a mage's assistance. There was a lag as the controls relayed their message to the engine room. Adi felt the *Sidereal* accelerate, though the response was unbalanced. She helped Wright steer toward the gap between the barrier isles. A thunderous boom echoed across the water and the *Sidereal* shuddered from prow to stern before settling deeper in the water. Adi banged her chest on the wheel and bit back a cry.

*That engine's gone.* She scrambled to stay on her feet.

Vista struggled to the helm. His left arm hung limp, and Adi saw bone protruding through the skin.

"Captain," he shouted over the driving rain, "the port engine flooded."

Adi fought the urge to scream and slammed her fist on the pilot's station. It was all sails, then, and they'd already lost one mast. "Djinnar's fiery blood. Bring the crew topside. Use as few of the remaining men as possible to secure the rigging. Have the rest load the cannons on the starboard side. The gate should be just past those isles. When we come around, I want a starboard volley to rake their rigging; give them something to think about."

Vista stared at her for a long moment until Adi wanted to slap the man.

"What is it?" she yelled over the din.

"The spin loader is stuck open."

"We have no stellarium; why is that a problem?"

Vista blinked at her again.

"By the Nine, man, I don't have time for this. *What?*"

"When you max out the speed level the Ainsley automatically opens the spin loaders to feed fuel straight into the core. With no spinners, it's malfunctioned, and the cores are still open."

A Stellarium Potential Injection Nodule, or spinner, held astral dust refined into stellarium for augmented engines. Like the focus, the existence of pre-refined astral dust made the mage's job easier. Even a few talented engineers without the ability to channel could manage spinners. The realization must have shown on her face because Vista opened his mouth to say more, then clamped it shut again. If seawater got into the core and mixed with the residual stellarium embedded in the transfer lines, the ship would explode. Even if water didn't get in, without an astral mage to close the core valves, the refined residual stellarium would leak out and detonate. Astral dust was harmless. Once refined into stellarium it was as volatile as the dynamite used by Behlian coal miners.

"Is there any other way to close the core?" she asked Vista. He shrugged and this made her angrier. "Well then get the damned crew up here."

Vista, accustomed to taking orders, jumped to attention before dashing down into the hold. At least Torrance's crew took orders well. Though, in her experience, even the surliest of crew members tended to fall in line when death was bearing down on them.

The *Sidereal* entered the gap between the barrier islands. The wind-driven waves buffeting the ship eased in the lee of the island and Adi muttered thanks to Phoebe, for the reprieve. The remaining crew poured up onto the deck. She watched, impressed at the speed and efficiency with which they moved on an unfamiliar ship. As soon as the cannon were loaded, she cranked hard on both rudders.

The flooded port side continued to lag, so the starboard turn was not as crisp as she'd hoped, still the *Sidereal* was much lither and lighter than its pursuer. Once the turn was executed, she gave the order to fire. The boom of the first cannon filled the air.

The stellarium-enhanced projectile shot across the water and tore through the starboard rigging of the *Dragonhammer*'s foresail. Adi's crew cheered.

The second cannon erupted in an explosion of gunpowder and hot metal, taking three crew members and part of the ship's railing with it. Either they had misloaded the weapon or whoever had been tasked with maintaining those cannons had been lax. There was not much call for cannons on a pleasure yacht.

The *Sidereal* passed behind the barrier islands. Another ragged cheer went up among the crew at the reprieve, but it trailed off when they saw what was ahead of them. The seaward side revealed the heaving, gray Heartspring Ocean.

There was no gate. Rain-lashed, white-capped waves struck them broadside now that they had left the protection of the inner bay. She, and the entire crew, realized they were doomed. Any second now their pursuers would pass through the gap and make quick work of them.

Wright still stood at her side at the pilot's station.

"What do we do, sir?" he shouted.

"Crewman Wright, who's my first officer?"

He pointed toward the bloody remains beside the broken cannon.

"Congratulations, you're now first mate, Wright."

"Thank you, sir," he said as he saluted. Adi tried hard not to roll her eyes. His formality ate valuable time.

"Take the helm. Where's Vista?"

"He's in the port engine room trying to close the spin core."

Adi hurried across the deck with practiced ease, hurdling over ropes and detritus, sure-footed and swift. Racing astral yachts on the Azure Sea during her childhood had taught her how to navigate a chaotic deck at speed. She could see faint, blue light emanating from the stairwell. Residual stellarium was leaking out of the open cores.

Belowdecks, the cacophony faded, the thunder and crashing waves were muffled by the thick timbers. In the engine room, water sloshed around Vista's thighs as he tried to find the leverage to adjust the heavy bolts that connected the feeder flaps to the fuel chute. Adi was familiar with most engines and her magical affinity helped them make sense to her. She'd often had to adjust on the fly. As a child, she had tinkered with the engines in the boathouse to avoid dealing with her father whenever he was home.

She grabbed a wrench and threw all her body weight onto the shaft. Between the two of them they managed about a quarter turn.

"The bolts are rusted," Vista said. "Whoever was in charge of maintenance on this luxury bucket ought to be fired."

"We did steal this bucket out of the repair yard."

"I suppose we did."

"Go topside, there's nothing more we can do here."

"I take it the gate has moved." It was not a question. "I heard the gates to Xys were weakening."

She hesitated, "I lost the gatemarker when my channeling failed. Go topside and help the gun crews. When that dreadnought comes around the island make sure we give 'em all the hell we can."

"What are you going to do?"

"I'm going to the captain's quarters. Hopefully, there's a gatemarker, or at least some charts, among his affects."

*And I must find that star key.*

Vista nodded and strode toward the ladder. Adi stepped back into the hallway and struggled to breathe. All the stellarium in the air made it difficult. Standing beside the open core made her feel like she was treading water in a storm, something they would all soon be doing if she couldn't find the star key. Adi had expected to have plenty of time to search the ship once they were away from Tyre. Now she had to look for it during the heat of battle if they wanted to have any hope of escaping.

The captain's quarters featured all the trappings of a high chancellor. Lush purple carpets covered the floor. The luxury looked strange given the circumstances. All the Empire's denizens, criminal and otherwise, knew the high chancellor's ruthless and vengeful reputation. If there had been any way out from under the Blood Queen's thumb without stealing from the high chancellor Adi would have taken it.

She flexed her knees as Wright turned the ship to bring the cannons broadside. The *Dragonhammer* must have emerged from the barrier islands. *Wright's a good helmsman.*

A moment later cannons boomed, followed by a ragged cheer.

Adi focused on her search. She pulled out every drawer of the heavy desk, dumping the contents onto the pitching floor. No star key. Next she checked the armoire. It contained no clothing, but there was a locked drawer at the bottom. She hammered against the flimsy catch with the hilt of her sword until it snapped. Inside were two pairs of boots and a box with four gold spyres, twenty copparchs, and a small fortune in obsidian thieves' glass.

*What is Chancellor Vanguard doing with so much black-market currency?*

She grabbed the spyres and a handful of glass and stuffed them into a belt pouch. If they didn't find a gate soon, it wouldn't matter how many fortunes were hidden on the ship. Two spinners rolled back and forth in the bottom of the drawer, one half-empty. They weren't enough to make a difference in the engine room, but Adi tucked them into her belt anyway.

She searched the rest of the room, slicing chair cushions, overturning tables, and rifling through cabinets. Periodically, the cannons roared above her. Glancing out the window, she could tell they were headed deeper into the ocean, but it wouldn't be long before the *Dragonhammer* overtook the *Sidereal*.

Adi looked around the room, defeated. No star key. For the first time, she began to wonder whether she should take her chances in the ocean or allow their pursuers to take her captive. If the dreadnought did not blow them to smithereens and she somehow survived the boarding party, she doubted she would end up in a prison cell. The Thalian penal code prescribed hanging for ship thieves and pirates. Plus, the authorities would know she worked for the Blood Queen once they spotted the iron collar that hung heavy around her neck. It would be an interlunar incident.

She could not let herself get captured. But she was not too keen on fighting to the death, either. She could imagine Ajax's smug look if she did not return. Even though he was a long astral tunnel away, she balled her fists with the desire to punch the expression off his face.

*Could the gate's absence be a consequence of Xys's decaying orbit? Vista seems to think so.*

A cannonball punched through the window of the cabin. The shell hit the heavy armoire, which shattered into several pieces. Red goo splashed across the floor. Adi watched in horror as the fuse burned down to nothing, waiting for the inevitable explosion that would end everything.

It didn't come. The fuse snuffed out without igniting the flammable goo.

*They're using exploding shells. They want to kill us and sink this ship.* There would be no cell, no Thalian penal colony. They would be burned alive or drown.

A large oil portrait of High Chancellor Vanguard banged against the wall in the rolling of the ship. She watched it swing open and slam shut,

*It's on hinges. There's a compartment behind the painting.*

Adi bounded across the room and broke the flimsy lock with the butt of her sword. Inside lay a golden filigree box made of rosewood burl and inlaid with precious stones and mother-of-pearl. She opened the box and gasped. It was the most ornate star key Adi had ever seen. They were saved! She laughed despite everything, clutching the box to her chest as she ran for the helm.

The deck was in chaos. One of the exploding shells had struck the forward mast near the crow's nest and was raining fire down upon the crew. She smelled burning flesh and her stomach heaved. She could not tell how many men were left, but the remaining starboard cannon was still firing. She saw Vista ramming the rod home with his good arm. Wright was still at the pilot's station though blood poured freely from a cut above his left eye.

Behind them, the *Dragonhammer* closed. Their main deck was much higher than the *Sidereal* and she saw soldiers gathering on the foredeck. A boarding party. If the officers on that ship knew what Adi had stolen, they would be desperate to retrieve it and kill everyone on board.

*How did the Blood Queen know the Thalians had such a device?*

The Society of Astrologia certainly could not have known, or they would be in Thail negotiating for its return.

Thunder boomed and a broadside wave nearly swept Adi off her feet as she danced across the deck toward the pilot's station. She set the rosewood box on the panel and opened it. Wright's eyes widened.

"That's a star key!" he exclaimed.

Adi grinned. Then she glanced behind her and her grin vanished. She shouted to the remaining crew, "Prepare to be boarded!"

Wright opened the panel below the port for the gatemarker and connected leads to the star key. A small glass bell held a dragonstone which, when powered by stellarium, would rotate and turn the complex mechanism. It looked like the innards of an oversized pocket watch. It would take more astral dust than Adi could channel by herself to use the star key to create a gate. Gates were governed by a second type of magic, aetherial magic, illegal on all seven moons of the Empire due to its harmful consequences. The star key acted as a kind of translator between aether and astral dust, allowing someone like Adi to manifest limited aetherial powers. Still, it would require the concentrated stellarium of a spinner to give her enough power to utilize the delicate instrument. Their planned hydrogate was missing, but with a little luck Adi might summon another.

Despite the storm, Adi felt the shadow of the *Dragonhammer* fall over them. Moments later grappling hooks thudded into the railing.

"To arms!" she shouted at the crew. "Enemy on the stern!"

"We need a spinner," Wright shouted at her.

Adi produced one of the two she had salvaged from the captain's quarters.

"Where did you find that?" he asked.

"Below, in the chancellor's quarters."

"Can you use it?"

Adi watched behind Wright as soldiers from the *Dragonhammer* slid down the grapple lines. The truth was she didn't know. If her wildling astral magic wasn't strong enough, even with the aid of the spinner, she could open a gate to the gods knew where or strand her dwindling crew forever in the void.

"We have to repel the boarders," Adi said, more to buy herself time to think. "I don't want any Imperial soldiers to accompany us back to Xys."

Wright grimaced and nodded.

Soldiers clambered over the stern railing. Vista charged them, roaring and swinging his massive mace with his one good arm. The heavy iron head sank deep into a man's torso, driving him over the edge and into the water. They had to cut the grappling lines fast. Wright released the wheel and turned toward the fray, his knives glinting in a strobe of lightning. A wave hit the ship broadside and it rocked to starboard. Adi's attention was on the fight, so she failed to brace herself. The violent sway of the *Sidereal* knocked her off her feet. She rolled across the spar deck until her head cracked against the remnants of the mizzenmast. The world spun and she struggled to maintain consciousness.

She recovered as the fight raged on. Wright managed to cut the grappling lines, but a dozen men had crossed to the *Sidereal* and stood between her and her dwindling crew.

Adi buried her sword in a soldier's neck while his attention was on Wright. The man crumpled to the deck. A second man brought the shaft of his spear up to defend against her blow. Adi's dragonstone pulsed, the astral gem embedded in the hilt of her sword flared to life, adding force to her blade. The sword broke through the wooden shaft and she buried it in the man's stomach. The soldier died clutching his entrails.

She turned toward a third soldier. He punched her hard across the jaw. Her head whipped sideways and she lost her tenuous grip on her sword. She recovered and swung her fist into the man's face. It was a glancing blow, but enough to unbalance him. She tackled him around the waist and they both went down. He cried out as a chunk of wood from the mizzenmast pierced his shoulder. Adi landed on top of him. He brought his hands up to protect himself. Adi drew the dagger from her boot and slit his throat.

She stood and braced against the rocking of the ship as the rain lashed at her. Three men remained between her and the pilot's station, but they were ready now; focused on her.

*So much for dispatching the boarders first. I must get back to the star key.*

She kept one eye on the navigator's station where Wright was defending the helm and the star key. Wright's knives whirled as he dispatched one of the soldiers with a slash across the thigh. A second soldier kicked him from behind and Wright sprawled across the panel. His weight broke the spinner and its cerulean contents leaked onto the slippery deck.

Adi was out of time. In seconds, the stellarium leaking from the spinner would ignite in a fiery ball of death.

Two soldiers rushed her. She fell onto her back under the onslaught. She kneed one attacker in the groin. His breath whooshed out of him, and he rolled off her. She stabbed the second man with her dagger. The blade entered under his chin and she felt it punch through his jaw. He spasmed and then went limp. Adi retrieved her scimitar, scrambled to her feet, and drove it into the first soldier's torso. He stilled.

Adi detected the sulfurous tang of incendiary stellarium despite the lashing storm. She did not hesitate. Flames licked up the side of the navigator's station, teasing the edges of Wright's trousers, and threatened to damage the star key. Adi rushed up the steps to the stern deck two at a time. She withdrew the one remaining spinner from her belt. It was partially depleted, but it would have to be enough.

The leaking stellarium exploded. She threw her body over the navigator's station to protect the star key. Astral fire scorched her back. Adi gritted her teeth against the searing pain as she drew in astral dust to push the flames away and jammed the spinner into the input beside the star key. She dropped her sword, and with the spinner in one hand and the star key in the other Adi opened herself to a raging torrent of magic. Colors popped along the edges of her vision and a great howling wind threatened to tear her away from the navigator's station.

She held on as her feet lifted from the deck. Never had she felt such power, nor channeled so much stellarium. This was no ordinary star key. The colors exploded and resolved into unfamiliar landscapes, as if she were falling through levels of a tall tower, each one populated by a different pastoral landscape. The ominous thrum of heavy wings filled her ears, and she instinctively flinched away.

*What was happening?*

She had never experienced a trip into the void like this. The gas giant Solo, the ringed goddess, appeared then blinked out of existence. It reappeared as the center of a great eye into which Adi fell, screaming.

When she awoke, she was lying on her back beside the navigator's station. The sounds of the battle and storm were gone, the howling winds were absent. Millions of stars twinkled overhead, the laneway shimmered, and the oppressive quiet of the void embraced them. Wright was leaning over her, concern on his pinched, Grym face.

His voice resolved into comprehensible words. "Captain are you all right?"

Adi nodded, propped herself up on one elbow, then turned away and vomited on the deck. She had heard of casting sickness, when an astral mage drew in more power than their bodies were capable of processing but had never experienced it before. Too many occurrences could cause astralium necrosis. Adi shuddered at the thought. With Wright's aid, she rose unsteadily to her feet.

*Dragonhammer* was gone. Only one Thalian soldier remained, an officer. Seeing he was outnumbered and inside a void laneway, he dropped his sword, fell to his knees, and put his hands behind his head in the universal gesture of surrender.

The star key had worked, opening an interlunar gate right beneath them. Adi's body tingled with residual magic. Feeling slowly returned to her extremities as if she had been plunged into an icy bay only to be hauled out and warmed by a roaring bonfire. They were no longer at the mouth of the Heartspring Ocean on the border of the Thalian Empire on Tyre. They were in the void, hurtling toward the moon Xys and the Blood Queen.

# CHAPTER THREE

# ADI CRESTONE

## MOON OF XYS, MILLSDAY, 27TH OF HEBE

Adi and her small crew secured the Thalian officer with rope from the *Sidereal*'s destroyed rigging. Of the twelve members of Torrance's crew only Adi and three others remained: Chief Engineer Vista Sommers, First Officer Peter Wright, and a crewman named Joshua Mung. They were a sorry lot. Wright bled from a head wound, Vista's left arm hung uselessly, and Joshua walked with a heavy limp. The side of her face where she'd been punched was swelling and her hands and wrists were red and puffy from fire gel burns. She could feel numerous splinters in her shoulders and neck where the detritus from the explosion had embedded itself. Fires still smoldered on the *Sidereal* and the port engine core continued leaking stellarium.

The trip from Tyre to Xys was a short one, so they exited the channel of void and stars in minutes. Adi expected a calm transition through corresponding hydrogates. During a normal trip, one moment they would be sailing across the Heartspring Ocean, then briefly on a mirrored sea of stars, then they would arrive on the Boiled Sea of Xys. This time, though, the ship sailed out of the stars into the scorched air about two fathoms above a cresting dune thirty yards from the sea.

Adi experienced a brief sensation of floating before the ship dropped onto the sand. Everyone on deck fell hard, swearing at this further insult to their injuries. Timbers creaked and groaned as the beached ship settled, listing to starboard, but the hull did not crack. Wright threw a line down and they disembarked.

The calm waters of the Boiled Sea appeared frozen in place, so still was the wind. In every other direction stretched the desert. Far to the northwest, Adi could make out the smokestacks and haze of a large city, Solvigant. The Wandering City was currently in

Veria. A hundred yards away, a pair of fishermen were preparing a boat. They stared at the small coterie of pirates, their mouths agape. Adi secured the star key in its rosewood box, tucked it under one arm, then waved to the pair.

The two men waved back. As Adi and her crew drew closer, she saw they were not two men but rather a man and a young boy. *Perhaps father and son.*

"Hail Solo, friends," Adi called when they were still ten yards off.

"Hail Solo," they responded. The boy's voice carried more enthusiasm than his father's did.

"Not much to catch any more from what I hear," Adi said.

The people of Xys referred to this body of water by its historical name: the Windlass Sea. Xys was dying and its oceans were fading with it. The Windlass Sea had been shrinking and its remaining waters were a cesspool of sulfurous waste. Travelers from elsewhere now called it the Boiled Sea. Any fish remaining were usually inedible.

"We caught three stripers only yesterday," the man said, optimistic, as fishermen tended to be.

"Could only eat one," the boy complained, kicking the sand.

Adi saw their hunger and despair. She tried another tack. "I'm Captain Adi Crestone. My apologies for the dramatic intrusion. Could you tell me where we are?"

The older man started to speak but the boy cut in, "My friends call me Ion. Are you a real pirate?"

Adi considered the bedraggled men arrayed behind her. They all looked as if they could collapse at any moment. Except of course their prisoner, who appeared unharmed, with only a red splotch on one cheek where Adi had slapped him while trying to get his name. The officer hadn't spoken since his surrender.

"I am." Adi pointed. "That's my ship, the *Sidereal*."

As if on cue, the open core of the port engine exploded. Everyone on the beach ducked. The pirates turned to watch the multicolored fireball expand and dissipate in the desert air. Bright sparks shot across the sand. The ship shuddered and settled farther onto its shattered flank.

Ion gawped.

"Wouldn't have thought such a short drop would do that," the older man said.

"We had a bit of engine trouble before the passage," Adi said. Anxious to redirect the conversation, she asked the boy, "How old are you?" He was malnourished, but he looked close to fifteen, the same age as her son, Lucas.

"Twelve," Ion said, still watching the ship.

"And is this your father?"

Ion shook his head. "My grandfather."

"Castes is just over that dune," the old man said, pointing north. He laid a hand on the boy's shoulder and pulled him closer. "There's an overnight terrane that will take you to Solvigant."

Adi had never been to Castes. Most of her time in Solvigant had been when it was in Zaff. Another gout of flame burst from the *Sidereal*, licking out of the hatches onto the deck.

"Bad day to be a pirate," the man said. "Where did you come from?"

Adi ignored the question. Instead, she inspected the boy. He drew back from her bloodied face, but his eyes didn't leave hers. To Adi's surprise, the boy's blue irises were shot through with faint red lines.

*The boy is a mage,* Adi realized, *or could be. When had the Society of Astrologia last sent a Justice of the Stars to a backwater like Castes to enlist students?*

"I have a son about your age," she said.

Ion looked around.

"He's on Tyre," she said.

"What's his name?"

"Lucas. I haven't seen him for some time." *Now why did I say that?* Adi wondered.

"Why not?"

Adi looked away, tears stinging her eyes. "Thank you for the directions." She straightened, ruffled the boy's hair, and imagined what Lucas might look like now. She pulled a spyre from her belt pouch. The thieves' glass would not do the fishermen any good. Xys was firmly in the Empire and the grandfather did not seem the type to frequent Solvigant's black markets.

The grandfather's eyes widened at the sight of the coin. He held it gingerly as if it would disappear.

"Buy a few meals that aren't from this tepid sea." Adi said.

"Thank you, ma'am—Captain," he said.

Adi adjusted her hold on the rosewood box, took one last look at the boy, and tossed him a heavy piece of thieves' glass despite herself.

"Pirate loot."

The four sailors of the late ship *Sidereal* and their prisoner headed over the dunes to Castes. It took them over an hour to trek the two miles to town. Between their injuries and the shifting sands, every step was frustrating. Sweat ran in rivulets from every crease and fold of their bodies and the midday heat rippled the air, making it difficult to see.

Castes consisted of a main street with four dusty buildings and a terrane depot. They passed a tavern, a general store, a post office, and a guardhouse, half-collapsed from a recent earthquake. At the end of the main street was a small temple to the Nine Gods. It was the most ornate building in town, and seemed out of place amid the brown, sandy landscape.

Adi and her party headed straight for the terrane platform. She wanted nothing to do with the town guards, or the townspeople for that matter. What would they say to four bloody pirates and a bound man? Thankfully, few folks were about in the heat of the day. The terrane was a steam-powered cousin of the trains on the moons Maxon, Tyre, or Behl, but outfitted for the desert climate of Xys. Instead of metal wheels and iron tracks, each terrane car sported a dozen wide wooden wheels that floated on the sand. This allowed it to move at speed across the desert while adjusting its track to the location of the peripatetic city of Solvigant.

Two stevedores were busy loading heavy wooden crates into one of the boxcars while a pair of businessmen in suits, gold pocket-watch chains draped across their chests, stood in the shadow of the station smoking pipes. Both glistened with sweat, and one fanned himself with a bowler. Adi offered the stevedores a fair handful of thieves' glass so her party could board the boxcar away from prying eyes. Once they were settled, she used the sleeves of her shirt to fashion a bandage for Wright. She put her own captain's hat on his head and sent him into town to fetch water from the well. He returned carrying a large wooden bucket. Water sloshed over the sides as he climbed back into the boxcar. Adi resisted the urge to upend the bucket over her head as she took a long drink. It was warm and full of grit, but delicious. Once everyone had drunk their fill, Adi used the remainder to wash the rest of the fire gel from her hands.

She felt eyes on her and saw the Thalian officer staring at her head. Adi realized the blue roots of her hair showed under the bleached white. She plucked her hat from Wright's head and shoved it onto hers. She did not need word getting back to House Azure that one of their scions was running around Xys wearing the Blood Queen's collar. She had hidden from her father for fifteen years. She was not about to ruin it now with a stupid mistake.

Adi waited until the terrane left the station before tending to Vista's wound. She directed Wright to hold the engineer from behind. The shriek of the whistle and the sandy susurrations of the wheels as they gathered speed covered the sounds of his screams when she pulled the bone back into place. When Adi looked up from her work, all three crewmen were looking at her, their eyes wide. She fought the urge to look over her shoulder.

"What?" she said, breaking the silence.

"Capt'n Torrance never would've known to do that, or might not of wanted to," Josh said.

"Captain Torrance is dead," Adi said. She had only been sailing with them for the two weeks it took to travel from the small port of Salve near where Solvigant was currently located, across part of the Boiled Sea, and through the gate to Tyre to steal the *Sidereal*.

"Thanks," Vista said, his face pale with pain, as Adi fashioned a sling from the remains of her jacket.

"You did well back there," she said. "What happened wasn't your fault." Adi felt exposed without jacket and shirt sleeves and pulled her arms around her torso. Her left arm was densely tattooed with images of a boat upon a roiling sea, surrounded by the arcane symbols of the astral magi, an homage to a past life.

"We'll get you to a proper doctor in Solvigant. Till then keep it still."

"Where'd you learn how to do that?" Josh asked.

"Yes, where *did* you become such a healer?" asked their captive. There was a derisive sneer plastered on his face.

*He recognizes my tattoos.* There was too much glee in his eyes for a man in his position. Adi resisted the urge to slap him again.

"Here and there." She shrugged. She owed him no explanation. Pirates were a sordid lot with checkered histories most would rather not reveal. Their captive did not press the point.

Adi leaned against the wall of the rocking boxcar. Through the gaps in the planks, she could see it was twilight. She let the rhythm of the train work into her body as she took inventory: two gold spyres, twenty copparchs, and about a half-weight of thieves' glass, a star key, and an officer to ransom.

*Just a few hours away from freedom.* She had been indentured to the Blood Queen for three years. *Once I hand the Blood Queen the star key my debts are paid.* She fell into an unburdened sleep.

# CHAPTER FOUR

# ADI CRESTONE

## MOON OF XYS, TYRSDAY, 28TH OF HEBE

The high-pitched shriek of brakes woke Adi. The terrane was approaching Solvigant's terminal. She grabbed one of her daggers and eyed their captive. He sat poised, body swaying with the terrane. She envied him. He had come through the battle unscathed, his brown hair still combed to one side. He looked rested, his mussed clothing the only indication he had undertaken any recent physical exertion. Worse, he still did not look afraid. He watched her with the same bemused expression he had worn since his capture.

*It's the confidence of nobility,* she thought. Only some wealthy noble's son had the audacity to jump moons with pirates confident in the knowledge that when someone more important than Adi realized who he was they would send him home to avoid an awkward political incident. *That means good ransom money.* She grinned at him, imagining the coin he might be worth. He must have seen something of her intention in her eyes because for the first time since his capture his confidence flickered briefly. *The star key will settle my debts, the ransom will set me up off moon.*

The train arrived in Solvigant an hour before dawn. Solo, the great gas giant with her rocky rings, dominated the sky. The planet, the physical incarnation of the goddess Solo, was a constant ominous reminder of how little time the moon Xys had left as it spiraled slowly planetward.

She waited until the carriage passengers disembarked before leading her crew from the boxcar toward a rear exit in the terrane yard. Adi was in her element now. She'd made a home for herself in Solvigant and felt she knew all its various moods and twisted alleyways. The city had completed a full pilgrimage, what the priests called a *peripatesis,* since her arrival fifteen years prior. She had developed a local's knack for rediscovering her old haunts each time the city settled in a new location.

Adi and her crew exited the terrane yard. They limped and gasped as they surrounded their elegant prisoner, stumbling down an embankment and under a bridge before emerging onto a broader avenue. Adi woke a sleeping carriage driver and paid him extra to take them to one of her safe houses. "Safe house" was a grandiose term for the dilapidated shack, but it was sturdy enough to function as a cell for her nobleman. She was already thinking about how to discover which Thalian family he might belong to so she could scale her ransom demands accordingly. She was certain the Blood Queen and her minions did not know about this safehouse. Adi did not want anyone cutting in on her nest egg once she traded freedom for the star key. Joshua Mung, sporting only mild bruises and a slight limp, volunteered to guard the prisoner.

The next stop was the physicker. Adi left Vista and Wright on the threshold of the Doctors Vake with their last gold spyre. She bid farewell to them and the carriage driver, since he refused to take thieves glass, and began the long walk across Solvigant's Vocce quarter to Drake's Apothecary. Balthasar, the proprietor, was an old friend, and she hoped to learn something about the star key before handing it over.

Goldwynd Alley was quiet at sunrise. The narrow street was home to numerous retailers and apothecaries which catered to the arcane, astral mages—whether members of the Society of Astrologia or not—alchemists, collectors, affinity races like Dragons and Seraphim, and even the occasional snake oil salesmen made their way to Goldwynd Alley for supplies. The numerous apothecaries, boutiques, and paraphernalia shops would not open for several more hours, so Adi stood alone on the wooden boardwalk.

Outside Drake's Apothecary, she felt the familiar resonance of powerful artifacts vibrate her dragonstone like a second heartbeat. Balthasar sold stones and relics, pipes and vessels, herbs and poultices, through which a mage could access stellarium, aether, and void for various purposes. Adi rapped on the door with her sore knuckles, waited a few moments, then rapped once more. Just as she was about to go around to the back steps that led up to Balthasar's living quarters, she heard the rasp and *thunk* of iron bolts. The proprietor opened the heavy door.

Balthasar Balefire stood stooped in the doorway and yawned, too tall in his human form for standard doors. The air around him shimmered in the periphery of her vision, as it did for all Dragons in their humanoid form. He was clad in flannel pajamas and adjusted his horn-rimmed glasses. Though his eyes gleamed gold, Adi saw milky patches clouding the edges. He smiled when he saw her.

"Hail, Solo," he greeted her.

"Hail, Solo," she parroted.

"Adi, come in, come in. I'm just boiling the water for tea. But your face... you look terrible. What happened?"

Adi returned the smile and brushed away a concerned hand. Bale's eyes settled briefly on the ornate star key.

"Hello, Bale, good to see you." Bale was a friendly nickname from his childhood for those who tired of the mouthful that was Balthasar. Adi had not been alive then, but after spending so many nights around his hearth listening to old stories the nickname had stuck. "Got any coffee?"

"Gods no, can't stand the stuff," Bale snorted. This affectionate exchange was traditional for them. Bale teased her for her coffee addiction and she knew the scent of the ground beans made him sneeze uncontrollably, so he never allowed the stuff in his home. They both laughed then embraced. Adi winced at the pain in her ribs and face. Balthasar must have felt it because he let her go.

"Come inside, girl, and clean yourself up while I make us some breakfast."

Adi entered the cluttered shop and the familiar smells of sage, lemon verbena, and mahogany flooded her nose. She took a deep breath, reveling in the aromatic jumble, then she sneezed. Shelves along one side of the small shop bowed under the weight of jars that held hundreds of kinds of dried herbs and flowers, from wheat grass seed to exotic Ankhimian leather flower. On the other side were a hodgepodge of hats, pipes, boxes, pouches, staves, wands, and a plethora of other arcane objects gathered in teetering piles in the gloom of the shuttered windows. Adi felt at home.

*How many nights did I spend cataloging and organizing these objects?* By the looks of things, Bale needed help.

"There's still warm water in the wash tub upstairs. Clean your face while I investigate whether the chickens have done their duty." His ornate jade cane tapped across the floor as he ducked his white-haired head under another lintel into the rooms beyond. Adi gathered a pinch of lavender, a bundle of sage, and a handful of fragrant Maxonian stonewort before climbing the back stairs that led to Bale's apartments. The washbasin was indeed still warm, and Adi chucked the herbs into the steaming water before plunging her arms and face into the ceramic basin.

When she finally came up for air, dried blood tinted the water. The stonewort stung but she valued its antiseptic properties. She patted her face dry, wincing as she touched the cuts where shrapnel from the explosions on the *Sidereal* had lacerated her face. Her memory offered an unwelcome flash of Captain Torrance's shattered body.

*Was that just yesterday?* Adi shuddered. She was so tired. Downstairs, a screen door banged. Adi tensed, wondering if the Blood Queen's soldiers had spotted her on her walk across the city. Then she heard the familiar banging and clanking of Bale in the kitchen. On her way downstairs, she glanced into Rehka's old room. The twin bed was crammed into one corner and covered with crates of diverse sizes. Dust motes danced in the greasy sunbeams that penetrated the small, soot-stained window.

*No one has slept in here for some time,* Adi thought.

She crept into the room, wincing when the floorboards groaned. Adi opened the closet. Under a box marked "Miscellany" sat a folded stack of sweaters. Adi removed the scraps of her own shirt and replaced it with a green sweater. She inhaled the scent of wool, cedar, and curry. The shirt smelled nothing like Rehka, but it comforted her, nonetheless.

"Breakfast," Bale bellowed from downstairs.

Adi hastened from the room and joined him in the kitchen. Numerous springs, gears, and clockwork mechanisms covered the table, on which stood a large bronze torso with its chest plate removed. Adi ate her eggs as she leaned against the wooden countertop. Bale's eyes widened when he noticed Adi was wearing his daughter's sweater, but he said nothing.

She motioned toward the torso with her fork. "Is that a golem?"

"Was," Balthasar said between mouthfuls.

Adi never watched Dragons while they ate. Despite their sophistication and power, they still wolfed their meals like the predators they were.

"Where's the rest of him?"

"Don't have much use for a golem," Balthasar said slurping, his mouth full. "Not many can afford the initial investment. Of those who can, most can't stomach the maintenance costs. On the rare occasion I come across one, I usually scrap it out."

Golems were rare on Xys. Her father had owned one, but Adi didn't remember much about it. The idea of selling a body piecemeal—even a soulless, metal body—made her queasy. She set her fork on her plate.

"How's Rehka?" Adi asked.

Bale set his bowl on the counter beside an unruly stack of dirty dishes.

"I told you, I'm not playing messenger between the two of you anymore."

"I know, sorry." Adi cast her eyes down in contrition. "No messages. I was just wondering if you'd spoken to her recently."

"She came through about a month ago on her way to Flynt to visit her mother."

"She's touring?"

Bale nodded, "Playing gigs as part of a larger traveling show. She might be on Tyre now. I don't remember her schedule."

"Tell her—" she started to say, but before Bale could object Adi corrected herself. "I'm glad she's all right."

Balthasar made a guttural sound that might have been a draconic word unsuited to his human form. Adi sensed exasperation mixed with affection.

She set her eggs down and let the silence stretch between them.

*I wish I could tell her how*—Adi quashed the thought. There was so much to say but this was not the time or place.

"I came to get your opinion on an artifact," Adi said. *Dragons could be so damn patient.* "Nothing to do with Rehka."

"I wondered why you stopped by," he said, his sternness replaced with curiosity.

Adi offered the rosewood box to Bale, who took it in both hands. He made another draconic sound, one Adi recognized as a delighted grunt.

"Need my other glasses," he said and disappeared into the dim store. Adi fought an irrational surge of panic that he might flee with the star key. He returned moments later, a heavy leather apron over his pajamas and his reading glasses replaced with jeweler's spectacles that bristled with rotating side lenses of varying magnifications. Bale brushed aside the clutter on the table, sending a few springs and gears to the floor where they bounced and rolled in all directions. He pulled up a stool and sat, his long fingers tracing the inlaid finery. Bale hummed in a way that reminded Adi of a purring cat.

He swiveled a magnifying lens in front of his left eye and opened the box as if it might contain a venomous serpent. Adi watched over his shoulder as he produced a set of small screwdrivers from a flannel breast pocket and addressed the tiny set screws. The tangle of copper wiring looked even more convoluted than she remembered. The gem at the device's center sat dark and quiet. Bale held his breath as he lifted the apparatus from its housing. He smiled, the aqueous shimmer around him glistening.

"Well?" Adi asked.

Bale held up a hand. He slid the box to one side and raised the machine up to the weak light, rotating it to get a better look at the underside. He mumbled under his breath in draconic. Adi caught an occasional word but did not understand what he was saying, though he was more excited than she'd seen him in a long while.

Adi picked up her eggs and wandered back into the shop. Between mouthfuls, she re-alphabetized the jars of herbs. Bale would work on his own schedule. When she finished with the herbs, she lit a fire in the small hearth and began dusting with a scrap of cloth. The air in the room thickened, making her eyes run and her nose itch. She flung open the shutters.

*When did someone last clean this place?* Adi was organizing a display case of wands by size and wood type when Bale let out a "Whoop!" Adi collided with him as he emerged.

"Come up to the study," he told her, more excitement in his voice than she had ever heard. He had returned the device inside the rosewood box and was clutching it with trembling hands.

Adi followed him upstairs. "What is it?"

The study was organized if not clean. Bale spent his time here poring over manuscripts, catalogs, and engineering manuals to document the items that flowed through his shop. Even for a Dragon, one of the affinity races, magic was a broad, complicated world, riddled with unsolved mysteries, even for its very capable practitioners.

"Don't hold out on me, Bale."

"It's an astrolabe," he said, his finger running across book spines until he found the title he wanted and slipped it from the shelf. He plopped it down on the desk, rattling one of the moons on an intricate, hand-carved orrery that consumed most of the desk space.

"I've used astrolabes to navigate on ships, this doesn't look like those."

"Well, if I'm right, it's only *part* of an astrolabe."

"It still doesn't look like anything—"

Balthasar raised a hand to silence her. "Ah here it is. Apyreon." There was an awkward pause before Adi realized he was struggling to read the small text underneath the heading.

"May I?"

"Please." He removed the jeweler's glasses and rubbed the bridge of his nose. "My eyes aren't what they once were."

Adi read aloud from the indicated paragraph. "Apyreon. Built in the laboratory of Anaximander Mastrionardus Pallantier Stormfire on Seniphet, it is believed to have been the catalyst for the first major interlunar diaspora. Its capabilities were contested by

Karisian scholars and the Society of Astrologia in the Sakow Dialogues, but it is believed to grant a knowledgeable user access to realms lunar, interstellar, and celestial. A common myth amongst metallic Dragons states that the god Pallantier himself helped Anaximander create such a device, unbeknownst to the other Avernian gods. It is thought that Apyreon was destroyed during the Chamomile Rebellion. The Draconic scholar Claudius Mercer's *Schema and Diagrammata* does contain one plausible construction. He also suggests that in addition to aether, stellarium, and void, the device operated on a fourth unknown substance, though Constantius, et al. disagree."

The paragraph ended. "That's it?" Adi was not impressed. "I already knew it could make gates."

"You did?"

"How do you think I got here?"

Bale's face fell. "You were able to open a gate without aetherial magic?"

"Aether is illegal to possess and I have no affinity for it anyway. I hotwired it into a navigation panel and augmented my own power with a spinner. It's all I had."

"That's not supposed to be possible." He tilted the artifact in a shaft of weak sunlight. "This aether gem is unlike any I've ever seen, though. I've never come across one with so few impurities. The royal stockpile in Thail might contain two or three of this caliber, or the vaults on Flynt near the mine, but I dare say most artificers alive today couldn't refine the aether to such a flawless state."

Adi thought about it. Aether gems were mined and refined at a unique location on the moon of Flynt, home of Dragons, where every step of the process was scrutinized by the Kuxalim, a fanatic order of Dragon monks loyal to the empress and her descendants. "What about a Nefeshi stone weaver?"

"Perhaps..." There was a hitch in Bale's voice. "But I know of none currently in existence."

Adi sighed. She had yet to encounter any of the legendary Nefeshi, the elemental children of Solo, let alone a stone weaver."

*What is the Blood Queen planning to do with such a powerful star key?*

Bale eyed her, his eyes suddenly clouded, his face suspicious. "Where did you get this?"

"I stole it from High Chancellor Vanguard as an assignment for the Blood Queen."

*"What?"* Bale's eyes widened and he clenched his jaw. "You intend to hand this over to Sasha Riven?"

"It pays my debts. I'll be able get this stupid collar removed and I'm free. Free to go my own way. Free to be with my son."

"The Blood Queen would be able go anywhere she liked whenever she liked. To all ten moons, the divine realms and beyond. This is Sojourner tech."

"You keep saying 'beyond.' What do you mean 'beyond'? Ten moons, that's all. Solo?"

In response, Bale turned his attention to the orrery. The great, ringed goddess Solo stood in the middle, her ten children arranged around her in their orbits. He cranked a lever as he spoke, causing the moons to move slowly around the central planet.

"Ten moons, it is true, but Solo is not the only goddess in the solar system. Other planets orbit the central star, and each light in the sky is another star which could contain its own planets with their own moons. What's more, this multiplicity of stars, planets, and moons exists within just one plane. What we live on, these moons and such, comprise the terrestrial plane. The space between the stars is the astral plane, what we call the void. Dragons partially inhabit the aetherial plane, Pyrea. This is where the reptilian body of my Dragon resides while I maintain this human form and vice versa. It is what allows Dragons to harvest aether for sorcery and alchemical use. That in turn is why the emperor always takes a Dragon wife to seal the compact between Dragons and the Empire and maintain control of aether gems. That aetherial plane separates the other planes from the celestial ones, of which there are at least two: the netherworld Basalt and heavenly Avernus. Scholars and mystics have suggested the existence of others, elemental planes, planes of void, et cetera, but nothing has ever been proven. Anaximander was a first generation Kratoi, descended from the Sojourners himself. This astrolabe could open gates to other World Systems."

"What's your point?" Adi said.

"Apyreon would allow the Blood Queen not only to travel between Solo's moons but anywhere in the universe. To the heavens themselves and into the vastness of the infinite. In the old tongue, 'Apyreon' means infinite, limitless. I believe it's a power beyond what even the gods possess."

Adi swallowed and sat heavily in an overstuffed chair, sending up a plume of dust. "What are you suggesting I do? The Blood Queen is sure to have had spies at the terrane station. She knows I'm in the city. If I don't turn Apyreon over to her, she'll have Ajax or one of her other generals hunt me down. She'll still get the device and I'll be dead."

Bale shrugged, conceding the point.

"How do you know this contraption is Apyreon?"

"The box," he said tracing the inlay with one gentle finger. "This ornamentation is a star chart. Though unfamiliar to me, it matches the description of Apyreon in Heidel's *Telestaria*." Bale gestured to a second large tome. "Plus, it appears to combine with a second artifact. Legend refers to this second piece, Tethysteon."

"There's another piece?" Adi said, hope in her voice. "Perhaps the Blood Queen does not have this other piece? Maybe Apyreon's power is limited without it?"

"Perhaps." Bale flipped the machine upside down, "Look at these six indentations. It appears as if something in addition to the aether gem interfaces with the device."

Adi studied the points Bale indicated. The openings had delicate internal topography, female openings for matching male connectors. She wasn't much of an engineer unless they were talking about ships.

"I still have to give it to the Blood Queen," Adi said. "I doubt she'd be satisfied if I pretended I didn't have it. She would not grant me freedom from my indenture. I would only get more missions, accrue more interest, and increase my debt. I've got to get out from under this, Bale."

The Dragon did not respond.

"I can steal it back once I'm free," Adi suggested. "Or go after Tethysteon to prevent Riven from ever acquiring it. I can't do anything to oppose her while I wear this stupid collar."

Bale turned the machine over in his hands, considering.

The idea of traveling through the astral plane to other stars, or even to Avernus itself to visit the gods did not motivate Adi as much as the ability to walk down the street without people staring and whispering of the Blood Queen. That said, her pulse quickened at the idea of a skeleton key to the universe.

*I could collect Lucas and we could run somewhere the Blood Queen would never find us. Out of the very World System. But a life on the run was hardly a life for a fifteen-year-old boy.*

"My freedom is worth more than some legend," Adi said at last. "Real, tangible freedom, not the embodied ideal of it sitting in some museum where the Blood Queen will probably steal it anyway."

Bale relented. He inserted the machine into its housing and tightened the set screws one by one. He closed the case, gave it a reverent stroke, and pushed it across to Adi.

"Promise me something," he said as Adi picked up the device and slipped it into her satchel.

"What?"

"When you have your freedom, leave Rehka to hers. My daughter is happy. She's moving on. She doesn't need the drama and darkness that dogs your heels."

Adi's knee-jerk reaction was to be offended, but she recognized that Bale had good reasons for his request.

*This was expected.* She licked her lips. "Fine, I promise."

"Very well," Balthasar said, ignoring the tension now dense between them.

Adi knew it was time for her to leave. *I have eaten his food, taken his hospitality, and asked him to part with a legendary artifact. Not to mention Rehka. I have overstayed my welcome.* She rose, but Bale stayed where he was.

"Thank you, Balthasar," she said from the doorway.

"Take care of yourself," he said, his voice rough.

When Adi stood once more in the dry morning air of Goldwynd Alley, she looked back and saw Bale watching her from the window of his study. She waved. He waved back, then pulled the curtains closed.

# CHAPTER FIVE

# ADI CRESTONE

## MOON OF XYS, TYRSDAY, 28TH OF HEBE

Adi left Goldwynd Alley and walked through the sandy streets of the metropolis. Pink-hued sunlight was just beginning to cut through the gaps between buildings, chasing away the stars. Adi knew the sunlight would be dim at this point in Xys's orbit. Solo obscured much of it, but she welcomed the sunrise. The sea battle with the Thalians felt distant. Around her, shopkeepers were unshuttering their windows and loading carts for market. Even though the moon was falling apart around them, life went on. Goods had to be bought and sold, bills had to be paid.

Adi fingered the collar around her neck once more. *When the sun rises next, I will be free.*

Apyreon, resting in the leather satchel over her shoulder, would settle all her debts with the Blood Queen. Her ransomed captive would put money in her pocket. She would be free to return to her son. She could buy out Iris's contract and get off this dying moon. Her relationship with Iris was still new, but already Adi could feel herself falling for the woman. The three of them could find a place outside the Empire to make a fresh start.

*What will the Blood Queen do with Apyreon?* Guilt tugged at the edges of her dreams, but Adi shook it off. *Let her do whatever she likes. I owe the World System nothing.*

She was imagining her new life when she entered the warehouse district and turned into a narrow alley, a shortcut to the Red Wyrm, the night club that was the Blood Queen's seat of power. Two men stepped into her path. Both appeared gaunt and malnourished with only a handful of teeth between them. Their gums bled, indicating scurvy. Adi knew the terrors of scurvy.

She raised her hands in greeting. "Hail Solo, gents, I got nothing for you."

Adi realized two other figures, a man and a woman, had closed off the alley behind her. She spotted the White Rabbit tattoo on the necks of the toughs in front of her.

*Djinnar's blood!* Gang-affiliated thugs were harder to scare off.

"Hail Solo." The first man raised his cudgel to her chin and used it to turn her head one way then the other. An inflamed, puss-filled sore on his lower lip quivered when he spoke. "You look like you lost a fight."

"Our opponents didn't survive." Adi put more confidence into her voice than she felt. Taking on four thugs, even scrawny ones, was a challenge, and she was injured and exhausted.

"What's in the bag?" the pimpled man asked.

"You got any food?" the second man piped up. He was younger and seemed to be in slightly better condition than his partner. *The White Rabbit isn't taking care of its men.*

Adi rooted around in her belt pouches, hoping she might have a few rations from her time on Tyre, but she had nothing.

"What happened to your face," the younger man asked.

Adi didn't answer.

"You service some client badly and he took it out on'ya face?"

"I'm not a whore!"

"I bet you work at the Rose House."

"Rose House don't hire whores with busted faces," Pimple said, "or collars of indenture. She works at the Rusty Nail or some other blackhole."

"Whores don't carry swords," the younger man said, "and she got a dragonstone. She's a mage."

"Shut up," said a thug behind Adi. The woman. "It don't matter what she is, just take her things and let's go. The guards'll be by soon."

"This is Blood Queen territory," Adi snarled. "I'm an indenture. You're poaching. You steal from me and the Blood Queen will have her revenge."

Pimple twitched but didn't back down. "That bloody wench'll get hers soon enough."

*What is he talking about? Is this hubris or does he know something?*

"If you ain't got nothing," he continued, "I'll do you right here and see what kinda whore you are." He gestured for Adi to remove the sweater.

"How about you run off and I don't tell the Blood Queen that White Rabbit is trespassing?"

"How 'bout you don't say shit and we don't kill ya." Pimple said, reaching for her breast. Adi swatted his hand away. The younger man reached for the satchel at her shoulder. Adi twisted away but the strap came free and the rosewood box clattered onto the cobblestones. Its jeweled inlay glimmered in the early morning light. For a moment, no one moved then chaos erupted.

The young man dove for the box and Adi kicked him across the jaw. He screamed and went sprawling. She started to draw her sword, but a cold knife was pressed against the nape of her neck. Adi raised her hands as if to capitulate. Instead she reached around, grabbed the wrist, and twisted until something snapped. Her assailant, the woman, yelped and the knife skittered away. The young man reached for the box again as strong arms grabbed her from behind. She managed to stomp the young man's hand hard enough to snap bones and the box tumbled away.

*Surely city guards will hear this racket, or Blood Queen lackeys.*

The man pinning her arms lifted her off the ground and tried to toss her. Adi's dragonstone flared as she drew in astral dust. She felt her blood convert it to stellarium and she suddenly became too heavy for her assailant to lift. He grunted in surprise and released her. Adi dropped to her knees, the magical weight was crushing her. She released her grip on the dust, but the flow did not relent. She worried her wildling nature would crush her. Then the magic ebbed away, and her normal weight returned.

Apyreon lay on the ground. She snatched it up and drew her scimitar in one fluid motion. The blade bit deep into the abdomen of the young male assailant. He screamed and dropped to his knees, clutching his stomach. Adi turned to run when Pimple's cudgel connected with her stomach. The blow drove the wind from her body. She collapsed against the wall of a building, her vision going gray at the edges as her sword skittered away. While she gasped, trying to catch her breath, Pimple plucked the box from limp fingers then backhanded her across her swollen face. She nearly passed out. He crouched in front of her.

"How about a kiss?" he said, puckering his lips. The sore released more pus.

Adi spit in his face and hissed, "Don't you touch me."

Pimple wiped the spittle from his face and kissed her so hard she thought he'd crack the back of her skull on the wall. He squeezed her left breast and she winced.

Adi tried to bite him, but he slipped away, laughing. "Better than Rictor's wife."

"Shut your mouth," said the young man, Rictor.

Adi's breath was coming back and she gasped, "By Djinnar's fury I'm going to kill you."

Pimple kicked her hard and she slid down the wall until her face lay on the ground. The air was filled with the high shriek of a guard's whistle.

*Praise Solo they're here.* A second whistle accompanied the sound of booted feet.

"Let's go," Rictor said. Pimple scooped up the leather satchel and dropped Apyreon into it. The four White Rabbits bolted around the far corner.

The two guards hoisted her up, shouting questions she could not understand. The blood was rushing in her ears as she stared down the empty alley where the White Rabbits had fled with her hard-won freedom.

# CHAPTER SIX

# 1ON RUCINARE

## MOON OF XYS, TYRSDAY, 28TH OF HEBE

Ion sighed and shifted his weight in the boat, making it rock.

"Sit still," his grandfather hissed. Ion fumbled his fishing rod, dropping the heavy reel onto the bottom boards. He scrambled after it and hefted it so fast the hook popped out of the water and arced overhead, trailing spray. Thankfully, it did not catch either of them.

"Settle down, lad! You want to capsize us?"

"Sorry." Ion tucked the rod between his knees and rebaited the hook. The heat of the late spring afternoon pressed down on him. Reflected sunlight from the flat, silent surface of the Boiled Sea glared at him.

"What's on your mind, boy?"

Ion pulled the thieves' glass from his pocket and held Captain Crestone's gift up to the light.

His grandfather chuckled. "Thinking about pirates, are we?"

Ion nodded. "I want to be one."

"Not much call for pirates on the Boiled Sea."

"I don't want to be a pirate *here*. I want to leave this stupid place."

"This place is our home."

Ion groaned. *How many times have we had this conversation?* "It can be *your* home."

He gazed at the horizon and wondered what lay beyond it. He had never dreamed of being a pirate, but yesterday the beautiful captain and her fiery ship had dropped from the sky. Now wanderlust refused Ion any peace. It chivvied him to go anywhere, to be anything except a dying fisherman in a dying town on a stupid, dying moon. The Empire was huge, encompassing seven moons, and that wasn't even all of Solo's children. He wanted to see it, and not just see it, but be someone—a notorious pirate.

His grandfather reeled in his empty line. "Maybe I'll try a water skipper."

"We don't have any."

"Millipede larvae it is then." His grandfather took a swig from the canteen and passed it to Ion, who drank several swallows. "Slow down, Ion, we've got a few hours left yet, and no dinner to speak of."

Ion's stomach rumbled in protest, and he wiped his chin with the back of his free hand. He handed the canteen back to his grandfather and cast his line.

"We could use the money she gave us for a meal."

"That money's for something special. If we spend it on food, we'll be hungry again in a few days."

"I'm hungry now."

His grandfather reached into a soiled pocket and produced a bit of dried fish from an oily cloth. Ion munched it, though the salt crust made him thirstier.

"We could use it for terrane tickets."

"Where would we go?"

"To Solvigant, of course. It might be enough to get off-moon."

"What would we do in Solvigant? We're fisherman."

"I'm sure we could find work."

"And where would we stay? We'd be homeless. Here we have a roof over our heads and enough food in our bellies to keep going."

"We could go to Saba or Maxon or Tyre. They all have oceans and rivers with actual fish in them." An idea occurred to Ion, "We could save the money and row out to one of the hydrogates."

His grandfather recoiled at the thought of traveling the void. "I have never risked the void and I see no reason to now."

Ion huffed, exasperated. Suddenly, his line went taught, the reel spinning out line, yanked by a fish on the run. Ion whooped and jerked the rod up to set the hook deeper. Then he began to reel it in. The pole bent double. Ion braced his bare feet against the gunwale to avoid being pulled overboard.

"It must be a big one!"

His grandfather laughed. "A feast tonight."

Ion played the fish, letting out line and reeling it in, tiring the creature so he could bring it to their landing net. Sweat beaded on his brow, and his palms were slick on the rod. He blinked drops from his eyes. The fish was close now. Their little boat leaned to port. Ion could see the lithe silver form under the water now, and when he pulled hard he could get it to break the surface.

"Not too fast now," his grandfather cried. "Patience. Be patient."

"I think it's a mackerel."

Ion heaved upward once more on the rod while reeling in more line. His grandfather made his way to the gunwale, net in hand, poised to heave the muscular fish into the boat.

The line snapped.

Ion tumbled backward, banging his head against the center thwart. He leapt to his feet in time to see the gleaming fish leap and writhe on its way to the safety of deeper water.

"Djinnar's blood!" Ion cursed.

"Watch your language."

Ion cursed again and hurled his rod into the bottom of the boat. It clattered against the bait bucket and tackle box.

"I hate being a fisherman! I hate Castes. I hate this godforsaken dying moon, and I hate you!" Ion sat down hard on the stern sheets, crossing his arms in mute protest.

His grandfather set the oars in the rowlocks and they rowed back to shore in silence. His grandfather's pace was slow, and Ion's anger was spent by the time the bow scraped against sand in the shallows. Feeling guilty but not ready to apologize, Ion jumped into the warm, knee-deep water and hauled the boat onto dry land above the tide line. He did not wait for his grandfather to tie off the skiff, but fled toward their hut, his eyes stinging with tears.

Inside their dingy dwelling, he dropped onto his pallet and rolled to face the wall. Through cracks in the battered boards, he watched his grandfather walk from the shore. He stood outside for a long time, tacklebox in one hand, the two rods in the other. Finally, Ion could take no more. He stood, intending to go outside and apologize.

"Bah," his grandfather said to no one. Ion heard his grandfather set the tackle box and rods on the stoop before turning down the dune toward town.

Ion waited on the stoop as the afternoon faded into evening and the sunlight waned. He had cleaned and organized their entire cabin. He even took the faded rug they used to cover the holes in the floor out to the line and beat the sand from it with their soup ladle. His fingers ached from gripping the wood handle. Still his grandfather had not returned.

Ion's stomach growled in protest. He did not know whether it was hunger or guilt that gnawed at him. Perhaps both.

*Why did I say that?* Ion thought. *He's all I have.*

Ion did hate Castes and fishing, but he loved his grandfather. His grandfather had been there since his parents abandoned them.

*Did Grandfather leave? Did I drive him away like I did my parents?*

Ion had no idea why his parents had disappeared from Castes one summer night, but in his darker moments he blamed himself. The first stars of twilight twinkled on the distant horizon when he could no longer handle the anticipation and trudged into town.

He found his grandfather at the old bar counter inside the general store, sipping a mug of tepid ale. A sack of groceries sat beside him on an empty stool. Ion sidled up on the other side and took a seat. Alicia, the shopkeeper's wife, was busy dusting shelves of commodities no one would purchase.

"What'll it be, lad," his grandfather said when Ion was settled. The old man's words were slurred and he rocked dangerously on his stool, so Ion knew it was not his first pint.

"Mead?"

"One mead, please, Alicia."

"The boy's too young, Atticus," the woman chided. "I've got some sarsaparilla, but no ice I'm afraid."

"She says you're too young, Ion. Sarsaparilla okay?"

"Yeah, that's good." Ion said, his voice small.

Alicia disappeared into the back. Ion heard the rattle of glass bottles followed by the hiss of one being opened. She returned and set it in front of him. Ion's grandfather offered up one of the coins.

"This one's on the house." She smiled and reached across the bar to ruffle Ion's hair. Normally, Ion hated that, but tonight he was too distracted by his grandfather's dour mood.

Ion took a sip to wet his mouth. The brown liquid was warm and much of the carbonation was gone, but it was sweet enough that Ion didn't care. He set the bottle on the counter with a *thud*.

"I'm sorry, Grandpa. I didn't mean it. I was angry about the fish."

"I know."

"I mean it. I don't hate you. You're all I've got."

"I know, lad."

"Please don't leave me." The words were out before Ion could reel them back in. His grandfather turned toward him, his eyes shining. The old man sniffled. He took Ion's hands in his and Ion stared at the loose mottled skin.

"I'll never leave you Ion, you hear me?"

Ion choked on a sob.

"I'll never leave you," grandfather said again.

They stood and embraced. Ion squeezed hard with his skinny twelve-year-old arms while his grandfather rubbed his back. They stood that way for a long time, until Alicia coughed.

"I ought to close up," she said, "and you two ought to go home and eat. Your grandfather bought some delicious treats."

Ion released his grandfather and wiped his nose on his tattered shirt.

"Yes, ma'am. Thank you." He picked up the sack of groceries. It was heavier than he'd expected. His grandfather stumbled the first few steps and Ion realized the man was quite tipsy. He took his grandfather's hand and they made their way back to their hut.

Ion helped his grandfather to their only chair. It was fully dark now and the cold desert night clung to them. He built a driftwood fire in the hearth and rummaged through the sack of food. It contained a moldy onion, a potato, two wilted carrots, a mealy apple, and a small cut of meat, maybe cow, maybe goat. Ion couldn't tell from the scent. It was a feast. It was more food than they'd had in months. He couldn't remember the last time he'd had red meat. His grandfather must have spent all the money.

He diced it all and cooked everything together in their only pot. When it was done, he ladled the stew into their bowls. They sat together on the stoop and watched the meteors streak from Solo's rings. The stew warmed their bones. Ion almost complained that his stomach hurt, until he realized that he felt odd because he was full. He leaned against his grandfather and yawned.

"I'm sure I'll land that mackerel tomorrow," Ion said.

"I know you will."

"Thank you, for staying with me. I can be a fisherman. I'm sure the Empire has enough pirates. Castes only has two fishermen. This town needs us."

His grandfather laughed. "We all count on each other."

Ion rose and pulled the thieves' glass from his pocket. He gazed at it in the orange light of Solo and then hurled it down the dune toward the sea.

"What d'ya do that for?" his grandfather asked.

"It seems like a dangerous thing."

His grandfather rose and ruffled his hair. Ion spluttered and pushed his hand away, laughing. Back inside their shed, he helped his grandfather undress and lay down on the pallet. Ion laid beside him so their backs were touching. In moments, his grandfather was snoring, but Ion laid awake for a long while feeling the rhythm of his grandfather's breathing.

He wished he hadn't tossed away the thieves' glass, but it felt like the right thing to do. He could survive Castes as long as he had his grandfather. Ion's mother used to sing a song, "The Valley of Eld," and Ion fell asleep singing it to himself.

He awoke to light streaming in through the cabin window. The angle of the sun's rays told him it was late morning. Usually, they were down at the shore shoving off by now. Ion rolled over on the pallet, but his grandfather was gone. Panicked, the boy leapt up.

"You all right, lad?" his grandfather asked from his chair beside the hearth.

Ion let out his breath. "I thought you left."

"I told you, I won't ever be doin' that to you."

The boy stepped over to him, picked up the hardened piece of driftwood, and poked at last night's ashes.

"I know. Are we fishing today?"

"Of course we are. We don't fish, we don't eat. I just wanted to give you a minute."

The two began their morning routine. Ion restrung his fishing rod and organized the tackle box while his grandfather inspected the nets and poked around the woodpile for bait. Then they descended the dune toward the Boiled Sea. Ion cast furtive glances back and forth to see if he could spot the obsidian coin glinting in the sun. He could not. By the time they reached the boat he was sweating. The day promised to be hot, the water still as glass, not good fishing conditions. Their quarry would dive deep to avoid the heat of the surface water.

His grandfather climbed aboard and settled himself at the oars. Ion picked up the anchor and tossed it over the gunwale before pushing their small skiff into the breakers and clambering aboard.

"I took a walk this morning," his grandfather said, "to clear my head. I haven't had a hangover since your parents left." He cleared his throat and paused his rowing. From his pocket he produced the small dark coin and pressed it into Ion's palm.

"It's okay to dream, lad. A man needs something to do while he fishes."

# CHAPTER SEVEN

# ADI CRESTONE

## MOON OF XYS, TYRSDAY, 28TH OF HEBE

The interrogation room at the city watch station was unadorned stone. Adi sat manacled and the shackles were locked to a loop of metal protruding from the roughhewn table. The large wooden door swung open on ancient rusty hinges and a Faelani entered carrying several rolls of parchment under one arm. Behind him was a tall human woman carrying three cups of steaming liquid in her large hands.

"I'm Senior Inspector Solomon Broc," said the Faelani. The chair across from Adi squeaked when he sat. He was a badger, the black and white fur of his face neatly waxed, and he wore an eyepatch that partially obscured a scar across his right cheek and forehead. "This is my partner, Watchman Becca Henge."

Watchman Henge set the three cups on the table to reveal a dark liquid, coffee.

Adi jangled the irons. "Do you always shackle assault victims?"

"Standard procedure for persons who come into the station wearing one of the Blood Queen's collars, I'm afraid."

"It's not—" Adi began.

"As I am, however, a senior inspector," Broc said over Adi's objection, "I am permitted some latitude." He produced a key from his vest pocket and unlocked the manacles. Adi rubbed her wrists, her gratitude plain to see. She picked up a coffee and savored the aroma. It was a luxury rarely available to pirates.

*A senior inspector? There are a dozen in the whole city watch. Why is he interested in me?*

"That was a hell of a beating you took. We're going to have the garrison physicker clean you up after a few brief questions."

"Am I under arrest?"

"You should be," Henge's voice was unexpectedly high considering her tall frame. She was easily six feet and broad of shoulder. An imposing woman, her hair was cut in a tight bob that framed her face. She leaned against the far corner of the room, trying not to make the confined space feel overcrowded.

"Are you related to the politician, Vincent Henge?" Adi asked.

Henge flushed, which was answer enough for Adi.

"One senior inspector and one nepotism hire." Adi scoffed.

"You criminal, b—" Henge started.

Broc *tsk*ed her comment away. "We just need a statement about the assault. We can start with your name."

"Captain Adi Crestone."

"Captain of what?" Henge's voice was scornful.

Adi adjusted her tricorn, which had miraculously survived the attack firmly affixed to her head. "I'm in the market for a new ship."

"Let's get back to the matter at hand," Broc said. "Tell us about the men who attacked you in the Vocce Quarter this morning. What were you doing there?"

"Does it matter?"

"Just trying to get the whole picture," Broc said.

"Are their certain activities that justify being assaulted?" Adi asked.

"Bein' a thug for the Blood Queen?" Henge suggested.

"Thank you, Watchman Henge," Broc said. "Please confine your personal feelings to your personal time."

Henge scoffed but stopped talking. There was silence until Adi realized Broc was still waiting for an answer.

"I've been off moon for two weeks. I just returned and was on my way to check-in." *I can be a little honest. They'll track the bastards down for me.*

"Where were you?" Henge asked.

"Maxon." Adi felt no compunction about lying to the partner.

"Doing what?" Henge pressed.

"I don't see how that's relevant."

"When did you come back?" Broc asked.

"Yesterday on the *Maxon Lancer*." The dirigible *Maxon Lancer* made the run between Xys and Maxon twice daily and carried huge crowds. It would take the city watch some time to check her alibi. Time she needed to retrieve Apyreon.

"Your assailants, you knew them?" Broc asked.

"Not before this morning. They were White Rabbit."

"Could your assault be connected to whatever you were doing on Maxon?"

*Nice try,* Adi thought. "No."

Broc sighed and scratched under the eyepatch with one clawed finger.

"Just a coincidence then?" Henge said.

"Can I have some more coffee?" Adi asked.

"Henge, would you please oblige the lady."

Becca Henge looked as if she might protest, but she grudgingly picked up Adi's empty cup and left the room.

"I'm not trying to trip you up, Captain," Broc said. "I just need to know what's coming down the pike. Over the last two weeks, I've had several White Rabbit hits all over the city. The morgue has two Talon thugs, half a dozen Blood Queen soldiers, and a city watchman on slabs. Now you've been attacked."

"I don't know anything about that." It was the truth. *What is going on?* When Broc didn't say anything, Adi reiterated, "I've been off moon."

Broc waited.

*Did the White Rabbits know about Apyreon? Have they started a war over it already?* "I'm just indentured. They wouldn't tell me even if something was going on. I take orders until my debts are paid. You know how it works."

The door squealed and Henge re-entered. Broc pivoted his line of questioning.

"Can you describe the men who attacked you?"

"Three men, one woman. I sliced the younger man up good. One of the men, a bigger guy with crooked teeth, they called Rictor. The man in charge looked ill, his breath smelled terrible, and he had some large, pus-filled sore on his left lip." Adi saw a flicker of recognition in Henge's eyes. The coffee was hot and delicious.

"You know who he is." Adi said.

"Why do you think that?" Broc asked.

"Because your partner has a terrible poker face for a future inspector" Adi sneered.

Henge leaned in close, but Broc put a restraining hand on her shoulder.

"Recognition in the eyes followed by defensiveness—dead giveaways. What's his name?"

"No." Broc was emphatic. "I'll not hand that over to you so you or any other Blood Queen thugs can play vigilante."

*They're after bigger fish,* Adi realized. *Pimple was an informant, which meant the city watch had made deals.*

"You give me his name and I'll tell you if I learn anything about what the White Rabbits are up to." Adi said, surprised at herself. She had no love for the Blood Queen, but volunteering to give up information was not how Adi had expected this conversation to play out. *I was so close to getting out.* Adi feared the Blood Queen's wrath when she learned her indenture had lost Apyreon within blocks of the Red Wyrm. *Maybe the watch can help me out.*

She watched Broc. The lengthening silence told her he was considering it.

"Inspector, you can't. I know he was your partner, but you can't," Henge insisted.

"The dead watchman was your partner? Doesn't bode well for Henge."

"Shut up," Henge said.

"No," Broc said at the same time. "No, no deal. I'll catch him." His voice was low, lethal. "You're sure these White Rabbit toughs had no reason to attack you?"

"No reason," Adi said.

"Because if I find out they had a reason and you didn't tell me, then you stop being a victim and start being a person of interest."

"Wrong place, wrong time," Adi said firmly.

"I'll make *you* an offer," Broc said. "If you find out anything about your attackers you tell me."

"That's only half a deal. What do I get out of it?"

"Next time we round up a bunch of Blood Queen soldiers just for generally being criminals, I'll make sure you aren't one of them."

"Inspector, you can't." Henge said.

"Quiet, Henge," Broc finally snapped at her. "Do we have a deal, Captain Crestone?" Adi nodded.

"Your free pass is only good if you actually provide any information, understand?"

"I understand."

"All right then," Broc said rising from the seat and collecting his documents. "Off you go to the physicker. Try to lay low and heal up, you look like shit."

"Can I get another cup of coffee?"

# CHAPTER EIGHT

# ADI CRESTONE

## MOON OF XYS, TYRSDAY, 28TH OF HEBE

Deal struck and wounds tended, the watch released Adi into Torhan's Square. No map of Solvigant existed because every time the city moved its denizens reconstituted it differently. While the central core of the city was prescribed by law, citizens hustled and bribed to get good real estate on a first-come, first-served basis. There was a whole legitimate market for advance couriers to hold positions, and a whole black market to try and thwart them. The open-air market called Torhan's Square was an unofficial tradition among Solvigantians. Torhan's limestone statue crowned the fountain at the center of the square after every peripatesis. Named after an Ankhim general who put down a long-forgotten insurrection, it was always a neutral space for the city's criminal element. Everyone had their fingers in the economics of Solvigant's largest market, so it benefited everyone to mind their manners.

Torhan's Market was a bustling hive in the middle of the afternoon. People and races from the ten moons of the World System haggled and bartered over goods as diverse as the shoppers. Adi could hear the drone of their myriad voices several blocks away. She allowed herself to get lost in the incomprehensible chant of commerce. Framed as it was by tall buildings, the wind swirled around the square, mixing the complex intensity of the spice merchants' wares, the cloying odors of the wool dyers, and the sulfurous fumes of the smiths and metalworkers. The air carried the aromas of one trade into another, so the blacksmiths smelled of cardamom and the wool dyers of the mesquite wood in the forge fires.

Adi was starving, but she had little money left. Of the cache she'd discovered in the captain's quarters on the *Sidereal*, only the copparchs remained. The watch had relieved her of the illegal currency that was thieves' glass. The copparchs would not go far. Her meager breakfast with Bale seemed ages ago. Street vendors turned skewers of lamb and bakers pounded dough into disks before casting them into wood-fired ovens. Her mouth watered, her stomach squirmed, and she felt dizzy.

She spotted a silk merchant's stall where a string trio was playing a lively tune. When the song ended and everyone applauded, she nicked a blue paisley scarf and tied it around her neck over the Blood Queen's collar. The disguise wouldn't hold up under close inspection, but it was better than walking the streets with a sign around her neck.

She wove through the press of bodies. The population of Solvigant was mostly human, but here she saw short, stout Grym, several types of Faelani, a few tall, willowy women who were Dragons in their anthropoid form, hulking Ankhim, and half a dozen Seraphim, one in the full green shroud of the Daughters of Darak. Gaping like a Maxonian tourist, she bumped into a man arguing over the price of a finely glazed terracotta urn. The small coin purse she had liberated held three spyres. Immediately, she traded one of the coins for two skewers of lamb, a stack of fresh pita, and a small bag of chocolates.

She was so hungry she forgot to haggle when the stall keeper quoted her the outrageous foreigners' price, she simply paid it. He seemed more disappointed than elated at the overpayment as he handed her the food. She shoved scalding, oily pieces of meat into her mouth, a slight moan of pleasure escaped her lips. Surprise crossed the stall keeper's face. He was probably butchering alley dog and charging a premium for lamb, but that did not bother Adi.

Next she purchased a flask of dreadful wasake, a cheap liquor distilled from Gaashian sugar cane. It made her eyes water, but the pain of her bruised ribs lessened after two long pulls. She also purchased a few extra bandages, an herbal poultice good for disinfecting wounds, and a small dagger. It felt good to be armed once more, safer given whatever bold plan of action the White Rabbits were hatching.

At the end of her little shopping spree, Adi's spirits felt lighter. Her stomach was full, she thought the scarf complimented her green eyes, and the wasake obscured the pain in her body and blurred the sharp edges of her situation.

She was royally screwed. The Blood Queen's soldiers would be looking for her now that she had missed her rendezvous. She needed to get off the streets.

Stella's Echo was in an alley off the main square, where the buildings blocked most of the sunlight so that no matter the time of day, it appeared to be early evening inside the brothel. There were few patrons around this early, and most of the girls were lounging in the bar playing cards or dicing. Stella bustled behind the bar, organizing and inventorying the various bottles of liquor. She was Faelani, a five-foot-tall arctic fox, whose muzzle fur was thinning with age. She wore jangling gold bracelets with matching gold hoops in her ears. She had a dark mole on her left cheek that was partially obscured by her whiskers. The neckline of her green cashmere dress swooped low revealing ample furry cleavage.

"Hello, Stella," Adi greeted her.

"Adison." Stella's voice was warm and low. "Welcome. Work or pleasure?"

Adi smiled and laid her remaining coins on the bar with a deliberate slap. "Pleasure."

Stella surveyed Adi's bandages, her burned hands, and her pained expression. "Good, because I can't sell your services when you look like that."

Adi laughed as she slid behind the bar to embrace Stella. They hugged for a long moment, Adi grateful for the fox's warmth and affection. When Adi finally released the Faelani woman, Stella's hand went gingerly to Adi's bandaged cheek.

"What happened?"

"Rigors of the job."

Stella *tsk*ed, looking at the two meager copparchs on the bar. She pushed Adi away playfully.

"Ack! What am I supposed to do with these?"

"Your finest wine." Adi swept her hand at the gleaming row of green bottles on the top rack.

"This won't buy you much more than middling wine I'm afraid." She sniffed Adi's breath. "Is that *wasake*? Dear child, what are you doing?" Stella plucked the flask from Adi's belt and dumped the remaining liquid into the slop bucket.

"Hey! I paid good money for that," Adi protested.

"Oh yeah? Who's money?"

Adi laughed, "Good point."

Stella grabbed a bottle of wine from a middle shelf and poured Adi a glass. Adi's coins disappeared into an apron pouch.

"Is Iris working?" Adi asked.

"Child, how are you going to afford Iris? You just spent all your money on that glass of wine you're sloshing around."

"Put it on my tab," Adi suggested.

"When are you going to pay your tab?" A bit of the good humor leached out of Stella's voice.

"I'm good for it," Adi promised.

"You could work it off."

"I don't do that anymore." Adi went cold as soon as the words left her mouth. She had insulted the woman. *Don't tell a brothel owner that whoring is beneath you. It's especially rich coming from a pirate captain beholden to an organized crime boss.*

Adi downed her wine to cover the awkwardness and Stella refilled the cup.

"You were safer when you worked here," Stella said.

"I'm fine," Adi lied and knew the lie didn't penetrate. She squirmed under Stella's concerned regard as the alcohol impaired her sensibilities. Sure, Stella had helped her out of a tight spot, but that didn't mean she got to mother her. *I've made it fine so far without a mother.* With less alcohol in her system she would have debated the meaning of "just fine," but not today. Stella must have sensed the nerve she'd touched because she dropped it.

"Iris is off tonight, you can check her room," Stella said and refilled Adi's wine once more. Adi turned toward the stairs, but Stella's soft hand grabbed her wrist.

"Child, the Blood Queen is looking for you."

Adi tried to focus her eyes on the woman, the edges of whose face was now blurry. "I can handle it."

Stella released her wrist. "Be careful, Adison."

Adi made her way up the stairs and knocked on Iris's suite door. Calling it a suite was a bit of a stretch. Stella's Echo did okay for itself, but it was quite different from the upscale brothels in the Bergahn Quarter. The room held a bed barely large enough for two people, a nightstand, a washbasin, and an armoire. Gauzy curtains hung over one window, diffusing the late afternoon sun. Sage burned on the nightstand, obscuring the other, less pleasant odors of the brothel.

Iris was sprawled on the bed, wearing a linen shift, reading a book, smoking a pipe. She smiled and put the book away when Adi entered the room. Her eyes wandered over Iris's olive complexion and ample curves, the strands of curly brown hair that stuck to her forehead in the heat of the late afternoon.

"Adi, how are—what happened to your face?"

Adi grimaced. "That bad?"

Iris laughed, though Adi sensed an edge of concern. "You haven't bathed? Should I be flattered or disgusted?"

*And me in Rehka's sweater,* Adi thought.

There were no mirrors in the room, but Adi could imagine her bedraggled state. "I suppose it will be more difficult than usual to seduce you."

"You don't have to seduce a whore," Iris said.

"You know I don't see you that way." Adi and Iris had been dating on Iris's off nights since early Dar'an. It was late Hebe now, so a little over eight weeks.

"I know."

"What are you reading?"

"*Maxon Laird and the Revenge of Skull Island*. You left it here."

Adi set her tricorn captain's hat on a bedpost. "I managed to hang onto the most important piece of the costume." She grinned and pulled off the sweater. Iris's eyes went to her breasts as she offered Adi the pipe. Iris's glances were filled with desire and appreciation and Adi was flattered. She didn't smoke often, but today she took the proffered pipe with eager hands. Adi took a long pull, coughed, tried again, and exhaled a quick rush of smoke. Her shoulders and back relaxed. Between the wasake and the tobacco, she struggled to keep her eyes open. She hadn't slept well in days. The rocking and rollicking terrane car had hardly been refreshing.

Iris stood up from the bed, unfolding her matronly figure. She embraced Adi, her whole body pressing against hers. Adi allowed herself to be held, allowed Iris to take her weight. She stroked her hair and Adi nuzzled her neck.

"Read to me?" Adi asked and the two women lay down on the pallet, Adi's head in the crook of Iris's shoulder.

"From the beginning?"

"No, from wherever you are. I've read it enough times that I'll know it."

Iris stroked Adi's head. "I'm glad you're back. We need to bleach your hair tomorrow; your blue roots are showing."

Adi nodded, yawned, and nestled further into Iris's chest. Iris began reading the creased adventure novel. The hero, Maxon Laird, was lost in the catacombs beneath Skull Island, while the tide came in and filled the caverns. Adi was asleep after three pages.

Her dreams were shallow and chaotic, full of indiscernible gray figures who emerged briefly from a darker fog. At some point during the night, Adi awoke to shouts coming from the hallway. Her mind felt thick and slow. Iris was at the door, peering through a crack. Adi could hear Stella's voice, high and acrimonious.

"I won't allow you to harass my clients! She's not here! Don't touch that!" followed by violent curses. The Blood Queen's goons had found her. Glass shattered downstairs and the argument grew louder. With all the grace and speed of the risen dead, Adi stood. She retrieved her pants and underclothes. Iris handed her the sweater.

"Warm for four weeks into Hebe."

"My shirt got ruined."

Iris handed Adi a man's white linen shirt. "Here."

"I can't take this."

Stella's Echo was hardly a wealthy brothel and Iris gave most of her excess money to the Daughters of Light, Phoebe's clerics. The shirt was half of her wardrobe.

"It's hot outside, you'll sweat through that knit in moments while running."

"I'm not running," Adi said, feeling reckless.

"Then at least go to the Blood Queen with a clean shirt."

Adi shrugged and pulled the tunic on. It was too large for her, but it was cooler than Rehka's old sweater. She tucked the dagger into her waistband. There was no water on the nightstand, so she took a swig of stale wine and grimaced at the foul taste. It woke her up though. She kissed Iris on the cheek and opened the door into the hallway.

"No tip?" Iris joked.

Adi smiled at her. "I don't have any money."

"Of course not." Iris rolled her eyes, then shut and bolted the door.

# CHAPTER NINE

# ADI CRESTONE

## MOON OF XYS, TYRSDAY, 28TH OF HEBE

Two of the Blood Queen's henchmen dragged Adi down the stairs and stuffed her into a carriage. From their triangular tattoos she recognized them as beholden to Petry, the Lord of Pain, one of the Blood Queen's generals. They dropped a moldy black hood over her face, which made her face itch. She could smell their sweat and leather through the cloth. Neither spoke. The carriage bounced along the rutted road at speed. Her arms were bound behind her, which made it difficult to catch herself each time it swayed and lurched, so she braced herself with her legs. By the time the carriage slowed, tendrils of pain lanced through her cramped calves.

They stopped and Adi heard the pulsating beat of timpani drums underneath a spritely gittern and a lyre. Adi tasted the sharp tang of grease, and the deep drone of idling airship engines reverberated in her chest.

*The Red Wyrm.*

Her escorts shoved her from the carriage. She tripped twice as neither man offered her assistance on the unfolded steps. She winced, rising on tiptoe and dropping down to stretch her sore muscles.

"Would you be so kind as to remove this hood?" Adi asked. *I will not let the Blood Queen see my fear.*

They did not respond, but a meaty hand landed on her shoulder and steered her through a door into the bowels of the building. The Red Wyrm was the Blood Queen's premier nightclub. She paid handsome bribes to senior wardens to ensure there was always room for the club beside the airship terminal after each peripatesis. Through the Red Wyrm, the Blood Queen Sasha Riven smuggled weapons, drugs, endangered species, and any other interlunar contraband she acquired. All manner of persons from across Solvigant's socioeconomic spectrum could find an audience at the Red Wyrm. Adi had spent many nights at the club over the years. It was common to see a handful of Xyssian congressional delegates, a shipping magnate or two, speaking in hushed tones to agents of the Blood Queen, comfortable in their anonymity amongst so many greaseballs looking for a fix and a good time. And tonight was no different, the revelry was in full swing. The resonant bass notes of the timpani shook the room, the strings shrilled in her ears.

*I'm hungover.*

Bodies jostled her and elbows shoved her from side to side. She felt a wave of vertigo as the two men led her across the crowded room. The clash of shouting voices fused into an incomprehensible babble. Loona smoke swirled through the air. Even though the hood stifled her breathing, Adi hoped the heavy cloth would filter out some of the intoxicating smoke. People called the addicts lunatics or loonies.

Someone spilled their cold drink down Adi's shirt.

*Djinnar's blood, I just got this one.* She stumbled and went down hard on her knees on the wooden floor. The thugs jerked her to her feet and shoved her forward through the press of bodies. Adi knew that no one here would give her a second glance. The Red Wyrm was the Blood Queen's royal court. Everyone knew it was safest to ignore what happened around them.

Adi's escort bounced her off a doorframe, then pushed her down onto a worn leather chair. The door clicked shut behind them, muffling the club's cacophony. Adi tensed when she heard the hiss of a blade being drawn from a scabbard. Its wielder sliced the rope binding her wrists. She rubbed them, wincing at the pins and needles as blood returned to her numb fingers. A hand yanked the hood away and Adi blinked at the onslaught of warm light.

A figure dressed in a dark three-piece suit with a two-tone black paisley vest sat behind a massive wooden desk. His shoulders sported velvet epaulets from which hung leather strands strung with polished bones that swayed when he shifted.

"Ajax!" Adi offered her fiercest grin.

The Lord of Bones put down the magnifying glass with which he'd been perusing a ledger book and studied her.

"Captain Adison Crestone. You *are* calling yourself 'captain' again are you not?" He punctuated the "are" by snapping the ledger shut. Adi forced her hands to lay quiet in her lap instead of fingering the collar at her neck. Ajax saw her flinch and smiled. The edges of his square teeth were stained violet by lacweed. He waited for Adi to speak. She refused. Bored with their silent contest, Ajax stood, the bones jangling and clinking like a desiccated wind chime.

"Let's see, Lucius Torrance and his crew, deceased. The *Sidereal*, a smoldering wreck. The star key lost to White Rabbits. And you, hiding instead of reporting to this court." He ticked each failure off on a gloved finger as he approached her. "Such a disappointment. How will you pay off your debts now?" He crouched before her, so they were eye to eye.

"How do you know about the White Rabbits?" she asked.

Ajax waved the question away with a tinkling flick of his hand.

"The Blood Queen is quite angry with you."

Adi shivered. The realization that she would likely not leave this meeting alive settled heavy in her stomach.

"Do you always toy with your prey before the kill?" Adi asked.

The Lord of Bones looked offended. "What? No. Nothing like that." He rose and took a folded piece of parchment from the desk.

"Get on with it then. You can skip the sermon."

Ajax chuckled. "You're not going to die today, Adi Crestone, at least not by the Blood Queen's order. The universe"—he gestured vaguely—"may have other plans."

Adi exhaled and stood. The two guards tensed but Ajax motioned them to stay put. The office had two windows that overlooked the interior of the Red Wyrm. Adi walked to one and gazed out, steadying herself on its sill. She hoped Ajax could not see her tremble.

Colored light swept the open room, greens and yellows, blues and reds, as a complex geared mechanism rotated stained glass in front of shimmering oil lanterns. Below her a packed crowd writhed together to the pulsating rhythms of the music. A young Grym woman sang in the harsh tones of her native tongue. Around the perimeter of the dance floor, all manner of folk crowded the tables. Adi watched lips move in earnest conversation, customers gesticulated and raised toasts, grabbed serving women, and enjoyed their raucous evening under the watchful eye of the Blood Queen and her minions.

All the races were present: Grym, Ankhim, Humans, Seraphim, Faelani, even a pair of Draconic males. That such a diverse population could lay aside animosities here at the Red Wyrm testified to the power and reach of the Blood Queen. Adi did not see Sasha Riven holding court from her red upholstered throne. She did see two men wearing white armbands that marked them as Xyssian congressional delegates sitting in a corner speaking with Xevon Topstay, the chancellor of the Treasury.

*We are vultures,* Adi thought. *So many vultures picking over the carcass of a dying moon.* She noted with relief that neither of the delegates was Xander Marrion. He had his faults, but he hadn't yet descended into the mud with the rest of them.

*I'm getting distracted.* She had been so certain that she would die tonight that she had no backup plan. Now that she knew she would live, her mind cast about for an alternate strategy.

"Fascinating, isn't it?" Ajax said. He stood next to her, watching her as she watched the revelers below.

"I can't remember the last time I felt free enough to dance." She fingered the collar at her neck before remembering to whom she was speaking. She coughed to cover up her awkwardness. This time the Lord of Bones didn't laugh at her.

"People only want the idea of freedom," Ajax said, "Actual freedom crushes people under the weight of all that possibility."

Adi said nothing. She resented the revelers. They seemed unencumbered compared to the weight of the collar she wore. It bothered her that Ajax's observation affected her so.

"What does the Blood Queen want me to do? I have no ship, no star key, and no funds to pay my debts. Yet she wants me alive. She must expect me to do something for her."

"The Blood Queen does not expect, she commands." The Lord of Bones's voice was severe.

"I wanted the illusion of a choice," Adi said.

Ajax eyed her for a long moment. "The Blood Queen commands you to recover the star key, Apyreon."

"I can't say I'm surprised. But why me?"

"You lost it, it is your responsibility to recover it." Ajax's smile discomforted her.

"What will she do with it?" Adi asked before she could stop herself.

"None of your business."

"And if I refuse?"

"Let's consider your options." Ajax reached up and tapped Adi's collar. It took all her control not to flinch away.

"Get someone else. Give me a few days to pay off my debts and then I'll be done with the Blood Queen."

Ajax smirked. "Have you come into some money? Anything recovered from the *Sidereal* belongs to the Blood Queen."

*Technically, it came from Dragonhammer.* She just needed a few days to ransom her captive officer. "What do you care where it came from?"

Ajax's fingers traced the line of her collar, down the leather thong of her necklace, and came to rest on Adi's dragonstone. She fought down the revulsion of his rough yellow nails on her breastbone.

"Money may remove your collar"—his fingers closed on the cold hunk of jade and before Adi could react he yanked it free—"but only Apyreon will return your dragonstone."

"Djinnar's blood, Ajax," Adi shouted, forgetting where they were and who he was. "I need that. I'm no good to the Blood Queen without my abilities."

Ajax slapped her so hard, her head bounced off the windowpane and her vision blurred. "Failure does not go unpunished, Adison, and once again you have failed to hold up your end of the bargain."

Adi stepped forward, prepared to take a swing at the Lord of Bones, but her thug escorts were upon her. Each grasped an arm as she struggled to land a blow on Ajax's smug face. He produced a wrought-iron key from his pocket, tossed Adi's dragonstone into an open drawer, shut it, and locked it.

Adi slumped. Her eyes fixed on the drawer. An astral mage bonded with just one dragonstone in their lives. Without it, Adi would experience excruciating pain any time she tried to channel stellarium. Already she could feel her power receding from her, the sparkling presence of astral dust fading from her sight.

*How long will it be before the sickness takes root?*

"So, I must retrieve Apyreon or be cut off from my magic forever." Adi tried to imagine what would happen to her in those circumstances. *Would it really be so awful?* Adi ran through the symptoms of astralia necrosis: debilitating arthritis, anemia, blood poisoning, brain death. *Yes, it would be awful.*

Ajax waited.

"Maybe I don't need it," Adi lied. Her dragonstone was no good to Ajax either, since it was attuned only to her. She would end up living her final days in searing pain in a Society hospital on Karis, but she would be free of Xyssian gangsters. That she briefly considered it was testament to her hatred for Ajax and the Blood Queen, of the depth of her spite.

"The Blood Queen said you would require further motivation." Ajax motioned to the goons, who released her. Adi rubbed her shoulders and feeling slowly returned to her strained joints. Ajax handed over the folded parchment.

Adi opened it and it took a moment to register what she was looking at. It was a chart containing classes and marks. Adi's breath caught. Her knees threatened to give way beneath her. It was Lucas's report card. Adi gripped the parchment in a white-knuckled hand, observed its double creases, held it up to the dim light of the office. She clutched at the sill of the window as her world spun. The watermark... it was the quill and gear of the Thail Engineering Academy. This was no fake.

*Lucas! How had the Blood Queen discovered her son? But, of course, she had discovered him.*

The Lord of Bones watched her, his eyes gleaming. Adi wanted to collapse. She wanted to lunge at him and gouge out his poisonous, arrogant eyes. She held herself still. Ajax shrugged and returned to his desk.

"The choice is now yours. You will either recover Apyreon and regain your dragon-stone, or my personal soldiers, the Osmen, will kill your son."

Adi imagined a world where she threw herself at Ajax and begged him to leave her son out of all this. She would spend her life in service to the Blood Queen if she promised to leave Adi's son alone. She suppressed a shameful flicker of anger that she had a son to be used against her in this way.

She flinched at a sharp knock on the door.

"Enter," Ajax called.

The door opened on silent hinges and a Seraph entered, all smooth curves and sharp blades.

"Palestrina," Ajax smiled, "so good of you to stop by."

Palestrina, the Lady of Spiders, was another of the Blood Queen's generals. She stood, unshrouded, her wings folded, but Adi saw the wicked talons at the tips of the delicate bones. White leather armor ornamented with hooks and spikes lined the leading edges and crests. She inclined her head in greeting.

"I was unaware you had company." The Seraph's mellifluous voice was at odds with her filed teeth.

"Adi was just leaving. Weren't you, Adison?"

Adi studied Palestrina. She'd never met the Lady of Spiders before, only heard the ghastly rumors about her. *Two of Sasha's generals at the Red Wyrm at the same time. Something is happening.*

"Adison Crestone," Palestrina purred. "I've heard of you and your...misfortunes."

Adi blinked, but her lack of reaction seemed to irritate both Ajax and Palestrina. The Lord of Bones gestured to Adi's escort.

"Return her to wherever you found her." As Adi passed him, he said, "Have Apyreon when I see you next. The longer it is out of our hands, the more expensive it will be for you."

Adi nodded, clutching the fine paper against her damp palm. Palestrina snapped her fangs as Adi passed and she jumped. Palestrina laughed.

"Not the stalwart captain I had expected."

Adi faced forward, intent on the open door. She was thinking about Lucas in Thail, about where they could flee. *On which moon was the Blood Queen's hold weakest?*

The gangster's influence was as wide as the emperor's. With heavy hands on her shoulders, she stumbled down a back staircase. They shoved her back into the carriage, though they did not hood her or accompany her. She wanted to scream. She needed to slow her breathing. She needed to think. She had not seen Lucas in eight years. He was fifteen now, she knew, and in danger. She needed—

Adi didn't know where to begin.

# Chapter Ten
# THEO VANGUARD
## Moon of Xys, Lensday, 29th of Hebe

The rope bit into Theo's wrists as he reached for his boot knife. Outside, his captor lit a cigarette and leaned against the shed. The pirate Crestone had identified him as Josh Mung. The door was cracked open enough that Mung could turn his head and peer in, but no one from the street could see the man bound and gagged inside. Theo did not know Captain Crestone's intentions. He had expected ransom negotiations to begin as soon as they had reached Solvigant, but she'd deposited him here with no word of their intentions and Theo was done waiting. He had fulfilled his side of the traditional transaction by surrendering, but now he was honor-bound to escape.

He was hungry. Mung had doled out periodic ladles of water, but no food. The fact that Mung had eaten nothing, either, suggested that Captain Crestone's plans had gone sideways. It was time to leave. Theo had slept poorly, dozing off only for severe cramps in his wrists and shoulders wake him. Frequent small tremors shook the dirt floor, symptoms of the moon's stress as Solo pulled her child Xys into a lethal embrace.

Mung, to his credit, had stood his post the entire time Crestone had been absent. But his concern showed as he paced further and further from the shed, muttering under his breath. Mung rolled cigarettes until he'd smoked all his tobacco. Now he flicked his lighter open and shut in a steady rhythm that Theo heard while he dozed.

He had dreamed of his father's estates in Balan outside of Thail, as a boy bouncing a ball off the stone façade of the grand fireplace. *Ping*. His father, Simon Vanguard, entering the room with two of Theo's older brothers. *Ping*. His father producing a pipe and puffing in thought while Theo's brothers argued. *Ping*. That was odd. *Ping*. His father didn't smoke. *Ping.* That was one of Theo's vices. He'd awoken to find Mung staring at him, the golden lighter in hand. Open. *Ping.* Shut. *Ping.* Open.

Mung slouched against the building in the weak daylight. Straining against the pain, Theo grasped the hilt of the small blade in his boot. His calf cramped again and he bit into the soggy gag to keep from screaming. He straightened his leg to ease the muscles, but now he had his knife. Mung turned at the scuffle of Theo's boot on the wood floor. Theo stared back. Mung looked away first. Theo switched the knife to his right hand, turned it, and sawed at the hemp rope. As strands frayed and parted the tension in his wrists eased.

"Mmmmm," Theo said into the fabric.

"Shut up," Mung said without turning.

Theo moaned again.

*"What?"* Mung glanced over his shoulder. Theo gestured with one foot toward the bucket of water. Mung sighed, flicked the lighter closed, and entered the hovel. When he bent over the bucket, Theo kicked out hard, causing the water to splash in his captor's face. Before Mung could wipe the grimy liquid from his eyes, Theo was on him, right hand clamped on Mung's mouth, left hand stabbing up between his ribs, once, twice, three times. Mung screamed against Theo's hand, elbows flailing. The fourth stab missed its mark, bouncing off a rib. Mung flung himself backward so Theo crashed hard into the wall. Weak as he was from his captivity, the force of the blow drove the wind from him and black spots popped in his vision. Mung bit down on Theo's palm and he screamed into the gag. Mung spun away and the two men faced each other.

Blood dripped from the wounds in Mung's side. Theo's right palm was on fire. Mung charged him, but faltered on the last step, gasping as his injured lung failed. Theo danced aside and his captor crashed into a set of rickety shelves, one of which held the smoky oil lamp. It sailed through the narrow space, trailing an arc of oil, and shattered on the floor.

Theo thrust his blade at Mung's throat. Mung deflected the blow, but a new slice on his forearm bled freely. Flames licked at the hem of his trousers and smoke quickly filled the small space. Theo struggled to breathe around the gag, but dared not take time to remove it. He looked toward the door. Mung followed his gaze and blocked the exit. Flame climbed his left leg, following the splatter of oil up the cloth.

Theo charged him. The rotten door gave way under the weight of the two men as they crashed into it and landed in the alley, shattered planks flying. Theo's elbow banged hard against a stone and his knife skittered away. He rolled onto Mung and knelt on the man's chest, punching him in the face and neck. The man tried to block with his arms, but one was trapped in the wreckage. Theo punched the stab wounds and Mung cried out, his body bucking. Theo hit him again, and Mung went limp. Theo rolled off him and clawed at the gag. He undid the knot and crouched, panting, beside his unconscious captor. His calves and thighs cramped, objecting to a day of confinement ending in frenetic gymnastics. Behind him the fire crackled up the walls of the hovel.

He had to get away from here before someone noticed the smoke and came to investigate. Theo steadied his breathing, stood, and retrieved his knife. Mung moaned, so Theo opened the big artery on the side of the pirate's neck. He cleaned his knife on the sailor's shirt, returned it to the sheath in his boot, then lifted Mung's body and heaved it into the hungry fire.

His right hand felt as though he was holding it to the flame. The skin of his palm was jagged and torn where Mung had bitten him. Debris from the alley had stuck to the wound. It was a dangerous injury. He picked up the gag and wrapped his hand to stanch the bleeding.

He needed food and clean water, but first he needed to leave the scene. A bell at the end of the block rang out, summoning the fire brigade. Flames engulfed the hovel, and smoke rose above the surrounding buildings. Theo knew he was in Solvigant, but he'd never been here before, and did not know where to find help. He exited the alley onto the busy street where a bucket brigade was already forming.

Theo paused to gape at the ringed giant dominating the sky. No other moon had a view like this, glorious and terrifying. Given the crowds and the diffuse sunlight, it had to be late morning, though Theo could not see the sun itself. Debris from Solo's rings burned bright in the moon's atmosphere, streaks of blue white against the pale colors of the mother planet. All around him Xyssian citizens were going about their daily lives, oblivious—or resigned—to the impending destruction of their home.

An aerogate floated above the city, its outer rings oscillating, its shimmering interior distorting the view between Xys and Solo. The bow of a massive cargo dirigible emerged from it, its props pulling it forward. The sight of the ship brought Theo back to reality. A cluster of city watchmen eyed him. Perhaps they recognized his uniform. Stories of Solvigant's corruption were legendary throughout the Empire. Theo did not want to trust local law enforcement, who might be on the payroll of some gangster. He needed Imperial troops. He set out at a confident walk, the best disguise when you did not belong somewhere. The watchmen did not follow.

He needed a change of clothes but had no money with which to purchase any. He wandered the streets, avoiding major thoroughfares. He'd grown up in the ordered grid of Thail, seat of the Solan Emperor, so the haphazard streets of this city baffled him. Some streets trailed off into narrow alleys or unfurled into wide boulevards. The blocks had no uniform size or shape. He wondered how anyone learned Solvigant's layout. Where the city of Thail on his home moon of Tyre was all carved stone, brick, and soaring glass, the City Peripatetic was wood, plaster, and mud brick. Axles protruded from walls where he expected cornerstones, the roofs were fabric where he expected slate. Many of the buildings in this section of the city were little more than tents, ready to be pulled up and mobilized in a matter of hours.

Theo turned into another narrow alley. Tenants had strung laundry lines between two small buildings to allow their clothing to dry in the dusty air. With a furtive glance to ensure no one paid him any mind, Theo snatched a shirt and trousers from a low-hanging line. Using a riderless surrey for cover, he quickly changed his clothes. He folded his uniform and tucked it under one arm. A beggar watched him from a wooden stoop but said nothing.

The governor of Xys was married to Theo's cousin. If he could find the governor's manse he could get word to his father.

*What will my father do? Does he think I'm dead?* Theo was the youngest of five brothers. His father, Simon Vanguard, usually approached him with weary apathy sharpened by chronic disappointment. Theo stood to inherit little, so over his father's strident objections he'd made a career of the Solan Navy. There, his skill and self-discipline carried more weight than his family name, and he rose through the ranks to first officer of the HMS *Dragonhammer*. This fact made him immensely proud, though his father never acknowledged it. Simon Vanguard would certainly take notice now that Blood Queen agents had stolen Apyreon from under his nose.

*And I failed to stop them,* Theo thought. He wondered where he might find Captain Crestone. After he sent word to his father, the first order of business was to discover where the Blood Queen's minions gathered. If his quarry wasn't there, someone would know where to find her. Theo hoped he could complete the mission and recover Apyreon before his father did something rash, like invade Solvigant. But he wouldn't do that.

*Would he? Probably not.* It would raise too many questions. While Theo was not privy to all his father's plans for Apyreon, he knew the existence of the artifact was still a secret from the Solan Emperor. Open war between the emperor's high chancellor and a lunar governor over secret artifacts would infuriate Emperor Callire and be met with lethal punishment.

For the first time, Theo wondered if the governor might be involved. Corruption lived like a parasite throughout Solvigant. The influence of Solvigant's crime lords had spread beyond the Wandering City, gaining footholds in other parts of the World System, in and out of the Solan Emperor's holdings.

*Could Governor Gambol be involved? His cousin?* He had only met Tabitha Loire, now Tabitha Gambol, on three occasions that he could remember. Once was on his thirteenth birthday, when his father had invited all their relatives to Theo's coming-of-age ceremony. The second was at Tabi's fifteenth birthday and her betrothal to Eliott Gambol, then a First Order Diplomat, and the third was at her wedding ten years ago. He knew her more by reputation than actual acquaintance. She'd be in her late twenties, with two or three children commanding much of her time. Hardly the sort to be involved in criminal intrigue.

The savory aroma of baked bread and sweet fruit roused Theo from his musings. He was reminded that he hadn't eaten in two days, since he'd boarded the *Dragonhammer* to ambush the *Sidereal*. He entered the bakery to the tinkle of bells before remembering he had nothing with which to purchase or even barter a pie. In the moments it took for the baker to appear, he considered stealing one.

*I could demand one as a noble of the Solan Court.* Theo quickly dismissed the idea. The baker appeared from the kitchen in the back and frowned as she took in the unwashed customer in ill-fitting clothes.

"I don't do charity," she said.

*No one would believe my claims of nobility anyway,* Theo realized. Saliva coated his mouth, his stomach twisted and growled, betraying his hunger. "Can you direct me to the governor's mansion, please?"

The woman laughed, then stopped. "You're serious?"

Theo nodded, trying not to look directly at the pies.

"Where are you from?"

"Thail." He had no reason to lie.

"Uh-huh. And you're what? Lost?"

"Quite turned around." Theo tried to sound casual. "It's my first time in Solvigant, not much order to it." He winced. *Don't insult her home.*

Hands on her hips, she sighed and muttered something that sounded like "loonies." "Head toward the aeroport. From here take your first two rights and you'll see the terminal tower rising above the buildings. Make for it. Make a left on Torhan when you reach the tower, and follow it until you reach Congress Park."

"Thank you," Theo said and left the shop. Two right turns later he saw the tower, a hodgepodge of wooden scaffolding with dirigibles floating nearby. It was the most ramshackle excuse for an airship terminal Theo had ever seen. *It's a wonder the propeller downwash from incoming ships doesn't knock it over.* Theo continued down the broad avenue in the direction of the tower and the distant drone of engines. He hoped his cousin and her household were excellent cooks.

# CHAPTER ELEVEN

# ADI CRESTONE

## MOON OF XYS, LENSDAY, 29TH OF HEBE

Adi had spent the remainder of the night in a rocking chair on the porch of Stella's Echo, refusing all offers of aid. She needed a plan, but every way she ran it she was trapped. She paced the narrow alley. Recovering Apyreon from the White Rabbits was her only path forward to protect her son. She stopped pacing and gazed at the familiar buildings as if this were her first time in Solvigant. The orange-hued light of dawn had not reached the shadow where she stood. She could feel the oily blackness of it pressing against her lungs. She took several slow, deep breaths and the knot in her chest eased.

*The Blood Queen knows about Lucas,* Adi thought for the three hundredth time since departing the Red Wyrm. *That changes everything.* She dismissed Apyreon, her dragon-stone, her own debts and freedom, and focused on her son.

Her son. *I must save my son.*

To do that, she would have to face him. It was a prospect as terrifying as losing him forever.

Adi considered retreating into Stella's Echo for a drink to take the edge off, but she had no money and a small voice in the back of her mind said, *You wouldn't stop with one anyway.*

Money. She needed a hefty amount if she was going to run. She couldn't book passage to Tyre without coin. She would need fake papers for herself and Lucas. She would need to set them up somewhere on Aleph or Maxon. That would involve time and bribes, all of which cost money.

*Maybe Iris would come.*

She made her decision. Adi would return to the safehouse, force her captive to reveal his heritage, then she would ransom him. She would use the money to collect Lucas and run. It was the best scheme she had.

*Ransoming him will take too long—slavers.* She would haul him over to Ryland's scrapyard and sell him to the Order of the Talon. Slavery was illegal on all ten moons, yet a robust black market for slaves existed in the World System. Adi had sold people into slavery before, though she did not relish it. When she and Rehka had captained the *Snowcrest* they occasionally sold the crew of captured ships. Merchant vessels needed scullers, militaries needed infantry, brothels needed mistresses, and criminal organizations needed henchmen. Its illicit nature ensured a tidy profit and kept the price of ransom high. The Blood Queen did a small trade in slaves, but Adi couldn't risk alerting Ajax or Palestrina. The only good thing about the White Rabbits was that they avoided the slave trade. That left the Order of the Talon.

With renewed purpose, if not renewed calm, Adi started across Solvigant's Iudex Quarter toward the safe house where she'd left Josh Mung to guard over her captive. The walk was long, and it looked like it would be another sweltering day. The warmth of Solvigant when it was in Veria mingled with the stench of the tanneries and the sulfurous coal smoke of the ore refineries. The shrill ring of blacksmiths' hammers striking anvils punctuated the bass rumble of the flour and textile mills. The city was waking up, stretching, groaning, taking on another day oblivious to the anchor that burdened Adi's steps. She wanted to run, but she walked.

*I'm being followed.* She used an unnecessary turn to glance back. One of the Blood Queen's thugs from the carriage sauntered twenty yards back. She ducked into a mercantile shop, startling the young woman who was opening it for the day.

"Can I help you?" the girl said. "What happened to your face?"

Adi guessed the shopkeeper was about fourteen.

"I'm fine. It's an old injury," Adi lied despite the oozing bandages. "Just browsing." There was a display of cast-iron pans behind the window. She pretended to peruse them while looking across the street at her tail. He was watching her in the reflection of the window of a haberdashery. Adi exited the mercantile and continued along the street. The man followed. Adi wandered through Solvigant's haphazard streets and considered her options.

*They'll watch me until Apyreon is returned.* She browsed a selection of bright scarves. *If they see me selling to Talon operatives, they'll know I'm planning to run.* It would be difficult to hide her intent. Best to remove the Blood Queen's eyes and ears.

Adi turned left onto a street lined with taverns. She was in the Pernix Quarter now, her safe house further away with every block. A pair of humans and a large orange Ankhim worked, elevated on scaffolding to repair the facade of one of the inns. The rigors of living in a moving city meant buildings required repair after the stress of relocation.

Adi ducked down an alley and found what she was looking for—a heavy length of scrap wood. Her tail came jogging around the corner, afraid he'd lost his mark.

"Hello there." Adi smiled and swung her makeshift club. The wood connected with the side of his skull, breaking in half from the force of the blow. The man collapsed. Adi tried to drag him deeper into the alley, but her bruised ribs protested so she let him lie where he fell. She returned to the main thoroughfare and resumed her walk. An hour later, she reached the sorry street where the safe house stood. A crowd was gathered in the street to observe a roiling black column of smoke. Adi's heart sank. She stepped around a brougham wagon with barred windows bearing the torch and stars emblem of the city watch. A white and red carriage from the physicker's guild stood in front of it.

Adi pushed her way through the gathered crowd until she reached the constable posted to deflect curious bystanders chatting with a butcher in a blood-stained apron. Both men gesticulated at something across the street. Adi walked past them with an air of a local resident. Four watchmen were pawing through the charred remains of her safehouse. Medics in their pristine white robes had pulled a body from the smoldering wreckage. Adi recognized the gray shirt and tan trousers as her crewman Josh Mung.

She walked past the scene, then approached a watchman.

"What happened to him?"

"What, who are you? You're not supposed to be here," he replied.

"Did he die in the fire?"

"Nope. Someone slit his throat and intended to hide their crime," a familiar voice said.

"Inspector Broc."

"Adison Crestone. Do you know this man?"

"Captain," Adi corrected.

"Excuse me?"

"It's Captain Crestone, and no, I don't know the man."

"Ah, yes. Captain of which ship? Oh, never mind, it doesn't matter."

"Is he the only body?"

"Were you expecting others?" Inspector Broc was calm, but his eye, black and beady, was sharp.

"I have friends who live on this street."

The inspector studied her. "He appears to be the only casualty."

Adi kept her face composed despite the dread churning her guts.

*How will I afford to flee now?* Then she berated herself for not feeling bad about Mung. Inspector Broc must have noticed this hitch in her reaction.

"Interesting that we run into each other twice in as many days."

"I was attacked!"

"So, it would seem." His eye flicked to her collar. "What are you doing here today?"

"I was at the butcher's when all the commotion started across the street."

"The butcher's?"

Adi pointed at the aproned man speaking with the constable.

"I see. And what did you purchase?"

"Excuse me?"

"At the butcher's. What did you purchase."

"Nothing, I was interrupted."

"What were you going to purchase."

"A rasher of bacon." Adi said, an edge of anger creeping into her voice.

"A rasher of bacon."

"Yes."

"A rasher of bacon," he repeated.

Adi wanted to slap the man. *What is he on about?*

His smile was all canines. "Very well, you may go." Adi started walking away. "Ah, Captain Crestone," Inspector Broc called. She turned and he flipped a coin in her direction. She caught it. One silver tower.

"For the bacon," he said. "Yesterday, you were robbed of all your money. And if I'm to call you 'Captain,' you can call me *senior* inspector."

Adi's cheeks flushed scarlet. She nodded at him, then set off down the street. The safe house contained nothing worth salvaging. Her captive was no longer captive, he was out there in the city.

*Will he come looking for me?*

Adi pushed thoughts of ransom aside. Inspector Broc's jurisdiction didn't extend off-moon. Whatever suspicions he might have of her were of no consequence. Soon, she'd either be dead or off-moon, or both.

*What would her captive do?* Would he race to the airship terminal or the shipyard and arrange passage home? Would he tell his story to the city watch? A nobleman would have connections in the Xyssian Congress. Perhaps he would take refuge at the Thalian Embassy? Depending on how blue his blood ran he might even request an audience with the governor. Adi could hardly kidnap him in broad daylight from the halls of Congress.

Then Adi groaned. There was one more person Adi could ask for money.

*I'd rather sell my own teeth than beg him for more scraps.* Yet even as she thought it, she knew she would ask.

# CHAPTER TWELVE
# ADI CRESTONE
## MOON OF XYS, LENSDAY, 29TH OF HEBE

A di's boot heels clicked a fast rhythm as she crossed the red marble flagstones of the Xyssian congressional building. Above her the intricate blue marble dome rose lofty and wide. The serene, sculpted faces of former governors and noteworthy congressional speakers watched over the small throng of morning visitors with pupil-less eyes. In the center of the great hall, a larger-than-life statue of the current Solan Emperor, Justus Solaric Callire IV, loomed, bedecked in cuirass and toga, leaning gracefully upon the Lance of the Future Moon. Tesserae of colored light ornamented his gray body and plinth where the morning light filtered through variegated stained-glass windows.

Adi preferred to visit Xander at his manse, currently near the outskirts of Solvigant. The congressional building's sheer mass oppressed Adi as no other building in the mobile city did. The paradox of its ornate stone construction spoke to the money and power that allowed it to move across the moon. She glanced over her shoulder at a group of city watchmen, expecting them to stop her. A few watched her from the periphery as she crossed the hall. She imagined a supplicant wearing the Blood Queen's collar of indenture didn't often visit here. She adjusted her scarf over the rough metal. It was her right, however, as a citizen of Solvigant to have access to her elected representatives, or at least someone from their large staff.

Had she requested an appointment, Xander's formidable secretary would suddenly discover a reason the congressman's schedule prevented him from meeting with her. Today, it was imperative that she catch Xander unaware. She couldn't allow him time to prepare for this conversation. This was the only way she could be certain he hadn't revealed Lucas's existence to the Blood Queen and her minions.

*If he told her, I'll*—that thought was the extent of her plan. She couldn't very well murder a congressional delegate. *What would it mean for Lucas if he lost his benefactor?* She pushed these thoughts aside and focused on her anger, the anger that she pretended was not fear.

Xander's office was on the third floor. She waited until the security staff was preoccupied with a group of Daughters of Light, women who devoted themselves to worship the Goddess of Light, Phoebe, daughter of Solo. The guards who had noticed her entry were now on the opposite side of the great hall. Adi slipped under a heavy, velvet rope and ran up an ancillary flight of stairs.

The stairs curved around the outside of the circular great hall. At each landing Adi waited for a ten count to make sure no one emerged from any of the doorways before she scampered past. The third-floor hallway bustled with activity as staff members, suppliants, and errand boys hustled back and forth, preoccupied with their various missions, each confident of its vital importance to greasing the wheels of state. Now that she had made it this far, no one noticed her. She was another cog in the machine, another drone in the hive. No one questioned her when Adi took a wrong turn down a green-carpeted hallway and had to double back.

The situation changed when she arrived at Xander's office. Adi set her shoulders and flung open the door. Melanie Krimpet, Xander's chief secretary and the oldest daughter of Viscount Toller Krimpet, recognized Adi. Melanie rushed to block the inner office door, which was shut.

"You can't go in there," Ms. Krimpet said as she snapped to attention in front of the door handle. Adi uttered a low, guttural snarl, her fists clenched, knuckles white. Melanie raised her hands as if to offer resistance. Adi thought she might have to punch the woman, but Ms. Krimpet faltered under Adi's glare. Adi shoved her aside, then plunged through the door.

"That's why it's imperative we hold the vote before the end of the month."

Xander was speaking to an ornately dressed cleric. The cleric yelped when the door slammed against the stone wall of the small office. Xander took two strides across the room, his hand resting on an ivory drawer pull. Recognition crossed his face, and the drawer remained shut.

"Adi! what in the Nine Gods—" he began.

"You know this woman?" the cleric said, attempting to mask his damaged composure under his stern tone. Adi recognized the man as Archdeacon Limon Heilig, the head of the Church of the Nine on Xys. She knew him by reputation and had seen him speak in the Temple of the Nine on holy days. He took in her bruised face and ill-fitting clothes with disdain and an arrogant sniff. Adi made the sign of the Ring and executed a brief curtsy. Then she glanced around the room, looking for a sentry. There wasn't one.

"We need to talk, Xander." No one moved. Adi watched Xander's eyes. She saw surprise, shock, even mild amusement, but he had not been expecting her. There was no fear, no premonition of a reckoning. *He's not guilty. The Blood Queen's information didn't come from him.* Adi's anger eased but her voice stayed firm. "Now."

Xander straightened his cravat. "Father, if you would excuse us. I apologize for the intrusion, but I have an... unexpected scheduling conflict."

The cleric puffed out his chest, preparing to object. Adi took one purposeful step forward and his protest deflated into a huff.

"I see that, Congressman. I will report this treatment to the Brotherhood." He glanced at Adi's poorly concealed collar.

"Do what you must," Xander said, but his eyes held Adi's.

Affronted that Xander hadn't defended him in front of this shabby ruffian, the cleric moved toward the door. Adi shifted to one side, but he was forced to squeeze around her. She shut the door behind the cleric, and when she looked back at Xander she saw his rage.

"What, Adi? You can't just barge into my office whenever you want. Certainly not with that!" He pointed at her collar. "I have a reputation. Now the clergy will suspect me of consorting with the Blood Queen. How, by Solo's divine fury, did you get in here anyway? Where's Melanie? I swear if you've harmed a member of my staff, I'll have you arrested. In fact, I'm half inclined to call the guard and have you arrested anyway. Do you know who that was? No of course you don't. Why would you? Some people have more going on in their lives than fixing your pathetic messes. I swear. I know I owe you, but I don't owe you this. There's a limit to what I can do, to what I will do because of the sins of my brother. Why don't you make his life miserable? He's the one who deserves it."

Adi waited until he paused to catch his breath.

"Well?" he said at last.

"The Blood Queen knows of Lucas."

Xander deflated. "What? How?"

"I thought you could tell me."

He collapsed into the leather chair. "You don't think I...?"

Adi was certain he was telling the truth, but she needed clear confirmation. She placed her hands on his desk and leaned forward. He shrank back.

"Did you tell her about Lucas?"

"No. I would never. I don't speak with the Blood Queen at all. Unlike some of my colleagues, I have nothing to do with the criminal element in this city."

"Did you tell Sasha Riven about my son to hurt me?"

Xander rose. "I would never give up my son to that filth."

"He's not your son."

"As you're so keen to remind me," he said through clenched teeth.

Adi was sure now. She had hurt Xander, and he hadn't flinched. He was not the informant.

"You're sure she knows?" Xander's voice was soft now.

Adi nodded, fighting back unwelcome tears. She bit one knuckle before dropping her hand, embarrassed at her weakness. She sank into the chair opposite Xander's desk.

"Ajax has Osmen on Tyre monitoring him. He's not safe. You must help me get to him."

"Wouldn't that put him in greater danger?"

"There must be somewhere I can take him that's safe. Our son—*my* son is in danger."

"I'm only his father when it's convenient for you."

"I know. I'm sorry." *He's more of Lucas's parent than I am,* Adi thought, swallowing the old guilt. She could see Xander agreed with her, though he had the grace not to say it.

On Adi's thirteenth birthday, her father had betrothed her to Xander Marrion, the eldest son of the Sabaian duke of Viridia, and heir to the family fortune. As far as Adi knew, her father had never come looking for her when she ran away at fifteen. But Xander had. He'd spent three years scouring four moons before he found her on Xys. She had refused to return with him, and he had chosen to stay. He told his father he wanted to make a different life for himself away from the brutal infighting of the Sabaian court and had been disinherited for his troubles.

"What should I do?" Adi asked. "I need to go to him."

"The minute the Blood Queen learns you're on an airship to Tyre, Lucas will be in danger."

"He's in danger now!"

Ms. Krimpet poked her head into the office. "Sir, your next appointment is here."

"He can wait," Xander said.

"Sir, it's—"

"I said he can wait." He slapped his hand on the desk to emphasize the point, then caught himself. "I'm sorry, Melanie. Please offer the governor's envoy whatever refreshment he'll take and apologize on my behalf. I'll be with him momentarily."

Melanie nodded and closed the door.

"Really?" Adi had little experience in the political realm but knew that one did not keep the governor's envoy waiting.

Xander waved his hand. "It's nothing. Why is the Blood Queen using Lucas to threaten you?"

Adi bristled, then bit back a sharp retort. She gripped the chair's carved arms.

"Well?" Xander was distracted now, his glance flicking to the door as if he could see into the waiting room beyond.

"When you found me here on Xys all those years ago, why didn't you tell anyone?"

"You asked me not to."

"Your father disinherited you and my father forbade you from returning to Saba."

"I'm well aware of my misfortune on your behalf," Xander snapped. His shoulders dropped. "I was in love with you, and our betrothal was part of my duty to my family."

"Duty is the leading cause of death among the nobility. And do you love me now?"

"What does this have to do with anything?"

Adi waited.

Xander nodded. "You know I do."

Half of Adi soared at his admission, honored by the sacrifice Xander had made for her freedom. The other half recoiled. When Xander was himself, he was proud and confident, a good statesman. Now that the danger to Lucas made Xander vulnerable, his face changed and she saw his younger brother Hubert, the man who had stolen her innocence. Someday, she would wring Hubert's neck.

She almost told Xander everything then, her honesty spurred on by his. But then she felt the two halves of herself reconverge and the logic of her situation took over. If she confessed to Xander that she'd acquired a powerful star key for the Blood Queen and subsequently lost it, she didn't know what he'd do, but martial law and door-to-door searches were within his ability.

"She wants me to acquire an artifact." Adi paused and considered how far she wanted to go with the truth. She didn't want to put Xander in too untenable a position, nor did she want to engage his instinct toward heroism at the gravity of her task.

"Where is it?"

"It's here in Solvigant. Stuart Royal has it."

"The leader of the White Rabbits?"

"The one and only."

"No mean feat. Royal and his goons are well protected in the Warrens. I understand the city watch has little presence there."

*You have no idea,* Adi thought.

"What does she want with the artifact? What is it?"

"No idea," Adi lied, "The Blood Queen does not share her plans with low level indentures."

"I suppose you need money?"

Adi nodded.

"Of course you do." He sighed and his defensive bulwarks returned. "If only you'd asked for help before letting Ajax clamp that hideous thing around your neck, then we wouldn't be in this mess."

*We?* Adi started to say it aloud but stopped. He was entangled in her mistakes. "Despite your ideas to the contrary, I have some pride." Xander held up his hands in surrender. Adi pressed on, though it hurt her to say it. "I know how much you've sacrificed for me, and if we weren't worried over Lucas's safety I wouldn't ask now."

She hoped Xander couldn't detect her lies. She really needed money to locate Apyreon. There would be bribes to pay, gear to assemble, and, gods, she needed a stiff drink. Her mind strayed back to Stella's Echo and Iris's pallet.

"Do you really think Sasha Riven will let you go when she holds so much power over you?" Xander asked.

"What choice do I have?"

Xander sighed. His shoulders slumped. "How much do you need?"

"One hundred gold spyres should do it."

His eyes widened. It wasn't a huge sum, but it wasn't a small one either.

"Finding a magical astrolabe in a corrupt city of millions isn't cheap," Adi said. "And I've lost all my gear."

Xander shook his head. "There is another way around all this."

"No, Xan, we've been over this. We're not betrothed anymore." Adi adjusted her collar, which suddenly chafed.

"I'll have Melanie draw up a withdrawal notice."

"She likes you, you know."

"What? Who?"

"Melanie." Adi had seen the way Melanie watched Xander. Adi had deduced that they weren't sleeping together, but Melanie was an attractive woman and the eldest daughter of a viscount with no sons. If they married, Xander would inherit when Melanie's father passed. For a Xyssian congressional delegate, banned from his home and stripped of his titles, Xander could do worse.

Xander dismissed this with a wave of his hand. She sensed he was preoccupied by thoughts of Lucas and the governor's envoy. A tentative knock came from the other side of the door.

Xander stood, leaned across the desk, and put a hand on Adi's. She fought the urge to pull away.

"Lucas is *your* son. Make this right, Adi, for all of us."

Adi stood, knocking the chair aside in her haste to hide fresh tears. *When did I become someone who cries all the time?*

"You've given Lucas the chance for a good life on Tyre," Adi managed, her eyes on the parqueted floor. "I have to protect that."

She quickly strode from the room, dodging around the governor's envoy who was standing pensively on the far side of the door. She handed Xander's withdrawal slip to Melanie, who read it and frowned, then stepped to the safe on the far wall of the reception area and began to cycle through the combination.

"If you're not going to marry him," Melanie said, "you could stop begging for his money."

Adi flushed deep crimson and swallowed her anger. *This is for Lucas. Wasn't it always though?*

"This is the last time," Adi said.

Melanie clicked her tongue, skeptical.

"I swear it," Adi continued, and realized she meant it. When this business with Lucas and Apyreon was over, she would cut ties with Xander for good. She knew it was the only way he would move on.

Adi took a step forward as Melanie counted coins into a leather satchel. "You know Xander is a good man, a loyal man. He doesn't love me the way he thinks he does. He needs someone who can reciprocate his feelings. He needs someone deserving."

Melanie turned and thrust the heavy purse toward her. "Are you suggesting that's me?"

"I've seen the way you look at him."

"And I've seen the way he looks at you. If you honestly think he doesn't love you, you're as delusional as he is and you two deserve each other."

Adi cleared her throat. "He will learn to love someone else."

Melanie scowled hands on her hips. "You tell yourself whatever you need to feel better about manipulating a good man. Every time you walk in here, every time you visit his estate, every time you reject his proposals, he dies a little bit. You're killing that man."

"I'm not—"

Melanie held up a hand. "Take your blood money and go. Congressman Marrion has a busy afternoon. Funding whores who play pirate is no longer on the schedule."

Adi had been called a whore before, most especially during her time at the Echo. Under normal circumstances it was an invitation to fight. She clenched her fists until her knuckles whitened, but she dared not strike Melanie in Xander's office.

Instead, she curtsied, her mouth in a tight line as she ground her teeth. "You're right of course."

Hot tears welled at the corners of her eyes, and she excused herself and fled back to the safety of Stella's Echo. Outside, a fitful wind blew, the precursor to an approaching sandstorm.

## Chapter Thirteen
# THEO VANGUARD
### MOON OF XYS, LENSDAY, 29TH OF HEBE

Wind blew between the buildings, buffeting Theo as he turned down Torhan toward Congress Park. In the distance, strange russet storm clouds rose from the ground rather than building in the sky. By the time he arrived at the incongruous green park, traces of grit swirled in the air and caught in the corners of his lips and eyes. Theo had never experienced a sandstorm. He hoped he would be safe indoors before it struck.

The governor's mansion was a rambling, single-story wooden structure; a mansion more by sprawl than by grandeur. The eastern portion of the roof sagged, while the central hall was encased in scaffolding. Everywhere, Theo saw indications of the building's mobility. The structure consisted of separate cubic sections that joined together. The exterior sported the intricate ornamentation common to most castles, but it lacked conventional defensive structures and stonework, though skilled carpenters had created crenelations along the eaves, thick enough that they might be able act as gun emplacements if needed. Gargoyles yawned with gaping maws from dry gutters.

Citizens of Solvigant could petition their elected representatives, but they did not have access to the governor's mansion. The avenue had emptied as the storm advanced, and the two guards at the gate were crouched in their respective sentry booths, eyeing the sky and muttering. Theo approached the large gate whose abundant vine-and-leaf iron work looked out of place here on the edge of the desert. One of the sentries stopped him. The man was a member of the elite Ring Guard tasked with protecting the Solan Emperor, the seven governors, the emperor's chancellors, and members of the royal family. Theo halted as instructed before the short Grym and executed a smart salute. He knew better than to underestimate the fighting prowess of a Grym despite its diminutive stature.

"State your business, sir." The guard's reluctance to step into the abrasive wind to deal with this newcomer put an edge on his voice.

"Theo Vanguard of House Vanguard to see Her Lady Tabitha Gambol."

The Grym looked Theo up and down and snorted. "Is the lady expecting you?"

"She is not." Theo took his uniform from under his arm and removed one of the silver epaulets that indicated his rank. "Please provide this to her ladyship should she require proof of my station."

The Grym coughed to hide his surprise, stamped the haft of his polearm in the dust, and offered a brisk salute.

"Sir! Apologies, sir. I—"

"I do not presently look the part, Corporal. No need to apologize."

The Grym signaled for his partner to wait with the visitor before disappearing into the house.

Theo waited. The storm was upon them. Skiffs of wind-whipped sand hissed along the street and against the closed shutters of the palace. Theo waved the other sentry back into the shelter of his booth. He worried that Tabitha would refuse to see him.

*What's your backup plan Theo?* He didn't have one. His self-recrimination stopped when the Grym soldier returned and hustled him through the gate.

"The Lady Gambol welcomes you, sir, and bids you join her in the parlor."

Theo released a long breath, annoyed by the grit on his tongue.

"Lead the way," he said gesturing to the soldier. They hurried across the grassy court-yard. It was a bleak garden, lacking plantings and shrubs. The grass was coarse and losing its battle against the encroaching sand. Theo felt a sharp pang of homesickness. He remembered the lush lawns and formal gardens of Tyre which invited one to nap amid shady glades.

The soldier rapped on the heavy front doors. They opened inward and a maidservant, no older than sixteen, curtsied.

"Welcome, Sir Vanguard. This way, please."

Theo bowed and stepped into the foyer, grateful to be out of the ferocious wind. He stomped his boots and tried to brush the sand from his clothing so he would not track it deeper into the corridor. The maidservant took a lamp from its sconce and guided him through another doorway. Theo hastened to follow.

The foyer and hall were broader and more open than he had expected. Thick tapestries lined the floors, oil lamps burned in their sconces and reflected warm light across half a dozen polished suits of armor. Servants bustled to and fro from a door in the rear. Judging from the savory aromas of thyme and baked apples, Theo thought it must be the kitchen. Theo's stomach growled loudly enough that the maidservant's eyes widened in surprise before she blushed and looked away. A gust of wind slammed the shutters as he passed a closed window.

The house rambled, like the city which surrounded it. Theo wondered if they arranged the cubic sections the same way after each parapatesis. He lost his sense of direction in the maze of hallways and corridors.

*How big is this place, anyway?* he thought. At last, the maid knocked softly on a half-open door.

"Enter," came a woman's voice from within.

Theo stepped into the room and coughed to hide his shock. The woman sitting on the blue upholstered chair was his cousin, but she had diminished since her wedding a decade ago. She was so pale and thin that triangular hollows above her collarbones framed her throat. Her high cheekbones, once rosy, held no color, and even her expression looked brittle. She dabbed at the sweat on her face and neck with a silk handkerchief held in delicate fingers. Even from across the room in dim light, Theo could discern the blue veins lacing the backs of her hands and the sharp knobs of her wrist bones jutting from her cuffs. Yet her green eyes still shone with intelligence and interest just as he had remembered.

A physicker in pristine white robes snapped closed the clasps on his bag.

"I'll see you next week, Lady Gambol," he said, collecting his hat from a side table.

"Thank you, Dr. Mallory." Tabitha rose unsteadily to her feet and curtsied. Theo bowed. Then they both laughed at their own formalities and embraced. Her skin felt hot against Theo's palms and when he kissed her cheek.

"Theo! What an unexpected delight." Tabi took a step back and looked him over. "Uncle did not inform us that you were coming."

"I had not planned to be here. I was kidnapped by pirates on Tyre and brought to Xys by force."

"By the Nine, Theo, are you all right?"

"I'm starving and I could use a wash, but otherwise I'm no worse for wear." Theo turned and spoke to the departing physicker. "Dr. Mallory, is it? Would you have a moment to inspect this wound?" Theo extended his hand toward the man who *tsk*ed at the bloody bandage.

"Of course he will," Tabitha said, "Maybelle, hurry to the kitchens and bring our guest something to eat."

The maidservant curtsied and disappeared from the parlor.

"Have a seat here, please, sir." The physicker indicated a brocade divan. Theo sat. Tabitha dropped back into her own seat, dabbing her forehead and upper lip with her handkerchief.

Dr. Mallory knelt beside Theo, who winced and clenched his teeth as the man snipped the makeshift bandage and gingerly pried it off the clotted wound.

Tabitha said, "What a dreadful adventure you've had, cousin, I cannot imagine. But you escaped?"

"Yes, I did. I suspect the pirate captain who captured me met with some mishap, as she left and did not return for two days. The guard set to watch me grew tired and I seized the opportunity. They meant to ransom me—" Theo hissed and bit back a harsh word.

The physicker had sterilized a pair of tweezers in candle flame and was picking debris from the gash. Theo curled his toes inside his boots and concentrated on breathing slowly through his nose and holding still so the man could work. Next, Dr. Mallory trimmed the dead, ragged edges of the skin, then smeared a reeking green salve into the wound. It stung as badly as it smelled.

"'Tis a bad place for a slash, sir," Dr. Mallory said. "And your opponent's blade was none too sharp, so the cut is not clean; sutures would not hold." He rummaged in his bag and brought out four rolls of white bandage. "Keep it covered. Soak and change the bandage every day—if you take it off wet it will not tear off the scab. Let it dry, apply the salve, and bind it again. I'm afraid I only have these four rolls with me, but it will get you started." He opened Theo's hand until it was flat and began to wrap it.

"Have you spoken to your father yet? Does he know you were abducted?" Tabitha asked.

Theo focused on her face to distract himself from the physicker's work. "No, I had no way to reach him. I was at a loss after my escape until I recalled you had wed Governor Gambol and would be in residence here. I came straightaway to ask for his assistance." His hand burned. Theo wanted to clench it into a fist, but Dr. Mallory's clever wrapping prevented that. "But, Tabi, I had not heard you were ill. Is there anything I can do for you?"

Tabitha looked away, plucking at the lace of her cuffs. "Dr. Mallory says it's Feverfire sickness. When we arrived here after the wedding, Solvigant was in Amar. The disease is known there, though rare."

"The Nine's curse, Tabi, have you been ill all these years?"

Lady Gambol coughed into her sweat-stained handkerchief. "I'm afraid so."

"Why haven't you written? Have you seen the Astral physickers at the temple on Karis? Spoken to a Dragon healer?"

Theo saw Doctor Mallory's shoulders stiffen as he packed his bag and closed it. Decorum prevented him from speaking unless addressed. Theo recalled the animosity between the different sects of physickers and realized his misstep.

"Of course, cousin," Tabi reassured him. "But there is nothing to be done for Feverfire, I'm afraid. They can only make me comfortable and slow its advance."

"Tabi, I'm sorry. Are your children at risk?"

"I have no children, cousin. The disease prevents it."

"But your husband—" Theo bit back the rest of his remark before he made another misstep.

"Has other pursuits." Tabitha's eyes moved to the door where Maybelle appeared carrying a tray with several covered dishes and a steaming teapot.

Dr. Mallory stood and Theo looked back at him. "I appreciate your rapid treatment, Doctor."

Mallory again picked up his hat and bag and inclined his head, accepting Theo's thanks. "You must flex that hand several times per day, sir. The cut spared the tendons, but the scar may make that hand stiff if you're not careful. Have Lady Gambol contact me if you require anything further."

"Indeed."

"Maybelle, please escort Dr. Mallory to the kitchen. He can wait out the storm here and must want some dinner by now."

"Thank you, my lady." The physicker bowed to Tabitha and Maybelle led him out past a footman and a kitchen girl who entered with a small table. In moments they had laid out a full place setting for Theo's meal. When he sat, the footman uncovered the dishes.

"Will that be all, sir?"

"Yes, this is splendid." Theo fell to and Tabi dismissed the staff.

*What the house lacks in opulence they more than make up for in hospitality,* Theo thought.

"I beg your pardon, cousin," Theo said looking up from his food "Two days as an unfed captive has given me the manners of a Dragon." He wiped the grease from his chin with a monogramed napkin. His bandaged right hand made managing his knife difficult.

"By the Nine, Theo, please tuck in. I only wish my husband and I had known of your predicament sooner; we would have alerted the city watch."

They heard a crisp knock, and a male voice said, "Tabi? Dear, are you all right?"

"Eliot, my love, we have an unexpected visitor."

The door opened and the governor of Xys, Eliot Gambol entered. Theo scrambled to his feet and saluted the governor. Tabitha stood, leaning against the arm of the couch. Theo caught the warmth in her expression when she looked at her husband and hoped Lord Gambol was worthy of his cousin's devotion.

Gambol was short for a human male, barely a hand's breadth above five feet, and stocky, once well-muscled but now subsiding into fat, his active days behind him and long years at a desk taking their toll. Yet his posture remained impeccable, his chest broad and shoulders straight. Theo thought the governor must be a generation older than his wife. His gray hair stuck out in unruly tufts, which he smoothed with one palm every few minutes.

"I heard you had company," Eliot said.

"This is my cousin, First Officer Theo Vanguard, fifth son of High Chancellor Simon Vanguard of Tyre."

Gambol displayed a flicker of displeasure at the mention of the high chancellor.

Theo inclined his head to his host. "A pleasure, sir, Many thanks for your generous hospitality. I apologize for my disheveled appearance, but I have had a few challenging days."

Eliot Gambol took in Theo—his ill-fitting peasant's garb, the smears of lamb grease still on his cheeks, the bandaged hand—and clicked his tongue. Then he looked at Tabitha.

"My darling, our dinner guests have arrived. Do you feel well enough to join us this evening?"

Theo thought the man's tone indicated that he preferred his wife to say no. The rules of formal dining, however, demanded the lady's presence.

Tabi curtsied. "Of course, husband. Would you have the servants set a place for my cousin, please?"

The governor's attention returned to Theo. His nostrils flared and Theo suspected that the governor could smell the smoke, gunpowder, dried blood, sweat, and alley filth Theo had accumulated over the previous days. "Do you have something more suitable to wear, young man?"

"No, sir. My uniform did not survive my recent battle and captivity intact." Theo smiled. The governor did not.

Gambol harrumphed. "We will see what we can do. I'll have a footman attend you for a bath. We'll find you proper attire. Someone will be with you shortly." He turned his back on Theo and offered his wife an arm. "If you would accompany me to the dining room my dear."

"Of course." Tabitha needed his support as they walked from the room. She looked slight and fragile beside the old soldier, and Theo fretted that the vivacious girl he'd known in his youth was now so impaired.

A footman arrived just as Theo was gulping down the last of his cider.

"If you would follow me, sir, we will dress you for dinner."

Theo took a hasty hot bath. He longed for a soak but worried about arriving too late for the formal meal. When he was finished the footman presented him with a pile of clothing.

"Apologies, sir, we do not have an exact match for your height."

"We shall make do," Theo said, blotting the last of the water from his hair and pushed it back out of his eyes.

Theo donned formal white breeches, a shirt with a cummerbund, and a red dinner jacket. The frilled collar of the shirt made him feel foppish and it was tight at the biceps and across his shoulders. The breeches were too short, but his boots were high and hid this problem, and he had to fight the urge to pull down at the crotch. He salvaged the Anchor, the Bear, and the Dolphin from his uniform, symbols of the Royal Navy, House Vanguard, and his rank respectively, and affixed them to his lapel.

He combed his hair and pulled on his boots, which he saw had been cleaned and polished as he bathed.

*This will have to do.* Then Theo yawned, as though being warm, clean, and dry suddenly released days of accumulated fatigue.

*I hope I don't fall asleep in my soup.*

Theo followed the footman through the twisting corridors of the mansion toward the dining hall. His stomach growled again.

# CHAPTER FOURTEEN

# ION RUCINARE

## MOON OF XYS, LENSDAY, 29TH OF HEBE

I on heaved against the weight of the rowboat, dragging it from the breakers of the Boiled Sea onto the sandy shoreline. Thunderheads towered far out over the water. Though the storm was still some distance off, he could make out the occasional bolt of lightning as it sliced downward toward the choppy sea. He knew better than to get caught out in a gale such as that. On his first day fishing alone, Ion was determined to be extra careful.

Sweat dripped into his eyes, and he wiped it away with one tattered sleeve. Behind him the wreckage of the *Sidereal* smoldered. Its astral components kept the fire alive long after the wooden structure was reduced to ash. Ion was relieved to see his grandfather making his unsteady way down the boardwalk from Castes, leaning heavily on his cane. The boy yanked his catch from the boat. Considering that most days they caught nothing, two skipjacks and a snapper were an impressive catch. The skipjacks were small, stretching from his wrist to the tip of his index finger, and the snapper barely fit in the palm of his hand. Still, his stomach rumbled in anticipation of the meager feast.

"Look, Grandpa!" Ion held up the fish for the man's perusal. His grandfather was pale, his skin clammy even in the intense heat of the desert in mid-afternoon. The great, ringed planet Solo scorched them like ants under a magnifying glass.

"Great work, Ion, that's a good haul." His grandfather coughed and smacked his chest. "And all by yourself."

Ion stood up straight. "I pulled both oars, too."

"You're turning into a strong lad," his grandfather said. It was a pleasant falsehood. Living at the edge of civilization on a dying moon had reduced them to tanned skin, sinew, and bones. His grandfather ruffled Ion's hair. "Guess what I found to accompany them?"

"What?"

"Beans."

Ion's face fell. "I hate beans."

"But—" Then his grandfather produced an oily handkerchief from a threadbare pocket. He unwrapped it like a prize, and in his palm was a one-inch cube of pork fat.

"Bacon!" Ion cried with a whoop and bounce. "Where?"

"Alicia, the general store owner's wife, owed me a favor."

Ion whooped again, "I told you that pirate treasure was good luck."

His grandfather smiled. "So you did. Come on, let's get those fish back to the house before they cook out here." He coughed again, then spat a gob of phlegm into the sand.

Ion slung his catch over his shoulder, took his grandfather's elbow to steady him, and the two made their way up the boardwalk toward Castes and their small wooden shack.

Castes had never been a large town. Despite its oceanfront location, it was too far into the desert to merit consideration as a pilgrimage site for Solvigant. Instead, it had functioned as a small oasis along the translunar terrane line so steam-powered terranes could stop and fill their boilers. A gaiagate migrated through the edges of town, so people from other moons could arrive in Castes and catch the terrane to Solvigant. Unfortunately, the other end of the gate migrated through an equally run-down backwater on Karis, so few travelers used it.

There had once been a modest dock for a distant hydrogate when the Boiled Sea was known as the Windlass Sea. But since Pallantier's disappearance had forced Xys into its slow, final descent into the Mother's embrace, no one on the other end of the gate was willing to risk the journey.

Ion watched as the older man gutted and prepped the fish with a sharp knife and deft hands. Ion poked at the cook fire with a gnarled length of the ubiquitous mesquite wood. "Grandpa?"

"Yes?"

"Why don't we go to Solvigant? Everything here is dying."

"Everything in Solvigant dies, too. The whole moon is finished, you know, not just Castes."

"I know, but there's people in the city"—his stomach rumbled—"and food."

"We have food here."

Ion eyed the meager fish. It was not the first time he had pressed his grandfather on this issue. He heard the shrill whistle of a terrane pulling into Castes Station. The towns east of Castes were long abandoned, so the terrane ran only between here and Solvigant. When the city moved, the terrane would alter course, stopping in Castes less frequently for a decade or so until the city returned to Veria. If Xys lasted that long.

"We could leave Xys. I heard Gaash has snow sometimes. I'd love to see snow."

"Who told you that?"

"Cornyn."

Cornyn was the town drunk. He was harmless enough and could usually be found on the steps of the old Temple of the Nine, singing, drinking, or muttering to himself.

"I told you to stay away from Coryn."

"Grandpa, there's only twenty people in town. You've told me to stay away from most of them."

"As well you should." His grandfather punctuated the point with his filleting knife.

Ion sighed and stirred the beans. The rich oils of cooking pig fat made his mouth water. "I hate it here."

His grandfather stopped carving the fish. "I grew up here. It's a respectable town."

"Maybe it was. There's not even a school here. Djinnar's blood, I'm the only kid in the whole place."

"Watch your language."

"Sorry," Ion said and lowered his voice, "but it's true."

"What was good enough for your grandpa isn't good enough for you?"

"It wasn't good enough for my parents."

"Their absence has nothing to do with you or Castes."

Ion hunched and scuffed the dirt floor with one foot. Every day they fished. On good days, they cooked and ate their meager catch. Most days they had the same conversation.

"Where are they?"

"I don't know."

Ion sighed and shuffled outside to hide his tears. The shack stood atop a small hillock on the boundary between the sparse grass of the oasis and the ever-encroaching sand. Its only redeeming quality was the view. To the left he could watch the storm rage over the Boiled Sea. To the right, the distant sun set over Castes. Ion flipped the thieves glass Captain Crestone had given him between dirty fingers.

*Pirate booty. Enough to leave this stupid place,* he thought. Every night since the pretty pirate and her bedraggled crew had passed through Castes, he had dreamed himself on the seas of Tyre or Maxon or Gaash. *Pirate King Ion,* people would say, *please, it's all the gold we have,* or *please, a kiss from the pirate king* and he would bestow it with a laugh. *Oh, Ion,* Captain Crestone would say, *I'm lucky to count you as one of my crew.* Then she would kiss him on top of his head, ruffle his hair, and he would pretend to hate it.

But each day he woke, pulled on his much-mended trousers and thin shirt, and went down to the boat for another day of fishing. He longed to get away from this dying moon to a place where food was plentiful and he could go to school. But he couldn't leave his grandfather, who, the Nine curse him, would never leave his hometown.

Ion had managed his fantasies until real pirate treasure sat heavily in his pocket, undeniable proof of the World System beyond this wretched place.

The wind had picked up, whisking sand off the dune crests and stinging Ion's bare shins. A flash of lightning illuminated a small boat, sails unfurled, running at full speed before the storm. It was headed toward their beach.

"Grandpa!"

"Not now, Ion, the fish are almost done."

"Grandpa, there's a boat."

"What?" His grandfather stepped outside. "Fools must've used the hydrogate."

"I thought it was closed."

"Not closed, just no reason to use it. There's plenty of other gates connecting Xys and Tyre much closer to Solvigant."

The two watched the boat buck and wallow when it reached the surf zone. It dropped its sails and oars thrashed the turbulent water, driving it toward shore.

"Should we go down and help?" Ion asked.

"Better to mind our own business."

"They could be in trouble." *They could be more pirates!*

"They know what they're about—" Grandfather started, but Ion bolted down the hill, taking the shortcut down the dune face, leaping and sliding toward the beach.

He arrived a few moments before the ship landed. He saw no name painted on the gunwales, no blazon on the slack sails. The crew ran it hard against the shingle until the prow plowed through sand and the ship shuddered to a stop. Ion scampered backward to avoid being run over.

A rope ladder dropped from the port bow and four men landed on the beach. They spoke the common tongue with thick Tyrian accents.

The sailors were two men and two Ankhim. They wore loose, gray robes wet from the distant storm over the hydrogate. The Ankhim were gray, darker than their robes, their skin marking them as Cavern Clan. White tattooed lines in no discernible pattern were etched into their skin, peeking out from sleeves and above collars.

A fifth man wore full-length black robes with a hood pulled over his head. He wore the forehead, nose, and upper jaw of a gleaming human skull over his face so that only his chin was visible, which was obscured by a great beard that fell all the way to his belly. To Ion, he was a figure out of legend and fit neatly into the boy's ongoing fantasies about adventure.

"You're a void mage!" Ion said, bouncing on his toes.

The whole party turned at the sound of his voice. The two men reached for the short swords secured in scabbards on their leather belts. Ion froze, his hands clammy despite the evening heat.

The void mage motioned with one hand and the men relaxed. He approached Ion and knelt, so the sockets of his bone mask were level with Ion's eyes. Ion stepped back, poised to run. Up close, the man smelled like the air after a lightning strike. The hair on the nape of his neck and arms rose and he felt queasy. He met the mage's green shattered eyes through the mask. They were human and unkind. Ion trembled, and he told himself that it was just a man beneath the costume.

"Who are you, boy?" The mage's voice was soft, and reassured Ion.

"Ion."

"What are you doing here on the beach?"

"That's my fishing boat."

The mage looked at the boat, then out at the storm-tossed waters. "A brave lad to sail that."

"Thank you, sir."

The mage closed his hand on Ion's wrist, holding him in place. Ion tried to pull away and the grip tightened.

"Let go of the boy," Ion's grandfather gasped, breathless from hurrying down the boardwalk.

Ion tried again to free himself, but the mage was strong.

"Have you seen any pirates recently, Ion?" the mage asked.

"No." Ion's voice cracked. He hated that.

The void mage looked past Ion toward the wreck of the *Sidereal*.

"Are you sure?"

"I'm sure."

"Let go of him," his grandfather hissed.

The mage ignored him and reached into Ion's pocket. He removed the thieves' glass.

"Where did you get this?"

"Hey! That's mine!" Ion reached for it, but the mage snatched it away.

"Were you paid for your silence?"

Ion didn't understand. He saw his one chance to escape Xys with his grandfather disappear inside the mage's black robes.

"I'm going to ask you again," the void mage said, "and if you lie to me, my man here will kill your grandpa." A robed sailor seized the old man, clamping one arm across his chest and holding a dagger against his fragile neck.

"You wouldn't," Ion sniffled.

"Test me, boy, and find out. Who came on that ship?" The mage gestured toward the *Sidereal*.

Ion glared defiantly at the shattered pupils behind the bone mask. The void mage sighed and the man holding Ion's grandfather slid the knife along his throat. Crimson blood spilled down his chest and soaked into his shirt. The man's knees buckled and air bubbles appeared in the blood.

"No!" Ion shrieked. His grandfather pitched forward onto the sand, his blood staining it brown. Ion tried to run to him, but the mage held him fast.

"Who came through on that ship?"

Ion could barely see through his tears. "A lady," he sobbed, "with three pirates and another man." The grip on Ion's wrist hurt now.

"Tell me about this other man."

"He wore a black uniform." Ion choked on his tears and was unable to take a deep breath. "He was all tied up. I don't know who he was. They didn't talk about him."

"Good boy," the mage said as he released Ion.

Ion staggered backward and tripped over his grandfather's body. He threw himself on the man, weeping. A shadow fell across him, but Ion was too grief-stricken to care that they might kill him next. His parents had abandoned him, and his grandfather was murdered. He was truly alone now.

"Where were they headed?" the mage asked from above.

"They boarded the terrane for Solvigant three days ago," Ion said between sobs.

The mage stood and sniffed the air like a dog seeking scraps.

An Ankhim addressed the crew in Tyrian and two men jogged toward the *Sidereal*'s remains. The others clambered onto their boat then returned moments later with bulging rucksacks. An Ankhim threw a large anchor down onto the sand.

Ion huddled over his grandfather's corpse. The two men returned from the *Sidereal* and reported to the mage. The crew headed toward the boardwalk and Castes, but the mage hung back. He crouched again in front of Ion.

"Tell no one you have seen us. Is that clear, Ion?"

"Who would I tell?"

"If anyone learns of my arrival, I'll hold you responsible. I'll flay them alive while you watch. Then I'll kill you. Do you know what it means to flay someone, Ion?"

Ion shook his head.

"It means I'll take a knife and peel off all their skin, and we'll see what's underneath."

Ion whimpered and hid his face in his grandfather's shirt. The mage grasped the boy's chin and forced him to meet his eyes.

"Leave me alone," Ion whimpered.

"Can I trust you to stay silent?"

Ion nodded.

The mage slapped him. "Let me hear you say it, boy."

Ion felt blood on his chin. "Yes, sir."

The mage patted Ion's cheek and stood, then pressed the thieves' glass back into Ion's palm.

"Good lad."

# CHAPTER FIFTEEN
# THEO VANGUARD
## MOON OF XYS, LENSDAY, 29TH OF HEBE

The dining hall was warm and brightly lit, in contrast to the dim interior of the parlor. Even the wind from the sandstorm outside seemed diminished, the incessant rasp now a subtle susurration. Governor Gambol sat at the head of the table, his features framed by the glow of firelight from a stone hearth. Tabitha sat to his left, stirring her soup and listing slightly. Theo could see that it took all her concentration to remain upright in the chair. A place had been reserved for him beside her.

Conversation halted when the servant announced Theo.

"Sir Vanguard, welcome," the governor said, gesturing toward the vacant seat. "Please, join us."

Theo sat as a footman placed a steaming bowl of onion soup before him.

"I thank you for your hospitality, Governor," Theo said before laying his napkin in his lap.

"An officer in the Imperial Navy! Your father must be proud," said the man sitting across from Theo. There was a slight mocking edge to his voice. He was handsome, with green eyes and a strong jawline, though patchy stubble obscured it. His eyes were quite close together, which gave his entire face a subtle, pinched expression.

"Theo, this gentleman is the recently appointed Sabaian Ambassador to Xys, Hubert Marrion. This lovely young woman is his wife, Lady Beatrice Marrion of House Azure."

*Lady Marrion is lovely,* Theo thought, *with blue hair like Crestone.*

Gambol continued, "The loyal servant of the people on Hubert's left is his older brother, Xyssian Congressional Delegate Xander Marrion."

"A pleasure to make your acquaintance." Theo inclined his head to each as Governor Gambol made the introductions. "Thank you, Lord Governor, for the opportunity to join your esteemed table."

"The pleasure is mine," Gambol said. "I am delighted you escaped your ordeal unscathed."

Theo sat and tucked into the soup.

"As I was saying," Xander Marion began, "the Parliamentarian is prepared to introduce a motion of peripatesis for consideration as early as Cordsday."

Hubert *tsk*ed, though only Theo and Beatrice noticed.

"Out of the question," Gambol said before Xander finished speaking.

Xander rolled his eyes. "Why not? Solvigant has been in Veria long enough."

Theo could tell that this was not the first time they'd had this conversation.

"I do not disagree with the necessity of peripatesis," Gambol said, "but what you're proposing opposes centuries of church doctrine. In addition, a Cordsday introduction would mean taking auspices the following day, on Djinnday, and one does not take the auspices on the day reserved for the God of Destruction. Any other day would be acceptable—for the normal auspices for a *normal* peripatesis. Father Heilig, the archdeacon, would be apoplectic."

Xander sighed, his soup untouched. Servants began clearing the bowls.

"What is it you're proposing?" Theo asked.

"To move the city to—" Xander began.

"Beyond the prescribed route," Hubert interrupted, his sonorous voice taking on a patronizing tone.

"I would like," Xander said, his tone firm, "Solvigant to move to Ourania."

"And that's controversial?" Theo asked.

Gambol interrupted, "It is off the pilgrimage path completely."

Xander addressed Theo. "The trajectories of the gates are shifting, becoming more erratic. Amar would be suicidal with these daily moonquakes. Gamb is too remote, and Iman doesn't have access to any water gates. In two months, there will be a rare conjunction of gates—aero, hydro, and gaia—at Ourania. It is our last chance to evacuate the people of Xys."

"Rumors and tall tales," Hubert said dismissively to his brother.

"I experienced it myself," Theo said. "The pirates who apprehended me intended to use the hydrogate outside the Barrier Isles. It has always passed through there, though it is seldom utilized anymore because it opens into the Boiled Sea. I hate to admit, but had the gate been where it was supposed to be, the pirates would have escaped before we had a chance to board. I've never seen anything like it."

"Commander Vanguard is correct," Xander said. "Reports come in everyday from the ferry companies and shipping firms. The closer Xys comes to Solo, the more erratic the gates. The Caretakers outside Orrin report they have seen no gates in a fortnight."

The servants returned with covered plates for each guest. A footman lifted each dome to reveal half a roasted chicken. Tabitha coughed into the silence while the conversation waited for the servants to retreat. Her cough was thick and full of mucus. Theo resisted the urge to place a concerned hand on her forearm.

"Djinnar ordained the path of peripatesis based on the fluctuations of stellarium," Hubert said. "The Solan Emperor, Nine bless him, recognized the importance of Solvigant's pilgrimage when he annexed Xys into his empire. Are you suggesting that you know better than gods and emperors?"

"We are in this mess because Pallantier has abandoned this moon," Xander replied. "I believe the gods would not want us all to die here."

"If the gates are erratic, the stellarium waves must be also," Hubert said. "The city might not survive the pilgrimage. We should not deviate and invoke the ire of the gods because the pilgrimage is suddenly inconvenient. No one wants Pallantier and Djinnar to begin a Third Avernian War."

"Enough." The governor waved a hand at Hubert, cutting off his retort. Gambol spoke through a mouthful of chicken. "You have both made your positions clear."

"My brother," Hubert said, addressing Theo with a conspiratorial wink from across the table, "always so quick to play the hero. Wants to be a martyr that one."

Xander frowned as he sliced meat from bone, ignoring Hubert. Although Xander was the older brother, Hubert's position with the Solan Diplomatic Corps meant that he outranked Xander. Theo suspected Hubert was enjoying every minute of this authority.

"Why the haste, brother?" Hubert asked, spraying crumbs from a bite of dinner roll. "It could be generations before Xys returns to the Mother."

"Or it could be months," Xander insisted. "The quakes are becoming worse and more frequent. Debris from her rings illuminates our skies night and day, the seas are foul, the livestock are starving, the gates are behaving more erratically, their orbits breaking down. How bad must it get before we take it seriously? Today, senior members of the Alchemist's

Guild informed me that when Xys gets too close to Solo, the gates may stop working entirely."

"Hacks," Gambol interjected. "There is no proof of that. The Alchemical Guild is full of fearful fools hoping to conjure great fortunes out of thin air. Do you have any proof of this?"

"I spoke with Master Moreland of the Alchemists Guild yesterday," Xander said. "Their researchers on Karis have connected the erratic behavior of the gates to fluctuating amounts of astral dust. Quantities of astral dust in the atmosphere increase with a moon's proximity to Solo and interfere with the stability of the aether that holds the gates together."

Conversation halted again as the footmen circulated to top up wine glasses.

When they left, Beatrice said, "It will not take generations." All eyes turned to her. She stared at her plate, pushing peas and chicken around with her fork.

She was young, Theo realized, in her late teens. Her blue hair hung long and straight, the front locks braided with small gems to frame her cherubic face. A net of iridescent pearls had been draped over her hair and twinkled like stars in the lamplight.

"You have the gift of House Azure," Tabitha said, leaning forward with interest.

Beatrice nodded, flicking her aqueous eyes up to Tabitha's for a moment before returning her gaze to the tablecloth.

"You're a prophet," Theo said. He had never met anyone with this gift.

"How long do we have?" the governor asked.

When Beatrice said nothing, Hubert hissed something unintelligible into her ear and she flinched.

"I don't know," she said tremulously.

"What do you mean?" the governor pressed.

"It doesn't work that way," Beatrice whispered as she shuddered under the combined weight of everyone's attention.

"I don't experience time and memory the way the rest of you do," she mumbled. "In order that my power not rival that of the gods, the Prophets of House Azure have little control over their gift. I see events without the context of past, present, or future, and without the ability to distinguish between what will happen or what could happen, what did happen or what could have happened. It is a curse more than a blessing."

Tabi reached across the table and grasped Beatrice's hand. The young woman gasped at the contact but did not pull away.

"Is this true?" the governor asked.

Beatrice nodded. "I have seen the moon fall into Solo many times in many ways, but they are always there."

"They?" Tabitha pressed.

Beatrice indicated Xander, then Theo.

Theo choked on a bite of carrot. "Me?"

"Prophecy is a gift of demigods, not the Children of Solo," Hubert said. "We must not reward their connivances by giving credence to their lies."

"It is no lie!" The vehemence in Beatrice's voice surprised them all.

"What does Commander Vanguard have to do with any of this?" Xander asked.

Beatrice flushed. She had abandoned her fork and clutched her napkin in both hands, twisting it. "I don't know, sir."

"There is an awful lot that you don't know." Hubert's voice had a serrated quality. He speared the last piece of chicken from his plate and gestured with it. "I can assure you, being married to the woman, that her fits and visions only create confusion."

Xander ignored Hubert with the skill of an older sibling. "What *are* you doing here, Commander Vanguard?"

"It's an embarrassing story, I'm afraid," Theo began. Tabitha squeezed his knee under the table and Theo took confidence from the gesture. "Two days ago, as first officer of the HMS *Dragonhammer*, I was pursuing pirates who had stolen a ship which belonged to my father. I led the boarding party, but they managed to flee through a hydrogate to Xys. I was bound and held somewhere in the city until I realized they had no intention of ransoming me, so I escaped and came here to beg succor from my cousin, the Lady Gambol, and her lord husband."

Xander looked as though he might be ill.

"So, you will return home?" Hubert asked.

"Once I see the pirates brought to justice," Theo said. *And once I recover Apyreon for my father.*

"Did you know these pirates?" Xander asked. "How many are there?"

"Only four survived, now three. Their leader had hair like the Lady Beatrice Faide but bleached it white to hide the natural color."

"The pirate captain is from House Azure?" Xander interjected. "Are you sure?"

"I wasn't," Theo said, "until I met the Lady Faide here this evening."

"What was the name of the ship?" Xander inquired.

"The *Sidereal*." Xander had paled, but Hubert looked oddly delighted. Theo realized there was a larger story here. He asked, "Are either of you familiar with this woman, being from Saba yourselves, the seat of House Azure?"

"No," Xander said.

"I am an officer of the Empire," Hubert said evenly. "I do not consort with pirates."

Theo wanted to press them, but decided the governor's dinner table was not the right place.

"We are very glad you're safe, cousin," Tabitha said looking from Theo to her husband.

The governor nodded. "Quite right. It sounds like a harrowing ordeal, though nothing too difficult for a young Imperial Navy officer." The governor was clearly uninterested in blue-haired pirates.

The staff removed their plates, and conversation drifted to the storm outside, shipping delays, and the effect of the heat on gardens.

To Theo's delight, dessert was sticky toffee pudding, one of his favorites. He tucked in, avoiding the gazes of the two Marion brothers.

"Husband," Tabi said, "may I offer some advice."

Eliot Gambol waved a hand granting her permission as he chewed his pudding.

"Xander's parliamentary motion seems well-intentioned, if unorthodox. If the choice truly is between saving the people of Solvigant and defying centuries of religious doctrine, it is fitting to consult the gods."

"What do you mean?"

"The disappearance of Pallantier, God of Creation, caused Xys's orbital decay. I propose that you send an emissary to consult with his brother Djinnar, God of Destruction, in his temple on Maxon. He imposed this pilgrimage upon us as part of the divine peace after the Second Avernian War. Perhaps he would agree to a compromise whereby both the people can be saved and the gods' wishes upheld."

"An interesting proposition," the governor said, caramel sauce dripping from his fork. "I am inclined to permit the Parliamentarian to introduce Xander's bill. Congress will debate the bill if our delegation to Djinnar's temple receives the god's blessing."

It was Xander's turn to object. "Governor, we may not have enough time."

"Whatever time we may or may not have on this moon, we will not use it to ridicule the gods. Those of us who do survive this catastrophe still have to live in a World System governed by their powers."

"Who will comprise the delegation?" Tabitha asked.

"Who better to commune with an enigmatic god than one with part of their gifts. Lady Faide, would you be willing to make the journey?" Gambol said.

"My wife couldn't possibly—" Hubert started saying at the same moment Beatrice nodded emphatically and said, "Yes, please!"

Hubert looked as though he'd bitten his tongue, but he had no grounds on which to oppose the governor's invitation.

"Lord Hubert, in your capacity as diplomat, you are needed here. I am in the debt of Lord Marrion and Lord Daniel Faide, the patriarch of House Azure, for agreeing to host so many of the refugees from Solvigant. You will be needed here during the planning process. If we can move Solvigant to Ourania, I want the refuge sites on Saba to be ready."

"Theo," the governor continued, "it is wonderfully fortuitous that such an able-bodied soldier would appear at a time when I have a delegation in need of a military escort."

"I couldn't possibly," Theo exclaimed, "I must finish my duties here and return to my post."

"Theo," the governor fixed him with a stern gaze.

"Yes, sir?"

"Are you not an officer of the Imperial Navy?"

"I am, sir."

"And am I not the representative of Imperial power on Xys?"

"You are, sir."

"In exchange for my hospitality, I require you to escort the delegation to Maxon. I will inform your father of your good health, and your commanding officer of your new assignment. You may return to the *Dragonhammer* once this mission is complete. Understood?"

"Yes, sir." Theo executed an awkward salute while seated.

"I will request that Father Heilig provide a suitable emissary from the Sons of Destruction to accompany you. Djinnar should be more amenable to our entreaties if the request comes from one of his own clerics."

"Yes, Governor, of course," Theo acquiesced.

"Very well," the governor said. "That's settled." He ate the last large bite of his dessert and nodded at the footman to pour him coffee.

Theo cleared his throat "My lord, might I have two days to conclude my business here? That is, to file a report with the city watch and see a doctor." He held up his bandaged hand.

"I will grant you one better. Today is Lensday. Embarking in four days on Djinnday is auspicious, is it not, for a group intending to visit the eponymous celestial? Xander can introduce his bill, and Father Heilig can read the auspices on Solanday."

With a cognitive click, Theo realized that Governor Gambol had assembled this plan the moment Theo had appeared on his doorstep. *Clever man.* Only Tabi seemed pleased with the outcome of their dinner.

*A good compromise is one in which no party is happy,* Theo's father had often said, though in practice he always got exactly what he wanted. *Four days to find Apyreon in the metropolis of Solvigant. It's not much time.*

Theo's belly was full, however, and the warmth of the room made him drowsy. He would be no good on the hunt if he didn't get some sleep and he was grateful when Gambol allowed him to excuse himself before the sherry and cigars. Tabitha led him through the tangle of sprawling rooms to where he had cleaned up earlier. He had planned to stay awake ruminating on the various motives and reactions around the table, but he was asleep before the servants finished dousing the lights.

# CHAPTER SIXTEEN

# ADI CRESTONE

## MOON OF XYS, LENSDAY, 29TH OF HEBE

S ounds of revelry from downstairs woke Adi. Light reflected from Solo cut the darkness, filtered through the gauzy curtains of Iris's little room. Groggy, Adi groped toward where Iris's sleeping form ought to be, but she was not there. A tremor, stronger than usual, woke her further. Downstairs, the night-time revelry of the brothel paused. Next door a woman's moans hitched while everyone waited to see if the shaking would subside. The tremor eased, the band struck up a bawdy tune, and the sounds of pleasure resumed.

Adi rose and stretched in front of the window. The night air was warm and dry. Dust devils swirled amongst the empty market stalls of Torhan Square below. Scattered silhouettes of people moved through the city, laughing or whispering, in ones and two and threes. Some carried torches, others moved in the semi-darkness. Clear skies to the east revealed the delicate shifting lines of Solvigant's nocturnal meteor shower. She spotted the yellow orb of Tyre, the red and green flicker of Aleph, and the blue moon of Saba, low near the horizon.

The moment of peace suffused Adi's body like a light breeze. To the west, smoke from refineries drifted across the sky, dark streaks against the backdrop of Solo. The phosphorescent edges of an aerogate floated above the city, its perfect circle contrasting with the jumbled angular skyline of Solvigant. The muscles in Adi's shoulders relaxed for the first time since setting foot in Thail with Captain Torrance and her crew. She breathed in the night air and when she exhaled, she imagined all her concerns and worries flowing out of her body. Watching the nightlife of her adopted city let her forget about Xander, about Mung and the escaped officer, about the collar around her neck, about Broc and

Henge, and about her lost dragonstone. But though it eased, she could not forget her fear of Lucas's safety. No amount of nostalgia could subvert motherhood.

Adi considered wrapping Iris's thin blanket around her shoulders and stepping out onto the balcony. She couldn't remember the last time she'd been alone like this. As tempting as the night was, the voices and merriment below called to her. Instead of stewing alone with her thoughts on the roof she pulled on her stained trousers and the oversized shirt to join the party in the bar. She used the blue paisley scarf to tie up her hair and conceal her roots.

*I need to bleach it,* Adi thought as she opened the door to the narrow hallway.

Raquel, one of Stella's new girls, stood in the doorway across the hall in a green robe with a faded houndstooth pattern accepting money from a satisfied male customer. Coins clinked in Raquel's palm. The man turned at the sound of the door opening and he eyed her up and down, his eyes still hungry, but he made no offer. Her voluminous shirt hid most of her body, and she returned his gaze with hostility. A lot of time had passed since Adi had last been sized up by a potential client, and she shivered when he turned away. In a brothel, one erected stout walls between body and mind. In the years since Adi had left Stella's Echo for the promise of piratical adventure, her walls had eroded.

The man clomped down the stairs.

"Hey, Adi," Raquel said.

"What time is it?"

"Almost midnight."

"Where's Iris?"

"Working off site." Raquel smiled. "Apparently Dansko has taken a shine to pleasant Iris."

"Dansko?" Adi said, drawing a blank.

"One of the congressional delegates, heads up one of the smaller parties, I don't remember which one."

"Well, good for Iris," Adi said, unsure how she felt. "Must pay well."

"It must."

Adi turned to leave. She knew Iris was a working girl, Adi had been one herself for a pair of years after coming of legal age on her eighteenth birthday. Still, she did not like imagining Iris at work.

*I have deeper feelings for her than I realized,* Adi thought. "I need a drink."

Raquel grabbed Adi's wrist. "I haven't got any further commitments. Fancy a game of ahric? I got a new deck."

Adi smiled but pulled her hand free. "I—thank you, but I'm too tired."

"Just keep me company then." The invitation in Raquel's voice morphed into something else, something firmer, a warning.

*That doesn't make any sense,* Adi thought. "I can't. Too much on my mind."

Raquel opened her mouth as if to say something but only sighed. "Goodnight, Adi."

Adi started down the stairs. Raquel's door shut behind her. She had to move aside so another of Stella's girls could lead a client upstairs, his cheeks ruddy with drink.

The tavern was crowded with patrons and prostitutes alike. Most of them packed the floor in front of the rickety stage. Adi could not see the musicians but appreciated the folksy rhythms of their strings and horns. She picked her way through the crowd toward the bar, where Stella was bustling back and forth, filling cups of ale from two large barrels along the back wall. Verdun, the hulking Ankhim brewer, was sitting at the bar, mug in hand, his bald head moving with the rhythm of the song, his skin the color of fresh basil.

Adi recognized the music "The Grasses of Galberd Valley," a popular Gaashian folk song. At the counter, Adi motioned Stella for a pint. Stella rolled her eyes but poured the frothy brew into a clean tankard and set it before Adi.

"That'll be a half tower."

Adi choked on the first sip. "A *half tower*? When did you start price gouging?"

Stella laughed. "Since the moon started falling into the Mother. Turns out people will pay a tidy sum to forget their impending destructions."

Adi reached into her pocket and set a gold spyre on the bar.

Stella looked startled, but the coin disappeared. She quirked a brow at Adi. "You sure you want to be down here tonight?"

Adi set down her ale, savoring Verdun's excellent work.

"First Raquel and now you. What's going on? Is the Blood Queen singing later?"

Stella frowned and held her eyes. Adi looked away.

She took another healthy slug of ale. "The musicians sound good."

Stella patted Adi's hand. "Take it easy, at least."

Melinda the Ancient sat at her usual place near the end of the bar. A glass of mead, untouched, waited on the counter before the woman. Melinda had been sitting in that exact spot at Stella's Echo since before Adi and Lucas first arrived. She'd been ancient then, now she looked decrepit. Her rheumy eyes were completely white, and her swollen knuckles appeared incapable of curling around the stem of the wine glass. Adi had never seen Melinda drink the mead.

*It could be the same glass from fifteen years ago,* Adi mused as she squeezed in beside her at the crowded bar. "Hello, Melinda."

"Adison!" Melinda's voice creaked and rattled but Adi heard her delight at their meeting. The woman turned her blind eyes toward Adi and grasped one of her hands. Melinda's thin, white hair stuck out in all directions as if charged by static.

"You seem diminished, girl. Are you all right?"

Had anyone else called Adi "girl" after she'd downed a pint and a half, fisticuffs might follow. But Adi took it from Melinda, feeling the warmth intended.

"I'm all right," she said.

"You've lost your dragonstone."

Adi's hand went to her neck. "What? How did you know?"

"I've known you too long for secrets." Melinda smiled. "I thought you might come down this evening."

"You did? I wasn't sure if you knew I was here."

"Oh, I know everything I need to from this stool here. Stella is most accommodating, you know. To let an old woman decompose on one of her bar stools."

Adi laughed. "She plays tough, but thankfully for us both, Stella is a kind soul." Adi ordered a second pint, enjoying the light-headedness the alcohol brought on. She had never felt at home, not really, but sitting beside Melinda in Stella's Echo on a busy Valeday night came close.

"Plus," Adi added, "you don't smell like you're decomposing. I figure you'll live forever. Stella says you've been sitting here since before this place was a tavern."

A sound like colliding river stones came from Melinda's throat and Adi took it as laughter.

"Mayhap I have."

They sat in silence.

Verdun ambled over to shake Adi's hand. "Adi, good to see you. You working for Stella again?"

"No, just passing through."

Verdun sighed. "Pity. The old madam may not admit it, but she misses you when you're gone."

"What?" Stella exclaimed, "Verdun, what are you telling people about me?"

Verdun's laughter was deep. He slapped Adi on the back so hard she nearly spilled her beer.

"Just reminding this one that there are a few people in the World System who enjoy seeing her."

Iris appeared and squeezed in beside Adi. "Only a few though."

Adi put her arm around the woman's waist. The ale made the blood run hot in her veins. "You're back!" Adi realized she was relieved.

"Dansko's prowess isn't what he'd like it to be."

Adi laughed. "A drink for the beautiful lady, and another for me, of course." Adi was sober enough to sense the tension in those beside her.

Iris nuzzled Adi's neck, planting delicate kisses in its curve. "Why don't we go upstairs?"

"After another drink."

Iris slid a hand up Adi's thigh, "Why wait?"

"Because I'm here with all of you and I want to enjoy it. Then I'm going to enjoy you." Adi kissed Iris, felt her lips part sweetly under the pressure from hers. When she pulled away, they were both flushed. Her companions had fallen silent.

"What?" Adi said, her voice loud. Slowly, notes from a single lute floated over the crowd. Adi followed everyone's eyes toward the stage, where the musician stood plucking an ornate, inlaid lute. Adi knew that instrument, knew every piece of the pattern, every fret, the bright areas of the grain polished by finger pressure. She recognized the dulcet chords of "To the Vale I Go to Find Thee." Adi had scrimped and saved to buy that lute as a gift for a musician who was starting a tour of the seven moons in the Solan Empire with a prestigious Seraph musical company.

"Rehka!" Adi cried out over the song. Rehka continued playing, her eyes locked on Adi's.

Adi dropped her hands from Iris's and the whole tavern shrank until Adi was alone with Rehka, hearing their song for the first time in three years. The song ended and the myriad sounds of the crowded tavern intruded once more: low conversations, the clink of tankards, the sound of wooden chairs scraping across floorboards warped by peripatesis. There was a smattering of applause and Adi applauded earnestly, as drunk people do. As the band struck up the next tune, Rehka stepped down from the elevated stage. Patrons parted as she moved across the tavern until she stood before Adi. Iris, Verdun, and Stella had vanished. Only Melinda remained, on her stool behind Adi, mead untouched.

"Rehka," Adi breathed, her chest tight.

"Hello, Adi."

"Rehka, I—" Adi leapt from her stool and embraced the woman. Rehka was Dragon-tall, so Adi's head pressed firmly against the woman's sternum. She patted Adi awkwardly on the back. Adi pulled away and looked up at her. "It's wonderful to see you."

"Is it?" Rehka's eyes glanced toward the stairs where Iris had retreated, abashed.

Heat flooded Adi's cheeks. "You don't get to be angry with me."

Rehka's grin infuriated Adi, "Oh? How should I feel?"

Adi gripped her mug with white-knuckled fingers. "You betrayed me."

"And what was that?" Rehka pointed toward the stairs where Iris had fled.

"Iris cares for me as more than a means to an end."

Rehka stiffened. Adi tensed.

"What are you doing here?" Adi asked as Rehka only stood, sputtering.

"Playing music."

"Aren't you a little famous for Lensday nights at Stella's Echo?"

"Better famous than infamous."

Adi fingered the collar around her neck. "If you're determined to fight, can we at least go outside? I'd rather not give all these patrons a second show."

Rehka motioned toward the door. "By all means"

Adi watched Rehka pace before Stella's Echo under a clear night sky.

Adi's mind felt thick and foggy. *I wish I hadn't drunk so much. How many times have I imagined seeing her again? And now I have nothing to say.*

"Iris?" Rehka asked.

"What about her?"

"You're with her?"

"No. I—"

"It certainly seemed like it."

"And what if I am?" Adi didn't want to be obstinate, but she felt out of control. And she could fight; fighting was familiar enough.

"She's a whore!"

"They're all whores. I used to be a *whore.*" Adi spat out the word.

"That's not the point."

"Then what is the point?"

Rehka growled. "You could do better."

"You don't know anything about Iris."

"I don't need to."

"No, your baseless judgment is pretty clear."

Rehka crossed her arms over her chest. "That's not what I meant."

"You seem to be having a difficult time saying what you *do* mean."

"That's because I miss—"

"Because what?" Adi blurted. "Because I could do better? Have better? Have *you*? *You* left *me*, remember?"

"That's because you—"

"Enough!" Adi shouted. "I don't need to be reminded of how everything is my fault."

Rehka's shoulders drooped.

"You still haven't answered my question." Adi said. "What are you doing here? And don't say you're playing a gig."

"I'm here on assignment," Rehka said.

"I might have guessed," Adi scoffed. "Your little mercenary club. Chewing me out was just a bonus."

"The Water Knives."

"What?"

"My mercenary club."

"Wait, are you here for Stella? Verdun? Me? Are you offering reconciliation before you stab me in the back?"

Rehka laughed. "Don't flatter yourself. For being a former prostitute and a self-styled pirate, you have a dim view of mercenaries."

"I don't kill for money."

Rehka stopped laughing, "No, you just lie on your back and spread your legs for it, that's better."

Adi punched her. It was difficult to punch someone so much taller than her, but Adi managed.

Rehka's head snapped to the side at the unexpected blow and blood flowed from a split lip. She stepped back to put distance between them. "Someone knows about Apyreon."

The sudden change of topic threw Adi. She shook her head. "What?"

Rehka wiped the blood from her chin "Someone approached the Water Knives. They knew all about Apyreon, about Lucas, and some ship called the *Sidereal*."

"How could anyone know that? Who was it?"

Rehka shrugged "I don't know."

"You don't know? How could you not know?"

Rehka was unperturbed. "It's standard. I usually don't know who hires us. Plausible deniability and all that if we fail."

"So, we're in a race?"

"Not at all. I was hired to help you find it."

Again, Adi struggled to find traction. "You were?"

"They requested me, specifically."

"And when we find it?"

"I am to let you recover it."

"To hand it over to the Blood Queen?"

"I guess. Those are the end of my instructions."

"You can't."

"I certainly can. I'm up for promotion after this assignment. I don't get to turn down jobs. You think I wanted this one?"

"I promised Bale I would leave you alone."

"A hard promise to make."

Adi gazed at her. "Yes. Yes, it was." Her voice cracked.

Rehka's anger visibly cooled. "How is my father?"

"Go visit him yourself."

They stood in silence for several moments.

"This doesn't make any sense," Adi said.

Rehka shrugged. Her nonchalance made Adi flush.

"Sleep it off, Adi. You only get one free punch. We can talk more in the morning when I come by to pick you up."

"Come pick me up?"

"For the search. No point in wasting any time together."

Adi nodded. Her mind was racing as fast as three pints in a brief time would allow. *Who knew? Xander? Was there a faction of the Blood Queen's soldiers working against Sasha Riven? Who else could have so much information?*

"Get some sleep," Rehka insisted.

Adi turned to go inside.

"Adi," Rehka called after her, "if I were hired to kill you, I'd do it while I looked you in the eyes. Fair is fair after all."

"That's not fair. My responsibilities to Lucas and yours to your Dragon are not the same."

"Are they not?"

Adi felt as if she'd been punched. Rehka turned away before Adi let out a hoarse scream and tackled the tall woman from behind. They went down hard on the cobblestones. They rolled, each struggling for purchase against the other. Rehka emerged on top, and she struck Adi in the face. Adi brought her forearms up as a shield and tried to buck the woman off, but Rehka was too tall and her weight pressed the breath from Adi's lungs. Adi finally managed to get a leg up and push Rehka away, reversing their positions. Rehka's right arm was pinned beneath Adi's leg, and she got in several satisfying jabs to Rehka's face and midsection.

Rehka levered her hips and Adi tumbled onto the street. They scrambled to their feet and faced each other, breathing heavily.

Adi wiped spittle from her chin. "How dare you come here. As if I need your help."

"You need all the help you can get," Rehka said, panting.

Adi charged and the two women tangled in a flurry of limbs. Rehka's height gave her the advantage and Adi grunted as the larger woman's bony knee connected with Adi's stomach. Rehka hooked an arm under Adi's armpit, pivoted, drove forward, and tossed Adi over her shoulder. Adi flew through the air and landed hard on her back but managed to keep her breath. She rolled away before Rehka could stomp down on her and got to her feet in time to dodge under Rehka's next swing. Adi landed a satisfying blow to Rehka's kidney and started to swing again, but she was suddenly flying backward through the air.

Verdun had a hold of her. A man Adi did not recognize leapt in front of Rehka and urged her backward. Adi flailed against the hulking Ankhim without success.

"Calm down," he was saying, "you'll alert the watch."

Adi didn't care. The strength of her anger blurred her vision and dulled her thinking. Verdun continued his whispered consolation. His grip did not loosen. Rehka watched them, the stranger still pushing her back. Verdun held Adi until she lost all strength in her limbs. She slumped against him. Unbidden tears sprang into her eyes, and she was suddenly sobbing into the green man's chest, her shoulders heaving.

"Get yourself together," Rehka growled.

Adi did not acknowledge her.

"I'll be back in the morning."

# CHAPTER SEVENTEEN
# ADI CRESTONE
## MOON OF XYS, VALEDAY, 30TH OF HEBE

"Wake up," a woman whispered.

"Go away," Adi moaned. Her head pounded. Even through her eyelids, the morning light was too bright.

"Wake up."

Lips found the hollow of Adi's shoulder. Delicate kisses moved down her collarbone. A soft hand cupped one exposed breast and Adi felt her nipples stiffen. The lips, accompanied by trailing fingertips, moved down Adi's stomach to her hips, then to the inside of her thighs. A warm tongue found the wetness between her legs. Adi grasped a head covered in tight curls, moaning as her partner slid two slender fingers inside her. The pleasure of those fingers took the edge off the pounding hangover. The tongue played back and forth, the fingers found that delicate internal spot and applied pressure. Adi rocked her hips to match the fingers' rhythm.

"Oh gods, yes," she moaned. The fingers quickened. Adi clenched her teeth to contain a cry. Her legs squeezed the woman's body.

*It has been so long.*

"Please, don't stop," she gasped and arched her back, moaning as climax overtook her and spots of color exploded behind her eyelids. Her legs spasmed then relaxed, and her body went slack.

"Rehka, I've missed you," Adi said when she could breathe again. She opened her eyes to see Iris's face inches from her own. "Oh shit, I'm sorry," Adi croaked. Her head throbbed and nausea roiled her insides. She pushed herself up on one elbow and swallowed hard.

"By the Nine Gods, Iris, what was that?" Her hangover slammed back worse than before, and it was all too much: too bright, too loud, too much to process. *What happened last night after I left Rehka?*

Iris stood and smiled, unperturbed at being mistaken for someone else. She snagged her cotton bathrobe from the floor and tossed it around her shoulders.

"I believe that was the notorious Captain Crestone in orgasm." Iris sat in front of a tarnished mirror and began tidying her curls.

Adi's brain felt as limp as the rest of her. She struggled to recall what had happened after her conversation with Rehka and found hazy images of a dance with Verdun, sloppy kisses with Iris on the way to the outhouse, several more pints of ale, a few shots of some rotgut liquor, the pressure of Iris's hips against her own. Adi sat up, pulling the thin blanket around herself, and bracing against the pain in her temples.

"What happened last night?" Adi asked. She saw Iris's shoulders stiffen. "Did we—?" She could not muster enough spit to swallow and her voice was raw. "I mean, I shouldn't have."

"Why? Because of Rehka?" Iris snorted, studying Adi through the mirror.

"I'm sorry, Iris." Adi rubbed her gritty eyes. "Gods, do you have any water?"

"In the pitcher beside bed."

Adi poured herself a glass, drained it, poured another. Iris, her robe open, knelt on the bed, straddling Adi.

"You and Rehka are done, Adison. You've been done for three years. We've all known it, and you confirmed it again last night. You're the only one who doesn't seem to know."

Adi took in Iris's unmarred olive skin, her perfect breasts, the thick patch of dark hair between her legs, the upturned lips, the button nose. She was beautiful.

"Seeing her again threw me," Adi said.

"Threw you right against me. We were getting along quite well until she showed up. When you came back inside, I just picked up where we left off."

*I was too far gone,* Adi thought. "That's fair." She laid a hand on Iris's cheek. "And you're as good as you are gorgeous. I don't deserve you."

"It's not about what you deserve." She kissed Adi. Adi kissed her back but kept it light. Iris pulled back, a question in her eyes.

Adi ran a hand along one cheek, down her neck to Iris's shoulders. The woman shivered. Then Adi placed both hands on Iris's collarbones and pushed her aside, giving her shoulders a squeeze of reassurance. Iris pouted, but relented, tying her robe shut.

"Fine, at least let me get you ready," Iris said.

"Ready? Ready for what?"

"Rehka is downstairs waiting for you."

"She is? For how long?"

Iris shrugged.

"Why didn't you tell me sooner?"

"And ruin the morning? No."

Iris's room contained an old oak wardrobe. She pulled open both doors to reveal an eclectic assortment of clothing piled in heaps rather than hung from the wardrobe's upper rod. She began rummaging through the garments, holding onto some, tossing others onto the floor behind her.

"We can at least make you look the part," Iris said.

"What part is that?"

"A pirate captain that Rehka wishes she could have."

"Iris, I'm sorry," Adi said. "I didn't mean to offend you."

"Why would I be offended, Adi? I'm a prostitute and we had sex, that's it. Great sex, too, I might add, which is not something this prostitute gets to say very often. I'll have Stella put it on your tab."

As Iris flung clothing about the room in her search for specific items, Adi could see the tension in her back. Iris turned toward her, clutching a shirt and breeches, her knuckles pale, her jaw set.

*I've hurt her,* Adi thought. *Another person damaged by knowing me, dammit.*

Iris dropped the clothes in front of her. Adi slipped on the black breeches with faded white pinstripes, cinching them with a wide, black leather belt. Iris handed her a white shirt. It fit better than the previous one, though Iris was bigger in the bust than Adi. Next, Iris passed her a matching black and gold vest. Adi tied the blue scarf once more around her neck, and Iris settled Adi's prize tricorn hat on her head.

"Needs one more thing." Iris bustled out of the room. She returned a moment later with a green doublet with azure trim.

"Iris, that's beautiful. Where did you get it? I can't take this." The coat fit her as if made to her measure, and the azure trim was the same blue as the hair she had hidden.

"A gift. Stella got it for you when you first set sail, but you disappeared before she could give it to you. Since you returned, the time hasn't been right. It smells terrible of mothballs and cedar chests. Stella wanted to give it to you herself, but I insisted."

"I can't take this," Adi repeated.

"It's not polite to refuse a gift, Adison. We may be prostitutes here, but we're still folk with feelings."

Adi regarded herself in the cracked mirror. It was a beautiful coat, and it was the first time in a long time she'd looked like the pirate captain she claimed to be.

"Thank you, Iris. It's perfect." Adi brushed her cheek with a kiss.

Iris stiffened and drew back. "I need to clean this up." She turned her back on Adi and began snatching handfuls of diaphanous garments from the floor and bed and stuffing them back into the wardrobe.

There was a knock on the door.

"Who is it?" Iris asked.

Verdun opened the door. there were no locks on any of the brothel rooms.

"Good morning," he said. Adi winced. "Rehka is pacing downstairs. I've held her off as long as I can."

"Thank you, Verdun," Adi said. She polished off a second glass of water. She tried to refill it for a third, but the pitcher was empty.

"I see Iris gave you the coat. You look splendid. Very commanding. I asked her to wait until I could be there, but she insisted. She's quite fond of you, you know."

Adi flushed. "I'm ready."

She adjusted her hat to a rakish angle and stepped into the hallway. Verdun and Iris followed. Adi descended the steps with one hand clutching the railing as the loud world spun.

The tavern was empty now except for Stella and Rehka.

Adi said, "Stella, this coat is perfect." She spun to show it off and tripped over her own feet. Verdun saved her from pitching face-first onto the floor.

"Hair of the dog please, barkeep," Adi said.

"I think you've had enough," Rehka replied, acid in her voice.

"Dragons don't get hangovers?" Adi asked.

Rehka flinched. "I'm still cut off from my Dragon."

Adi grinned, though part of her recoiled at hurting Rehka.

Instead, Stella poured her a huge mug of coffee. "I'm glad you like the coat, dear."

Adi eyed the coffee, wishing it was something else, but it smelled amazing. She surrendered and sipped it as quickly as its heat would allow.

Rehka stood apart, looking every inch the mercenary. She wore brown breeches over tooled leather boots, a loose-fitting shirt cut low under crossed bandoliers, one sporting a full set of knives, the other, cartridges for the two pistols that hung beside her hips. A blue embroidered jacket completed the ensemble. Her blond hair was cut short beneath a pointed felt hat. An awkward moment passed as they both realized they looked good together.

"Where's the lute?" Adi asked.

"Where are your boots?" Rehka asked in response.

Adi shrugged, glancing down at her worn shoes. "Still shopping for the perfect pair. Do I get any weapons?"

"I have none to spare."

"Figures."

"We should get going," Rehka said, "to save your son and all that."

Adi flinched, chastened. "After you." She followed Rehka outside.

Ten paces out the door, Adi heard Iris call her. She turned to see the woman sprinting barefoot across the street toward them. Iris skidded to a stop and kissed her full and hard on the lips. Before Adi could decide how to respond, Iris pulled away. "See you soon," she said and bolted back into Stella's Echo.

"See you soon," Rehka said, her voice laced with scorn.

Adi's feelings for Iris were conflicted, but she had no trouble coming to the woman's defense "I don't remember you being so petty."

"You used to be better about keeping your mind on the mission."

*I didn't know you were waiting for me,* Adi wanted to snap back but swallowed it. If she started another argument now it would prove Rehka's point. Instead, she asked, "Where do we start?"

The two women started toward Torhan Square.

"The Warrens."

"Are you serious? That's a terrible plan."

"Do you have a better one?"

"I'm not walking into the heart of White Rabbit territory. Did you forget I'm wearing a collar of indenture?"

"How could I forget."

"Djinnar's blood, Rehka, it's not like you gave me much choice." Rehka's long strides forced Adi to trot beside her, every step jarring her aching head.

"You made your own bed."

Adi flexed her fingers.

"You've already used up your free punch."

"The Water Knives could have sent anyone else."

Rehka rounded on her. "I was requested. It's not like I want to be here."

"So you say."

"You think I'm lying?"

"I don't know," Adi said. "You show up here unannounced employed by some un-known client and knowing more than I do about my own situation. You even have a plan. But Lucas is my problem. Apyreon is my problem."

"Keep your voice down. I was hired, that's it. That's all I know."

Adi's dry mouth and nausea made it hard to argue further. She was afraid she'd have to stop and throw up if this got any worse.

"How do you know that the Blood Queen knows about Lucas?" Adi asked.

Rehka eyed her as they strode through the busy market square.

Adi slapped her forehead. "Phoebe's light, you have someone watching Lucas too. Am I the only one not spying on my son?"

"Apparently."

Adi grabbed Rehka's elbow and spun her around. The tall woman yanked her arm free but something about Adi's expression changed her tone from rebuke to reassurance.

"Adi, I swear. If I knew who the client was, I would tell you. I care about Lucas, too."

Adi accepted the conversational shift with relief. Arguing with Rehka was like death by a thousand cuts. Her tongue was as good as one of the knives secured to her bandolier, but Adi did not appreciate that talent when it was aimed at her.

"I don't want to fight you, Rehka. If you're here to help, help me. I need it. Just save the holier-than-thou judgmental crap. I have enough to worry about without some self-righteous, half-Dragon mercenary following me around trying to prove a point."

"Half-Dragon?"

Adi took a step back. "I'm sorry. I didn't mean it. It just slipped out." Adi watched as Rehka decided whether to take offense. The woman sighed and shook her head, then picked up her pace. Adi hurried to stay with her.

"My plan had two parts," Adi said, panting. "Phase one: get drunk and wallow in self-pity. Phase two: collect Lucas on Tyre and run. Phase one worked perfectly. That suggests a high probability of success with phase two."

Rehka shortened her stride so Adi could catch her breath. "Let's put some thought into that second part. You're right, we can't just storm into the Warrens and demand the White Rabbits hand over the spoils from a mugging outside their territory. And you can't run from the Blood Queen. Being on the lam from Sasha Riven is no life for young boy."

"He's fifteen now," Adi said.

"Wow. I haven't seen him in so long. I miss him."

"Me too." Adi allowed herself to sink into the memory of ten years ago, listening to her bright boy's excited plans for the new ship model sent by his mysterious uncle. He longed to sail the moons with her. When she glanced over at Rehka, Adi saw that her eyes were moist. Rehka put a hand on her shoulder.

"What do you want to do?"

Adi thought for a moment. "The Iron Dirigible."

"What's that?"

"It's a tavern near where I was attacked. White Rabbits and Blood Queen soldiers sometimes parlay there. It's likely Rictor and the others spent some of the night there before stumbling upon me. If so, someone will have seen them. I won't stand out there either."

"It's a start."

"I could use a drink anyway," Adi said.

"As long as it's coffee. I need you sober and focused. I don't have time for wrathful, spurned Adi."

Her insult twisted Adi's stomach. "Whatever."

Rehka gave her a genuine smile for the first time. "Come on, I'll buy you a coffee on the way, and some breakfast too."

"That's great. Because I'm starving... and broke."

Rehka rolled her eyes, but they were softer now. They turned down the boulevard that led to the Iron Dirigible.

# CHAPTER EIGHTEEN

# ION RUCINARE

## MOON OF XYS, VALEDAY, 30TH OF HEBE

Ion woke beside the corpse of his grandfather, blood and sand stuck to the side of face. His clothes were stiff, and sand lice crawled across his scalp. He did not remember falling asleep. His dry lips were stuck together, and they bled when he opened his mouth. He was so thirsty.

*How long have I been here?* he wondered. Then he remembered the void mage and the callous gesture that had torn open his grandfather's throat. Ion shivered despite the heat. The prow of the murderer's ship loomed a few yards away. A bedraggled seagull called out to him from the port gunwale. The crashing waves fell inches short of his toes. The tide was going out. There was something he knew he needed to do, but he couldn't put his finger on it. He shielded his eyes against the sun's glare and looked back at his grandfather. Thankfully, the old man was lying face down.

*That was it,* he realized.

He needed to bury the body. But where and with what? Then he had an idea.

The rickety hut stood upon the dune as if nothing had happened, as if the whole World System had not changed utterly overnight for him. He made it three paces before he vomited on the sand. There was little left in his stomach but acid and bile, but the convulsions squeezed his belly. Ion lay on his side, his arms wrapped around his stomach, waiting for the spasm to pass.

When he was able to stand again, he stumbled up the dune to their hut. Last night's fire had burned down to ash. The forgotten food was cold and covered in sand flies. The thought of food brought a fresh wave of dry heaves. He climbed into the pallet, hoping he would wake from this nightmare to find his grandfather snoring beside him. Ion pressed his head into the straw and squeezed his eyes shut. When he could bear it no longer, he opened them.

He was still alone. Clumps of bloody sand fell from his face onto the pallet. His loneliness and grief angered him. He leapt from the pallet, took hold of his grandfather's chair, and smashed it against the hearth, against the pallet, against their small table, against the ramshackle shelves laden with fishing gear. When his fury abated, he looked around at all their meager possessions, now broken and strewn across the floor. He had also knocked over the water bucket, so he could not clean himself. No matter. He was alone now, there was no one to care how he looked.

Slowly, he picked through the debris and packed his few personal belongings and whatever food he could scrounge from the hut into his pack. He removed the rusty machete from behind the shelves where his grandfather had hidden it. The blade once belonged to Ion's father, but had not seen use since the man had disappeared. Ion searched through the detritus until he located the flint and steel they used to light the hearth and placed them in his pocket. Finally, he returned to the beach, knelt beside his grandfather, and said a prayer to each of the gods to welcome his grandfather's spirit into holy Avernus.

When that was done, he took hold of his grandfather's ankles and dragged him toward the ship. The body was heavier than he expected. Even after years of undernourishment and hard labor, it took all of Ion's strength to move the body down the beach. He was sweating when he finally reached the shadow of the void mage's vessel. The breaking waves tugged at his grandfather's trousers.

Ion climbed the ladder to the deck of the ship and located a coil of rope. He ran it through a block and tackle and tossed one end over the side. He descended the ladder and secured the rope under his grandfather's armpits. The wound in the old man's neck was deep and his head lolled dangerously from side to side. Ion tried not to look at it, but it was difficult not to be horrified at the severed muscles and tendons. When he finished tying off the rope he ascended to the foredeck once more and hauled his grandfather up.

Despite the mechanical advantage, the task was more than Ion could manage. Well before the body reached the gunwale, Ion's muscles were screaming in protest. Sand chafed his hands and armpits. Rivulets of sweat ran down his face, stinging his eyes before dripping from his chin. The corpse was halfway up when Ion lost his grip. The rope slipped, burning his palms. Ion cried out as he heard the splash below. He paced the deck swearing and cursing, kicking anything that wasn't tied down into the sea. When he regained control of himself, he removed his shirt and tore it in half, then wrapped each half around a hand. Once his hands were protected, he repositioned himself near a row of belaying pins, so he could tie it off when he got tired.

His grandfather was heavier now, his clothes and hair soaked with foul water of the Boiled Sea. Eventually, between the padding and the pins, Ion was able to haul his grandfather level with the starboard railing. He glanced at the sun and saw it was much lower in the sky. He used a boat hook and the boom to which the block and tackle were attached to maneuver his grandfather's body onto the foredeck.

Finally, he dragged his grandfather across the deck into the rear cabin. He searched the drawers of the captain's desk but discovered nothing valuable. He took a pair of hooded lanterns from their hooks and shattered them, soaking the small cabin in fuel. Then he struck sparks with his flint and steel, igniting the flammable oil.

Ion retreated to the foredeck and watched the smoke billow from the stern. Flames licked at the doorway to the cabin and the pitch sealing the beams began to sizzle and pop. When the flames advanced on the helm, Ion retreated from the ship. He stood in the shallows, the thieves' glass gripped tightly in one hand, and watched the flames climb toward the reefed sails.

He wanted to stay and watch the ship until it was reduced to a charred wreck, but he was worried the conflagration would attract attention, and he did not want to have to explain himself. The terrane for Solvigant would leave soon and he intended to be on it. He was leaving Castes. His grandfather was dead, his parents had been gone for years, even Pallantier, the God of Creation had abandoned this moon. His only option was to find Captain Crestone and get off Xys. He imagined he would be just one more pirate with a sordid past no one spoke of, and that was fine with him.

Ion walked the long way around the dune to avoid encountering anyone from town who might come to investigate the blaze. He wondered if the void mage would realize what had happened when he returned for his ship.

*Let him come,* Ion thought, *I have nothing left to lose.*

Ion arrived in Castes at dinner time. His stomach growled as he stood outside the general store debating his next move. He needed food and a fresh shirt, but he had no money left. He thought of Alicia's kindness, the free sarsaparilla, and knew he could not steal from her. He stopped at the well, pulled up a bucket of water, and dumped it over his head.

"What are you doing?"

Ion turned and saw Cornyn, the town drunk, watching him. Ion did not know how old the man was, but the hairs of his unruly beard were just beginning to turn gray. He wore a soiled white shirt and tan breaches. A healthy assortment of overstuffed pouches hung from a thick belt, and he carried a metal flask in one hand.

"Where's your grandfather?" Cornyn asked when Ion didn't respond.

Ion opened his mouth but couldn't form the answer. He gave up and shook his head.

"You leavin'?"

"Yeah," Ion croaked. He dropped the bucket into the well and hauled it up again.

"Good for you." Cornyn took a pull on the flask, "Ain't nothing for a young boy here anyway."

"Not anymore."

"You got any money?"

Ion stiffened and shook his head. *Was he being robbed?*

Cornyn took another pull from the flask. "Where you gonna go?"

"Where are you from?"

"Pashull. It's a mining town on Behl."

"I'm going there."

Cornyn laughed. "Nobody goes there. It's nothing but miners, slavers, and blasted rock. It might be worse than here."

"Why'd you leave?"

"My contract was up, and I was done breaking rocks for the glory of the Empire. You could go to Aleph. I hear the Sea of Zog is a fisherman's paradise."

"My grandfather was the fisherman."

Cornyn nodded as if Ion had said something profound, then he reached into one of his pouches and produced two silver towers. Ion gawped as the drunkard pressed them into his hand.

"For the terrane and a new shirt. A half-naked runaway is sure to draw attention."

"Where'd you get the money?"

"I didn't steal it if that's what you're askin'," Cornyn huffed. "Miner's pension."

"I can't pay you back."

"You already have, son. Your grandfather was a decent man. Just promise me you'll find a place better'n this. Somewhere that the Empire hasn't ground down or that the gods haven't forsaken."

Ion nodded. "I promise."

The terrane steam whistle shrieked. Ion jumped.

"Run along then. You ain't got much time."

"Thank you," Ion said, and he stepped forward and hugged the man. Cornyn stiffened and did not return the gesture.

Instead, he said, "Be careful out there, you can't often get by on the kindness of strangers."

"Thank you, sir, I will."

Fifteen minutes later, Ion was sitting in an empty terrane coach wearing a fresh shirt and holding a full canteen. The steam whistle shrieked once more, and the terrane jerked forward. Ion snacked on a tin of nuts he'd recovered from their cabin. It was their cabin no more. His grandfather would never set foot inside again, and Ion had no intention of ever returning to Castes. Still, he watched tearfully as the only home he'd ever known dwindled in the distance.

He wanted to cry, to grieve for his grandfather, but he felt twisted and wrung out. He suppressed a pang of guilt at leaving the town his grandfather had loved. He would never understand what the old man had seen in the place, though he had told Ion that once it had been a proper town and the sea had been filled with the nets of numerous fishermen. There had been taverns, a school, and a temple, but by the time Ion's parents had left, those had all closed and the sea had earned a new name. His grandfather had loved the old Castes, so Ion tried to love the ghost of it. He couldn't, but it would remain special. It would always be his home. Then he closed his eyes and wept until the gentle rocking of the carriage crossing the desert lulled him to sleep.

The terrane rolled on toward Solvigant.

# CHAPTER NINETEEN
# ADI CRESTONE
## MOON OF XYS, VALEDAY, 30TH OF HEBE

"I need to make a stop," Rehka said.

"What about Apyreon?" Adi asked.

"There will still be gang members at the Iron Dirigible when we're done."

"What is it?"

Rehka looked down her nose at Adi, but did not respond.

*Still playing her cards too close*, Adi thought. It had gotten them in trouble on multiple occasions.

Adi followed the Dragon woman through the twisting streets of Solvigant. The morning air was already hot and dry. A light breeze carried sand and the smells of engine grease and spiced roasted meat. Adi's stomach rumbled, but she kept her head down. The sand in the air forced both women to don their goggles to protect their eyes.

*A sandstorm is the last thing I need.*

Rehka stopped at a cutlery. The tradesman's apprentice, a young boy five years younger than Lucas had just finished prepping the whetstone. The cutler, a wizened man with a long white beard, appeared ancient next to his apprentice. He was also a clunker; his left leg ended below the knee. An intricate metal skeleton was attached below the kneecap and functioned as a foot. Despite the elegant prosthesis, he walked with a pronounced limp.

When Rehka produced several knives in need of sharpening, Adi worried the cutler's beard would wrap itself around the whetstone. It did not. While they were there, Adi spent some of Xander's money on a cutlass, a boot knife, and a jambiya, then watched out the window as they waited for Rehka's blades to be finished.

"Have you heard anything?" Rehka said to the cutler.

"Diana arrived last night from Highgaard on the *Fairplay*." The cutler's voice was soft, barely above a whisper. Adi took a step back from the window to hear their conversation better.

"Did she bring the Fieldstone?" Rehka asked.

Adi's curiosity was piqued. She had no idea what a fieldstone might be.

The cutler shrugged, which seemed to irritate Rehka. "Well?"

"I didn't see it," the cutler said. "But she said she would, so she did. She is a dangerous woman, but not an untrustworthy one, in my experience."

"I've made arrangements to acquire the manual. I want to perform the rite as soon as possible."

Adi sighed in exasperation. Only priests and alchemists performed rites, and this tradesman was no priest.

"The moon, Flynt, is in the western quadrangle in a fortnight. That will be your best chance to enter Pyrea."

Adi coughed to cover her surprise. *Rehka's still looking for her Dragon.*

Rehka's eyes flicked to Adi, who tried to appear nonchalant. Rehka's conversation with the cutler ceased and there was only the sound of metal against the whetstone.

Adi resented the delay, and she was tense. Rehka had been all hustle and hurry to leave Stella's Echo, but now that they were out in the city, all her haste had evaporated.

*I wonder if she wanted to be away from Iris,* Adi thought. *Rehka can hardly fault me for moving on. But have I moved on?*

Adi remembered that day three years ago, standing on the dock outside the port city of Kelian on Behl waiting for Rehka, but already certain her lover wouldn't return. The temptation for Rehka was too great. Adi knew what it was like to feel less than whole. She had been carving off pieces of herself since childhood and leaving them behind. Her mother had taken the first piece when she'd suddenly died of typhoid. The bony knuckles on the back of her father's hand had knocked loose several more pieces over the years. Hubert had taken a large piece, then her leaving home, Stephan's death, homelessness in Solvigant, violent clients at Stella's Echo, and her separation from Lucas. Adi knew what it was like to feel less than whole, but that hadn't lessened the sting of Rehka's betrayal.

When Adi had seen Behlian soldiers marching down the hill from Kelian's coastal fortress, she had known for sure that Rehka had sold them out. The Imperial Navy detachment at Kelian had pursued the *Snowcrest* for a week. Though the pirates had eventually outrun their pursuers, it was in no thanks to Captain Crestone. Adi had spent the week veering wildly back and forth between drunkenness, rage, and desolation. Rehka's love had held the remaining pieces of Adi together and the betrayal had shattered her. With Iris, Adi had begun to put herself back together. But with Rehka's return, Adi could feel all those delicate fissures reopening.

*But she hasn't changed. Rehka's priority is still her Dragon.*

Across the street from the cutler stood a man in a bowler hat. He leaned against a gas lamp and watched Adi. His attention ended her reverie. The combination of lean muscle and confidence indicated the man was a soldier, though Adi saw no obvious signs of affiliation. She recognized him as the man who had helped break up the fight the night before.

"Finished," Rehka announced, coming to stand beside Adi, who flinched in surprise. If Rehka noticed, she did not acknowledge it or the man's presence. Adi's stomach rumbled.

"Breakfast?" she asked. She would not give Rehka the satisfaction of showing her impatience to get to the Iron Dirigible. Plus, if there was going to be fighting involved, she wanted a clear head.

Rehka nodded and they departed the shop. Adi marked the man in the bowler as he trailed fifty paces behind them. She followed Rehka once more, distracted by their tail, and paid no attention to where Rehka led her.

"Here we are," she said.

Adi looked up and saw the swinging shingle of the Crook & Vine.

"Not here," Adi protested.

"This was our café," Rehka said.

"Was. Years ago." Adi kept her voice flat, but inside she was a storm of emotions. A decade prior, before the *Snowcrest*, in the heady days when their relationship was a new and vibrant thing, they had frequented the Crook & Vine. Rehka had often performed there. And it was here that they had met Captain Grint of the *Snowcrest*.

A look of pain flickered across Rehka's face, but the Dragon pushed it away. Adi sighed. Across the street, the man in the hat watched them. He made little effort to blend in.

"We're being followed," Adi said, changing the subject.

Rehka looked across the street and waved. The man grinned and waved back but did not approach.

"That's Duncan, my first lieutenant," Rehka said. "He's part of my crew."

"Your crew? He's a Water Knife?"

"He is."

"What's he doing here?"

"Security. Plus, we might need some help if things go bad at the Iron Dirigible."

Adi scratched the inflamed skin beneath the edges of her collar.

"How many mercenaries are with you?"

"Today, just Duncan. But my squad is a dozen." Rehka indicated the tattoo on her left bicep. "I'm a captain now."

Adi heard the pride in Rehka's voice. It made her angry.

*Of course, Rehka has a squad. Phoebe's Light, does anything phase this woman?* She always came out ahead. Adi wanted to bash her face in or kiss her. She was not sure which and that only made her more irritable.

"We can go somewhere else," Rehka said. Adi heard uncertainty in the Dragon's voice.

"It's fine. Let's eat" Adi said, teeth gritted. She walked into the tavern without waiting for Rehka to follow.

It was like stepping back in time. Everything inside the Crook & Vine appeared exactly as it had been years ago when Adi last entered the place. Ornate, weathered Tyrian rugs covered and softened the warped boards of the floor. Bucolic faded tapestries of vineyards, shepherds, and musicians hung over the canvas walls, which snapped lightly in the wind. A stage stood empty in the back corner, and a stew pot simmered over coals in the middle of the room spreading the odor of turmeric and cardamom throughout the tavern.

The early morning hour meant that only three other customers were patronizing the establishment. One of them, a young man in his twenties with a black eye snored loudly in a booth, sleeping off whatever trouble he had gotten himself into the night before. At a table near the bar, two elderly women nursed bowls of stew. The older human's rich but faded garb marked her as a merchant who had once been wealthier. The other, a Grym woman, was her house servant.

Adi slid into a booth near the door and signaled for the tavernkeeper. Rehka plopped down across from her with a sigh.

"You don't seem very happy to see me," Rehka said.

"What did you expect?" Adi snapped. "That I'd be locked in a high tower pining away and waiting for your return."

"Honestly, I thought you might try to kill me."

"The thought has crossed my mind."

Rehka flushed. "I won't go easy on you."

The tavernkeeper approached the table. Adi did not recognize the young gray Ankhim from her previous visits. She ordered a bowl of stew, and Rehka did the same. Adi waited until the tavernkeeper was out of earshot.

"You thought I would be glad to see you?"

"I hoped."

"You left me. You betrayed me, betrayed our crew, and for what?" Adi's voice cracked. The snoring man hitched, and the two women cast curious glances their way. Adi lowered her voice. "I waited for you as long as I could."

"Oh really? How long before you crawled into Iris's bed?"

Adi vibrated with irritation. "No. You don't get to judge me for finding someone else. Iris cares about me. She isn't using me to go after something else that she really wants."

"Can you blame me?"

"Of course."

"Adi"—Rehka placed her hands on Adi's who snatched them away—"I'm a Dragon without a Dragon, half a person. I found a lead, a way to reconnect. I had to take it."

"You could have taken me with you."

Rehka blanched. They fell silent again as the tavernkeeper placed steaming bowls of stew before each of them. Despite her anger, Adi was famished and started devouring the savory meal.

"I couldn't have." Rehka said, her stew untouched.

"Why not?"

Rehka looked away but didn't answer.

"More secrets," Adi scoffed.

"I wanted to," Rehka insisted. Believe me, I got no pleasure from lying to you. I had a lead to reconnect with my Dragon form in Pyrea and I took it. There was no other choice."

"And did it work?"

"No."

Adi could tell Rehka wanted her to ask about the details of her adventure, but she refused to give her that satisfaction. She had no desire to be regaled with Rehka's stories of adventure while Adi had been picking up the pieces of her shattered life.

"No," Adi said. "Of course it didn't work. How many false leads will you follow?"

"All of them."

"Despite your parents and scholars and priests and the Airene and whoever else telling you it is impossible to reconnect to your Dragon form?" Adi set her spoon down and regarded Rehka. "So, nothing's changed?"

"How could it?"

"You show up in my life after a betrayal like that, and expect me to run back into your arms until you take off again on your next futile lead?" Adi was truly angry now.

"You don't know what it's like to spend your whole life as half a person."

Adi stood. "How dare you!"

"Adi, I—"

"You think I don't know loss? I gave up my child for you."

"Adi, sit down. You're causing a scene."

Adi brandished her spoon in front of Rehka's nose. "Good, that will get it through that thick wall of arrogance between your skull and your brain. I nearly died. You sold me out to the Imperial Navy. If they had run down the *Snowcrest* they would have killed the whole crew. When you didn't come back, I tried to take my own life. Twice! And here you sit, bewildered that I didn't willingly leap into your waiting arms. Curses on you, Rehka. I gave up everything for you and you betrayed me. And for what? Djinnar's blood, you're not a Dragon anymore and you're not going to be. I loved you and you threw our whole lives back in my face. I was your Selene. You were my Maxon Laird."

"I'm a Dragon!" Rehka shouted, "I'm not supposed to be stuck in this human skin. I'm supposed to be more. This—This is not enough."

"It was enough for me! You had a choice, Rehka. I would've followed you to the edges of the World System on your stupid journey, if only you had asked me. But you didn't. You left me behind. You used me until you found something you wanted more."

"Adi, that's not true."

"Then why didn't you take me with you?"

"The places I had to go, Adi, I couldn't, in good conscience, ask you to follow me."

"You could have told me. You could have given me a choice. Or at least said goodbye. Instead, you were willing to trade away my life, my love. And for what? Look at you. You're no closer to being whole than when you left me. You should want me back. No one else will love you like I did, would follow you to the ends of the System, like I would've. Now you're broken *and* alone. Just like me."

Tears clouded Adi's vision and she felt as though she might be sick. She was shaking with rage and her speech had left her breathless. She yelled in incoherent rage and pain and chucked her spoon at Rehka's face. It clattered against the booth, spraying flecks of stew across a nearby tapestry, and fell harmlessly into the seat beside Rehka. Adi stormed out of the tavern only to run smack into Duncan. He grabbed at her wrists, but Adi twisted away. He stumbled but managed to grab Adi around the waist from behind.

"You're not going anywhere," Duncan growled.

Adi struggled and flailed but could not reach her attacker. Rehka emerged from the Crook & Vine still holding her coin purse. To Adi's satisfaction, Rehka had to blink away tears before regaining control of herself. Duncan got his arms around Adi's, pinning her elbows to her sides, grunting with the effort. Adi stamped down on his foot. Duncan cried out but did not let go.

"Enough, Adi," Rehka barked. Despite herself, Adi stilled. "I have a job to do, no matter how unpleasant your little tantrums make it. I am going to help you recover Apyreon. It's my job, never mind that it will save both your life and Lucas's." Rehka stuck her finger in Adi's face. "You haven't changed either. You're still the same selfish whore when you want to be. The little noblewoman from Saba who ran away from Daddy because she thinks she has a monopoly on pain. Grow up, Adi. You're no hero and you're far from the only broken person in the World System. Yes, I hoped that I would come find you as a whole Dragon and share my whole self with you, but you're a selfish child, Adi Crestone, and I was delusional to think anything else. You're done with me? Fine, be done. Run to Iris. Tell her what a mean Dragon your ex-lover is. But now, right now, shut up and think about Lucas."

Adi went slack. She knew Rehka was trying to hurt her. She had cut Rehka deeply and the woman wanted revenge. But knowing that did not make her words any less painful. She shrugged off Duncan's hold. He must have sensed the fight leave her because he let her go. Adi swallowed and blinked away tears, resisting the urge to sneak in a parting shot. She cleared her throat and straightened her weapons, stalling until she was in control of herself once more.

"All right," Adi said at last. "Let's go."

Rehka nodded.

"But lose Duncan. I'm not your prisoner. I'm your ally until this is done and then I never want to see you again."

Rehka sighed.

"You sure boss? I can stick around in case she runs," Duncan said.

"She won't run," Rehka said. "Go back to headquarters and wait for my message."

Adi took several deep breaths to calm herself further. Duncan looked her up and down as if making certain she was defeated, then he offered Rehka a salute, turned on his heels, and trotted off down the street. Adi and Rehka headed in the opposite direction, toward the warehouse district and the Iron Dirigible.

# CHAPTER TWENTY

# ADI CRESTONE

## MOON OF XYS, VALEDAY, 30TH OF HEBE

A di rapped five times on the metal door of the Iron Dirigible, paused, then knocked twice more. The speakeasy grille slid aside, revealing a pair of dark blue eyes and a turquoise brow.

*An aquatic Ankhim*, Adi thought. *Unusual on Xys.*

"Hail Solo," Adi said, standing on tiptoe so the bouncer could see the Blood Queen's collar around her neck.

The grille slid shut. An iron bolt scraped, then the door swung inward on creaky hinges. The Ankhim filled the doorway, tattooed muscles rippling in the morning light. Thick clouds of pungent smoke rolled around him and out the door. Adi detected both the leathery musk of hookahs and the burnt sugar of loona.

The bouncer eyed them. "What's your business?"

"Blood Queen business," Adi said.

"With a Water Knife mercenary?" Skepticism tinted the bouncer's husky voice.

*How did he know that?* Adi wondered. Then she noticed Rehka had removed her jacket in the morning heat, revealing three wavy lines tattooed on her left bicep.

"I don't remember the Blood Queen's business being any of yours," Adi said.

The bouncer's muscles tensed. "No Dragons."

"She's no Dragon," Adi lied.

The bouncer took in Rehka. "Tall enough."

"No aura," Rehka said, her voice flat.

The bouncer was large, even for an Ankhim. Adi had never seen him before. He took two steps toward Rehka and inhaled deeply. Adi had no idea what he might be sniffing for, but when he stepped back, he was relaxed.

"Fine," he said. "No weapons."

"Are you serious!?" Adi protested "Since when?"

The bouncer crossed his arms.

Rehka removed her bandoliers, then her pistols. She produced half a dozen blades from various scabbards secreted on her body. When she finished, she took a step toward the door. The Ankhim puffed out his chest, his eyes on her boots. Rehka sighed and removed a long boot knife from an ankle sheath. The bouncer scooped up the weapons and glared at Adi.

She shrugged. "I've got none."

The bouncer waited in silence.

Adi opened her coat to remove her newly purchased armaments.

The Ankhim grunted and stepped aside, allowing them to enter. "Stay out of Charity section," he said as they stepped into the dim foyer. There was a complex clatter as he deposited all their weapons in a wooden crate.

"What's going on in Charity?" Adi asked.

"I don't remember the business of the *proprietor* being any of yours."

*Fair enough,* Adi thought. The bouncer's comment let her know Tabrin Wik was here. *Interesting.*

The entryway of the Iron Dirigible lacked both charm and décor. Beyond it, the bartender leaned on the counter, cleaning his long nails with a knife. Half a dozen White Rabbits sat around a table. One of them was dealing cards. Adi didn't recognize any of them from her mugging. An older bald man sat on one of the barstools, half asleep. The inside of his left wrist carried the eagle and sickle tattoo that marked assassins for the Order of the Talon.

Adi felt nine pairs of eyes sweep over them, decide they were not yet a threat, and move on. The card dealer never paused in her duties. The azure Ankhim resumed his position on a heavy stool beside the door.

Once, the Iron Dirigible had been a storehouse for Vescovite Iron Smelting. But when Xys began to drop toward Solo, the metal magnate Alexei Vescovite had relocated his operation to the moon Behl. It was hard enough to run a complicated manufacturing business in a peripatetic city, but the geologic mayhem caused by Xys' descent had made it next to impossible.

The proprietor of the Iron Dirigible, Tabrin Wik, was a well-known antiquities dealer. He converted the maze of storage rooms into a bar where White Rabbit, Blood Queen, and Water Knife gang members, Talon operatives, and more could find a moment's respite from the constant internecine struggles. He and his staff encouraged neutrality, but brawls were known to still occur. The far end of the room was curved in a rough semi-circle with four doors marked Faith, Hope, Grace, and Charity. All the doors stood open except Charity.

"Something's going on," Rehka whispered in Adi's ear. She nodded in agreement and made her way to the bar.

"Hail Solo," Adi told the barkeep. "Two pints."

"Hail Solo," the barkeep muttered and selected two questionably clean mugs.

"It's a little early, Adi," Rehka hissed.

"It's a bar, Rehka, you won't get very far without spending a little coin."

The barkeep set two pints of murky brown liquid in front of them. Adi overpaid. The coins disappeared into the man's apron.

"You seen a White Rabbit in here, bald, sick-looking, big sore on his lower lip?" she asked.

"Nope," the barkeep replied, keeping his eyes on the card game.

Adi described Rictor, the tall assailant. When the barkeep still didn't respond, she sighed and placed another coin on the table. The man's fingers pounced like a hungry creature and the coin disappeared into his apron, but he remained silent. Adi was weighing the consequences of starting a fight with the bartender, when his shifting eyes slowly locked onto the door to Charity for a second before he stepped away.

*Of course.*

"Thank you, friend." She took a sip of her beer and immediately spit it back into the glass and shuddered. Turpentine and swamp muck. She set down her mug and smiled at the man. "Delicious."

The barkeep snorted. "Whatever you're here to do, keep it civil or take it outside."

Adi turned and leaned against the bar.

"Rictor's here," she whispered to Rehka.

"Who?"

"One of the guys who attacked me. If we can find him, we get a lead on"—Adi swallowed—"on the device."

"Where is he?"

She nodded once toward Charity's closed door. "Where do you think?"

Rehka sighed. "Naturally."

"We need a distraction."

Rehka laughed. "I suppose you want me to pick a fight, unarmed, with six White Rabbits and that bison of a bouncer while you sneak into Charity?"

"The thought did cross my mind."

"I'm good, but not that good."

They were considering plans of action when five knocks, then two more sounded on the metal door. The bouncer stood and slid open the grille. After a moment's consideration he opened it and allowed three more White Rabbit goons inside.

Adi recognized the woman from the group who'd attacked her. Adi kept her face turned away to prevent her former assailant the same recognition. The newcomers stopped and chatted in hushed tones with the card players before entering Grace. Adi counted to five then gestured with her beer glass for Rehka to join her.

The two women followed the goons at a distance down the twisting corridor. Every ten paces, a curtained doorway opened on alternating sides of the hallway. Many of them were empty this early in the day. One contained three women sleeping on overstuffed cushions, embers used to light a long loona pipe smoldered on a brazier. Another room contained a group of kids in their late teens gathered around a hookah, guzzling the terrible ale. Adi guessed they'd been going all night. At the end of the hallway, the White Rabbits opened a door. A bright bar of sunlight cut through the smoky air.

"Back doors," Adi said. "How handy."

Rehka nodded. "I doubt gangsters congregate in a bar with only one entrance and exit."

"Can I help you?" a woman's voice interrupted their hushed conversation.

Adi saw her assailant returning down the hallway.

"You followin' us?" the woman asked. Suddenly, Adi missed her weapons. When the blonde, mousy woman was three paces away, she recognized Adi.

"You—" the woman began.

Adi didn't wait for her to finish. She smashed her beer glass into the woman's face and felt her nose break. Adi followed the hit with a knee to the stomach. When the woman doubled over, Rehka clobbered her on the chin.

The White Rabbit thug shrieked as beer, blood, and glass splattered the walls and floor and collapsed onto her side, clutching her nose. Adi crouched beside her and picked up a triangular piece of broken glass. The woman gasped as she tried to stanch the blood from her broken nose. Adi stroked the shard lightly across the woman's cheek.

"Where're the others?"

"Djinnar's curses!" she retorted, spraying bloody spit.

Adi added a shallow slice to the woman's damaged face.

"What's going on in Charity?" Rehka asked. Adi held the shard up to the woman's eye. When she tried to scramble away, Rehka stomped her ankle.

"Don't make me ask you again."

The woman's defiance collapsed. "Rictor and Royal are meeting with Wik."

"Stuart Royal? Is the leader of the White Rabbits here? Away from his hideout in the Warrens?"

The woman realized she'd said too much.

Rehka pressed down on the trapped ankle. "What are they meeting about?"

The woman's eyes flicked to Adi, then settled on Rehka. When the White Rabbit said nothing, Rehka lifted her leg to stomp again. The woman cried out, then clamped her mouth shut. She was shaking all over now.

"I think they're discussing what they stole from me," Adi said. "Maybe Wik recognized it."

"What's going on here?" The Ankhimian bouncer filled the hallway behind them.

"Time to go," Adi said. She released her grip on the woman and let the glass shard clatter to the floor. She and Rehka dashed for the back door and burst into the alley. Adi expected a fight with the other two White Rabbit goons, but the alley was empty.

"It must be Apyreon," Adi said, "Stuart Royal would never leave the Warrens for anything less."

Behind them the bouncer stepped through the doorway, the woman two steps behind him, blood still streaming down her face. She took a small pistol from her belt.

"Run!" Adi shouted. Rehka needed no further prompting and they bolted down the alley to the main street. Adi saw a musket ball ricochet off a wall ahead of them just as the bark of a flintlock rang in her ears. She and Rehka jumped away from each other and added erratic dodges to their headlong rush.

The two women rounded the corner into the main street, breathing hard. A few people glanced in their direction, but most kept their heads down. Another pistol shot reverberated through the quiet morning. Adi looked down the street and saw two city watchmen alerted by the sound. The bouncer and the White Rabbit woman emerged from the alley.

"Let's split up," Adi said. "Meet back here in half an hour."

"Are you crazy?" Rehka exclaimed, "We can't go back in there."

"We must. Apyreon is there. My attackers are there. Trust me, Rehka."

Rehka eyed her and Adi expected further argument, but the city watchmen were shouting now. Adi pushed Rehka toward the other side of the street.

"Just go!" Without waiting for a response Adi sprinted toward the city watchmen. She heard another shot from the pistol.

The shockwave of their running battle rolled into the early morning traffic. People panicked, scattering in all directions with their children or their loads. Dogs barked and joined the chase. A team of heavy horses spooked when Rehka vaulted over a whiffle-tree, passing between their great haunches and their wagon, bounding forward into the frightened crowd. Adi spotted two more watchmen emerging from a side street, weapons drawn. She bowled into the first two. One of them went down hard, but the other managed to grab her wrist. His grip spun Adi around, killing her momentum. Her heel struck a lose cobblestone and she fell backward. The watchman pounced on her, pinning her arms above her head.

"Help me!" she gasped over the pain in her tail bone. "They're trying to kill me!"

"You attacked me," he hissed. "Stop struggling."

A shadow fell across them and Adi realized the bouncer from the Iron Dirigible had caught up to her.

"She assaulted another customer," the bouncer snarled. "I want her arrested."

*Djinnar's blood,* Adi thought, *the bouncer's smarter than he looks.*

"He's lying," Adi grunted. She could not see Rehka or the White Rabbit woman anywhere. The two other watchmen arrived and succeeded in shoving the massive Ankhim back.

The man who'd brought Adi down stood and offered her a hand. She took it and rose, stifling a gasp of pain as she brushed grit off her clothing. Her new doublet was undamaged. When she stooped to retrieve her hat, the watchman grasped her upper arm.

"You're both under arrest until we determine what happened."

"I want to speak with Senior Inspector Broc," Adi said to the captain of the squad.

"You're a rat!" The bouncer lunged for her, dragging the watchmen along.

"You're an informant of his?" one asked.

Adi nodded.

"If you're lying, I'm going to let this giant pound you into the street, understand?"

"Just find Broc."

The captain nodded to one of the others, who ran to fetch the inspector. Adi sat on the curb of the street to wait.

# CHAPTER TWENTY-ONE
# THEO VANGUARD

## MOON OF XYS, VALEDAY, 30TH OF HEBE

Theo awoke with a shout, arms and legs twisted in sweat-soaked sheets. Warm light filtered through linen curtains. It took several long breaths before he remembered he was in a guest room in Governor Gambol's sprawling estate in the heart of Solvigant. And he had three days to find Captain Crestone and Apyreon before escorting the governor's delegation to Djinnar's temple on Maxon. In a city the size of Solvigant, that wasn't much time.

The thought of visiting the God of Destruction reminded Theo of his dream. He'd been floating on the sea, amid flotsam from a wrecked ship. He knew nothing of the dream ship or its destruction, but hundreds of bleached bones bobbed and swirled in the water around him. A bony hand slapped the broken wood, and the upper half of a skeleton pulled itself onto the raft. He had tried to kick it off, but the skeleton held on, thrashing and biting. Theo was certain the creature was hunting him.

He shivered despite the dry heat in the bedroom. He didn't often remember his dreams, and even when he did he never put much stock into such things. His mother, the Nine bless her, was always consulting psychics, physickers, alchemists, and anyone else bold enough to charge the high lady for a peek behind the astral curtain. Theo, while less brutal toward her than his brothers, still rolled his eyes whenever she came to him, convinced of some impending danger.

He pushed the dream and the sheets aside and rose from the four-poster bed. He relieved himself in the empty chamber pot and discovered fresh clothes had been left out for him on a table beside the wardrobe. He unwrapped the bandage on his left hand and winced at the fiery edges of the wound. He dutifully spread the physicker's salve into the bite and replaced the bandages. With the wound redressed, he buttoned his cuffs and peered into the hallway. A servant was standing at attention outside the door, waiting for her guest to appear.

The woman, old enough to be his mother, curtsied. "Good morning, m'lord."

Theo nodded in return.

"The governor requests your company for breakfast at your convenience."

"Lead the way," Theo replied and followed the stout woman through the many corridors of the palace. "What time is it?"

"The clock struck a quarter past ten a few minutes ago."

Theo chastised himself. *I slept through most of the morning.*

The servant led him out a back door into a spacious garden. To the left, water gurgled through a stone fountain. Squat palms crowned in broad fronds provided shade for a wrought-iron table. Governor Eliot Gambol sat in one chair, his half-eaten breakfast perched precariously on a stack of papers. Beside him, holding a steaming cup of coffee, sat a Faelani squirrel. His red, tufted ears twitched as Governor Gambol laughed at something Theo could not hear.

"Commander Theo Vanguard," the servant announced.

The governor and the squirrel looked at Theo and smiled. Theo had seen Faelani before but was unaccustomed to the number present in Solvigant. They tended to eschew crowded urban centers like the capital of the Empire yet seemed quite at home in the City Peripatetic.

Theo sat in the indicated chair as another servant, a middle-aged man, bustled out from the nearby kitchen and placed Theo's breakfast in front of him.

"Theo," Gambol began, "this is Arthur Volaticus, Archdeacon Heilig's emissary from the Sons of Destruction. He is to accompany you on the pilgrimage."

Theo coughed to cover his surprise. Given the archdeacon's reported displeasure concerning the delegation, Theo had expected Heilig to send the most dour, stuffy priest he could find.

Volaticus extended a hand across the table. Theo wiped sausage grease on his napkin before shaking the Faelani's... *Paw? Hand?* The wiry fur tickled his palm as the short claws brushed against his wrist.

"A pleasure to meet you, Father," Theo said.

The squirrel laughed, a chittering sound with a hint of wry humor.

"Please, call me Art, Commander. We who follow Djinnar aren't big on formality." Art took a sip of his coffee.

"Very well, Art, please call me Theo."

The squirrel nodded with approval. Theo studied the priest. Art wore light leather armor over a white tunic. A green traveling cloak flowed from his shoulders, clasped with a silver skull and crossbones, the emblem of the Sons of Destruction. A wide leather belt hung with bags and pouches prevented him from sitting back in the chair. The glowing plume of his red tail rose behind him, the tip flicking as he spoke. An amethyst dragonstone hung from a metal chain around his neck. Theo noticed the sides of the tunic and armor were modified to accommodate large folds of skin under Art's armpits.

"Not what you expected?" Art winked at Theo.

"No," Theo admitted.

"You're exactly who I expected," Art said. "A soldier and the youngest son of Simon Vanguard."

Theo was unsure how to interpret the remark. *Good thing my father isn't present to hear this priest skip all his honorifics.*

"Art wanted to speak with the Lady Faide before your departure," Governor Gambol explained. "He is recently returned from Highgaard, where he was running an errand for me. He was briefing me on the details."

"Please"—Theo gestured—"don't stop on my account."

"We had just finished," Gambol said.

"And how is the Lady Faide this morning?" Theo said to fill the awkward silence that followed.

"Still abed it seems," Art said.

"The ambassador and his wife have accommodations here?"

"The Sabaian Embassy sustained damage in the last significant tremor," the governor said. "They'll stay here until the reconstruction is complete." Gambol sipped his coffee. "I spoke with your father this morning."

Theo set down his fork. "You did? I mean, what news from my father?"

"He expressed his gratitude and relief that you're here and safe. He had little to say about the ship—the *Sidereal* was it?—that was stolen, except that he seemed quite put out by it. He wanted me to pass this along to you." The governor shuffled through the stack of papers and produced an envelope which he slid across the table to Theo.

"You saw him?" Theo asked, not touching the letter.

"I've already been to Tyre and back this morning. Governor's and chancellor's prerogative."

Theo nodded.

"He'll be here himself in two days, just before your own departure,"

"He will? Why?" He must have looked confused because Governor Gambol smiled.

"Who knows all the reasons that drive the emperor and his chancellors."

"Did you speak to him of my leadership of the delegation to Djinnar?"

Gambol nodded. "I did. He approved of your appointment. He even offered the use of his personal vessel, *Penumbra*."

Theo leaned back in his chair, eyes wide.

"You did not expect this?"

"I expected the loss of the *Sidereal* to anger him."

Gambol smiled. "Oh, he is angry."

"Is that why he's coming here?"

Gambol tapped a fat finger on the envelope, "Perhaps you should read for yourself."

Theo reached for the letter just as a servant cleared his throat and announced, "The Lady Beatrice Marrion and her husband Ambassador Hubert Marrion."

The three men rose and bowed at the presence of a lady. This morning, Beatrice wore a simple green gown that, with her blue hair and blue eyes, made her look like a water spirit.

*She brings such beauty to this dry place,* Theo thought. Her husband's pasty face suggested that he was suffering the consequences of a sybaritic evening. He squinted against the bright morning light.

"Gentlemen, good morning," Hubert said, and shook each of their hands in turn. Beatrice curtsied, her eyes fixed on the ground. She said nothing, but blushed when Theo said,

"Good morning, Lady Faide."

"It's Marrion," Hubert corrected him.

"Apologies, Ambassador, of course," Theo said.

The couple sat and the rest waited while servants placed plates of eggs, bacon, and a popular local dish called corn pudding. Once the flurry of activity died down, Gambol leaned forward and laid a hand on Beatrice's on arm.

"Are you finding your accommodations acceptable?"

Beatrice swallowed. "Yes, Governor, the rooms are lovely."

"If a bit drafty," Hubert added.

"It is a challenge," Gambol said. "The pilgrimages are hard on the city. The work to keep a structure such as this one in the appropriate shape for its purpose never ends. I will send carpenters this afternoon to inspect your rooms and make any necessary repairs. If that is to your satisfaction?"

"It is," Hubert said. "Thank you."

"What news from Saba this morning?" Gambol asked.

"My father, Lord Tobias Marrion, sends his regards. From Governor Faide, I have heard little since my arrival, though my courier is due this afternoon."

Theo shifted, already bored by the bureaucratic conversation that did not include him. He tried not to stare at the Lady Marrion while she ate beside her husband. Her movements were timid and delicate, like a hummingbird. Theo wondered why a woman with her abilities was not seated at the right hand of the emperor, why she lived without titles, yoked to an arrogant second-tier nobleman.

"Lady Marrion," Art said when there was a lull in the conversation, "I wondered if I might ask you about the content of your visions. If that is not too forward?"

Beatrice looked up from her plate, startled. "You are from the Sons of Destruction?"

"I am."

"You want to know about Pallantier?"

"Have you seen anything?"

"Why do you want to know?"

"Until Pallantier's disappearance, the Sons of Destruction and the Daughters of Creation shared an affinity, as our patron gods are twins. In Solvigant, we share two halves of the same temple. Now the doors to the Temple of Creation are barred, the windows shuttered. No one has seen or spoken to any of the Daughters in twenty years. Our abbot has had no correspondence from their prioress. I recently visited our brethren in Oringrad on Highgaard and they report the same. Lady Naima Korex, the High Sister, has not reported to the Emperor's Council, nor has High Brother Maynard received any correspondence."

"The God of Creation has been missing for two decades," Hubert said, "The seclusion of the Daughters is old news."

"Something has changed, husband, or Brother Volaticus would not be asking."

Art cleared his throat, clearly uncomfortable with the malice that simmered between Lord and Lady Marrion. "Indeed, it has. We assumed the Sisters were in seclusion, a kind of mourning for the missing god. Still, they are mortal creatures who must eat and sleep, who fall ill and create waste. Servants were often seen in the marketplaces buying food, medicines, or clothing. Tradesmen came to oversee temple maintenance, and doctors visited. Two weeks ago, all activities at the Temple of Creation in Solvigant ceased. No one has seen anyone associated with the temple in a fortnight. The temple in Oringrad reports the same as of ten days ago, and yesterday we received word from Thail that as of two days ago, the temple there has fallen silent. No one is tending to the eternal flame. I expect to find a similar situation when the delegation arrives in Planktown on Maxon."

"I'm not sure how I can help," Beatrice said. "I seldom observe the gods in my visions."

"If you have seen anything that might explain the recent changes, it could be useful," Art pressed.

"I record all my visions for posterity at my father's request. Sometimes they are like dreams that fade quickly upon waking. I will consult it, and if I find anything I will report to you."

Hubert scoffed but said nothing.

"What of Djinnar?" Gambol asked. "Have the Sons of Destruction beseeched the god for the whereabouts of his sibling?"

"We have many times, and will continue to do so," Art said. "Djinnar still grants us his favors, but he is quiet. There have been no new edicts or prophecies since Pallantier's disappearance. High Brother Maynard sent several envoys to Maxon in the early years to question Djinnar at his House, but none were successful."

"What happened to them?" Theo asked.

"Two did not return. Two others returned, and both now reside in the Temple of Destruction in Thail. One is silent, the other babbles incessant nonsense. After Brother Vincent returned amid the throes of madness, we sent no further envoys. The Sons of Destruction's ranks have thinned since the disappearance of Pallantier, and I think the High Brother did not want to risk losing anymore priests. I sent a formal inquiry to the High Brother, that I might interview him before our delegation departs, but have received no answer as of yet."

Everyone was silent while they digested this information.

"What of me?" Theo blurted. All eyes at the table turned toward him.

"I beg your pardon?" Beatrice asked.

"At dinner you said the congressman and I witnessed the destruction of Xys. Is there more you can tell me?"

"There is not. But do not fear, I said you were present, not that you were responsible."

Theo sighed. He had not even thought of that as a possibility but felt immense relief despite himself.

"I did have a vision last night," Beatrice said. "Of Xys." Theo leaned forward. The governor stopped shuffling through his papers and listened.

"I wandered the bowels of Xys accompanied by the people of Solvigant. I lead them through a vast network of caves."

"There is no such network," the governor interjected.

"Sometimes it was a sandstone cavern, other times we wandered in the bowels of a great machine."

"What happened?" Gambol pressed. "Where did you go?"

"That is all. We simply wandered. The people were thirsty and tired, but they followed me though I knew not where I was leading them. I followed someone, but they were always too far ahead for me to make out any details of the person."

Theo watched as Beatrice relayed her vision. She seemed to grow tired even speaking about it. Her shoulders slumped and Theo noticed makeup hiding dark circles under her eyes. Governor Gambol continued to drill her about the details of her vision, but nothing she said seemed to satisfy him or reveal anything more of significance.

"Perhaps the Lady Marrion would appreciate a respite from this interrogation," Theo said. The governor looked up at him, a reprimand on his tongue, which he bit off when he remembered to whom he was speaking. It often happened that the long shadow of his father protected him, and part of Theo resented it.

"Governor, might we delay this line of questioning? The lady seems tired. Xys will not fall into the Mother today. You could query her again at some other time." Theo's audacity at reprimanding the governor surprised even himself. He could see the stolid man considering his response. There were few people in the Imperial bureaucracy above the governor, and Theo was not technically one of them. The governor would be within his rights to reprimand him, regardless of who Theo's father was.

Theo was saved from chastisement when another servant scurried into the garden and whispered in the governor's ear.

Gambol rose. "If you will excuse me, representatives of the city watch would like a word. I will see them in my office. My Lady Marrion, if I have caused you any discomfort, I apologize. Commander Vanguard, we will speak of this later."

Everyone stood as the governor followed the servant across the gardens into the mansion. Hubert glared at Theo over an empty breakfast plate as an awkward silence settled over the quartet. Theo wanted a reason to excuse himself but could think of nothing appropriate. He did not look forward to a future dressing-down by the governor. Theo could not meet Beatrice's gaze.

Art said, "We might take in the sights of Solvigant, Commander Vanguard. You haven't much time here before the delegation departs, and the governor informed me it was your first time in our wandering city. It would be my honor to show you the Temple of Destruction while we discuss some of the details of our upcoming journey."

Theo jumped at the opportunity, grateful for the chance to excuse himself and flee the breakfast table. He rose so quickly that he bumped into the table, causing the dishes to rattle.

"A splendid idea, Art, though I should say good morning to my cousin before we depart."

# CHAPTER TWENTY-TWO

# ADI CRESTONE

## MOON OF XYS, VALEDAY, 30TH OF HEBE

"Stuart Royal is out of the Warrens," Adi repeated.

"Did you see him?" Becca Henge loomed over her.

Adi ignored the woman and spoke to Broc, who leaned against the counter of the blacksmith's shop he'd commandeered for his interrogation. He avoided Adi's gaze, focusing on the Iron Dirigible a few blocks away.

"How often does that happen?" Adi said. "You're missing a huge opportunity." They had clamped her manacle chain to the floor vise. She shifted, testing the limits of her mobility.

"Got somewhere to be?" Henge sneered.

"I haven't done anything wrong," Adi hissed through clenched teeth.

"You assaulted two watchmen while fleeing the scene of a crime."

"I went to them for help after I was attacked in the Iron Dirigible."

"And what were you doing there?"

"Gathering information for Broc."

Henge snorted. "Of course, one meeting with the great Senior Inspector Broc and you're one of the good guys."

"You're an idiot," Adi snarled. "I've met those folks you call the good guys when I was delivering their bribes. The Blood Queen paid for that Alephian crystal decanter in your father's office."

Anger flashed in Henge's eyes and Adi was certain the officer was going to slap her.

Broc's sonorous tenor interrupted Henge's retort. "The Blood Queen would find it quite convenient if I captured her chief rival."

Adi leaned toward him. "A White Rabbit who attacked me is in there. White Rabbits killed your partner, Broc."

"The city watch is an instrument of justice, not vengeance. We are not a tool for criminal organizations to gain power over one another."

Adi thought of all the crooked guards and politicians she had seen coming and going from the Red Wyrm over the years and tried another angle.

"You said something is going on. The White Rabbits are bolder, murdering targets all over the city, including your partner. Now Stuart Royal has come out of the Warrens for the first time in years. You could wait for the inevitable gang war, or you can raid the Iron Dirigible and arrest Royal right now."

"Sir," Henge said, "the Iron Dirigible is a labyrinth of hallways and storage rooms. It would be suicide to raid it without a full brigade. The gangs can hold that hellhole against us with only a few men."

"You've been inside the Dirigible?" Adi asked. "Maybe I underestimated you, Henge. You don't look like a loony. Or maybe lacweed is your drug of choice."

Henge shot her a withering glance.

"Enough." Broc held up a furred hand. Adi noticed the polished tips of his sharpened claws. "Henge, have the men outside set up a perimeter around the Dirigible. Put two men on the alley and get some crossbowmen on the roof across the street. No one goes in or out without our knowledge. You're right, we can't go in, but Captain Crestone has a point. We don't know when we'll get another chance at Royal. We must grab him when he comes out."

"What about her?"

"She stays with me. I need her to identify Rictor and the woman who shot at her."

Adi grinned at Henge and offered her manacled hands to Broc. He shook his head.

"Manacles stay on." Adi slumped. "You stay closer to me than my shadow. If you disappear or if I discover you've played me, our deal is off and you go to jail."

"On what charges?" Adi protested.

"I'll have no problem coming up with a few that'll stick."

"It's like you don't trust me."

It was Broc's turn to laugh. "That would be true. Let's go."

Under Broc's supervision, Adi instructed two guards in street clothes on the coded knock and password so they could monitor the premises from within. City watch carriages were parked at each end of the street. One held watchmen ready to block the street if necessary. Broc, Adi, and Henge climbed into the other. Adi found herself crammed onto the rear bench between two large watchmen, while Broc and Henge trained a spyglass on the front door.

*Where is Rehka?* Adi wondered. She had no idea how much time had elapsed since they'd split up, but it felt like almost two hours. *I hope Royal didn't slip away before Broc set up his perimeter.*

"What's going on?" Adi asked. She could only see a mere sliver of the front door through the carriage window.

"Our men just went inside," Broc reported. "Now we wait."

Time oozed by. Twice Broc asked her to peer through the spyglass at departing customers, but neither man was Rictor. The second time, Adi scanned the street. Beyond the other carriage she saw Rehka sitting at a café table. When Broc realized she wasn't watching the door, he snatched the glass away and trained it where she'd been looking.

"Who's that?"

"Who?"

"That woman?"

"Never seen her before."

Broc clearly did not believe her, but he didn't press the issue. They continued to wait. Adi hummed "To the Valley I Go." She could not carry a tune.

"Shut up," Henge grumbled.

"I'm bored," Adi said.

"Quiet," Broc said, "We have company."

Adi craned her neck to peer out the small window. Two carriages clopped toward them. The larger one was drawn by four black horses decorated as if for a state funeral. Red velvet curtains obscured the windows. The driver wore a coat with tails, and Adi spotted a collar of indenture to the Blood Queen.

"Why by the gods?" Adi whispered. *Why would the Blood Queen come here in broad daylight?*

The other carriage wobbled along behind, one wheel misaligned. The driver slumped on his seat, reins slack in his hands. The roan mares hitched to it were lean and uneasy.

"Someone's coming out of the Dirigible," Henge said. Adi couldn't see past Broc's head.

"Who is it?" she asked.

"Royal," Broc said. "Let's go."

An Ankhim signaled the nearest crossbowman, who relayed the signal to the second watch carriage.

"Go!" Broc shouted, and he and Henge burst from the carriage. Adi followed close behind while the two Ankhim stayed near the carriage to block the exit to the street. Adi saw soldiers pouring from the other carriage. She glanced toward the café but could no longer pick out Rehka.

Stuart Royal stood in the middle of the street, which was now devoid of bystanders, arms held over his head. Adi had never seen the Faelani before; he was a short white rabbit. His ears made him taller than Broc, but he was lightly built and would be no match for the badger. One of Royal's ears stood tall, but the top half of the other hung crumpled. He wore a tailored waistcoat and breeches. His broad feet were bare on the cobbles. Over his shoulder was Adi's bag and she could see one corner of the rosewood box through the open top.

*Apyreon.*

"Senior Inspector Broc," Royal drawled, "a pleasant surprise."

"Stuart Royal, you are under arrest for the murder of Senior Inspector Damgaard."

Royal eyed the manacles Broc was carrying.

"I'm surprised you're sober enough to be here," Stuart said. His harsh voice clashed with his face's delicate leporidae features and his twitching nose. He lowered his arms and rotated on his heels to survey the situation. His good ear rotated, tracking the sounds of the watchmen on the street and the roofs. His eyes paused on the Blood Queen's carriage. "Very thorough. Is the great Senior Inspector Broc reduced to carrying out the Blood Queen's bidding?"

"I have no arrangement with Riven," Broc growled.

The door to the Iron Dirigible opened, revealing the six White Rabbits from the card game, led by Rictor. Between them they held the two officers Broc had sent inside. They had been beaten bloody, and one of them had to be dragged, both legs broken. Rictor brandished a short sword.

"Let them go," Broc ordered.

"Perhaps we can make a trade? Their lives for mine."

Adi still detected no movement from the Blood Queen's carriage. She shrank into the shadows inside her own carriage. If Sasha Riven spotted Adi in the watch's custody, the Blood Queen would consider her a compromised asset and have her killed.

"I don't negotiate with gangsters," Broc said.

"Then more watchmen will die," Royal said. His casual brutality unnerved Adi. Surrounded by city watchmen and a vicious rival, he looked as comfortable as if he were sitting in his own living room deep in the Warrens.

"If you kill those men, Royal, your life and the lives of your men are forfeit."

"Senior Inspector Broc, you are so confident. Your late partner was confident, too. Though I see they promoted you to his position. I suppose congratulations are in order."

Broc took two steps forward, his fists clenched.

*Royal is baiting him,* Adi realized. *And it's working.*

"Order your men to stand down Royal."

Royal laughed and Adi caught the glimmer of an ivory dragonstone hanging from a thick chain around his neck.

*Djinnar's blood, he's a mage!*

Adi's eyes flicked from Royal to Rictor to the mob of White Rabbits standing behind him to the Blood Queen's silent carriage then back to Royal. Adi wanted to wipe the sweat from her forehead, but didn't dare cause her manacles to rattle.

Boots pounded on cobblestones and, too late, she realized what was about to happen.

"Rehka, no!" Adi jumped out of the carriage and shouted at the mercenary. Rehka was running at breakneck speed down the street. She blew past the city watchmen to slam into Royal from behind, flattening the leader of the White Rabbits onto the hard-packed road. The rosewood box slipped out of the bag and skidded away.

Rehka ignored Royal and dove for the box, but the leader of the White Rabbits was faster. He rolled onto his back and kicked her hard with both powerful feet. She rolled across the cobbles, swearing.

"Take him!" Broc shouted.

"Save Royal!" Rictor bellowed.

"Rekha!" Adi screamed into the din.

Two crossbow bolts whizzed over the fray and struck with a *thunk* into the torso of a White Rabbit goon, hurling him into his fellows. The goons and the watch closed in a blur of steel, flesh, and claws. Broc and Royal faced off in the middle of the street. Rehka scrambled up and lunged toward Rictor, who was sprinting for the box. Henge shouted for more guards. The Iron Dirigible's door banged open and six more White Rabbits poured onto the street. Adi recognized Pimple among the newcomers and her stomach tightened, her palms were sweaty.

*This is no time for revenge. I must get Apyreon.*

Weaponless and manacled, Adi dashed toward Rictor. He bent to pick up the rose-wood box and she leapt onto his back, dropping her manacle chain across his throat. She yanked the chain taut and Rictor snapped upright, his sword flailing. Adi twisted, dodging the blade as she tightened the chain. The manacles bit deep into her burned wrists.

Adi screamed to release the pain. Rictor's sword clattered to the street as he fought against the chain. She threw her weight back and brought him down. Gasping, he groped for his sword. Rehka snatched the hilt away and kicked him hard in the ribs. He slumped onto the cobbles, unconscious. Adi maintained the chokehold for several more seconds to ensure he stayed down, then she untangled herself and stood.

Rehka thrust the rosewood box at her.

"I'm going to get our weapons," Rehka said. "Then we'll get the hell out of here."

Adi nodded and looked to where Broc and Royal were still facing off. Around them, watchmen and White Rabbits fought, each side preventing the other from aiding their leader.

Adi scooped up Rictor's abandoned sword and slid it into her belt. She ran toward Henge, who held the key to her manacles.

"Henge," Adi shouted as she skidded to a stop. "Unlock me."

"Yeah, right," Henge said, applying a tourniquet to a wounded guard.

"I'm no good to you in this fight."

"Go back to the carriage and wait," Henge ordered.

"You're about to be slaughtered!"

"We can handle a few White Rabbit thugs."

"Royal's a mage!"

"He is?" Henge looked toward Broc and Royal. The Faelani thrust and parried with a rapier. Broc could not get his dagger inside Royal's guard. Royal fought with eerie coolness and poise, while Broc was already panting, his lightness and speed fading against his opponent's agility and fitness.

The ivory dragonstone around Royal's neck glowed with an oily white light. Broc parried, parried again, then lunged. The dragonstone pulsed and Broc's dagger halted in midair. The shock threw Broc off balance. Royal kicked Broc in the chest and drove him back. The inspector scrambled to stay on his feet, his red face twisted in pain.

Behind them, Rehka emerged, fully armed once more, holding Adi's weapons in a bundle. She surveyed the scene and froze. Adi followed her gaze past Broc's carriage.

Jogging toward them was a gray-robed acolyte of Kade, the God of Chaos, the Pretender. Behind them, Adi saw dark robes and a bone-white mask.

*A void mage! They answer directly to the emperor. Whose side are they on?*

"Henge, we have to leave now!" Adi shouted.

"Not until we have Royal in custody."

Adi considered clocking Henge on the back of the head and snatching the keys.

"There's a god-cursed void mage coming. Give me the keys, Henge. At least give me a fighting chance."

Henge looked where Adi was pointing. The acolytes were only half a block from Broc's carriage.

"Djinnar's blood!" Henge fumbled the keys from her belt. "If you abandon us, Crestone, I will hunt you down and kill you myself."

"Fine," Adi agreed. Henge inserted the key and the lock clicked open. Adi looked up at Rehka.

*Of course it gets worse.*

Palestrina, the Blood Queen's general, was emerging from the Blood Queen's carriage. The Lady of Spiders took in the melee as the Blood Queen's carriage retreated from the fray. To Adi's right, the void mage's acolytes engaged the Ankhimian watchmen. Adi watched in horror as bulbous tumors swelled upon the skin of one of the watchmen. Steam spurted from his body and his skin crackled. The soldier exploded with a teakettle scream. Smoking flesh smacked wetly against the buildings on both sides of the street. The other watchman bolted, but the leading acolyte cut him down.

Thunder echoed across the cloudless sky as an iridescent wave of force erupted from Royal's dragonstone, knocking Broc backward twenty feet to slam into the gangster's waiting carriage. Wood crunched as the inspector's solid body caved in the side of the rickety chassis.

The horses bucked and skittered but the driver kept them in hand. Broc slumped beneath the carriage. If the horses took off, Broc would be crushed.

Adi heard Rehka and Palestrina yelling at each other.

"Henge, get Broc!" Adi shouted. She tucked the box under one arm, drew her sword and ran toward Rehka.

Adi saw Palestrina spread her chiropteran wings, talons glimmering in the sunlight.

*What is Palestrina doing here?* Adi realized the Seraph was looking at Royal as the Lady of Spiders drew a shotel from her belt. *This is an assassination. The Blood Queen knew Royal was out of the Warrens, too.*

"Rehka!" Adi shouted. "Let her take Royal down!" She pointed at the White Rabbit, who stood transfixed by the incoming void mage.

Rehka and Adi fled into the Dirigible, heading for the back alley.

# CHAPTER TWENTY-THREE

# ADI CRESTONE

## MOON OF XYS, VALEDAY, 30TH OF HEBE

Adi and Rehka were alone in the Iron Dirigible. The muffled sounds of steel ringing against steel punctuated the low boom of magical explosions. Tables and chairs had been flung aside when the White Rabbits had bolted outside. Everyone else had fled. Adi and Rehka took a moment to catch their breath. She took her bundle of weapons from Rehka and replaced them in their sheaths.

"Why did you charge Royal?" Adi demanded. "You should have let the watch handle it."

"Then the watch would have Apyreon. I couldn't let that happen."

Adi was silent. Rehka was right. If the city watch learned of Apyreon, her task would become a lot harder.

"Who was that?" Rehka panted.

"Palestrina, the Lady of Spiders. One of the Blood Queen's generals."

"What's she doing here? I thought it was your task to retrieve Apyreon."

"I don't think her presence here has anything to do with Apyreon."

"Then what?"

"My guess is that Sasha Riven learned Stuart Royal was leaving the Warrens and saw an opportunity to take out the competition."

"An assassination?"

Adi shrugged and hefted the rosewood box. All six sides of the wooden cube were crisscrossed with delicate engravings and mother-of-pearl circles so that it looked like the cosmos itself.

*If you held it up to the sky at night, the box would almost disappear,* Adi thought, turning the cube in her hands. The craftsmanship was so fine it took her several rotations to identify the faint seam indicating the split between the lid and the body. She placed her fingers on top of the cube and pulled the lid free.

"Djinnar's blood," Adi swore.

"What's wrong?"

"It's empty." Adi held out the two pieces of the rosewood cube.

Rehka uttered a string of harsh, draconic invectives. Adi studied the polished metal brackets into which the set screws should have been affixed. Except Apyreon, screws and all, was absent from its housing.

"W-who has it?" Rehka stammered.

"How should I know?"

The metal door to the Iron Dirigible blew off its hinges and shot straight into the room like a rectangular missile. Adi and Rehka dove in opposite directions. Adi leapt over the bar and saw Rehka dive behind the overturned card table. The heavy door demolished the furniture in its path before it clanged against the back wall and then clattered to the floor in a cloud of debris.

Adi peered over the countertop as the void mage strode into the room. From the shadows in the hallway of Hope, a White Rabbit woman charged the sorcerer, her face bloody, pistols firing. The lead shot curved away from the mage and struck the wall behind him. He did not flinch at the fury of the woman's onslaught.

An acolyte bounded forward from behind the mage, bloody sword drawn. The woman flung her pistols at him. He dodged one but the other connected with his shoulder. In one smooth motion, he side-stepped her assault and swung his sword horizontally at shoulder height. Adi gasped as the woman's head parted from her neck, blood spurting from the arteries. Her head hit the ground and rolled toward Rehka. The momentum of the woman's charge carried the rest of her body into the far wall, where it struck before slumping to the floor.

Rehka rose from beneath the card table, two knives drawn, two already sailing toward the mage. Hot, white lightning burst from his hands and the knives exploded into ash and dust leaving a searing afterimage in Adi's eyes. Rehka loosed the two knives, even as she reached for two more.

*She's even faster than I remember,* Adi thought. The second set of blades whizzed toward the acolyte. He parried the first, but his return stroke was too slow and the second buried itself to the hilt in the gap between his collarbones. The acolyte staggered, dropping his sword so he could use both hands to grasp the dagger's hilt. He yanked it out, wobbled, then collapsed onto his face, blood spurting from the wound. They all watched him convulse twice then go limp.

Adi cast about behind the bar for anything she could throw at the mage, because there was no way she was going to go after him with a blade. She hurled a mug, and another bolt of searing lightning blinded her as the mug disintegrated. Adi hurled more, but the afterimage streaks in her vision made it hard to aim.

The void mage did not bother parrying. He let a few of the mugs sail past, even let one hit him square in the chest. When Adi had exhausted her supply of ceramic ammunition, she paused. She heard the hiss and cackle of the mage's laughter in the sudden silence.

Adi vaulted the bar, drawing Rictor's short sword. Rehka charged from the other direction. They'd outflank the bastard.

"Enough!" the mage bellowed.

Adi's body continued moving forward, but the sword stuck in mid-air, pulling her off balance. She let go of it and, scrambling to stay upright, crashed into Rehka. They went down together in a tangle of limbs.

The void mage loomed over them, the polished bone mask reflecting the light of the sputtering oil lamps. He was still laughing, a sound she knew would haunt her forever.

"A commendable effort," he said, his voice hoarse and oddly quiet. Rehka's daggers and Adi's sword hung in the air. Adi wished for her own magic, but astral magic was the magic of engineers. Void magic was all fire and lightning, combat magic, and Adi had no idea how to counter it, even if she been able to use her abilities.

The void mage retrieved the rosewood cube and its discarded lid. He fit the two pieces back together and admired it. He did not bother to keep an eye on the two women.

*We are no threat to him,* Adi realized. This raised the hair on the back of her neck. She untangled herself and eased Rehka to the floor. The force of their collision had stunned her, and her face was slack. Adi's tricorn lay several feet away. The mage approached them on silent feet. Behind him, through the open doorway, Adi could see city watchmen and White Rabbits in close combat.

The mage's shadow fell across her and she flinched.

"Where is the device?"

"I don't know." Adi positioned herself in front of Rehka. "The box was empty."

The mage's pale green dragonstone flared as it pulled in void particulates. Crooked lightning arced from the mage's left palm and struck Rehka in the chest. She screamed and thrashed.

"No!" Adi shouted. "We don't have it. The box was empty."

The mage paused and looked at her. He sent a second bolt sizzling into Rehka. Adi smelled the sharp tang of burnt flesh. Rehka twitched, then went still.

"Stop it!" Adi screamed again. She reached deep for her own latent magic, but her wellspring of power was like a lake under several inches of ice. She fought to grasp it despite the pain of raw power searing her veins and slammed it into the mage's solar plexus. He doubled over as his breath was forced out of his lungs. It was not something she had known she could do. She gasped at the fading glow in the veins of her arms.

*What was that?*

Nausea from the resonance of channeling astral dust without her dragonstone overwhelmed her surprise. She scrambled to her feet and stood over Rehka. The mage leaned on his staff, coughing. His mask had fallen to the floor beside the rosewood box.

*Human,* Adi thought, *or what's left of one.*

The void mage snatched up his mask and replaced it. She met his gaze, sickened by his black irises shot through with glints of green lightning. Void magic consumed him. Everyone knew about the high cost of void magic. It came from Kade, the God of Chaos, and its power distorted a user's will and unraveled their sanity.

Adi braced for the next attack.

His dragonstone glowed again and Adi felt hot tingling as her trousers burned. The fabric peeled back and her exposed skin erupted into hundreds of roiling, tumescent lumps. Her flesh stretched and swelled, some of the pustules burst. She itched all over, and the sores caused terrible, piercing pain. Adi dropped to her hands and knees, grunting and screaming.

Amid her torture, she heard heavy steps at the front of the Dirigible's hall. Through tears of pain, she saw Palestrina swing her shotel at the mage. He parried with his staff and fired a bolt at his tall opponent.

The itching stopped so fast that Adi collapsed and gasped in relief. Her clothes were intact, her skin unblemished.

*What kind of sick illusion was that?*

Adi wiped her face with her hands and slid closer to Rekha, who had not stirred. The Lady of Spiders and the void mage fought across the littered floor of the tavern, the former wielding magic along with her curved blades. The mage fought with fire, and soon the walls were covered in splashes of flame as the old wood absorbed the deflected blows.

"Get out of here!" Palestrina shouted at Adi. The Seraph screamed as a bolt of lightning seared the thin membrane of one wing. Adi crawled toward the rosewood box, but the mage kicked it, hard, and sent it skating across the room.

"Forget the empty box," Palestrina ordered. "Royal has Apyreon."

Adi stood and picked up her tricorn. Rehka moaned. She slid her arms under Rehka's shoulders and knees. With a determined effort she stood. Rehka was tall but light, her body adapted for flight, though she had only once taken her Dragon form. Fire consumed the Iron Dirigible and smoke dimmed the room, lit sporadically by flashes of magic.

Adi stumbled toward Grace and the back door they had discovered earlier. Rehka shifted and Adi nearly dropped her. She recovered but jarred her shoulder hard against a door frame. She fled through the twisting halls past the empty rooms. Once, the whole building shook and Adi fell to her knees. She heaved them both up and kept going, gasping with relief when the bright door to the alley appeared. Rehka felt heavier by the moment, but Adi willed herself forward, holding her breath against the acrid, oily smoke rolling down the hallway.

The door gave way under one ferocious kick and Adi blinked in the daylight. Far behind her, Palestrina screamed. A gout of flame exploded through the roof. Adi saw no watchmen. She hoisted Rehka higher in her arms and hustled away from the street battle raging in front of the bar.

*Where should we go?* she wondered. *The hospital? The Water Knife guild hall?* Adi turned left at the mouth of the alley. She'd already decided. Cradling Rehka in her arms, she walked down the street as fast as she could. People parted in concern when they saw her carrying the unconscious Dragon. No one tried to stop her. Then an elderly grocer offered her his empty market cart, which Adi gratefully accepted. Her arms were numb except where the lacerations stung, and her shoulders trembled. She placed Rehka in the cart, arranging her long limbs with care.

"Can you get us to Goldwynd Alley?" she asked the grocer.

# CHAPTER TWENTY-FOUR

# ION RUCINARE

## MOON OF XYS, VALEDAY, 30TH OF HEBE

Ion stood on the terrane platform in the blistering heat of the Solvigant afternoon, his mouth agape, surrounded by hundreds of people from all the World System's races and moons. They bustled to and fro, oblivious to the rural lad from nearby Castes. His parents had brought him to the city once when he was four and needed a doctor for a terrible, phlegmatic cough. Ion remembered the painful hacking of his chest, but few memories of the bustling metropolis survived the dual filters of childhood and fever.

*How will I ever find Captain Crestone in this,* he wondered.

The steam engine whistled behind him, signaling its impending departure. Ion gripped the exterior grab bar and put one foot back onto the terrane, but didn't hoist himself up, caught by indecision.

"I can't go back." *Castes has nothing for me now,* he thought tearfully.

During the overnight ride from Castes to Solvigant, his grief had ebbed and flowed, receding only to return with renewed force. The truth was that Ion would never have been able to leave his grandfather behind while he lived. There was some relief in his death, which came in guilt-stricken waves.

*Would he be angry with me for leaving? Sad?* They'd both been abandoned when Ion's parents had left all those years before. Ion felt his departure was a double betrayal. Yesterday, he and his grandfather had had each other. Now Ion was alone, and his grandfather slain by the void mage's acolyte.

Ion removed the thieves' glass from his pocket. The dark edges were already smoother where he'd rubbed it to soothe his anxiety. He shivered despite the heat, remembering the harsh voice of the void mage threatening to torture him, and worse.

*Why am I here? Why am I doing this?* But he already knew the answer. It was why he'd finally summoned the courage to leave. *To run away. I am a runaway.* His parents had given up on him and left, his grandfather was dead, the very ground beneath his feet was giving up on every inhabitant of Xys. When Captain Crestone had leveled that green gaze at him, the proffered coin in her outstretched palm, Ion had seen his own potential reflected at him. The captain was his key to adventure and his ticket off this dry, dead moon.

*I will count for something.*

Ion released the grab bar and stepped back from the boarding stairs onto the platform. He had no idea where to begin his search but leaving the terrane station seemed a reasonable first step.

*Where do pirates hang out?*

Ion followed the teeming crowd toward an exit. Once outside the station, the jostling crowd thinned, and he was able to breathe more freely. The massive wooden tower of the aeroport rose on stone foundations on the opposite side of the hard-packed street. He craned his neck to see the numerous dirigibles docked at all levels of the structure. Aerogates floated lazily along their orbital paths and Ion whistled as a massive cargo dirigible emerged from a shimmering gate.

Music drifted from the dark doorway of a nearby tavern. Ion studied the cracked sign hanging over the entrance: *The Red Wyrm.* There had never been enough children in Castes to warrant a school, so his grandfather had taught Ion his letters, but there was scant reading material in the backwater he'd just left. He swallowed hard.

*How could all of this be just a few hours' ride from home?*

Around him people hustled, strode, shoved, and staggered. Surreys, hackneys, and stagecoaches vied for position with pedestrians and mounted folk in the dusty street. The hot morning air reeked with the stink of sweaty bodies, sewage, manure, and rotten food. The din of carts, hawkers, and conversations drifted over the deeper rumble and clanking from buildings with smokestacks and piles of coal near huge sliding doors. He vibrated with the underlying pulse and beat of the city.

His stomach growled. The hut's small pantry had contained so little and Ion had loaded it all into his pack. He'd eaten the raisins and crackers last night on the train. Across the road, a street cart vendor peddled sizzling skewers of meat. Ion studied the traffic and when he saw a break in the flow he darted into the street. He made it three paces when a shrill whistle made him freeze.

"Make way, make way!" a rough voice shouted.

Ion was too short to see the speaker or determine its direction. A second blast of the whistle, much closer this time, spooked him deeper into traffic.

"Make way!" the man hollered. "Make way!"

A contingent of twenty armor-clad Imperial soldiers plowed between the carts and pedestrians on his left, scattering people and vehicles. Ahead of them, an officer on horseback repeatedly blew his whistle. His horse's neck was spattered with sweat and its huge feet struck and stomped to disperse the crowd. The battalion was jogging along, managing to maintain their formation even as they left chaos in their wake. A thick, brown hand grasped Ion by his collar and hoisted him skyward moments before the booted feet of the soldiers passed where he'd been standing. The hand deposited him safely on the driver's seat of a buckboard. Ion twisted to look up at his savior, an immense, sand-colored Ankhim. The large desert dweller said something Ion could not understand. They both turned their attention back to the soldiers trooping past.

The aeroport was built on higher ground than much of the rest of the city, and from his perch Ion saw a turbulent sea of wood, canvas, and terracotta. A faint boom echoed over the street and a great gout of dark flame erupted from a distant warehouse. Oddly, the fire seemed to drink in the light rather than expel it.

*Is that normal?* Ion wondered. A surprised grunt from his rescuer suggested it was not.

Many of the people in the street looked around in alarm, though others did not spare it a glance. The battalion of soldiers broke into a run, turning onto an adjacent street that would take them closer to the explosion.

The desert Ankhim repeated his remark to Ion. He shook his head and gave a friendly shrug.

"Thank you," he said, waving and jumping down to the street.

Ion wove through the snarled traffic toward that dazzling aroma. But when he reached the place where he had seen the kabob merchant, he discovered the cart had moved on, leaving only its scent to tease him. His stomach twisted in protest.

*How can there be so many people?*

A sharp tug on his backpack threw Ion off balance. To his horror, the straps slipped easily from his shoulders. He whirled and saw two boys smaller than himself racing away with his pack suspended between them.

"Hey!" Ion called after them, "That's mine."

He gave chase, but the thieves were swift and agile. Ion pelted along, heart and legs pounding, but he could not match his quarry's ability to move through the crowd. He bumped into shoulders and parcels, pushcarts and bundles. Several people swatted at him, a few managed to connect. Slaps stung his back and rump. The two thieves flowed through the crowd like water, flexible and supple as they slipped past every obstacle.

Sweat poured down Ion's face and back. He nearly lost them when they ducked into a narrow alley. He found them when they paused to chuck his pack over a fence and scrambled up broken crates to follow it. Ion was hungry, but countless days pulling oars on the Boiled Sea gave him strength and endurance. He bounded up the crates and vaulted the fence in time to see his assailants turn onto another busy avenue. Ion followed, no longer bothering to shout.

He gained on them, only to lose his advantage when they slipped through an iron gate he had to climb over. They left the business district and main markets behind, skirted residential areas and tore through vacant lots. They led Ion onto dim, narrow streets with few doorways and abundant rubbish. Once he had to leap over a man sleeping off his drink in the shadows of stacked barrels. Twice Ion almost caught them, but both times they eluded his outstretched fingers.

Eventually, he lost them in a neighborhood of stained canvas tents and makeshift wooden lean-tos. They were there one moment and then they were gone. Ion jogged on, peering between the tattered homes hoping to catch a glimpse of them. A huge dog lunged at him, and only the rope on its collar kept it from catching Ion's leg as he scrambled backward. Finally, he stopped, hands on his knees, and gasped through the pain of a stitch burning in his side. Sweat, tears, and snot ran down his face. They were gone, and everything he owned had disappeared with them.

He had been in the city for less than two hours and it had cost him all he had. Thirst arrived, sharp and angry.

*Where can I get water here?* Ion wondered. He did not remember seeing any public pumps. *Do they sell it? What do people who have no money do?* He reached into his pocket for the thieves' glass and felt a glimmer of relief when his fingers found the familiar shape.

*Not that I know how to spend it.*

A group of pale tattooed men were watching him from a street corner and Ion decided it was unwise to linger. He had no idea how to return to the train station, but the street on his left widened into a broader road, and beyond it was a busy thoroughfare. He walked as briskly as he could toward that brighter road.

He passed a ramshackle wooden shop selling cast-iron objects: pots and pans, hinges and latches, horseshoes, wheel rims, and pipes in many diameters and lengths. The shopkeeper, a short, stout Grym woman, frowned at Ion and his threadbare, sweat-soaked clothing. The next building was corrugated steel with a canvas awning to shade the man working in front of it. He sat behind a sturdy table made from crates and was focused on carving neat lines into a small block of wood with a delicate blade.

*Typeface,* Ion realized. *He's cutting a printing block.* The weekly newspaper in Castes had shut down two years ago. Ion had broken into the abandoned office several times to explore it. He loved the smell of the ink and the intricate, complicated fitting of the heavy steel printing press.

The man looked up and met Ion's gaze. Ion saw an iron collar on the man's neck, identical to the one Captain Crestone wore.

"Hail Solo. Excuse me, sir, are you a pirate?"

The man's hissing laughter made Ion uneasy. "Hail Solo. Is that some kind of joke, boy?"

"Your collar, sir, do you crew with Captain Crestone?"

"Did someone put you up to this? I'm busy." The man gestured with ink-stained fingers to the trays of type blocks stacked neatly on shelves nearby. Still, he chuckled.

Ion barreled on, "No, sir. I'm looking for a woman with a collar like yours. She's a pirate and she's got blue hair. Well, it's dyed white, but the roots are blue, and she has a tricorn hat, and a pirate ship, though the ship is... damaged, but she's looking for crewmen and I've come to join up." Ion took a breath. "Except I've never been to Solvigant before, and some thieves stole my backpack." His knees were shaking, so he plopped down in the shade. "And I'm so thirsty but I don't know where people get water. Hungry, too..." Ion's voice petered out at the end of his speech, and he sighed.

The typesetter quirked an eyebrow at him. "A pirate from House Azure needs your help?"

Ion nodded, raking his soaked bangs away from his forehead. A familiar aroma drew his eyes toward the back wall where a coddle pot was simmering over low embers. He jerked his eyes away, not wanting to be rude.

The man huffed and stood, stretching his back. He stepped over to a barrel and dipped a small mug of water from it. He passed this to Ion, who drained it in two swallows. The man filled it again, and then a third time.

"Better?"

"Yessir. Thank you, sir. I can't pay you, though."

"No one should have to buy water on a day this hot," the man mumbled. He stepped to the fire and ladled greasy, brown liquid from the pot into a cracked ceramic bowl. He handed the stew to Ion. "That's the best story from a street urchin I've heard in some time."

"I'm not a street urchin," Ion gargled around a mouthful of scalding soup.

"Well, I'm not a pirate. So, I guess we're both wrong."

Ion slumped his shoulders. The man flicked the metal collar with his fingernail and it made a dull *tink*.

"This is a collar of indenture to the Blood Queen."

"Who's that?" Ion took another slurp of the oddly viscous liquid. It tasted worse than Grandfather's coddle stew, a thing Ion hadn't thought possible. But at this moment, he didn't care. "Who's the Blood Queen? What's indenture?"

"You definitely aren't a street urchin."

"What d'you mean?"

The typecutter just waved one mottled hand as if that were answer enough and watched as Ion licked the bowl.

"The food's a one-time deal, understand?"

"Yessir." Ion passed the crockery back to him. "Thank you. That was wonderful."

"Desperation makes almost anything delicious, don't it?" The man set the bowl back in its place near the fire and settled onto his stool. "This collar means I owe money to the kind of people you never want to owe money to."

"I see," Ion said, though he didn't. "Where can I find other people who owe money?"

The man gestured broadly. "All over the city. No one place."

Despite the food in his belly, or perhaps because of it, Ion felt queasy. The man idly stroked his chin, adding to the ink and wood shavings in his razor stubble.

"You could check out Duneharrow. But that's no safe place for a lone kid."

"What's Duneharrow?"

"It's the debtor's prison. Your captain must be a poor pirate if she's bearing the Blood Queen's collar, but someone there might know her."

"She's a great pirate," Ion said.

The typecutter didn't argue. He stroked his blade on the whetstone and stropped it on his apron.

"Duneharrow is a big, wooden monstrosity on the northern edge of the Warrens. Mind that you stay outta *those* streets. Them White Rabbits would snap up a lad like you."

"White Rabbits? What's a rabbit?"

The typecutter shook his head. "Where'd you come from, boy?"

"Castes."

"Djinnar's blood. That's right on the Boiled Sea, ain't it?"

"Born and raised there. We fish there." Ion paused. "Or we used to. The fish are mostly gone now or gone wrong."

"You couldn't pay me to eat anything from those waters. But there was a time, way before you came into the world, when that was a graceful place, and the finest restaurants bought what those fisherfolk caught."

Ion gawped. "Really?" His grandfather had said as much, but the boy figured it was a tall tale. There was a reason his parents gave up and fled.

"Yes, really. No wonder you liked the stew." The man examined the block with a lens, then started to carve again. "I could direct you to Duneharrow, but I think you'd have better luck at the Iron Dirigible. It's neutral ground for the gangs, and you're less likely to fall foul of a predator there."

Ion listened as the man described the way to the Dirigible. The route was convoluted, but Ion repeated each step back to him.

"Keep your eyes open, kid."

"It's not like I have anything left to lose."

"You do, son, you do. But let's hope it doesn't come to that."

Ion got to his feet, relieved that the rest had steadied him. He had the second wind he needed to find his pirate captain.

"Thank you for everything, sir. Someday I can pay you back or return the favor."

The typecutter did not look up. "Maybe so. Or you can help someone else whose lot is worse than your own. Now git, I have work to do."

Ion turned east into the sun and set out, reciting the directions to himself as he jogged along.

# CHAPTER TWENTY-FIVE
# THEO VANGUARD
## MOON OF XYS, VALEDAY, 30TH OF HEBE

Theo and Art stood outside the gate of the governor's mansion awaiting a hansom cab, when the front door opened, and a servant ushered a large badger out. Theo watched as the Faelani exchanged final words with the governor. Though Theo could not hear the exchange across the garden, the badger seemed nervous. His ears were flat and he turned a worn bowler over in his hands. The governor gesticulated broadly and poked the badger in the chest with a fat finger.

"I think he's in trouble," Theo said conspiratorially to Art.

"That's Senior Inspector Solomon Broc," Art replied.

"Should I know him?"

"There are only a dozen or so senior inspectors in all Solvigant. Only the city watch commanders out rank him."

"None of that seems to intimidate Gambol."

"I do not think the governor is a man to be easily intimidated. Broc's partner was Senior Inspector Joe Damgaard."

"Was?"

"The city watch raided a warehouse in the Warrens two months ago. Damgaard was killed."

Theo watched the badger with a new appreciation. He suppressed the urge to cross the garden and defend the inspector, but he did not need another reason to draw the governor's ire. He and Art watched as Broc bowed low before Gambol shut the door. The badger turned toward them, and Theo laughed in surprise. The inspector was not cowed at all. He set his hat at a jaunty angle and brushed the tips of his ears with clawed forepaws. He walked toward them, and Theo half-expected the Faelani to be whistling when he arrived.

"Good morning, Inspector," Theo said, when the watchman approached.

Broc had one good eye. The other was covered by an eyepatch and a thick pink scar protruded from the top and bottom. He surveyed the unlikely pair.

"You must be Theo Vanguard," Broc said at last.

"Yes, sir. A pleasure to make your acquaintance."

"You saw that exchange I suppose?"

"Seems the governor is going to have a bad day."

"Who is this?" Broc motioned to Art.

"Arthur Volaticus, Inspector," Art said, "Neophyte from the Sons of Destruction. It's a pleasure, Inspector. Your reputation precedes you."

Broc frowned. "Yes, unfortunately it often does."

"May we inquire about the nature of your visit?" Theo asked.

"You were First Officer on the HMS *Dragonhammer*, if I am correctly informed," Broc said. Theo glanced reflexively at his shoulders, where the epaulets of his uniform announced his rank, but he was not wearing his uniform.

"How did you know?"

"I spoke with your father prior to coming here."

"You did?" Theo was incredulous. *Has everyone spoken to my father?* It made him feel like a child in a room where all the adults were whispering about him. "What did he say?"

"He expressed his relief that you escaped those pirates unharmed."

Theo held up his injured hand, "Not entirely unscathed."

"I am sorry to hear of it," Broc said, but the formality in his tone suggested that he was apathetic at best. Broc continued, "This morning, we attempted to apprehend Stuart Royal, leader of the White Rabbits, at an establishment in neutral gang territory called the Iron Dirigible."

"Who is Stuart Royal?"

"The leader of the White Rabbits," Art cut in. Theo's expression remained confused. "One of three gangs that vies for supremacy in Solvigant."

"It sounds as though you were unsuccessful," Theo said.

"We were. Our efforts to bring Royal to justice were interrupted by a void mage. I understand your brother is a void mage."

"If you spoke to my father, you know that he is." *He's testing me,* Theo realized, *he wants to see if I'll lie about something he already knows.* "Is this an interrogation? Should I engage a solicitor? I escaped from pirates; I was not aware that was against the law. Nor am I my brother's keeper, responsible for his actions."

"So, it was your brother?"

"I have no idea. We have not spoken in some time. He does not inform me of his responsibilities to the emperor."

"Your father said the same thing."

"You question the word of the high chancellor?"

Broc grinned, revealing two rows of gleaming teeth, "The Empire pays me to question everyone. Tell me again how you escaped the pirates?"

"I never said."

The brougham arrived at that moment. The driver dismounted and opened the door for Theo and his companions.

"Where are you headed?" Broc asked.

"Brother Volaticus wanted to show me the Temple of Destruction."

"I wonder if you might take a detour with me."

"I'm not sure we have time, we—"

Broc cut him off. "I would appreciate the benefit of your insight into the situation. Something about the wreckage might indicate your brother's involvement. In the meantime, you could regale me with your story of heroism and escape."

Theo saw no way out of the Inspector's invitation without insulting him. Theo had no reason to be suspicious of the Faelani, but there was something about his demeanor. Theo was sure the badger was suspicious of him for some reason he could not yet put his finger on.

"Very well." Theo indicated the carriage. "After you."

The trio climbed into the cab and the springs groaned. Between Art's tail and the badger's stout frame, the ride was crowded.

Broc waited until the driver closed the door and the carriage started down the lane. Then he turned to Theo with an expectant eye. "So, how did you escape?"

"The pirates held me in a ramshackle safehouse. I expected them to ransom me immediately, but when they did not, I overpowered my guard and fled here. Governor Gambol's wife is my cousin."

"Your guard," Broc pressed, "you killed him. Then you burned the safehouse."

Theo groaned, "You already knew."

Art was watching Theo intently.

"I wanted only to overpower the man and flee. When he persisted in coming after me, I had no choice. I broke no laws."

"You seem very knowledgeable of the letter of the law." Theo heard menace in the Faelani's voice.

Theo said, "If you intend to accuse me of something, then do so. Stop wasting my time asking questions you already know the answers to."

Broc cleared his throat. "It seems the Blood Queen's forces learned of Royal's trip outside the Warrens and used the opportunity as an assassination attempt. I wonder, Commander Vanguard, if you have had any interaction with her representatives?"

"The Blood Queen is another of the gang leaders," Art offered.

"How would I know?" Theo protested.

"The pirate," Broc asked, "was it a woman? Did she wear an iron collar?"

"Yes, on both counts. Captain Crestone, they called her. What do you know of her?"

Broc waved the question away. "Very little."

Theo was not convinced. "I believe I have been more than forthcoming."

"Captain Adison Crestone is what's known as an indenture. They all wear iron collars. It's a symbol of their forced allegiance to Sasha Riven, the Blood Queen."

"You know her?" The brougham jostled over a bump. Theo had to hang onto the door handle to keep from being thrown into Art.

"Since yesterday," Broc admitted. "We brought her into a watch station after White Rabbit thugs assaulted her. Do you know why she was interested in your father's pleasure yacht?"

"No idea," Theo said. He felt his response was too quick, so he hastened to add, "I understand greed drives piracy. My father's yacht was a beautiful prototype."

"Do you know where it is now?"

"It's a smoldering wreck outside a dead-end town called Castes, I believe."

Broc stroked his chin, "How did it get there?"

Theo saw the trap and remained silent. The brougham rumbled to a stop and the springs groaned as the driver dismounted and opened the door for his charges. Theo looked to Broc.

"I assume the city watch is paying for this detour?"

Broc growled but took the requisite coins from his pocket and paid the driver. Theo stretched. *A void mage from the emperor, his father's impending arrival, the letter.* He sensed the schemes of his father in all of this and knew it must be connected to Apyreon, though he did not yet know how.

The remains of the Iron Dirigible reminded Theo of some great metal beast divested of its wooden exoskeleton. Iron girders jutted from piles of scorched and shattered beams. City watchmen poked through the wreckage from the morning's battle.

*I've seen coastal villages survive bombardment with less damage than this tavern,* Theo thought.

Watchmen cleared the streets and oversaw groups of workers moving rubble onto buckboards to be hauled away by horses and camels. Some soldiers combed through the remains as if searching for something, while others brought buckets of water from a nearby well to douse the green-tinted flames still licking at one edge of the building. Smoke and steam combined in the still morning air and shrouded the scene. Groups of curious onlookers at either end of the closed street gawked and murmured to one another.

*I wonder what they're looking for?* Theo thought. The smoldering fires were eerily dark and seemed to absorb light rather than to emit it, indicative of a void mage's magic. *Did father send Isaiah or did the emperor? Either way the emperor also knows of Apyreon.*

"I gather that this fellow Stuart Royal doesn't often make an appearance?" Theo asked as they walked toward what had once been the entrance to the Iron Dirigible.

Art said, "Stuart Royal's headquarters are deep in an impoverished part of the city called the Warrens. He rarely ventures out from there."

"What would entice him to risk leaving?" Theo asked. *Does Broc already know about Apyreon? Is he waiting to see if I'll confirm something else he already knows?*

Broc shrugged. "We've seen an uptick in gang violence in the last two weeks. We're still investigating the cause, but these things do flair up from time to time."

*That predates the arrival of Apyreon on Xys,* Theo thought. *But its arrival might have escalated the conflict. What are the gangs up to?*

Theo felt Broc's eyes on him. He was going to have to play some of his cards if he wanted information from the Faelani inspector.

"Any evidence Crestone participated in this?" Theo asked, gesturing toward the shattered building.

"She reported Royal's location to the watch," Broc said.

"Captain Crestone is an informant?"

Broc considered Theo. He had not known that the gaze of a one-eyed badger could carry so much weight. "Here are the events as I understand them. Captain Crestone stole High Chancellor Vanguard's yacht. The HMS *Dragonhammer* interrupted the theft and attempted to commandeer the vessel. It failed and you ended up here. I have several questions about that part. On her way to rendezvous with the Blood Queen, Crestone was ambushed, though she reported nothing stolen. Royal, the leader of those men that ambushed her, risked leaving the Warrens and came here to the Iron Dirigible. Do you know of the Iron Dirigible?"

Theo shook his head.

"The proprietor is a notorious antiquities dealer named Tabrin Wik."

Theo hesitated as he searched for a reasonable answer. "So, Royal had something to sell."

"Something so valuable that he risked assassination by leaving the Warrens. Were there valuable items on the ship that required fencing? Has Chancellor Vanguard reported the theft to the Tyrian watch?"

*This inspector is sharp.* Theo was accustomed to captains of the Tyrian city watch and the royal guard kowtowing to his father, not grilling aristocrats as though suspecting them of crimes.

Theo tried to change the subject. "I imagine the void mage wrought most of this destruction."

"Why would you assume that?" Broc asked.

"I've encountered the aftermath of their powers before."

Both Broc and Art were quiet for a long moment, their bright animal eyes locked on him.

"Is this your brother's work?" Broc asked at length.

"How should I know? It's not like he leaves a calling card," Theo lied.

"Your father," Broc mused, "loses a luxury yacht containing valuable items. Your father, high chancellor to the emperor, has a connection to the void mages through your brother, so your father sends him here to retrieve said item, or items. Something valuable enough to pique Stuart Royal's interest and draw him out of the Warrens."

"An interesting theory."

"What is it?"

"What is what?"

"The item your father wants retrieved."

"I don't know what you're talking about."

"And if I think you're lying?" Broc asked.

Theo puffed out his chest as a prelude to the offended royal routine. Or he could pull rank as a first officer of a Royal Navy vessel. But he was interrupted when a lanky woman ran up to Broc.

"Inspector Broc," she said. "They found her." She offered a tardy salute. Broc shot her a warning look, which the woman missed.

"Henge—" Broc started, but the woman continued.

"Horace and Morelund saw Crestone and the mercenary on a wagon turning onto Goldwynd Alley, they—"

"Henge!" Broc shouted. Henge flushed, noticing Theo and Art for the first time.

"Apologies, sir." Henge stood at attention, chastened.

Broc turned to him. "First Officer Vanguard, I believe you are unwilling to assist me with this inquiry." He waved a hand to dismiss Theo's objections before he could make them. "Consider this a formal report filed with the city watch about your father's yacht. I'll take it from here and report what we find to you. You will return to the governor's palace and wait for my updates, understood?"

Gone was the fumbling, embarrassed inspector from the mansion. Broc stood erect, poised on the balls of his feet, his hackles bristled.

"Preparations for the pilgrimage require I move about the city."

"Are you disobeying a directive of the city watch?"

"I was unaware the city watch of Solvigant could make such demands of the nobility. Unless you're going to arrest me, I will move about the city as is necessary."

Broc sighed and scratched at his eye patch. "Very well, the carriage will take you both back. Pray to the Nine that I do not discover you mixed up in all this." With that, Broc and Henge hurried off.

Art turned to Theo, "So, Goldwynd Alley?"

Theo smiled. He barely knew the Faelani priest from the Sons of Destruction, had no idea what his angle might be, but he liked him.

"Yes, indeed," Theo said. "Lead the way."

# Chapter Twenty-Six

# ADI CRESTONE

## Moon of Xys, Valeday, 30th of Hebe

Adi offered the wagon driver one of Xander's gold spyres to deliver Rehka to her father, Bale. When the man objected to the strange nature of the task, Adi pressed a second coin into his outstretched palm. It hurt Adi to part with so much at once, but she needed to know Rehka was safe and well cared for, and she knew she wasn't ready to face Bale. Two days earlier she had promised him Rehka would be uninvolved in her dealings. Now they were in the thick of it having joined the fray for reasons of her own. Adi doubted Bale would be interested in the nuances of her defense.

Adi watched from a distant alley as the buckboard made its way toward Drake's Apothecary. The wagon halted in front of Bale's shop and the driver entered the cluttered establishment. Bale and the wagon driver emerged moments later to unload Rehka's unconscious body. Once, Bale glanced down the street in Adi's direction and she ducked out of sight.

*Did he see me?* Adi wondered. If he did, he didn't come after her. Adi took several long breaths to slow her heartbeat. Guilt flared in her gut.

She had little time to waste, so after a few more minutes she risked peeking out of the alley. The buckboard was gone. Bale was nowhere in sight. Adi sighed. Phoebe, Goddess of Light, should curse her for her cowardice. She considered running down the street and falling at Bale's knees, but she couldn't convince her feet to move in that direction. Rehka was safe now. Adi had seen to that, at least. She had so much to accomplish before Apyreon's trail went cold.

*When my son is free from the threat of the Blood Queen's retribution, all of this will be worth it.* Adi swallowed against the rising doubt.

First, she reviewed her information. Stuart Royal knew about Apyreon. That must be the reason he was bold enough to leave the Warrens. Rictor or Pimple must have recognized the object as an item of importance and sent word to Royal.

*But why not take it directly to the Warrens?*

The White Rabbit woman had said Royal was meeting with the proprietor of the Iron Dirigible, Tabrin Wik, who was also an antiquities dealer. Maybe he knew something about Apyreon. Adi had once met the proprietor and knew that he was Grym and a clunker. The right side of his face had been replaced with a brass plate and a fancy metal eye. Royal figured he could retrieve the artifact in neutral territory. Now that the Iron Dirigible was a smoldering ruin, Adi had no clue how to locate Wik. She couldn't venture into the Warrens after Royal, not with the Blood Queen's collar of indenture around her neck.

Then that blood forsaken void mage had joined the fray. That meant the emperor was involved somehow. Many powerful mages in the Society of Astrologia feared the void mages. Adi's hand drifted to where her dragonstone had hung. She could not have defeated him even if she'd had it, wildling trained as she was.

*Maybe Ajax would loan mine back to me so I can complete this assignment?* Adi immediately pushed the ridiculous thought aside. The whole point of collateral was to motivate the debtor, and Adi had nothing else of value to offer in place of it.

*Not that I want any help from either Ajax or Palestrina.* She wanted to be as far away from the Blood Queen and her minions as possible. Palestrina had saved her life, and Rehka's. Adi didn't know what to think about that, didn't want to think about what she might owe the savage, batlike Seraph.

*What to do?*

Adi balled her fists against the alley wall behind her. Rictor might know where Apyreon was since he had been in the meeting with Royal. It was likely the city watch took him into custody after Adi choked him into unconsciousness. They'd hold him, with any other captured White Rabbits, at Opus Station since it had the largest jail near the Iron Dirigible.

*How do I get to him?*

She couldn't go to Broc without telling him about Apyreon. Even if she did, Adi doubted the senior inspector would let her interrogate Rictor. Xander might be able to pull some strings, but then she would have to confess her lies about her situation and why she'd needed the money.

That left infiltrating the Opus guard station after dark. It was risky, the station would be busy after all the action at the Iron Dirigible. If she were caught it would end her deal with Broc. She'd go to jail and all hopes of recovering Apyreon and saving her son would vanish along with her freedom. The Blood Queen wouldn't let her live peacefully incarcerated, either. People had tried to use the law to hide from her before and it had never ended well for them. Adi shivered at the thought of being murdered in Duneharrow by a Blood Queen agent.

The solution to that problem was simple: Don't get caught.

*I'm going to need some help.*

Adi hated asking for help. No one at Stella's Echo would help her. Rather, Stella and Iris would try their best to talk her out of it. Adi loathed the idea of involving others, but this situation was out of hand. There had been a Talon operative at the Iron Dirigible. Soon, all three gangs would be at each other's throats for such a powerful artifact.

Then Adi knew where to go. She would return to the physicker and see if Wright and Vista of Captain Torrance's old crew were up for another adventure. She'd have to pay them from her limited funds, but she had no other options.

Adi exhaled loudly and stepped from the narrow side street onto Goldwynd Alley... and collided with a Faelani squirrel in a green cloak holding a quarterstaff. Her shoulder struck his, bouncing her back. The Faelani snapped his tail sideways and kept his balance. Adi fell against a shop's façade and sat hard on a deep windowsill. Her hat tumbled from her head.

When he recovered himself, the squirrel bowed low.

"I beg your pardon, madam. I did not see you there."

Adi nodded her head in mute response. She was too busy looking at the Faelani's companion. His clothing was different, a blue coat with brass buttons over a light vest and pleated trousers, yet she immediately recognized his face.

*The officer from the* Dragonhammer. *The captive. The one who killed Mung.*

Adi saw recognition dawn in his brown eyes. Reflexively, her hands covered the blue roots of her hair, though she knew it was already too late. The officer's hand closed around the hilt of a short sword. The ornate pommel bore the crest of Governor Gambol himself.

"Djinnar's b—" was all Adi got out before her former prisoner pounced. He drew the sword and set its tip between Adi's ribs. He and the Faelani used their bodies to shield the weapon from the few passersby on the street.

"Where is it?" he hissed.

"I don't know what you're talking about," Adi said.

"This is Captain Crestone?" the Faelani asked. "She really is from House Azure."

Adi tensed further at the mention of her family. *What do these two know about me?*

"You know perfectly well what I'm talking about," the officer insisted.

"I was paid to steal a ship, that's all," Adi lied.

"Are you a prophet, too, like your sister?" the squirrel asked.

The officer glanced sideways at the Faelani, brows raised in confusion.

"What sister?" *Who, by the void, is this guy?* Adi wondered.

"What are you getting at?" the officer asked his companion.

"A prophet and a pirate, intriguing," the squirrel continued as if he hadn't heard either question.

"I'm no prophet," Adi said.

"Just Azurian then." The squirrel *tsk*ed in disappointment.

"Where's the rosewood box from my father's cabin?" the officer pressed. Adi saw the Faelani's eyes flicker with delight. She recognized the clasp on his cloak as the emblem of the Sons of Destruction. He was an itinerant priest.

*What was he doing with a Tyrian officer?*

The sword pressed into her ribs and Adi turned her attention back to the officer.

"You're one of Vanguard's sons," Adi reasoned.

The officer flushed, realizing his mistake.

"The *Sidereal* is a smoldering wreck outside of Castes," Adi said, an idea forming in her mind. "I don't have the artifact."

Adi's eyes flicked back to the Faelani. He was watching the officer intently.

*He doesn't know,* Adi realized. *The Faelani doesn't know what this is all about.*

"I know you took it," the officer insisted, "Otherwise you never would have escaped the *Dragonhammer*. You used the device, or else I'd still be in Thail, and you'd be marching to the gallows."

Adi only shrugged, trying to appear nonchalant.

"Tell me," he insisted. "What you did with it!"

"Or what?" Adi snarled. "You'll kill me? Then where will you be?"

"Where is the device?" He pressed the sword harder against her ribs.

Adi hid her wince behind a toothy grin. "Did you lose one of Daddy's trinkets? I bet he's terribly angry." Despite the sword, Adi put her hands on her hips and cocked her head in what she hoped was a mocking gesture.

She thought he might stab her then. Rage and embarrassment warred on his face, and she felt the pressure increase at the sword's point. Adi sucked in a breath. It hurt.

"What did she steal?" the Faelani asked.

His question brought the officer back to himself as the man realized his predicament. Whatever story he had told his Faelani companion about why he needed to track down the blue-haired pirate, it had not included Apyreon. Adi's mind raced.

*How do I turn this to my advantage?* With a pang of regret, she realized she missed Rehka and her myriad knives.

"Your father must not have much faith in your abilities to retrieve it if he had the emperor send a void mage. They're not exactly subtle."

The officer huffed and looked between Adi and his Faelani companion.

"If you're going to run me through in the middle of the street," Adi continued, "you'd best get on with it before a watch patrol comes this way."

"Tell me the location of my father's device and I'll let you be on your way," the officer said.

"Fine," Adi agreed. "I've had nothing but grief since I took that stupid ship."

The officer stepped back, startled, as if expecting her to protest.

"Put the sword away," Adi said. "What's your name?"

He sheathed his sword while Adi stooped to pick up her tricorn.

"Where's Apyreon?"

Adi winced. *So much for subtlety.*

Adi gestured toward the Faelani. "Who's this?"

The squirrel extended a paw. "Arthur Volaticus of the Sons of Destruction. People call me Art."

Adi shook the proffered paw. "A pleasure." She turned to the officer. "See, not so hard. You know my name. If we're going to retrieve Apyreon, I'm going to have to call you something."

"Tell me where it is. I'll retrieve it without the help of pirates."

Adi brushed the road dust off her hat and placed it atop her head, then straightened the sleeves of her coat, waiting.

"Commander Theo Vanguard," he said at last. "How did you lose it?" Adi heard a hint of anguish in his voice.

"Pleasure to meet you, Theo. Well, not a pleasure exactly, but it's a relief to have a name to curse to the gods. And I didn't lose it; someone stole it from me."

Theo sighed. "Who?"

"You going to run off to stab that person? As much as I might appreciate your assistance in killing my assailant, I'll pass."

"Who has it?" Theo pressed. "It's better that I find them before that void mage does."

Adi considered the truth of this. "All right, Theo, I'll make you a deal."

"I don't make deals with pirates."

"I don't see that you have much of a choice. You want to retrieve Apyreon for Daddy, I need money."

"Of course you do."

"I'm not much of a pirate with this collar of indenture. I need to clear my debts, leave Xys, and find a new ship. You wrecked my other one."

"That was my father's ship. You stole it."

Adi shrugged as if to say, *"Don't get hung up on the details."*

"Who sent you?"

Adi pointed to the collar around her neck. When Theo looked blankly at her, Adi rolled her eyes.

"That's a collar of indenture," Art said, "for the Blood Queen Sasha Riven."

"You'd think an officer of the Royal Navy would know more about the empire he's paid to keep in line," Adi said.

"Indenture?" Theo asked.

"I owe her a lot of money," Adi said. "You agree to pay my debts to Riven and I'll help you reclaim your precious Apyreon."

"I'm not paying off a gangster."

"Don't tell me the Vanguards are broke,. Adi smiled. "You killed my crewman and denied me my ransom. I need that money."

"Where's Apyreon?" Theo asked, but Adi saw his resolve was weakening.

She cocked an eyebrow at Theo and waited.

"If I pay your debts how do I know you'll keep up your end of the bargain?"

"A fair question. You don't, I am a pirate after all. But if I don't, you have permission to chase me down and use the pointy end of that sword you're so keen on. Believe me, I have no interest in the device. Too many dangerous people know it's here in Solvigant. The Blood Queen, the White Rabbits, a cursed void mage, your father, and the emperor, for Solo's sake. And now the Sons of Destruction and anyone else you've told. I want it out of the city. It draws too much attention to a lowly pirate captain. Do we have a deal?"

Adi held out her hand to shake and seal the deal. She was sure Theo would never betray his father by paying off a pirate's debts to a gangster, but that was fine. She had no intention of handing Apyreon over to him once they retrieved it. She didn't give a damn about Theo and his pathetic need to please his father. She needed it to ensure Lucas's safety.

*It doesn't matter. We'll play each other and worry about where the dust settles once we've retrieved Apyreon from the White Rabbits.*

Bandages muffled Theo's grip on her hand. Adi squeezed and saw him wince. She yanked him off balance and landed a hard left hook on his jaw. Theo reeled backward, arms whirling for balance. He reached for his sword.

"That's for Joshua Mung." Adi said, massaging her knuckles. She waited to see if Theo would draw his weapon. She gripped the hilt of the jambiya at her belt.

"You tied me up and put me in a shack," Theo said.

"You tried to kill me."

"You were supposed to ransom me."

"You were supposed to be patient. I don't think impatience is a laudable character trait in the Royal Navy." Adi didn't give Theo time to respond. "Meet me at the Red Wyrm tonight after sundown." Then she turned her back on the two.

Theo grabbed her wrist. "You don't leave my sight."

Adi twisted free of his grasp. "We're hardly an inconspicuous group—a Faelani from the Sons of Destruction, a Tyrian naval officer, and a Blood Queen indenture. We'll meet at the Red Wyrm and go over the plan to retrieve Apyreon. No one will bother us there."

"Where are you going?" Theo asked, but Adi was already moving away.

"To get the rest of my crew. We'll need more than the three of us to infiltrate a city watch jailhouse."

*"What?"* Theo spluttered.

Art laughed uproariously, slapping his furry knees with his paws.

"Crestone!" Theo said and for the first time, as Adi started to round the corner, and she heard the crack of authority in his voice. She paused and looked at him over her shoulder. "We're not part of your crew."

Adi stuck out her arm to hail a nearby hansom cab.

"You're the one making deals with gangsters." She climbed into the coach, "Ivy Street please," she said to the driver.

Feeling lighter than she had since before commandeering the *Sidereal* in Tyre, Adi blew the two companions a kiss as the hansom rumbled away. Volaticus was still laughing as the two men faded from view.

# Chapter Twenty-Seven

# ADI CRESTONE

## Moon of Xys, Valeday, 30th of Hebe

A shingle painted with a caduceus swayed in a light breeze outside Dr. Vake's clinic. Delicate bells tinkled when Adi entered. She wrinkled her nose at the salubrious aromas of alcohol and herbs. Deborah Vake leapt up from a stack of cushions piled high in one corner, book in hand. The tan woman jangled with several pounds of silver and pewter jewelry. A feather made of delicate strips of amethyst pinned to her lapel marked her as a matron of the wayfaring Passerines.

"Adi," Deborah said and embraced her. Adi winced. Her ribs and jaw were still quite sore. It had only been three days since the battle on the deck of the *Sidereal* and only two since her mugging. Adi looked in the mirror over Deborah's shoulder and saw that the left side of her jaw was still quite swollen. Adi hugged her back.

"Dr. Vake, good to see you."

Deborah clicked her tongue and put a hand on each of Adi's shoulders. "Don't be so formal. Only patients call me that." She took a hard look at Adi's jaw. "Are you checking in?"

"No." Adi stepped back to put some space between them. "I'm here to see about my crewmen. You didn't kill them, did you?"

Deborah swatted her playfully with the book. "Both are recovering well, though their injuries were severe. I'm not sure they'll both be thrilled to see you. Well, only the Grym is still here. The other checked himself out this morning. Vista, his name was. You seem wounded. Let me look at you. I've got an exam room open."

Adi heard footsteps on the wooden stairs near the back of the room as the other Dr. Vake descended. Roald Vake was a diminutive man who wore thick glasses and a waxed mustache much too large for the sharp, delicate planes of his face.

"Roald," Adi said moving across the room to hug him, "a pleasure to see you as well. Thank you for taking care of my crewmen."

"It's Dr. Vake," Roald said, polishing his glasses. He sighed. "Good to see you, Adi. You're always good for business." The three of them laughed.

"How's Lucas?" Deborah asked, "Have you spoken with him recently?"

Adi felt the blood drain from her face even as she tried to maintain a neutral expression.

"He's fine. He doesn't write often. You know teenagers. Or at least that's what Stella tells me to keep me from worrying in the long silences between letters."

Deborah threw up her hands. "Don't I know it. That Stella is a brilliant woman. I can hardly keep track of the little ones we've got around here, and now Lizbeth, my oldest, is married and pregnant, as is Val. I'm going to be a second mother and a grandmother at the same time. Can you believe it?"

Adi shook her head, "Val?"

"Valence Mina, or Val Vake now. Roald and I took her as a second wife last spring."

"I want to hear all about the romance," Adi said.

"All in good time, dear. Let's get you checked out. There are lacerations and burns on your wrists. Still kindling the flame for that dangerous Dragon Rehka?" Deborah said.

"Hey!" Adi huffed. "No, I'm not."

"Never good for you," Deborah said, "though we saw you more often when you were with her."

"I'm sorry, Adi." Roald shook his head. "My first wife is ever a busybody."

Deborah feigned offense. "I care about our clients. It's human decency."

"It's all right. I'd best see to my crewman first." Adi slipped Deborah's hand from where the physicker had taken her elbow to steer her through a curtained doorway toward the examination rooms.

"He's in the kitchen." Roald pointed through a pair of saloon style doors in the wall beneath the stairs. Neither of the Vakes followed.

Wright had his back to Adi and was scrubbing dishes with a horsehair brush over a wooden basin. Heavy bandages, wrapped to accommodate his pointed ears, leaked green, foul-smelling ointment and obscured the left side of his head. Though tall for a Grym, Adi was reminded how short he was; the top of his head was level with her collarbones.

"I wasn't sure you'd come back," Wright said without turning around.

"I'm your captain,"

"Capt'n Torrance was my captain."

"Torrance is dead. His command passed to me the moment that cannonball blew him off the deck."

Wright lowered the scrub brush and turned to face Adi. The bandages covered his left eye and most of his forehead.

*That cut must have been worse than it looked,* Adi thought.

"It got infected," he said, when he saw where she was looking. "I might lose sight in the eye. The Vakes offered to let me stay. I suppose to pay off some of the debt you saddled me with."

"I left two spyres."

"Hardly enough for this, let alone Vista's arm."

"It's all I had. You'd both be dead otherwise."

"Dead's better than in debt," he insisted.

Adi tapped her collar. "We'll agree to disagree."

"What was that all about anyway? Why did the Tyrians send an Imperial battlecruiser to recover a stupid pleasure yacht?"

"That was... unforeseen," Adi admitted.

"I'll say, but you didn't answer my question."

"The answer to that question is reserved for crew members."

When Wright said nothing, Adi tried another tactic. "How long were you with Captain Torrance?"

"About a year."

"Was he a good captain?"

"Better'n most, worse than a few. Do you even have a ship?"

Adi winced at the reminder. "Not currently, but that's never stopped me before."

He pointed at her collar with the scrub brush. "I don't want to work for the Blood Queen."

"I don't want to work for the Blood Queen either. This is my last job. Once I recover Apyreon, my days of indenture are through."

"Apyreon?"

"The formal name of the star key we got from the *Sidereal*. It's what Riven was after." Adi shrugged, hoping it looked nonchalant. "And as my first mate you're entitled to the whole tale." She stepped toward him, her hand outstretched to shake his. "Are you my first mate?"

Wright shook her hand, his grip light and skin clammy from the dishwater.

"That's what the Blood Queen was really after."

"It is."

Wright sighed. "Why'd Torrance go and steal the whole cursed ship then?"

"He was a pirate. It was there for the taking."

Wright laughed at that. "I've never been first mate to a land-locked pirate."

Adi laughed with him. "A temporary setback."

Wright's expression grew serious. "I'll help you as much as I can with these injuries, but if you don't lose that collar after we recover Apyreon, I'm out." Wright dropped her hand.

Adi nodded gravely. "It's so much more than a star key, Wright. I'll tell you all about it on the way to see Vista. Where is he, by the way?"

Wright shook his head. "As soon as he was able, he left for home. I don't think he's going to be happy to see you."

"Where's home?" Adi pressed.

"He has a family on the western edge of Solvigant; a wife and two or three kids."

"Vista?"

"You say that like you knew him for more than two weeks."

"Well, in two weeks you'd think he'd have said something about his family."

Wright only shrugged.

Together they returned to the foyer. Deborah insisted Adi sit for an exam. An hour later, Adi and Wright were on the street hailing another hansom. The same foul ointment shading Wright's bandages was now smeared across her face. A thick bandage was wound around her ribs under her clothing. Despite all her protestations about a captain being treated in front of her first mate, Deborah had been implacable.

*I do feel much better,* Adi thought. The bandage around her torso provided support and made it less painful to move despite its encumbering presence. Adi paid the Vakes five spyres for their care of her, Wright, and Vista, and promised to come for dinner sometime soon and meet Val, and to bring Lucas next time he visited her. Lucas had never visited in the ten years since she'd abandoned him, but it was a nice fiction. Then they said their farewells.

On the street, Adi and Wright flagged down a cab. As the hansom was rumbling along the hard-packed earth of Solvigant's streets, Adi filled in Wright on everything that had transpired since she'd left him at the physickers. She omitted the parts about Iris and Rehka and Xander Marrion's involvement. She embellished the mugging in the warehouse district, but otherwise it was everything and the truth.

The cab deposited them at the intersection of five streets in the Ironhorse District, so-called for the massive rail yard foundries that built the steam-powered terranes that once crisscrossed Xys. When Adi first arrived in Solvigant all those years ago, there had been eight foundries here. After fifteen years, only two of them remained. All the others had either gone broke or moved off-moon. The once-thriving neighborhoods were falling into disrepair. Looking around at the ramshackle state of the houses, Adi worried that many of these folks would not make the next peripatesis. Not all Solvigant's citizens could keep up with its migrations.

Ironhorse was Talon territory. Adi removed the blue scarf from her pocket, the one she'd pilfered from Torhan market two days prior and tied it over the collar like an ascot.

"Where does he live?" she asked.

"Somewhere down this way, I think," Wright said.

"You don't know?"

"We were shipmates together on a pirate vessel. He didn't exactly have us all over for dinner. Vista disappeared when we were on shore leave. Didn't hang out in the taverns."

"You did?"

"I don't have anyone waiting on me." Wright shrugged. He shouldered his pack and started down the street in the direction he'd indicated.

Adi followed.

They knocked on a dozen doors before one of the denizens was kind enough to point them in the right direction. Adi and Wright backtracked to a different street and walked several more blocks. It was late afternoon when they knocked on Vista's door. The rosy light of sunset was blooming on the horizon.

*It'll be dark soon. We're running out of time to return to the Red Wyrm and make our plans with Theo and Art.*

A young, dark-haired girl opened the door, one hand on the latch, the thumb of the other in her mouth. She could only be Vista's daughter. She had the same, gray-toned skin as the mountain Ankhim and was unusually broad across the shoulders for a child. Her father arrived moments later. His weathered bulk filled the doorway behind his daughter.

Adi stifled a gasp when she saw the stump of Vista's arm. The Vakes had amputated his left arm just above the elbow. Wright had told her this during their ride to Ironhorse, but seeing it made Adi queasy with guilt. Vista leaned heavily on a cane, his face tense with pain. He stepped between Adi and his daughter and began to close the door. It was Wright who intervened, placing his booted foot inside to hold the door open.

"Hear her out, Vista," Wright said.

"I've got nothing to say to that woman," Vista said and spat in the dirt of the street. Three children were gathered behind him now, peering between his legs and around his waist, two girls and a young boy, none older than five.

*When did he have time to sire such a brood?* Adi wondered. The life of a pirate was hardly conducive to a relationship, let alone an entire family. The two men argued, but Adi paid little attention, instead watching the children watch her.

"I lost my arm for some stuffy lord's pleasure yacht, a yacht we left a smoldering wreck outside Castes," Vista snarled.

Adi had dreaded this conversation since leaving the physicker's. She'd run through various strategies to convince him to join back up, but now that she was standing in front of him and staring at his children, all her entreaties felt self-seeking and insincere.

*How can I ask him to sacrifice more?*

Adi was content to let Wright lay the groundwork for this battle. She guessed it would be a few minutes before her first mate softened Vista up enough to even speak to her. Despite Wright's reluctance to join her crew back in the kitchen, he fell easily into the role of first mate.

*I can't wait until there are deck planks under our feet once more.*

Adi knelt in the sandy street, so she was eye level with the oldest daughter. Adi waved. The girl waved back shyly. Adi grinned. It made her face hurt, and the tooth she'd lost fighting on the deck of the *Sidereal* left an embarrassing hole on the lower right side, but the girl smiled back and took half a step out from behind her father's knee.

"Hey there," Adi said softly, "what's your name?"

The two men continued arguing above her. The girl remained silent.

"I bet you're happy to have your dad home," Adi said.

The girl nodded once. Her grip on Vista's trousers tightened.

"My name's Adi."

"I'm Sapph!" the little boy exclaimed.

The sound of his voice brought everyone up short. Vista and Wright looked down at where Adi crouched a few feet away from the children.

"Step away from them." Vista's voice was low, menacing.

Adi held up her hands. "You have beautiful children."

"What of it?" Vista snarled, clearly trying to work out her ploy.

"No angle, just beautiful children. I envy you."

"You do?" Vista took a protective step to block his kids. Adi sighed and stood.

"I have a son; his name is Lucas. He'll be sixteen next month." Adi swallowed. "If he lives that long."

"What do you mean?" Vista's eyes narrowed.

"It wasn't about the ship," Adi said, her eyes still on the children, "It was never about the ship. The Blood Queen was after a star key. A special artifact called Apyreon." Adi laughed nervously.

"My pirate days are over," Vista said in the tone of one who'd said it many times and would say it many more.

"I'm sorry about your arm," Adi said. She wanted to keep changing the subject, keep him on his toes. "By the Nine, I'm glad the Vakes were able to save your life. It looks like they used Passerine magic to mend the wounds a bit faster, too."

Vista's eyes grew cloudy, and he shrugged. "I suppose."

"I need your help."

"I told you, I'm done."

Adi met Vista's eyes for the first time. "What makes you think I want a one-armed engineer on my crew?" She forced iron into her tone.

"Capt'n—" Wright interjected.

Adi saw Vista's gray cheeks flush and the Ankhim snarled, "I can—"

Adi cut him off. "If it weren't for me, you'd be dead. Bled out on the train from Castes. I left you at the Vake's because I knew they could help you. You should thank me!"

"*Thank you?* Captain Torrance would never have taken that job if not for—"

Adi cut him off again. "I have to save my son!"

A few people from nearby homes poked inquisitive heads out open windows.

Vista stepped back in surprise. Sapph squealed as his father's bare foot bumped his own. Vista patted the boy's head, making shushing and cooing sounds. Adi could see the pain in his face at not being able to pick up his son.

Adi continued, "His name is Lucas, and if I don't retrieve Apyreon—" Adi choked, swallowed, and grabbed a hold of herself. "If I don't, the Blood Queen will kill my son."

"I have my own children to worry about. I can't help you."

Adi lowered her voice "Be that as it may, we are headed to the Red Wyrm. Then, before the midnight shift change, we infiltrate Opus Station. There's a White Rabbit thug inside who knows Apyreon's location."

Vista considered Adi for a long moment.

"If you want to stay here with your family, I won't blame you. But if you stay here because you feel useless, then curse you. If the Blood Queen kills my son while you sulk in Ironhorse after I saved your life, I'll come back here and kill you myself."

The children's eyes went wide. The middle daughter began to cry. Vista slammed the door in their faces.

"That went well," Wright said.

Adi waited. Five minutes elapsed, then ten. Adi pounded on the door and they heard two bolts thud into place.

Adi turned away. "He's not coming."

Wright nodded. "The Red Wyrm?"

Adi blinked away the tears forming at the corners of her eyes. *Some captain I'm turning into, berating a one-armed man in front of his children.*

"Let's hope four of us will be enough," she said.

# Chapter Twenty-Eight

# THEO VANGUARD

## Moon of Xys, Valeday, 30th of Hebe

"Have you ever visited a god before?" Theo asked Art. The two sat across from one another at a corner table in the Red Wyrm. It was early enough in the evening that the tavern was still quiet. The band had just arrived and many of the tables were still empty.

"No, I haven't," Art said. He set his large beer mug down on the table with a thud and wiped foam from his upper lip. Theo's beer sat untouched. Art checked a pocket watch. "She's late."

"If she shows up at all," Theo said. "She probably just sent us here to get us out of the way." *Could she have double-crossed us already?* Theo had no intention of honoring his end of the bargain. *Deals with pirates aren't binding.* "So, why are you visiting the temple of Djinnar now?"

"All delegations to the god's temple require a representative from the Sons of Destruction." Art eyed Theo's tankard. "Do you really think she'd stand us up? She needs our help."

Theo snorted. "Yes, but why you? Father Heilig was not thrilled that the governor ordered this trip."

"So, you expected someone more… obstructive? Are you going to drink that?"

Theo shrugged.

Art picked up Theo's beer and took a long pull. He smacked his lips and said, "Father Heilig is hoping Djinnar, God of Destruction, will refuse me."

"Why would he hope that?"

"I've failed the Bane Rite twice now." Art took another deep draught.

"What's the Bane Rite?"

"All novice priests of Djinnar must pass the Bane Rite to progress from neophyte to acolyte. If you fail twice, you must seek permission from the god himself for a third attempt. If He denies me, then I am kicked out of the ranks. If He permits it and I fail, then I will be killed for profaning the god."

"Sounds suitably destructive."

"Father Heilig hopes that I will either be denied a third attempt and thus Djinnar will not entreat with the delegation, or that the God of Destruction will grant me an exception and I will fail a third time. Dead, I will be unable to assist the delegation's negotiations."

"So, your failure is the delegation's failure, and your failure is nearly assured?"

"Precisely."

"If we fail to speak with the god?"

"Then Father Heilig will insist that Solvigant proceed along its prescribed pilgrimage route. Instead of skipping ahead to Ourania, Solvigant will move to Amar. There, seismic activity will destroy the city and we will miss our opportunity to evacuate."

"Does he want Solvigant to be destroyed?"

Art shrugged and took another drink. "He fears departing from divine tradition."

"Tell me more about the Bane Rites."

"They are part of the Annihilation Mysteries."

"The Sons of Destruction do like their apocalyptic jargon."

"I'll get us another round." Art stood and made his way toward the bar.

Theo removed his father's letter from his vest pocket and considered it. "Theodore" was written on the outside in his father's familiar cursive script. Theo flipped it over. The seal depicting the owl of the office of high chancellor gleamed in red wax. Theo tapped the thick cream envelope against his thumbnail. At the bar, Art was in conversation with a human bartender clad in revealing red leathers. Theo swore through his teeth and tore open the letter:

*Theodore,*

*Your brother Paul was slain in battle against Eldarians on Maxon outside Ft. Kaspar. His military funeral took place in Thail on Tyrsday, Hebe 28th.*

Theo put down the letter. That was the day after the *Sidereal* was taken. He'd been a captive in a shed while his older brother was laid to rest. That meant his father had known of Paul's death before sending the *Dragonhammer* in pursuit of the *Sidereal*. He had not seen his brother in a year. It was customary for the eldest brother of a noble family to spend time as a military officer, but Paul should never have been anywhere near the front lines. Theo waited to feel grief for his brother's death, but it did not come. He read on.

*Dante's pursuits prohibit him from filling your brother's position.*

That was a polite way of saying that Dante's criminal activities kept him in prison more days than he was out, even though High Chancellor Simon Vanguard as his father.

*Isaiah's station as void mage is too valuable to the family. Upon Paul's demise, I named Joshua my heir. He will inherit my titles and responsibilities in Tyre. Isaiah will recover my artifact. You are to resign your naval commission and return to run the family estates in Balan. Your mother has arranged for you to immediately wed Lady Hannah Valefyre. Congratulations. The Nine have Blessed You, despite your failures.*

*I will arrive in Solvigant Djinnday Luxor 2nd on the* Penumbra. *We will speak of this delegation then.*

*Lord Simon Vanguard, High Chancellor to Astral Emperor Justus Solaric Callire IV.*

Theo reread the letter twice, then crumpled it into a ball. The Vanguard family was in chaos. Paul was dead. Dante in prison, Isaiah a void mage, and now Joshua—*Joshua*—was his father's heir. Of all Lord Vanguard's sons, Joshua most resembled their mother. He had been a child of delicate sensibilities and precarious health. An indifferent student and unfit for military service, he pursued pointless, eccentric interests. Like his mother, Joshua preferred the advice of soothsayers and mystics to physickers and scholars.

*My obstacles to inheritance have significantly diminished.* The thought turned Theo's stomach. His father's station was not a thing Theo wanted. *Or is it? Has it simply seemed so far away that I forced myself to stop wanting it? And I never wanted it at the expense of my brother's life.*

Theo did not want to resign his naval commission. He liked the *Dragonhammer*. He hoped to be captain someday. Maybe when he had enough experience, he would get a fleet command. He was a good officer.

The Lady Valefyre was of a noble, pseudo-Dragon family, a cousin of His Majesty Emperor Callire IV. She was also sixteen years old, and Theo had barely interacted with her at court. She was twelve when Theo joined the navy. Unbidden, an image of Beatrice Faide flashed in his mind. He shook his head to clear it. He wanted to grieve for Paul, yet he felt more unease than sorrow. He resented his father's arrogance. Generals in the Imperial Army treated their soldiers with more respect when giving orders.

*Why is Father coming to Solvigant?*

"Here we are," Art said as he thumped two full tankards onto the table. Theo looked up, startled to see Art standing with Captain Crestone and another survivor of the *Sidereal*, a Grym sailor, his pointed ears poking out from beneath the thick bandages on his head.

"Are you all right?" asked Art, "you're rather pale."

"I'm fine," Theo said. He held the note over the candle in the center of the table. In a few heartbeats, the flame had consumed the letter and its ominous tidings.

Adi plopped into a chair beside him, grinning.

"Espionage and intrigue, is it?"

Theo tossed the last flaming scrap of the letter onto the floor and ground the ashes beneath his boot heel.

"This is my first mate, Peter Wright," Adi said. "You remember him from the *Sidereal*, don't you?"

Wright tipped his hat to Theo and the Faelani.

"Arthur Volaticus, neophyte from the Sons of Destruction," Art said.

Theo was unsure how much he wanted Art to know about this operation.

"Art, maybe you should find somewhere else to be? I don't want to get you in trouble." Theo's voice was flat. He was still reeling over the letter and Crestone's energetic tone disoriented him.

Art bristled, but Crestone put a hand on his arm. "To recover Apyreon, we need all hands, and paws, on deck." Adi addressed Art, "The whereabouts of Apyreon after that affair at the Iron Dirigible are known to a White Rabbit goon named Rictor, who is imprisoned at Opus Station."

Wright opened his mouth to say something, but Crestone raised a hand to silence him.

"Does the plan involve more sucker-punching of Imperial Naval officers?" Theo asked woodenly.

"You deserved that," Crestone replied. "Who's to say you won't earn yourself another down the road?"

Theo tried to focus on the present moment rather than the daunting news of his father's impending arrival. In three short days, his life had taken so many sharp turns. He rubbed his jaw and shrugged.

"You need to work on that left hook," Theo said.

Crestone gave him a jaunty, mocking grin missing one tooth. "The plan," she began, "starts with Wright."

Wright cleared his throat. "I will file a report at Opus Station that Stuart Royal and a large squad of White Rabbits are planning to move on the Red Wyrm. I will tell the watch that the Blood Queen and Devlin Seneschal are meeting at the Red Wyrm and Royal wants to take out the competition."

"Who's Devlin Seneschal?" Theo asked.

"He's one of the four claws of the Order of the Talon," Crestone said. "The Talon has four leaders. Devlin is the same rank as the other three, but it's well known that he's the most powerful."

"He's meeting with Riven? Why?"

Crestone rolled her eyes. "Keep up, Vanguard. He's not. But the watch is already on high alert. Gang violence has been rising for weeks. After this morning's debacle at the Iron Dirigible, the watch will be keen on any leads, and they'll want to avoid another humiliation. The lure of having all three gang leaders in one place is too large to ignore."

"How do you know all this?" Art asked.

"What kind of pirate would I be if I didn't know my home waters?"

"You're a desert pirate now," Theo chided.

"I did well enough on the water to steal *Sidereal*."

"That was blind luck," Theo said. Crestone blinked at him and raised one eyebrow.

Theo explained. "You owe your success to Apyreon, not to your cunning. You got lucky. How did you figure out how to use it, by the way?"

"I'm a wildling astral mage." Crestone said by way of explanation. "And your father left two spinners aboard."

"You're full of surprises." Theo's eyed Adi's chest. "Where's your dragonstone?"

"I lost it."

Theo sighed. "Of course you did."

"May I continue with the plan?"

"By all means, Captain Crestone. What happens next?" Theo sipped his beer and studied the far wall, his expression bored. Out of the corner of his eye he saw Crestone glare at him.

"Wright's report will clear out Opus Station. They'll overcompensate for this morning's failure. Plus, they've already seen Royal and Palestrina fighting in the street in front of the Blood Queen's carriage."

"Planning a coup?" a sly, feminine voice interjected.

All four of them jumped at the intrusion. Crestone clamped her hands over her face in exasperation. Wright blanched and froze in his chair. Theo gaped at the winged woman standing behind Crestone. The newcomer was tall and lithe, her gray skin stretched taut over delicate bones, batlike wings folded behind her. Theo noticed hooks and barbs on the leading edges. Petite black horns grew from either side of her forehead.

"You're a Seraph." Theo said.

"You're very observant," the woman said and pulled over a chair from a nearby table.

"What do you want, Palestrina?" Crestone sounded petulant.

"I heard it was all hands on deck."

"How long have you been listening?"

"Adi, nothing gets said in the Red Wyrm that I don't know about."

"What do you want?"

"I told you, I'm here to help with the parts of the plan that you've forgotten."

"What are you talking about?"

"You continue and I'll fill in the inevitable gaps."

Crestone twitched. She drained half her tankard. Theo knew he'd been swimming in deep water, now he worried they would close over his head.

*How many criminals will I have to associate with to recover Apyreon? I should let Isaiah deal with it.*

Yet, despite Theo's anger at his father's orders, he still wanted to recover the device. No matter what happened when his father arrived, he refused to give the man anything else to use as leverage against him.

The confidence faded from Crestone's voice as she continued. "Most of the watchmen will head here immediately, leaving a skeleton crew to man Opus Station. Theo and I—"

"And me," Palestrina said.

Crestone fidgeted with the collar around her neck. "Fine. Theo, Palestrina, and I will use the opportunity to sneak in, find, and interrogate Rictor."

"What about me?" Art asked, unconcerned by Palestrina's presence.

Adi reached inside her jacket and removed a stick of dynamite. Everyone at the table leaned away. A few eyes from other tables widened in surprise, but it was the Red Wyrm after all. It was better for everyone not to see anything at the Blood Queen's headquarters. The other customers quickly looked away from Theo's party and resumed their conversations.

"Where did you get that?" Theo asked.

"Wright and I nicked it on the way here from an old mining depot in the Ironhorse District. That's why we were late." She handed the dynamite to Art, who took it with just his claw-tips. "Once the street is full of city watchmen you'll set this off in the alley. The watch will assume Royal is making his move and raid the Red Wyrm."

"I don't think the Blood Queen would approve of this plan," Palestrina said.

"The Blood Queen will get what she wants on my terms," Crestone snapped. "If she wanted a more genial plan she shouldn't have threatened my son."

Crestone flushed and Theo realized that she'd said more than she'd meant to. Adi handed Art two spyres.

"After the explosion, hire a hansom cab outside the aeroport and wait in the alley east of Opus Station. At midnight, we'll all meet there. Theo, Palestrina, and I will have Apyreon's location. In the morning, we can plan our next move."

"I'll bring the rosewood box," Palestrina said.

"Rosewood box?" Theo asked.

"The container for your precious Apyreon was separated from the device. The watch confiscated it after the brawl at the Iron Dirigible. They're holding it as evidence at Opus Station. While you're interrogating Rictor, I'll steal it back. I told you, Adi, that you'd forget something."

"I would prefer to retrieve Apyreon without becoming one of Solvigant's most wanted," Theo said. "Breaking into a watch post, interrogating a man in custody, stealing from the impound, and setting off an explosion—even as a diversion... people could get hurt."

Crestone raised an eyebrow. "You have a better idea?"

"I'm an officer of the Imperial Navy. Can't I just ask the watch to give me five minutes with the prisoner?"

"And what reason would you give for needing to converse with a White Rabbit thug?" Crestone said. "You'd have to tell them about Apyreon. How would you interrogate him under the eye of the watch? They won't let you touch him. Even if he did give up the location, the watch would insist on recovering it, and when they discover what it can do? What then? Do you think they'll just hand it over? Plus, the watch is full of soldiers working double duty for the gangs. If Royal gets word we're coming for the device, he'll disappear inside the Warrens and our search will be futile."

"I'm an officer of the Imperial Navy—"

"So, you keep saying," Wright grumbled.

"I took an oath to uphold the law of the Empire."

"And yet here you sit," Crestone said, "plotting with two pirates, one of the Blood Queen's generals, and a Son of Destruction on how best to infiltrate a watch post."

Theo looked to each of them in turn, trying to work up enough spit in his dry mouth for a sharp retort.

"She's right," Art said. "If you want to learn the whereabouts of this device without tipping off Royal, this is your only chance."

"What if this Rictor won't give up the location?" Theo asked.

"You leave that to me," Crestone said, a hint of glee in her green eyes.

Theo sighed. *I wish this wasn't so important to me. Why is it so important to me?*

"When do we start?" Theo asked, resigned.

"What time is it?"

Art checked his pocket watch again. "10:30."

Crestone drained her beer and stood. "Right now."

# CHAPTER TWENTY-NINE

# ADI CRESTONE

## MOON OF XYS, VALEDAY, 30TH OF HEBE

B reaking into Opus Station proved easier than Adi had expected. The Iron Dirigible incident had wound the city watch tight. Twenty minutes after Wright filed his report, two squadrons of city watchmen in full battle armor loaded into wagons and clattered away toward the Red Wyrm. A few minutes after that the Imperial military attaché for the station galloped off in the opposite direction.

"Let's hope your friend Art is a wily one. He's going to have lots of company," Adi said.

"I barely know him." Theo sounded petulant. He'd been sulking since they left the Red Wyrm.

Adi waited until Wright slipped his guard and emerged from the station. Then she led Theo inside. The front office was empty. Through a narrow window into an adjacent office, Adi could see two watchmen conversing, leaning over a city map. As they crept down the hallway, she saw a third officer sitting with her back to them. Adi opened the side door to the station to let Palestrina in. A wind gust banged the door shut behind the Seraph.

Approaching footsteps echoed through the hallway, so they ducked into a dark storage closet. Squashed together among the mops and brooms, Adi had to lean against Theo to avoid Palestrina's wing talons.

*I wish Rehka was here instead of Theo*, Adi thought. *She's the stealthiest person I know.*

The footsteps receded, and they cautiously exited the closet. At an intersection Palestrina moved left on her errand. Despite her awkward height and wings, she moved so silently that it made Adi shiver. Adi and Theo turned right, toward a stout iron door that led to the jail. She eased it open, grateful the watch kept the hinges oiled. She made sure to shut it behind them.

To Adi's delight, when she peered into the sentry's nook, the Grym watchman was snoring in her chair, the remains of her dinner on the desk. Adi stepped behind her, clamped one hand over her mouth and the other around her neck. The watchman bucked against Adi's grip. It took two full minutes of squeezing the Grym's muscular neck to knock her out. Adi used the woman's cuffs to anchor her to her desk then slipped the keys from the woman's belt and motioned for Theo to follow.

The jail cells were cages, independent of the structure of the building. Each cage had hinged sides held together by iron cotter pins so they could be folded for transport. Every cage held multiple prisoners that had been herded into the center and shackled to a bolt in the floor.

*Peripatesis must be a nightmare for the watchmen,* Adi thought. *There must be thirty White Rabbits here.*

The conversation among the inmates ceased when an armed Blood Queen indenture entered the cell block. Adi scanned the faces, looking for Rictor. Unlike the others, he had a cell to himself near the back of the room.

*I wonder if he's one of Royal's generals.*

Adi strode toward him with measured steps, as if interrogating him in front of thirty of his comrades had always been part of the plan. She opened Rictor's cell, then tossed the keys to Theo.

"If anyone else talks," she said to him, "slit their throats."

Theo nodded gravely but she was under no illusions that he would follow that order. She hoped no one would call her bluff. They all stared fixedly at Theo's gleaming military blade, the shield and pen emblazoned on its pommel. Adi smiled, wondering what their audience thought about her traveling with an emissary of the governor.

Adi addressed the big man. His manacled hands rested easy in his lap. "Rictor, is it?"

"Ah, Sasha's little pirate. Are you here to kill me?" he asked.

Adi unsheathed her blade. "Not if you tell me what I want to know."

Rictor snorted.

"You stole something from me, from the Blood Queen herself, and she wants it back."

"Doesn't sound like me," Rictor said.

"So, you and three friends didn't mug a woman in the Blood Queen's warehouse district? That must've been another Rictor."

"Must've been." He spat tobacco juice onto the floor through yellow teeth.

"Where'd I get this then?" Adi raised the sword point to his throat.

Rictor snorted. "You're the one who carved up Polly's face. She got a musket ball with your name on it."

"Polly is, sadly, no longer with us," Adi said.

"You killed her?"

"One of the void mage's acolytes decapitated her." *I'm stalling.* She didn't know if any of these White Rabbits knew about Apyreon, thought it seemed as if everyone in the World System had known about the device except Adi. She did not want to broadcast any more information about it here. Outside, the wind gusted, rattling the jail's walls. Drafts blew through cracks, whirling dust through the room and making the small flames sputter in their sconces.

"Where is Royal taking the device?"

"So, you people can try to kill him again? I saw the bat lady at the Dirigible. No chance."

"Tell me or my colleague will start killing your friends one by one, then you."

Rictor laughed.

"Do it." She ordered Theo. He stared at her, brows raised.

"Your boy don't have the guts," Rictor said.

Adi stormed towards Theo.

"Take one into the hallway, knock him out, cut him, and bloody your sword," she hissed.

"Which one?"

"It doesn't matter." Adi glared at him and pushed him toward the closest cell. Theo unlocked it. Adi eyed a grizzled woman, trembling from loona withdrawal. "Her."

The woman cowered. Adi steered Theo into the cell so he could unlock the prisoner's shackles. He hoisted her by one arm and dragged her down the aisle to the hall. The loonie whimpered and writhed but could not break Theo's grip.

Adi checked her pocket watch as she waited. They had to be out before shift change at midnight or before those two squadrons realized Wright had filed a false report.

Rictor studied her, a thin, amused smile on his face.

*Bring a boy to do woman's work,* Adi thought.

Theo returned, his face pale and his sword glittering red. Adi returned to Rictor, who grinned at her. *Cheeky bastard.*

"Take another," she ordered.

Theo understood his role now and pounced on a brown-skinned desert Ankhim, dragging him away. Adi heard sounds of a scuffle. Theo returned faster this time, panting. His eyes looked too bright.

"Should we start killing them in front of you?" she asked Rictor.

He shrugged, but Adi noticed the inmates looking between Rictor and Theo. Some whispered together, noticing the pommel of Theo's sword.

*They're wondering if the governor let us in here.*

She loomed over Rictor and snarled, "Where's Royal taking the device?"

Rictor inspected his ragged nails.

Adi pressed the tip of her blade between Rictor's shoulder and collar bone. He grunted as she shoved the sword into the muscle.

"I don't know," he said, leaning as far away as his shackles allowed.

*Progress,* Adi thought. *From silence to denial.*

"Where?"

"I don't know, I swear." Pain replaced confidence in Rictor's voice. Adi shoved the blade deeper.

"Shall I disable this arm forever? Then I can do the other one." Adi saw Rictor blanch, and he clenched his jaw against a scream.

Theo stood beside her. Gone was the queasy unease with his task. It had been replaced with fevered anticipation. Adi wasn't sure she liked the look. Her sword jerked deeper into Rictor's shoulder.

"Tell us where," Theo growled.

Rictor's breaths came fast now and he moaned. Adi reckoned he'd tell her the truth soon.

*We're running out of time,* she thought. *If Rictor doesn't know, the device is as good as gone.*

"Royal needed Wik to help him sell the device," she said. "Who's he selling it to? Where's the sale?"

One of the inmates took advantage of Adi and Theo's inattention and shouted for the sentry. Other voices joined in.

*The influence of Theo's sword is waning.*

"I don't know," Rictor croaked. Adi increased the pressure on the sword. Rictor gasped.

"Who?"

Rictor shook his head and Adi leaned on the blade again.

"Buyer's anonymous," Rictor said, "We were setting the terms, fixing the location."

"Someone has to represent the buyer," Adi said. She twitched the blade and Rictor cried out. *Shift change is minutes away. I hope Art's explosion has diverted those squadrons.* "Who?"

Rictor started to speak through his ragged gasps.

"Water Kn—"

Theo lunged and grabbed Rictor by the throat. The sudden move threw Adi off balance and her sword slid deeper than she had intended. Theo clamped his hand on Rictor's windpipe, cutting off his scream.

"You want water?" Theo snarled. "You should have thought of that before you stole from my father."

Confusion overcame the agony on Rictor's face for a moment. It was well known the governor had no children.

"Theo," Adi said. He did not relent. *Something's snapped.*

"He's coming here," Theo said. "He's coming to enact his revenge, on me, on you, on Crestone here. On all of us. You can stop him. You can save us all. Just tell us where the device is. Tell us!"

Adi smacked Theo's forearm. "He can't speak if he can't breathe."

He ignored her, and his eyes were wild.

"Tell us!" Theo squeezed. Rictor's face purpled, his eyes bulged. His shackled hands jerked and rattled as he tried to reach his throat. Adi withdrew her sword from his shoulder.

"Theo, he doesn't know. We need to leave." Adi pulled hard on the man's upper arm.

"Quiet, Crestone," Theo snapped. "He knows. He knows or he wouldn't be in here."

"You're killing him."

Rictor's legs thrashed. His manacled hands clawed at Theo's wrist. Theo's strong grip did not waver.

Then Rictor's words clicked.

*Water Knives! That's what Rictor was trying to say. Rehka! Curse the Nine!*

"Theo, I know where the device is," Adi said, throwing her weight against him. All the inmates were shouting now. In seconds, watchmen would arrive.

Theo shook her off. He snarled into Rictor's blotchy face, "Where is Apyreon?"

"Theo, I know!" Adi shouted over the din of the other inmates.

"He's coming for his revenge," Theo said. "Tell us and save yourself. Don't let him ruin your life too."

*Who is he talking about?* Adi grappled with Theo from behind. He was tall and wide and did not respond to her frantic efforts.

"Theo, we need to go *now*!" Adi reached for her pocket watch to check how much time they had before shift change. Before she could flip it open, Theo drove the governor's sword into Rictor's chest just below the sternum. Adi heard wood splinter as the honed blade punched through Rictor's back and into the floor. Theo drove it to the hilt. Rictor's eyes widened and blood bubbled from his mouth.

"Djinnar's blood, Theo, what did you do?" Adi shouted.

The other inmates howled with rage. The door to the cellblock banged open and Adi jumped. The sudden *clang* of the studded iron broke through Theo's rage. A city watchman loomed in the doorway, his sword drawn.

"What's going on in here?"

Adi glanced around. There were no other exits from the cellblock. Theo tried to extract his sword, but it was stuck between Rictor's ribs and the floor. He looked at Adi and she saw the shocked fear of a traumatized child who's just realized what he's done. Theo placed a booted foot on Rictor's torso and pulled. The sword did not budge.

The watchman strode into the room. "Who are you?"

*We are so screwed.*

Palestrina's nimble form rose behind the watchman, wings mantled.

"Don't!" Adi cried, but too late.

Palestrina's shotel flashed and the watchman crumpled.

"That's twice in one day I've saved your life," the Lady of Spiders said, unperturbed. "Time to go."

Adi wanted to protest. She wanted to check on the watchman even though bright red arterial blood spurted from his wound. She wanted to smack Theo, the damned fool.

*What was that tantrum about? Who's coming for revenge?*

But Palestrina was right, they had to move. They had seconds before more watchmen arrived. Theo braced his feet and heaved at his sword again. Adi grabbed the back of his belt and hauled him away from Rictor, then she slapped him hard.

"We have to go," she hissed.

Theo nodded, his eyes glazed. Palestrina led them toward the side exit. The shouts of the inmates blended with the booted clamor of returning watchmen. Rounding a corner,

Palestrina bowled over an unsuspecting watchman. Adi vaulted him, dragging Theo by one elbow. They slammed through the side door and bolted out into the warm night air. Wright and Art were waiting on a dilapidated buckboard.

Palestrina removed the rosewood box from a sack and thrust it at Adi. Another small parcel fell from the sack, but Palestrina scooped it up before Adi saw more than a flash of amber gemstones in the reflected light of Solo. Wind gusted around them.

"Thank you," Adi panted.

"I hope you got what you needed."

"I did."

"Your idiot officer just made this harder for you."

"He did."

"Go get that artifact and get the hell off Xys." With that, Palestrina leapt into the sky, vanishing on silent wings.

"Djinnar's blood!" Adi shoved Theo toward the wagon. "Get in." They clambered into the bed of the buckboard and she heaved a tarp over herself and Theo. "Wright, get us out of here."

"Aye, aye, Captain." Wright flicked the reins on the swaybacked mare and she set off at a stiff trot. The whistles of the city watch echoed along the streets and alleys. Grit rattled off the tarp and peppered Adi's face.

Wright drove the mare through random streets. No one followed them. When they reached one of the night markets, Adi told Wright to halt. She slipped from the buckboard, clutching her prize.

"Drop these two outside the governor's palace." Adi leaned in so only Wright could hear. "Come by the Echo tomorrow afternoon."

Wright nodded.

"Where are you going?" Theo asked. "What about Apyreon?"

"You've proved yourself incompetent," Adi's anger bit off the words, "I'll contact you when I've recovered it. Go secure my money."

"What do you mean?"

"A certain inspector will put two and two together and I'll be a fugitive thanks to your tantrum back there."

Before Theo could protest, she set off down the street, taking a meandering path to Stella's Echo.

*The proprietor of the Iron Dirigible is brokering a sale for Apyreon between Royal's White Rabbits and the Water Knives. Does Rehka know? Has she been playing me the whole time?*

There were so many scenarios and implications. The adrenaline of their work at Opus Station was wearing off and she started to droop. Her jaw ached and the bandages around her torso and arm needed changing. She needed sleep.

Iris was perched on a barstool sipping tea when Adi stumbled into the Echo. Her eyebrows rose as she took in Adi's condition.

"Let's get you to bed," Iris said, guiding her upstairs. Adi was asleep before Iris pulled off her boots.

## CHAPTER THIRTY

# THEO VANGUARD

## MOON OF XYS, CORDSDAY, 31ST OF HEBE

The wind increased as they crossed Solvigant in the dark, until sand was whipping against the tarp. It was difficult to converse over the rising storm, though Theo had nothing to say to Crestone's first mate. Wright deposited Theo two blocks from the governor's mansion. Art, who looked stricken, did not speak to either of them. He disembarked near the temple precinct. Sand stung Theo's face and eyes as he sought refuge in the first lighted doorway he encountered.

The Thistledown Brothel catered to the elite and government officials who had daytime business with the governor or at the Xyssian congressional building. Despite the early morning hour, a handful of patrons occupied tables, speaking in hushed tones. An elderly man in a bespoke suit played calm melodies on a grand piano. Now and then a moan or burst of laughter drifted down the spiral staircase across the room, though thick draperies and plush cushions muffled most of the noise. Even the storm outside faded away under the music and tobacco smoke.

Theo pushed past a young blonde woman in a sheer silver chemise. The thin fabric revealed rather than concealed, inviting the imagination to survey the intricate tattoos that covered every inch of her skin except her face, which floated pale above fragile shoulders. Theo sat at the imposing wood bar and ordered a double whiskey from a petite red-headed woman. He drained it and ordered another. Liquor would cause him to forget the night's events much faster than companionship.

Theo brought the glass to his lips, but the woman put a hand on his arm. "Easy there, soldier."

Theo sipped the amber liquid, relishing the burn as it snaked down his throat.

"How did you know," he asked, "that I am a soldier?"

"You sit ramrod straight, as if strapped to a board."

"I see." He sipped again, forcing himself to slouch.

"Let me guess"—she eyed him up and down—"not an infantryman, not mounted cavalry... a navy man."

Theo was impressed. "How did you know?"

"You don't have the arrogance of an infantry man, nor the calluses of the cavalry. You have that distant look of a navy officer, always thinking about a different port than the one you're in. Plus, the insignia on your lapel."

"Well done." He felt the alcohol fraying his concentration.

"Cigar?" she offered him a box. Theo took one. She lit it for him, blowing on the end of it to kindle the flame.

Theo took a deep drag, then doubled over, coughing. When he regained control of his breathing, he looked back at her, his eyes watering. She smiled at him. Theo drained the rest of his whiskey. He watched her as she moved around behind the bar, pouring drinks for other patrons. She wore a blue apron over a green silk skirt. Her back was an explosion of freckles against the white of her skin. Theo's pulse quickened despite his exhaustion and the effects of the whiskey.

"There's something you should know," she said when she brought him a fresh drink.

"What's that?"

"I don't do soldiers."

Theo needed a moment to decipher what she meant.

"Why not?"

"They've often been deprived for too long, and it makes them aggressive. I don't do sad guys either."

"Sad?"

Her green eyes flicked down to his third double.

"Ah," he said. He stirred the ice in his drink with an idle finger.

The tattooed blonde suddenly appeared at his side and purred against his ear, "I love soldiers."

Theo couldn't remember how much money the governor had loaned him, but it was enough. He reached for his coin purse.

A woman shrieked upstairs. The piano stopped. All eyes fixed on a woman stumbling down the steep stairs wrapped in a bloody sheet, one hand pressed against her cheek.

"Get away from me!" she shouted.

Two bouncers rose and moved toward the stairs. Theo tried to rise, but his feet got tangled around the foot rail and he fell hard on his tail bone. The tattooed woman laughed even as she helped him to his feet.

"Stupid whore!" a man shouted, his boots ringing on the metal stairs. Theo leaned against the bar and the woman for balance as Hubert Marrion clomped down the stairs brandishing a small knife.

The two bouncers were on him before he reached the bottom. One punched him hard in the stomach while the other disarmed the young noble.

"Do you know him?" the woman on Theo's arm asked.

"He's the Sabaian ambassador, Shir Hubert Marrion," Theo slurred.

"Unhand me!" Hubert shouted, twisting in their grip. "I will see you both hanged."

The bouncers ignored his rant. One on either side, they maneuvered Hubert toward the exit. The injured prostitute sobbed in the arms of an older, gray-haired woman.

*The madam,* Theo thought.

The door to the Thistledown banged open and everyone jumped. Sand streamed in from the storm outside.

There was a chorus of "Close the door!"

The Lady Beatrice Marrion stood there, framed in the gaslights. She wore a heavy coat over a wind-swept nightgown. "Hubert Marrion, shame on you!"

Theo winced as he saw not just anger in those brilliant blue eyes, but shame.

Hubert went limp in the arms of his assailants. "Ah, my lady wife. Will you please explain to these men that I meant no disrespect."

Beatrice quivered, her eyes darting to the wounded woman. "You've overstayed your welcome. It's time to go home," she said through clenched teeth.

"I'll leave when I get what I paid for," Hubert snapped.

"You'll leave immediately," the bartender said, "or we'll summon the Imperial Guards."

Hubert scowled at her and Theo appreciated the presence of the bouncers to keep the man contained. Beatrice stalked across the room and slapped Hubert's face.

"You're embarrassing yourself," she hissed. "This is not diplomatic behavior."

Hubert stiffened at the rebuke but stopped struggling. The bouncers released him and he staggered. Beatrice slung one of his arms over her shoulders and steered Hubert toward the door. He was more drunk than Theo had realized, and high too from the glassy look in his eyes. Beatrice looked around the room in a silent plea for help. Her eyes widened when she saw Theo.

Theo had an arm around the waist of the tattooed woman. He dropped it.

She lifted an expectant eyebrow at him. It made him queasy. "Sir Vanguard?"

He placed several spyres on the bar and, walking with exaggerated care, he went to her. Theo hoisted Hubert by his other arm. The diplomat mumbled. Theo concentrated on putting one foot in front of the other as the trio made their way out the door and into the howling sandstorm.

The two blocks between the Thistledown and the governor's palace revealed both Theo's inebriation and his exhaustion. At the gate, Theo slumped against the iron rails and fought the urge to retch. To his relief, a pair of Ring guards saw them and jogged from their shelter to assist.

Once inside, Theo sat beside the embers of the kitchen fire sipping from a tankard of water. Hubert and Beatrice had retired to their rooms. Tabitha sat across from him, the bones of her face a sharp contrast to the plush robe drawn over her night clothes. He itched from the sand that managed to get into every crack and orifice of his body. It ground between his teeth as he devoured a small plate of meat and cheese the cook had produced from one of the larders. He had lost track of how late it was. Theo debated telling Tabi everything.

*I killed a man in cold blood,* Theo imagined himself saying, *with your husband's sword while wearing my military insignia.*

He had no idea how his cousin would react. There was respect, but was there love between Tabitha and the governor? There would be no children to continue his legacy. Still, given Tabi's fragile health, her social situation benefited from her marriage to Elliot. She would never be without shelter and medical care even if she had to deal with her husband's indifference. Theo wondered if he ought to accept his own situation, to follow the orders in his father's note.

*So what if Lady Valefyre is seven years younger than I am? I can't fault her for her age.*

In truth, his resentment of his unsolicited betrothal came easier than any anger at his father for inflicting it on him. The nobility of the Solan Empire rarely married for love. Theo had hoped that, as the youngest of five sons, he could escape the frivolous and spiteful games men like his father played with power and prestige.

"You don't have to stay up," Theo said to Tabi. "I can make my way to the baths and bed. I'm sorry for disturbing you at such an hour."

"The illness prevents me from lying comfortably in bed. I spend most nights propped up beside the fire."

"Thank you for waking the cook." Theo's appetite embarrassed him given the events of the previous day.

"What happened, Theo? You look as though you've aged several years in one evening."

Theo opened his mouth to explain but shut it before he could formulate any words. Tabitha watched him, her gaze patient and kind.

"You don't strike me as the type to frequent the Thistledown."

"I received some troubling news from my father," Theo said. "I'm ashamed to say it took me by surprise."

"Is he all right?"

"He's fine."

*How do I explain in a way she'll understand?* Theo wondered.

"When my father betrothed me to the governor I tried to take my own life on three occasions."

Theo gaped at his cousin. "You did?"

"I did. I thought I was in love with Lord Turnbull's middle son, and he with me. I thought that if the two of us couldn't be together then I didn't want to be alive."

"What changed your mind?"

Tabi yawned. "Life is bigger than childhood love. I have a duty to my family and the Empire."

"My father has no qualms sacrificing the rest of us to increase his power. We are expected to comply for the good of *his* authority."

Tabi nodded, a knowing expression on her face.

"I just wish he gave more thought to our lives. I dislike feeling like a game piece."

A woman cleared her throat, and Beatrice Marrion entered the dim kitchen.

Both Tabitha and Theo rose and bowed. "My lady."

Beatrice flushed. "Please do not rise on my account."

"It is customary, my lady," Tabitha said before taking her seat once more.

"I am sorry that you had to see your husband in such a state this evening," Theo said.

Warning flashed in Tabi's eyes.

Beatrice sat and smoothed her robe. "My husband is a man of substantial and volatile appetites, Sir Vanguard. But what about you? Does the cliché of the sailor apply to you?"

Theo rearranged cheese crumbs on his plate. "I don't know what you mean."

"A woman in every port, a handful of bastards strewn across the various moons?"

Theo reddened. "No, milady. I'm a confirmed bachelor, or I was until this evening."

"Congratulations," Beatrice said, her voice flat. "Who is the fortunate woman?"

"I have been informed that I am betrothed to the young Lady Hannah Valefyre."

"A noble family. I have met Lady Valefyre and her mother, the Dragon Liza Poison-heart-Valefyre. I suppose you were celebrating at the Thistledown?"

"No, I only took refuge there from the storm."

"You did not accompany my husband?"

"I had no idea he was there until—until the incident." Theo avoided eye contact.

"You spent the evening with my half-sister?"

Theo coughed, bringing his hand to his mouth too late for propriety. "I beg your pardon?"

"I think I will retire," Tabi said. "The less I know about your dealings with pirates the better. Governor Gambol and I must entertain a congressional delegation in a few hours. I do encourage you both to get some sleep."

Theo rose again and bowed as his cousin left the kitchen.

"How did you know?" Theo asked when Tabi's footsteps faded away.

"Rumors of blue-haired pirates only point to one woman." Beatrice cut a slice of cheese. Theo caught her scent, fresh rain over the ocean.

"I would like to bring her to justice."

"Would you?"

*What does she know?* Theo wondered.

"We are all children forced to live in a world our parents created," Beatrice said.

"What do you mean?"

"It is the nature of a prophet to know little about the world and much about the cosmos."

*What is she trying to tell me?* Theo wondered. "Do you enjoy being a prophet?"

"I don't understand the question."

"Last night you told me that I would be present at the destruction of Xys. Is there more you can tell me?"

Beatrice took his hand and inspected the palm. Her hands were soft but cool. Theo held himself still, alarmed at his quickening pulse. She traced the lines of his palm with idle strokes of her fingertips and he shivered.

After several minutes she said, "There is no more I will tell you."

"Can Xys's destruction be prevented?"

"Do you want to prevent it?"

Theo shrugged. "I don't want innocent citizens of the Empire to die."

"From my perspective, Xys is both already destroyed and newly formed by Solo."

"Your husband said you experience time differently."

"My husband is a fool." She said it with such ferocity that Theo balked. "For the rest of you events form a chain, a progression of cause and effect. My gift means that I stand at the center of a sun from which time radiates out in all directions."

Theo nodded, though he did not understand.

"You killed a man tonight."

Theo's hands twitched. He could still feel the hilt of the sword against his palm as he fought to wrench it free from the floor and Rictor's body.

"Like every soldier death is all around you. Did you know Xys is sacred to Pallantier, the God of Creation?'"

"Yes, each god prefers their own moon."

"Do they?" Beatrice seemed amused, though Theo had no idea why.

"What are you getting at?"

"Do you have a patron deity?"

"All Imperial soldiers beseech Yeom, God of Civilization."

"Do you?"

Theo rose. "It's been a long day, milady, and I am not comfortable with this line of questioning."

"What is my half-sister like?"

"She is a pirate in every sense of the word."

Beatrice nodded as if she had expected such an answer.

"I bid you goodnight, Lady Marrion."

As he stepped past her, she grabbed his arm and their eyes met. "You know, Commander, you cannot lose what you do not already have."

"I am too tired for riddles."

"The truth is obvious. It is reality that confuses you. Goodnight, Theo." Beatrice released his wrist.

"Goodnight." Theo said, flustered.

He did not bathe, but stumbled through the sprawling hallways to his room, where he collapsed into the sheets. Rictor's visage, slack in death, his bloody torso pinned to the ground, haunted Theo's dreams. In the darkness he heard laughter. Though he had never spoken to the young woman, he knew it was Hannah Valefyre and the Lady Marrion.

# CHAPTER THIRTY-ONE
# THEO VANGUARD

## MOON OF XYS, CORDSDAY, 31ST OF HEBE

T heo woke from unpleasant dreams. He checked his watch. It was three in the morning. He rolled over and sighed. Ocher light from Solo glowed around the edges of the curtains.

Images of Rictor's death replayed themselves in his mind. *Where had that flood of anger come from?* Theo did not know what to expect in the way of consequences. *Will the city watch come for me? The Imperial Guard?* And one thought would not leave his mind, no matter how hard he squeezed his eyes shut. *I am a murderer.*

He tried to rationalize it: Rictor was a gangster, a thug, a criminal. Theo had done Solvigant a favor ridding it of just another street tough. No one would miss Rictor, and whatever future evils the vile man might have committed he could no longer perpetrate. No one knew how many people he had saved from that White Rabbit goon.

But overall, Theo's convictions rang hollow.

*I am no more than a bloodthirsty pirate, like Crestone.*

Thoughts of Adi led to thoughts of her half-sister, Beatrice. He remembered the look of shock and disappointment on her face when she had recognized him in the Thistledown. He recalled her disgust directed toward her husband. Theo knew Hubert's type: aggressive, arrogant, lecherous, and controlling. His brother Paul had been that way toward his wife Mary.

*Had been.* Theo still could not wrap his head around his brother's death. He wondered how Mary and her two young daughters fared. Emotion stirred in him then when he thought about his sister-in-law, widowed at twenty-five. Theo was only twenty-three and would soon be married himself. He could not imagine marrying, fathering children, and becoming a widower in so short a span.

Theo could no longer lay abed. The thought of his impending nuptials drove him from the comfort of thick blankets. He sloshed tepid water on his face from the washbasin and toweled himself dry. When he had been unable to sleep on the *Dragonhammer* he practiced sword forms on the officer's deck. He had lost his own sword, and the sword Governor Gambol had loaned him he had left behind in Rictor's body.

Theo pulled on his shirt and laced up his breeches. He considered returning to the Thistledown. Good whiskey and a naked woman might be enough to distract him. It had worked before. The tattooed blonde with the green eyes had enticed him. He was ambivalent about tattoos, but her boldness had stirred something in him.

*She's a prostitute. Boldness earns coin in that line of work.*

Beatrice's disapproving expression floated across his mind's eye. Even angry, her poise and intelligence compelled him. He would not return to the Thistledown. Whiskey, however, was an excellent idea. His hand throbbed and his thoughts were dark with murder and desire. Whiskey was the perfect thing to smother dangerous memories.

He slipped into the hallway so as not to rouse the staff. It took him several moments to orient himself to the rambling palace. Theo remembered a crystal decanter on the sideboard behind the dining room table, but he did not remember the route back to that room. Twice he lost his way, stumbling first into a dark sitting room and then an empty bedroom. At last, he reached the dining room. He heard servants at work in the nearby kitchen.

*Is it that close to breakfast?* Theo wondered. He wanted the empty silence of the meandering palace to last. Theo grabbed the decanter and a crystal goblet.

"Pour two."

The woman's voice startled him and he dropped the glass. It shattered on the floor and Theo winced. The kitchen servants ceased their whispered conversation. He whirled and saw Beatrice standing in the doorway wearing a satin robe over a loose shift. She grinned at him as though they were two children caught committing mischief. The kitchen door swung open and a young cook poked her head out.

"What's goin' on here? Who's there?"

"I dropped a glass," Theo explained, "I apologize for my clumsiness."

The girl's eyes traveled from Theo to Beatrice. Theo saw disapproval there, but the cook did not voice it.

"I'll get a broom," she said.

Theo and Beatrice waited in silence while the cook swept up the shards of glassware.

"Can I get you anything?" the cook asked.

"No, thank you," Theo said. He considered asking her to keep this encounter to herself, but decided that would look suspicious.

Once the servant retreated into the kitchen, Theo selected two glasses from the cabinet.

"Can't sleep?" he asked Beatrice over his shoulder.

"A common side effect of prophetic vision."

Theo was intrigued. "You had a vision this evening?" he asked before realizing it might be a rude question. He cleared his throat, then set the two glasses on the corner of the table and poured the liquor. He poured himself a healthy double and pushed the other glass down the table toward Beatrice.

"I am sorry," he said, "I meant no offense."

She flashed him another smile, sadder this time. "I saw nothing that made any sense to me."

Theo studied her and realized *she is lying*. He decided not to press the issue. Her visions were none of his business. Instead, he motioned toward the double doors leading out to the veranda. "Shall we retire to the patio?"

She stifled a laugh and nodded. Theo drew back the bolt and opened the door. He followed Beatrice outside, tumbler in one hand, decanter in the other. The sandstorm had abated and the cobalt light of the moon Highgaard, the moon closest to Xys, blended with the red sands to create a haunting purple hue that bathed the landscape. The wind had cleared out the coal smoke and Solvigant lay spread before them. Theo saw the city with a new clarity. The flickering glow of gas lamps and the running lights of dirigibles spread out to the horizon. Theo had spent much of his time in Thail, the Imperial capital. It, too, was a beautiful city, but one outlined by the harsh angles of stone façades and the imposing architectural trappings of an empire that stretched across the better part of seven moons.

"It is a beautiful city," Beatrice said coming to stand beside him at the veranda's railing. She sipped her whiskey and gazed out at the City Peripatetic. Behind them, Solo and her rings loomed large, but in this moment, the Mother's presence did not feel menacing to Theo.

"She is," Theo agreed, though his gaze was fixed on Beatrice and not out toward the sprawling maze of Solvigant. Beatrice realized this and flushed.

"You flatter me, sir," she said, brushing a stray strand of blue hair behind her ear.

Theo cleared his throat. "My apologies. I spoke out of turn. I meant no impropriety or offense." The whiskey dried his mouth, so he took another ample swig.

"No offense taken. You are not the first man to compliment me."

"Your husband, I hope."

Theo realized his mistake as she turned away. Then she changed the subject. "How does it feel to lead the delegation to the God of Destruction?"

Theo refilled both their glasses while he thought about his answer. He was starting to feel lightheaded from his first drink and he sloshed the liquor. Drops landed on Beatrice's outstretched hand and he reddened when he realized he had nothing to offer her to wipe it away. Laughing, Beatrice licked away the drops. Theo's pulse quickened.

"I've never met a noblewoman like you."

"What do you mean?"

"The women I know are trained to endure the world with stiffness and rigor, all while appealing to their husband's appetites."

"Well, I'm not a noblewoman."

"Your father is Lord Daniel Faide, patriarch of one of the four great houses. Your husband is a nobleman and an ambassador."

"My mother is a wayfaring Passerine. My father did not acknowledge her until I passed the Crucible. My prophetic ability allows me and my mother to masquerade as nobility."

Theo struggled to respond. In the world of Imperial politics, men and women would kill, manipulate, and screw anyone they thought might give them a social leg up. If there were titles involved, all other alliances were null and void. The cavalier way Beatrice dismissed his whole framework for the world excited him in a strange way.

"You haven't answered my question," she pressed when he was silent too long. "About the delegation."

"It seems a grand adventure."

"Is that why you volunteered? To go on an adventure?"

"Isn't that what every young officer wants, an opportunity to prove himself?"

"What about Solvigant's fate? Djinnar must agree to alter the city's pilgrimage path."

"Yes. I want to save the people of Solvigant, of course."

Beatrice studied him. Theo fought a rising wave of hiccups.

*She seems much older than her years,* he thought and emptied his glass. A warm buzz played behind his temples and along the length of his spine. He recognized the drunkenness for what it was.

"So, Theo, the young, exuberant naval officer, wants to go on an adventure, is that it?"

Theo heard the sharp tone of her voice, and he grew serious. He gazed out at the city and said, "I want to do something I choose to do. It is a luxury the sons of House Vanguard have not had."

"What do you mean?"

"My father sees us not as sons but as tools to extend the influence of his own power. But it's killing us. He's like a carpenter who does not care for his equipment. My brother Paul was a hammer, Dante a chisel, Joshua—" Theo stumbled on the extended metaphor. He waved his glass angrily at the city. "Now Paul is dead, Dante is in prison, Joshua is a broken husk of a man, and Isaiah is the horror he is. My father did this to us."

"What about you?"

Theo turned to look at her. Her robe had slipped open and he could see goosebumps on the upper curve of her breasts. Her eyes met his. He cleared his throat and looked away.

"My father has selected a wife for me. I am to leave the navy, marry, and take my place at our estates in Balan." To his surprise, Theo had to blink away sudden tears. Beatrice put a reassuring hand on his arm.

"That doesn't sound so terrible," she said.

"It's not what *I* want." Theo was aware the statement made him sound like a whiny brat, but the whiskey had dulled his ability to care. "I've never met my betrothed, and I don't want to be sidelined in Balan."

"Ah, you want to be in the action. You want to move the pieces around the board, not unlike your father."

Theo flushed, angry at the comparison. "I don't want to be like him at all."

"You're a good man, Theo."

"And my father isn't?" he shook his head. "I'm sorry. I don't know why I feel the need to defend him when I've disparaged him in front of you."

"He is your father. You're allowed to disparage your own parents."

"I can't help feeling like I'll be a prisoner. Even if it's a beautiful estate, it's still a prison. I wonder if he's trying to hold his last fit heir captive. Yet I don't want to die because of my father's schemes." A thought occurred to him. "You said you saw me with that congressman, Xander, watching Xys's destruction. Have you seen me married, running Balan?"

A part of his whiskey-addled mind recognized that he was overstepping again, but he barreled ahead anyway. He stared at her, waiting for her response, crossing his fingers that he might find release and hope in her answer.

"I cannot offer you the solace you desire," she said at last. "At least not in the way you hope. My abilities don't respond to specific questions. Believe me, I've tried. I know little about your future besides what I've already told you. I can only offer consolation through our shared experiences."

Theo looked puzzled. Beatrice pressed on.

"I know something about being used for what I can provide to those more powerful in my life, like my father. I have learned, Theo, that we're all prisoners. Some of us have the luxury of designing our own enclosures, but most of us make do with wherever we find ourselves incarcerated. Those of us willing to work within the confines of our situation often excel and find comfort in unexpected places."

Theo refilled their glasses and contemplated her words.

"Tabi said something similar."

"Lady Gambol is an intelligent woman. People underestimate her because of her condition, but they are wrong to do so."

Theo nodded. "How do you do it? How do you women smile and bear it and make do?"

"We don't grow up with any illusions that we have a choice."

"I don't understand."

"Boys grow up expecting to be leaders, knights, and lords. Imperial society grooms girls for supporting roles, marries us off, and expects that we will dedicate ourselves to our husbands and sons. We cannot lament the loss of an autonomy we never had."

Theo let out a long breath. "You never asked for your life, to be a prophet or to be married to Hubert. Your father made those decisions for you."

"If I had not manifested my prophetic ability my father would have disposed of me. But, otherwise, you're correct."

"I imagine you had many suitors on Saba."

Beatrice laughed. It reminded Theo of the soft chime of his mother's rotating pendulum clock. He and Joshua used to hide in her study so they could hear those exquisite bells chime the hour. Theo did not have many fond memories of his brothers, but that was one.

"Most men avoid powerful women. Especially women they believe can see their hidden foibles," Beatrice said.

*Most men are blind,* Theo thought, trying not to stare at her cherubic face.

"Plus," she continued, "I was promised to Hubert at birth."

"Even for the Imperial nobility, that seems young."

"House Azure and House Marrion have a complicated, intertwined history."

"What do you mean?"

"How familiar are you with the stories of the Sojourners?"

"I know that one, Selene, carried the surname Faide. Did they not found the four noble houses, Vanguard, Phaeton, Laird, and Faide?" Theo searched his brain for more facts. He wanted to impress this enigmatic woman, but he could not remember any more of the grade-school history lessons.

Beatrice nodded. "That's right. Kade Vanguard and Selene Faide were partners. They had two children, Aner and Bella. The other Sojourners, Arthur Phaeton and Penelope Laird, had three children, Maxon, Felix, and Rosalyn. We call this second generation of five children the Kratoi. Aner married the beautiful Seraph Valerie Balaxandros, their son Abram Vanguard founded the house that bears his name. Bella loved only her brother, Aner. They used the realm of Basalt for their illicit trysts, and it is there that Bella gave birth to the demigods, Droth and Kelek, who remain trapped on Saba by the power of the Crucible.

"Of the Phaeton/Laird union, more is known. Felix Phaeton married a human woman, Sarah Pella. Their son Felix II founded House Phaeton. Rosalyn fell in love with a wealthy Dragon named Jasper Valefyre. When her parents forbade the marriage, she ran away. They lived on Flynt and had six children. Their oldest daughter Phaedra founded House Valefyre; their other children founded the five major draconic houses."

"What about Maxon Laird, their eldest?" Theo asked.

"Maxon never married. His life is a mystery, woven of conflicting stories and accounts. It is those same accounts that inspired the Maxon Laird novels my sister and I loved so much."

"Crestone?"

Beatrice nodded.

Theo rubbed his temples. "What does this have to do you and Hubert?"

"According to certain stories, Maxon was suave and debonair and seduced men and women alike into his bed, married and unmarried. But his most famous is his aunt, Sojourner Selene Faide."

Theo choked. "He slept with his *aunt*?"

"Yes. Depending on which accounts you read, he was either a charming devil or the two really loved one another. They had two children, Lily and Thomas. Lily married Andre Marrion, but their marriage was a loveless one. She disappeared after bearing a son. Little is known of her after that. She may have been the first prophet; it is impossible to know. Thomas Faide claimed Kade as his father to legitimize his status as a Kratoi. He married and his wife bore ten children, and he founded House Faide. All these centuries later, my father believes that the potential for prophetic ability increases when the Faide and Marrion lines breed."

Theo paid more attention to the subtle movement of Beatrice's lips than her genealogy lesson. Her upper lip had a pronounced bow in the middle and delicate dimples framed her mouth. The name Valefyre shook him from his reverie and brought him back to the moment.

"Breed is such a terrible word," he said. "Horses breed."

"Noblewomen breed."

Theo shook his head, distracted by the curve of her throat. "You should be able to pursue your own goals, follow your own dreams. Djinnar's blood, you're a prophet!"

Beatrice smiled, "That's a first."

"What?"

"The curse, 'Djinnar's blood.' You have been cavorting with pirates."

Theo did not want to talk about Crestone. Thoughts of Crestone brought back images of dark blood spilling from Rictor's abdomen. Theo took a long draw of his whiskey. He realized Beatrice was closer. Her glass sat empty on a nearby table. He could smell the fine liquor on her breath and something floral on her skin. The two scents combined in a heady way.

Beatrice leaned into him. "This delegation will give you leverage with your father. If you succeed, you'll be the hero of Solvigant. That ought to come with some bargaining power. Has your father ever visited a god?"

Theo shook his head and licked his lips. "I don't think so. What about you? If you could follow your own path, where would it lead?"

Beatrice gazed at him. "I've been thinking about that. I want to visit with my sister. For all her faults and foibles, she is her own woman. There's a lesson in that for me, for both of us."

"A lesson?"

"I have no idea what I want. I've never given myself permission to think about it before. I waited for my father or Hubert or the gods to tell me what they wanted. I will have to think about that. I will have to build up the courage. I will have to practice."

"Practice?"

Beatrice kissed him. Theo's breath caught. Her lips were hesitant, so he opened his mouth to hers in encouragement. They kissed until they had to stop and breathe. Theo ran the back of his fingers along the side of her face, then drew her close once more. Her own hand came up to cradle the back of his head. He was thrilled at the sensation of her body pressing against him. Her movements were cautious, her hands searching. Theo tried to encourage her, but he too was giddy with the sensation of her touch and not well-practiced in such affairs.

*An affair? Is that what this is?* Theo wondered but did not allow himself to answer. He quashed all thoughts of Hubert and consequences. This elegant, blue-haired prophetic woman, whose presence titillated him whenever they occupied the same room was holding him, kissing him, because she wanted to—she wanted *him*.

Theo lost his balance and stumbled backward. He sat down hard in a patio chair. They laughed awkwardly and Beatrice let her robe fall from her shoulders before coming to sit on Theo's lap. Between luxurious kisses, Theo reached out and pushed the veranda door closed. He didn't want any of the house staff witnessing. Beatrice pulled his shirt over his head and ran her hands across his chest and torso before leaning into him once more. Theo placed kisses on those perfect lips, on the bump of her throat, and the nape of her neck until she shivered and moaned.

She shifted and straddled him.

Theo surrendered.

# Chapter Thirty-Two
# ADI CRESTONE
## Moon of Xys, Cordsday, 31st of Hebe

Adi awoke to muted red light and the sibilant hiss of sand brushing against the shutters. Last night's storm had brough another behind it. She was alone in Iris's room. The Echo was quiet. Adi smiled when she saw a mug of coffee on the side table beside the pallet. She groaned when she picked up the chilly mug.

*How long have I been asleep?*

Adi rummaged through her discarded clothes until she found her watch. It was mid-day!

"Djinnar's blood," she cursed. She chugged the coffee, gagging on the tepid acidity. Bending down to pull on her clothes, she gasped at the pain in her ribs. Her jaw felt more swollen than it had been yesterday, and the cuts on her wrists oozed. She stank and itched. She couldn't confront Rehka without bathing first.

A moment of panic struck her as she remembered the rosewood box. She stood, wincing as her ankles and knees popped. Adi scanned the small bedroom and saw Apyreon's box sitting askew on Iris's dressing table, its lid open. Adi picked up the delicate box and traced the swooping lines of the mother-of-pearl inlay with one finger. Her agitated pulse settled.

She set the box down and opened the wardrobe. She selected a green chemise and slipped it on. Gathering her clothes, she went downstairs. The tavern was dim, all the windows shuttered against the storm. A few candles lit the room and Melinda snored from the leather chair beside the banked fire. With the shutters closed, the tavern was sweltering. The homey aroma of roasting meat lured Adi to the kitchen. She noticed sausages roasting on the wood stove. Adi said good morning to Warwick the cook, then nicked two sausages and a bundle of sage when he turned away to tend rising dough. They were perfect, seasoned with fennel and thyme and their skins popped when Adi bit them. Grease ran down her chin.

There were still embers beneath the cistern in the bathroom. Adi stoked the coals and added more wood. She filled a basin, scrubbed her clothes, and hung them near the fire to dry while she waited for the water to heat. When it was hot, she scooped it into the wooden tub. She gasped with pleasure as she lowered herself into the bath. She scrubbed her injured body with delicate strokes. The water turned murky with sand and dried blood. She drained the tub and refilled it. This time she threw in the sage from the kitchen and a handful of dried lavender Stella kept beneath a floorboard for just this purpose, though none of the girls were supposed to know about it.

Adi was dozing in the warm, scented water when someone knocked on the door and entered.

"I'll have to find a new hiding place for the lavender," Stella said.

Adi smiled, but did not open her eyes. "I won't tell anyone."

"You were out late."

"Mmm hmm."

"Everything all right?"

"At this moment, perfect."

"An Inspector Solomon Broc came by this morning and asked after you. I told him you weren't here, but I wouldn't be surprised if he came back with an Arbiter's Notice of Inspection this afternoon. I expect the storm might slow them down a bit."

Adi's opened her eyes and sighed. "That was quick."

"What are you mixed up in, Adi?"

"Where is everyone?"

"You mean where is Iris?"

Adi said nothing.

"Cordsday Rite, then the market, I think," Stella said.

"She's attends the Cordsday services?"

"Careful with that one, Adi. She cares for you a great deal, and she's sensitive for a working girl."

Adi shifted deeper in the water. Stella put down her laundry and perched on the edge of the tub. She wet some soap and began scrubbing Adi's hair. Adi moaned at the feel of Stella's fingers on her scalp.

"I noticed Rehka didn't return with you."

"Playing matchmaker? No, she's laid up at her father's."

"She's injured? Badly?"

"I hope not," Adi said. "You don't like her."

"Just protecting my girls."

"From me or Rehka?"

"You and Rehka have changed since you met all those years ago."

"Not that much."

Stella huffed and ladled water over Adi's head to clear the soap. "I heard reports that the Iron Dirigible was destroyed yesterday. Some say it was the Blood Queen, some say the emperor sent a void mage to Solvigant. There are also rumors that an agent for the governor murdered a prisoner and two city watchmen at Opus Station."

Adi sat up and looked at Stella. "Are you asking me if I was involved?"

"Oh, I'm certain you were involved," Stella said. "I'm asking if you're all right."

Adi's shoulders slumped as her defensiveness evaporated. She sank below the surface for a final rinse, then rose and wiped water from her eyes. The collar of indenture sat heavy around her neck.

"This is it, Stella," she said.

"What do you mean?"

"Soon I'll be free of the Blood Queen. Lucas and I will be free and we'll have a fresh start."

Stella smiled and shook her head. "You know, Adi, there are people who care about you here. People who love you, people you can trust with whatever"—Stella gestured expansively—"with whatever this is that you're mixed up in."

Adi climbed out of the tub. "I know."

"Do you?" Stella handed her a towel.

"I just—" Adi started, then gulped. "I'm tired of putting other people in danger."

"Just Rehka?"

"Rehka puts herself in danger. She's her own woman."

"And Iris isn't? Meera and I? We've risked our lives for you before. You're one of my girls, Adi, even though you ran away to play pirate on distant moons."

Adi nodded and blinked to clear her eyes. "Thank you, Stella. I know. Please, just give me some time to get things sorted. I'll tell you everything then."

Stella observed her, hands on hips, a stern vulpine gaze. "Very well, Adi. We trust you even if you don't trust us. You don't have to be in this fight alone." She turned to go, and Adi knew she had hurt the woman's feelings.

At the door, Stella turned and appraised Adi once more. "You know, Iris is stronger than you think." Then she was out the door before Adi could decide how to respond.

By early afternoon, Adi was ready to cross town to Goldwynd Alley and see Rehka. Adi had washed her clothes, bleached her hair, and brushed out her new jacket. The second storm had abated as Adi enjoyed a hot lunch, joined by several of Stella's girls, and chatted with Melinda. The frail woman was remarkably well-informed for someone who rarely left the Echo. Her hearing must still be acute because she caught so much gossip from the patrons of the bar. Adi wondered how old the woman was, and felt a pang of sadness that the Echo would lose some large, undefined part of itself when Melinda passed. It was enough to fill her with nostalgia for the life she'd left behind when she ran away with Rehka.

She departed the Echo with reluctant footsteps. The sandstorm was still strong enough that Adi opted for a carriage instead of walking. She had left the rosewood box on Iris's dressing table, along with a note of thanks for taking care of her last night.

Adi did not know how to feel about Iris. Between the whirlwind return of Rehka, the threat to Lucas, and the hope of ending her indenture, she didn't have time to feel anything else and could not invest in a new relationship. But that didn't stop the fluttering jitters every time she and Iris were together.

As the carriage rattled toward Rehka and answers, toward Bale and broken promises, all of the fear and anxiety of her situation came crashing back.

*I should have brought Wright as a distraction,* Adi thought. Then she reminded herself that he was her first mate, not her emotional support Grym.

Adi opened the door to Drake's Apothecary and the bell clattered. Bale appeared from the back. His expression hardened when he saw Adi.

"You're not welcome here, Adison."

"Bale, please, I need to speak with Rehka."

"You need to leave."

"I can't. Lucas is in danger."

Bale lowered his thick brows. "You promised me you'd leave her out of this."

"She came to me, Bale. I swear."

"Adi's right." Rehka appeared from the back rooms of the house. "The Knives' job required me to find her."

Adi rushed across the room and embraced Rehka. She felt the woman wince in pain and released her.

"You're all right?" Adi's knees felt watery.

"You mean you volunteered to find Adi?" Bale inquired, his voice stern.

Rehka grimaced. Adi remembered why she was there, and her heart clenched. She needed to know the Water Knives' role in all this. She took several awkward steps back.

*Will Rehka betray me again?* Adi was unsure whether that was a thought or a prayer. Perhaps both.

"The Doctors Vake came by this morning to check up on Rehka," Bale said. "They brought this with them." He handed Adi a rolled-up parchment.

Rehka peered over Adi's shoulder as she unrolled it. The upper half of the parchment contained a reasonable sketch of Adi's likeness including her tricorn and the collar of indenture. Below, it read:

WANTED:

Adison Crestone

In connection with the events Valeday, 30th of Hebe

at the Iron Dirigible and Opus Station.

Report to city watch if found.

Do not approach. Armed and Dangerous. Reward.

*Broc moves fast,* Adi thought. *Thank the Nine for this storm.* Few people would be out looking for her today.

"They forgot 'Captain,'" Adi complained. It was easy to sound confident with Rehka beside her. A decade together on the high seas as pirates and lovers meant they'd run into their share of lawmen.

"How big do you think the reward is?" Rehka asked. Adi shoved her.

"Ow!" Rehka whined. "I was electrocuted then bludgeoned by a flying pirate, remember?"

"You did this to her?" Bale said.

"No, Dad," Rehka said. "I told you the void mage used her against me. It wasn't her fault."

Bale's eyes darted back and forth between the two women. "Void mages, gangs, Seraphim, and now you're a wanted woman. What's going on, Adi?"

"Apyreon," Adi said. "It's a hot commodity in Solvigant right now."

"You gave it to the Blood Queen. Why is that your problem?"

Adi flushed, "I lost it in a mugging before I could deliver it."

"And now you have to recover it or Riven will hurt Lucas?" Bale, said, immediately connecting the artifact with her earlier statement.

Adi nodded. "Someone hired the Water Knives to recover it, too. Thus, Rehka. I really am sorry, Bale. I had intended to honor my promise."

Rehka's brows shot up and her eyes glinted with hurt.

"Rehka, can we talk?" Adi pressed.

Before her father could protest, Rehka agreed. She took Adi's hand and led her upstairs to their old room. Rehka reclined against the headboard and Adi sat at the foot of the long, narrow bed.

"Is that my sweater?" Rehka asked.

Adi looked down, "Yeah, I borrowed it. I came here when I returned to Solvigant from Thail. I figured Bale would know something about Apyreon."

"Did he?"

"He's the one who identified it as Apyreon. I thought it was just a fancy star key."

"You had no idea you were stealing one of the most powerful and mysterious devices from Anaximander's workshop?"

Adi shook her head. "I was sent to steal a trinket for the Blood Queen." Adi paused and touched Rekha's bruised face. "I'm glad you're all right."

"You too, Adi. It sounds like you had a busy evening."

Adi stared at the bed covers, one finger tracing idle circles.

Rehka coughed. "What happened at Opus Station?"

Adi met her gaze. "I need to ask you something."

Rehka stiffened, the soft light in her eyes stained with concern.

"Tabrin Wik is brokering a sale of Apyreon between Stuart Royal and—"

"The Water Knives," Rehka finished.

"So, you knew? You didn't tell me? I risked my life and the lives of other people last night at Opus Station to get that information and *you knew*."

"Adi, I'm sorry. It's complicated." Rehka leaned forward and grasped Adi by the arm.

Adi snatched her arm away and grimaced in pain as Rehka's fingers brushed her wrists.

"Two men are dead, Rehka, one of them a city watchman. When were you going to tell me? After the sale?"

"Adi—"

She stood. "You realize if that sale goes through it will become that much harder to recover Apyreon and save Lucas? Did you think about that?"

The tall Dragon shrank against the headboard.

"Did you even care about that?" Adi shouted.

A knock on the door.

"Go away," Rehka said, and Bale's footsteps retreated. "Adi, listen to me, okay? Just listen."

"Yes, I volunteered, and yes, I didn't tell you everything, but I had good reasons."

"My son—" Adi continued.

"Adi, sit down and listen," Rehka growled, hinting at her Draconic heritage.

Adi sat.

"Let me explain," Rehka said. "I knew Apyreon was in Lord Simon Vanguard's possession. I had no idea the Blood Queen was making a play for it."

*She's still holding something back,* Adi realized.

Rehka continued. "I didn't know you were involved until I spotted you on Thail."

"You had me followed?"

"I needed to know what the Blood Queen was up to. I was completely surprised when Duncan saw you casing the maintenance dock where the *Sidereal* was anchored. You had Captain Torrance's crew with you, so I figured it would be safer to let you steal it."

Adi huffed. "I undertake the difficult theft, and you get the satisfaction of stealing it from me?"

"I hoped we could come to an arrangement."

"Like what? Apyreon would have ended my indenture. I would have been free." Adi's voice broke.

Rehka held up her hands, "Let me finish, please."

Adi snorted, biting back her anger and hurt.

"The storm and the *Dragonhammer* prevented me from intercepting you. I never thought you'd figure out how to use it."

Adi smiled despite herself. "You never give me enough credit."

"When I returned to Solvigant and discovered Apyreon was lost to Royal, the plan changed. It was decided a team of Water Knife assassins would buy the artifact for the client. In the meantime, I was to contact you and if we could locate it before Tabrin Wik set up the sale then the Water Knives could avoid paying for it."

Adi took it all in.

"When I learned about Lucas, everything changed again. I wanted to help you find the device for his sake. I swear. It was never my intention to risk either you or Lucas."

"But you did," Adi said, her voice soft.

Rehka hung her head and tears glistened on her cheeks.

"Rehka," Adi said.

Rehka sniffled and looked up at her. One detail from the story bothered Adi.

*Who knew that Apyreon was in Lord Vanguard's possession? Was the Blood Queen hedging her bets if I failed?* Adi wondered. *Was a Blood Queen minion leaking information to the Water Knives?*

"Rehka, who is the client?"

Rehka began to cry in earnest. She reached out and grabbed Adi's hands. "It doesn't matter."

"Who?"

Rehka slumped further. "I don't know. That's why I didn't want to tell you."

Adi said nothing and stared out the tiny window.

"Adi, I'm sorry."

"Is it Palestrina?" Adi said.

"I don't know."

"I don't believe you."

"I didn't even know what Apyreon could do. It was just a job!"

Adi rounded on her. "Just a job. It's my life, Rehka, and my son's life. Did you think about that?"

"The client promised a new lead on connecting with my Dragon form."

Adi threw up her hands. "Of course they did. You haven't learned anything. You didn't even question it, just believed them."

"I have to believe."

Another knock at Rehka's door.

"Not now, Dad," Rehka said.

Bale opened the door and leaned in.

"Dad, I said—"

"There's an Inspector Becca Henge downstairs asking after Adison."

Adi and Rehka's gaped. Rehka rose from the bed.

"Go out the back, Adi. We'll tell her you're not here."

"You need to go to the Water Knives and find out where the sale is happening. And then *you need to tell me*," Adi hissed.

Rehka nodded.

"Promise me, Rehka."

"I promise. Where will I find you?"

"At the Echo."

"Won't they come for you there?"

"Not without an arbiter's notice, which they won't get during the Cordsday Rite."

"Adi, please forgive me," Rehka whined.

"Make this right. Get me that information and then we'll talk."

"I'll go distract Henge. Wait a few minutes then slip out the back." Without warning, Rehka grabbed Adi's face in both hands and kissed her. Adi froze, the pain in her bruised jaw receding in her shock. Rehka released her.

"I'll make this right, Adi. I love you." She clomped down the stairs, leaving a bewildered Adi and a furious Bale.

Rehka's voice drifted up the stairs, "Inspector Henge, how can I help you?"

Adi removed her boots and held them in one hand. She waited, listening to the conversation below. Then, with Balthasar leading to take credit for any sound on the stairs Adi tiptoed into the kitchen and out the back door.

The sandstorm was beginning to dissipate.

# CHAPTER THIRTY-THREE

# ION RUCINARE

## MOON OF XYS, CORDSDAY, 31ST OF HEBE

Ion spent a fitful night huddling inside the dilapidated stack of an ore smelter beside the remains of the Iron Dirigible. The yips of distant coyotes and the sporadic barrage of conversation from late night pedestrians kept jolting him awake. Between the unfamiliar noises, the hunger pangs, and the haunting images of his grandfather's murder, Ion finally gave up on sleep. He built a small fire from scraps of broken furniture to pass the time.

The sandstorm brightened as the sun rose, but visibility did not improve. He was accustomed to being underfed and malnourished, but starvation was new. The former was a consistent dull ache that he could drown out with activity. The latter was an angry fist constricting and twisting his stomach. He had not eaten since the generosity of the typesetter, and he had vomited most of that thick stew onto the street a few hours later. He needed to eat, but he had no money. He needed to find Captain Crestone, but the Dirigible, now a smoldering wreckage, had been his only lead.

Hunger and boredom drove Ion out into the storm. He had found strips of stained linen in the rubble of a room and tied one around his nose and mouth. It stank of stale beer, but it kept him from inhaling too much sand. The gritty wind stung his eyes and forehead, but his goggles had been in his stolen pack. Ion squinted, angled his face away from the onslaught, and pressed on.

He wandered through the street, keeping his back to the prevailing wind whenever possible. The storm did not prevent many people from going about their day. Lanterns from shop windows brightened the streets. He stayed close to the buildings because he could not see the traffic until it was upon him. Shapes loomed out of the murk too close for him to dodge: a wagon with mules, a gang of men, a blacksmith with a sledgehammer on his shoulder.

He had fished in worse conditions. Yet sandstorms in Castes were usually trivial affairs, the storm having spent most of its wrath before reaching the sea.

*Is it storming in Castes?*

Twice Ion considered stealing food, but the street vendors had taken the morning off, hoping the storm would dissipate before the busier afternoon and evening meals. Ion pressed his face against the window of a produce merchant. He salivated against the glass until the shopkeeper chased him off with a broom. A man emerged from a bakery and dropped some bread. The wind taunted Ion with the scent of the magnificent yeasty loaf, but the man scooped it up and brushed it off rather than leaving it in the gutter for Ion to scavenge.

The typesetter had mentioned that Captain Crestone, if apprehended, would be held in Duneharrow, the debtor's prison on the edge of the Warrens. Ion had no idea where Duneharrow or the Warrens were, and few of those who passed appeared inclined to offer aid. Ion had a brief, terrifying vision of wandering the streets of Solvigant in the driving sand until he collapsed.

He entered a butcher shop and felt faint as he breathed in the succulent aromas of roasted goat and pork. Behind the counter a tan Ankhim woman in an apron was cutting apart a pig shoulder with a sharp cleaver.

Ion cleared his throat. "Excuse me, ma'am, do you have any work in trade for a meal?"

The butcher turned and took him in. "Scat, you! I got no charity for street urchins."

"But, ma'am—" He longed to be inside out of the sand with a full belly.

"Git!" The woman waved the bloody cleaver and Ion left.

Ion tried another bakery, two cheese shops, and a tavern kitchen with similar results. The opportunity to steal a large, fragrant rind presented itself in the second cheese shop, but Ion could not bring himself to take it.

*What would Crestone do?* Ion thought and squeezed the thieves' glass in his pocket. *She's a pirate captain. She would take what she wanted at sword point.* Ion had no sword, nor any training in its use.

As he was leaving another tavern, his hunger mingled with a growing despair, when he saw a wall of notices. Pinned fresh atop the older sheets was a picture of Captain Crestone. The likeness was not identical, but Ion had spent the last three days and nights dreaming of that face, building imaginary lives around that person. Ion would know it anywhere.

Hers was the face of freedom from Castes, of freedom from hunger and unimportance. Beneath the sketch was a bit of text.

He tore the notice from its nail and returned to the tavern keeper. Before the man could shoo him away a second time, Ion slapped the flyer on the bar.

"Can you direct me to the closest watch station?"

The tavern keeper sighed and scanned the notice. His annoyance faded when he reached the word "Reward."

"You know something about this, kid?"

"How do I report to the city watch?"

"Any station will help you. I can take you there for three-quarters of the reward."

For the first time since coming to Solvigant, Ion was in his element. He had often haggled the price of fish at the general store in Castes.

"Ten percent."

"Half."

"Half and roast beef."

"Half and coddle," the tavern keeper said.

"Coddle now, and it's a deal."

They shook hands and Ion scrambled onto a barstool.

"A full portion," Ion said when the tavern keeper put only one meager ladle's worth in the bowl. The man scowled so Ion, despite the pain in his belly, started to climb off the stool to leave. The gambit worked. The tavern keeper filled the bowl and even provided a square of fresh cornbread from the kitchen.

"Better be a good reward," the man grumbled. He stacked tankards and watched as Ion gobbled down the whole bowl.

*To ensure I don't eat and run, no doubt.* Ion knew.

When the coddle was gone, Ion used the dry bread to soak up the remainder, then licked the bowl clean. The tavern keeper huffed in exasperation, but Ion paid him no mind.

"I'm ready," he said, when not a scrap of stew or bread remained.

"Lars, I'm going out," the tavern keeper yelled into the kitchen.

Outside, the storm was breaking up and the wind carried less sand. Ion winced when he spotted the city watch post on the corner adjacent to the tavern. He had not seen it through the murk, but the warm food in his belly kept him from complaining.

The tavern keeper laid the notice on the counter in front of the watchman. "This young lad would like to make a report on Captain Crestone."

"Get in line," the watchman said, his tone flattened by boredom. He motioned toward a room where twenty assorted people stood or sat. Some read the daily paper, others napped, several chatted with their fellows in muted tones.

"Who are they?" Ion asked.

"They're all waiting to give their statement."

The tavern keeper snorted.

"They all know Captain Crestone?" Ion asked.

"Claim to. Whenever headquarters prints 'Reward' on a notice, they crawl out like sand lice. Half of them were in here last week, and the week before that."

"I don't have time for this," the tavern keeper said.

"I'll wait," Ion said. He had nowhere else to go. "I'll come back when I've finished."

The tavern keeper sized Ion up. Apparently, he decided that either Ion's word was good or that it wasn't worth the hassle. The man couldn't ask the watchman about the reward without giving away his own stake in the matter.

"Fine." He shrugged and left.

Ion ventured into the waiting room and made himself comfortable. With a full belly after two fitful nights, he fell asleep sprawled across three chairs.

Late in the afternoon another watchman woke him. The storm was over and through the window in the waiting room Ion could see Solo rising above the horizon as the distant sun sunk lower. The green orb of the moon Gaash and the blue orb of Highgaard shone in the crowded sky.

"Good nap?" the watchman asked. "It's your turn."

"Excuse me?" Ion said wiping sleep from his eyes. His hair was full of sand and he itched all over.

"The inspector will see you now."

Ion followed the watchman into a small room with a table and three chairs. There was a bolt in the floor.

Ion swallowed. "Am I in trouble?"

"Not at all." The inspector, a Faelani badger, motioned for Ion to take the seat across from him. "I'm Senior Inspector Solomon Broc. You can call me Sol. The watchman on duty says you have information about Adison Crestone."

"I understand there's a reward," Ion said.

Sol's smile was thin. He scratched at his eyepatch and rubbed his nose. Ion noticed the scar above his left eye.

"If the information you provide helps me find Crestone, there is a small reward, yes. What do you know?"

"Do you have any food?"

"Reese, see if there are any biscuits still beside the coffee," Sol addressed the watchman.

"He's an urchin, sir, a freeloader," Reese said. "I'm sure he doesn't know anything. He's just taking advantage of our hospitality."

"Nevertheless, please check," Broc said.

The watchman left the room. Ion perched on the edge of the hard seat. Sol turned to Ion, his quill ready over his notebook.

"What's your name?"

"Ion Rucinare. I'm trying to find Captain Crestone so I can join her crew. I don't wanna get her in trouble, sir."

"She's gotten herself into trouble, son," Broc said. "And there are better occupations for a willing lad than piracy."

Ion swung his feet, studying his battered shoes. "She was nice to me. I don't want her to get hurt."

"Both willing and noble, then. Let's just say that we both want to find the captain, shall we? When was she kind to you?"

"I was pulling my boat up after fishing on Millsday, when she fell out of the sky."

"Wait. Where was your boat?" Sol asked.

"Castes, that's where I live, or used to, before I ran away."

"You ran away recently?"

"Two nights ago, to find the captain."

"You fish the Boiled Sea?" Broc asked. "That's a lost cause."

Ion nodded. "It's not much, but it kept us fed. Mostly."

"Hold on," Broc scribbled furiously, "you said she fell out of the sky."

"Grandpa and I were pulling up the boat when an aerogate appeared above a nearby dune and the wreck of a ship fell through."

"Do you remember the name of the ship?"

"The *Sidereal*."

Sol leaned forward.

"It wasn't a particularly good ship though. It exploded a few minutes after she disembarked."

"Was anyone with her?"

"There was an Ankhim, his arm was broken, and a Grym man with a face wound. He was bleeding something awful. She had a man in chains, too."

"Tell me about the man in chains."

"He wore a black uniform."

Sol scribbled in his notebook. "You spoke with Captain Crestone?"

"I told her where to catch the terrane."

"Why do you want to find her?"

He flushed and looked down at the table. "I need to warn her about the void mage."

Broc's eye widened. "You know about the void mage?"

"He came through the old hydrogate the next day." Ion gulped, remembering the mage's broken voice and shattered eyes. And his violence.

"Did he say anything to you?" Henge said.

"He killed my grandfather."

"I'm sorry, son. When we're done here, I'll show you where to file a report for compensation from the Imperial coffers. I must ask, though, do you know where the void mage is now?"

"I burned his boat as a pyre for my grandfather." Ion began to cry.

"Where are you parents?"

Ion cried harder. "They left when I was four."

Broc shifted, uncomfortable. "I'm sorry, son."

Ion nodded and wiped his nose with his shirt. "Is that good enough for the reward? I could really use the money. My backpack was stolen when I got off the terrane and I don't have anything." He hoped he wasn't begging. Pirates didn't beg.

"I'll need to look into your story."

Ion fished in his pocket and took out the thieves' glass Captain Crestone had given him. "She gave me pirate treasure."

Sol reached for it, but Ion snatched it away.

"It's mine."

Sol held up both hands. "I'll give it back."

Ion hesitated then handed over the coin. Sol inspected both sides and passed it back. He shut his notebook.

"I must go now and check into your story. This has been helpful."

"Can I come?" Ion asked.

"No, son. But you can wait here. I'll make sure Reese feeds you, and when I get back I'll see to it that you have a place to go."

Ion was disappointed despite his victory. If Sol found Crestone, he wanted to be there. Then he felt the chill of remorse.

"Are you gonna arrest her?"

"Yes, son, I am. I need to ask her questions, and she refuses to come in and answer them," Broc said. The badger's head tilted as he regarded Ion. "I know you want to talk to her again, but that may not be possible."

"If she answers your questions, will you let her go?"

"That depends on her answers. Ion, if we gave you the fare would you take the terrane back to Castes?"

Ion did not hesitate. "No, sir. I want to stay in the city. There's nothing for me in Castes anymore."

"You'll need to find work. Honest work. It might not pay as much as the other kind, but it would be steady and safe. I'll ask around for you. If you're still here when I return, I can suggest something. Stay nearby, lad, I'll be back soon."

# CHAPTER THIRTY-FOUR

# ADI CRESTONE

## MOON OF XYS, CORDSDAY, 31ST OF HEBE

Adi sat propped against the stone surround of the fireplace in Stella's Echo. She held the rosewood box in one hand, her fingers idly tracing the inlay. Iris lay stretched out along the hearth, her head on Adi's right thigh. Melinda sat in a chair by the fireplace, an untouched glass of mead before her. Verdun and his assistant were maneuvering a new barrel onto the back bar. Stella sat at her usual table near the stairs, her account book was open, but she was chewing her pen instead of scribbling entries. Three of Stella's other girls were playing a subdued game of ahric with Wright at a nearby table. The Echo would open for the evening's business in less than an hour, and everyone was enjoying the calm before the whirlwind.

"Waiting for Rehka?" Iris asked with a yawn. Adi stopped bouncing her free leg.

"Waiting for the information she's bringing," Adi said. Her mind wandered back to Bale's shop on Goldwynd Alley and Rehka's renewed declaration of love.

*Where was that years ago when I needed it? Do I want to hear it now?* Adi wondered.

The answer was unequivocally yes, but it wasn't accompanied by the light and joy she once thought it would bring. Rehka had lied about her reasons for reappearing in Adi's life and about the Water Knives' involvement in the whole Apyreon affair.

*How can Rehka confess her love for me while she lies to me? Is this another manipulation?*

Adi wanted to pace about the room but couldn't bring herself to disturb Iris.

"Do you know any good stories?" Iris asked.

"Excuse me?"

"You spent a decade as a pirate. You must have a few good tales of your adventures."

Adi thought for a long moment. All her stories included Rehka and declarations of love among the mayhem, but she did not want to hurt Iris by telling her that kind of tale.

"When Lucas was a boy," Adi said, "I used to tell him Maxon Laird stories."

"Those old adventure rags?"

"My caretaker Stephan used to tell them to me."

"Caretaker?" Iris smiled. "How elegant."

"My mother was dead and my father had no time for stories. Stephan was more a parent to me than either of them."

"What happened to him?"

"He died of pneumonia contracted while helping me escape my father."

Iris' smile faded. "I'm sorry."

Adi shrugged as if her childhood still didn't haunt her, as if she didn't carry it as hard and heavy as the collar of indenture.

"It was a long time ago."

"I love a good Maxon Laird story," Melinda said.

Adi looked up in surprise. She had almost forgotten the old woman was there. The overstuffed chair nearly swallowed her bony frame. Her rheumy eyes followed Adi's fingers as they traced the rosewood box.

Maxon Laird was the subject of many adventure novels written before Adi was born. In the books he was an alchemist and adventurer, the grandson of the Sojourners Arthur and Penelope. Legend held that the Sojourners had traveled from another World System, far away from Solo and her lunar children. They had brought knowledge of aether, a magic apart from that which required using astral dust. Then the Solan emperors outlawed the destructive aethereal techniques. The Sojourners left the World System after Kade overthrew Corendar as God of Chaos. The Sojourner's descendants, the Kratoi, remained and were rumored to possess special abilities.

Most denizens of the World System knew only legends about the Kratoi. Only a few dusty scholars studied the actual historical remnants. When Adi and Rehka had run away to become pirates, the first mate had claimed lineage from the Sojourner Penelope. When he'd been drinking, he claimed that he could fly short distances. One night, while drunk, he leapt from the crow's nest to prove it. He hit the rigging before crashing on the foredeck and snapped his neck.

As mythic figures, the Kratoi lived in the collective imagination. The moon Maxon had been called Seniphet before the first Lunar Emperor Solaric Callire had renamed it after the hero. Adi loved the stories as a girl. Each time she finished one of the small volumes, Stephan had presented her with another, until she had all forty lovingly cataloged on a shelf in her bedroom. She knew most of them by heart. She had shared fragments of the tales with Lucas as he lay beside her on their pallet. She had told those stories to shipmates during long watches of the night. She had even compared the bold Rehka to Maxon, and herself to his love interest, the indomitable Selene.

*Adi, I love you.* Rehka's words echoed through Adi's head again.

"Where are you?" Iris asked, stroking Adi's cheek.

Adi looked down and forced a smile. "Just thinking which story I should tell you. You've heard about Maxon and the Diamond of Kaphir?"

"I never read the books." Iris shook her head and blushed. "I only recently learned to read. Stella taught me."

"And now you read damn well," Stella piped up.

Adi couldn't imagine her childhood without reading. Without the Maxon Laird books and yacht racing, there would have been no respite from the overbearing violence of her father. Adi knew illiteracy was common in the World System, and that she had been lucky that Stephan had taught her.

Adi cleared her throat and set the rosewood box down on the hearth.

"For three days and nights, Maxon Laird had driven his ship, *Sophos*, through spring storms in pursuit of Braden Houndstooth. The evil Highgaard Baron Houndstooth had stolen both the beautiful Selene and the Diamond of Kaphir and retreated to his fortress outside of Drang.

"Maxon's crew was exhausted, battered, and bloody from the pursuit across the Jade Sea. If the storm did not pass before they reached the rocks of Battersea, *Sophos* would be dashed to pieces on that wicked shore. Maxon had not slept since Houndstooth had stolen Selene. Her cries as the baron's men had dragged her away echoed in Maxon's ears over the roar of thunder and crash of waves all around them.

"He gripped the helm, forcing the rudder this way and that, navigating the rise and fall of the towering swells with incomparable deftness. In the moments when the sound of the gale diminished, his crew heard him laughing and cursing, undaunted by the pounding storm.

"On the fourth day, the storm abated. The bedraggled crew wrung out their sopping garments and trimmed the sails. Their spirits soared, only to be brought low when they saw the towering Battersea rocks which had shredded many a hapless vessel. Behind the rocks rose great, granite cliffs, and atop those loomed the impenetrable fortress of Drang.

"When the baron's men spotted the *Sophos* speeding toward the coastline they unleashed a barrage of cannon fire so dense the water among the rocks churned as if alive with a thousand leaping fish. The men despaired. What could they do? Not even the great sea-faring skills of their captain, the Kratoi Maxon Laird, could save them from such a fierce fusillade."

Adi coughed, her mouth dry. "Verdun, a pint of your newest please."

Melinda continued studying the rosewood box. It unnerved Adi.

*Why is she so transfixed by it? Or is she somewhere else, remembering a different time?*

Adi took a long swallow of the proffered ale and smacked her lips.

"What happened?" Iris said.

"What do you mean?"

Iris poked her in the ribs. "To the crew of the *Sophos*!"

"Ah." Adi took another long pull of ale. "Maxon had to land on that perilous shore. So, he sailed the *Sophos* into the Battersea rocks. Cannonballs caromed around them, smashing through the deck and masts. The ship took on water, and soon the cry arose to abandon her. The men dove overboard, taking their chances in the churning water. Maxon took up his tricorn, kicked off his boots, and dove into the roiling sea. One of the gifts he possessed as a grandson of the Sojourners was the ability to swim as nimbly as a dolphin and to hold his breath for long minutes. He streaked beneath the waves as if his feet were webbed and soon emerged near the base of the cliff.

"The granite cliffs rose vertically, with no track or trail. Yet Maxon found small niches and narrow cracks. He climbed until his fingers bled, his shoulders ached, and his legs shook. Once, he glanced down at the distant waves and vertigo threatened to cast him back into the sea, but he thought of his beloved Selene. He thought of the Diamond of Kaphir, which he needed to open the gateway to the realm of the Sojourners. He wanted Selene to see the land of his ancestors.

"This renewed his strength, and he scrambled to the top of the cliffs to the fortress of Drang."

"Wait," Iris interrupted, "what about his crew? Are they all dead? They can't climb like a Kratoi. What kind of captain would abandon his crew that way?"

"The hero Maxon Laird is driven by love and family to explore the World System and thwart evil like the Baron Braden Houndstooth."

"But is he a good man?" Iris pressed.

"Of course he's a good man. He's Maxon Laird!" A note of irritation crept into Adi's voice. "Are you going to let me tell the story?"

Iris flushed, abashed.

Everyone in the bar was listening to Adi now. She opened her mouth to continue, but Melinda interrupted. "Did you know that the name Maxon is a bastardization in the human tongue of another name in the proto-draconic language? It's pronounced Animaxondorthon and survives in modern day draconian as Anaximander."

Adi gaped at the old woman. Bale had claimed Apyreon was created by an alchemist by that name, whose ancient workshop still stood on the moon of Flynt.

"Melinda," Stella said, "I had no idea you were such a scholar of languages."

Melinda sniffed. "I'm not so old that there were no universities to attend when I was a teen."

Before Adi could respond, the door to Stella's Echo banged open. She moved so Iris now lay on the hearth and stood, hand on her sword. She expected Senior Inspector Broc and a contingent of city watch to rush in and arrest her. They must have found an arbiter willing to sign a Writ of Inspection, even on a Cordsday.

Instead, Rehka stormed in breathing heavily, blood smeared across the front of her shirt. She took in the scene, and Adi saw her face harden.

"I see you're all hard at work this afternoon," Rehka snapped.

"Waiting on you," Adi shot back. "Which I wouldn't have to do if you'd just told me the whole truth in the beginning."

Stella took Rehka by the arm. "What happened, child? Are you all right? You're covered in blood."

"It's not mine," Rehka said while allowing herself to be led, limping slightly from her earlier wounds to a chair at an empty table. "Two White Rabbit thugs recognized me from the Iron Dirigible and tried to settle the score."

"What did you find out?" Adi asked, Melinda's comment momentarily forgotten.

"May I have a glass of water?"

"Rehka!" Adi snarled.

Rehka waited until Verdun's assistant produced the water. She drained the glass and asked for another. Adi tapped her foot and tried not to explode.

"The sale is two nights from today," Rehka said at last, setting down her empty cup. "Ten o'clock in the evening at Alhambra's."

"Alhambra's? Djinnar's blood, why there?"

Rehka shrugged. "Probably because no one would expect it to be there."

"But that cargo aeroport is operated by the Order of the Talon," Adi said.

"I know. Why aren't you more concerned?"

"You asked for the location of the meet. I went to my superiors and got you the location. Stuart Royal is meeting a Water Knife emissary for the exchange."

"Who's the emissary?"

"I don't know."

"Security?"

Rehka shrugged again. Adi wanted to shake her. "Tight, I'm assuming," Rehka said. "After Palestrina attempted to assassinate him at the Iron Dirigible, I can't imagine Royal will travel unaccompanied. The Water Knives are mercenaries, they have a cynical view of loyalty and always plan for betrayal from some quarter."

Adi's laugh was tainted by bitterness and anger. Rehka winced.

"Meera," Stella called down the hall to the launderess. "Could you bring a clean shirt? One long enough to fit a Dragon, please."

"Thank you, Stella," Rehka said and peeled off her bandoliers and soiled shirt. The blood had soaked through and stained the bra beneath. Burned skin from the void mage's bolts covered her chest and shoulders. Adi stared, then realized she was staring, met Rehka's eyes and looked away. Meera appeared moments later with a clean shirt.

Adi cast her mind elsewhere. Leyala Fedhani, another of the four Talons, ran Alhambra's. It was a minor aeroport on the outskirts of the city that served mining craft from the moon Behl. Adi knew Fedhani only by reputation. She was said to be young and exceptionally beautiful, but diminutive with Nefesh or Grym in her bloodline. She was from Behl and trained under the famous Master Koriki, a legend in hand-to-hand combat with common and exotic weapons.

*Why would they meet at Alhambra's?* Adi wondered again but then decided it didn't matter. If that's where Apyreon would be then that was where she had to go. She had no idea how she would go about nicking the device from a dozen White Rabbit goons and a contingent of Water Knife mercenaries.

As if reading her mind, Rehka said, "There will be too many soldiers at the sale, too many variables. It would be better to wait and steal it from the buyer later."

"No, I can't risk it. Who knows what your mystery buyer's plans are? I owe Apyreon to the Blood Queen now."

"Do you have a better idea?" Rehka asked. "Preferably one where we don't all get killed because you made a hasty decision."

Adi ignored the jibe. "Wright, we're going to need an ally." Peter Wright had long before put his cards down to listen to Adi's story.

"Aye, Captain. Who did you have in mind?"

"Dervish Machineworks."

"That's Devlin Seneschal's place," Rehka said. "He's a Talon."

"Exactly," Adi said. "He'll think Leyala is conducting business without cutting him in. The Talons are always scheming against one another. It's the reason the Blood Queen can run the city mostly without their interference. We'll make him a deal."

"What deal?" Rehka pressed.

"Djinnar's blood, woman, I don't have all the answers. We'll come up with something on the way."

"Need I remind you there's a warrant out for your arrest. You should lay low until the sale. Let me or Wright run errands for you."

"Devlin won't deal with you," Adi said.

"And he'll deal with you?"

Adi tapped her collar. "Blood Queen emissary."

"Adi, what—" Stella, Rehka, and Iris all began at once, but Adi held up both hands to silence their objections.

"I know it's a risk, but I can't let Apyreon slip away, not when it means I'd forfeit my son's life."

"Adi, you can't," Rehka said meekly.

"You're not a mother," Adi snapped. Rehka flushed and Adi immediately felt guilty. "I'm sorry, Rehka, but it's true. If you were, you'd understand. Besides, you'll protect me. It's a matter of time before Broc returns with a Writ of Inspection. I'll be harder to find if I'm on the move."

Rehka looked away. "After the last few days, are we in any state to do this?"

Adi grabbed her coat from the back of a chair and made for the door.

"Wright, let's go," Adi said.

"Aye, Captain."

Rehka stood, shrugging her bandoliers over the clean shirt.

"Adi, be careful," Iris called after her.

Adi flashed her best grin, missing tooth and all.

"Always am." Then she and Wright were out the door, Rehka trailing in their wake.

# CHAPTER THIRTY-FIVE

# THEO VANGUARD

## MOON OF XYS, CORDSDAY, 31ST OF HEBE

The storm abated by mid-afternoon. Theo sipped tea on the patio of the governor's mansion while a small army of servants cleared the sand from the expansive gardens. Art had not yet returned and Theo was disappointed. He wanted to speak with someone who had witnessed his crime. Beatrice claimed to understand but speaking with the prophet only clouded Theo's head further.

Hubert and Beatrice had been arguing in the dining room when Theo's desire for lunch overcame his reticence to leave his room. Silence fell when Theo appeared. It was clear Hubert blamed Theo for part of the previous night's humiliation. Theo had hoped the diplomat would not remember his drunken behavior at the Thistledown. Theo flushed at the memory of Beatrice's body pressed against his just a few hours ago. He avoided eye contact with Hubert fearing he would give himself away; he had slept with the wife of a married man. Theo arranged for lunch on the veranda and beat a hasty retreat from the dining room.

*What's the city watch doing right now?* Theo wondered. *They must have the governor's sword. It's only a matter of time before Broc arrives asking awkward questions.*

Theo had never witnessed a court martial during his naval career, and he was not keen on the first one being his own. Still, he couldn't imagine what story he might tell to explain the presence of the sword in Opus Station. He considered reporting the sword had been stolen, except it was not his property, which might make that awkward. He had no desire to answer uncomfortable questions in a watch station. If Crestone was right, a watchman in the secret employ of the White Rabbits might use the opportunity for revenge.

*Let them come here and question me in the comfort of the governor's mansion.*

A servant approached, his lean face sweaty and eyes wide.

"What's wrong?" Theo asked.

"You have a—a rather unusual guest requesting the favor of your presence, sir."

Theo raised an eyebrow. "Who is it?"

"He says he is your brother, sir. But he is also"—he servant leaned in and whispered—"a void mage."

Theo sighed. *Isaiah has found me at last.*

"Is the governor in residence?"

"No, sir, he and the Lady Gambol are not yet back from the congressional office."

"The mage is indeed my brother. Please show him in."

The servant gave him a crisp nod, steeled himself, and disappeared back into the house.

Theo rose to embrace his brother when the servant returned with the void mage on his heels. Isaiah's body looked waifish, his shoulder blades prominent and his frame birdlike, as if he might crumble should Theo squeeze too hard. Isaiah's beard was too large for his face. Theo had tried, and failed, to love this brother, whose strange proclivities even in childhood had kept Theo distant. He looked away when Isaiah removed his hood and mask. The shattered black pupils, sick gray skin stretched tight over his skull, and the few wisps of hair remaining on his scalp erased Theo's memory of the quiet, dark-haired boy he had been.

"It's good to see you, Theo." Isaiah said, releasing the embrace. His voice sounded abrasive and ill-used.

"And you," Theo said, though he did not mean it.

"You've had word from our father?"

"He wrote that Paul was slain on Maxon." Theo could not read Isaiah's emotions in his broken eyes. If he looked into them for more than a moment, the flecks of pupil floating in the iris rearranged themselves.

"You missed his funeral."

"I only learned about his death yesterday." Theo willed grief to materialize, but the intervening hours had not generated any.

"You didn't miss much."

"He was our brother."

"And now he is dead."

Theo felt strange defending Paul, who was—had been—just as arrogant and power-hungry as their father. The two had deserved each other, as Theo had told himself the night he enlisted in the Imperial Navy.

"Why do the void mages show disrespect for the dead?" Theo asked.

A smile warped Isaiah's thin lips. "We acolytes of Kade, God of Chaos, approach death differently."

Theo wanted an explanation, but Isaiah changed the subject. "You had an exciting Valeday, I understand."

"As did you. I saw the remains of the Iron Dirigible."

Isaiah dismissed this with a wave of his hand, as if destroying a city block was unremarkable.

"What were you doing there?" Theo said.

"Cleaning up your mess."

"Who sent you to Xys?"

"I'm a void mage, Theo, we answer only to the emperor." Isaiah's tone was playful. "Everyone knows that."

"So, the emperor wants Apyreon?"

Isaiah glanced around at the mention of the device, but there were no servants within earshot.

"He does."

Theo bristled. "If Father, or you, had informed *Dragonhammer* that we needed to guard *Sidereal* in particular, we would have been more effective keeping it in Thail."

"Perhaps."

Theo lowered his voice. "How long has the emperor known of Apyreon? Did Father tell him or did he learn about it elsewhere? Why was Father keeping it secret? What are you dragging me into?"

Isaiah laughed, a sound like a coughing fit. "Never fear, dear brother, soon you will be safely ensconced on our estates in Balan making vainglorious miniature versions of yourself on that darling new wife of yours."

"Are Father and the emperor at odds?" Theo asked. *Does Father's ambition know no limit?*

"The high chancellor does many things in service of the Empire's longevity, things with which the emperor himself does not always agree with or know about."

"What is that supposed to mean?"

"It is better you don't concern yourself with the petty machinations of court."

*I am a victim of those machinations,* Theo thought. *They are hardly petty.*

"You have business with the governor?" Theo asked.

"No."

"Why did you come here then?"

"To see you, brother."

"I will not get between Father and Emperor Callire."

"That's not why I came."

Theo cleared his throat. "Why then? Why is Father coming here?"

"Only dutiful sons are privy to his plans in their entirety, and perhaps not even then. Father consists only of ire and complex schemes. He will tell you when he arrives. Who else knows of the device?"

"Why does it matter?"

"It is important that the legend of Apyreon remain legendary. There are too many factions in Solvigant and the Empire who would go to war over a device that gives its wielder the power to travel outside the World System. It grants the power of the Sojourners themselves."

"It's too late to save the legend. The Blood Queen ordered Captain Crestone to steal the device. Then she lost it to another gang faction, the White Rabbits. After your debacle at the Iron Dirigible, most of the criminal elements in this city are aware that Apyreon exists. Father should have trusted me to recover the device in secret rather than sending an agent of chaos into this powder keg of a city."

It was difficult to say when Isaiah made eye contact, but Theo felt his gaze now, and there was anger in that stare.

"I am sorry to interrupt," said Lady Gambol entering the veranda. "I heard we had a visitor from the emperor himself and that there are now two of my cousins taking tea in my house."

Isaiah rose, took Tabitha's hand, and bowed. "Lady Gambol, cousin, it is a delight to see you. I apologize for the unannounced visit."

"No need. Will you be staying with us? Shall I have the servants prepare a room? Do you sleep?"

Theo marveled at her aplomb when faced with such a hideous visitor. Tabitha pulled her hand away and took a step backward.

"We are more human than rumor would have you believe," Isaiah said, chuckling. "And no, thank you, I have accommodations elsewhere in the city. I came to say hello to my brother. Did he inform you that our oldest brother Paul passed away?"

Tabitha looked from Isaiah to Theo.

"My apologies, Tabi," Theo said, "I only learned late last night."

"Tabi?" Isaiah asked, raising his eyebrows. "I'm glad you two are getting to know each other."

Tabitha ignored the jest in Isaiah's voice. "You have another visitor, Theo. Inspector Broc from the city watch has returned."

"I will go speak with him. If you two will excuse me," Theo said.

"We will not," Isaiah said, "have him join us."

Theo glared at his brother.

Tabitha looked at them both and shrugged. "Very well."

A trembling servant refreshed the tea and biscuits and fled. Broc entered, trailed by Becca Henge, and the five of them sat around the table on the veranda, each waiting for someone else to speak first. Henge kept glancing at the void mage, who fixed her with a steady, bemused gaze. Theo stared at the gleaming governor's sword lying across Broc's lap.

"Commander Vanguard, your hand is healing well I hope." Broc said at last.

Theo flexed his bandaged right hand. "Not quick enough for my liking."

"You ought to get more rest. I understand you visited the Thistledown last night."

"To escape the storm."

"So, you were out in the city prior to visiting the brothel?"

"My brother escaped the bonds of pirates and saved our father a substantial sum in ransom, no thanks to the city watch," Isaiah said. "Is it a crime to seek comfort in whores?"

"Your *brother*?" Henge croaked.

"You're a Vanguard?" Broc asked.

"Isaiah Vanguard, First Order void mage."

*First Order?* Theo studied his brother. *When was he promoted?*

"May I ask what you're doing in my city?"

"It is my lord husband's city, Inspector," Tabitha said.

"My apologies, milady," Broc said, "a figure of speech that we at the watch often use unintentionally. We take pride in our work under your husband for the glory of the Empire."

Tabitha nodded, appeased.

"So?" Broc turned back to Isaiah.

"You may not ask, Inspector," Isaiah replied.

Broc scratched at the scar over his eye.

"The Lady Tabitha Gambol reported this sword as stolen this morning," Broc said hefting the sword.

"She did?" Theo said.

"I did," Tabitha said. "Thank you for returning it. It is an heirloom prized by my lord husband. Where did you find it?"

Theo clenched his jaw.

"We pulled it from the body of a White Rabbit goon. This goon was killed while incarcerated in Opus Station near the Iron Dirigible. There is blood on the hilt, as if the wielder were injured."

"What's your point, Inspector?" Isaiah asked.

"You were at the battle outside the bar," Broc said to the void mage.

Henge leaned in. "You murdered two city watchmen."

Isaiah ignored her. "You may appeal to the emperor for a stipend for their families and restitution for the watch."

"They were friends of mine," Henge growled.

Isaiah looked the woman up and down. "I doubt it."

Henge shifted, but Broc placed a restraining hand on her shoulder.

"Sit down, Henge," Broc's voice was a low snarl.

Isaiah laughed. "Yes, sit."

Henge looked between the two, then sat.

"You also visited the aftermath at the Dirigible, Commander Vanguard."

"You escorted me there," Theo said.

"The governor loaned you this important family heirloom, if I'm not mistaken."

Theo swallowed, "No. I mean, yes, he did."

"So, when exactly did you lose it?"

"It's embarrassing."

"But you did lose it, correct? You have a penchant for losing important objects."

Theo ignored the insinuation. "Crestone took it from me."

"You saw her? You were supposed to report to me if that occurred."

Before Theo could answer, Isaiah interjected, "My brother is young and impulsive. He was held captive by this woman for two days, then he lost the governor's property while trying to get revenge—" Isaiah *tsk*ed, as if that explained everything.

"Thank you for returning the sword, Inspector," Tabitha said again.

"Of course, milady." Broc handed her the weapon, hilt first. He stood and wiped his hands on his trousers. His eyebrows lowered and he addressed Theo. "Adison Crestone is officially a fugitive. Notices went up this morning. Witnesses at Opus Station say they saw her, the Lady of Spiders, and another Blood Queen thug murder the White Rabbit at Opus Station. Commander, if you encounter her again and do not report it, you will be aiding and abetting a fugitive and I will turn you over to a naval tribunal for court-martial. Is that clear?"

"Yes, sir."

"Crestone is extremely dangerous. The governor wants her found and detained. You could be in danger. People do desperate things when they're cornered. We can't have criminals murdering people with Gambol family heirlooms. I hear you are leaving us in two days, so hopefully the threat will be short-lived."

Broc flared his whiskers and quivered, then he turned his attention to the void mage. "Your business is your own, but I want a record of everywhere you go, everyone you speak to, and every building you level. You can be certain we will send the emperor an invoice for every spyre, tower, and copparch. We may live on a dying moon, but we are a proud city, and we do not offer our streets up for whatever violent game the emperor and his chancellors are playing." Broc drained his tea. "Lady Gambol, I thank you for your hospitality."

He turned on his heels and strode from the table before a servant could approach to lead him out. Henge hurried after him without taking formal leave.

*The inspector has a temper,* Theo thought.

"Inspector!" Isaiah called after the retreating Broc. Broc stopped and faced the group once more.

"Hail Solo!" Isaiah cried.

Broc stiffened but returned the salute. "Hail Solo." Then he was gone.

Isaiah waved to the departing Henge. She flinched as if struck and quickened her pace. Isaiah stood, "Come, brother, we have much to do before Father's arrival."

"We do?"

"We do. Cousin, I apologize, but Theo and I must beg your leave."

Tabitha considered the sword rather than the void mage.

"Do as you will," she said. "My lord husband would appreciate it, however, if you left the rest of the taverns of the city standing."

"Only the taverns?"

Tabitha's smile was formal and cold. "Do whatever it is you were sent here to do while inflicting minimal damage and leave the moment it is complete.

"As you wish, cousin." Isaiah made a mocking bow and ushered Theo off the veranda.

# CHAPTER THIRTY-SIX

# ADI CRESTONE

## MOON OF XYS, CORDSDAY, 31ST OF HEBE

Talon operatives had been following them for several blocks by the time the trio arrived at the outskirts of Devlin Seneschal's stronghold. Adi took it as a good sign that though the observers made no effort to hide their presence from the trio, they did nothing to prevent their approach. Now that Adi was standing on the threshold of the vast, rumbling factory, she hesitated. It was time to come up with the next steps in her plan.

*What can I offer Devlin?*

Dervish Machine Works was an incoherent accretion of buildings that belched coal smoke from a battalion of chimneys as diverse as they were abundant. The entire street upon which Adi stood vibrated from the great engines and belts spinning within. Two flywheels could be seen turning through wide slots in the walls of the largest building, their silent, stately rotations at odds with their size and power. The dissonant, reverberating music of hammers on anvils rang through the morning air accompanied by shouts of foremen and crews in a staccato counterpoint.

All around Adi, Wright, and Rehka men and women in hard hats and soot-covered clothes hustled between the buildings. Bridges linked the upper floors of steel-paneled buildings. The rusty walls shimmered from the intense heat of the smelters within. The air reeked of bubbling pitch and machine oil. Adi covered her face with her scarf to avoid inhaling the fine black particulates swirling through the complex like a perverse snow. The cacophony was so intense that Adi reconsidered her plan to recruit Devlin Seneschal, but Rehka tapped her shoulder and pointed toward an open door.

A man approached them and bowed low. His slick bald head featured tattoos of two sinuous black Dragons. He wielded a walking stick with a hammer on the upper end and a metal spike on the other. An ornate necklace of feathers and bird skulls dangled against his stained linen shirt. It hung low when he bowed and Adi guessed it was an indication of office.

"We're here to see Devlin Seneschal," Adi shouted over the din.

"Of course you are, Captain Crestone, of course. We are expecting you. I am Oto the Anvil. Please follow me." The man turned and strode away before Adi could respond. She rushed to keep pace with his long strides. He led them through a canvas flap into one of the nearby buildings. They wound through a series of hallways before descending metal stairs into an earthen tunnel.

*The whole compound must be connected underground,* Adi realized. *A huge task in a city that relocates every few years.*

"You knew I was coming?" Adi asked when the grinding roar of the machine works faded to a dull rumble in the subterranean passageways.

"The Talon knows all things in Solvigant."

"I doubt that," Rehka said from behind Adi.

Oto the Anvil stopped and rounded on them, one eyebrow raised, a tight grip on his staff. "You would insult the Talon within his own walls?"

"We would not," Adi said hurriedly.

Oto's face relaxed into a smile and he resumed walking.

Adi shot Rehka a pointed glance, but the mercenary offered no sign of apology. They walked through the corridors dimly lit by oil lamps, passing side tunnels which gave Adi the impression they were wandering through a labyrinth. Sweat trickled between her shoulder blades and all their faces glistened.

*We must be nearing the smelters and crucibles.* The close quarters, stale air, stink, and heat reminded Adi of the perilous threshold her younger self had been forced to cross so she could be evaluated. Her pulse quickened and the blood drained from her face, her breathing was fast and shallow. Now and then the clamor above them rained clods of earth onto their heads. The reek of grease and machine oil reminded her of the camphor odor of Droth the Minotaur.

*I need to get out of here.* Adi struggled to slow her breathing. She tripped and would have sprawled onto the sandy floor if Rehka hadn't caught her shoulders. Adi smiled weakly at the woman and Wright pretended not to notice. Oto charged ahead, oblivious of Adi's increasing discomfort.

They traveled below Dervish Machineworks until Adi had lost all sense of time and direction. The scheming part of her brain knew Oto was deliberately confusing them so that when they arrived before Devlin Seneschal they would feel trapped and unable to flee. But recognizing the stratagem did not prevent it from working. It reminded her of the crucible when she was ten years old. She kept glancing over her shoulder to ensure Droth and Kelek, Djinnar's children, weren't following them. Her breaths became shallow and fast. Oto turned another corner, then they were climbing again. As Adi ascended several flights of stairs, the air cooled and her breathing eased. Finally, their escort paused before a metal blast door. He spun its wheel and it opened silently on oiled bearings.

The quartet emerged into a large warehouse bathed in grimy light that filtered in through opaque glass high above. Panels of waxed canvas provided a yellow-stained illumination. Their wind-rippled surfaces did peculiar things to the shadows. Craftspeople in blue-gray coveralls carried trays of smoking-hot rivets to teams assembling the framework of a massive machine. Others hustled tools and parts to their colleagues, occasionally a group carried a subassembly past on their shoulders, reminding Adi of a millipede. The logic of the room's cranes, pulleys, shafts, and steampipes was beyond her, but the speed of the work and the organization of the teams indicated a single mind orchestrated the entire enterprise. For all she could tell, these workers were marrying the World System's largest pipe organ with some hellish war contraption.

*Too bad it's so loud I can't think.* She still had no coherent plan.

At the center of the room, Devlin Seneschal was commanding everything from a raised dais. Adi had never met him before, but it could be no one else. He stood beside a tall metal cylinder, his head bowed in conversation with two men in hard hats. Oto picked his way across the crowded room, deftly avoiding the worker traffic. Adi's party scampered to keep up with him.

She had not expected Devlin to be a Seraph. Palestrina unnerved Adi and she did not relish dealing with another of the strange creatures. Oto halted the small troupe at the base of the dais and waited for Devlin to finish his conversation before clearing his throat to announce their presence. Devlin turned intense yellow eyes to the company and Adi took an involuntary step back.

Devlin Seneschal was shorter and stockier than Palestrina. Where she was lithe, supple, gray grace, he was stocky, scarred, blue muscle. His right arm was larger than his left, and his wings—Adi gaped. The long, thin bones of his wings remained, but the leathery membrane stretched between the bones was a ragged lattice of holes, more skin missing than present. Devlin wore suspenders to hold up brown breeches, and his naked torso sported hundreds of tiny pale scars. Some were blade marks, but most were round burns or puckered paths left by flying hot metal. His hard hat perched on the back of his head, directly behind his twisted, black horns. Around his neck hung a large claw on a leather thong. This marked him as one of the four Talons. Devlin smiled at Adi and her crew. His teeth were dazzling white against his dark blue lips. Unlike Palestrina, he had not filed them to accentuate their natural points.

"Captain Crestone, welcome to Dervish Machineworks." Devlin gestured around the cavernous workroom. The soft tenor of his voice surprised Adi and she wondered whether this Xyssian gangster had a beautiful singing voice.

"You were expecting me?" Adi asked. Devlin picked up a piece of parchment from the table and waved it in Adi's direction. She recognized it as one of her wanted posters.

"You've developed the sort of reputation that encourages people to flee. If you want to be smuggled away, who better to run to than smugglers."

*So, the great Devlin Seneschal does not know everything.* Adi felt a measure of her confidence return.

"I didn't come here to run."

"You sure? For the right price, the Order of the Talon can help you disappear. No one would be able to find you, not Rehka, not the city watch, not the Blood Queen's debt collectors, not even Lord Daniel Faide, your doting father."

Vertigo hit Adi and she had to grab the platform's lower rail to keep from pitching forward.

*He knows who I am?* She swallowed and closed her eyes for a long moment. When she opened them, the world had steadied. Devlin studied her. His round yellow eyes reminded Adi of a Tyrian owl. He waited for her to say something but she did not trust her voice, so she studied him in return.

"Captain Crestone doesn't run," Wright said.

Devlin relaxed. His smile returned. "I thought not. Otherwise, you would have run to my associate, Fedhani, since she controls the aeroport. I'm just a man with a big hammer. Come here, Adison."

Adi picked her way up the three steps to the platform. Rehka and Wright moved to follow, but Oto the Anvil used his staff to block their way. Rehka protested, but Adi shook her head. The Dragon coiled like a spring, but did not pounce. Wright's attention snapped between his captain's drama and the marvelous mechanical wonderland around them.

*Wright has some inkling of what Devlin is building,* Adi thought.

Now that Adi was standing on the platform, she realized Devlin was only a few inches taller than her. The table to her right was covered in plans and diagrams. Adi recognized the script as seraphic, though she could not decipher it. She saw that the large metal cylinder was open. Inside, a metal chair faced an array of dials, gauges, levers, buttons, and grips.

"What is all this?" Adi couldn't help but be curious.

"This, Adison, this is the work of gods."

"You are a religious man?"

"Who would not be when they walk among us? Who would not be a zealot in a religion which requires no faith? You do not believe in the gods?"

"I do not doubt their existence," Adi said, unsure how their conversation had taken a theological turn, "but neither would I consider myself a zealot. I honor Phoebe, Goddess of Light most often, but I wouldn't consider myself an adherent of the others."

"Interesting," Devlin said and seemed sincere.

Adi suddenly felt very self-conscious, as if she had to justify herself. "They've never seen fit to help me, so I make my own way."

"I understand." Devlin flexed his perforated wings. "So, what can I do for you, Adison Crestone? If you didn't come here to run away and you're not a theologian, I'm not sure we have much to talk about."

"How do you know so much about me?"

"It is my business to know all I can about my enemies."

"I am not your enemy."

Devlin's eyes settled on Adi's collar, "The Blood Queen is not my ally."

"I do not come on behalf of the Blood Queen."

"I know."

"You do? How?"

Devlin waved a clawed hand dismissively. "Ajax told me you were smarter than this."

"Ajax? The Lord of Bones was here?"

"About an hour ago."

"What did he want?"

"What do you think he wanted?"

Adi wanted to pound the table in frustration. *I don't have time for this man's games.*

"Think, Adison. You came here for the same reason anyone comes here."

"Please"—she stopped, then took a moment to compose herself. "What do you mean?"

On the stairs, Oto tensed. The moment passed and Devlin placed a hand on Adi's shoulder. She flinched and he laughed.

"You came here to make a deal. That's why all desperate people come here."

"Ajax was desperate?" Adi wondered aloud.

"Oh, he tried to hide it, but I saw through the armor of his clanking bones and bellicose threats."

"What did he want?"

"That wouldn't be very sporting of me, would it? No, you tell me what you want, and I'll decide whether to help you or honor the deal I made with your superiors."

*What are Ajax and Palestrina up to? Are the generals fighting?* Adi swallowed hard to stay focused. "I need your help."

Devlin opened his arms in an expansive gesture. "I know, Adison."

She wanted to shout, *"Stop using my name!"* but thought it would sound petty.

Adi sighed. Telling the truth was her best option. "Two nights from now, the White Rabbits are selling an artifact to Water Knife mercenaries. The sale is taking place at Alhambra's under the auspices of Talon Leyala Fedhani."

"Who do the Water Knives represent?"

"Can they not represent themselves?"

"Mercenaries never do."

"I don't know," Adi mumbled. Her mouth was dry.

"Rehka?" Seneschal asked, but Rehka shook her head.

"You knew about the sale?" Adi asked.

To her surprise, Devlin laughed. "Contrary to what Oto tells guests about me, I do not know everything."

Adi felt a surge of hope. "That's proof then. Fedhani is gathering influence from powerful off-moon nobles without you. She must be planning to move against you."

"Fedhani is always planning to move against me. What about this artifact?"

"That's not part of the deal."

"So, you want me to do what exactly?"

"Raid the sale. Show Fedhani you are not to be trifled with."

"Why would you want Fedhani to fail?"

"I don't care about Fedhani. I will use the uproar to steal the artifact."

"For the Blood Queen?"

Adi hesitated, then nodded.

"Tell me about the artifact."

Adi shook her head. "Not part of the deal."

"How do I know this is not a ploy by the Blood Queen to weaken two Talons at once? I take Fedhani down a notch and the Blood Queen receives some artifact that wields power over me."

Adi said nothing.

"Your silence is proof this is so," Devlin said. "I will not do this thing for you."

"What did Ajax promise you?" Adi pressed.

"He wanted to purchase the plans to this machine."

"You said no,"

"He offered a staggering sum."

"But you said no."

Devlin's laugh was dry. "I said no. This work is not for sale. This machine will be my legacy. I considered it. There is little Ajax could do with the plans if he had them."

"What can I offer you to help me?"

"Can you offer an incredible sum? My legacy is proving quite expensive to construct."

Adi tapped her collar. "I'm afraid all my income is promised elsewhere. I can offer you my services."

"And what services would those be, Adison? Your services as a pirate? A thief? A prostitute? No, I am well satisfied on all accounts."

"Then I am afraid I have nothing to bargain with." Adi turned toward the stairs and prepared to leave. Convincing Devlin to help had always been a long shot.

"I heard about your activities at Opus Station," Devlin said. Adi struggled to follow his non sequitur.

She gestured toward the wanted poster. "Everyone has."

"I heard you tortured and murdered a man in cold blood."

Adi flushed, "You don't know everything."

Devlin held up his hands, "I meant no offense, Adison. I just need to know, are you a murderer? You may not be a zealot, but you seem to me a partisan at least. Can you kill in cold blood without knowing why?"

Adi swallowed hard. She thought about Lucas, unharmed, reunited with his mother, herself freed from her indenture. "Who are we talking about?"

Devlin leaned close and whispered a name in Adi's ear. Adi blanched.

"No! I can't. You're insane." *I don't kill people who have saved my life.*

Devlin shrugged. "If I help you recover the artifact from Alhambra's I need to ensure the Blood Queen is weakened."

Adi looked to Rehka for help. There was empathy, but no understanding on the mercenary's face.

"It's impossible. I'm no fan, but I couldn't," Adi said.

"Farewell, then, Adison Crestone. Oto, please see our guests out."

Adi descended the stairs on shaky legs. Oto gestured and two workers opened a door on the far side of the room. Daylight flooded into the warehouse and Adi felt relieved that she would not have to return through the tunnels.

"Oh, Adison." Devlin called after them, "don't come back. You can refuse me once in my own home, but twice and I'd have to take offense."

Adi faced him. She thought once more about Lucas and about being horribly outgunned at Alhambra's. Her shoulders slumped.

She swore under her breath. "All right, Devlin. You help me recover the artifact and I'll kill Palestrina, Lady of Spiders."

Devlin clapped his hands in delight, his yellow eyes flashing. "Splendid. I knew you'd come around, Adison."

"If I fail? I'll already have the artifact."

"If Palestrina doesn't kill you, then I will. A life for a life, Adison."

Adi grimaced and followed Rehka and Wright out the door.

# Chapter Thirty-Seven

# ADI CRESTONE

## Moon of Xys, Cordsday, 31st of Hebe

Adi stood alone on the quiet street three blocks from Dervish Machineworks. Rehka had left, mentioning confidential Water Knife business. Adi did not mind. She wanted to keep their relationship professional, something Adi found challenging when Rehka was breathing down her neck. Over Wright's protestations, she sent him away to gather supplies from another safehouse. Adi wanted to be alone with her thoughts. Her encounter with Devlin Seneschal had left her jittery and high on adrenaline. She thought about returning to Stella's Echo. A couple of tankards of Verdun's finest would settle her nerves. The warrant for her arrest made that prospect difficult; not impossible, but risky.

Adi walked east without a destination in mind and tried to calm her roiling thoughts. Her indenture, the threats to Lucas, the return of Rehka, deals and debts to gangsters, and the pain of her own injuries all combined to create a great ball of pressure inside her chest that made her feel as if she would explode. She wanted to scream. She wanted to cry. She wanted to get drunk and punch a stranger in the face. But none of those things would improve her situation, and she knew they would not ease the pressure, either. She wandered toward the eastern periphery of Solvigant, watching her boots scuff the dust from the street.

When she finally looked up she smiled. Her heart knew what she needed even if her brain did not. She was standing before the ornate facade of the Wandering Mausoleum. She would visit Stephan, tell him all her woes, and then risk returning to the Echo. She felt calmer around Iris. The pressure eased in anticipation of this safe confessional.

A bell tinkled when she opened the door of the mausoleum and stepped onto the wood parquet floor. Adi entered a quiet hall filled with light from clerestory windows. No ornament distracted visitors from the contemplation of their requested icon. A father and his daughter sat on a bench, crying as they gazed at a tiny painting in the father's hands. Two Ankhimian women whispered over their icon on a bench near the front window.

Behind a simple counter sat one of the Sons of Destruction, a devotee of Djinnar. He read a book and did not look up when Adi approached. The chair next to him was empty. Two decades ago, one of the Daughters of Creation would have occupied it, but since Pallantier had disappeared his clerics had sequestered themselves.

"Good morning," Adi said.

The cleric, a young boy in his late teens, reached for his bookmark, harrumphing at the interruption. He stood, stretched, and set the book on the counter: *Maxon Laird in Rogue Shadows*. Adi smiled.

"One of my favorites," she said, gesturing toward the cover. A dashing, dark-haired Maxon Laird brandished a torch at dark, humanoid shapes. The cleric yawned and shrugged. The unadorned skull pin on his collar marked him as a neophyte.

"I borrowed it from my roommate. It's not very realistic."

Adi bristled at this insult to the novel.

"Who would you like to see?" The boy's tone suggested that her need for his assistance annoyed him.

"Stephan Crestone."

"One moment." The boy ambled toward the doorway to the vault. Adi leaned her elbows on the counter.

*How long has it been?* she wondered. *Not since my indenture. I didn't want to explain the collar to him.* Stephan had been her manservant since her mother died. His loyalty to her had been the one reliable element in her home life. After Hubert raped her and Adi's subsequent realization that she was pregnant, Stephan had not objected when she told him she was running away. Instead, he had helped her prepare and plan. It would not do to fail and have Lord Daniel Faide catch her. Her father's anger often outweighed his judgment in such matters.

When they set their plan in motion, Stephan had accompanied her, risking his own life. He would not allow his pregnant charge to travel alone and unmoored across the World System. Using aliases, they stowed away on a Behlian cargo freighter bound for Solvigant. Their paltry berth had been cold and damp, and the food poor and tainted. Stephan contracted a cough. Even after their arrival in the dry heat of Xys he worsened until he died two weeks later. With only enough money for two more nights at an inn, Adi was soon on the streets, alone and grieving. Her pregnancy had just started to show.

"Here you are," the cleric said when he returned with a miniature portrait that fit in her palm. Adi reached for it, but the boy eluded her grasp. She blinked at him, momentarily confused, until she saw him nod toward the donation box. Adi rolled her eyes and sighed, but he did not relent. She took a silver tower from her pouch and it fell with a clink into the receptacle. The boy handed her the icon.

"Bring it back in an hour."

*I'll bring it back when I'm done,* Adi thought. She flashed her wolfish smile at him, pleased when he blanched. Clutching the icon close, Adi walked through the back door into the mausoleum's rock garden. She sat on a bench away from the handful of other visitors and contemplated the painting. It was a decent approximation of Stephan's smiling face. She hadn't been able to commission the likeness until she had established herself at Stella's Echo and saved up her coin. The mausoleum's artists were skilled in translating descriptions into sketches the bereaved recognized as their loved ones. Those with the resources for proper funerary practice had the artist visit the undertaker's rooms, and some even sat for their portraits while they lived.

When Stephan died, Adi was forced to abandon his body in their room at the Black-stone Inn. At the time, Solvigant was in Gamb. Stephan's unclaimed body passed into the hands of the Caretakers, permanent residents who cared for each of the city's pilgrimage sites. They guarded and maintained those buildings which did not move along the peripatetic path. They cared for the aeroport towers, factories dependent on heavy machinery, infrastructure, government buildings, and the cemeteries. Whenever Solivagant was in Gamb, Adi visited Stephan's unmarked grave. She had done this twice since arriving on Xys.

Families who wanted to visit with their dear departed throughout the pilgrimage had prevailed upon the city to build the Wandering Mausoleum. It was a repository of all the icons entrusted to it with a small endowment, and it traveled the pilgrimage route along with the rest of Solvigant. Adi visited Stephan's painted presence often in those early days, telling him stories of her exploits as well as admitting her defeats to his silent, unjudging face. Adi wondered if he had been the last selfless person in the World System. Everyone else wanted to claim a piece of her.

A shadow fell across Adi's lap. "I thought I might find you here."

Startled, Adi looked up to see Xander Marrion. He was the only one who knew about Stephan. For reasons Adi could never explain, she had left Stephan out of the story of her escape from Saba when she had told it to Rehka. Stephan belonged only to Adi. Of all the emotional wounds she had received in her life, his death was the one that had never scabbed over. Xander had met Stephan when he had chaperoned their visits after the formal announcement of their betrothal.

"Hello, Xan." Adi patted the empty bench beside her. "Care to sit?"

Xander sat. Together they contemplated Stephan's image in silence for long moments.

"He was a good man, a loyal servant," Xander said.

"He was my champion."

Xander shifted on the bench.

"You've been looking for me?" Adi asked.

"I wanted to make sure you were all right. I checked the city watch rolls and saw they hadn't yet arrested you. You weren't at Stella's. This was my next best guess."

"You went by the Echo?" This surprised Adi. Xander had not set foot in the Echo in twelve years. He had appeared there on Adi's eighteenth birthday, gallant and hopeful, triumphant that he had located and would rescue his fiancée. Adi had sent him away, humiliated.

"This is serious, Adi. I asked a contact about Senior Inspector Broc. He is as tenacious as they come. The Blood Queen is using Lucas to manipulate you, and I know you would move the celestial realms for your boy. What are you involved in?"

Adi exhaled and ran a finger along Stephan's painted face. She considered being honest with Xander.

*I could tell him about Apyreon, the* Sidereal, *all of it, but what good will it do?*

Xander would want to insert himself as the hero. Adi knew he would risk everything to save her and Lucas. And that was the problem. He had built a life for himself in Solvigant after his irate father disinherited him and banished him from Saba. He had suffered that punishment to be near her. Adi would not allow him to give up his accomplishments and livelihood twice. If the city watch discovered Xander was aiding and abetting a fugitive, it would create a scandal. He could lose his property, his office as congressman, even his interlunar visa. If he tried to save Lucas by removing him from his school in Thail, Ajax's spies might harm her son. Just by sitting next to her at the mausoleum, he was endangering his career.

Xander was a good person. The people of Solvigant needed him in their corner. He might even be governor one day. If—

*If the moon doesn't fall apart before then,* Adi thought.

Xander watched her, patient and kind.

"I can't involve you, Xander, you know that."

"You came to my office. I'm already involved."

"I came before I was a fugitive. I was just a constituent then. It's different now, don't pretend it isn't. If someone recognizes us, you could lose everything."

"I care about you. I care about Lucas. I wish you would let me help you."

Adi tensed. "Xander, don't ask me again."

"Marry me, Adi. Let me help you, let me be a father to Lucas. With my contacts and influence, I can protect you from the city watch and the Blood Queen. We could leave the Empire."

"I could never compromise you like that." The Blood Queen would be delighted to corrupt another congressman. Adi did not want to think about what Sasha Riven might demand of Xander to end Adi's indenture. "You would lose everything."

"I don't care. We could leave Solvigant. We could return to Saba, our family ties would protect us."

"I'll never return to Saba."

"Fine. We could move to the moon of Gaash. Lucas could finish his schooling at the academy in Glyff. When he graduates then we can decide what to do next."

"What would you do in Glyff? It's a backwater."

Xander shrugged. "I don't know. Be a fisherman."

Adi laughed, imagining Xander cutting bait. "I wouldn't do that to you."

"You're not forcing me to do anything. I'm volunteering."

"You wrecked your life once for me over a decade ago. I won't allow you to do it twice."

"If you and Lucas are with me, my life wouldn't be ruined."

Adi hated it when Xander got this way. He had proposed a dozen times over the years. She could only shut him down by hurting him. Again.

"I don't love you, Xan."

"That doesn't matter."

"You're lying."

"You might love me, given time."

Adi sighed and gripped Stephan's icon in white-knuckled fingers. "I've never loved a man that way."

"Have you ever tried?"

"As kind and noble as you are, Xander, you represent everything I left behind on Saba: my father, my failed Crucible test, your brother Hubert, even you. The girl I was, Adison Faide, she's dead. Hubert murdered her. I will never be that person again. I'm not sure I ever was that person."

"Is this about Rehka?"

Adi growled in frustration. "Rehka abandoned me. She left me to die, and for nothing." Adi reined in her temper. "No, it's not about Rehka. You deserve a life, Xander. You deserve to be with someone who loves you, shares your goals, and wants a whole passel of kids. You're a born leader. Solvigant needs politicians like you. The Empire needs public servants like you. Besides, fishing would bore you to tears."

Xander gave her a weak smile. "It's true. I don't know the difference between a trout and a barracuda."

They sat in silence.

"Not many people in my life have been as kind to me as you have," Adi said. "You sacrificed your life on Saba so I could remake my life here on Xys. I built this life, I must salvage it. I can't spend my life in your shadow and shielding me endangers you."

"What about Lucas? What about what he needs?"

Adi's patience flared into anger. "Don't you lecture me about what Lucas needs. I'm his mother." She glared at Xander, daring him to comment on her approach to motherhood.

"He would be safe, no longer a cat's paw of the Blood Queen."

*This cannot go on,* Adi thought and prepared to deliver her coup de grâce. "No, he would be yours."

"What are you talking about?"

"Listen to yourself. You're using my son as leverage to get what you want!" A pair of visitors to the mausoleum looked toward them when Adi raised her voice.

"That's not what I'm doing."

"Isn't it?" Adi hissed. "My whole life you've pursued this plan, and I've said no every time. That will never change. I am no longer your betrothed. Lucas is not your son. I'm eternally grateful for your support, but, by Phoebe's light, move on. Live your own life and stop trying to dictate mine. No one—not gangsters, not lovers, not politicians—no one gets to use my son against me."

Xander swallowed hard. He was holding a delicate silver band between tense fingers. She had not noticed him take it out. It was a fine wedding band. Adi softened, placing her hand over his.

"You're a good person, Xan. Save this for a good woman who loves you. But it's not me."

Xander snarled and snatched his hand away. He stood and turned on her. "You spurn me, after everything I've done for you? After everything I've given up for you?"

Adi knew he was lashing out, hurt and angry, but that did not lessen the sting in his words.

"I have hidden you from your father, given up my life on Saba, and paid for Lucas's education while you gallivant around the World System playing pirate. If it weren't for me your father would have you caged in a basement as breeding stock for more of his precious prophets."

"That's enough, Xander."

"I rescued you. I saved you. You tried to do it on your own, but you've failed. I will save you and Lucas, again, but you owe me this."

"Enough!" Adi shouted, rising to her feet. The other visitors in the rock garden quickly retreated into the main hall of the mausoleum. *The cleric will be here soon to kick us out.* "I don't owe you love, Xan. I don't owe you my life, and I have not failed until I lie bleeding out in the sands of Solvigant. I will live my life the way *I* choose."

Xander deflated, his eyes downcast. The neophyte cleric from the Sons of Destruction hustled over to them.

"Is there a problem here?" he asked.

"No problem," Adi said. She shoved the icon into the boy's hands. "I was just leaving." Adi took two steps and Xander grabbed her arm.

"Adi, please—"

She twisted free of his grasp. "Don't touch me. Your days as my knight in shining armor are over. I don't want to see you anymore."

Xander shrank into himself. Adi hated herself for berating him in public, but she had to end this.

*He will heal,* she knew, *and he'll find someone worthy of him.*

She spat in the sand at his feet. "And stay away from Lucas."

Xander stood dumbstruck. Adi did not give him time to regroup. She fled the mausoleum at a brisk walk. She glanced back before rounding a corner. Xander stood outside the entryway. He did not follow her.

# CHAPTER THIRTY-EIGHT
# THEO VANGUARD
## MOON OF XYS, CORDSDAY, 31ST OF HEBE

T heo followed Isaiah up the short flight of heavy stone steps to the Void Temple. His brother beat the smooth brass knocker against the door. There was a pause, then the door swung inward on silent hinges. There was no one on the other side. Theo suppressed a shudder as he crossed the threshold. It was his first visit to such a temple. While he knew the rumors of void mage rituals to be just that—mostly—he still listened for distant cries of pain.

The south transept was a perfect square lit by a channel of liquid fire cut across the stone wall at waist height on either side. The lower wall was polished black stone that reflected the light in strange, wavering shapes.

*Obsidian,* Theo realized. He had never seen so much of it in one place, and so skillfully worked.

On either side of the room above the fire line hung two massive paintings depicting the night sky. Dark blue lines connected the white stars to create constellations Theo did not recognize. There were no moons in either painting and Solo was conspicuously absent.

In the middle of the opposite wall, a mallet hung beside a large, gleaming gong. On either side of the gong was a door. Above Theo's head, wisps of blue-black smoke glowed against the ceiling, though its source was a mystery.

Theo stared at the hard stone surfaces. "The temple moves during peripatesis?"

"In a manner of speaking."

"What does that mean?"

"Come," Isaiah said, "we haven't much time." He opened the left door and gestured for Theo to follow.

The large adjoining room was circular. In the dim light and haze of curling smoke, Theo had to squint to see the other side. He felt as if he was standing inside a massive stone drum. Granite columns formed a ring around a central reflecting pool. Thorned vines decorated the capitals, and torches burned from protruding sconces. Bookshelves lined the perimeter of the room and were heavily laden with dusty tomes. Theo and Isaiah were alone.

"Where is everyone?" Theo asked.

"This library is a sanctum for void mages. I am currently its only occupant on Solvigant." Isaiah slid a thin volume from a shelf and consulted its table of contents.

"How many void mages are there?"

"Maybe thirty, I'm not sure." Isaiah paged through the book.

"You were promoted."

Isaiah snapped the book shut, replaced it on the shelf and selected another one. He grinned at Theo, who shuddered at the incongruity of his expression framed by the skull mask.

"I ascended to the rank, yes. Promotions are for the military," he said with a derisive sneer.

Theo approached the reflecting pool. The water was clear and he saw the pool contained a dozen brilliant yellow fish who cruised in slow curves around one another. Streaks of white tile shimmered beneath them like lightning bolts. Theo extended a finger to ripple the surface of the pool.

"Don't touch that."

Theo withdrew his finger. Above the pool hung another painting of an unfamiliar night sky.

*Not a painting*, Theo realized as a meteor whizzed across the image. As he studied the stars, he saw slow movement, as if a great ovoid form moved behind that sky, distorting the starfield as it traveled.

"Are all Void Temples this—strange?" Theo asked.

Isaiah looked up from the volume in his hands. "What do you mean?"

Theo opened his arms to the austere library. "Temples to the other gods are built to accommodate worshippers, to welcome adherents, to convey the beneficence of a god. Here I feel as if I'm raiding a tomb."

"People confuse the void, a great cosmic absence, with death. That is understandable, but wrong. Both death and the void trade on our fear of the unknown. Kade is a monster who scares us because he is not a child of Solo. Before Kade, Corendar was the father of Solo's children. Like Solo, he has always existed. He is not a descendant." The last phrase held the heaviness of ritual.

"You call your god a monster, yet you do not fear the void?" Theo asked.

"Every monster diminishes when illuminated."

"You told me once that void mages are scientists studying Kades's realm, Basalt."

"I say we void mages learn to see in the dark." Isaiah shelved the book he was holding and moved along the curve of the room to another shelf.

"What are you looking for?"

"Have you heard of Marya Ghent?"

"Who?" A flick of new color caught Theo's attention. The fish in the reflecting pool were now a vibrant pink.

"One of Celeste's granddaughters, an explorer and diviner."

"Celeste of Sojourner fame?" Theo watched the fish to see if they would change again. "I thought she and her husband were only legends."

"Legends are accretions of antiquity and ignorance."

"When did you become such a poet?" Theo looked up to see his brother watching him. Isaiah chuckled. "When I got promoted."

"Did this Marya Ghent write a book which you are now looking for and which will help us recover father's artifact?"

"No."

"Then why are we here?"

"Bonding as brothers."

"The infamous First Order void mage Isaiah Vanguard wants to spend quality time with his younger brother. I'm flattered but unconvinced. Why are we here?"

Isaiah grinned. Even across the dim room, his teeth shone bright white.

"The book has nothing to do with Apyreon," Isaiah said.

"I ask again, what are we doing here?"

"Here it is." Isaiah plucked out a book, crossed the room, and handed Theo a slender red volume.

"*House Valefyre*," Theo read. "Very funny. Did you bring me here just to mock me?"

"Father would make you lord of the Balan Estates. You would spend your days a wealthy and powerful man. You would sire strong children on the beautiful Lady Valefyre, raising them to be as noble as you think yourself to be. Is that such a terrible fate?"

Isaiah returned to browsing the bookshelves. Theo looked down. The fish in the reflecting pool were now powder blue.

"Father wants me out of the way." Theo winced as he heard the petulance in his voice.

"There are certainly less luxurious ways of accomplishing that goal."

"You and father are planning something and Apyreon is a part of it. Whatever it is, you're willing to risk sedition charges by coming here as a void mage without the emperor's knowledge. Let me help."

"Was losing the *Sidereal* your idea of helping?"

"If I had known the stakes, I could have better protected the yacht."

"Are you so willing to prove yourself to father that you'd betray the emperor? Didn't you take an oath as a naval officer to uphold the integrity of the Solan Empire?"

"For once, I'd appreciate a choice in the matter."

"Did you know that House Valefyre claims Ghent as a distant relative?"

Theo stared expressionless. "Who?"

"Celeste's daughter, Marya Ghent, the diviner. The one I was telling you about before you started complaining about how unfair the life of a noble son is."

"What does that have to do with anything?"

"Nothing, really, except that there are no other known diviners in the Valefyre bloodline."

"What is a diviner anyway?" Theo thumbed through the book without really seeing any of the pages.

"A diviner identifies wrinkles in the fabric of the World System."

"Wrinkles?"

"Places where the fabric of this mortal realm is thin."

Theo was losing patience. "You enjoy doling out your superior knowledge in chunks too small to be useful. Why is that important?"

"I appreciate your recognition that my knowledge is superior."

"Those of us who risk our lives for the Empire seldom have time to waste in libraries. Get to the point."

"The Solan Church recognizes three realms which are—?"

"Celestial Avernus, the Mortal Realm, and dark Basalt," Theo said, reciting the tidbit from grammar school.

"Precisely, and between the realms?"

"Void."

"And?"

Theo shook his head.

"Aether," Isaiah said. "Raw aether is found in the void and occurs nowhere else. Think of the thin areas sussed out by a diviner as aetherial mineshafts. Aether was central to the magic of the Sojourners and the Kratoi."

"Aether magic is forbidden in the Empire."

Isaiah shook his head. "And you wonder why Father never gives you a choice."

"Kade and Aether are connected, then. The God of the Void and a substance found only within his domain."

"Indeed. You're catching on."

"What's the connection?"

"For that answer, you'd have to become a First Order void mage."

Theo sighed in exasperation. His brother had always flaunted the esoteric learning of void mages. It was both arrogant and annoying.

"And aether, or diviners, or Ghent relates to Apyreon?"

"Only tangentially. Talk at court is that the Lady Valefyre is quite the scholar. You may have to read more books, brother."

"Can we focus on recovering Father's device rather than on my pending nuptials?"

"Rumors also claim that she is quite enthusiastic about the match."

"She is barely sixteen."

"You're twenty-three, Theo. Father is older than mother by a larger margin. Besides, she is quite smitten with you."

"We met once, four years ago. I don't think we even spoke to one another."

Isaiah shrugged and took another book from a shelf. "You will have a lifetime to get to know one another. Besides, it's not like you can marry Beatrice. She is already married to that lummox Hubert and Father and Lord Faide are not currently on the best of terms."

Theo made a choking sound. "What? No."

"I hear the attraction in your voice when you speak of her."

Theo paced around the rim of the pool.

"Here it is." Isaiah stood on tiptoe, struggling to reach a dark blue volume from a top shelf. For a moment, Theo's brother looked small and vulnerable. Then the moment was gone. Theo looked down at the fish which were bright yellow once more.

"What is it?"

"Ghent's journal containing her notes on her visit to Flynt."

"That's important?"

"The Solan Church is wrong about the three realms," Isaiah said while thumbing through the book. "There are at least four. Pyrea, where the dragon forms reside, is the fourth. This proves it." He waggled the book. Theo arched an eyebrow.

"Ghent is the only known non-Dragon to ever witness Xiamentarisia."

"Which is?"

"It's the Dragon coming-of-age ceremony."

"I thought we were trying to find Apyreon, not write a research paper on Dragon adolescence."

"Are all naval officers so obtuse?"

"Aether, Dragon rituals, diviners, and the Kratoi are not my areas of expertise."

"No, I suppose not." Isaiah seemed disappointed. "You wouldn't know that Apyreon was built by the Dragon artificer Anaximander then. Let's go."

"Where?"

"To a café. I'm starving." Isaiah rubbed his stomach.

"Do the Dragons want Apyreon, too?"

"No, they don't. Well one might. Patience, brother. Trust me." Isaiah laughed, his voice a cascade of sharp gravel. Theo handed him the Valefyre book.

"No, consider that an engagement present. You'll learn something about your future wife."

"You're an asshole."

"I'm a First Order void mage."

"Same thing."

Isaiah eyed Theo for a long moment, then turned and made for a door on the other side of the room. Theo followed him, holding the small book. The fish in the reflecting pool shone the green of fresh limes.

"That's not the way we came in." Theo said.

"I know."

The door opened onto a ramp that spiraled upward. Theo could not remember descending into the temple at any point and was disoriented when, after climbing for several minutes, the two brothers emerged at street level in a nondescript alley. Theo felt no closer to Apyreon than before his brother had arrived.

*Be a good boy, get married, sire a brood of children, run your estates.* The contemptuous voice in his mind was his father's. Theo shook his head to clear it and stumbled over a short curb. *Why do I need to understand so badly? To be included? Am I rejecting a blessing in disguise?*

If Theo wanted to know what Isaiah and his father were up to, he would have to be patient. He resolved to listen and wait and hoped that one of them would give something away that connected all the pieces.

*As if I have any other choice.*

# CHAPTER THIRTY-NINE
# ADI CRESTONE
## MOON OF XYS, CORDSDAY, 31ST OF HEBE

Adi hailed a cab, anxious to be away from the Wandering Mausoleum and Xander. The brougham driver charged a full silver tower to cart Adi across town to Stella's Echo. Irate, Adi fumed inside the cab. Still, she had no choice but to spend the money Xander had given her.

*I just need enough to book passage to Tyre, to Lucas. It would be so much less complicated if she just ran.*

Adi remembered a Maxon Laird story wherein Laird, penniless and disinherited, successfully took on an entire smuggling ring. He managed to win the heart of a local princess in the process, while appearing to never break a sweat.

*But I didn't inherit powers from the Kratoi.* She rubbed the cold collar and felt the absence of her dragonstone. No part of her plan involved storming the Red Wyrm to steal it back from the Lord of Bones.

*If I can hand over Apyreon to the Blood Queen, this will all be over.* Adi recognized the naïveté of that thought. It would never be over. The Blood Queen would never release Adi, not when the gangster held so much leverage over her. Even if the collar came off, Lucas would never again be safe on Tyre. Her magic would be forever encased behind an impenetrable wall of pain.

*What was it Captain Torrance used to say? When you have a tiger by the balls you don't let go, you squeeze harder. Am I the tiger?* Adi had never seen one. She laughed aloud to herself from the comfort of the brougham. Maxon Laird never made deals with criminals, never made promises he had no intention of keeping. *That's why they write books about him and not about me.*

Adi took stock of her situation. In two days, Stuart Royal would meet with Water Knife mercenaries to sell the artifact. Adi knew her plan was weak: to create chaos and take advantage of it. Seneschal and Fedhani would distract each other. That would give her an opportunity to steal Apyreon from Royal before it fell into the hands of Rehka's mysterious client.

*It's a terrible plan. Too many variables. What about the void mage? Theo? Broc and the city watch?*

There was nothing to be done about the void mage. She could manage Theo. Adi just had to evade the city watch for two days. She would deliver Apyreon to the Blood Queen, lose the collar, and leave Xys with all speed to Lucas at the Thail Engineering Academy.

*But what about Palestrina?*

She had promised Devlin Seneschal that she would kill the Seraph in exchange for his help. The idea made Adi queasy. As unnerving as the chiropteran woman was, Palestrina had saved Adi's life at Opus Station. She was also one of the Blood Queen's generals. Killing Palestrina would make a mortal enemy of the Blood Queen. Adi had never accepted a contract on a life before. Rehka was the mercenary, not her.

*I wish Rehka was here. Or do I?* Adi had no time to sort out her tangled feelings for the woman. After three years, Rehka reappeared on a contract she'd taken because it involved Adi. Rehka had professed her love for Adi on the steps of Bale's shop. Adi remembered when such declarations sent delicious chills down her spine and curled her toes. Now she was merely confused. She wanted to feel the delight but found only tepid caution.

Sitting alone in the carriage, she realized how tired she was. All her injuries ached and her eyes felt heavy. Adi yawned, leaned her head against the swaying coach and fell asleep.

"Your stop, miss." The cab driver was shaking Adi's shoulder. Adi blinked and stretched, bringing the world back into focus. The driver looked peeved. Adi guessed it was not his first attempt to wake her. She stifled a yawn and climbed out of the cab. Her weariness was deeper now than it had been when she had fallen asleep. Adi walked down the alley toward the Echo.

Iris was sitting on the narrow front porch puffing on a calabash.

"You smoke a pipe midafternoon?" Adi asked.

"You're not the only one with vices, Adi." Iris grinned, leaned her head back, exposing the elegant length of her throat, and released three perfect smoke rings.

"Impressive. Pair that with drinking rum and you would make a dashing pirate."

"Don't you have to know something about sailing a ship?"

"Not really," Adi said. "It's mostly smoking and drinking."

"I've never been on a sea-going ship."

"That is a travesty which must be rectified. But first, I need a cup of coffee and a pint."

"Both?" Iris laughed with her entire body, her dark curls bouncing.

"Why not?"

"A fair question." Iris's expression turned serious. "There's someone here to see you."

Adi braced herself, wary. "Broc? Did someone turn me in?"

Iris shook her head. "She's waiting for you in my room. Stella didn't want any of the clients to see her."

"Who is this mystery woman?"

"I wouldn't want to ruin the surprise."

Adi studied Iris's face. There were no clues there and trepidation replaced Adi's curiosity.

"Thank you, Iris." Inside, a handful of patrons were bellied up to the bar. Melinda sat beside the fire. Stella wiped glasses. Meera emerged from the back carrying a load of clean laundry and shot Adi a significant look.

"Iris spoke with you?" Stella said.

"Why the intrigue?"

"It's by request."

Adi needed liquid reinforcement. She ordered a pint and drained it in one go. At the top of the stairs, Adi knocked on Iris's door.

"Adi?" came a woman's voice from inside.

"Aye, Captain Crestone," Adi replied.

"Come in."

Adi hesitated, counted to five, and opened the door. "You!" she spluttered.

Beatrice rose from her seat beside Iris's dressing table. "I thought if they told you it was me you'd refuse to see me."

Adi stared at her half-sister. Their resemblance was remarkable. Beatrice was taller and her face was dappled with freckles, but otherwise she was the image of Adi ten years ago.

"I had heard Lord Faide found a prophet. What are you doing here? Did our father send you? Does he know I'm here?"

Beatrice flushed. "No. I came on my own. I wanted to meet you." Beatrice stepped toward Adi, her arms open for an embrace. Adi took an involuntary step back. Beatrice's face darkened and she dropped her arms. "I'm sorry for surprising you like this. I should go." Beatrice started for the door, but Adi was in the way. The two did an awkward tap dance before Adi shifted to let Beatrice pass. She was on the stairs before Adi recovered.

"Wait," Adi called. "Come back, please."

Beatrice paused, looking up. There were tears on her cheeks.

"I'm sorry. You surprised me."

Beatrice wiped her eyes with a hankie, sniffled, and returned to the room. Adi perched on the edge of Iris's pallet while Beatrice resumed her seat beside the dressing table. The two women gazed at each other, then looked away.

"Theo told me you were here, with Hu—with your husband," Adi said when she could no longer handle the silence.

"I thought you wouldn't want to see me."

"I'm honestly not sure I do."

"I wouldn't blame you. After all our father put you through, I wouldn't blame you for cutting ties with everything and everyone associated with House Azure."

Adi admired Beatrice's vibrant blue hair.

*She wears it so boldly.* Adi ran a hand through her own hair, bleached white and dry from the treatment.

"How old are you?" Adi asked.

"Twenty."

"Why don't I remember you?"

"Father didn't bring me into the house until I was ten. Until I—"

"Until you entered the Crucible."

Beatrice nodded.

"Who's your mother?"

"Officially, Lady Phyllis Heathwood. Our father married her about a year after you ran away. My real mother is a wayfaring Passerine. Hence the freckles," Beatrice waved a hand in front of her face. "Sorry, I don't know why I'm crying." She blew her nose and steadied herself. "Father refused to recognize me unless I had the gift."

"So, it's true, you are a prophet."

Beatrice nodded. "Not an exceptionally good one. Reading the histories of the Faide prophets, I am the weakest of them."

Adi felt cold. She wanted to wrap up in Iris's blankets to keep her teeth from chattering. The two women watched each other.

"We look so much alike," Adi started. "I feel like I'm looking at me in another life."

"I'm sorry, Adi. I must remind you of all the horrors of home."

Adi did not know what to say or to feel. This woman, her half-sister, was like a strange dream. Beatrice was living the life their father had wanted for Adi, a prophet daughter married to a Marrion. The thought of Hubert made Adi shudder.

*Does this woman know the monster in her bed? She must. Hubert Marrion is not a subtle predator.*

"I'm sorry," Adi said, "I didn't mean to insult you. I have a lot on my mind and you're like a dream." Adi thought she ought to be elated. Here was another person who understood the terrors and trauma of her childhood, someone who had experienced it herself. Beatrice had descended into the Crucible, faced Droth and Kelek and whatever else lurked down there, had endured the controlling and unpredictable rage of Lord Daniel Faide, and now endured the petty wrath of her husband, Hubert Marrion. Both Adi and Beatrice had entered the forge fires of House Azure. Adi had emerged brittle, broken, and discarded, while Beatrice emerged tougher and alloyed.

"Will you tell our father about me?" Adi asked.

"I would never," Beatrice swore.

Adi studied her face and decided she was telling the truth. "Thank you."

The two women fell silent once more.

"What are you doing on Xys?" Adi asked.

"Hubert was appointed Sabaian Ambassador to Xys. He and the governor are discussing refugee colonies."

"What refugees?"

"For the people of Solvigant."

With all the crises in her own life, Adi had forgotten about the doomed moon.

"Father never lets anything go."

"What do you mean?"

"I built a new life on this moon and Saba is sucking it back."

"What life is that?"

"My life," Adi snapped.

Beatrice shrank away but did not back down. "You live in hiding, wanted by the authorities and at the whim of a gangster. When was the last time you saw your son?"

"What do you know about Lucas? Does Hubert know anything?"

"I'm a prophet, Adi, I often know things people think are hidden. And no, Hubert is unaware."

"Do you have any children?"

"No."

"Good."

Beatrice narrowed her eyes. "What do you mean good?"

"Hubert is a monster. He doesn't need any more offspring running around."

"He has offspring?"

Adi's grin was wicked. "The prophet doesn't know all the secrets."

"That's not how it works."

"I wouldn't know. But you are a stepmother."

Adi waited for Beatrice to connect the dots.

"Hubert is Lucas's father?"

Adi nodded, worried she was about to be sick to her stomach.

"I don't understand."

"I ran away from Lord Faide, yes," Adi said. "But I also ran because Hubert raped me and I ended up pregnant with his child. I didn't know what Daniel would do when he found out his daughter, who has none of the family gifts, was carrying a bastard."

"Hubert doesn't know?"

"No."

"Xander?"

"Xander knows. He's been a surrogate father for Lucas. He pays for Lucas's education and looks out for him when I can't."

"Why are you telling me this?"

"You should know the type of man you're married to."

"I do know," Beatrice's voice held a subtle edge of menace. Adi realized the woman was hugging herself, unconsciously rubbing her ribs.

"Do you want me to kill him?"

Beatrice blanched. "What? No! I just came to meet you."

"I thought not." She tried not to sound disappointed. "I'm a pirate, not an assassin." *Palestrina aside.*

"Don't they both murder for money?"

Adi winced. "There is a distinction. I was tired of living under the shadow of House Azure. I needed my own adventures, my own life. I wanted my own Maxon Laird story."

"I don't judge you, Adison. I read those books too."

Adi watched Beatrice. Her half-sister was two people: one a demure, traumatized twenty-year-old child; the other a hardened prophet privy to mysteries of time and the World System.

"Everyone judges the prostitute-turned-pirate. Especially those who insist they do not."

"I truly don't."

"What's it like?" Adi asked.

"What do you mean?"

"Being a prophet, what's it like? My entire childhood it was the sole focus of my life."

Beatrice shifted in her seat, twisting the silk handkerchief. "If life is stumbling forward blindly through a dark cave, I have a sputtering lantern. When it works, I can see a short way ahead or behind, but it is difficult to discern between shadows and reality. I can see both the veins of gold in the stone and the monsters lurking in the recesses. When the lantern goes out, it is dark again and I stumble on like everyone else."

"It sounds like the Crucible."

"I never left the Crucible." The haunted look in Beatrice's eyes kept Adi from pressing further.

"The darkness is better," Beatrice said. "I wish I didn't have a lantern at all. I wish lanterns did not exist. Yet having had the light, I crave it. I beg the gods to let the lantern illuminate the world. I am an addict who cannot control my fix."

"I know what it is like to love something that also kills you."

"I suppose you do."

"Can I ask you about the future?"

Beatrice tucked the sodden hankie into her reticule, ignoring Adi's question. "When you're chastising yourself for being a prostitute-turned-pirate, you should add hypocrite to the list."

"Excuse me?"

"You assumed that I came here to ask you to kill Hubert, to use you. That made you angry. But I have never discussed my abilities with anyone, not Hubert, and never Father. I have no friends to confide in. Now you ask me to prophesize, you want to use me."

Adi flushed, ashamed, but pressed on. "Please. I need to know if my son—your step-son—will be safe. I don't care about the rest of it—Apyreon, indenture, Rehka, or any of it. Just tell me if Lucas will be all right." Adi had a sudden thought. "But I don't want to know if he isn't safe, just lie to me."

Beatrice's smile was full of pity, but Adi did not care. "You render my answer useless, then. If I say 'yes, he is safe' you do not know if I am telling the truth or lying because you asked me to. Why bother with your question at all?

"I need reassurance. There are so many variables. I must believe it will all be worth it." Adi felt her eyes prickle with tears.

"I wish I had news for you, Adi, I do, but I have seen nothing of Lucas's fate."

"Nothing?"

"I would tell you if I had seen him. I would never come between you and the knowledge of your son. I will tell you what I have seen."

"I have seen Xys destroyed by the rocky rings of Solo as Xander and Theo watch. I have seen a void mage walk across the surface of a star. I have seen a young woman decapitate a soldier. I have seen a faceless Seraph crucified upside down. I have seen the Blood Queen twice, once ascending the Imperial throne and once burned by Dragon's breath and melting into the very rocks beneath her feet. I have seen myself big with child while nursing another. I have seen that Faelani downstairs, Stella, in full battle regalia, and I have seen Droth the Minotaur freed from the Crucible and killing mages at the Astral temple on Karis. I have seen Hubert leading a great armada through the stars. These are the things that currently haunt my dreams, both waking and asleep."

Adi swallowed hard. "Are all these things that will come to pass?"

Beatrice shrugged. "Not necessarily. The gods show me possibilities, but I have no way to discern which are probable."

"These visions come all the time?"

"I have no control over when the gods illuminate my lantern."

"I'm sorry."

"For what?"

"For the visions, for our father, for using you. For all of it."

Beatrice sighed. "It's all right. I am a tool, Adi, and tools are meant to be used. I am sure you spent years feeling like a failure because you couldn't manifest prophetic abilities. The truth is you won. You got to grow up to be a whole, imperfect, disaster of a person, but a person, nonetheless. You should be more grateful."

Adi flushed, chastened.

"I meant what I said," Beatrice went on, "I do not judge you. Who am I to judge anyone? I only want to provide you with perspective."

"Maybe I could help you," Adi offered. "I can help you get away from Hubert and Lord Faide."

"You can call him father."

"He is no longer my father. You may call him whatever you wish. I escaped; I could help you do the same."

Beatrice shook her head. "You have not escaped. You may not live in our father's house, but you still live in his shadow, afraid, in a prison of your own making. I would not have you build such a cell for me."

Adi was too surprised to be offended. "I loved my life."

"For a while."

"For a while," Adi admitted. It was unnerving to talk to a prophet, she decided, especially when that prophet knew so much about her childhood. "The seven years Rehka and I were on that ship, sailing the seas of the World System, was true liberty. We had freedom, love, and adventure. It was tough, but it was ours. We were the masters of our own fates. I'll get back there one day."

Beatrice's smile did not reach her eyes. "I'm sure you will." She stood. "I should get going."

"What about you? What will you do? Will I see you again?"

"Do you want to see me again?"

"I do," Adi said, and meant it.

"Theo is escorting me to the Temple of Destruction on Maxon to visit Djinnar. We are part of an embassy to beg favor from the god to alter the city's path and to learn what we may of Pallantier's fate."

"Theo is leading the delegation?"

"The governor appointed him commander of the delegation two nights ago."

"I will be sailing for Tyre late on Djinnday. You could accompany me."

"Hubert is opposed to my journey. The only reason I have permission to leave is through the governor's explicit invitation. Hubert cannot refuse it. There is no chance he'd allow me to accompany you. I will not live my life as a fugitive from my father's wrath and my husband's scorn. I will help you make amends with Father if you like. He would protect you and Lucas from the Blood Queen."

"I need no help from that man." Adi was crestfallen. "Nothing will keep me from leaving for Tyre once I hand over Apyreon."

"Be that as it may, I have seen you."

"You have? Doing what? Where?"

"I have seen you sailing between great whirring cogs and spinning flywheels surrounded by Dragons."

"I don't understand."

"Neither do I," Beatrice admitted. "I rarely do."

Adi stood. "It was good to meet you, Beatrice Marrion." She nearly choked on the surname but pushed it through.

"And you, Adison Crestone."

"It's captain." Adi tried to smile. "Just knowing you're real, that you survived what I could not, it gives me hope. I'm glad you came."

"I am, too."

Adi closed the gap between them and embraced her half-sister. It was a stilted hug, and Beatrice's arms were stiff across Adi's back. When they released one another, they both laughed and avoided eye contact.

"We'll get better at it," Adi said.

"I hope so," Beatrice replied and left.

Adi sank back down onto the pallet, exhausted. The evening sun filtered through the diaphanous curtains of the small window. She heard a muffled knock, and Iris entered carrying two steaming mugs of coffee.

"Are you all right?" she asked.

"I'm fine," Adi replied then immediately burst into tears. Iris set the mugs aside and folded Adi into her arms. Adi wept into Iris's chest, great heaving sobs, while Iris rocked her and made soft shushing sounds.

# CHAPTER FORTY

# THEO VANGUARD

## MOON OF XYS, CORDSDAY, 31ST OF HEBE

Theo and Isaiah occupied a corner booth in the Copper Fox, a blue-collar tavern three blocks from Dervish Machine Works. It was mid-afternoon and the tavern was quiet. Half a dozen patrons situated themselves across the room from the void mage. They spoke in hushed tones and pretended not to notice the dark robes and bone mask.

Isaiah nursed a beer, reading the book he had taken from the Void Temple. Splotches of ale dotted the table where the trembling tavern keeper's hand sloshed foam over the tankard's rim. Theo was well into his second pint. Isaiah licked one gnarled finger and turned the page. Theo wanted to get up and pace the room but worried the other patrons might faint or bolt if the void mage's companion came anywhere near them.

He refused to open the book of Valefyre genealogy on principle. Studying his betrothed's lineage would be a small defeat and could lead to a cascade failure. The result would be a sheepish Theo, molded to the indomitable will of his father.

"You still haven't told me why Father is coming to Xys," Theo said, "If he sent you to recover Apyreon, why does he need to be here?"

Isaiah eyed Theo over the top of the book but said nothing.

"Why House Valefyre anyway?" Theo pressed. "He must want something from them. Otherwise, he would court Azure, Heathwood, or Gregor or one of the other major Imperial Houses. What do you know of the Valefyre dowry?"

Isaiah turned another page and did not look up.

"Do you really read so fast?" Theo prodded.

Isaiah dog-eared the page and closed the book. "You are most impatient, brother."

"What are we waiting for?"

"Who."

"Excuse me?"

"You asked what we are waiting for, and it's a 'who.'"

"Who, then?"

Isaiah removed the skull mask, set it on the table, and rubbed his temples. "Can I trust you, brother?"

Theo was taken aback. He had never trusted the machinations of Isaiah or their father. Or their oldest brother, Paul. He was cut from the same ambitious cloth as Lord Vanguard.

*Had been cut.* Theo reminded himself. It had never occurred to him that his older brothers might not trust him.

"Of course," Theo said.

"Don't look so offended."

Theo tried to hold the gaze of Isaiah's distorted pupils but he had to look away.

"You're so eager," Isaiah continued, "it makes you seem young."

"You're only two years older than me."

Isaiah rubbed his knuckles the same way arthritic old cannoneers did. "Pain stretches time in odd ways."

"I don't know what that means."

"Pray to all the gods, dear brother, that you never do."

"You still haven't answered my question."

"Which one? You asked several."

"Any of them," Theo snarled. "I'm sailing blind here."

"Keep your voice down." Isaiah sipped his beer. Theo's knee bounced. He was unable to keep his foot still. "To your first question," Isaiah continued, "House Valefyre is a perfectly reputable house. Fifth sons do not marry into major houses, not even fifth sons of chancellors. The dowry is considerable but contains nothing but Imperial coin. As for what Father wants from House Valefyre, I was hoping you could tell me."

"How would I know?"

Isaiah tapped the slender red book on the table before Theo. "Father has become obsessed with antiquity, the house lineages, and the devices of Anaximander. Whatever he wants, there are clues in that book."

"Why don't you read it then?"

"I don't care what dusty artifact or tidbit of knowledge he hopes to glean from your marriage to Hannah Valefyre. She's not to be my wife. To your other questions, I do read fast. I read even faster when not peppered with inane questions. Why is Father coming himself? I have no idea."

Theo snorted.

"He doesn't tell me everything either. But his rival, Governor Faide, also seeks the device. I suppose Father wants to ensure that he secures the device and drives a wedge between any Gambol/Faide alliance. If our dear cousin Tabi dies, we don't want any Gambol offspring from a new wife betrothed to any Faide heirs."

"We don't?"

"We don't. Finally, my informant."

"Informant?"

"That's who we're waiting on. My informant is going to arrive here at any moment and provide me with the location of Apyreon." Isaiah's voice cracked. Its ragged quality suggested the conversation had cost him. "Satisfied?"

Theo nodded, his hands toying with the book.

"You're disappointed," Isaiah noted. "You would rather find the White Rabbits and bash their heads in until they give up information. How did that go for you in Opus Station?"

"I don't know what you're talking about."

"I heard you tortured and killed a man in cold blood, in a fit of pique. I had no idea my little brother had such a temper."

"Keep your voice down." It was Theo's turn to rasp the command. "Crestone did the killing."

Isaiah chuckled. "You're a terrible liar."

"I'm telling the truth!" Theo's stomach clenched with guilt.

"If you are—and you're not, but let's pretend you are—then a bruised and battered pirate girl stole a ship, a priceless magical artifact, and your sword, wounding your hand in the process." Isaiah gestured at Theo's bandaged hand. "You're either a terrible soldier or a terrible liar. Perhaps both."

Theo opened his mouth to protest further but Isaiah held up a hand to silence him. The void mage's altered eyes focused on the tavern's door. "My informant is here. I'm trusting you with this, brother. Keep your mouth shut until she's gone."

Theo's back was to the door, but he heard the creak of rusty hinges followed by the steady footfalls of leather-soled boots. A slender shadow fell across the table.

"May I sit?" she asked. The woman was tall as a Dragon but lacked the usual shimmer. Bandoliers packed with throwing knives and bullets crisscrossed her chest, and her sleeveless shirt revealed the bicep tattoo of a Water Knife mercenary captain. A purple bruise on her chin indicated she had recently been punched in the jaw. Her green gaze flicked between the brothers. Theo scooted over on the bench and the woman sat.

"Rehka," Isaiah crooned, "good of you to join us."

"I don't have much time," the woman snapped. "Who is this?" She poked a thumb at Theo.

"This is Commander Theo Vanguard of the HMS *Dragonhammer*."

"What's he doing here? I wasn't aware we would have company. I don't like surprises."

"Theo is my brother. We are out celebrating his impending nuptials. Now, are you going to tell me where my artifact is? That was the deal, Rehka, was it not?"

The mercenary nodded, but she was staring at Theo. His brother's pale face and bizarre eyes did not affect her the way Theo had seen it cow so many others.

"Wait," she said to Theo, "you're the prisoner from the *Sidereal*?"

Theo bristled, "What do you know about that?"

Rehka ignored him. "You killed Rictor. You're the reason there's a warrant out for Adi's arrest! The Imperial Guard will get involved now."

Before Theo could respond, Rehka pounced. Her bony forearm slammed into his neck and pinned him against the wall. The pressure forced his head into an awkward position where he could not see his attacker. He grabbed her arm and felt a blade's cold bite press into his thigh.

"Don't move," she growled. Theo froze.

"Rehka" Isaiah chided, "release the officer."

Rehka leaned harder into Theo's neck. He spluttered, unable to turn his head. "Give me a good reason," she said through clenched teeth.

"What are you going to do with him?"

"Clear Adison's name."

"Even if the city watch believed your accusation that a decorated Imperial Naval officer whose father is high chancellor murdered a man in a jail cell, what do you think would happen?" Isaiah replaced his mask and cleared his throat. "Adison is a child playing with forces she doesn't understand. Better to look after yourself. That's why you're here, isn't it? Your passion for the wayward pirate is commendable but misplaced."

"Adi is not to be harmed," Rehka insisted. Theo gurgled and tried to shift his weight, but she pressed the knife more firmly against his femoral artery. "I said, don't move."

"Adison's safety is not part of our deal."

"I'm changing the deal. Swear on the void that no harm will come to Adi."

"I will not. There are too many players I cannot control."

"Then I will tell you nothing."

Isaiah shrugged. "I will speak to my acolytes. My followers will not harm your dear captain."

Black dots filled Theo's vision as he struggled to draw breath. He smacked a hand on the table.

"Please release him," Isaiah said. "He can't flee. You are between him and the door, after all. Or you can kill him to assuage the guilt of your betrayal."

Rehka's arm eased slightly and Theo gasped.

"I would never betray Adison." Rehka's voice was fierce.

Theo looked down the bridge of his nose at his brother. Isaiah drained his beer, anointing the teeth of his mask with foam. Then he picked up his book from the table.

"Yet here you sit," he crooned.

Rehka tensed. Theo sensed her indecision. The woman cared for the pirate, but something had driven her into his brother's terrible orbit.

*Should I feel loyalty to Crestone?* Theo wondered. *She did what a commanding officer should do at Opus Station by taking responsibility for my error. We shook hands on a deal, Apyreon for debts paid off.* Guilt threatened to overwhelm Theo once more, but his struggle to breathe and the cavalier way his brother gambled with his life kept him focused.

*Crestone is a pirate and a thief. She may be planning to betray me. I'm supposed to be better than her,* Theo's conscience reminded him, but he shoved the thought away. If Rehka didn't kill him, he could wallow in guilt later.

Isaiah's dragonstone pulsed and fire danced from the fingers of one hand. The fire traveled around the void mage's palm then settled atop his index and middle fingers.

"If you do kill him," Isaiah said holding the book above the conjured flames, "our deal is off."

Theo smelled the reek of scorching leather. Rehka pressed the blade into Theo's thigh.

"Stop it," she growled.

"That is entirely your choice." Isaiah said.

*Can't he blast this woman from her seat?* "Please," Theo whispered.

Rehka surrendered, releasing him. Theo caught himself and leaned over the table gulping air and massaging his aching throat. The knife disappeared back into her bandolier as Theo glared at his brother. The flames around Isaiah's fingertips vanished and he slid the book across the table to Rehka, who snatched it up. The damage to the cover was superficial.

"Marya Ghent's travels to Flynt," Isaiah said. "Perhaps you'll find something in there that will elucidate your—condition."

Rehka flipped through the pages, then ran her forefinger down the table of contents.

"What is your connection to Crestone?" Theo asked.

Rehka did not respond.

"Rehka and Adi were companions," Isaiah said. "They crewed a pirate ship together. They were lovers once upon a time."

"Lovers?"

"I apologize, Rehka, I had no idea my brother was so close-minded."

"Shut up," Rehka said.

"Th-that's not what I meant," Theo stammered.

Isaiah waved a dismissive hand. Theo chafed at his brother's schemes. This woman loved Crestone and Isaiah was manipulating that affection.

*What am I thinking? This woman is a mercenary who loves a pirate. She just nearly killed me. Why do I even care?* But the concern was there, nonetheless. Theo could not deny it. *I am not cut out for these games. Maybe I should be banished to an estate to raise children.*

"Your turn," Isaiah said to Rehka. "Where's Lady Brixton's necklace?"

Theo stared at his brother in alarm.

"If I don't tell you?"

"I provide you with the book, you provide me with the details of the necklace's whereabouts."

"I have what I want," Rehka said. "What's to stop me from walking out of here?"

"You'd be a greasy smear on the wall before you could leave that bench," Isaiah said. Theo found Isaiah's matter-of-fact tone disquieting. The mage continued, "Stop wasting my time and tell me who has it."

The two stared each other for a long moment. Trapped in the corner of the booth, Theo could only watch and brace for impact.

"Palestrina," Rehka said at last. "She nicked it from Opus Station while your brother was busy torturing people."

"The Lady of Spiders has it? Interesting. Where do I find her?"

"The Red Wyrm. It's a night club near the aeroport, the court of the Blood Queen."

Theo could stand it no longer. "You're not here to recover Apyreon?" Isaiah gave him a warning look, but Theo pressed on. "What new game is this? Who is Lady Brixton? What is the significance of this necklace?"

"The Lady Brixton is a pompous windbag, who thinks her extensive charity work makes up for her insufferable manner. She is married to Viscount Nigel Brixton, a minor Xyssian noble house. She matters insofar as she was in possession of this artifact."

"What is it?"

Isaiah paused, searching for the right words. "It is important only if you are a void mage, and you are not."

"What about Apy—"

"Silence!" Isaiah barked. Theo's mouth slammed shut. Rehka sat up straighter, her eyes fearful.

*Is he using void magic on me?* Theo wondered. The tension in his jaw eased, and he rubbed feeling back into it.

Rehka found her voice first. "What about the rest of our deal?"

"Tell me about the exchange with Apyreon."

"That wasn't—"

Isaiah held up a hand to silence her. "Tell me. Will Palestrina be there?"

"The exchange is set for Leyala Fedhani's aeroport, Alhambra, Djinnday at eleven at night. I do not expect Palestrina to be present. The Blood Queen has tasked Adi alone with the artifact's recovery."

Isaiah removed a small notebook bound with a length of cord from his robe. He untied the cord and turned several pages.

"There are six Osmen in Thail keeping tabs on Adi's son."

"Curse the void," Rehka swore. "Ajax."

"Language, Rehka." The void mage smiled. "Yes, it is my understanding that the Blood Queen's bone warriors answer to Ajax. He calls himself the Lord of Bones, does he not?"

"Your acolytes will take care of them?"

Isaiah nodded. "If your information proves correct, when I acquire the necklace my acolytes will eliminate the threat to Adi's boy."

*Crestone is protecting a son?* Theo needed a moment to consider this.

"Adi has recruited Devlin Seneschal to help her recover Apyreon. He'll be there in force to ensure Fedhani doesn't eclipse him."

"Does Palestrina know of Senechal's involvement?"

"Why would she?"

"They have a history, you know."

Rehka's expression was one of confusion. "I don't think Adi would involve Palestrina. She wants to be finished with the Blood Queen and her generals."

"Excellent." Isaiah steepled his fingers beneath his chin, thinking. Theo could only guess what.

"That's all I know."

"Fair enough. This arrangement has worked out well for you. Soon you'll be a Dragon again, and you've assuaged your guilt at betraying your lover by protecting her son. All the while securing a hefty sum for your mercenary guild. Adi underestimates you."

Rehka ground her teeth, tucked the book under an arm, and stood. "If we're done here?"

Isaiah stood and offered his hand. "A pleasure doing business with you Captain Balefire."

The mercenary spurned the proffered hand, turned on her heel, and stormed from the Copper Fox.

"What, by the Nine Gods, was that?" Theo exploded when Rehka had disappeared. "Maybe a heads-up next time before you gamble with my life."

"She wasn't going to kill you. She had to look tough in front of the scary void mage. That woman is desperate to recover her Dragon form. Desperate people can justify anything."

"You don't think that's cruel?"

"Of course, it's cruel," Isaiah snapped. There was real anger in his voice. "Life is cruel, brother. Grow up."

Theo shrank back from Isaiah's rage. "What now?"

"Now, you will return to the governor's mansion and wait. I'll come for you tomorrow afternoon when Father arrives."

Theo swallowed. In the excitement, he had forgotten all about Lord Vanguard's impending arrival. "What are you going to do?"

Isaiah stood, "I have to catch a ferry off-moon."

"What? Where?"

"All in good time, brother. See you tomorrow. Remember"—Isaiah tapped the little red book—"do your homework."

With that Isaiah strode from the tavern, leaving Theo alone to wonder and brood.

# CHAPTER FORTY-ONE
# ION RUCINARE
## MOON OF XYS, CORDSDAY, 31ST OF HEBE

I on was sitting on the station steps when Inspector Broc returned. His face was drawn in a tight scowl. Broc's assistant, Henge, was absent.

"Inspector—" Ion began, but the Faelani ignored him, stomping into the station. Ion followed as Broc disappeared down the hallway. The desk sergeant prohibited Ion from following, so he stood in the lobby of the station, unsure how to proceed. Down the hall he heard shouts and the crash of metal against the wooden floor. Ion sighed and returned to the steps. He had nowhere to go. Broc had returned in a foul mood and without Captain Crestone, which meant no reward for the young street urchin.

*Am I a street urchin?* It was a phrase the watchman Reese had used during his inter-rogation, one Ion was unfamiliar with, but he had said it with such vitriol he knew it was unkind.

He struggled to figure out his next move. Night was encroaching as Solo moved between Xys and the distant sun. The planet's ruddy orange light deepened the shadows. Ion shivered. City watchmen regularly moved in and out of the station, but none of them gave any heed to the lost boy, the street urchin. Broc did not appear. The street before him remained quiet. Most citizens of Solvigant were at home or in the temples on this Cordsday holiday.

*I should go home,* Ion thought. This was turning into a different sort of adventure from the one he had imagined. He had expected to swashbuckle his way through Solvigant with a jolly pirate crew under the command of the beautiful Captain Crestone. *How does one swashbuckle, anyway?*

He had expected to sleep in the swaying comfort of a hammock below decks, not in hard-packed alleys or in dilapidated factories. Broc had offered him terrane fare and Ion had turned it down. This time he would accept. He had left his grandfather cremated beside the Boiled Sea. He had left his village to face the chaos of a dying moon. The tavern keeper's coddle had transformed the gnawing hunger into creeping guilt. He thought he was being selfish. When his parents had disappeared from Castes, Ion had spent years furious at their selfishness. He was his parents' son. He had done the same once he was no longer able to stomach the difficult fisherman's life. At least there he had a roof over his head and knew how to scrape together an existence, albeit a meager one. The memory of his grandfather's murder rose up in his mind.

*There is nothing for me in Castes.*

"You're still here." He jumped as Broc's voice cut into his ruminations. He had not heard the Faelani approach.

"Yes, sir, Did you find the captain?"

Broc shook his head and sat beside him on the stairs. The inspector withdrew a small leather flask from his pocket and took a long pull. "I did not find the captain today."

Ion let out a relieved sigh he had not known he had been holding.

"She made quite an impression on you," Broc said.

Ion shrugged trying to be casual. "No reward then?"

"I'm afraid not. But tomorrow I'll talk to a blacksmith I know, see if he's interested in hiring a headstrong young lad."

"I think I want to go home."

Broc took another drink from the flask and belched. "Excuse me."

"I need to go home and help the people of Castes. Would you still give me money for the terrane?"

The inspector was silent. Ion turned to look at him to see if he had fallen asleep. Broc was staring out at the street watching a young man light the streetlamps.

"I would, but there's nothing for you in Castes. Xys is dying and places like Castes are the first fatalities."

Ion nodded. The thought of sleeping in their hut on the dune without his grandfather seemed unbearable. *What about Alicia? Or Cornyn? The town still needs fishermen.*

Broc stood. "And tonight?"

"What do you mean?"

"The return terrane to Castes only runs on Millsday, that's two days from now. What will you do in the meantime?"

Ion drew up his knees, crossed his arms over them, and hung his head. "Sleep on the street." Then he had an idea. "You could arrest me. I could stay in a cell until it was time to catch the terrane."

"I don't have enough cells to give you your own, and I do not trust the other inmates to leave you be. Besides, if I charged you with a crime, I couldn't just drop the charges two days later, you'd have to see it through."

"I understand."

Broc took another pull from the flask. Ion stared at the inspector's leather boots, the buckles were polished to a high shine despite the constant sand and dust of the city.

At last Broc broke the silence. "You can stay with me."

"What?" Ion said, confused.

"I have a spare settee, if you can behave yourself until Millsday."

Ion knew the polite response was to decline, or at least to put up some resistance. He ought to say something like *"No, thank you, I couldn't possibly"* but the thought of living two more nights on the streets of Solvigant subverted all thoughts of propriety. Instead, he leapt to his feet and embraced the watchman. Broc grunted his surprise and fumbled the flask.

"Thank you, sir," Ion said into the Faelani's waistcoat. "Thank you. I can behave. I will."

Broc stoppered the flask, then put both paws on Ion's shoulders and pushed the boy away. "That's quite enough. You're welcome."

Ion wiped moisture from the corners of his eyes and sniffed. Broc opened his mouth to say more, then shut it. Ion watched the inspector descend the stairs to the street and hail a cab. The brougham came to a halt before the badger and Broc looked over his shoulder at Ion.

"You coming?"

Ion wiped snot from his nose with his sleeve and scrambled down the stairs and vaulted into the cab. "Yes, sir, thank you sir."

"That's enough gratitude," Broc said once they had settled in the wagon. The driver flicked the reins at the drab mare and the brougham jerked forward. Ion shut his mouth and blushed, looking sheepishly out the window. He had not realized he was still tripping over himself, offering his profuse thanks to the watchman.

From the comfort of the cab, Ion watched the copper-hued city of Solvigant roll by. Without resources, he had felt as though each unfamiliar building was the jagged tooth of a great maw about to close over him, each unknown passerby a potential danger. Now, the closed door of the coach may as well have been a fortress wall. Ion felt safe for the first time since arriving on the terrane platform two days earlier. Those two days felt like two years, but suddenly everything seemed to snap back into place. Solvigant looked warm and inviting through the leaded glass windowpane. He saw the people for who they were, merchants, traders, craftsmen, and factory workers. He imagined them on their way home to families at the end of a long day, engaged in merry conversation with their peers on the street. People waved to one another in greeting or purchased food to take home for dinner. Ion watched with rapt attention as Solvigant transformed before his eyes from a menace into a vibrant, thriving city.

He was disappointed when the cab halted before a line of wooden row houses. He could have watched the city roll by all night.

"Here we are." Broc motioned for Ion to open the door and climb down from the cab. Broc paid the fare, and the brougham rumbled off, its iron-shod wheels clacking on cobblestone.

Ion followed Broc to one of the row houses where he removed a key from his belt and opened a heavy iron lock below the door latch. He pushed the door inward and motioned for Ion to go on ahead. For the first time since receiving his invitation to stay with the inspector, Ion hesitated. The house yawned dark and silent before him.

*What if Broc is not a good man? What if he wants something from me? I don't have anything.*

Ion reassured himself that a senior inspector at the city watch must be a good person and stepped bravely across the threshold. Broc followed and shut the door. The house was completely dark, and Ion waited expectantly as Broc fumbled with drawers in the blackness. After a long minute, an oil lamp flared to life. Ion blinked against the sudden flame and looked around. They were standing in an entry hallway that led to a small sitting room. To the left he saw the vague outlines of a stove in another room.

*That must be the kitchen,* he thought.

A staircase led to a second story where canvas walls flapped idly in a gentle breeze. Dried flowers drooped in a vase on a low table, their fallen petals making a mess on the floor. A spider had built a cobweb amongst the stems. A yellowed envelope stuck in the vase revealed a red wax seal, the image of a claw broken in half where Broc had opened the card.

Broc motioned down the hallway toward the sitting room. "You're through there."

The row house felt like a mansion to Ion who had spent his entire life sharing a one-room shack with his grandfather and he gaped as he walked down the hallway. The sitting room had a couch and two chairs before an empty fireplace. Behind the couch stood a low table. On the table sat a wooden box left open to reveal a neat assortment of badges and medals. A half-empty bottle of whiskey sat beside it and a framed tintype photograph of Broc and another man in uniform looking serious, staring straight ahead into the camera.

"Who's that?" Ion picked up the photo and pointed to the man.

"That's my partner."

"I thought Henge was your partner."

"She is now," Broc said, and the inspector's voice took on a gruff note. "That's Joseph, my old partner."

"What happened to him?"

"He's dead."

"How?" The question was out of Ion's mouth before he had time to consider the propriety of it.

"White Rabbits killed him."

"The gang?"

Broc nodded. He took the tintype from Ion's fingers and placed it back down on the table.

"Sorry."

Broc changed the subject. "You can sleep on the settee. I'll get a fire going in a minute. You hungry?"

"Yes, sir." Ion shook his head with enthusiasm. "Very hungry."

Broc smiled thinly and retreated to the kitchen. Ion took one last look at the tintype and followed. The kitchen consisted of a small counter beside a wood-burning stove, a table with two chairs, one piled high with folders and rolled parchment, and a rack upon which hung an assortment of cast-iron cookware. Ion goggled at the selection. He and his grandfather had had only one battered skillet between them, stained with the char of years of cooking fish over an open stove.

Broc opened an ice chest and removed a hunk of white cheese and mottled log of cured meat. He cut thin strips off both and laid them directly onto the table. Ion snatched them up as quickly as Broc sliced them.

"Delicious," Ion said, his mouth full.

"Save some for me," Broc admonished, "and don't make yourself sick. I'm not cleaning up after you."

Ion slowed the pace he shoveled food into his face.

"Where are your parents?"

Ion shrugged, his appetite suddenly flagging.

"You don't know?"

"They ran off to Solvigant when I was four."

"They didn't take you with them?"

Ion shook his head. "What's that?"

Broc held a round red fruit. "It's a tomato."

"Is it good?"

Broc sliced off part of the tomato and handed it to Ion. He took a bite and promptly spit it out into his hand. Broc laughed for the first time Ion could remember. It was a resonant, happy sound and Ion laughed too despite the foul taste in his mouth.

"Gross," Ion said.

"More for me, then," Broc smiled and bit into the tomato like an apple. Ion wrinkled his nose.

"Are you here looking for your parents?"

Ion shook his head. "No. They never looked back for me."

Broc took another bite of the tomato and leaned on the counter.

"What were their names?" he asked.

"How old are you?" Ion asked instead. He did not want to talk about his parents. What few memories he possessed of them were his alone.

The question surprised Broc and Ion grinned. He enjoyed surprising a senior inspector of the city watch.

"I was a boy when Stanislav Stagheart fought at Owlspear, so a little less than fifty I think."

Ion had never heard of Stagheart or Owlspear, but fifty had to be as ancient as his grandpa.

"Where's your family?" Ion asked. "I thought all old people had families, a wife and kids and stuff."

"Not every old person it seems. Come, it's late. I'll pull out some bedding for you."

Broc trod up the creaky stairs and returned with an armload of blankets. Ion started a fire in the sitting room hearth. Soon, wood crackled, and Ion was swaddled comfortably in thick blankets on the couch. The desert city was often quite cold at night. Broc eyed him and took another pull from the flask at his hip.

"I'll be back in a bit," the Faelani said.

"Wait, where are you going?"

"To the tavern down the street. I do my best thinking there."

"You're just going to leave me here?"

"Go to sleep,"

"I'm not tired."

Broc smiled ruefully. "Just stay in the house then. Don't go wandering out in the dark. You know where the food is. I'll get you up in the morning. I have a list of chores you can do. My hospitality isn't free."

Ion groaned theatrically and Broc laughed again.

"Don't steal anything," Broc said.

"I won't," Ion responded, a bit offended. In the kitchen it had felt like they might become friends.

Broc looked as if he might say something else but turned and trudged back down the hallway.

"Broc!" Ion called after him.

Broc's voice floated back to Ion. "Don't tell me a brave runaway like you is scared?"

"Good night."

Ion heard the jangle of keys and the creak of door hinges before the front door snicked shut. The boy was asleep before the inspector made it down the front steps. Curled in woolen blankets beside the fire, Ion dreamed of catching huge fish on a beautiful crystal ocean.

# Chapter Forty-Two

# ADI CRESTONE

## Moon of Xys, Cordsday, 31st of Hebe

Adi was wrung out. She and Iris were sitting on her pallet. Below them, the tavern filled up with the evening's clients. Raucous male voices floated up the stairs, some blurred by drink and most boasting of their prowess. Adi did not miss her life as one of Stella's working girls, but it was one of the few times she remembered feeling protected. The girls looked out for one another, and matronly Stella looked out for all of them.

*I should tell Stella how much that meant to me.*

"I'm sorry," Adi said. "I had no idea seeing my sister would affect me that way."

"It's all right." Iris's voice was sleepy. "Family is the best at catching us by surprise."

"I've spent fifteen years running from House Azure. I've rebuilt my life from the wreckage my father made of me. When I saw her, saw Beatrice, standing there it felt as if I'd been running in place. She is everything I was expected to be."

"You're Captain Adi Crestone, feared pirate and fierce mother. That's a legacy and a life you can be proud of."

Adi nestled into the hollow of Iris's collarbone. "I haven't captained a ship in three years, and I haven't seen my son in seven." Tears threatened to overwhelm her again. "What kind of legacy is that?"

"You're doing your best." Iris kissed the top of Adi's head. "You rejected life in a noble house and live amongst us common folk. Ours is a hard life."

"And sometimes just as cruel. What an idiot I am."

"I admire you for it."

"You do?"

"What would have happened if you'd stayed?"

"Father would never have let me keep a child of rape, born out of wedlock."

"Then you saved your son's life before he was even born."

Adi smiled at this kindness. Family was a taboo subject among the women of Stella's Echo. They were not ashamed of their work, but many of their relatives were. A woman gave up her relatives when she came to the Echo, exchanged her old family for a new one. That transition was easier if the old family went unmentioned. Adi was an exception. From Lucas to Rehka and now Beatrice, Adi's past spilled into her present. Iris had seen some of her scars, and Adi wondered if that meant Iris would show a few of her own.

"What about your family?" Adi asked.

"I was born on Highgaard," Iris said. "A small village near the equator called Akroté. My father harvested lumber, and my mother spun cotton into yarn. When I was ten, consumption struck our village. My mother was one of the first to succumb. My father never really recovered. He grew depressed and listless. Finally, the foreman had no choice but to let him go. Money was tight and my father sold my sister and me to the Daughters of Light."

Adi sat up to look Iris in the eye. "You were a nun? If only your Sisters could see you now."

Iris smiled but did not laugh as Adi had hoped. "The Daughters sent us to a monastery on Behl, offering aid and succor to the miners there. I received my citizenship and was educated in the worship of Phoebe, Goddess of Light." Iris made the sign of the Ring. "My sister and I spent a dozen happy years there."

"Where is your sister now?"

"My sister is a diplomat and a politician. She worked her way into leadership of the order and was promoted to Abbess at Luxandra Abbey on Tyre."

"I've seen Luxandra Abbey." Adi said with reverence. "It's beautiful."

"I have not. My sister invited me several times to join her there, but I declined. After a while, she grew tired of asking."

"Why didn't you join her?"

"I met a man. We fell in love and were married. I left the Daughters of Light and moved into his house. He was a structural engineer for a large silver mine. He did well and I wanted to move my father in with us. But he had used the money from selling us on drink and when it was gone he hung himself. I hadn't known."

"I'm sorry, Iris." Adi shifted and stroked her arm.

"I'm not. He was craven and he took the coward's road. Now my sister and I will never see him in celestial Avernus in the next life."

"What about your husband?"

"After five years, I was unable to conceive a child, so he left me for another woman. I was devastated. I even thought about following in my father's footsteps." She blinked away tears. "The Daughters of Light wouldn't take me back, not even with my sister's intervention. So, I came to Xys to start a new life. I worked as a server in a tavern until it became a White Rabbit establishment. I didn't want any part of the gangs. One of the other serving girls got a job at a brothel and offered me a spot. I took it without knowing what I was getting into. The owner was a louse and a drunkard. He beat us, soiled the merchandise, and carried on in a despicable manner." Iris scoffed, her eyes distant. "One night, Stella and Verdun came in to settle a dispute between the two brothels. I never heard the details, but Stella saw how weak and undernourished I was and bought my contract on the spot." Iris shrugged.

Adi hadn't expected such a story. "You're an impressive woman, Iris."

"As are you, Adi, despite being too hard on yourself. You're not the only one struggling to overcome your past, you know. If you let people in once and a while, you might see that."

"I let someone in once. It ended badly."

"Rehka?"

Adi nodded.

"Has it ended?"

Adi leaned against the wall and ran her hands over her face. "I thought it had."

Iris waited for her to continue.

"Three years ago, Rehka betrayed me and ran off with an alchemist who claimed he could restore her connection to her Dragon. That broke me. I continued as captain of the *Snowcrest* for another year, but we weren't successful. Then we took heavy cannon fire on Behl, and I couldn't afford the repairs. I took out a loan from the Blood Queen. When I couldn't pay that either, I became indentured." Adi tapped a dirty fingernail on her collar. "I never heard from Rehka until she showed up here on Lensday."

"And now?"

"She says she still loves me, but—"

"But what? Do you love her?"

Adi opened her mouth, closed it again, and shrugged. "She abandoned me three years ago, and then she lied about her reasons for returning. I don't think I can love a woman I don't trust."

"You're a wise woman, Adi Crestone."

Adi grinned, then wanting to lighten the mood, said, "I was called many things during my time on the *Snowcrest*, Adi the Wise was never one of them."

Iris chuckled. "What did they call you?"

Adi leaned her head back. "Do you have anything to drink?"

Iris rose and took a wineskin from a drawer in her makeup table.

"Hiding the good stuff, are you?"

"Hardly, it's leftover communion wine from last Valeday service. The Daughters of Phoebe may not take me back, but the local temple is understaffed so they let me help with the services."

"You stole this from nuns?" Adi laughed as Iris poured two glasses.

She grinned at Adi. "Don't tell."

"They called me Crestone the Scourge on Karis," Adi sipped the wine. It was a white that tasted of pears and sun fruit.

"They did not!"

"They did. On Aleph, a judge once referred to me as Adi Bonestealer."

Iris covered her mouth in mock terror. "How frightening,"

"It's a long story."

They continued along that vein for some time, laughing and drinking through the evening hours. When the room grew dark, Iris lit the lantern. The wineskin was soon empty, and the two women stayed on Iris's pallet trading stories of pirates and nuns. Adi could not remember the last time she'd felt so lighthearted or laughed so much. All thoughts of Beatrice, her family, and dire prophecies faded into a haze of tipsy nostalgia, along with thoughts of Rehka, debts, and responsibilities. Through the open window Adi heard a distant clock tower chime midnight.

"I guess you don't have to work?" Adi asked.

"I asked Stella for the night off."

"Doesn't that mean you'll have to work Valeday and miss services?"

Iris nodded. "It's not a big deal. When Beatrice came, I knew she had to be related to you. I know family is a sore spot, just like for the rest of us. I wanted to make sure you were okay."

Adi flushed from the wine and Iris's concern. "Thank you."

Iris leaned in and kissed Adi, who overcame her surprise and returned the kiss. Iris's lips were moist and pliable. She moved closer, straddling Adi, cupping her neck with a delicate hand, moving her hips against Adi's. Adi gave herself over to the rhythm of it, burying her fingers in Iris's thick curls. Iris nipped Adi's lip, and her breath caught in her chest.

Then Iris pulled away. "You're going to leave, aren't you?"

"What?"

"Once this business at Alhambra's is finished, you'll go to Tyre."

"I have to," Adi said. "I must make sure Lucas is safe from the Blood Queen, and it's time I reconnected with my son."

"Take me with you."

Adi leaned back so fast that she struck the back of her head against the wall. She winced.

"I'm done being one of Stella's girls," Iris said, "I want to go with you. I could finally visit my sister."

Adi saw determination in Iris's amber eyes. "Why?"

"Because I like you, Adi Crestone, and because you need someone to remind you that you're not alone."

"I can't buy out your contract from Stella."

"I can deal with Stella. Will you take me with you?"

Adi had no idea what Rehka's plans were after Alhambra's and discovered that, at that moment at least, she did not care. The memory of Rehka professing her love on the steps of Bale's shop did not move Adi.

"Yes, I will," Adi said.

"I want to be asked like a proper girl."

Adi leaned forward to press her forehead against Iris's. "Will you come with me to Tyre?"

Iris squealed with delight. Adi laughed. They kissed with renewed vigor until Adi's teeth hurt. She pulled Iris's loose shirt over her head and ran her hands over that perfect olive skin. She kissed the nape of Iris's neck, the hollow in her shoulders, her breasts, and bit playfully at one nipple. Iris gasped then moaned with pleasure.

They made love then on Iris's pallet, and afterward Adi fell into a deep and dreamless sleep.

# CHAPTER FORTY-THREE

# THEO VANGUARD

## MOON OF XYS, SOLANDAY, 1ST OF LUXOR

Theo awoke to a flurry of activity at the governor's mansion, so he had a late breakfast in his rooms to avoid the commotion. When he finally ventured forth, the long meandering hallways were full of people. Soldiers stood straighter at their posts in their starched dress uniforms. Servers and cooks bustled back and forth, and Theo caught the savory aroma of roasting boar. Tabitha sat in a wheelchair in the banquet hall, directing a small army of servants as they decorated the hall. They hung garlands and banners, laid tablecloths, polished glassware, and lit the expansive silver chandelier which hung from stout roof beams high above.

"Tabi," Theo said over the din, "what's the occasion?"

"My lord husband desires to feast the delegation to Djinnar before tomorrow's departure. The entire delegation will attend, along with our honored guests."

Theo observed that all the decorations were the alternating midnight and sky blue of the sibling gods Djinnar and Pallantier, gods of destruction and creation, respectively. The two were opposite sides of a coin, their worship and rituals often combined.

It would be a day of introductions and farewells. His father would arrive on the HMS *Penumbra* accompanied by Lady Hannah Valefyre. He would have one day with his betrothed before the delegation's departure.

*What will we say to each other?* Theo wondered. He realized he had little clue how long the trip to Djinnar's residence on Maxon would take. *A week? A month? What about the wedding?* He pushed thoughts of Hannah Valefyre aside.

"The high chancellor is the honored guest?" Theo asked.

His cousin grimaced. "Your father and his entourage arrived early this morning."

"He wasn't supposed to arrive until this afternoon."

"I think he enjoys arriving early and throwing everyone into a panic."

"That does sound like him." Theo meant it as a joke, but it landed flat. "Is he here, now?" Theo glanced around, worried that his father might suddenly stride into the room. It would be their first face-to-face meeting in four years. Theo needed time to prepare himself.

"No, he and Lord Gambol are meeting with several congressional representatives in the small chamber of Congress. The Lady Valefyre is here, however, in the statue garden."

Theo decided to avoid the statue garden.

"Dinner begins at four," Tabi continued. "Your father requests your presence in Lord Gambol's study for lunch. Are you all right, Theo? You're paler than I am."

Theo nodded, his gaze unfocused. He considered fleeing the palace.

*Where would I go? The Thistledown? A hurried charter off-moon? I have no money.*

Theo had disobeyed a direct order from his father only once before when he had enlisted as a naval officer in training. He had not visited his father's estate in the royal city of Thail since. It was not difficult to stay away. The navy often sent Theo on long assignments, and Lord Vanguard only summoned his sons when he needed something from them. Tonight was his first summons since that time. Now he was expected to do his filial duty.

*What about Beatrice?* Theo wondered, then chastised himself. *She was never yours to lose.*

"Theo?" Tabi repeated.

"I'm fine," Theo said. His head was spinning. The suddenness of it all left him numb and paralyzed, a startled animal. He had received the letter only two days ago.

"The Lady Valefyre would love to meet you," Tabi said. "A first introduction without your father present would be a fortuitous thing."

"I should prepare for dinner. I ran all over the city yesterday with my brother. I need to bathe and tend my injury, then dress for dinner. Have you seen my father? Is he wearing mourning?"

"He is. I'll have hot water brought to your rooms." Tabitha put a hand on his arm. "There are worse fates than the love of a beautiful woman and wealthy estates, Theo."

He looked down at his cousin, abashed. Here she was, so weak that she needed a wheelchair and yet so strong. Theo knew that the billowing sleeves of her dress hid the red, inflamed skin of Feverfire. She was childless, her husband had debauched tastes, and she was relegated to this dying, desert moon.

He sighed and gave a slight bow. "You are right of course, cousin. I beg your pardon; it has been a long week."

"No apology necessary. Go, prepare for dinner. I will delay the Lady Valefyre a while."

Theo excused himself, but on his way out of the banquet hall, he nearly collided with Arthur Volaticus.

"Theo!" the Faelani squirrel beamed. "You must meet my family."

"Art," Theo mustered false enthusiasm. "What are you doing here?"

"The governor invited the members of the delegations and their families to spend the day on the grounds." Behind the acolyte of the Sons of Destruction was clustered a scurry of Faelani squirrels. Art gestured to the golden-furred woman holding a young kit tight to her breast. "This is my wife, Violet. Violet, this is Sir Theo Vanguard."

She did her best to curtsy and flicked her tail. "A pleasure, Sir Vanguard. Thank you for undertaking this journey with my husband and keeping him safe."

"Call me Theo, please."

"I told you, beloved, we are only going to Maxon. We're barely leaving the Empire. There's nothing to worry about."

"Be that as it may, I feel better knowing Theo accompanies you." She shifted from foot to foot, a shy person awed by a tall stranger. Art rescued Theo from speaking by introducing his children.

"This is my oldest, Arthur Volaticus III."

Theo extended his hand. "Pleasure to meet you, Art."

"Please call me Arthur," the lad said, his chin high and tail stiff. His tufted ears twitched even though he stood at attention. Theo guessed him to be twelve or thirteen.

Art laughed. "He is insistent on that point. The next is my daughter Bella."

Bella curtsied and her tail quivered.

"This one, who insists on carrying her stuffy everywhere and sucking her thumb is Mary."

Mary curtsied without removing her thumb from her mouth and nearly tripped on the hem of her dress. She met Theo's eyes, though. Hers were curious and confident, which surprised him.

"Pleased to meet you, Mary," Theo said, giving her a small bow.

"And our youngest there is Thomas, after my father-in-law."

"You have a beautiful family, Art. It is a pleasure to meet you all, but I must beg your pardon, I need to prepare for the festivities." Theo extricated himself from the eager family of squirrels and fled down the hall toward his rooms. Twice he got lost in the winding corridors of the palace but eventually found his accommodation. There was already hot water steaming in the bath and a fire in the hearth. Theo's formal family suit with its heraldic touches hung in the wardrobe. Lord Vanguard must have brought it with him. His flesh prickled at the thought of his father's servants in his rooms when Theo was out. Not that Theo possessed anything on Xys. Still, it felt like a violation.

He stripped off his clothes and lowered himself into the bath with an audible sigh. He would have a few moments of peace before the evening. The wound on his hand—the bite from Crestone's goon—burned. He unwound the bandage to reveal it, covered in the green paste the physicker had given him. Even so, the edges were red and puffy. He closed his hand into a fist to fight the stiffness and wondered if he should call for the physicker.

*No time,* he decided.

The servants had added salt and fragrant oils to the bath and the warm water relaxed him. Theo inhaled and enjoyed his guilty pleasure; baths were not available on a naval vessel. Theo visited bathhouses whenever they were in port, though he hid this habit from his men, who would have given him no end of grief had they discovered his penchant for womanly bathing. He missed his men, missed the direct life of a battleship. There were chores to do, a strict hierarchy, life's missions were handed down by orders from leadership. Theo had strict parameters for all his decision-making, thanks to extensive military protocols.

Never had he felt as adrift as he did these past few days. The choice between discipline and chaos on a naval ship was an easy one, and, so far, for Theo, never a life-threatening one. Now he was juggling conflicting orders from his father and Governor Gambol. His father, as high chancellor, would try to ensure that his preferences prevailed. But the real conflict was between his father's commands and Theo's wishes.

He dozed in the bath until a knock at the door awakened him. Before he could respond, the door opened and Beatrice entered. Her blue hair was disheveled and her eyes were red-rimmed and puffy from crying. Theo started to stand and bow, until he remembered where he was. He quickly sat so the water covered him and flushed; his towel was out of reach. The Lady Marrion ignored Theo's embarrassment and took a shaky seat facing him.

"Lady Marrion, perhaps you might give me a moment?"

"I went to visit my sister last night."

Theo blinked, then realized what she had said. "Crestone?"

Beatrice nodded. "She lives in a brothel near Torhan Square. After our... conversation, I needed to see her. I wanted to practice seeking the things I want, like a relationship with my sister. My husband had men follow me, and now Adi's cover is blown. He says he will report her location to the authorities."

"Crestone is a pirate and a thief."

"She's my sister!"

"She wears a Blood Queen collar of indenture."

"She's going to think I betrayed her."

"She left me to starve in a dilapidated shed. I have no affection for Crestone. Why are you telling me this?"

Beatrice wrung her hands and stared at him. "Because I thought you would understand."

Theo stared back, transfixed by her brilliant blue eyes, the curve of her jaw. The tears only made her more beautiful. Theo sat forward and took her face in his hands. He kissed the tears on her cheeks. She nuzzled against him despite his wet skin. Theo relaxed against her.

This wasn't about his feelings toward Crestone, and he understood a thing or two about complicated sibling relationships.

"Would you hand me that towel?" Theo asked when Beatrice's tears finally stopped.

She obliged and turned her back to him as he stood, water running off his body, and stepped from the tub. He was grateful for the adjacent dressing screen. He dried himself, wondering what time it was. Despite their previous assignation, he was anxious about her seeing him naked in the full light of the room.

Beatrice's voice quavered. "I'm sorry, I have no one else to tell."

Theo knocked his injured hand against the screen. "Djinnar's blood."

"I will leave you. My apologies."

"No, Beatrice, please excuse me. It's only my hand. I fear the edges of the wound are infected."

"Shall I summon the physicker?"

"What time is it?"

"Half past eleven."

Theo swore again, this time under his breath. He was supposed to meet his father in Lord Gambol's study in a quarter of an hour. Theo was not dressed and it would take him at least five minutes to navigate the palace. He was going to be late. No one, especially not a younger son, made the chancellor wait. "No time."

He wrapped the towel around his waist and emerged from behind the screen. He could feel Beatrice's eyes on him as he made his way to the wardrobe. Theo did not usually feel abashed by his nudity. Sailors often bathed in the sea or stripped down on brutally hot days, but he had never been sized up by a noble woman, much less a married one. He had been with women before, but always in brothels and always in the dark. He was acutely aware of the light reflecting off his damp skin as he avoided glancing in Beatrice's direction. Once he retrieved his suit, he retreated behind the screen once more.

"What should I do?" Beatrice asked.

"Crestone is a criminal," Theo insisted. "Her warrant is a consequence of her own actions." Theo felt guilt rise in him once more like bile. If Theo had not murdered the man in Opus Station, the city watch might not have issued their warrant. Crestone was going to take the fall for Theo's crime. Ironic, as she doubtless had many crimes of her own.

*She held me prisoner,* Theo reminded himself and *embarrassed the* Dragonhammer.

"They would be within the law to execute her," Beatrice said.

Theo pulled on his pants. "For killing a White Rabbit thug?"

"It's murder in the eyes of the law. A watchman is dead."

Beatrice paced the flagstones before the fireplace.

*For the city watch, it is two birds with one stone,* Theo thought. Theo wanted to clean and wrap the wound before pulling his shirtsleeve over it. The physicker's ointment sat on a stand beside the tub. He emerged from behind the screen, hunched as if that would hide his naked torso. He picked up the bottle but had difficulty unstoppering it.

"Let me help," Beatrice insisted taking the bottle from him. "Show it to me."

Theo held out his hand. Beatrice removed a small knife from her bodice and prodded the inflamed edges of the bite. Theo winced and sucked in a breath.

"It's not too bad." She took a washcloth from the stand, dipped it in the bath water, then began to gently puncture the infected regions, wiping away the pus with the cloth. Theo felt both pain and relief. A small laugh escaped his lips.

"What?" Beatrice's eyes were focused on the wound.

"You're not what I expected."

"What did you expect?"

"I pictured prophets as austere matrons who only speak in riddles, never concerning themselves with the problems of mere mortals."

Beatrice snorted and clear snot left from her crying escaped one nostril. Since Beatrice's hands were occupied, he took his handkerchief from his trouser pocket and wiped it away. She looked up, startled. The knife slipped into the flesh of Theo's thumb.

"By the void!" he swore and drew back his hand, sucking at the beading blood.

"I'm sorry!" Beatrice cried. "You surprised me."

Theo took his hand from his mouth. "I'm sorry. I shouldn't have touched you like that."

Her smile was weak as he placed the handkerchief in her outstretched hand. "Thank you."

Beatrice unstoppered the ointment.

"I'll finish."

She dabbed the foul-smelling green goo onto his palm. "We're not so aloof as all that," Beatrice said, picking up their conversation where they left off. "I'm a mere mortal like the rest of you lowly folk."

"I am learning that. I know one of the Ring Guard here, a Grym sergeant who served briefly on the *Dragonhammer*. I could ask her to deliver a message to Crestone. I wouldn't ask her to deliver it to Crestone directly, aiding and abetting a fugitive would put the sergeant's station at risk, but she could get it to an intermediary."

"Stella Volpes," Beatrice said immediately. "She runs the Echo, the brothel where Adi stays. Tell her to expect a raucous city watch presence this afternoon. Please hurry, I don't know if Hubert has already sent runners to the watch, but if not, he will soon. He'll be delighted if Adi is captured." Beatrice shuddered but finished wrapping a fresh bandage around Theo's hand.

"What is Hubert's interest in all this?"

"He has a... history with my sister. You will send the sergeant?"

He coughed. He felt queasy at the mention of Lord Marrion. "I will."

*Now I'm aiding and abetting a fugitive. One who has taken on the burden of my own crime. One whose hand is forced by the danger to her son. She can't recover Apyreon for me if she's in jail, and I know Isaiah is up to something else.*

He started when Beatrice placed her free hand on his cheek. Her fingers were cool and he leaned into her palm. He stared at her lips and shivered, remembering them pressed against his skin.

"Thank you, Theo." They stared at each other for a long moment. It felt wonderful to be her knight in shining armor. He wanted to kiss her.

*How can Hubert be such a fool?*

A crash of dishes shattered the silence. Theo quickly stepped away from Beatrice. On the threshold of the open door stood a young woman. She wore a white dress, with a blue sash to honor the divinities. A silver tea tray lay dashed at her feet. She gaped at them, her face was as red as her hair, which cascaded in loose curls to her waist. Theo had only seen her once four years earlier at a ball in Thail the night he snuck off to enlist.

It was Hannah Valefyre.

"My lady," Theo said, bowing low and composing himself. "Please forgive me, this is not as it seems."

"It *seems* the Lady Marrion attends you in the bath." Valefyre's voice trembled and tears glinted at the corners of her green eyes.

"I wounded my hand," Theo said. "Lady Marrion was kind enough to clean and dress it." Theo held up the bandaged hand for his betrothed to see.

"There are no physicker's available?"

"No, my lady," Beatrice said. It did not help that it was clear she had been crying a few minutes before.

"When you didn't come introduce yourself in the statue garden, I thought I would surprise you and escort you to your father," Valefyre said. "I see that was a mistake."

"Lady, please," Beatrice insisted. "We—"

"I don't want to hear it." There was rage in her voice now. Her furious gaze traveled from Beatrice to Theo and back again. Then she kicked the teapot across the room, spraying hot water across the carpet. Hannah shrieked and fled from the room.

Theo and Beatrice winced.

She started toward the door and said, "I should go. I am sorry about this. Please don't forget about the sergeant."

Theo nodded. "I won't."

He rushed to don the rest of his uniform and finished just as the palace clock chimed noon.

# CHAPTER FORTY-FOUR

# ADI CRESTONE

## MOON OF XYS, SOLANDAY, 1ST OF LUXOR

Iris and Adi enjoyed a leisurely morning in bed. When they finally joined the others downstairs in the Echo's tavern, it was lunch time. Adi's wounds hurt, but she felt more refreshed than she had since accepting the Apyreon job over two weeks ago. The early afternoon air seemed cleaner, the sunlight through the windows crisp and inviting.

"It's a relief to see you looking happy," Stella said from behind the bar counter. Iris grinned and Adi flushed. Stella looked amused.

"I didn't expect it in the midst of all this," Adi said taking Iris's hand. "But I'm happy."

There was a sharp knock at the door and Verdun answered it. Adi tensed; her joy replaced by fear. She peered beyond the Ankhim brewer and saw a stout Grym woman. She wore a cloak, but underneath Adi discerned the insignia of the Ring Guard.

*They sent not just Imperial soldiers, but elite Imperial soldiers,* she realized. Her weapons were upstairs.

Verdun finished his conversation and shut the door with slow deliberation and turned to face the group. He nodded curtly to Stella.

"You need to leave, Adi," Stella said.

The few patrons in for lunch looked up, concern on their faces.

"Are you throwing me out?"

"That was a sergeant of the Ring Guard," Verdun said. "She informed me that the city watch is on their way here to arrest you."

"Why would a soldier do that?"

"Apparently, Theo Vanguard sent her."

Iris clung to Adi as she stood.

*Why would Theo warn me?* she wondered.

Stella said, "Run to one of your safe houses. I would hide you if I could, but I can't have the city watch tearing up my business."

Adi quickly pulled on her boots. She had to lay low somewhere until the sale tomorrow night. She had a safe house near Duneharrow, an abandoned guard post from when the debtor's prison held more inmates. She looked out the front window.

"Djinnar's blood," Adi swore, "they're here."

Iris pushed Adi aside to peer into the street. A whole contingent, twenty soldiers, were coming down the alley toward Stella's Echo. Henge led the company.

Adi clambered upstairs to collect her things. Her body and mind felt sluggish.

*The happiness was a nice fiction,* she thought.

Angry fists pounded on the door.

Adi raced back into the tavern and headed for the back door. *Time to go.*

Two patrons looked up in surprise when Adi plowed into their table, tipping their mugs of ale to the floor. She hurdled the foamy mess as light reflecting off armor glinted over the dimpled glass panes of the front windows. Adi bolted down the back hallway, past Stella's rooms, the laundry, and the bath to the rear exit. Adi opened the door, revealing half a dozen Imperial Guards. There was a moment's hesitation as each side recovered from their surprise. Adi found her wits a split second faster and slammed the door shut in a soldier's face.

Adi backtracked through the tavern. Angry voices were demanding to know what was happening. A patron called for a fresh drink on the house as Adi had spilled his previous one. She missed the turn up the back stairs and collided with him. He fell onto the table, split it in half, and hit the floor. Wood fragments and beer foam scattered everywhere.

"Sorry," Adi gasped and leapt up the stairs.

Henge's shrill voice cut through the clamor. "Adison Crestone, you are under arrest. By the authority of the city watch—"

Iris stood at the top of the stairs holding Adi's tricorn. "You forgot your hat."

"After her!" Henge shouted from below.

"Thank you, Iris." Adi kissed the woman, snatched up her hat, and bolted down the hallway. Vivian's room was at the end, and her balcony had a ladder to the street that was used in case of emergencies. Adi hoped the city watch had not put troops there.

She kicked open Vivian's door with a grunt. Vivian was mending her clothing. She shrieked in surprise and dropped her needle and thread.

"Adi, what in the void!?"

Adi pried up the window. "Sorry, Viv. I need a quick exit." She stepped onto the balcony and surveyed the alley. No watchmen waited. She glanced down the hallway through Vivian's open door in time to see Henge reach the top of the stairs.

"Adi, stop!" she bellowed when she saw her.

Adi swung onto the ladder and scrambled down.

*Where to run? First I need to lose the watch, then I can go to the safe house by Duneharrow.* Adi took off down the alley as Henge emerged onto the balcony. She rounded the corner and realized she would have to pass the front door of the Echo. She hoped all the watchmen were inside.

Arms and legs pumping, the adrenaline of the chase masking the pain of her bruised ribs, Adi ran. Behind her, the door to Stella's Echo banged open and Henge yelled, "Stop, Crestone!"

Adi ran faster.

*I only need forty-eight hours. Just. Two. Days.* She struggled for breath. *Then I'll be gone.*

Two city watchmen stepped out of the end of the alley, cutting off Adi's route to the main street, and Henge's long, loping strides covered twice the ground of Adi's frantic, unsteady ones.

On her right, Adi's spotted the side door to a restaurant. She whispered a prayer to the Goddess Phoebe that the door was unlocked. It was. Inside, four cooks were preparing meals for the patrons. One sweated over a stone hearth, rotating a large sizzling spit of lamb.

Adi knocked over a young man carrying a stack of dishes to the washbasin. She grabbed a set of shelves to keep her feet. The weight of it kept Adi upright, but her momentum tipped the shelves forward. Everything crashed onto the floor, pots and pans flew, and several ceramic vessels containing dry rice and shell beans shattered, their contents spilling across the kitchen. The cooks shouted, and one tried to grab Adi, but she dodged him.

Henge appeared in the doorway, panting, but had to pick her way over the fallen shelves and the slippery rice-strewn floor. Adi dashed into the dining room. It was full of lunch customers. Adi squeezed between bodies, tables, and chairs, apologizing as she went.

She finally burst out the front doorway and onto the main street. She paused to gulp in a deep lungful of fresh air. The two city watchmen from the alley spotted her and charged. One called, "You there!"

Adi ran. Behind her, the *clomp-clomp* of booted feet blurred as other watchmen joined the chase.

What she needed was a distraction. *The market!*

She made a sharp left into an alley packed with trash cans. The watchmen made the turn, so Adi heaved over several metal cans, spilling trash across the path behind her. She emerged onto another broad avenue with more traffic and sprang between vehicles. She tried to dodge an oncoming brougham but tripped and sprawled to the street. Adi threw herself sideways to avoid the crushing hooves and wheels and rolled through something hot and squishy.

*Horseshit.*

"Djinnar's blood," Adi swore, then she was up and running again. The shouts of her pursuers grew louder as she reached the far side of the street. There was more foot traffic here, and she spied the dense crowd of the marketgoers ahead of her. If she could get into the milling throng, she could disappear.

Adi stumbled again on an uneven cobblestone but caught herself on a lamppost. She leaned against it. Her lungs burned. A stitch in her side grew more uncomfortable by the second and her battered ribs ached, but she pressed on. She was so close.

A blow across the back of Adi's head made lights explode in her vision. Her feet kept churning, but her upper body went limp and she collapsed, thrashing. A blurry shopkeeper stood over her, holding a broomstick. He had seen the chase and decided to assist the watchmen. Darkness crept into the edges of Adi's vision.

Adi spotted Henge, her face flush with triumph and exertion. Two more soldiers bounded up and loomed over Adi. They hauled her to her feet, but her knees would not cooperate, so they had to hold her up between them. Henge laughed and looked as if she might hit Adi in retaliation for the pursuit. Adi blinked and shook her head, frantic. Her eyes would not focus.

*I do not have time to be arrested. I must do something!* But she could not think straight. Her head pounded. She wanted a piece of that smug shopkeeper.

Henge arrived, panting, with several more watchmen. One of them shackled Adi's wrists as another removed Adi's sword from her belt and patted her down for more weapons. They waited in the street surrounded by curious onlookers as the jail wagon pulled by two gray mares rolled toward them. When it arrived, watchmen escorted Adi to the back and tossed her inside. A length of chain secured her manacles to the floor. The watchmen shut the door and the carriage rolled away.

# CHAPTER FORTY-FIVE

# THEO VANGUARD

## MOON OF XYS, SOLANDAY, 1ST OF LUXOR

Theo stood outside Governor Gambol's office, hand poised to knock. His father stood on the other side of that door. The trajectory of Theo's life would be different after this conversation. For four years, his father had seemed a distant looming sentinel. Now the high chancellor was on Xys expecting Theo to play the role of dutiful son.

He took a deep breath and knocked.

"Enter!" A delicate rasp underlaid his father's powerful voice. The man was aging. This brief reminder that his father was mortal, that he was not omniscient, steeled Theo's nerves. He opened the door.

Lord Simon Vanguard, high chancellor to the Solan emperor, patriarch of House Vanguard, stood over the governor's heavy desk flipping through a thick stack of vellum documents. His dark hair was still cropped short in the military style, the ends of his ample mustache waxed and impeccably curled, but now everything was shot through with white. Theo bit back a gasp. He belatedly realized his father was staring at him over severe square spectacles waiting for the expected obeisance.

Theo cleared his throat, dropped to one knee, and lowered his gaze.

"High Chancellor," Theo intoned, "I am honored to be in your presence. Welcome to Xys... Father."

Silence stretched between them for so long that Theo broke tradition and looked up. Simon Vanguard met his gaze, but his expression was unreadable. Theo noticed the large lapel pin gleaming on his father's shirt. It was the symbol of his office, an amber Solo with rings of meteorite.

"You're late," said his father, gesturing toward the ticking grandfather clock near the door. Theo took his father's speech as an invitation to stand.

"Sorry, Father." Theo kept his voice low.

He glanced around. The study was empty except for the two of them. A large oil painting hung over the mantel of a dark fireplace.

"Are you?" his father asked.

"Am I what?

"Honored to be in my presence?"

"Of course, Father. It is only that I expected you later this evening."

Lord Vanguard sat in the governor's large chair. He motioned for Theo to take a seat across the desk. Theo sat. The leather upholstery creaked as he tried to make himself comfortable under his father's scrutiny. After a few moments, Theo gave up.

"I received your letter," Theo said to break his father's judgmental gaze. "Why are you here? I will retrieve Apyreon. I learned the details of its whereabouts yesterday. There is no need for you to involve yourself."

Lord Vanguard glanced surreptitiously around the room.

"The emperor has asked me to personally investigate the extent of the damage wreaked on Xys as a consequence of its decaying orbit."

"Are there not engineers and geologists who could be trusted? Why send the chancellor?"

"He is punishing me."

"Why?"

Lord Vanguard removed and polished his reading glasses. "Despite your belligerent insistence on joining the navy, you are still my son, loyal to me and House Vanguard."

Theo nodded automatically. "Is that a question?"

"As my dutiful son, I am trusting you with information that, should it leave your confidence, will result in the execution of both of us."

Theo swallowed and his voice cracked as he said, "You speak of treason to an officer in the Imperial Navy."

His father waved a dismissive hand. "You're done playing officer. It is time to do the work of real men." Theo opened his mouth to object, but his father spoke over him. "The emperor wants Xys destroyed."

"How can that be?"

"He will use Apyreon to accelerate its destruction. That is why I hid it away. He knows I do not approve of this and he suspects that I am working against him.

"Does he know Apyreon is lost?"

"I assume your brother Isaiah has reported it, which is why he is here."

Theo swallowed. Four years of absence from Imperial court intrigues and now he was thrown into the thick of it. "Isaiah is here on other business. He is working with Water Knife mercenaries to procure a necklace that once belonged to a Lady Brixton."

The high chancellor considered this while dozens of questions whirled through Theo's mind. He had spent the last two days wishing to be taken into his father's confidence. Now that he had, he wished only for the simplicity of command on the *Dragonhammer*.

"What does the emperor stand to gain by destroying Xys?"

To Theo's surprise, he saw sorrow on his father's face. "That is the reason I did not object to being sent here. I hope to learn the answer to that question myself. The emperor is corresponding with one of Solvigant's gang lords, a Devlin Seneschal."

"Does Isaiah know?"

"Your brother is the messenger between the emperor and this thug. I cannot trust him with this, and neither can you. His time as a void mage has... estranged him from the family. His only loyalty is to the emperor."

Theo rose from his chair, walked to Governor Gambol's liquor cabinet, and poured them both a stiff drink. His father took a timid sip. "You have met Lady Valefyre, I understand."

Theo blushed and held up his wounded hand. "Lady Marrion was only assisting me in the care of my injury."

"I assume you require no further help from Lady Marrion?"

"No, Father. Of course not." Theo uttered the words without thinking. So many thoughts were churning through his head that he couldn't single one out.

Lord Vanguard waved a hand. "It is done then. You will make up with your betrothed tonight at dinner."

"Make up? I hardly know the woman. She is a child, Father."

"She is sixteen. Your mother was fourteen when we wed."

Theo thought of the pale waif who was his mother, cowed and defeated after five sons, one now dead. She had found refuge in Passerine mysticism and opium and her eyes perpetually leaked tears. He thought of Tabi and her slow, painful death while her husband slept with all the young housemaids. Theo wanted no part of those fates. He wondered who warmed his father's bed these days, then pushed the thought aside.

*I will be better to Lady Valefyre,* Theo promised himself.

"What role does she have in all this?"

"A man risking his life for empire over emperor needs heirs."

"She is breeding stock then. I do not want a wife who is no better than a cow."

Lord Vanguard laughed. "I think you will find Lady Valefyre more to your liking than a common heifer. Plus, it is time for you to marry. If you're going to participate in court life, you must appear respectable. She may be young, but Lady Valefyre can teach you a thing or two about life in high society. And we need allies. If it comes to open hostility between me and the emperor, we need powerful allies."

Theo drained his glass to buy time to collect his thoughts. "What of Joshua?"

"Your brother is my heir. I need the emperor to believe I am growing old, more concerned with my House and grandchildren than in affairs of state. No one suspects a grandfather in his dotage of being a poisonous serpent in the grass. If all goes according to plan, neither the emperor nor his wife will ever suspect our involvement.

*"Our involvement."* The words echoed in Theo's mind. *I am involved now.*

"Joshua has no heirs," Theo pointed out. "It makes no sense that you would appoint him as yours."

His father grimaced. "Your brother will wed the young Lady Aretha Castleton in a fortnight."

Theo tried to imagine his brother siring children and failed.

"Governor Gambol has ordered me to accompany the embassy to Djinnar."

"I know, and I approve. We must do everything in our power to give Xys a chance to survive."

"Do you think Djinnar will allow it? What of Pallantier? Do you know where they are?"

His father shook his head. "I do not pretend to know the minds of the gods. If Djinnar himself comes to Xys's aid, the emperor can hardly carry out whatever plans he has for the moon's destruction."

Theo reeled at the idea of the emperor actively seeking to destroy one of the World System moons, one of Solo's children. *What could he hope to gain?*

Lord Vanguard handed Theo a letter. "Our time grows short. Governor Gambol will return soon. Sign this."

"What is it?"

"Your resignation from the navy."

Theo bristled. His father had not changed. Even when discussing treason, his father treated him like the child he had been at their last meeting.

"I do not want to leave the navy, Father," Theo said. "Can I not wed and remain an officer?"

Lord Vanguard laughed. "Our family does not need a dreadnought captain or a naval bureaucrat."

"Paul was a soldier." It was as close as Theo could come to saying *"Why didn't you tell me Paul was dead?"*

"Paul was a colonel." His father looked pained. "If he had returned from the Maxonian campaigns he would have been promoted to general and eventually been appointed to the military high command."

"I too could rise to high command."

"No!" Lord Vanguard slapped the desk. Theo flinched. "I will not allow it."

*Could it be he doesn't want to lose another son?* Theo wondered. *Is he afraid of losing me? Certainly not, considering the cavalier way he is risking my life now.*

Theo had never heard an emotional or encouraging word escape his father's lips for anyone other than his wife and Paul.

"I love the navy, Father. It is where I want to be. I will help you thwart Xys's destruction, but let Joshua run the estates."

"I have other plans for Joshua."

Theo wondered what his father had planned for Theo's slow, sentimental brother, but his father had plans for everyone and everything. Still, Theo could not imagine his brother holding his own in the Emperor's Council. Lady Castleton would run circles around him.

"If I refuse?"

There was danger in his father's laughter this time. "I am willing to consider your enlistment as nothing more than youthful exuberance. I am willing to forgive you for your trespasses against this family. I would make you Lord of Balan. The Balan Estates are the primary financial driver of House Vanguard. Without them, we would not have come so far, and we would be unable to continue to expand our influence. I would make you steward of these lands, master of the Vanguard purse strings, the caretaker of the foundation upon which all our fortunes are built. Is that so terrible?"

"No, Father, but it is not what I want."

"I do not care what you want!" Lord Vanguard shouted, his face purpling. Theo shrank back into the chair. His father took a deep breath and collected his thoughts. When he spoke again he was quieter, more controlled, "You will take this power I am giving you. You will marry Lady Valefyre and go to Balan. You will do your duty to me as head of House Vanguard or"—his father paused to run fingers through his hair—"or you will be disinherited, no longer a member of House Vanguard, no longer my son. And when the rings of Solo smash into Xys, you will gaze upon its destruction and know that it is your fault. You will know that it could have been avoided if you had agreed to do your god-cursed duty!"

Theo blanched as if struck. "Father, I—"

Lord Vanguard held up a hand to silence Theo. "Think carefully before you finish that sentence."

Theo opened his mouth to reply further, but there was a knock at the study door.

A servant's voice came from behind the stout wood. "Lord Vanguard. There is a senior inspector from the city watch requesting the presence of your son."

"Tell him to wait."

The door opened, and Theo saw it was one of his father's personal servants. Any of Gambol's men would have been flogged for presuming to open the door without being explicitly ordered to do so.

"What is it?" Lord Vanguard demanded.

"My lord, the inspector is here with a whole battalion of men and a warrant. He says you must produce Theo or he and his men will enter the palace and arrest him."

Lord Vanguard rose. Theo saw anger in the deep creases at the edges of his father's mouth.

"Who is this inspector?"

"He is Senior Inspector Solomon Broc," the servant replied.

"Theo, do you know this man?"

"Yes, Father," Theo replied, fear growing in the pit of his stomach. "He claims he is seeking the same pirate captain who stole your yacht, but he has been nothing but trouble for me and Isaiah."

*He is here to arrest me for murder.* Theo was certain of it. *He knows it was me and not Crestone.*

"We will have a word with this inspector," Lord Vanguard said, his voice clipped. "Theo, come with me."

Together they followed the servant through the sprawling corridors of the governor's mansion to the main entrance. Broc and his men were crammed into the small front courtyard.

"What is the meaning of this?" Lord Vanguard demanded without introduction. Broc looked the nobleman up and down, his eyes resting on the broach before widening in recognition. Broc dropped to one knee. His men, confused, followed suit.

"High Chancellor," Broc said doffing his hat, "I was not aware you were a guest here this evening."

"You have not answered my question, badger."

Broc bristled but did not rise to the bait. "I am afraid, my lord, that I have a warrant for the arrest of your son."

"What, me?" Theo burst out. "What for?"

"For your actions at Opus Station," Broc said.

"What actions?" Lord Vanguard demanded.

Broc was still on one knee. "Your son, accompanied by known pirate captain and Blood Queen gang member, Adison Crestone, participated in a raid on a city watch station two nights ago. Two men were killed, one a watchman, and certain objects were stolen from impound."

"You lie," Lord Vanguard hissed.

"I do not, my lord," Broc said.

"Theo, tell the inspector he is mistaken."

"I have numerous witnesses," Broc said.

"Criminals, I'm sure."

"And the half dozen city watchmen who pursued them from the station."

"Theo, tell the inspector he is mistaken."

Theo glanced over his shoulder toward the main entry. Lady Valefyre stood there watching, one hand braced against the door frame. Theo tried a weak smile. His betrothed did not smile back.

"Theo!" his father shouted.

Theo turned back to the inspector. He could deny it, but then he'd have to go inside and face a long afternoon with his father and Lady Valefyre while he contemplated treason and broken oaths. To heed his father was to accept his role as traitor to the emperor he had sworn to serve when he joined the navy.

*I killed a man in Opus Station*, Theo reminded himself.

"I was there," Theo said at last. "I was pursuing a lead in the problem you assigned me."

Broc rose and took a pair of manacles from his belt.

"You will not put those on my son." Lord Vanguard's voice was calm with fury. Theo wondered if his father might harm the inspector, even here in front of all these men. What would they do? The chancellor answered only to the emperor. Lord Vanguard may not be above the law, but he was as close as one might get in the Solan Empire. Did that grace extend to sons? It appeared not.

"I will come with you, Inspector," Theo said. "The manacles are not necessary."

"You will do no such thing!" spat Theo's father.

"Father, I will not spit in the eye of Xys's laws." Theo took a step towards Broc, a step away from the governor's mansion and all the obligations it now represented. He felt a sensation of relief.

He took another step.

Lord Vanguard grabbed his shoulder.

"You and your solicitor may visit first thing in the morning," Broc explained to his father. Theo wondered if he resisted, how many of Broc's men would obey their commanding officer and how many the chancellor. He did not want to find out. He did not want to start a brawl amongst the city watch on the governor's—his cousin's—doorstep.

"It will be all right, Father," Theo said with a calm he did not feel, "I will be fine for one night."

His father's hand dropped from his shoulder. "You will provide my son with his own cell."

"That is customary for nobility," Broc said, as if he regularly arrested elite members of the aristocracy. Theo took another step towards Broc.

"I am disappointed in you, Theo," Lord Vanguard said from behind him.

"I know, Father."

With that, Theo allowed the city watch to lead him through gate and toward a waiting prison coach.

"Hold please," the Lady Valefyre said when Theo had one foot on the step. Everyone turned their attention to the newcomer. "A word with my betrothed before you haul him away."

Broc glanced from one to the other, then shrugged. Theo thought the Faelani inspector had been prepared for the arrest to be much more difficult. Broc and the watchmen stepped away from the couple and averted their gazes. Theo could not meet Hannah's eyes.

*What could she want?*

She stood on tiptoe and kissed his cheek. "Take care, my betrothed."

Theo could only wonder. *What new game is this?*

"Fear not the darkness, my love, and hear the light within you," she said and placed one hand on his cheek. Her tone had all the seriousness and heavy benediction of a prayer, but it was not one with which Theo was familiar. He stared at her, confused and dumbfounded. He noticed a tattoo on the inside of her wrist: a stylized sun, a circle, and eight wavy lines, four long and four short.

"Let's go," Broc cut in.

Hannah Valefyre held Theo's face a moment longer, then turned back toward the palace. Theo watched her go as Broc read Theo's rights before ushering him into the coach.

# CHAPTER FORTY-SIX

# ADI CRESTONE

## MOON OF XYS, SOLANDAY, 1ST OF LUXOR

"You were supposed to bring me information about your attackers," Broc told Adi, "not exact revenge in a city watch station."

Adi rolled her shoulders. Her captors had not removed the manacles in the hours since her arrest or before dragging her into an interrogation room.

"Can I have a cup of coffee?" Adi asked.

"You're so cavalier about murder?" Henge sneered.

"I'm sure you're heartbroken. One less gang member in Solvigant."

"You want a medal?" Henge said. "A watchman is dead."

"I told you, Palestrina is responsible for his death. You know how to find the Red Wyrm?"

"Convenient, to be surrounded by murderers so you can keep your hands free of blood."

Adi laughed. "You're just jealous. Those laws really cramp your style, don't they? Given who your father is, I bet you could get away with murder. Are you a vigilante, Henge?"

"You're sick."

"Careful, Broc. Your partner wants to be a hero."

"Shut up," Henge said.

"Just be honest. You don't care about Rictor. You're embarrassed I snuck into your watch station."

"That's enough," Broc said. He rubbed the bridge of his furry nose.

"You look tired," Adi said.

"Henge, would you get us some coffee please?" Broc asked. Henge bristled then spat on the floor at Adi's feet and stomped out of the room toward the mess.

"Her self-righteousness is going to get you killed," Adi said.

Broc scratched under his eyepatch. "Tell me something I don't know."

"There are plenty of Blood Queen agents who won't be as friendly as I am."

"You hate her."

Adi grinned.

"So, you admit you're a Blood Queen agent?"

Adi snorted and rolled her eyes. They had shackled her hands to the table, so she inclined her neck to show Broc the inflamed skin around the edges of her collar.

"What powers of deductive reasoning you have."

Broc sighed and stood to pace the room.

"We have a lot to talk about," Broc said.

Adi's ears still rang from the shopkeeper's blow. She tried to rub the back of her head, but the manacles prevented her.

"I want to press charges against that shopkeeper."

"That shopkeeper is getting a reward for his assistance in the capture of a wanted fugitive."

"He can use it pay the physicker who treats me."

"We had a deal, Adison."

"It's not my fault you couldn't bring Royal in. He wasn't part of the deal anyway."

"You were supposed to come to me with any information about the White Rabbits."

"I did. The Iron Dirigible was your mess. How was I supposed to know there was a void mage in Solvigant?"

Broc sipped from his hip flask. "We had Rictor in custody until you murdered him."

"The world is a better place for it." Adi wanted to say that Theo Vanguard had killed Rictor, but the statement stuck in her throat. She had seen Broc bring Theo in and wondered if the guilt-ridden naval officer had confessed already.

"That's not a decision you get to make."

"You know I'm right. One less White Rabbit goon in the city is a good thing."

"And one less Blood Queen thug?"

Adi gritted her teeth.

Broc took another sip, then offered the flask to Adi. He had to tip it up so she could drink. Adi coughed as the harsh liquor burned her throat.

"You'll hang for this, Crestone."

"I doubt it, Inspector." Adi tried to stifle the fear in her voice. "You respect your job too much to make idle threats. Anyway, you should let Henge make them, she's better at it."

Broc sighed and put away the flask. "You came to me, remember? My men saved you from a beating in the warehouse district."

Adi closed her eyes, her head throbbing. "I owe my life to many people more powerful than you, Inspector."

"Since then," Broc continued, ignoring her interruption, "fights between White Rabbits, the Blood Queen's men, and Water Knife mercenaries have been breaking out all over the city, and you're always in the middle of it. I want to know what's going on."

"You're the inspector, you tell me."

"By Yeom's beard, there's a void mage in my city, looking for you. I could have left you out there for him to find."

"Leading me to the noose doesn't feel like a rescue."

"You murdered a man in cold blood in a watch station!" Broc growled. "I have a roomful of eyewitnesses who saw you cut Rictor down."

"They're lying and you know it."

"It won't matter."

"Because they're White Rabbits and I'm a Blood Queen indenture?"

"Because Commander Vanguard is the youngest son of the high chancellor. Why was he there with you? What are you two looking for?"

"What's in it for me?"

"I'll ask the arbiter for leniency in your sentencing; incarceration instead of the noose."

"No deal." Adi could tell Broc hated to be in the dark. She wanted to take full advantage of his discomfort. "Here are my terms: you let me go—"

Broc laughed. "Not a chance."

"Let me finish." Adi spat on the floor and she saw there was blood in the phlegm. She must have bitten her tongue when the shopkeeper whacked her. "Give me a day and a half to settle my affairs. Then I will turn myself in to you Millsday morning. You let me do that and I'll tell you everything."

"Even if I wanted to do that, Adi, which I don't, there's no way I could let you go. My superiors would have my job. But that is beside the point. I don't trust you. You only came to me about the Iron Dirigible when you realized you couldn't manage it yourself.

Then you made the whole watch look foolish at Opus Station when you broke into the evidence lockers and murdered Rictor.

"I didn't break any the evidence lockers," Adi insisted. *Palestrina!*

"I suppose it's a coincidence Lady Brixton's necklace went missing the same evening?"

"Djinnar's blood, Broc, I don't even know who Lady Brixton is. I didn't steal any necklaces."

Broc studied her. "Who did?"

Adi shrugged. "This is the first I'm hearing about that theft."

Broc chuffed in exasperation. "Here's the deal, Crestone, and it's the only deal, so listen carefully. You tell me what is going on or you hang tomorrow."

"If I'm going to the gallows," Adi shot back, "I would rather go sooner than later. Give me a day and a half of freedom, then you can hang me." Inside, Adi reeled. She had to figure a way out of this. The sale was tomorrow and without Apyreon there was no guarantee for Lucas's safety.

"What are you so afraid of?" Broc asked. "Why not just tell me?"

"Are you a priest of Strolen, Inspector, that I should confess my sins before I die?"

"If you don't tell me what's happening, I have no choice but to let you hang. You've been at the center of every incident this week. I must conclude that if I remove you from the equation things will calm down."

Adi laughed at this. "I don't know what the end game is here, but I do know it's much bigger than me."

"What do you mean?"

"There's a *void mage* in Solvigant. They only answer to the emperor. If they're involved it's bigger than me, bigger than you. You said so yourself, the gang violence started weeks ago. I arrived on Millsday."

"If you're worried about the void mage, I can keep you safe."

"No, you can't. I saw him boil your watchmen from the inside out at the Iron Dirigible."

"We don't have much time, Adison. Arbiters, lawyers, and watch leadership are about to become involved and I'll lose whatever ability I have to protect you. They want to make an example of criminals who kill under their noses. You've embarrassed them, and city watch leadership doesn't like to be embarrassed."

Adi sat in silence for a while, then said, "Come with me."

"What?"

"Be my escort until Millsday morning."

Broc rubbed his whiskers. "Believe it or not, Crestone, I have better things to do than run around the city with criminals all day."

"No, you'd rather chase after them, clueless about their true intentions." Adi could tell the inspector was intrigued.

"No. Your proposal breaks every protocol. Even if I thought it was a good idea, and it isn't, my bosses would never allow it. How about you tell me your relationship with Congressman Marrion instead?"

"Why do you want to know?"

"So, you *do* have a relationship with him?"

"You know I do or you wouldn't be asking."

"He's in the lobby and has requested to speak with you."

Adi paled. "I have no connection to the congressman. I don't want to speak with him."

"Does he work for the Blood Queen?"

"Xander?" Adi said, her surprise evident. "Never."

"How would you know?"

"I've never seen him round the Red Wyrm."

Broc suppressed a yawn.

"You need sleep, Inspector," Adi said. "Why don't we pick this up later?"

"You'll be dead tomorrow. The hangman has little patience and the city watch has less for criminals who embarrass them."

"Are they really such fragile men?"

"You murdered two men under their noses."

"We both know I didn't wield either blade."

They were silent for a moment as they stared at one another. Henge returned with two mugs. She set one in front of Broc and the other where Adi could not reach it with her shackled hands. After watching Adi struggle, Broc pushed it into her hands. Adi leaned in to slurp from the rim of the cup. She chuckled after the first swallow.

"Something funny?" Henge asked.

"Thank you for the coffee," Adi said. Henge opened her mouth to fire back but closed it again when Adi said nothing further.

"If you didn't go to Opus Station to murder Rictor, why were you there? And why were you there with Theo Vanguard?" Broc asked.

Adi scowled at the oily surface of her coffee.

"I'll tell you what I think: You stole a pleasure yacht from Lord Vanguard, but I don't think the theft was really about the ship."

"I'm a pirate," Adi said.

"Not a very good one," Henge said.

Adi blinked. Her vision briefly bifurcated. *I wonder if the shopkeeper gave me a concussion.* "You're awfully hard on a woman chained to a table."

Broc returned to his chair, ignoring their banter.

"There was something on that ship," Broc said.

"How do you figure?" Adi replied.

"Why else would you and Commander Vanguard team up?"

"We're not teamed up."

"Whatever you want to call it. You and Theo were after the same thing. What is it?"

"Why would I tell you that?"

"So, you were looking for something."

Adi grimaced, realizing her mistake.

"You're going to hang for the events at Opus Station. High Chancellor Vanguard is pressing charges over the theft of the *Sidereal.* Either you plan to run, or whatever affairs you must settle for the Blood Queen will kill you."

*Broc is good.* Adi sipped her coffee and considered her answer. *If I tell him, I must tell him everything. Lucas, Apyreon, the device's potential, Rehka... Everything, and I must do it in front of Henge.* Adi was developing a grudging admiration for Broc, but she didn't trust Henge, or the city watch. *If I talk, the Blood Queen will learn of it.*

"You'll have to trust me," Adi said.

"Trust requires reciprocity. Tell me what you were doing at Opus Station and who you're protecting with your silence and I will consider giving you one day under city watch guard to get your affairs in order, if it doesn't involve any further illicit activity."

Henge's eyebrows shot up. "That's not procedure."

A knock at the door saved Adi from having to respond. A young city watchwoman leaned in and handed Henge a scrap of paper. She read it, sighed, and passed the note to Broc.

Broc chuffed and crumpled the note. "Tell him he has to wait until my interrogation is complete."

"He insists it must be now. He has a tight schedule."

Adi watched Broc. She could tell he wanted to say no, but the expression on his face indicated he couldn't.

"Send him in," Broc said. The watchman disappeared. "Congressman Marrion insists on seeing you, now."

"I have nothing to say to the congressman," Adi protested. "Send him away."

The door opened again and Xander Marrion entered. He cut an impressive figure in his full congressional uniform, a wide blue sash over russet jacket and trousers. The tailored jacket sported blue epaulets and accentuated his muscular physique. A dozen pins and medals glinted on the sash, and he held a russet cap with a blue brim under one arm.

*He's on his way to Congress,* Adi realized.

"Inspectors," Xander said greeting both Henge and Broc with a firm handshake.

*The consummate politician.*

"I apologize for interrupting your interrogation. I will keep this brief."

He waited, and there was an awkward pause until both inspectors realized Xander expected them to leave.

"I don't think you should be alone with the prisoner," Broc said.

Xander gave them his best politician's smile. "Your concern is noted, Inspector. Should anything happen to me I will not hold the watch responsible. She is chained after all. But I must insist on a few moments alone with the prisoner."

"That's against protocol, sir," Henge said.

"I can get a Writ of Injunction from watch command, if need be," Xander offered.

Henge blanched at the mention of the city watch high command.

"That won't be necessary." Broc stood and offered Xander his chair. "We will be right outside. If you need anything, just shout."

Xander sat "The prisoner seems sufficiently secured. I do not foresee any issues."

Adi caught a brief glimpse of two of Xander's personal guards as the inspectors left the room.

The door closed, leaving Adi alone with Xander.

"It's good to see you." Xander laid his hands over her shackled ones. Adi briefly allowed the contact, then pulled away.

"I cannot stay long. I am on my way to Congress to introduce the motion for peripatesis."

"Have you negotiated for my release?"

"You lied to me," Xander said. His voice was cold and flat, distant. Gone was the politician's warmth and charm.

Adi put her head on the table and sighed. Her crossed arms muffled her voice. "What do you want, Xander?"

"An explanation, Adi. You asked me for money to pay off your debts. Now I hear you're gallivanting around Solvigant with the Lady of Spiders murdering people. You told me you were going to recover a star key from White Rabbit thugs and be off to help Lucas. What was the money really for?"

Adi looked up. "It *is* to help Lucas."

"Liar. You were broke and needed money to finance your next binge. You don't care about Lucas. If you did, you'd visit him more than once a decade. This is about Adi being Adi. Then you cut me out, only to beg me to save you again. I'm done being your patron saint of lost causes."

Adi lowered her voice. She imagined Henge with her ear pressed to the other side of the door. "The star key is more than that. It's a unique ancient artifact with extensive powers. I had it and I lost it when those White Rabbit thugs jumped me in the warehouse district. I needed money to retrieve it, or Ajax's men are going to hurt Lucas. Royal has the device now, and that White Rabbit goon at Opus Station knew where. I wasn't lying about that part. Riven knows where Lucas is; she threatened his life."

Xander sat back taking it all in. "Does Lucas know?"

"I didn't want to scare him."

"You mean you didn't think he'd take you seriously or even read your letter."

Adi studied the wood grain of the table.

"When was the last time you saw him?"

"Three years ago," she mumbled. "When I left the *Snowcrest*."

"Let me ask it this way: When was the last time *he* saw *you*? When was the last time you visited him instead of lurking in the shadows at a distance?"

Adi shrugged. She didn't want to tell Xander that it had been seven years.

"He doesn't want to see me," she said instead. "But if you get me out of here, Xander, I'll go to him. I promise you won't have to worry about the two of us ever again."

A pained expression settled onto Xander's face. "You're a cruel woman, Adi Faide."

"It's Crestone."

Xander sighed. "Why do you think I'm here?"

"To get me out of here! I still have time to recover the artifact and save Lucas."

"I can't do that, Adison."

"Why not!?"

"The Blood Queen knows about Lucas. Do you think she will discard such leverage once this task is done? She owns you forever, Adi."

"What are you saying?"

"That Lucas will only be safe if you're free of the Blood Queen."

"What do you think I'm trying to do!" Then realization dawned on Adi. "You're going to let me hang."

"No!" Xander said.

"Then why are you here?"

Xander glanced nervously toward the door. It remained shut. He cleared his throat. "Marry me, Adi."

"Excuse me?"

"This is the last time I'll ask. Marry me, and I can make all of this go away."

Adi growled in exasperation. "No, Xander."

Xander took her hand. Adi tried to pull away, but he held on. "Listen to me, Adi. I know you do not love me, but we can help each other. Marry me and I will settle your debts with the Blood Queen. No more piracy, no more collar of indenture, and you can be a mother to Lucas. He can come here, go to school here. We can be a proper family."

"Xys is dying. Plus, it's about more than money now. The Blood Queen won't release me until the artifact, Apyreon, is in her possession."

"If this Apyreon is as powerful as you say, we must find another way. We can't give such an object to a dangerous criminal. Let me help you."

Adi's stomach churned and she felt sweat on her cold palms.

"You met with Sasha Riven," Adi said, terror building in her chest making it difficult to breathe.

"You're missing the point," Xander said.

"What did you offer her?"

"It doesn't matter."

Adi leaned as far from Xander as the manacles would allow.

"Adi, what in Djinnar's name?"

"What did you offer her?" Adi repeated.

Xander looked crestfallen. "Xys is dying. What do you think she wants? That is all I will say while sitting in a city watch station."

"Xander, you idiot! Do you think the Blood Queen will treat you any differently than she has me? You've given her leverage over a congressional delegate. Of course, she'd rather have you than me. You won't wear a collar, but you'll be indentured just the same."

"But you won't be!" Xander shouted. Adi flinched.

"I won't marry you, Xander. I'm sorry."

"Why not?"

"Because I don't love you."

"So?" His voice was rough with hurt.

"You love me."

"I never—"

"It's obvious, Xan. I would never do that to you. I would never saddle you with an unhappy marriage to a woman who doesn't love you and a son who's not yours. That's not freedom for either of us. You would be compromising everything for me." Xander blinked away tears and Adi saw anger there. She steeled herself.

"Stop being so selfish, Adi. You say you want to help Lucas, to save him, then, by Phoebe's blinding light, do it. You would be the wife of a lord. We could make a family, no more piracy. I am offering you your freedom, everything you claim to want, yet you throw it in my face. I gave up my family for you, my home."

"I would have to admit my lineage or you would lose your titles. Then my father would know where I am. Stop, Xander, just stop. I don't want anything from you."

He rose and loomed over the table. "You just want my money, is that it? I'm sure my brother has already written your father."

Adi hadn't considered that. She suddenly felt more trapped. "I don't want your money either. Do you think I enjoy traipsing through the congressional building and slinking into your office every time I need something?"

The door opened and Broc poked his head in. "Everything all right in here? I heard shouting."

"Get out," Xander growled.

Broc looked at Adi, who nodded. He left the room.

"I can still save you, Adi, save Lucas."

"I would rather serve out my sentence, than saddle us both with a lifetime of unhappiness."

"Your sentence is death, Adi. Death by hanging. Will you risk your life and the life of your son for your own pride."

"I don't want you to save me, Xan, just help me get out of here. Then I'll be out of your life and you can move on."

"You had no qualms asking me to play banker and long-distance father when you wanted to run off with Rehka to live like you were in one of those stupid Maxon Laird stories."

"I was a child, Xander. Rehka was the first person to ever ask me what I wanted!"

"You never wanted me."

"No, I didn't. I was twelve when my father betrothed me to you. No twelve-year-old knows what they want. Twelve-year-olds don't understand what betrothal means."

"I would have saved you from all of it, from your father, from the streets of Solvigant, from Stella's, from Rehka's pain. You have always rejected me."

"I don't love you, Xander."

"I don't care."

Adi recognized the lie, but she didn't call him on it.

"I do not care, Adi. I would still save you from everything, from yourself!"

"You didn't save me from Hubert," Adi snarled. She wanted to hurt him. She wanted him to leave. *How dare he come here and pretend to be a hero? As if my life could ever be as simple as his fantasy.*

"What did you say?"

"I said, you couldn't save me from your brother. He raped me. I bore his son. He took everything from me. Yet you stand here pretending to be my knight in shining armor trying to rescue me from all my bad decisions! How dare you!"

"Adi, I didn't mean—"

"Shut up," she roared at him. The door banged open. Henge and Broc burst in. Broc's hand was on the hilt of his dagger, but she ignored them both.

"You want to blame someone for ruining your perfect life? Look no further than that monster who is your brother. You want to be a hero? Go save someone else. I don't need you! I don't want you."

"You ungrateful... whore!" Xander spluttered. Adi flinched, expecting him to hit her, but he only slammed his fists onto the table. Adi's coffee sloshed out of the mug.

"Congressman, it's time for you to leave," Broc said.

"I'm not finished here," Xander snarled.

"Go, Xan," Adi said.

Xander looked at Broc and back to Adi. She had never seen Xander so angry.

"You'll never get your old life back, Xander. You've done enough, tried hard enough. The gods have been cruel to you, your family has been cruel to you. Make a new life. Forget about me."

Xander trembled with rage and humiliation and she could not predict what he might do next. She wished that she were not shackled to the furniture. She had never cut him so deeply.

"Go, Xander," she said again, her voice soft, resigned. "Build a life with someone who deserves you."

He reached inside his jacket and everyone tensed.

"Congressman..." Broc warned.

"Xander, don't," Adi pleaded.

But Xander merely withdrew a marriage contract. He wadded it up and threw it at Adi then stormed from the room.

"What, by the Nine gods, was that?" Henge asked. "Who are you, really?"

Adi could not answer. She was sobbing too hard, clutching the crumpled papers to her chest, dampening it with her tears.

"That's enough interrogation for now." Broc said.

Henge rolled her eyes, but Broc unlocked Adi's hands from the table and helped her stand. He was strong for his size. She leaned heavily against his shoulder as he escorted her back to her cell.

# Chapter Forty-Seven

# THEO VANGUARD

## Moon of Xys, Solanday, 1st of Luxor

Theo woke from a nap to the harsh light of the setting sun burning stripes onto his face through the barred window of his cell. He yawned, stretched, and pulled back the thin blanket. He had slept surprisingly well despite the lumpy mattress. A bucket of water stood inside the door. Theo gulped water from his hands, quenching his parched throat until runnels of water dripped from the corners of his mouth. He unwrapped the bandage on his left hand and winced as the inflamed edges of the wound caught. Then he rinsed his hands and face and dried them on his shirt. Without a fresh bandage or the physicker's ointment, Theo had no choice but to rewrap his palm with the old bandage.

"Excuse me," Theo said to the guard sitting on a stool outside the cell trying not to watch him too obviously.

"Yes, sir?" The guard, a young woman with dark hair, snapped to attention. Theo guessed she had only recently graduated from cadet to full watchman.

"It is 'my lord,'" Theo corrected her.

"Apologies, m'lord, I am unaccustomed to noble prisoners—er, guests." She blushed.

"Is there dinner to be had?"

"No kitchen at the post, my lord, but there may be some fruit in the mess."

Theo waved both hands to indicate she should go inquire. The guard hesitated briefly before disappearing through the far door. Theo heard the thud of her boot heels diminishing. When he was certain she was gone, he took the lid off the waste bucket in the back corner of his cell, emptied his bladder, and sighed in relief.

The door swung open, and Theo barely had time to lace his trousers before the guard entered holding a pair of oranges in one hand and a cup of coffee in the other. Theo took them and thanked her. She half-curtsied before remembering that he was, in fact, a prisoner.

Theo was finishing the second orange when the door opened again and Inspector Broc entered, trailed a moment later by his lanky partner Becca Henge and Theo's brother Isaiah. Theo's guard shot coffee from her nose at the sight of the void mage. She made the sign of the Ring and fled the room. The three newcomers did not notice and stood before Theo's door. Broc took one of eight keys that jangled at his belt and unlocked the cell.

"Sir Theo Vanguard," the Faelani inspector said, "you're free to go with apologies from the city watch for your brief incarceration."

Theo sat on his cot and stared at him. "What about Opus Station?"

Broc's attention kept sliding to the void mage. "I have a signed affidavit here indicating that you were acting as an agent for the chancellor."

Isaiah smiled at Theo beneath the skull mask, "The emperor thanks you for your service, brother."

Theo stood and stepped toward the strange trio. The situation baffled him. "I killed a man."

"Our witnesses—" Henge began, her voice tight.

"White Rabbit thugs," Isaiah cut in.

"—our witnesses claim Captain Crestone wielded the blade."

"You have her in custody?"

Broc nodded. "We do."

"What will happen to her?"

There was a long pause before Henge answered,

"She murdered a prisoner being held in custody in cold blood inside a watch station and a heroic member of the city watch. Not to mention resisting arrest, and she's a known affiliate of the Blood Queen. Crestone was also seen in the company of Palestrina, Lady of Spiders. Your father, Lord Simon Vanguard, is pressing charges for the theft of his yacht, the *Sidereal*. She will hang. As should you."

Theo thought Henge sounded excited at the prospect.

"Inspector," Isaiah said, chastising her.

Broc held up a hand to stifle any further disagreement. "The terms of your release, Sir Vanguard, are that you will leave Xys with the delegation and not return for one year."

Theo could not take his eyes off Isaiah. *Does he know about Father's plans?* It would be difficult for Theo to help save Xys if he were banished from the moon.

"Should you not abide by these terms," Broc went on, "you will be charged with violating a legal contract in contradiction to your charter as a naval officer. Do you understand?"

Theo nodded. Should he return to Xys before the year ended, he would be dishonorably discharged from the Imperial Navy.

*Father is forcing my hand,* Theo realized. Both Isaiah and his father were manipulating him, and Theo felt powerless to stop it. "I understand."

"Very well, then. You are free to go."

Theo cautiously stepped out of the cell.

*Captain Crestone is going to hang for me.*

Becca Henge opened the door to the room and motioned for the two men to lead the way.

Theo and Isaiah headed for the exit.

"I have one question," Broc said from behind them.

Theo turned.

"What was the nature of your mission?"

Theo was momentarily confused. "Mission?"

"For the chancellor."

"That is sensitive information," Isaiah interrupted. "It is not contained within our agreement for a reason."

Broc sighed and rubbed the bridge of his nose. "Were you successful?"

"Again, Inspector—" Isaiah said, but Broc cut him off.

"I only want to know if I should expect more of the chancellor's agents cavorting around Solvigant with known criminals, infiltrating watch stations, and murdering folks. That seems only fair to me."

Theo thought about telling Broc everything right there. The people of Solvigant deserved to know the emperor wanted to destroy their moon.

*I can't commit treason if I'm in jail.*

Isaiah took Theo's elbow with firm, cold fingers. "Come, brother. Father has prepared for your departure."

*I bet he has.*

"No, Inspector," Theo said. "I was not successful."

Isaiah hustled him from the room.

"You're not above the law," Henge hissed at the brothers as they walked past her. Isaiah paused to glare at the young inspector. He was shorter than Henge, but the power and myth of void mages rolled off him like a physical force. Henge thrust out her chin in defiance before wilting and looking away.

Isaiah smiled. "House Vanguard answers only to the emperor's justice, not to backwater yokels with tin badges."

Henge stiffened but did not reply. Theo and Isaiah left the room.

"Oh, Theo," Broc called. Theo hesitated, his back to the Faelani. "I have already filed a report with your superiors at Naval High Command. I expect they'll open an inquiry. And congratulations on your wedding. The Lady Valefyre seems a decent woman. You are a lucky man."

Theo's shoulders slumped and he allowed Isaiah to lead him down the hall.

Lady Valefyre was waiting for them at the entry to the station. Her russet hair was disheveled and she was fanning herself briskly with a white lace fan that matched the opalescent accents on her green dress.

"Where is Father?" Theo asked when it was apparent the chancellor had not personally come to the station.

"He has better things to do than deal with your self-righteous foolery," Isaiah hissed.

"It is good to see you unharmed, Theo," Lady Valefyre said. "I have heard dreadful stories about how petty watchman might treat a prisoner." His betrothed, Theo noticed, did nothing to acknowledge Isaiah's presence.

It was all Theo could do not to pull away under the soft press of her lips on his cheek.

"Thank you... Hannah," Theo managed as she took his arm in hers.

At that moment, Broc and Henge emerged from the hallway followed by a young boy. He was crying and tugging on Broc's waistcoat to get his attention. Theo watched the lad with a growing feeling of familiarity.

"You can't hang her, Sol" the boy said between sobs. "You can't."

Inspector Broc growled in embarrassment, "She made her own choices, son. She's a pirate and a gangster."

"You're the young lad from Castes. Ion wasn't it?" Theo said, dropping Hannah's arm and taking a step toward the lad.

The boy looked at them and shouted in alarm. He dove behind Broc, then peered out from behind the inspector's back.

"You're a monster! You killed my grandfather."

It took Theo a moment to realize the boy was looking at Isaiah, not him.

Isaiah's voice was full of menace. "You're the brat from Castes."

"You two have met?" Theo asked.

"Ion here provided directions when my men and I came ashore," Isaiah said.

"You were her prisoner," Ion said, recognition dawning on his face as he looked to Theo. "You both want to hurt Captain Crestone." The boy looked as if he might start wailing again at any moment. "They're going to hang her because of you!"

"She will hang because of her own choices," Broc insisted.

"I will take care of the lad," Isaiah said.

"No!" Ion shouted. "Don't send me with that man, Broc."

"You will do no such thing," Broc said.

"I speak with the voice of the emperor," Isaiah said, stepping forward. To his credit, Broc did not flinch.

"You bring a Writ of Release signed by the emperor himself and I will turn the boy over to you. Until then, he stays here."

Silence reigned in the watch station as everyone waited to see what the void mage would do. It was Theo who broke the tension.

He touched Isaiah's shoulder and said, "Come, brother, the boy is no threat to you."

Isaiah brushed aside the contact, but relented, his stance softening.

"Our carriage awaits," Lady Valefyre said from behind the brothers.

The three of them left the station and Broc followed them out.

"I am still waiting for compensation from the Imperial Treasury for the damage done to Solvigant at the Iron Dirigible," he said to Isaiah. "I will file a formal complaint if I do not receive it soon. I'll be adding a death benefits penalty for the life of that child's grandfather."

"Careful, Inspector," Isaiah replied. "You wouldn't want to share the same fate as your late partner."

Theo was already inside the carriage so could not see Broc's face, but he heard an unmistakable animal growl. Isaiah climbed in, shut the door, and waved at the furious Broc, who was still sputtering on the steps of the watch station.

The ride home was silent except for the wind that made the carriage creak on its springs. Hannah Valefyre sat beside Theo, his brother across from him. Theo noticed his two companions were reticent to make eye contact with one another. Isaiah kept clearing his throat as if to speak, but he would remain silent after a sideways glance at Lady Valefyre. Theo tried not to feel like he was heading to his own execution.

*I felt freer in a prison cell.*

His father had once again turned the situation to his advantage. While Theo was free from his immediate legal troubles, he now had no choice but to be complicit in his father's schemes. The formal inquiry would ruin his naval career, and if he betrayed his father they would both hang for treason. His father was a brilliant tactician, and for the first time Theo found some comfort in that admonition.

*Did he arrange for my arrest, assuming I would need convincing?* Theo knew he would drive himself mad with speculation. He sat between his brother and his betrothed and tried not to let the defeat show on his face.

They arrived back at the governor's mansion as the evening's festivities were ending. Tabi greeted them at the door, the first of Theo's relatives to look worried for him. She ordered servants to draw him a bath, to start the laundry, and to find food for her cousin. Her concern touched him. Theo excused himself from the entire company and wandered through the twisting corridors to his rooms.

As the leader of the delegation, he wondered if he ought to make an appearance, but he could not muster the enthusiasm to face a room of nobles and the high chancellor. He arrived at his rooms and sank gratefully into the waiting bath. He hoped Beatrice might come to inquire about him. He was eating a late dinner in his rooms when there came a timid knock at the door. When he opened it he saw it was not Beatrice, but Hannah who stood framed by the dim light of the hallway.

"Good evening," Theo said and waited while Hannah examined the empty room. "Would you like to come in?" She hesitated on the threshold, then stepped into the room. Her shoulders were stiff, and Theo could tell she was fighting the urge to wring her hands.

"Am I interrupting?" she asked.

"I was just finishing dinner. Thank you for coming to the station with my brother. I appreciate whatever role you played in helping to secure my release."

"You are my betrothed, it is my duty to support you, though I did not anticipate being betrothed to an adulterer accused of murder."

Theo blushed. He had not expected to be scolded by a sixteen-year-old girl. "I apologize, my lady. Things spiraled after the *Sidereal* was lost. I assure you, I intend to honor the marital arrangements my father has made."

Hannah sniffed. "I am glad you are no longer in prison. The nerve of that inspector."

"He was just doing his job."

"There are plenty of criminals in Solvigant with which he could occupy his time rather than harassing the nobility who hold this Empire together."

Theo struggled to discern whether Hannah was arrogant or naïve or both. "Well, as you said, that is behind me it seems. I leave for Maxon tomorrow. We will be wed in Thail when I return. Would you like to have dessert with me? Perhaps we might restart our acquaintance."

"I cannot," Hannah said, "one of us must represent you at the governor's feast, and you seem intent on hiding here. It is just as well. I have come to inform you that the high chancellor has arranged for us to be married tomorrow at the Temple of the Nine by Archdeacon Limon Heilig. Then I will accompany you to Maxon."

Theo choked. "You will?"

"I will be your wife. I understand we have a duty to provide heirs to House Vanguard with all haste. And..." she hesitated, swallowed, and found her voice again, "I will not allow my husband to spend weeks gallivanting around Maxon alone with the Lady Marrion."

Theo considered Hannah closely. Her lips trembled, and her red hair glowed in the firelight. She was the most imperious teenager Theo had yet met, though the list was short.

"You need have no fear, the Lady Marrion was—"

Hannah held up both hands for silence. There was such anger and hurt on her face that it brought Theo up short. Tabi had told Theo the girl had real feelings for him and was enthusiastic about the match. Theo had not thought that possible since they knew nothing of each other, but seeing the raw emotion play out on her face told him otherwise.

"I am going to give you the benefit of the doubt this time. You say you are faithful to the arrangements of your father, that it was a chance awkward meeting. I will accept your explanations. There are rumors at court that you are an honorable man, but I am no fool and I will not be made a cuckold."

Theo nodded, chastened but grateful. "I understand. Thank you, milady."

Hannah forced a smile. "I am glad we understand each other." Theo watched her don the emotional armor of court nobility. She stood on tiptoe and kissed him on the cheek. "I must return to the governor's feast. You have had a trying day. Rest. There will be plenty of time for us to get to know one another on our journey. You may even come to appreciate me as your wife."

"I have no doubt."

She looked him up and down, and Theo saw something much older in that gaze, more mature than her age suggested.

"Goodnight, my lord." Without waiting for Theo's response, she whirled in a rustle of skirts and was gone, leaving the door open. Theo shut it and collapsed back into his chair.

*Married tomorrow? If I was ever in control of the events in my life, I am not now.*

He awoke sometime during the night in a cold sweat. He had dreamed again of the sea of bones. The fire had burned out and the wind had blown open one of his windows. He must have left it unlatched this morning in his haste to visit his father. A headache was blossoming behind his temples. He wondered if there might be a decanter of whiskey on the sideboard but felt unmotivated to search.

He yelped when a slender hand took hold of his hair and pulled his head back. A moment later the cold steel of a blade rested beside his exposed neck. His eyes widened.

"You!" He strained against the grip. "What are you doing here?"

"You're going to help me free Crestone," Rehka said.

# Chapter Forty-Eight
# Theo Vanguard
## Moon of Xys, Djinnday, 2nd of Luxor

"This is still a terrible idea," Theo complained to Rehka.

"Thank you for sharing your opinion. Did I mention that I don't care what you think?" Rehka's words were sharp. "I am not going to let *her* hang for *your* crime."

They were sitting in a café three blocks from the station where the city watch was holding Adi. Theo could scarcely believe the turn of events his life had taken over the past week. He had gone from the first officer of an Imperial dreadnought to plotting a prison break with a mercenary and two pirates. Vista and Wright were all that was left of Adi's crew from *Sidereal*. Wright had been just as surprised to see the one-armed Ankhim as Theo had.

"I thought you were out of the game?" Wright had said when Vista joined them at the table.

Vista had shrugged. "She saved my life. I can't let her hang."

Wright had nodded and that had been the end of it.

*For a pirate,* Theo thought, *Crestone has saved a lot of lives. Mine included.* That's why he was here after all.

"What are we waiting for?" Theo asked Rehka. "The later it gets, the more people will be around."

Rehka looked toward the station and made a sign to a man in a bowler hat leaning against a lamppost. The mercenary checked her watch.

"It's time," Rehka said. "Theo, pay the bill."

"I don't have any money."

"You're a nobleman," Rehka growled.

"You kidnapped me from the governor's mansion at knife point. I had no chance to prepare."

Wright motioned for the server and handed her a pair of gold spyres. The server gasped in surprise.

"If anyone asks," Wright told her, "we were never here."

The Grym woman nodded enthusiastically. "I never seen you."

"Follow me," Rehka said.

Fifteen minutes later, they were crouched in the alley beside the watch station. Rehka clutched a crowbar.

"Does Adi know you sold her out to my brother?" Theo asked. Rehka's face was impassive, but her grip on the crowbar tightened.

"I had no choice. At least Lucas will be safe."

"You have more faith in my brother's word than I do. Even if his acolytes kill Ajax's men, do you think this gangster who calls herself the Queen of Blood will just leave him alone?"

Rehka looked at him with interest. Her gold-flecked green eyes and her height, even when in this position, marked her as a Dragon, but Theo still found her lack of shimmer odd. The air around other Dragons bent the light, indicating their connection to their reptilian form. They seemed unfocused, where Rehka's form was crisp.

"You don't trust your brother?"

Theo laughed. Rehka frowned and jabbed him in the ribs with a bony elbow.

"Kinship bonds the Vanguards," he said, "not trust."

"If he double crosses me—"

"You'll what? Fight a void mage? Another great plan. I'm beginning to learn how similar you two are."

"It's for Adi's own good. If she knew what I was doing, she'd understand."

"Yes, I'm sure it's pure altruism on your part. And if she'd understand, why the secrecy?"

"Why are you defending her? A week ago, you were her prisoner. She stole your father's yacht right out from under your nose."

"People who love each other don't go behind each other's backs."

"What do you know about it? You get your lover prescribed to you by your father." A movement in the street caught her attention. "Here come Vista and Wright," Rehka hissed, ending the conversation.

The two pirates slunk around the corner from the back of the station.

"Did you locate the cell?" Rehka asked.

Wright nodded. "Just off the back corner."

"Let's go."

They all followed Rehka behind the building. Halfway along the alley, a door squealed open and two watchmen emerged. The quartet ducked back around the corner. Theo heard the clunk of a trash bag deposited into a can, then the strike of a match. Moments later, he smelled pipe smoke.

"They could be there for an hour," Theo whispered.

Rehka shot him a look. They waited and listened to the two men's muffled conversation.

"Carrie nearly pissed herself when that void mage stormed in here yesterday."

"Aye, I woulda, too. I want no business with that demon."

Theo crouched against the timber wall of the station, his thighs cramping, and checked his pocket watch. Over a quarter of an hour had elapsed when Rehka handed Theo the crowbar and drew two knives from her belt. Alarmed, Theo placed a hand over hers.

"We're not killing watchmen. You take down innocent watchmen and I'm out."

"You run and I'll kill *you*."

"My brother would enjoy avenging my death." Theo thought that was a lie. Isaiah would find it burdensome if he bothered with it at all.

*Do I owe Paul vengeance?* Theo wondered.

Rehka snarled but sheathed the knives. A moment later, the door opened and the two men went back inside the station. Theo stood and shook the tension from his legs.

"Come on," Rehka hissed.

They ran to the far side of the building. There were no windows on this side of the station. Rehka swore.

"How do you know where she is?" Theo asked.

Vista pointed to a knothole in one of the boards. The knot itself had been knocked out. Now that Theo was looking he could see half a dozen places where the Ankhim had dislodged knotholes to peer inside.

*How had he done that without anyone hearing?*

Theo put his eye to the hole and he saw a body with bleached hair curled up on a cot. Crestone was snoring. Rehka pushed him out of the way to peer in.

"Adi!" she called through the hole. "Adi!"

Theo could not hear Crestone's half of the conversation, but Rehka explained to her that they were there to get her out.

"All right," Rehka said, stepping away at last, "hand me the crowbar."

She slid the flat end between two boards, working it in to give herself leverage. The dry wood cracked and the nails whined as she lifted the first narrow board free. The next board came away faster. Theo could see Crestone peering through the wall at her rescuers. Her eyes were red and puffy, her face tear-stained.

She sniffled. "Theo, what are you doing here?"

"He was overcome by guilt." Rehka handed Theo the crowbar. "Your turn."

"Right," he said, "it wasn't Rehka's blade against my neck." Theo leaned hard on the crowbar as the next board resisted.

Crestone laughed. "Thank you for coming for me, Rehka."

"I always will," Rehka answered.

*I will always... stab you in the back?* Theo thought. *Why do I care if she's loyal to Crestone or not?*

"Vista? Is that you?"

Vista smiled half-heartedly. "You brought me home to my family. When Wright told me you would hang, I couldn't stand by."

"Thank you, Vista," Adi said.

Theo managed to widen the gap by two more planks. The opening was almost big enough for Crestone to squeeze out.

"What is the meaning of this?" shouted a gruff voice.

Theo dropped the crowbar. Two city watchmen were marching toward them down the alley. They must have come through the rear door, their footsteps masked by the sound of tearing wood.

"Stop that at once!" a watchman shouted, "Jailbreak! Sound the alarm."

"Yes, sir!" The younger watchman sprang for the door. Rehka and Wright lunged at the first man.

"Rehka, don't!" he heard Crestone shout, but Rehka gave no indication she had heard. In three long strides, she was on the man, her knives drawn. The watchman gurgled and sank to his knees, blood pumping from several stab wounds. Wright threw a blade after the fleeing soldier, but it clanked off the open door and the watchman disappeared inside the station. Wright slammed his fist against the door. He and Vista wrestled the heavy trash containers across it to hold it closed. Even with one arm, the Ankhim was strong.

"Theo, finish the hole," Rehka shouted over the din. Theo hefted the crowbar and attacked the wall with renewed vigor.

*Father will disown me if I'm arrested twice in as many days. Why am I doing this?* Theo forced himself to focus on the work.

"Faster, Theo," Crestone said. "They're at the door." Inside the station a bell clanged.

Theo heard shouts of "Jailbreak!' and "To your posts!" Vista grasped a board and yanked it away. The construction of the watch station was solid, and he had to brace his feet against the wall to get any purchase. The back door shuddered as the watchmen inside fought to get it open. Wright, too small to help with the boards, waited with his knives drawn for the watchman to emerge.

"Watch your backs!" Crestone said.

Sweat dripped down Theo's face, blurring his vision. His injured hand throbbed with the strain of wielding the crowbar. He jammed the tool into another space between two boards and wiggled it back and forth to widen the gap. The board groaned, splintered, and finally fell away.

"That's going to have to be enough," Rehka said. They could see fingers and faces through a widening crack in the back door as the guards broke it apart. Wright sent another knife twirling end over end into the gap. A man screamed, and the mob pulled back from the door.

Crestone slipped her arms through the hole. Rehka grabbed one and Theo dropped the crowbar to grab the other. Crestone slipped her head into the alley and angled her shoulders to pass them through. The rough boards caught on her clothes, ripping the fabric and abrading her skin.

Theo glanced toward the main street. Watchmen were filing out of the station's entrance and running toward them.

"We'll be trapped," he shouted. "We've got to move."

Crestone's torso was free, and through the hole Theo saw a trio of watchmen opening the cell door, Inspector Broc among them.

"Pull!" Rehka shouted at Theo.

Crestone's thighs came through, but her knee banged against a board, and she cursed as her shins slid over the rough boards. Then progress stopped. Theo thought Crestone's boots were caught. He and Rehka grasped her shoulders and pulled harder. Adi screamed in pain. Theo realized Broc had grabbed Adi's ankles. He was incredibly strong and managed to pull Crestone backwards before Theo and Rehka braced themselves against the wall of the station.

Crestone thrashed and swore. Vista grabbed Crestone's collar and her friends heaved. A whole squad of watchmen was pelting toward them. Broc snarled and panted. Crestone kicked again and caught the inspector hard below his jaw. He cried out in Fae, Theo and Rehka fell backward, and Crestone landed on top of them. Vista pulled Crestone to her feet.

"Get up," Rehka shouted at Theo. "Run!"

A watchman crawled out of the shattered upper half of the back door. Wright, a knife in each hand, engaged the first two guards that arrived from the main street.

Theo scrambled to his feet. Crestone's clothing was torn and she was bleeding in several places. He grabbed her hand and they bolted down the alley. She stretched her legs to match his long stride. Behind him, Theo could hear the heavy footfalls of Rehka and Vista, and the quick patter of Wright's boots. Finally, the back door banged open, knocking down the garbage cans. More watchmen poured out.

Theo, Crestone, and Rehka rounded the corner of the station and emerged onto the main street just as Broc and Henge burst through the front door.

"Over there! After them!" Broc shouted. Henge bounded down the stairs. Then Broc did something Theo had never seen a Faelani do. He dropped to all fours and charged them like the badger he resembled. The inspector outpaced the running watchmen in seconds. He felt Crestone tense beside him. There was no way they could outrun that dark fury. The Faelani badger's claws gleamed in the sunlight as he sprinted toward them. Rehka had not allowed Theo to bring a weapon.

Broc leapt. Crestone gasped. And Rehka crashed into the inspector at full speed. They landed hard on the street, a rolling blur of steel knives and black claws. The watchmen surrounded them, closing off the street. Theo stood transfixed as the two combatants tumbled in the dust. He could not differentiate the grunts of effort from the cries of pain. The watchmen, too, looked on in a loose ring around their commander and the fugitives. No matter who emerged from that tumbling chaos of limbs, Broc or Rehka, the rescue had failed.

All eyes were locked on the combatants. They grappled and rolled, but neither managed to gain the upper hand. Rehka's height gave her leverage, but Broc's low center of gravity gave him stability. Neither pulled their punches and no holds were barred. Suddenly Broc was on top, straddling Rehka's stomach, his claws inches from her face.

One of Rehka's knives had pierced Broc's right bicep and the arm hung limp, the fur matted with blood. She gripped his left wrist in both hands, straining to protect herself from his talons.

"Yield!" Broc shouted.

"Rehka!" Crestone shouted. She tore across the open space and grabbed Broc's arm to try and pull his claws away. Broc's muscles bulged with the strain and his claws crept closer to Rehka's eyes.

"Get her off me!" Broc roared.

Two watchmen grasped Crestone by the arms, but Vista was suddenly there, helping her pull Broc away from Rehka. Without thinking, Theo ran back toward the fray. He caught the first watchman with a right cross on the jaw. The man stumbled and released his grip on Crestone. Theo heard a bugle's bright call cut through the mayhem, sounding a charge. Rehka's mercenary troops had joined the fray, their blue sashes marking them as Water Knives. Theo slammed his shield into a watchman's stomach, before driving his blade below the shoulder. A short watchman with a hooked nose took a mace in the face, blood spraying from his lips. Wright tackled the other soldier holding Crestone and helped free his captain.

Theo wished he had a weapon, but there was nothing he could do but pray to the gods and start throwing punches.

"Wright!" Theo shouted. "Get behind me. We've got to move Crestone out."

"What about Rehka?"

"Forget Rehka," Theo shouted. "Get Crestone out."

More watchmen poured in and the street echoed with the thud of boots, grunts, and curses. It was a storm of fists and feet. Without his sword, Theo had to close fast with each opponent to keep them from drawing their own blades. Blood pounded in his temples. His whole body hurt. A blow to his belly drove the wind out of his lungs, but he managed to keep his feet. Theo kicked his opponent in the chest, driving him backward, then followed with several quick jabs. He heard the watchman's jaw crack and pain exploded in his own knuckles. He sucked in a breath, and instantly another watchman was upon him.

Vista saved Theo this time. He was massaging his hand when a watchman tried to run him through. The Ankhim kicked the soldier hard, knocking the blade aside and giving Theo a chance to dance backward. He watched as the Ankhim grasped the watchman's head in one massive palm and twisted. There was a sharp crack and the watchman crumpled to the ground. Theo turned as more soldiers approached. He, Vista, and Wright were fighting with everything they had, but it wasn't going to be enough. There were too many watchmen and they were much better armed.

"Enough!" The shrill voice seemed far away. A kick landed in Theo's ribs, and he dropped to one knee. He blocked the follow up, grabbing his opponent's leg and pushing forward to tip the man backward.

"Enough! Stop!" Theo thought it was a woman shouting, then someone punched him in the kidney, and he fell onto the man under him. He rolled off, grabbing the watchman's sword. Theo's opponent hesitated when he saw the raised blade, then the watchman kicked Theo's sword hand. The blow landed on the injury and Theo screamed, the pain worse than anything he had ever felt. He dropped the sword and hunched around his hand. Vista landed a blow across the watchman's face, driving him back and giving Theo space to rise to one knee.

"Broc! Stop it! Enough!"

The desperate voice cracked, and Theo realized it was a child. Theo rolled again as his assailant tried to stomp him. He picked up the fallen blade in his off hand and drove it into the meat of the watchman's calf. He withdrew the blade and leaped to his feet. The injured watchman stumbled away clutching his leg.

"Enough! Stop!"

To his surprise, Crestone and Wright were beside him, each engaged in their own fight. Theo glanced around. There was no sign of Rehka or Inspector Broc. Then he spotted the child.

A skinny boy waded through the brawl, shrieking for Broc, pleading for the mayhem to stop. No one listened. Theo recognized Ion just as a watchmen cuffed the lad on a back swing. Ion fell to one knee, stunned. Theo surged toward him but there were too many combatants between him and the boy.

"Crestone!" Theo shouted over the din. Crestone punched a man in the gut and he doubled over. She followed up with a blow to his chin and the watchman dropped to the dusty street.

"What?" Crestone hollered back at Theo.

"The kid!" Theo said pointing.

Ion shuddered, blood trickling from a cut across his forehead. He pushed himself up, but he was unsteady on his feet.

"Enough!" the boy shouted again. "Stop it!" His voice broke from the paired strains of puberty and despair. Broc emerged from the fray. Rehka did, too, her face awash in blood.

The light flickered as if they were fighting in a dim room with a sputtering torch instead of in the middle of the street on a bright Djinnday morning. It happened again and several more brawlers noticed it.

Theo saw panic on Crestone's face. She was gaping at Ion, whose slender frame was now floating above the street, his arms flung wide. Daylight flickered again and the boy's eyes rolled back in his head. Vista pushed through the crowd toward the boy.

"Ion, don't!" It was Crestone.

Sparks of blue and green light swirled around the boy. Everyone was watching him now. Wind whipped down the street blowing dust into Theo's eyes. He shielded his face with his forearm. The gusts intensified, forcing Theo to lean into them so he would not fall over. Swirls of light circled Ion like a shoal of fish. Crestone shouted, but Theo could not understand her.

The lights flared, wrapping the boy in glaring green, then all the swirling strands dissolved into Ion's body. Shadow claimed the street.

Ion's body hurled light out in a great wave. It flung Theo ten feet across the street and over the sidewalk. He was slammed into a wall, glass shattered and wood creaked all around him. There were screams and thuds as the other combatants tumbled through the air and impacted against other buildings. Theo gasped, choking on the thick dust as another wave of light slammed into him.

The street exploded in variegated light then went dark.

# CHAPTER FORTY-NINE

# ADI CRESTONE

## MOON OF XYS, DJINNDAY, 2ND OF LUXOR

Adi stood, coughing and caked in dust. Her ears rang and she smelled the burnt tang of unfocused astral magic. She blinked against the oily midday sun and gathered her bearings. Ion's blast had flung her through the glass storefront of a mercantile. Part of the roof had collapsed and the rest sagged low, snapping and popping in warning. Adi could not locate the shopkeeper in the cluttered store so she made her way on shaky legs toward the front exit. Soon the city watch would recover and Adi wanted to be long gone.

As she stepped over a fallen roof beam, she looked down and saw Vista beneath the wreckage. She gasped. The splintered beam had impaled him. He was dead. Adi made the sign of the Ring and closed his eyes with gentle fingers. A spasm of grief threatened to overwhelm her as the image of Vista's children, hanging on him in the doorway, came to her. Adi dropped to one knee and embraced the corpse.

"I will make sure they are provided for," she whispered into deaf ears. There was no time for a proper goodbye. Vista had given his life to free Adi from the city watch. If she were recaptured his death would be in vain.

*I must keep moving.*

Adi pushed herself up and climbed through the hole at the front of the shop, careful not to cut her hands on the jagged glass still in the window frame. Her escape through the watch station wall had shredded her clothing. Thankfully, her beautiful new coat was back in Iris's room, forgotten during Adi's flight from the Echo.

Ion, looking small and lost, swayed in the middle of the street. Blood ran down the left side of his face from a cut along his hairline. Adi wondered that the child was still standing. When she had first discovered her innate ability, it had blown her across the room, and her eruption had not been half as powerful as Ion's blast. A few watchmen moved, tending their injured and extracting comrades buried in debris.

"Ion!" she croaked. He did not hear her. She swallowed and tried again, a bit louder. She did not want to draw the watchmen's attention. Ion recognized her voice and he turned his face toward her, his eyes unfocused.

"Captain Crestone?" he said. "Is that you? I can't see."

"Stay put. I'm coming to you." As much as Adi wanted to flee, she could not do so until all her rescuers were accounted for.

Beside her, she heard the clunk of metal and the groan of a familiar voice. She saw Theo. He had hit the chandler's shop next door to the mercantile. The shop's wall had stopped his flight and a streetlamp, ripped from its moorings lay across his lap. He was covered in oil from the lamp housing and could not get enough purchase on the heavy pole to push it off.

Adi crouched next to him. "Are you all right?"

"I think so," Theo replied. "Help me move this post."

Adi wrapped her arms around the shaft.

"Ready?"

Theo nodded. Adi stood, lifting the metal pedestal as far as she could and Theo pressed upward at the same time.

"Slide your legs out," she said through gritted teeth.

Theo pulled his legs free, and Adi eased the post down so it would not clatter. Theo staggered to his feet, his joints popping in protest. They were both filthy.

"Thanks."

"Vista's dead." Adi said.

"The fight or the blast? What was that, anyway?"

"A roof beam impaled him." She pointed over the wreckage at Ion. "He used wild astral magic without a dragonstone."

"Hold on, Ion, I'll be right there," Adi said. "Where's Rehka?"

Theo scanned the street. "I don't see her. She was fighting Broc."

"We have to find her and get out of here."

Behind her, fabric ripped, wood and shelving crashed to the floor, and the mercantile collapsed. The chandler's façade rattled, but the shop did not implode. The watch station across the street was a shattered ruin. Smoke and flames rose from one side and Adi heard the cries of prisoners and the rattling of cell doors.

She and Theo picked their way through the prone bodies.

Wright moaned from the middle of the street where he lay. Crestone rushed to his side, knelt, and shook him gently.

"Wright, are you okay? Get up, we have to move. It's not safe here."

His eyes fluttered open. The bandage on his head was caked in dust. He had numerous cuts on his chest and arms from his tumble through the street. "Captain?"

"Aye, it's me," Crestone said. "On your feet sailor."

Wright rolled onto one side and groaned. Theo offered him a hand, which he gratefully accepted. The pirate's eyes were unfocused and he teetered dangerously but managed to stay on his feet.

"I'll get the kid, you two find Rehka," Adi hissed.

A crowd had gathered at the far end of the street. Someone shouted for water. Dust and sand clogged the air, hiding Adi and Theo but slowing their search.

"Here," Theo said. He crouched and Wright hurried over. Adi couldn't help but watch, as the two men ministered to Rehka. The watchmen in their leather jerkins lay tangled with Rehka's mercenaries. A few stirred, but most were still.

Rehka lay unconscious on her back, the right side of her face a grisly mess. Broc's claws had shredded her right arm. Adi swallowed hard against her rising gorge. She had to look away and take a deep breath to settle her stomach. Wright held his hand over Rehka's face.

"She's breathing," he said.

Broc lay a few feet away, Rehka's knife piercing his bicep. Theo placed three fingers on his neck and found a strong pulse.

"Broc's alive. We need to put a tourniquet on Rehka's arm," Theo said.

"She'll lose the arm, if we do," Wright said.

"She'll die if we don't."

Adi stood paralyzed. *Rehka's arm!*

Theo removed his jacket and cast about for something sharp. He found a watchman's short sword nearby. He cut a strip of fabric from the jacket and wrapped it around Rehka's bicep. He used one of Wright's daggers to tighten it before tying it off. Rehka groaned, but did not open her eyes.

"Can you lift her?" Wright asked.

"Maybe. Help me get her into a sitting position and then I can hoist her over my shoulder."

Theo shifted the legs of a mercenary off Rehka's hips, then he noticed the unnatural angle of his neck. The man would never feel anything again. Theo groaned but managed to stand with the tall mercenary draped over his shoulder. She was so tall that her arms dangled past his knees.

"I won't be able carry her very far," Theo said, his voice tight.

"I'll help the captain with Ion," Wright said.

"The boy? Why? Let Broc take care of him."

"I have no idea how many watchmen were killed in that blast, but Ion can't be here when they figure out what happened. Head into that alley beside the chandler's, we'll catch up."

Theo picked his way back across the street, over the unconscious brawlers.

Adi forced herself to move. She grasped Ion's searching hands and he squeaked in surprise.

"It's okay. It's me. Captain Crestone."

"I can't see." Tears ran down his grimy face and blood soaked his collar.

"Don't worry. It's temporary."

"What happened?"

"You channeled astral magic."

He coughed. "I did? How?"

"I'll tell you all about it after we get out of here. I'm going to carry you across the street. You ready?"

Ion nodded. Adi cradled him in her arms. He was small for his age and light, all bone and gristle. After the battle, however, she was grateful for Wright's aid. She set the boy down on the sidewalk.

She spotted Theo at the far end of the alley, staggering under his draconic burden. "Take my hand. We need to hustle."

"Is Broc okay?"

"He will be, but he mustn't find us. We need to go."

"I've been looking for you."

"I know. Let's talk about that later."

"There's a void mage in Solvigant. He's looking for you."

"You came to warn me?" Adi bit back a laugh at the absurdity of this child's efforts on her behalf.

"I want to join your crew."

Adi's smile faded at the new tightness in her chest. She brought too much death to her crew. "We'll discuss it once we're safe."

They caught up to Theo at the far side of the alley. Runnels of sweat rinsed the dirt off his face.

"Do you have any water?" Adi asked him.

"I do," Ion said. He took a water skin from his belt and handed it to Adi. She drank and splashed some onto her face.

"Hey!" Theo said, "Share the wealth."

Adi squirted a stream into his mouth and he gulped it down, then she rinsed his face. The water only thinned the grime.

"Thank you," Theo said. She repeated the process with Ion, washing the cut enough to see if it was serious. The blood was clotting, and he wouldn't need stitches. Then it was Wright's turn until the skin was empty.

"We need to get off the street," Adi said. "We're too conspicuous to walk to the Echo."

"Why there?"

"I left some things behind when the watch arrested me. I need to get them."

"That's the first place they'll look for you when they get organized."

"Then we'll need to be quick. Do you have any money?"

"In my left trouser pocket."

Adi slid her hand in and fumbled about.

"Hey!" Theo hissed. "Careful."

"I thought you didn't have any money," Wright growled.

"Rehka kidnapped me. I wasn't also going to finance this insane plan, too."

Adi withdrew three silver towers and glanced both ways down the street. Passersby were focused on the watch station fire. Adi heard more shouting and the clang of the fire bell, but no one was pursuing them. At midday in a good neighborhood, she had no problem finding a brougham cab. She paid the driver one silver tower for the fare, and a second to keep quiet about his passengers. She gave Wright the third.

"Go to Drake's Apothecary and tell him to get to the Echo. Rehka needs him."

"Aye, Captain. Vista—" he began, but Adi cut him off.

"We'll talk about it later."

Wright nodded and left to hail another cab.

Adi helped Theo wrangle Rehka into the coach. The Dragon groaned but did not wake. Theo climbed in and arranged her on the seat. Adi helped Ion up the steps and climbed in last, closing the door behind her.

They arrived at Stella's Echo half an hour later, by which time Ion could discern some light and blocky gray shapes. Adi hoped his vision would return fully by evening. Rehka, on the other hand, shifted and groaned. Adi felt the pain of her injuries would wake her soon. It was hard for her to look at the narrow face without a rush of nausea. Rehka loved her and had come to rescue her.

*But what a high price Rehka paid. Scars are normal in her line of work, but she'll lose an arm, and I can never repay that.* She knew this was not a productive train of thought, but she careened down it nonetheless.

Their arrival at Stella's Echo sent the quiet midday brothel into a flurry of activity.

Iris brought the pallet down from her room while Verdun helped Theo unload Rehka. They laid the Dragon down beside the fireplace. Stella sent one of the girls to fetch the Vakes while Meera began cleaning Rehka's wounds. Vivian heated bathwater while another of Stella's girls searched for clean clothes. Stella sent a runner to Tabitha at the governor's mansion with news of Theo while Melinda gathered warm rags from the kitchen for Ion's crushing headache.

Exhausted, Adi sank into one of the overstuffed chairs beside the fireplace, near Rehka. She held Rehka's hand through Meera's ministrations until Dr. Deborah Vake arrived and exiled Adi to her bath. Theo and Ion had already taken their turns, so the water was tepid and murky. Adi did not care. She stripped off her clothes and sank into the washtub. When she re-emerged, Iris stood beside the tub, brush and soap in hand. Without a word, Adi allowed Iris to scrub her down, biting her lip and wincing every time the rough bristles crossed any of her many cuts and scrapes, but she made no complaint.

"Are you all right?" Iris asked.

Adi shook her head. "I don't think so. How's Rehka?"

"Dr. Vake gave her something to keep her asleep. It's going to take a while to clean her face. They'll have to take the arm below the elbow."

Adi buried her face in her hands. Iris set down the washing implements, pulling her toward the edge of the washtub, and gathered her into a hug. Adi floated there and tried to calm herself, tried to contain the guilt.

"It's not your fault, Adi," Iris said after a time.

"Yes, it is. She never should have been there." She felt darkness closing in around her and she was losing the struggle to keep it at bay.

"It's not your fault."

"You shouldn't fall in love with me, Iris. I break people." Adi thought of the rage, pain, and fury on Xander's face as he fled from the interrogation room. She thought about how many nights she had fallen asleep on the *Snowcrest* gazing into Rehka's gold-flecked green eyes. She thought of Vista's fatherless children.

"I'm not so foolish as to fall in love with you yet, Adi Crestone."

Stella entered the bathroom without knocking. There was blood on her apron, and she carried a container of dirty rags. "Get dressed. There's someone here to see you."

Adi pushed Iris away and tensed, ready to run.

*Has the watch regrouped already? I thought I'd have more time.*

At the stricken look on Adi's face, Stella said, "It's Lady Hannah Valefyre. She says she is Theo's betrothed."

"Is she alone?"

"Seems to be."

Adi rose and Iris handed her a towel.

"You left these," Iris said handing Adi a stack of folded clothes. On top was the sweater she had taken from Rehka's old room. She held it to her face and inhaled. It no longer held the dry aroma of reptile and mothballs, instead it smelled of the lavender soap Stella used.

"I washed it," Iris said. Adi tried to hide her disappointment. She knew she failed because Iris looked away, her cheeks and neck pink with embarrassment.

"Thank you, Iris." Adi said and dressed. She wrapped the towel around her head. "Bad form to keep a lady waiting."

They returned to the tavern.

*Lady Valefyre is quite young,* Adi realized. *She's only a year or two older than Lucas.*

Lady Valefyre bore herself like a noblewoman visiting a military hospital, concerned but aloof. Deborah and Roald Vake were leaning over Rehka, their shirts blood-stained to the elbows. In contrast, Lady Valefyre wore a starched blue dress with an ornate white petticoat showing beneath the hem. The blue bodice was trimmed in black with tiny mother-of-pearl beads that caught the light. The outfit was beautiful, but it had the effect of making her pale skin look almost translucent. Her red hair was done up in a tower of voluptuous curls with freed wisps around her slender ears. Adi remembered how hard it had been to move through the Sabaian court with her blue hair piled high. She did not envy the woman her trek across the city to the Echo.

Theo sat beside Lady Valefyre in a white shirt and tan breeches that must have belonged to Verdun. The huge green Ankhim brewer seldom wore a shirt, and this one was big enough to sail a small ship. Swimming in all that fabric, Theo looked even more childlike than his betrothed.

Adi joined them at the table. "Lady Valefyre, a surprise. You have an interesting sense of timing."

Valefyre sniffed, a handkerchief to her nose. "I came for Theo. To stop him from starting another foolish endeavor. Lady Marrion informed me he might be here."

Theo swallowed audibly.

"It's natural to worry about your betrothed. As you can see, apart from a few cuts and bruises, he made it through the entire debacle unscathed."

Theo shifted and cleared his throat as if to remind the women that he was right there, and that those cuts and bruises hurt. His hand throbbed.

"You defend his actions freeing a notorious criminal from incarceration?"

Adi studied Valefyre. She used the language of the aristocracy, but she spoke it as though from a script, repeating what she thought she was supposed to say.

"How old are you, Hannah?"

The woman started, unaccustomed to strangers addressing her by her given name. "It's Lady Valefyre, and my age is not relevant. Theo's father and I require Theo to honor the marriage agreement. I came to insure he is disabused of any notions of future gallivanting."

"Future gallivanting?" Adi considered and turned to Theo. "I spared you on the *Sidereal*. You saved me from the hangman. We're even. You need feel no further guilt on my account."

To Adi's surprise, Theo's shoulders drooped, his posture eased with relief.

"Thank you," he said.

"Well, regardless, I will not have my intended husband cavorting around the World System with pirates. Theo, I come with the marriage contract from your father."

"You are to be his lackey in addition to being my wife?" Theo's tone was sharp. Adi looked at Valefyre's face and caught the barest flinch.

"If you deny me," Valefyre said, "I will return home in disgrace, a spurned woman. My father will be lucky to marry me off to a wealthy merchant's son. If you expect me to be an ally, I will need a commitment from you. High Chancellor Vanguard instructed me to tell you that he will not ask again for your obedience."

Adi had almost forgotten the vapid concerns of nobility. Most nobles fell into their wealth and had no idea what to do with it. She sympathized with Valefyre. It would fall hard on her if Theo rejected her, while he would emerge unscathed, still welcome in high society.

*There are worse things than marrying a wealthy, self-made man,* she thought. *Fewer power politics for one.*

"My apologies," Theo said, "I thought only of my rancor for Father and not of your situation."

Lady Valefyre straightened, startled by Theo's apology.

"Thank you," she said. She reached into her reticule and removed a roll of paper.

Theo groaned. "Father *would* draw up a contract."

"Would you like to read it?"

"Not particularly."

Lady Valefyre sniffed into her handkerchief once more. Adi could not help herself.

"Do the vapors of our brothel offend your noble constitution?"

"I did not imagine spending the morning of my wedding day in a *bordello*," Lady Valefyre said.

Stella *tsk*ed from behind the bar. "Bordello?"

"You could leave," Adi said. "We're all very busy being criminals."

"What does the contract say?" Theo said to cut off further argument. Valefyre's green eyes fixed on Adi with smoldering rage so intense she had to look away. The color reminded her of Rehka's.

Valefyre unrolled the paper and began reading aloud.

"How about the main points?" Theo said.

"It's a standard marriage contract. You will marry me, lead the delegation to Djinnar, and return to run the Vanguard estates at Balan."

"I will assist my father in his... machinations, in other words," Theo said.

"When the delegation has completed its stated purpose, you will resign your officer commission with honors and return to Balan. If you do so, the high command will suspend their inquiry. Your father has graciously offered his personal ship, *Penumbra*, for the delegation's use."

"Must we name our eldest Simon also?" Theo said.

Valefyre cleared her throat, unhappy at being continually interrupted. "You will retire from the navy and the Vanguard coffers will rebuild both Opus Station and Bruto Station."

"Bruto?" Adi interjected.

"The one you destroyed this morning," Valefyre explained.

"Father spoke with watch command then."

"High Chancellor Vanguard is a busy and important man."

"What are his conditions? He's loaning the delegation *Penumbra*. He will expect something in return."

"We will be married—"

"I know that."

"—tonight by Father Heilig at the Temple of the Nine. And..." Lady Valefyre swallowed, "and you will no longer have any contact with *any* daughters of House Azure outside of those required by your duties as leader of the delegation."

Valefyre's eyes flicked to Adi.

*Did something happen between Beatrice and Theo?* Adi wondered. It was easy to forget that Beatrice was still a noble woman. *What does Valefyre know about me?*

"Very well," Theo said.

"You should be happier about your free pass out of trouble and off Xys," Adi said. "You get to marry this beautiful, intelligent woman and retire to one of the fanciest estates in the Solan Empire to live a life proper to your station. Much better than hanging beside me for freeing a prisoner and destroying a city watch station. Not to mention the murder of Rictor. Cheer up."

"You're right, of course," Theo said, his voice glum.

"Is marrying me really so terrible?" Lady Valefyre's voice hitched.

"No, it's—"

"I understand," Adi interjected. "It's not that he won't learn to care for you Lady Valefyre, it's that he was given no choice."

Theo looked at Adi with something approaching admiration. Adi stood and offered him her hand.

"Good luck, Commander Vanguard. The delegation will be safer for your presence."

Theo hesitated.

"Sign the damn papers," Adi growled.

Meera produced a quill and inkpot. Theo signed the marriage license then stood and shook Adi's hand.

"You're the most surprising pirate I've ever met."

"I'll take it."

"Lady Valefyre—excuse me, Lady Vanguard, shall we go?" Theo asked.

Hannah Valefyre rolled up the contract, rose, and took Theo's offered arm.

"Thank you, husband. My carriage will take us back to the governor's mansion. We must get you changed before the ceremony."

# CHAPTER FIFTY

# ADI CRESTONE

## MOON OF XYS, DJINNDAY, 2ND OF LUXOR

A di watched Lord and Lady Vanguard leave Stella's Echo. An acute pang of loneliness took her breath away. Stuart Royal would sell Apyreon to the White Rabbits in a few short hours and Adi was alone. Vista was dead, Theo was gone, and Rehka would be out of commission for a while. Wright was an admirable first mate, but not enough muscle for the coming fight. Plus, she needed someone to look after her friends at the Echo until she was off-moon and it was safe for them.

*If Rehka ever speaks to me again it will be one of Phoebe's miracles. If Bale doesn't murder me before his daughter has recovered.*

Her connection to the city watch was now irrevocably severed. Broc and Henge, who had been instrumental in the fiasco at the Iron Dirigible, would arrest her on sight. The Imperial Guard would be out looking for her.

*If they don't shoot me on sight. How many watchmen died in the brawl? From Ion's magic?*

She had to leave Stella's Echo. Broc would come for her the moment he was able, and the Echo was the first place he would search. Adi did not want to be the reason the watch dismantled these women's livelihoods. They did not deserve to be punished for her actions. Adi needed to be long gone before the law arrived.

But she needed help. She wanted the planks of a ship's deck beneath her feet and a steady crew. It had been so long since she had sailed any sea as a proper pirate. Captain Torrance's crew was dead, but there were taverns, brothels, and piers where Adi could gather a collection of scalawags willing to try their luck on a pirate ship. Except Adi had neither the time nor the coin to seek them out. For the first time since boarding the *Snowcrest* a decade earlier, the idea of sailing felt like an escape rather than freedom.

Adi would have to go on alone. She would infiltrate Alhambra's, a Talon stronghold, and acquire Apyreon before the Water Knife mercenaries took it off-moon. She just hoped Devlin Seneschal would honor his end of the bargain and bring his men. The chaos and confusion they would create was the only window of opportunity Adi would have.

*I could go to the Blood Queen for help,* Adi realized. *She would loan me men.*

She did not want to start a war between the gangs, and she doubted Sasha Riven would be pleased with such an outcome, even if Adi managed to recover Apyreon. Leyala Fedhani would have heavy security, Devlin would bring enough men to make a point, Stuart Royal would expand his entourage after the assassination attempt, and who knew how many mercenaries the Water Knives would send. If Adi arrived with a battalion of Blood Queen thugs, there would be war in the streets of Solvigant. The city watch would bring every able-bodied officer to that fight and the damage would not be limited to Alhambra's.

*If it saves Lucas, what do I care about chaos in the streets of Solvigant?*

But was not just the chaos and aftermath of a battle Adi feared. She would be headed to Tyre and Lucas before tensions in Solvigant really ignited. She could not tolerate the idea of owing the Blood Queen any more than she already did. Between the collar of indenture and the threat to Lucas and Xander, Adi could not ask Sasha Riven for help.

*Palestrina.* The thought made her tense and shiver for a moment. Adi needed help and she had a deal to keep with Talon Devlin Seneschal. If things at Alhambra's went sideways, Adi could ill afford to have both the Blood Queen and the Talon in hot pursuit.

*Has it come to this that I would strike a bargain with the person I'm obliged to assassinate?*

"Girl, are you all right?" Stella asked sliding a tankard of ale across the table toward Adi. She had not heard the madam sit down. Adi picked up the proffered ale and took a long drink.

"Thanks, Stella." Adi wiped her mouth with the back of her hand, then removed the towel wrapped around her wet hair. "I should get going."

Stella nodded, "Well, that one's on the house." Both women stood and Adi embraced Stella Volpes.

"I don't know when I'll be back," Adi said.

"Just visit when you can."

"It's going to be quite dangerous for me in Solvigant for a while."

"What's your plan?"

"Once I hand Apyreon over to the Blood Queen, I will go to Tyre to spend time with my son. I need to make sure he's safe. Broc doesn't know about Lucas, so I doubt the inspector will follow me off-moon. We'll head north just in case. Outside the hustle and bustle of Thail, away from the seat of the Empire. I'll write to you when we're settled and come back and visit when things cool off."

Adi stepped away.

Stella was misty-eyed. "It seems you've thought of everything."

Adi forced a smile. "I've survived on pirate skill this long."

"I'm still coming with you," Iris said from where she sat holding instruments for the Doctors Vake.

"I'm not sure that's safe," Adi began.

"I already bought out my contract. I can't very well stay here now."

"I'd take you on as an apprentice and third spouse," Dr. Deborah Vake said.

Roald spluttered, "Darling—"

"That's very kind," Iris said, curtailing more disagreement between the doctors as they sutured Rehka's face, "but Adi already promised to take me with her."

"I'm coming too," Ion said. He sat at the bar beside Melinda, his legs too short to reach the boot rail. "I came to join your crew, remember?"

"What does your grandfather have to say about you turning pirate?" Adi asked.

Tears filled Ion's eyes, and he looked away. "He's dead. The void mage and his acolytes killed him. So, I'm coming with you."

Before Adi could protest, the door to the Echo swung inward and Balthasar Drake strode into the brothel followed by a haggard Wright. Sharp lines of worry shadowed Bale's gaunt face and the air around him wavered with Draconic shimmer.

Adi swallowed hard. "Bale."

"Where is my daughter?" Bale asked. "What have you done to her now?" He rushed across the room toward the pallet. "Oh, Rehka." He moaned as he crouched beside her unconscious form and grasped her good hand.

"Please don't jostle the patient." Roald Vake's voice was calm as he pulled the needle and thread once more through the skin of Rehka's cheek.

Adi stood behind Balthasar and placed a hand on his shoulder to comfort him. The Dragon snarled and shrugged it away.

"What happened?" he repeated. "Wright only told me that there was a fight." He let go of Rehka and stood, glaring at Adi. His lanky frame towered two feet over her and his blue-gold eyes glinted like lightning over a stormy sea. "What trouble are you in?"

"I did nothing to her! You have the city watch to thank for those injuries. Inspector Broc in particular."

"Why was she fighting the city watch?"

Adi felt her anger slipping away, "She came to Bruto Station to rescue me. I would be climbing the gallows stairs right now if not for her."

"Figures," Bale huffed.

"She saved my life!"

"At what cost, Adi? So you can muck it up again? My daughter will lose her arm, and you, look at you, unscathed." The snarl in his voice matched the menace in his glare.

"If it wasn't for me she'd be dead."

"If it wasn't for you she never would have been in this mess."

"No, she'd probably be dead in some alchemist's basement after taking some poison he promised would transport her to Pyrea to reunite her with her missing Dragon."

"How dare you!?"

Adi's bruised ribs ached, as did the swelling in her jaw. Her whole body throbbed, battered and bruised by this morning's brawl. She was injured but knew that was not what Bale wanted to hear.

"I'm sorry, Bale." Adi said, with all the contrition she could muster. Rehka's loss would haunt Adi to the end of her days.

"You promised to stay away from her."

"*She* sought *me* out, Bale. She took a job knowing it would throw us together. *She* confessed her love for me on the stairs of your house. I never wanted any of this."

"You did not push her away. You're always taking from people, Adi. Money, hearts, my daughter's arm—You're a vortex of need sucking the happiness from whomever you touch." His dark eyes narrowed with rage and his shimmer intensified.

"Bale!" Stella's voice was sharp, her teeth bared. "That is enough. Adi is a daughter to me, and both of our daughters are alive because of Rehka's heroism. I know you're angry and scared, but I will have no more of that talk in my establishment."

Bale snarled, took a step towards Stella, and brandished his jade cane. Adi was too stunned by Stella's outburst to move. She knew Stella cared for her, and she cared for the Faelani madam who had rescued her fifteen years ago. But this? Adi thought she might faint or explode where she stood. She did not have room for it all, for Bale's anger, for Stella's love, for Iris's concern, for Ion's admiration, for Theo's grudging respect, for Xander's scorn. She could not hold it all.

Verdun stepped around the bar bearing the large mallet he used to drive taps into fresh barrels. He intercepted Bale on his course toward Stella.

"You're angry, Bale," Adi managed. "Don't take it out on Stella. If you want to take it out on someone, take it out on me. I'm right here."

Bale whirled toward her and for a moment she thought he meant to do just that. It was illegal for a Dragon to shift into its reptilian form inside the city, but the rage contorting Bale's face indicated he was beyond caring.

He raised the cane. "You've done nothing but bring harm and ruin upon my daughter. Since you returned with that cursed device, I have had to attend to my daughter's bedside twice. Twice!"

She flinched but did not move. If Bale found catharsis by thrashing her with the cane, Adi would accept the beating. She wanted it, even. She had never wanted to hurt Rehka. Despite her tangled emotions, the sight of Rehka's injured and unconscious body made her spiral into a dark well of self-pity. Bale's cane would expiate her. Adi braced for the impact.

But Bale did not strike her, instead he deflated, folding in on himself, his shimmering aura subsiding. Adi knew the Dragon had enough power, even in his human form, to level Stella's Echo with all of them inside it. She watched in awe as he reined in that power until it winked out.

Bale collapsed into the nearest chair.

Adi wanted to comfort him, to cry with him about Rehka's situation, but she dared not move. Iris was standing beside her, ready to jump in and deflect a blow should it come to that. Her legs trembled and Iris took her hand to steady her.

Bale's laugh was bitter. "I see you have already found someone else's life to ruin."

Iris opened her mouth to object, but Adi cut her off.

"What do you want from me, Bale?"

"I want you to stay away from my daughter."

"Doesn't she get a say in this? You're going to break Rehka's heart."

"You don't think I know that?" Bale snapped. "Honor your promise."

Adi lowered her head, "I'll do my best."

"You will stay away."

"I promise you that I won't seek Rehka out. But I'm not responsible for her actions."

"I will take her to Flynt," Bale said, "There are healers there more proficient in Draconic injuries."

Deborah Vake clicked her tongue but said nothing.

"I leave for Tyre tonight," Adi said. "I doubt our paths will cross again."

Bale looked up until his eyes met hers. "You still intend to give Apyreon to the Blood Queen?"

"I do."

"You shouldn't."

"If it will save my son, I intend to hand it over. You may hate me, Bale, but surely you can understand that. You stand here railing about your daughter. I'm a parent too."

Bale relented. "I visited the local chapter of the Society of Astrologia. They allowed me access to their library."

"How did you swing that?" Adi asked, curious despite herself. The mages of the Society were notoriously stingy with the vast knowledge they held in their libraries.

"What?" Bale seemed suddenly distant. "That? It doesn't matter, someone owed me a favor. Do you remember how I told you the device is like a skeleton key that can open gates whenever and to wherever you like?"

"I do."

"It can do that because it harnesses aetherial magic. Of the tripartite division of magic into stellarium, aether, and void, the gates are governed by this middle type. As you know, practicing aether magic is forbidden because of aether's role as the building blocks of the World System. Aether can be neither created nor destroyed. To open a new gate, a different one must be closed. If too many gates are closed without new ones being opened, the aether gets overexcited and the gates start behaving in unpredictable ways."

"You told me this when I came to your shop," Adi said. All traces of Bale the Dragon on the verge of losing control had been replaced by Bale the scholar, and Adi's mind struggled to keep pace with the abrupt transition.

"That is why we do not alter the gates but rather allow them to perambulate through their respective orbits. Altering them becomes too complicated. That is why aether magic is illegal: each spell pulls the life force of aether from another place to the location of the spell. The spellcaster has no control over where that aether comes from. It could be from a branch of a tree in a vast forest someone will never see or it could come from a small child."

"Get to the point, Bale. What does this have to do with Apyreon?"

"When you were organizing my shop, I studied the aether crystal under magnification. The crystallization pattern was unusual, so I sketched it out and compared it to Bodwin's *Geology*. It's not an aether crystal."

"It must be a stellarium gem, like the focus on a ship, otherwise I wouldn't have been able to use it. I have no affinity with aether."

"It is no focus. I have no idea how you were able to use it, but Bodwin calls it an Acadian bloodstone, though his exposition on them is brief as he was writing after Acadia's destruction by Kade."

"I've never heard of such a thing."

"Neither have I, but Bodwin references Galliger's *Astrogeology and Magical Affinity*."

"Get to the point, Bale. I can't stay here much longer," Adi interrupted.

"Right. Galliger theorizes that Acadian bloodstones date back to the creation of Solo's children, and in some instances can grant the wielder elemental powers that require no natural affinity."

"That's not possible," Adi said.

"If Riven were to acquire both pieces, it would grant her power the World System has never seen. Power to rival the very gods themselves. You must not give the Blood Queen this power. Go to Tyre, rescue your son, but do not give that power to a bloodthirsty gangster."

"If I go off-moon before handing over the device, she'll kill my son."

"Is there anyone you trust to send?"

"The only other person I'd trust with such a task is unconscious on that pallet over there, and I promised you I would no longer associate with her."

Bale sighed, the scholastic enthusiasm leeching away as he returned to the crisis of the moment.

"Please, Adi, think of the damage the Blood Queen could do with that power. She could destroy moons, she could consolidate all the power of the World System under her. No one is safe if she wields the full device. There must be another way."

"If I don't give it to the Blood Queen, it will go to the Water Knives and their client. That would be as bad and maybe worse, depending on who hired them. Let us pray to the Nine that neither of them already has the other half. Do you know where it might be?"

Bale shook his head. "The library's sources on the device are incomplete. I was fortunate to learn as much as I did."

"Thank you, Bale."

Rehka's father huffed as though remembering how angry he was with his daughter's former lover.

"I'm sorry about Rehka. I hope the healers on Flynt can help her."

"If she were connected to her Dragon, that would help her heal. But she isn't."

"She wants that more than anything," Adi said. "More than she ever wanted me."

Vivian burst into the Echo before Bale could respond. Her chest heaved with the exertion of running and her hair was disheveled. "Adi, you must go. There is a whole battalion of city watchmen and Imperial Guards headed this way. I've never seen so many!"

Adi sprang into action. She took her money pouch from her belt and handed it to Iris.

"The midnight coal freighter to Tyre leaves from aeroport berth sixty-two. Take this and buy three passenger tickets. Pay double and they won't ask for passports. If I'm not there when the freighter leaves, go ahead. I'll catch up. There's another in the early morning."

"Adi, I—"

Adi put a finger over Iris's lips. "I'm sorry, I don't have time. If you're not there, I'll understand."

She reached into the pouch, withdrew six copparchs, and handed them hurriedly to Bale.

"Adi!" There was real urgency in Vivian's voice. "You need to leave. They can't find you here."

Adi ignored her.

"What is this for?" Bale asked hefting the coins.

She motioned to Ion. "Passage to Karis for the boy."

"But I want to come with you!" Ion protested.

Adi crossed the room and took Ion by the hand. "I know. I appreciate everything you've done for me. But what happened today in the street outside Bruto Station, I can't help you with that. Only the mages at the Society of Astrologia will have answers for you. When you get there, ask for Elder Quinn Lillian, she owes me a favor."

"What for?"

"No time for that now."

"Adi!" The voice was Stella's. "I can see the watchmen."

"Wright, go with Iris. Keep her safe."

"I'm a pirate, not a babysitter."

"I go on Blood Queen business and I want to keep you out of it."

"But you're my captain." Wright's objection was halfhearted.

"Then obey my order."

Wright nodded.

"Adi, you must go now," Stella said.

"Ion and Rehka can't be here either."

"We'll hide them."

"They'll tear this place apart looking for me," Adi said. "It's too risky."

"I have a few secrets you haven't sussed out girl. But I can't risk *you* being found here. Now, out the back with you." Stella crossed to where Adi stood and embraced her. Then Stella turned her around and pushed her toward the kitchen. "Leave now."

Adi took one last look over her shoulder at the gathered crowd in the tavern of Stella's Echo. Bale and the Vakes were already lifting Rehka to follow Stella toward the bath. Adi grinned and waved at them as if she weren't running from the law before the epic debacle that would be Alhambra's. Then she turned and fled.

# CHAPTER FIFTY-ONE

# ION RUCINARE

## MOON OF XYS, DJINNDAY, 2ND OF LUXOR

Ion stood frozen with indecision in the middle of the tavern at Stella's Echo. He caught a glimpse of Captain Crestone's retreating back as she opened the rear alley door and disappeared into the glare of the late afternoon sun. He wanted to run after her. He had come here to join her crew. His grandfather was dead, he had run away from home and braved the streets of Solvigant as an urchin. Now she was gone. From the hallway beside the stairs, voices were shouting at him to run and hide.

*Captain Crestone does not run and hide,* he thought. *Sure, she's running now, but running toward danger, toward her son.* Ion was supposed to run and hide, but he would not. Resolute, he took two steps toward the kitchens before Verdun grabbed him his collar and lifted him off the ground.

"Let me go!" Ion shouted. "I have to help Crestone."

"Not today, son." The green Ankhim's voice was not as deep as Ion expected. Verdun tossed the boy over his massive shoulder as if Ion weighed nothing and hauled him down the hallway toward where the women bathed and did their laundry.

The great barrel tub still contained the grimy water from his bath, but Stella was draining the bathwater. There were no clothes to fit a twelve-year-old boy in a brothel, so Ion was wearing a black dress, the bottom pulled up and tied near his waist to form a baggy shalwar. The top hung especially loose as he had no breasts to fill out the extra fabric. Verdun set Ion down and began to push against the tub.

"Help me," Verdun called to Bale. Balthasar hesitated for a moment, then lowered Rehka's feet so his unconscious daughter hung limp between Deborah and Roald Vake.

"Stella," Verdun called as he strained against the weight of the tub. "Go change your clothes, you're covered in blood."

Ion gaped as under the combined strength of Verdun and Bale the washtub began to slide toward the far wall. Underneath, Ion could see the crescent edge of a dark hole. Verdun noticed it too, for he redoubled his efforts. Soon the thin curve of darkness widened into a crack large enough for Ion to squeeze through. He tiptoed forward and looked in. Beneath the washtub was a pit about six feet deep and four feet wide. Someone had built a timber frame with canvas siding to help keep the sand from filling it back in. Smoke rose out of it and Ion realized it must be connected to the stove that provided heat for the tub.

"Jump in, Bale," Verdun ordered. "Deborah, you and your husband lower Rehka down to him."

Balthasar climbed into the hole. He was so tall his head and neck emerged from the top. The two doctors carefully transferred their patient to her father, and he lowered her into the hole. The floor was not large enough for Rehka to lay flat, so Bale curled her into a fetal position, her bandaged face bright in the dim pit. Verdun offered his hand to Bale.

"I'll stay with her," Bale said.

"It's not big enough," Verdun said. "Climb out so Ion can get in. Hurry man!"

Balthasar hesitated, clearly reluctant to leave his unconscious daughter alone in a hole with a twelve-year-old boy. The sound of heavy knocking carried down the hallway from the tavern entrance.

"Open up!" the voice said. "Open for the city watch."

Ion thought he recognized the voice as Broc's, but it was angry and pained in a way that he had never heard before.

"Coming!" Meera shouted down the hall.

Bale took Verdun's hand and the Ankhim hauled the Dragon out.

"In you go," Verdun said to Ion.

"Can I have a light?" Ion asked.

"Afraid not. There are too many gaps in the floorboards around the washtub where it might shine through."

Ion hesitated. He did not like the idea of sitting in a dark hole with an injured Dragon, but neither did he relish the idea of facing Broc and his myriad watchmen.

"No time, lad," Verdun said. He scooped up Ion and lowered him into the pit. Before Ion could react, Verdun and Bale were pushing the now-empty washtub back into place.

Ion heard Verdun's voice. "You're here looking for Rehka. Understood?"

The washtub scraped into place, but there was no audible response from Bale. The pounding at the front door sounded once more. Ion heard splintering wood followed by a loud bang. At first, he feared the tub was about to fall on their heads, then he realized someone must have kicked open the front door.

The pit was not pitch black, as Ion had feared. The hole was slightly wider than the washtub, so gaps in the floorboards allowed in just enough light for him to discern Rehka's curled form. He shivered, though his heart was pounding and sweat beaded on his brow. At least he could see well enough not to step on the injured woman.

"Where's Crestone?" Broc's voice was loud inside the tavern.

"I'm sorry?" Meera's voice wavered and creaked.

"Adi Crestone, is she here?"

"I'm afraid I haven't seen her, sir, not in some time."

Ion heard footsteps, both heavy and light, moving about the washroom. The heavy ones must be Verdun, the lighter ones were one of Stella's girls. Ion heard the creak of rusty iron and then water splashing. Someone was working the pump. It was difficult to hear anything from the tavern over the wail of the pump handle, and Ion fought the urge to yell at whoever it was to stop. He wanted to hear what was happening.

Though the fire had been extinguished, smoke still stung Ion's eyes. He pulled the fabric of his collar up over his nose and mouth to keep from coughing. Water sloshed into the washtub and Ion had a moment of panic as someone poured the buckets from the pump into the washtub, filling it.

"What is the meaning of this?" Stella's voice, shrill with anger cut through the washroom noise, but Ion could not hear the response. His vision had still not completely returned and in the dim light the pit played tricks on him so that large blocky shapes seemed to float before him. They merged into one another, then drifted apart. Beside him Rehka began to moan softly. Ion clamped one hand over her mouth to try to dampen the sound. His thumb brushed her freshly sutured cheek. It still oozed blood and Ion snatched his hand away. Rehka moaned louder. Steeling himself, he laid his hand once more over her mouth, careful not to touch any of her seeping wounds.

Ion sat in the pit and listened to the water sloshing into the washtub above him. He had no way to keep track of the time, so his imagination stretched to fill the gap. The whole brothel creaked and groaned as dozens of pairs of booted feet tramped through the building hunting for Adi and her companions, hunting for him. Twice, watchmen came into the washroom to search. Both times Ion considered calling out.

*Surely Broc would understand that whatever I did was an accident. I never intended to harm anyone.*

Ion did not understand what he had done to cause such mayhem. One moment he had been calling for the fighting to stop, the next he was blind in the middle of the street, ears ringing. He felt ashamed. Whatever he had done, it was enough for Captain Crestone to send him away. It was enough that Inspector Broc, who had taken him in and tried to get him work, was now hunting him.

*Is something wrong with me?* Ion had no idea.

That unknown kept him from calling out. He did not know how Broc would react. Ion understood that he had killed people, killed Broc's people.

*I don't know how it happened. I don't know what I did.* His conscience was clear, but that did not stop a nauseous gnawing sensation from settling in the pit of his stomach.

*Does it even matter that it was an accident?*

Ion knew he couldn't give himself up without also exposing Rehka. Justice in her case was clear. Ion did not know the woman, but he saw how much Captain Crestone cared about her and that was enough to make Ion want to help her.

*Captain Crestone isn't sending me away. She's sending me on a mission. Go to Karis, find Quinn Lillian, and she'll tell me what to do. I can also help Bale transport Rehka to Flynt.* That last part had not been explicit, but Ion believed Crestone would approve.

Rehka moaned again. Ion tightened his grip on her mouth and tried not to cough. The residual smoke burned his eyes until they watered and his nose wouldn't stop dripping. Floorboards creaked above his head and Ion heard Broc's voice.

"What's going on in here?"

Ion looked through gaps in the wood at black stripes that were the bottom of Broc's boots.

"This is the washroom," Stella replied. "The women are preparing for work this evening, bathing and laundering sheets."

Ion had met Stella Volpes only an hour before, but he liked her. She had been gentle with him and was one of the only people in the aftermath of Bruto Station not to look at him as if he had grown a second head.

He wished someone had thought to leave him a water skin. He waited and fought the fear of being trapped. Broc's feet moved around the washtub and Ion imagined the Faelani badger sniffing, smelling him. For the first time, Ion was glad for the cloying smoke.

Watchmen entered the washroom to report they had found nothing, the brothel appeared empty of all traces of Crestone and her companions. Broc's feet turned to leave, and Ion coughed. Broc paused. One of Stella's girls began once more to work the squealing pump as Ion bit his lip to avoid another outburst. His throat burned. Tears ran down his cheeks. Rehka's moans became more frequent. The pump squealed overhead and water sloshed. Ion waited, waited, barely able to breathe. Broc finally left the washroom, and as soon as he heard the door swing shut, he doubled over in a fit of coughing.

"Are you all right?" A woman's voice Ion did not recognize floated down to him.

"The smoke is too thick," he said, his voice barely above a whisper. "I think it is bothering Rehka, too."

"We'll get you out of there as soon as the coast is clear."

Ion coughed again and wiped his eyes with his free hand.

At least an hour passed before anyone else spoke to Ion. Despite the discomfort of the pit, he was dozing by the time the women above him drained the washtub. The scrape of the heavy wooden barrel against the floor roused him. He looked up and blinked against the harsh light. Verdun and Bale gazed down at him, their faces hazy through the smoke and Ion's affected vision. Bale looked particularly concerned as his gaze traveled over his daughter as if looking for fresh injury. Ion felt a thrill as he realized he could see well enough to follow the Dragon's blue-gold eyes.

"Give me your hand." Verdun knelt beside the pit and extended a muscled green arm. Ion stood, his knees and shoulders popping in protest after crouching so long in the small space. He took Verdun's hand and the Ankhim hauled Ion out. Bale dropped into the pit and lifted Rehka. It took all three of them to maneuver the tall, limp woman out. By the time they had her laid out on the floor of the washroom, all three were panting.

"You mustn't go into the tavern," Verdun said to Ion. "Broc left four watchmen in case Crestone comes back. They have descriptions of you and Rehka as well."

"How do we get out?" Ion asked.

"We'll send you down the fire escape outside Vivian's room. There will be a carriage waiting to take you to the aeroport."

"Though, I suspect," Bale said, "that Broc and his men are already on their way. I'll get you and Rehka secured on a ship, then run home to gather supplies before rejoining you."

"What about Captain Crestone?" Ion asked.

Bale grimaced. "I wouldn't worry about her. She has a history of overcoming long odds. You'll be safe on Karis. I, too, know Lady Quinn Lillian. She'll look after you."

"I wish I could talk to Broc."

"I don't think that's a good idea," Verdun said. "He seems quite angry. I'm not sure he's ready to listen to whatever it is you feel compelled to say."

Sullen, Ion looked at the floor and nodded.

"I'll show you the back stairs and Vivian will clean you up."

Unfamiliar male voices drifted down the hallway. Ion assumed they were the remaining watchmen. Verdun led Ion up a narrow set of steps to the second floor and into a small bedroom at the end of the hall. Ion recognized Vivian as the woman who had given warning about the approaching watch. The light coming through her window was muted, the distant sun already below the horizon so that Solvigant was bathed in the orange glow of Solo.

"How long was I in the pit?" Ion asked.

"Two hours," Vivian said apologetically.

Ion coughed. "Please, ma'am, could I have some water?"

"Of course. Let's clean you up a bit, too." She poured him a glass of water from an ewer beside the bed, then moistened a cloth and wiped the soot from Ion's face. He waited while Bale and Verdun carried Rehka upstairs, where the Doctors Vake reexamined her injuries, dressing the remaining wounds. Ion tried not to stare at the stump of Rehka's arm.

A carriage waited for them in the alley driven by Verdun's assistant. As Ion climbed down from the fire escape, he realized the fellow could not be much older than he was, maybe fourteen.

"Hello," Ion said, mortified he was wearing a working girl's black dress. The lad looked him up and down but said nothing. Verdun wrapped a thick rope twice around Rehka's chest and under her armpits, then lowered her feet first into Balthasar's waiting arms. They did all of this in silence for fear of alerting the watchmen lurking just around the corner. No one came to investigate, however, and soon the carriage was rattling down the street toward the aeroport.

# CHAPTER FIFTY-TWO

# ADI CRESTONE

## MOON OF XYS, DJINNDAY, 2ND OF LUXOR

Stars were beginning to appear on the horizon by the time Adi rapped on the back door of the Red Wyrm. Five days ago, two meaty goons had led her here blindfolded and unwilling for a meeting with Ajax, the Lord of Bones. Today, Djinnday, she knocked on that same back-alley door. Adi needed to speak with Palestrina and had no other way of locating the Lady of Spiders except to look for her here.

She checked her watch. Two hours remained before the sale at Alhambra's. The sun had set over an hour ago and Adi had finally felt safe enough to come out of hiding. She had spent the afternoon in a safe house near Duneharrow, pacing up and down the ramshackle cottage, fretting. It felt good to be out in the open air, doing what needed to be done, even if that meant slinking through the shadows of Solvigant to the back door of the Red Wyrm.

The door opened to reveal one of the largest humans Adi had ever seen; his muscular frame filled the doorway. He wore dark green trousers and a white shirt from which the sleeves had been ripped off. His ears, nose, and lips were pitted with metal studs, and he sported an elongated, upside-down triangle tattoo, called a spike, which marked him as one of Petry's men. Petry Dogollon, the Lord of Pain, was the Blood Queen's third and last commander. Adi had never met him, all her assignments from the Blood Queen had come through Ajax, but she had heard of the pale giant Ankhim. If Palestrina was notorious for her secrets and spies, and Ajax for his cruelty and cunning, Petry was known to be a sadistic madman. His presence made people uncomfortable enough that the Blood Queen often sent him off-moon and kept him busy intimidating the many fingers of her smuggling operations into profitable efficiency.

"I'm here to see Palestrina," Adi said to the guard.

When he did not respond, Adi tried to squeeze past him, but he blocked her path with a massive arm.

"Who're you?" he slurred, and Adi realized part of the man's tongue was missing.

"The Lady of Spiders is expecting me, and she expects me to be discreet."

It took the big man a moment to catch up. "Gimme a name."

Adi sighed. "Adi Crestone." She hoped Petry Dogollon was somewhere far away and this goon was only here on some errand. The guard slammed the door shut and Adi heard his ponderous footsteps clunking up the stairs. Adi paced and waited. She was sure Broc would have watchmen keeping an eye on the front entrance, so she was loath to go around. Just when she had decided to risk it, the door clanged open and the huge man beckoned her inside. The distant throb of music from the front of the club vibrated through her boots. The evening festivities kicked off early on Djinnday.

Adi followed the brute up the steps and onto the landing. She exhaled with relief when she saw Ajax was not in his office, but it was cut off a moment later when the Spike opened the door across the hall to reveal a sumptuously appointed conference room. The first thing Adi noticed was the clock. She realized she had been able to hear it ticking and grinding as soon as she entered the building. Its gears and wheels took up an entire wall, so that the water flowed in an intricate spiral toward the center of the gear assembly which sat below the central drum dial. The water powering the chronological contraption flowed dark red through delicate glass tubing.

*Looks like blood,* Adi thought and her face blanched. Her father had possessed a water clock in their main reception hall. It was smaller than this one, but one thing Adi remembered about its workings was that it required a constant supply of water.

*Whose blood? Blood would clot. Maybe it's wine.*

Behind Adi a throat was cleared, and she turned to see *all three* of the Blood Queen's commanders occupying chairs. Adi thanked the Nine that the Blood Queen herself was not present.

The bones that draped Ajax jangled as he rose to greet her. "Adison, welcome. We were just speaking of you."

"You were?" Adi's mouth was dry.

"Palestrina was updating us on your progress recovering Apyreon for the Queen."

"She was?" Adi's gaze flicked to Palestrina. There was no emotion in the Seraph's features, no indication of either irritation or excitement at her intrusion. Adi did recognize the necklace Palestrina was wearing as the one she had dropped outside of Opus Station. Eight overlapping rings framed the center stone, alternating plain gold and gold set with pavé diamonds. The central stone itself was an oval amber topaz, easily eight to ten carats. It hung around her neck on a braided golden chain. Palestrina's cool eyes dared Adi to comment on the remarkable piece.

*That must be Lady Brixton's necklace Broc mentioned.*

"Who are you?" The soft voice was Petry's and sounded as if his throat had been lacerated on more than one occasion.

"Adison Crestone. A Blood Queen indenture."

She had thought the goon at the door was big, but Petry made Verdun look small. The high-backed chair upon which the commander sat creaked and groaned whenever the Lord of Pain shifted. Adi fought the urge to gape as she took him in. His shoulders were easily four feet wide and his thick neck rose like a column from his meaty chest, making his head look too small. He wore no shirt, displaying the dense Ankhimian battle tattoos on his smooth skin. And he was completely white.

*Albino,* Adi realized. He wore round goggles fitted close to his face to protect his telltale red eyes.

The Lord of Pain motioned to a seat beside Ajax. "Sit, Adi Crestone. Tell us of your progress."

Adi sat. The guard left the room, closing the door behind him. Unease made her mind go blank.

"Well?" Petry said after long moments when no one spoke. Adi jumped when he slapped the table. "Speak!"

She had no choice. She dared not lie to them for fear of what they might already know, and for fear of endangering Lucas further.

"Stuart Royal has Apyreon," Adi said, her voice cracking.

Palestrina waved an impatient hand and a servant appeared from a door behind her with a pitcher of water and four glasses. Adi's hands shook as she drained the entire glass.

"Royal is selling the device to Water Knife mercenaries tonight. The sale occurs at Alhambra's."

"Who do the mercenaries represent?" Ajax asked.

"I don't know."

"I'll have my spies in the guild look into it," Palestrina said.

"Interesting," Petry growled.

"You asked me to retrieve the device. I intend to do so."

"Then why are you here?" Palestrina asked.

Adi's eyes rested once more on the amber topaz nestled against the Seraph's throat. Palestrina caught the look and smiled.

"You like it? It was a gift."

"I saw one like it in the impound at Opus Station."

"What a coincidence!"

Adi willed herself to gaze around the table and make eye contact with each of the commanders. "I need help. If this device is so important to the Queen, I need backup."

"I thought you were sufficiently motivated," Ajax said.

"It's not about motivation. I would do anything for my son but sending me alone into a Talon lair to steal from the White Rabbits while trying to evade the Water Knives is suicide. I cannot succeed against those odds."

"You want soldiers?" Petry asked.

"No, I want to steal the device not start a war. Leyala Fedhani and Devlin Seneschal will be there in force, as will Royal after Palestrina's earlier assassination attempt. I assume the Water Knives, too, will assess the situation and respond with an appropriate number of soldiers to safeguard their client's asset. It's already a powder keg. If a squad of Blood Queen soldiers showed, it would be open war in the streets of Solvigant."

The Seraph's nostrils flared. "Seneschal will be there?"

"Then what *do* you want from us?" Petry asked in his coarse whisper.

The blood clock chimed a quarter past eight. The unexpected resonance of the bells startled her. Ajax smiled. Adi forced herself to face the Blood Queen's commanders, not peer over her shoulder at the menacing clock.

"You could return my dragonstone," Adi said.

Ajax chuckled, the dry bones rattling as his shoulders moved. "No."

"You would send me alone and unarmed?"

"Nice try," Ajax said. "You were an astral mage, Crestone. We're not sending you in as a mechanic. Besides, you have nothing to exchange. What could you offer us in return?"

Adi knew better than to take that bait.

"What about the void mage from the Iron Dirigible?" Palestrina asked.

"I haven't seen him since, but I assume he is also interested in Apyreon and aware of the sale."

"You haven't answered my question," Petry said. "What do you want?"

"I came to ask if Palestrina would accompany me."

The trio of commanders was silent.

"Why?" Palestrina said at length.

"You have unfinished business with Royal," Adi said. *And it would seem Seneschal as well,* but Adi kept that thought to herself. "Two of us can still sneak in. You're stealthier than I am anyway. You have astral magic and I've seen you wield those shotels."

"Perhaps I'll send in my men and acquire it without you," Petry cut in. "My Spikes are better equipped to manage the extraction anyway."

"That wasn't the deal," Adi protested.

"But this way my Queen gets the device and we get the continued pleasure of your service."

"No," Adi said with more vehemence than was proper given her status here. "I do this for you and I'm done. Lucas is safe, my indenture is paid, and my dragonstone comes back to me. That was the deal."

"I made no such deal." Petry said. "Did my Queen make such a deal with you, little pirate?"

"I dealt with her," Ajax said, and Adi caught the slightest quaver in his voice.

"A bad deal," Petry said.

"Nevertheless, it's the one I made and I will not have it said that I reneged." His voice had steadied.

Adi bit back a sigh of relief. When one operated outside the law, all you had was your word. If Ajax reneged on his deal he would lose face with the city's powerful criminal element, which meant the Blood Queen would lose face. If Adi knew anything about her anger, she knew the loss of honor to be intolerable.

"I will come with you," Palestrina said.

"You will?" Adi was unable to hide her relief. "I mean, thank you, Lady of Spiders."

Palestrina smirked.

"I will send six handpicked men with you," Petry said.

"That will not be necessary, Petry," Palestrina objected. "I have my own soldiers."

"I do not trust them," Petry said. He muttered something else under his breath that Adi did not catch. All three commanders stiffened, and Adi wondered exactly what the topic of conversation had been before her arrival.

"I will send six men," Petry repeated. "They will have no difficulty infiltrating Alhambra's with you. If you do not leave Alhambra's by eleven or my men do not signal that all

is well, I will invade with a larger force. If I catch any hint of the void mage, I will invade."
He rubbed his throat as if so much speech pained him.

Adi wanted to object but could not. Six Spikes would make the already challenging task of killing Palestrina that much more difficult. But Adi had no power at this table and she had no grounds to object without making Palestrina suspicious. She waited for Palestrina to protest, but the Lady of Spiders remained silent.

"Is that all, Adi?" Palestrina asked. Adi's head was swimming, her heart pumping at twice the tempo of the clock.

"Yes," Adi managed.

"Good. Petry, have your men meet us out front."

"That may not be the best idea," Adi said. "I made many enemies with the city watch today. I am sure there are a few out front watching for me."

Palestrina grimaced. "I will not allow them to arrest you. They are in no position to bring down the wrath of the Blood Queen."

Adi felt undercurrents in Palestrina's words.

*Do they know how powerful Apyreon can be? Do they have the other piece?*

Adi could think of no clever way to ask without giving the game away.

"What are you going to do in the meantime?" Ajax asked.

Palestrina's smile was all sharp teeth. "Adi and I have to visit the armory."

# CHAPTER FIFTY-THREE

# THEO VANGUARD

## MOON OF XYS, DJINNDAY, 2ND OF LUXOR

F ather Limon Heilig cleared his throat and the organ behind the lectern began to play. The marriage anthem echoed through the Temple of the Nine, rising into the high wooden dome painted with the investiture of the first Solan Emperor Solaric Callire by all nine of the Avernian gods.

Theo stared down the empty nave and waited for Hannah to appear. The marriage rite traditionally required someone to stand as Theo's witness. He had refused to allow his father the honor, and Isaiah had not returned from whatever errand he went on after their meeting with Rehka. Fortunately, Arthur Volaticus agreed to stand for Theo. Tabitha was present for Hannah. She sat behind the bride's station in her wheelchair, the rims chased in pearl, amethyst, and gold.

Hannah stepped from the narthex in a flowing white gown covered with opalescent glass beads that sparkled in the temple's torchlight. Her red hair, covered with a fine silver net, curled down her back.

*She is beautiful,* Theo thought as Hannah progressed toward him. Even with a grim expression on her face, she glowed from the powders and creams dabbed on her cheeks to give her pale skin a ruddy complexion. *Where did she find that dress?*

Theo suspected she had traveled to Xys with the dress, that his father and his bride had conspired to have the wedding here all along for reasons beyond Theo's comprehension. He knew there was a longer, more subtle game playing out around him. Not only was he an unwilling participant, but he did not know all the players or their respective goals, some of which had to conflict with one another. He disliked being a pawn.

*How many players are there? My father? Hannah? Isaiah? Emperor Callire? Others?*

Theo pushed the dark thoughts of hidden conspiracies aside and focused on his bride, now two-thirds of the way along the nave to where Theo stood in the chancel. Four Daughters of Light trailed behind Hannah, each holding a handful of the long satin train. Hannah wore a carmine sash with a ruby brooch. The latter a symbol of House Valefyre that she was leaving behind. The former indicated the bride's virginal status. Both symbols would be presented to Theo during the ceremony. As she approached the few spectators, she offered a faltering smile.

The guests sat in the first few rows. Art's wife struggled to contain their four squirming children. Governor Eliot Gambol stifled a yawn. Theo's father sat on the opposite side of the aisle with Commander Linton, chief officer of Solvigant's city watch. Beatrice Marrion sat rigid in the pew in front of the Seraph, beside Hubert, her eyes on Theo. The captain and crew of the *Penumbra* had a row to themselves. A half dozen Xyssian congressmen who owed favors to his father filled out the rest of the final row. As Xander was not among them, Theo did not recognize any of them.

Hannah stopped before him and handed her large bouquet to Tabitha. The Daughters of Light rolled up the train with deft fingers and unclipped it from her gown. Theo watched as Hannah's shoulders rose and fell with a long sigh before she turned to face him, a smile on her lips and moisture beading in the corners of her eyes. Theo took her hands in his as he had been instructed to do and tried to ease his stiff posture. At a signal from Father Heilig, the organ music concluded and the archbishop cleared his throat.

Theo paid little attention to Heilig's soliloquy on the virtues of marriage as articulated in the Book of Solo. He invoked each god in turn and expounded on the gifts each one bestowed upon pious young couples. Theo held Hannah's gaze in what he felt was a kind of apology for being so unfairly rude to this noble woman. It was the machinations of his father that irritated him, not her or her unwitting role in the aristocratic game. As a fifth son, Theo shared the same status on that board that Hannah held, and nothing he did would elevate him in his father's regard.

The women of House Azure intruded on Theo's thoughts. He could feel Beatrice's unwavering gaze boring into his shoulder blades. He told himself it was just the scratchy wool of his formal dress uniform, but he knew better. His pulse quickened when he remembered the sea salt and cinnamon smell of the prophet, the uncalloused palm of her hand caressing his cheek as she bandaged his injury. On cue, his palm twitched, the pressure of the white kid gloves making the wound ache. Hannah's eyes widened with fear that she had done something wrong and began to pull her hands away. Theo gripped her fingers and gave them a reassuring squeeze.

Hannah's reactions often confused Theo. When she had come for him at the Echo she had been the picture of haughty nobility and the overconfidence that came with that personage. Tonight, she vibrated like a hummingbird, poised to fly away at the slightest threat.

*She is only sixteen,* Theo reminded himself. *Still a child.*

Father Heilig droned on and Theo wanted to check his watch. The sale of Apyreon would be taking place soon.

*Where is Isaiah?*

Theo was hurt that his brother was not in attendance. It went beyond the petty sibling rivalries of "look at me, I'm doing my duty." Paul was dead, Dante was in prison, and Joshua, though the heir, had never understood the honor that motivated Theo. That left Isaiah, and while Theo would never understand his brother's allegiance to the void, he still felt more kinship toward Isaiah than he did to any of his other brothers. It could be they were both harnessed and subject to the driving hand of their father, but Theo wanted to imagine it was something more.

Father Heilig ceased speaking and a string quartet began to play. The traditional music for this part of the ceremony provided a gentler backdrop to the vows spoken by the participants. He knew the piece from other formal weddings he had attended but had never imagined he would hear the warmth of the cello and lilting melody of the violin and viola played for him, and certainly never under these circumstances.

It was time to complete the ritual. He fumbled at Hannah's brooch, unaccustomed to working with gloved fingers. Hannah made a small, nervous sound before Theo detached the pin and placed it in the box Art provided for this purpose. Hannah lifted her sash over the confection of her coiffured hair and Theo bowed low so she could place the fabric over his right shoulder and smooth it into place across his chest.

Next, Lord Simon Vanguard stepped forward. As Lord of House Vanguard, he draped the blue sash over Lady Valefyre's shoulder, bowed low, and kissed her hand. Theo did not look at him but kept his eyes and smile directed toward Hannah. Theo wanted her to feel his acceptance. He lifted the blue brooch symbolic of House Vanguard and pinned it to the new sash.

The exchange of rings, plain bands of gold, and vows followed. When the newlyweds returned to the Vanguard estates at Balan on Tyre, they would host a proper celebration with the two houses and exchange official rings. At that event, Theo would be expected to speak on the virtues of his wife. He was grateful that tonight, given their compressed timeline, they would only repeat the prescribed vows from the Book of Solo. Theo stuttered twice but made it through his part. Hannah's voice rang clear and confident, though Theo saw that the confidence did not extend to her eyes.

*What does she think of me? And why haven't I wondered about this before? I must look like a spoiled, petulant child.*

Finally, Father Heilig ordered them to kiss. Theo leaned in and met Hannah's lips, dry and firm, chapped from the desert air of Solvigant in Veria.

And they were wed. Together they turned and faced the gathered crowd. Everyone clapped except for the Volaticus children who were delighted when they realized their cheers echoed inside the high-ceilinged temple. Theo winked at them. The organ struck up the recessional and the newlyweds walked down the empty nave. The Daughters of Light rang bright brass bells and sang a celebratory song in a language Theo did not recognize. Behind them, the rest of the guests processed out.

As Theo and Hannah neared the main doors of the temple, he felt Hannah stiffen. Two city watchmen in dress uniforms stood on either side of the door holding ceremonial poleaxes. They banged the shafts twice on the floor and saluted Theo. He released Hannah's hand from his arm so he could return the salute and then apologized to her by reaching for her hand and holding it. The watchmen opened the doors to the temple steps.

Theo was surprised to see an entire platoon of city watchmen standing in the windy evening air. When the couple appeared, an artillery crew fired a volley of arquebuses and the watchmen cheered. Black and blue banners of House Vanguard, held aloft by the Lord Vanguard's personal guards, snapped on their poles. At the bottom of the steps, a gilded carriage waited. Theo shielded his bride from the wind as they made their way down the stairs. Hannah's delicate heels prevented her from hurrying.

Theo paused at the bottom of the stairs when he saw Senior Inspector Solomon Broc was holding the door for them. A few of the other nearby watchmen gave the inspector sideways glances, clearly wondering what the Faelani badger was going to do. Theo was relieved. If the inspector was here it meant he didn't know about what was going to happen at Alhambra's.

"Congratulations and farewell," Broc said gruffly as Theo approached. Broc's wide grin revealed all his white teeth.

"Thank you, Inspector." The couple waited before the open door, but Broc said nothing else.

Hannah broke the silence. "Will you help me into the carriage, husband?"

Theo steadied her as she mounted the narrow steps, then turned to Broc.

"I'm sorry, Inspector."

Broc let out a curt laugh. "What for?"

"For the way this all turned out."

"Crestone will still hang. There will just be one less body swinging next to her."

Theo opened his mouth to say more, but Broc pushed him into the carriage and shut the door.

"Enjoy your wedding night, young Lord Vanguard."

The driver snapped the reins and the carriage jolted forward. Theo looked back to see his father and Lady Marrion standing at the top of the steps, watching him depart.

Theo sat back in the carriage and closed his eyes. Until now, he had not considered his other wedding night duty. His father expected Hannah to be with child when the delegation returned from Maxon and certainly before the two of them returned to the Balan Estates. One of the ladies accompanying Hannah on the voyage was a skilled midwife, just in case. Though Theo's older brother Joshua was technically the heir, he remained unwed and childless. He did not think Joshua had any bastards. Theo did not either, but both Paul and Dante had more than enough for the rest of the family. Paul's wife Lucile had only borne two daughters when Paul had died fighting on Maxon. But their father would burn the family estates to the ground before he bestowed titles upon a bastard or a woman.

Their wedding night would happen aboard the *Penumbra*. Theo did not relish consummating their marriage in the cabin of a ship. He knew the quarters would be sumptuously appointed, but even so, there was little privacy on any sailing vessel. He knew this from his naval experience, overhearing his comrades and soldiers when they brought prostitutes aboard in every port. Theo had limited experience himself. He believed it was his duty as an officer to model noble behavior in port and at sea. At least the emperor had done away with the barbaric practice of having someone in the room to observe the consummation. He wondered how much Hannah was thinking about the hours ahead.

Hannah's voice intruded into his thoughts. "Was it truly so terrible?"

Theo opened his eyes and saw she had removed her shoes and the silver net from her hair. She had a handful of pins and was plucking more from the recesses of her curls.

He checked his watch. The *Penumbra* was scheduled to depart at eleven. It was a quarter to ten. Stuart Royal was walking into Alhambra's right now. Theo could not explain why he felt he ought to be there, why he still felt Aypreon was his responsibility. Theo turned his attention to Hannah and tried not to think about the drama unfolding elsewhere in the city. He had enough happening in his own life.

"No, it was fine. Just not what I expected."

"What did you expect?"

Theo tried to think of an answer that would not hurt Hannah's feelings. As much as Theo did not want this marriage, he could not bring himself to be cruel to this young woman.

"I didn't expect to get married in an empty church on Xys." Theo motioned to the dress. "You did, apparently."

"Your father thought it prudent to be prepared for any eventuality."

*She even sounds like him sometimes.* "Can we please not talk about my father?"

Hannah flushed. "Sorry."

"It's all right." Theo was chastened despite himself. He offered her his hand again.

She said, "I didn't expect to spend our honeymoon visiting the God of Destruction."

Theo chuckled and the tension in Hannah's body eased. An awkward pause followed his laughter then Hannah moved closer and nestled into his shoulder and Theo put a tentative arm around her. The carriage was smooth, its suspension built and reinforced for the rough roads of Solvigant.

Theo and Hannah glided along together toward the aeroport and the *Penumbra*.

# CHAPTER FIFTY-FOUR

# ADI CRESTONE

## MOON OF XYS, DJINNDAY, 2ND OF LUXOR

Adi crouched between a bronze foundry and a dark warehouse waiting for Palestrina to return. Across the street, Alhambra's was quiet. The aeroport had eight berths arranged equidistant from one another around a circular terminal. The terminal itself sat atop a four-story brick tower. The entire structure resembled a great toadstool. Adi could just make out the fin and upper portion of the gas envelope of a Behlian coal freighter moored on the far side. The other berths sat empty. Adi studied the distant glimmer of an aerogate to the northeast in case a ship emerged. Behind her, Petry's six Spikes shifted in their combat fatigues.

Adi checked her watch again, a quarter to eleven.

*Where is Palestrina?*

The Seraph had left five minutes ago to fly recon around the tower. A workman exited the foundry and struck a match to light a cigarette. Adi recoiled at the sudden flash, backing further into the gap between the two buildings. Leathery wings rustled and Palestrina dropped from the sky to stand beside Adi. The orange glow of Solo did not penetrate the narrow space, so she appeared as a winged shadow with luminous eyes. The Spikes shifted closer to hear Palestrina's report.

"There's an external ladder on the east side of the building," said the Lady of Spiders, "but it ends twenty feet off the ground. You could climb the terrane and jump from the top of a car. It's a bit far."

As much as Adi loathed the idea of soaring through the air in Palestrina's arms, Adi had to ask the question. "Could you lift me?"

"My wings aren't strong enough to carry you."

"Other entrances?"

"Fedhani's men are out in force. There are four Talon soldiers on the main entrance and another six on the freight entrance on the north side. There's a padlocked door on the east by the terrane, beneath the ladder. There are two soldiers stationed there. We'll have to take them out before anyone can attempt the jump."

"Let's go then," Adi said. "We don't have much time."

"Who's back there?" the foundry worker shouted toward them from the far end of the gap. The red glow of his cigarette hung loose from his lips. Before Adi could react, one of the Spikes slipped past her, clamped a meaty hand over the worker's face, spun him around, and snaked his other arm around the man's throat. The man struggled but he was no match for a trained fighter. The Spike dragged the foundry worker into the gap and snapped his neck.

"Coast is clear," the Spike growled.

Anger bubbled up in Adi's throat. She wanted to object, but there was no time.

*The first innocent casualty of the night. How many more will there be?* She forced herself to focus. *Apyreon is the priority. The Blood Queen is waiting.*

Adi pushed guilt and worry aside. Bale's warning echoed in her ears. That was a decision for later when she had the device in hand.

Palestrina followed Adi out of the gap and the Spikes ran ahead. The street was wide here to accommodate the numerous freight and triple box wagons required to load and unload cargo from the aeroport. The street was not, however, well lit, to Adi's relief. South of Alhambra's aeroport there was a hundred meters of open space cleared for vessels on approach. Solo's light stained it dimly orange. Overhead, the southeastern dock was illuminated for an impending arrival. Adi crouched low and ran, hoping that the two Talon guards did not look south.

Adi hurdled over the tight-lock coupler between two terrane boxcars. Her right foot banged against the draw gear, and she tumbled forward, twisting her ankle, but she rolled and came up on her feet. The numerous weapons she had acquired from the Red Wyrm's armory jangled. She swore under her breath. When she stood two of the Spikes grinned at her.

*The only thing worse than clumsiness is witnesses,* Adi thought.

She tested her weight on the turned ankle. She would limp tomorrow, but tonight she could manage. They made their way along the far side of the terrane, using its massive wheels and the bulk of its freight cars as cover until they were across from the iron door.

The two Talon soldiers shared a flask. Torches burned in sconces on the curved wall behind them. They spoke in hushed voices so Adi could not make out their conversation. One wore an ivory horn at his belt so he could alert other soldiers in the case of an attack.

"There's no way to sneak up on them," Adi said to the Spikes. Palestrina was above her somewhere, winging through the night sky toward the roof of the aeroport. One Spike removed a flintlock pistol from a holster.

"Too loud!" Adi hissed. She really needed Rehka and her throwing knives. Adi could swing a sword like any half-decent pirate, but archery eluded her. She checked her watch: ten minutes before the exchange.

Another Spike strung a longbow and spoke to his comrades in a stilted Ankhimian dialect. Adi did not understand, but she got the gist of his hand motions.

"When my men rush the guards, climb the terrane," he said to Adi in the common tongue.

"Rushing the guards seems a bad idea," Adi said, but the Spike ignored her, nocking an arrow. His men moved to either side of the freight car and waited.

The first arrow missed, but the men charged anyway. Adi knew she ought to be climbing the boxcar, but she could not look away. She cursed under her breath that these fools accompanied her.

The soldier was placing the horn to his lips when the second arrow took him in the throat. He fell to his knees and the horn tumbled into the sand. The second guard ran around the aeroport toward the freight entrance, but the Spikes were faster. When it was clear they would catch the soldier before he could warn his comrades, Adi climbed the freight car. There was no ladder, but there were enough framing boards that she could scale the sidewall. She swung up onto the boxcar. With its all-terrain wheels, the boxcar was tall enough that Adi was eye level with the bottom rung of the exterior ladder. It was, however, four meters away. She only had the width of the terrane car to get up to speed and her bruised ribs ached from the run and the climb.

*I can't jump that far.*

Adi followed the line of rungs as they ascended the tower then curved outward along the underbelly of the aeroport. Assuming she made the jump, it would be a challenging climb while hanging upside down along the curve of the wood. She flexed her fingers and backed up as far as she could. Then she had an idea.

She beckoned for two Spikes to join her on the roof. She positioned them on the ledge of the car, their hands laced together to form a basket. They quickly realized what Adi wanted and, though they looked skeptical, neither objected to the plan. She felt exposed standing up here and desperately wanted to be in the shadow of the building, so she quickly backed up and nodded to her companions.

She took three running steps, set her right foot in the basket, and the two men heaved. She soared through the air, arms flailing to keep her upright.

The ladder was so far away.

She was going to fall short.

Her magic would have made a leap like this possible, but instead the Lord of Bones was using her magical focus as a bookmark.

Adi stifled a cry as the fingers of her right hand curled around the bottom rung of the ladder. Her left hand missed its hold and the force of catching herself one-handed wrenched her shoulder. She braced her feet against the building and her left hand found purchase. She pulled herself up, pausing to catch her breath once her feet were on a rung. She swallowed to calm her pounding heart, shook out one hand at a time, and began to climb. At the junction where the vertical brick of the tower met the wooden curve of the terminal, she risked a downward glance. Two of the Spikes had made the jump using her basket technique, and two more waited on the terrane. Adi watched as the leader made his jump, landing easily, his hands on the fourth rung.

*The Lord of Pain trains his men well.* She immediately regretted the thought when she pictured Petry raiding the sale in an hour if she failed. *It will be a massacre.* But it also steeled her nerves, and she climbed out onto the curve of the terminal. The ladder was easier than it had looked from below. The curve was subtle and her feet only slipped once. When the wall between the two berths angled back to vertical Adi sighed with relief. Her hands and shoulders shook, but she climbed a bit higher before pausing to rest. She heard the swish of fabric and the creak of ropes behind her. Adi looked over her shoulder and saw a small dirigible sailing toward the berth on her left. She had not noticed the ship emerging from the distant aerogate while she concentrated on her climb. The mast above the gas bag flew the blue and white crossed swords of the Water Knives.

*So much for my stealthy approach,* she thought. *They can swat me like a moth on a wall.*

Adi climbed faster. She needed to get out of the ambient glow of the docking lanterns. The skiff was too distant for Adi to discern individual crew members ranging the deck. It looked like a Huxstable 135, which meant it was small, fast, and well-armed for its size. The fact that it was under backward thrust even though the sails were not reefed meant that there was at least one astral mage aboard.

A Spike peered over the lip of the curve below and she motioned him back down, pointing at the approaching vessel. She checked her watch: eleven o'clock, right on time.

The top of the aeroport terminal was easier to climb. The slope angle of the dome was so slight that Adi did not need the ladder, though it continued all the way to the top. At the center stood a short lighthouse, its paraboloidal mirror orbiting silently on its geared track around the central flame. Palestrina was waiting beside the base of a stellarium array. Its netting pulsed with a soft cerulean glow as it harvested the ambient astral dust from the night sky.

"It's beautiful up here," Adi said steadying herself against a lightning rod. The night was clear. There were few buildings in Solvigant this high and Adi relished the view as she looked back over the city. The compound dome of Congress with its impressive gold finial dominated the skyline. Solo with her glorious rings silhouetted it, as well as the clock tower in Congress Park.

She could see the distant smokestacks of Devlin Seneschal's foundry in the industrial zone and the massive stellarium array run by the Society of Astrologia at the south end of town. She could see the vast grounds of Duneharrow prison and the central aeroport tower rising above it all. Though she could not identify Stella's Echo in the vast, sprawling array of timber, brick, and canvas, she was able to find the distant glow of the night market in Torhan Square and knew that Stella's was nearby. Adi hoped Broc and his men had not ransacked it.

"There's something else," Palestrina said, once Adi had caught her breath. "I spoke with my contacts with the Water Knives: Rehka is not on assignment."

Adi reeled and leaned against the lighthouse for support. "What do you mean?"

"Rehka was suspended. She disappeared for a week in the middle of her last assignment. There's no job. The Water Knives aren't aware of Apyreon."

Adi felt sick. "That means Rehka is after the device."

"There is no buyer," Palestrina agreed. "Rehka and her crew are acting alone."

"Why would she do that? Why would she lie to me?"

Palestrina shrugged. Her nonchalance made Adi want to scream. *Maybe it won't be so hard to kill this woman.*

"Rehka's injured. Her father is putting her on a ship to Flynt." Adi needed time to process this information. Rehka had betrayed her again, only this time her old lover had endangered Lucas too. *If she weren't already on the verge of death, I might kill her myself.* Adi knew her rage was all bravado, but it felt good to pretend.

"You know Rehka," Palestrina pressed, "why would she do this?"

"Pyrea," Adi said without hesitation. *I should have known.* "Rehka intends to use Apyreon to travel to Pyrea and reconnect with her Dragon."

Four Spikes joined Adi and Palestrina on the roof and there was no more time for discussion. An older Scorpion 8 dirigible approached from the west. It was a Xyssian desert model with horizontal canvas side panels to shield its crew from the sun. There were no markings on its gunwale.

"That's Royal," Palestrina said. "Everyone's here except Devlin."

"He'll be late. The exchange should be underway before anyone crashes the party. I'll signal him with this flare." Adi pointed to the red tube secured in a belt loop. A distant tower chimed eleven bells.

She tried to suppress the grief at another betrayal by Rehka. She felt so stupid for getting caught up in the adventure, in the protestations of love, just as she always had. Rehka was no different than she was three years ago. It was easier for her to channel that grief into rage.

The lighthouse had a hatch that opened onto a set of spiral stairs. Adi crept down each step, placing her boots with care to prevent the metal grate from ringing with the impact. The stairs deposited her onto a large metal platform suspended near the ceiling of the terminal. She hunkered down to study the building, hidden from anyone standing below on the floor of the docking structure. A catwalk ran out from the platform toward every berth, like the legs of a spider. Each one terminated at a panel with the controls the stevedores used to lower and raise the drawbridge pier for the vessels that utilized this aeroport.

The pier to berth seven, where Royal's ship would soon arrive, was stuck halfway down. Adi saw two mechanics in brown coveralls on the catwalk working with a long spanner. They grunted with the effort of trying to free a jammed bolt.

*How did they get up here?* Adi wondered. *There must be stairs inside the walls of the tower like there are at the main aeroport. I wish I'd had time to reconnoiter this building. I have no idea how people can get into or out of here.* She saw no other ladders or stairs along the catwalk network that might lead to the floor below. Then she noticed a rope swing on a winch, cranked by a third mechanic down below.

One of the Spikes came down the steps behind her. Adi motioned for him to wait and pointed at the mechanics. The soldier nodded in acknowledgment. Adi noticed movement at the pier where the Water Knife Huxstable had docked. A score of mercenaries disembarked, along with several crates heavy enough to require porters with poles. She recognized Duncan by the worn bowler.

*Palestrina was right, I have been betrayed again.*

The mercenary escort headed for the stairs that would take them to the ground, which was when Adi spotted the steam-powered gatling gun mounted at the prow of the Huxstable.

*Heavy artillery!*

What little hope she had shrunk further.

The Water Knives reached the main floor and strode toward the center of the terminal where a woman in a red jumpsuit was waiting with twenty men.

*Leyala Fedhani.*

The men around her had the shaved, tattooed heads of Talon soldiers. They wore no armor but stood at attention holding long poleaxes. Slender swords hung in scabbards from their belts.

A grinding clatter echoed throughout the terminal, catching Adi's attention. The mechanics had managed to free the drawbridge pier at berth seven. It jerked and several gears slipped before the chains caught and controlled its descent. Royal's dirigible swung parallel to the pier and several deck ropes were tossed to waiting stevedores, who secured the ship. Stuart Royal disembarked. Adi had been correct. After Palestrina's assassination attempt, Royal was taking no chances. He was surrounded.

*There must be a hundred White Rabbit thugs down there.*

There was a hiss of steam and the gatling gun swiveled to cover the untidy platoon of gangsters. The White Rabbits made no move to retaliate, though they spread their ranks out so a volley from the gun might not fell as many. The dapper leporine crime lord marched forward. His men arranged themselves around him when he halted several yards from where Fedhani and the Water Knives waited.

*Where is the void mage? We must pull this off before he arrives and crashes the party.* Movement in her peripheral vision indicated that the mechanics were now using the rope swing to descend. She stepped toward the spiral stairs so the mechanic waiting for the swing's return would be less likely to see her, but two Spikes had arrived without waiting for her signal. The second mechanic grabbed his toolkit and started along the catwalk toward them. Adi froze. There was no cover for any of them.

The Spikes realized this and sprang into action. One stepped in front of Adi, pushing her behind the stairs. The other moved to her left trying to blend into the shadows until the mechanic had passed. It worked. The mechanic, not expecting company, missed the crouching Spike, and headed for berth one, where the coal freighter was docked. Adi guessed the coal from that ship was intended for the terrane outside. When the mechanic had passed, the Spike lunged, reached around the mechanic's face, and clamped one hand over the man's mouth. The Spike stabbed him repeatedly until he crumpled. Adi dove forward and caught the toolbox before it clattered onto the metal grating.

"Fool!" Adi's whisper was harsh.

The Spike realized his mistake and took the weight of the falling man under the shoulders and lowered him gently onto the grate. Blood soaked his coveralls. Adi lay prone, holding the toolbox.

"Stanch the blood with something before it drips through the grate."

Her eyes were glued to the scene below. No one was looking up. The noise of Royal's troops shuffling into position had muffled the fiasco on the catwalk. Adi swore a silent blue streak as she lowered the toolbox gently onto the grating. She stood and shoved the flare gun at the murderous Spike.

"Go signal Devlin," she ordered.

The Spike wanted to object, but Palestrina had come down the stairs and taken in the scene.

"Go!" Palestrina hissed. Chastened, the Spike returned to the roof of the terminal.

*I hope Devlin's close by.*

Adi sent up a prayer to Phoebe that her diversion would come soon.

# CHAPTER FIFTY-FIVE
# ADI CRESTONE
## MOON OF XYS, DJINNDAY, 2ND OF LUXOR

A di watched the exchange below unfold. In the middle of the terminal, Talon soldiers had placed a table and four chairs. Leyala Fedhani sat down and motioned for the others to join her. Next, Duncan took the seat intended for Rehka and Stuart Royal took the third chair. Royal held a cloth-wrapped bundle in one hand. A short man with half his face obscured by a metal plate fused to his flesh sat in the fourth. Adi knew the clunker as the proprietor of the Iron Dirigible, Tabrin Wik.

She could not hear their conversation and wondered what details of the transaction still needed to be settled. Duncan looked angry and was gesticulating at Fedhani and Tabrin with short, punchy gestures.

Royal slid the bundle across the table to the mercenary, who loosened the drawstrings and peered inside. He nodded, closed the bag, and signaled his crew.

*Apyreon, it must be! Where is Seneschal?*

The Spike she had sent to fire the flare returned from the roof. Together, the four Spikes took ropes from their packs, affixed them to the railing, and prepared to rappel into the fray.

The first mechanic reached the floor of the terminal, and his comrade sent the swing back up. In two minutes, the mechanics would be wondering about the whereabouts of the third man. Adi glanced at the dead man. Bright blood stained the cloth pressed against his kidneys.

Below, Royal rose from the table and went to examine the Water Knife chest. Adi's breath caught. The crates were not full of gold spyres. Even from this distance she could discern the oily gleam of polished metal. Royal grinned.

Adi's heart hammered. *Weapons! Rehka was paying off the White Rabbits with armaments.*

She recognized a Vermax automatic rifle though she had never seen one in action. Heavy and complicated, they were intended for entrenched fortifications. They were too expensive for any but formal armies. Adi had seen nothing of this magnitude in the armory at the Red Wyrm. She looked at Palestrina. Her scowl showed her level of rage that Royal would bring such weapons into Solvigant. If the White Rabbits had that kind of firepower, war between the gangs would be inevitable no matter what happened tonight.

Questions swirled through Adi's mind. *Why fight a gang war on a dying moon? Why was Rehka arming the White Rabbits? Why would the Order of the Talon allow the White Rabbits such a clear military advantage?*

Adi's watch showed half past eleven. Soon Petry's men would raid the aeroport. She needed Seneschal and his distraction right now.

"By the Nine," Adi hissed, "this will take too long. Where is Devlin?"

"He is notoriously unreliable," Palestrina whispered.

She wanted to ask Palestrina about that, but this was not the time. Seneschal's price for a distraction and Palestrina's reaction at the Red Wyrm suggested that there was history between the two Seraphim. Adi studied Palestrina.

*Can I really kill her?* Adi wondered. *She saved my life in Opus Station.* She owed her life to too many people.

"What is it?" Palestrina whispered.

"Nothing."

The four Spikes stood by their ropes, waiting for Palestrina's signal. A splotch of red hit the gauntlet of a Water Knife mercenary. Adi bit her lip to keep from crying out in dismay. The saturated cloth pressed against the dead mechanic's body dripped. Before Adi could move to stop it, another drop fell through the metal grating. This one struck the mercenary's arm. Another drop. It landed on his upturned face.

"Djinnar's fury!" he shouted. "Up there, on the catwalk."

The terminal rang with drawn swords.

Movement from berth one, where the Behlian coal freighter was docked, distracted Adi. Ten men wearing the gray robes of Chaos acolytes emerged from the dock, the void mage striding behind them. Adi swallowed. Every soldier in the room tensed and watched him. One void mage could not overpower everyone in the room, but no one wanted to engage him.

"Find Palestrina," the void mage shouted. His acolytes produced crossbows and sighted on the catwalk as the aeroport erupted into a confused medley of shouts and curses.

"Djinnar's blood!" Adi hissed. *He's not here for Apyreon.*

The Spikes hesitated, still waiting for Palestrina's command.

"Go!" Palestrina said and leapt from the catwalk, spreading her wings. The Spikes heaved themselves over the railing and slid down their ropes. Adi ran toward the mechanic's swing at the far end of the catwalk.

Two concussive blasts rocked the terminal. Adi grabbed the railing as the superstructure vibrated from the explosions. When the world stopped rocking, she looked down into a smoking hole in the outer wall of berth eight. Through it she could see a new dirigible broadside to the pier.

A series of muffled bangs sounded from the dirigible's main deck and Adi saw puffs of smoke drifting west off the gunwale. She expected cannonballs, but half a dozen boarding grapples shot through the hole in the pier and lodged their steel spikes in the wooden floor of the terminal. The lines went taught, anchoring the newcomers. The air buzzed as if filled with angry bees as Devlin's soldiers whizzed down the lines.

The initial explosion knocked one of the Spikes from his rappel. The fall was not far enough to kill him, but he hit the floor in a heap, clutching at his fractured leg.

*Focus,* Adi thought.

Stuart Royal stood amid a circle of men shouting orders over the din. Duncan headed toward his ship, gesturing wildly, Apyreon clutched in one hand.

Adi smiled. *Where are you off to?*

She took a deep breath to calm herself, got up, drew her sword, and stepped out onto the swing. She hit the swing's counterweight mechanism with her sword's pommel and it dropped fast. Adi bent her knees and rolled a split second before the swing crashed onto the terminal floor. She stopped in a crouch. Across the floor she heard a rush of steam followed by a grating, metallic whir.

*The gatling gun on the Water Knifes' Huxstable.* Adi dove behind a weapons crate, praying it held nothing explosive. Bullets sprayed from the spinning barrel at the fore deck of the dirigible and dozens of White Rabbits and Talon soldiers fell under the onslaught.

Two rounds ricocheted off Adi's crate. When the metallic whir slackened so the gunners could reload, Adi popped her head up. Two dozen men lay dead and numerous others were bleeding from bullet wounds. Royal clutched a bloody paw to one shoulder. Everywhere men were fighting. Fedhani's soldiers were engaged with Seneschal's, the acolytes tried to corral the Water Knives and drive them back toward their ship, to block the gatling gun's line of fire.

Adi saw Palestrina, shotels drawn, descend in front of Duncan. He parried a strike meant for his neck but dropped Apyreon in the process.

*That's my cue.*

She bolted from cover and sprinted toward the artifact on the floor. She closed half the distance when the grinding whir of the gatling gun resumed.

Adi leapt over an empty crate, almost striking two White Rabbits who were locking one of the Vermax belt guns onto its tripod. She lost sight of Apyreon. During their fight, either Duncan or Palestrina kicked the device away. Then Adi spotted it, changed course, and ran.

*I hope Apyreon's robust enough to survive this thrashing.*

She was close when a new shockwave blew her off her feet. A wave of void energy swept toward the Water Knife ship. The terminal lights dimmed for a moment and the gatling gun stopped. Adi saw the Void mage on one knee near the table. Expending enough Void magic to blow a ship in half must have been excruciating.

The aft deck of the Huxstable was gone and a wall of flames was licking up the central spar toward the hydrogen gas bag. Water Knife mercenaries heaved the windlass to open the gas ports and vent the hydrogen before it ignited in a giant ball of fire.

*Glad I'm on the opposite side of the terminal.*

The shock wave had sent Apyreon spinning across the floor. All around Adi men and women fought. Palestrina had left Duncan and was now focusing her energy on Royal. The two remaining Spikes flanked the Lady of Spiders, keeping White Rabbit thugs from distracting Palestrina.

Apyreon was near the Behlian coal freighter. She sprinted behind Seneschal's men, but Tabrin had seen it, too, and was crawling toward it.

Another concussive blast shook the base of the tower. The whole aeroport trembled and the catwalk above swayed. A pair of mooring cables ripped away from the ceiling. Adi managed to keep her feet and dove for Apyreon. Her hand closed over the cloth-wrapped bundle at the same moment as Tabrin's. She punched him on the fleshy side of his face. He grunted and rolled away, blood trickling from his nose.

*Gotta get outta here—*

Leyala Fedhani kicked Adi in the stomach. White spots exploded in her vision as she doubled over and dropped the device. Fedhani followed up with a wild punch at Adi's face, but she dodged just in time.

The Talon woman stood between Adi and all avenues of escape. One hand wore brass knuckles, and she held a punching dagger in the other. Adi drew her jambiya. Apyreon lay on the floor between them.

Adi swung her sword in a wide arc then dove for the device. Fedhani leapt back, kicked Apyreon away, and punched the dagger toward Adi's gut. Adi parried, but the blade nicked her stomach, drawing a thin line of blood. She bashed her sword's guard into Fedhani's chin. The woman stumbled back, but regained her balance, spat out a gob of blood, and charged Adi.

For long seconds, Adi fought off Fedhani's furious assault. Steel clashed against steel as Fedhani lashed out with the dagger and Adi parried. Adi had the longer reach, but Fedhani was faster. It was all Adi could do to block her and retreat toward the outer wall of the terminal.

Adi's numerous injuries ached in protest. Sweat trickled down her face. She had to fling her hair back and forth to keep it from obscuring her vision. Fedhani was panting but showed less fatigue. Their two blades connected again in a jarring clang that rattled Adi's teeth.

Fedhani's fist connected with Adi's ribs and the brass knuckles bit deep. Adi cried out and dropped to one knee. She used her shoulder to block the next punch, then drew a long boot knife. Fedhani's eyes widened as Adi drove the thin blade deep into the woman's thigh. She stumbled back, screaming and clutching her leg.

Suddenly, Fedhani's body jerked as an arrow sprouted from her shoulder. Adi saw Devlin Seneschal amid the fray nocking another arrow. Talon soldiers loyal to Fedhani charged Seneschal and his second arrow went wide. Devlin discarded the bow and engaged with the soldiers. Adi couldn't locate Apyreon in the melee. The wind had shifted and smoke from the burning Huxstable was blowing into the terminal, blurring the action.

Three White Rabbit goons finally managed to mount a Vermax repeater rifle on its tripod. They slid the steel ammunition belt into the feeder and clanged home the belt cover. The rifle swung around toward the main battle among the Talon soldiers, the Water Knives, and the void mage's men. Off to one side, Palestrina and two Spikes still fought Royal and a half dozen other White Rabbit soldiers.

"Palestrina!" Adi shouted, "Watch out!"

The Vermax spewed its first round, paused, spat, paused, and spat a third time. Palestrina leapt into the air, wings wide. The first bullets tore into one of the Spikes, spinning him so the second and third slugs took him in the stomach. The Spike dropped to his knees clutching his wounds, then he dropped face-first onto the terminal floor, blood spreading beneath him.

Hovering above the fray, Palestrina flung a shotel end over end, embedding it in the neck of the Vermax trigger man. Then she dive-bombed the two remaining soldiers. They scattered but Palestrina slashed one of them across the back. He fell forward and lay still. She yanked her shotel from the trigger man's neck and threw it into the back of the third man. Even with the blade sticking from his ribs, he spun to face his attacker. Palestrina slashed him across the face.

Two black missiles streaked across the room toward the Seraph.

*Bolts from the Void mage.*

The energy slammed into an amber shield of light two feet from Palestrina's face and the necklace at her throat glowed. Palestrina swung the Vermax toward the Void mage and emptied the entire belt in his direction. Fighting men and women hit the floor to avoid the deadly spray. Blood and wood splinters filled the air as the bullets struck home. Bullets that should have hit the Void mage evaporated in puffs of black smoke inches from his body.

Adi spotted Tabrin running for the terminal exit. Blood ran down his face and he clutched Apyreon to his chest. She gave chase. He flung open the door to the tower below, then halted, horror on his face. The Lord of Pain roared out of the door and into the terminal, his Spikes fanning out behind him. Adi skidded to a stop as Petry's charge threatened to overtake her. Tabrin held up his hands in a pleading gesture, but Petry swung his heavy battle axe and cleaved Tabrin's head from his shoulders. The corpse stumbled backward and Apyreon tumbled from his lifeless fingers.

Adi rushed toward it. *If Petry gets it, I'll lose everything.*

As the huge pale man reached for Apyreon, Adi drew a small flintlock pistol and fired it at his outstretched hand. Blood sprayed from the stubs of two fingers. He snatched his hand back and cried out. Adi slid across the smooth terminal decking, discarding the pistol to grab Apyreon. She jumped up and sprinted away, not pausing to gloat.

A cluster of Talon soldiers blocked Adi's path. She did not know which were loyal to Seneschal and which to Fedhani. One swiped at Adi with a poleaxe. She dropped to her knees, her momentum carrying her forward under the weapon's swing, and drove her scimitar into the man's stomach, embedding it in his ribs. She let it go. Two more Talon soldiers advanced, but Adi could not wield the dead man's poleaxe with Apyreon in her hand. Neither could she get inside the other men's guard, so she bolted in the other direction.

As she ran, she tucked Apyreon into her belt pouch. Ahead of her, several White Rabbits were dragging as many weapon crates as they could toward Royal's dirigible. Adi hurdled an abandoned crate and took a grenado from her bandolier.

*Thank the Nine for Palestrina's forethought,* Adi thought. Their trip to the armory in the Red Wyrm had been fruitful.

She took a match from a pocket, but her hands trembled. It took her three tries to light the match. She touched it to the grenado's fuse then lit a second from the sparking fuse. She rolled the first one toward the weapons crates. The second she hurled at the drawbridge pier.

White Rabbits scattered as the grenado arrived in their midst. Adi ducked back behind a crate. The first grenado burst, followed by secondary pops, whines, and screams as the ammunition in the crates erupted. The second grenado burst and Adi heard loud metal pings and the ringing clatter of a falling chain. She risked a peek over her crate. Bullets for the Vermax machine gun popped off like hot corn as the crate burned. At the pier, the second grenado had blown apart the lowering mechanism. Half of the drawbridge listed downward, dragging the dirigible's mooring ropes with it, and the White Rabbit ship tilted at a precarious angle.

Adi dropped back behind the crate as her Talon pursuers caught up to her. A poleaxe swung overhead and she grabbed the shaft and heaved. Her assailant lost his balance, stumbled into the crate, and released his grip on the weapon. Adi stood and deftly turned the long shaft around before burying the blade in the shoulder of another assailant. She jerked it free and smashed the pole into the face of the first man. He squealed, then Adi skewered him with the point of the blade.

The poleaxe was too cumbersome to wield in such crowded quarters. Adi tossed the weapon aside.

*Time to find an exit.*

She assessed the battle. Palestrina and Devlin were fighting near berth eight where his ship had breached the pier. Royal and his remaining soldiers were struggling to save their ship. Men cut the mooring ropes, while others pried open the remaining crates. It was faster to toss the individual weapons up onto the deck than to carry the crates up the shifting gangplank. On the far side of the terminal, the void mage dodged the blades of Water Knife mercenaries and blasted them with dark bolts of void magic. His obsidian dragonstone hung exposed around his neck, flaring a brilliant purple. Duncan suddenly erupted in a spray of blood, bone, and dark energy. Adi clenched her teeth against the urge to vomit.

She couldn't exit down through the tower because Petry's men held the door to those stairs. Flames from the Water Knife dirigible had spread to the pier. Adi considered jumping from the listing pier in berth seven as it groaned and tilted further downward. Even so, it was still a good thirty feet to the street below and she did not think she could safely fall that far. Her only option was to go back the way she had come. The grenado's blast had destroyed the mechanic's swing, but the ropes her Spike escorts had used to rappel from the catwalk were still there.

*I'd be an easy target while I'm climbing.* Smoke from the burning ship and crates had reduced visibility and obscured much of the catwalk. *It's my only option.*

Adi headed for the ropes. A pair of White Rabbit goons, cut off from the rest of their men, blocked her path. Adi recognized one of them as Pimple, the leader of the goons who had jumped her in the warehouse district a long week ago. He recognized her and grinned.

"Came back for another kiss?" he mocked. Adi swung her fist at him. The other man was faster and lashed out with a short sword. She dodged to the side, grabbed his wrist on the back swing, and dislocated his elbow. He dropped his sword, writhing and swearing.

Pimple landed a glancing blow on her ear. Her head rang and she staggered backward.

*Damn that hurt.* She had bitten her tongue and tasted blood. She ducked his next blow. Holding her jaw, she kicked the side of his knee. He stumbled, the momentum of his punch carrying him forward. Adi leapt onto his back and locked her arms around his neck. Pimple flailed, but Adi held on. He tried to buck her off, but she squeezed harder. He fell to his knees, his fingers scrabbling for purchase on her forearm as his nails tore out strips of skin.

Adi grunted but did not let go. Pimple pitched forward and crashed into the floor face-first. She released his neck and drew a dagger from her belt. He thrashed beneath her, gasping for air, but she kept him pinned with her legs. Using the fingers of her left hand, she found the gap in his cervical vertebrae and drove the blade home. Pimple gurgled and died. She stood and kicked the dead man hard in the ribs. Twice.

Adi regained control of herself. *Move! You don't have time for this.*

She grabbed the rope and began to climb. Adi had years of experience clambering up and down the rigging of ships both of air and sea. She knew how to wrap the rope around one thigh and thread it between her ankles to ease the weight on her shoulders as she scooted up the line. Even so, her whole body burned with the exertion. Her ribs ached where Fedhani's brass knuckles had connected. The pain in her jaw made her eyes water, so she struggled to see. All around her the sounds of steel on steel mingled with men's shouts and cries as the battle raged on.

The rope swung as she climbed. Two black bolts of void magic hissed past her.

One singed her ear and set her hair on fire. She smacked the side of her head to smother the flames and grimaced at the stink. She threw her weight sideways to increase the swing so she would be harder to hit. The motion made her queasy, so she closed her eyes and pulled herself higher.

Adi's palms and shoulders ached by the time she reached the catwalk. She gripped the railing and hauled herself over it, then collapsed, panting, on the catwalk. Another bolt from the void mage whizzed past, slicing through the railing where her hand had been only moments before. He could see her through the metal grating. She scrambled to her feet just as another bolt cut two of the catwalk's support struts. The metal groaned and the entire structure leaned toward berth one.

Adi looked down and saw Devlin Seneschal ascending the rope. He could not fly with his tattered wings, but he was strong and he pulled himself hand over hand. Palestrina landed on the spiral steps that led up to the roof hatch and the lighthouse.

*The void mage's bolts are meant for her, but why?*

"We have to get out of here," Adi shouted.

"Do you have the device?" Palestrina asked.

Adi nodded. Devlin neared the catwalk. Two Talon soldiers were climbing a second rope, and the void mage stood at the bottom of a third, preparing to begin his ascent. Adi took out her last dagger.

"Adi, let's go!" Palestrina said.

Adi hacked at Devlin's rope. If Devlin died, she was free of their deal. The strands popped and twanged. She figured the edge of the catwalk would sever it under his weight and turned to the ropes holding the Spikes and the void mage. But Devlin's rope did not break before he was able to get a hand on the railing. The catwalk shifted more as he clambered onto it. Adi and Palestrina scrambled up the stairs to the roof.

# CHAPTER FIFTY-SIX

# ADI CRESTONE

## MOON OF XYS, DJINNDAY, 2ND OF LUXOR

When they reached the top of Alhambra's, Adi bent over, wheezing and gasping. It hurt like hell to take a deep breath. Palestrina stood beside her, bleeding from a dozen shallow wounds. The amber topaz pendant glowed a dull yellow. The wind blew hard and hot from the northwest indicating a coming sandstorm. Adi needed to be on the freighter headed for Tyre before any dangerous weather shut down the main aeroport. She straightened and leaned against the lighthouse for support. Her whole body trembled.

But now the night sky was clear. Solo bathed Solvigant in warm, orange light. Stars twinkled at the edges of the horizon. To the south, hundreds of meteors streaked blue and white across the sky. As the moon's orbit decayed, its atmosphere brushed against the fringes of Solo's rings, providing Xys's inhabitants with an ominous light show.

"You have the device?" Palestrina asked.

"Why is a void mage chasing you?"

"He's not."

"Djinnar's blood," Adi panted, "I saw him. He didn't care about Apyreon, he was here for you."

"A story for another time. What did you promise Devlin?"

Adi shook her head. "A story for another time. Any ideas on how I can get down from here?"

The ladder she had climbed to get into the aeroport was too close to the flaming wreck of the Huxstable. Even in the stiff breeze the air smelled of almonds as Rehka's remaining crew on the dirigible raced to vent the hydrogen before it ignited. Adi wanted to be far away from Alhambra's before that happened.

"Give me Apyreon," Palestrina said. "I'll fly it down and meet you at the Red Wyrm."

"No chance," Adi said. "*I* hand it over to the Blood Queen. That was the deal."

"You're going to have to trust me."

"Why would I do that?"

"I saved you at Opus Station and the Iron Dirigible. I agreed to help you tonight, here at Alhambra's. Why would I do that only to betray you now?"

"You had your own agenda at Opus."

"Still, I could have allowed the city watch to catch you and Theo. I didn't. I told you about Rehka. I could have lied and spared you her betrayal. You need allies, Adi."

"I didn't have Apyreon then. Help me get down, then we'll go the Red Wyrm together."

"I already told you, I can't carry a person. Give me the device, then you can get out with Petry's men."

Palestrina extended an arm toward Adi. She looked at the Seraph's palm, open and inviting. Adi took the pouch containing Apyreon from her belt and held it in both hands. She was about to give it to her when she noticed the tattoo on Palestrina's wrist. It was a black sun surrounded by four rays of stylized light, like the cardinal markers on a compass. Between them were four curving rays. Adi had seen that tattoo before, and recently.

*Hannah Valefyre,* Adi realized. She pointed at the tattoo. "What is that?"

"This is hardly the time, Adi."

"I've seen that same tattoo on the wrist of a young noble woman."

Palestrina lunged. The move caught Adi flat-footed. She snatched the bag away, but Palestrina knocked it from her grasp. It tumbled along the curved roof of the terminal toward the wreckage of the Huxstable.

Before either woman could go after the device, the door from the catwalk banged open and Devlin Seneschal strode onto the roof. He was bleeding from several shallow wounds inflicted by Palestrina's shotels. Both women froze. He laughed when he saw them.

"I see I arrived just in time to help you seal our deal," he said to Adi.

Palestrina pointed a shotel at Seneschal. "You promised him my life, didn't you?"

"That was his price," Adi admitted.

Palestrina drew another blade. She took three steps backward along the curved rooftop of the terminal so neither Adi nor Devlin could get behind her.

"I will have my revenge, 'Trina." Devlin laughed again, then lunged at Palestrina. Devlin's long sword clanged once, then twice against Palestrina's shotels.

Adi ran for Apyreon. She was reaching for the device when the handle of one of Palestrina's shotels whacked her on the ankles. She sprawled and slid further down the roof. The blade slid past her down the roof's incline and disappeared over the edge. Adi glanced back toward the fight. Palestrina kicked Devlin in the chest and he stumbled backward. Palestrina leapt into the air, wings pumping hard.

Adi scrambled on hands and knees toward Apyreon, which near the top of pier five. Her hands closed over the pouch at the same time Palestrina alighted in front of her. The Seraph tore the cloth bag from Adi's clutching fingers.

"I'm sorry, Adi." Palestrina said, "I can't allow you to give Apyreon to the Blood Queen."

*"What?"*

"It's too dangerous."

"But—" Adi spluttered. "You're the Lady of Spiders, one of her commanders. That doesn't make any sense."

Devlin had recovered himself. Adi could hear his booted feet pounding up behind them.

"I follow the Dragon in this." Palestrina said.

*What does that mean? It doesn't matter. Apyreon is the only way to save Lucas.*

Adi lunged at the Lady of Spiders, tackling her around the waist. Palestrina stumbled and then the two women were tumbling down the terminal's roof. Palestrina flailed, trying to dislodge Adi. Adi clawed at the pouch in Palestrina's left hand. The two women rolled and picked up speed. Adi made a last grab for Apyreon and managed to wrench it from Palestrina's grasp. Then they plunged over the edge.

Adi landed hard on the canvas shade of pier five. She bounced twice, curled into a ball around the device. Palestrina hovered over her. Adi tried to stand, but the undulation of the slack canvas in the wind gave her no secure footing. Palestrina descended. Still on her back, Adi drew her last dagger. She had no leverage to lunge, and her sudden movement caused the cloth to heave more. Palestrina parried the feeble strike. Adi tried to rise once more, but Palestrina shoved her down. Above them she saw Devlin was trying to find a way down to them. Behind Devlin loomed the black figure of the void mage.

Palestrina stood over Adi, the canvas sagging under their combined weight. The Seraph pinned Adi's wrist under one foot and pried Apyreon away.

"What are you doing?" Adi shouted over the wind and the snapping of the canvas.

"I should kill you," the Lady of Spiders hissed. "You thought you could trade away my life."

"I just want to save my son!"

"The Blood Queen will only use the device for terror. No one is safe if she wields Apyreon. This device was meant for a higher purpose than greed and power."

"But Lucas—"

"I am sorry about your son." Palestrina glanced up to where Devlin was watching them with interest. "I know the pain of losing a child."

"Please, no," Adi cried.

"His life is not worth putting the World System at risk. The power of the Kratoi must never reach the Blood Queen."

"What are you talking about?"

Above them there was a flash of blue as Devlin leapt off the roof. He hit the canvas and rolled before coming to his feet, but the weight of all three of them on the canvas shade was too much, one of the support posts tore free of the building. Palestrina rose into the air as the canvas crumpled and the whole apparatus tilted downward. Adi slid, then rolled.

Missiles from the void mage snapped the second support and the whole canopy plummeted toward the ground. Adi flailed as the sensation of freefall pitched her stomach. A strong blue hand grabbed her left arm. Adi's fingers latched onto Devlin's. He had secured a grappling hook to one of the roof's towers before he jumped, now it was a lifeline for both. The rope was wrapped around his other arm, but he was slipping.

"Grab the rope," he shouted down at her. "It will hold you. I can't."

Adi saw that the rope dangling below Devlin reached all the way to the ground. She grabbed it and wrapped her legs around it then released Devlin's arm. The rope swayed but held. Devlin stopped sliding. Adi took a deep breath and lowered herself to the ground. Devlin waited until ten feet separated them and then he, too, descended.

Adi's limbs were trembling so violently that when her feet touched the ground she staggered. She and Devlin stood atop the pile of wood and canvas that had been the sunshade. Now that she was out of the fray, she could hear the emergency bells of Solvigant clanging.

"You need to get out of here," Adi said. "Those bells mean the city watch is summoning the Imperial Army garrison.

"What about Palestrina?" he asked.

"She took the device. She's gone."

"I held up my end of the deal. I lost good men up there. I expect you to hold up yours."

"I didn't recover the device," Adi said.

"That wasn't the deal. I created a distraction, it's not my fault you failed at your objective. Where is she headed?"

*I failed.* The realization hit Adi hard. *Lucas!* "I don't know. But I know someone who might."

*I must get to the* Penumbra *and question Valefyre before the delegation leaves.*

Adi checked her watch. It was almost midnight. The delegation should be gone already. Iris would be waiting for her.

*Maybe the wind delayed the delegation.*

"I need a horse," Adi shouted.

Devlin looked around and then pointed across the street. Several horses were hitched to the post outside a tavern. Talons were fighting Spikes near that doorway, but Adi did not care. She bolted, Devlin on her heels.

"If you're going after Palestrina," he shouted as they ran, "I'm coming with."

Adi selected a sleek animal, gathered the reins, and vaulted into the saddle. To her surprise Devlin leapt on behind her, wrapping his scarred arms around her torso. Sizzling bolts of void magic struck the hitching post. The horse reared and Adi struggled to hold on. Devlin's weight dragged her backward. She headed southward toward the heart of Solvigant, kicking the beast into a gallop.

# CHAPTER FIFTY-SEVEN

# ION RUCINARE

## MOON OF XYS, DJINNDAY, 2ND OF LUXOR

Ion stared up at the great tower of Solvigant's central aeroport. Blimps, dirigibles, and hybrid airships sailed in a loose swarm around the piers that sprouted from the central core. Solo's ruddy orange light near the southern horizon gave the ships an ominous appearance as they were lit from below. Ion saw a shower of meteors light up the sky with their blue and white tails.

The central aeroport was the tallest building in Solvigant. Due to Rehka's condition, the stevedores allowed Balthasar and his party to use the freight elevator. Rehka's stretcher and the three of them packed onto the lift platform amid a motley assortment of luggage and cargo. Most crates bore the twin crescent moons of the Society of Astrologia. Two massive, hairy beasts with long trunks and tusks were harnessed to a winch, the cables of which extended up through the core of the tower and back down to the freight elevator.

The beast's handler cracked a whip, and the sound made Ion flinch. The two animals grunted, then stepped forward along the circular track around the windlass. The lift platform, which had no rails, began to rise. Ion clutched Bale's long hand as the ground dwindled beneath them.

"What are those creatures?" Ion asked.

"Mammoths," one of the stevedores answered. "Imported from Highgaard."

"Mammoths," Ion repeated, memorizing the word.

"What do you know of Karis?" Bale asked him.

"It's in the Empire." Ion thought for a moment and then added, "And the Society of Astrologia is based there."

"That is the headquarters for the Society, yes. By Imperial decree it is also home to Astral Mages. Prior to the Empire, however, practitioners trained in all types of magic there. What else do you know?"

"The Society is headquartered in Caelia. The little folk live on Karis and it has its own small moon."

Bale chuckled. "Yes, Karis is the traditional home of the Nefeshi, though you'd be lucky to see one. They are a shy people. And Karis's moon Flynt is an important place."

Ion exclaimed, "It's the seat of the Dragon court! I heard that Dragons can take their reptilian forms on Karis and fly through the skies, free as birds. Is that true? Are you going to turn into a Dragon when we get there?"

"Me? No," Bale said. "I haven't taken my Dragon form in over a decade."

"Why not?"

"That's a story for when we're comfortable in our cabin."

Ion glanced over the edge of the elevator as they rose past floor upon floor. The mammoths looked horse-sized now. The drop was long. Ion took a step backward and closed his eyes when a wave of dizziness overtook him. He squeezed Bale's hand.

"Almost there," the stevedore said.

The elevator came to an abrupt halt, jarring Ion and causing the platform to sway slightly. The stevedore looked down and scowled.

The wide barn doors slid open and Ion looked out into level sixteen. Despite the late hour, crowds of passengers and dockworkers filled the deck. The stevedores tossed mooring cables to their counterparts inside, who secured the platform against the open doorway.

They exited the elevator and found themselves on the commercial side of a massive Karisian frigate. Around them, loaders shouted at one another as they moved boxes onto the ship via a pair of broad gangplanks and a large hoist. Several men raced past Bale's party pushing wheeled carts. They stacked them with the cargo and emptied the platform in short order.

Ion had to crane his neck to see the upper curve of the freighter's gas bag in its mesh of cables. The undercarriage had four stories. The upper two featured windows for passengers, the lower two had solid walls with entrances for loading and unloading cargo. He had only seen such massive ships from below as they glided silently over Castes on their way to and from Solvigant.

"It's huge!" Ion said. "Are we really sailing on that?"

"We are. Follow me." Bale hefted the head end of Rehka's stretcher, and a stevedore picked up the foot end. Ion trotted after the long-striding Dragon.

*It has six gangways!* Ion realized. Freight moved off the lower levels on two dedicated ramps and onto the ship on two more. The passenger gangways had several flights of steps to reach the various levels.

Balthasar and the stevedore maneuvered the stretcher up the steep gangway with great care, so they did not jar the sleeping patient. They exited the ramp on the third level and turned down an exterior walkway. Their berth was near the back of the ship. Ion heard the pulsating rumble of the astral engines.

The room was not lavish, but neither was it sparse. A pair of bunk beds flanked either side and there was enough room for a table and two chairs between them. Above the table was a picture of Karis and Flynt painted as if the artist had floated in the void. There were two windows, one a porthole set into the door, the other beside it, above a pair of shelves for luggage. Ion had no luggage, but he took his shoes off and placed them on the shelf while Bale situated Rehka in one of the lower bunks.

Ion squished his toes on the soft cabin floor.

"What is this?" he asked, gesturing to the floor. "It tickles."

Bale looked over at him and smiled. "That's carpet."

"Carpet," Ion repeated. "What's it for?"

"Comfort. So, you can do just what you're doing."

Ion wanted to lay down and put his whole body on the stuff. It felt better on his toes than any straw pallet he had ever slept on, even softer than Broc's settee.

"Why isn't it everywhere?"

"It's hard to keep carpet clean on a desert moon. I imagine it's also heavy and difficult to transport during a peripatesis."

"I want carpet in my house one day."

Balthasar smiled and drew the curtain over the window.

"I must run back to the apothecary. I need to grab medication, clothing, and a few other things for the journey. I need you to stay here and keep an eye on Rehka. Do you think you can stay in the cabin until I get back?"

"I want to explore the ship."

"You need to wait until we've left the aeroport. There are city watchmen out looking for you and Rehka. It's not safe until we put some distance between us and the city. Understand?"

Ion's shoulders slumped. "Yes, sir."

"Once we're underway, it should be safe to venture about the ship."

"How long will you be?"

"The ship leaves in an hour. I'll be back before then."

Ion nodded. "Okay, but hurry." Though it was bright and clean, being confined in the cabin with Rehka reminded him too much of the hole beneath the washtub. "What if she wakes up?"

"I don't think she will. The Doctors Vake gave her poppy and moonwort, so she should sleep through the night and much of the day tomorrow. If she does wake, try to calm her and let her know I'll be back soon. Lock the door behind me."

With that, Balthasar left. Ion slid the bolt into place, then he pushed one of the chairs over so he could kneel on it and watch the dock. The only way he could tell time had passed was the actions of the stevedores. They were no longer loading cargo onto the ship, and much of what they had unloaded had already gone down on the lift platform.

It was late and he was exhausted, but the excitement of an airship voyage thrummed through him. All around he could hear the shouts and the tread of heavy boots as the crew moved about the ship, preparing for its voyage. Several groups of elegantly dressed passengers walked past his window on the way to their berths. Bale had explained that the voyage would take three days. They would sail for two days to the nearest aerogate to Karis, then another day from that aerogate's terminus to the aeroport in Caelia.

Ion fidgeted, drumming his fingers on the porthole's rim. A porter walked by carrying a large purple valise. A woman in a matching purple gown followed him, holding her hoop skirt at an angle so as not to catch it on the walkway railing. In her other hand, she held a leash. A furry gray terrier pulled hard at the other end, bounding forward and then back, yipping and trembling. A few moments later, four monks in green habits passed, their wooden tree pendants identifying them as devotees of Darak, Goddess of Nature.

Ion ducked away from the window when two city watchmen trooped past. He crouched with his back to the cabin door and waited for them to knock.

*Did they see me? Do they know who I am?*

Ion held his breath when he heard voices outside. Someone wrapped his knuckles against the door. Ion did not answer.

"Hello," came a voice. "If you're in there, open up. I need to check passengers against the manifest."

Ion waited. The room was dark. The man knocked again and the door handle rattled. Ion tried to think of a story to give the watchmen, but his mind was blank.

*I wish Bale and I had thought of a cover story.*

Ion waited behind the door with bated breath until he heard footsteps receding on the walkway. He let out a long sigh and laid down on one of the bunks.

*Where is Bale?*

He must have dozed off because the rhythmic thrum of the engines woke him. The room was dark, and it took Ion a moment to remember he was on an airship headed for Karis.

"Bale?" he said. A wave of panic swept over him when no answer came. "Bale"

Silence.

Ion got up from the bed and went to the window. He saw dockworkers casting ropes off from the pier. At first, he thought the aeroport was moving away from the airship. Then he realized the airship was under thrust, moving away from the pier.

*We're leaving!* Ion realized. He threw back the bolt, opened the door, and stepped out onto the walkway.

"Bale!" There was no answer. A company of watchmen running across the pier toward the lobby of level sixteen distracted Ion. He ran along the walkway toward the prow of the ship to keep them in view. Another company of guards joined them. Then the ship cleared the pier.

"Back to your berth, lad," a stern male voice said.

Ion jumped. The crewman put one hand on Ion's shoulder to steady the boy.

"No passengers on the walkway during departure."

Ion turned away from Crestone's drama and faced the crewman. He wore black breeches and a black shirt under a red vest. He looked more like a porter than a pirate. "My friend missed our departure."

"My apologies, lad. The watch ordered us to cast off. The next freighter for Karis departs in twelve hours, they'll put him on that one. He'll only be half a day behind. Which cabin are you in?"

"I don't remember the number, but it's back that way."

Ion looked back toward the pier. He sent a prayer to the Nine not to abandon his clever captain and to look out for Bale.

He and the crewman trudged down the walkway toward Ion's berth. He'd left the door open in his hasty departure.

"When you hear three bells, it'll be safe to move about the ship. Breakfast is served in the galley from six to eight bells."

"Thank you, sir," Ion said, stepping into his cabin. When the crewman had strode on, Ion closed the door and threw the bolt. Rehka slept, snoring softly. The orange glow of Solo illuminated the diaphanous curtains. Ion took off the shalwar, folded it, and placed it on the shelf beside his shoes. He stripped a blanket from one bunk. In his skivvies, he curled up on the carpet at the foot of Rehka's bed. The carpet felt luxurious on his skin. It was thicker than he had realized, and he dug his fingers into the plush material.

Had Bale abandoned them? Ion felt very alone. His grandfather was dead in Castes. At Stella's, the captain had given him a mission but then left him to complete it. Now Bale was missing. Something must have happened.

*He wouldn't abandon his daughter.*

Ion had seen the concern on Bale's face. Though Ion did not remember seeing that expression on his own parents' faces, he recognized Bale's love and concern.

*I hope he's all right.*

Ion wept, chastising himself for the fear and uncertainty he felt. He was Ion of Castes. He had ridden the terrane; he had survived the streets of Solvigant and stopped a wild battle between watchmen and pirates. He had used magic and saved Crestone. He had a mission. He would survive this trip to Karis, too. Bale would come for them. Ion only had to wait.

The dangers of Solvigant faded behind him. Ion said another prayer to the Nine and fell asleep curled up on the carpet.

# CHAPTER FIFTY-EIGHT

# ADI CRESTONE

## MOON OF XYS, DJINNDAY, 2ND OF LUXOR

Adi pulled her horse to a skidding halt in front of the aeroport. Her hips ached from the pell-mell dash across Solvigant. Her back ached from Devlin's grip. Slipping from her sweat-soaked mount, Adi glanced up at the aeroport clocks. She said a prayer to Phoebe, Goddess of Light. If she sprinted, and with a little divine luck, she might catch the *Penumbra* before the delegation departed for Maxon. Hannah Valefyre was her only link to Palestrina and Apyreon. Adi had no plan for how she was going to interrogate Hannah.

*Theo will help,* Adi thought. She felt Apyreon slipping through her fingers. *Palestrina betrayed me. Rehka betrayed me. I am not good at putting faith in the right people.* The bitter thought brought bile to her throat.

"Adison Crestone," a familiar voice purred, "you look terrible."

Adi spun toward the jangle of desiccated bones. She had not heard the Lord of Bones and his men approach. Twelve Osmen, Ajax's personal guards, stood around her in a loose ring. Passenger traffic to and from the aeroport at this hour was light, and everyone gave the Blood Queen's soldiers a wide berth. Ajax stepped toward her and doffed his hat, a wide-brimmed black boater. The cords of dried bones draped over his dark suit rattled and clanked. He brushed sand from the hat and placed it back atop his head.

"And Talon Seneschal," Ajax continued, "an unexpected surprise."

"What do you want, Ajax?" Adi said. Behind him she spotted a pair of soldiers in the livery of House Vanguard watching from the aeroport entrance, their curiosity piqued. They did not intervene.

"The Blood Queen summons you." Ajax's voice hissed like a desert wind.

"I don't have time for you."

"You refuse your mistress's summons?"

*She's no mistress of mine!* Adi thought, but bit back the retort. "We are on her business now."

Ajax grinned, his perfect white teeth contrasting with his dark face. He gestured toward the Red Wyrm. "Talon Seneschal is on Blood Queen business?"

"Apyreon is slipping away!" Adi protested.

Ajax gestured behind them toward the Red Wyrm. "The Blood Queen awaits."

The aeroport clock tower struck midnight.

*The* Penumbra*!* Adi realized. She looked up at the airship piers. The *Penumbra* was not docked on this side. Two Osmen with bone daggers watched her from the entrance stairs.

"My only lead on the device is about to set sail for Maxon," she said. "Palestrina betrayed us. I need to get up there."

The Lord of Bones lunged at Adi and clamped his rough and calloused hand hard over her mouth. Adi was too startled to struggle. Seneschal made no move to help her. Adi felt a curved bone knife pressed against her torso. She sucked in a breath. This close, Ajax smelled of mahogany and chrysanthemums.

"Hush now," he said, "no secrets in the street." He took his hand from Adi's mouth and placed it on the back of her neck, turning her head toward the Red Wyrm. Adi wanted to scream, wanted to run, but she felt the bite of the blade against her ribs.

"Talon, if you would be so kind as to join us."

"Do I have a choice?" Devlin asked.

Ajax smiled. "You do not."

*It is too late,* Adi realized. *The* Penumbra *is gone and any leads to Apyreon with it.*

Adi slumped, defeated. Ajax pushed her toward the glowing maw of the Blood Queen's nightclub. It was closed, but vermilion and amber light spilled from the open doorway as if daring passersby to plumb its fiery depths. Ajax steered Adi inside. Osmen framed the door.

Adi crossed the threshold and dragged in a deep breath. She exhaled, trying to relax her muscles. The club was dim, only a handful of the gas lamps were lit. Candles burned along the bar top and on the empty tables, creating shadows that danced in erratic patterns. Ajax pushed Adi into a chair. He offered Devlin a chair then poured amber liquid into three glasses and offered them around. Adi gulped hers down and stilled her tapping foot. She hated to give Ajax the satisfaction of seeing her adjust the confining collar, but she had taken to doing so when nervous. She held out her empty glass and he refilled it. Adi sipped it this time. Already the first round was taking the edge off.

"Where is the Blood Queen?" she asked.

"She arrives in her own time," Ajax said.

"What does she want from me?" It was disconcerting to sit between the two rival gang lords. Devlin, the blue Seraph, and Ajax, dark as the grave.

Ajax swirled his drink, muttering under his breath in a language Adi did not recognize. The two men waited in silence. Adi listened to the clatter of ice in Ajax's glass, the crackling wood, the wind against the windowpanes and wondered if she would go insane. Adi had only seen the Blood Queen once before, when Ajax had fixed the collar around Adi's neck. In her panic, Adi had hyperventilated while an astral mage bound the two ends of the metal together. The Lord of Bones had watched while whistling a jaunty tune. The memory made Adi nauseous.

"Did Royal escape?" Adi asked to break the silence.

A flicker of muscle in Ajax's jawline was the only indication that he heard her. He continued to gaze into the fire and Adi suspected wasn't going to answer her when he said, "Reports indicate he did."

"With the weapons?"

"What weapons?"

"The exchange for Apyreon wasn't for gold, it was for high-powered, military grade armaments."

Ajax shrugged and sipped his whiskey.

"Any leads on Palestrina?"

"We're looking for her," he said.

"Where would she go?"

"To her people on Highgaard."

Adi knew the Seraphim claimed Highgaard as their home moon. She tried to imagine Palestrina as a child, tried to imagine what her parents might have been like, but came up with nothing. Everyone in Solvigant, Adi included, treated the Blood Queen's generals as if Basalt had spawned them from its depths.

*How could loving mothers have produced such cruel offspring?* Adi did not think Palestrina would go to Highgaard. Adi remembered her saying "I follow the Dragon in this" before flying away from Alhambra's smoking roof. Adi had no idea which Dragon Palestrina had meant, but the combination of her tattoo and the confession led Adi to believe this was not a Seraphic plot. *Hadn't Theo mentioned something about Hannah's relatives and Dragons?* Adi couldn't remember the details now.

Upstairs a doorway opened, scraping across the wooden floor. Adi tensed. She followed the footfalls with her ears as they approached the stairs. There were multiple pairs, one lighter than the others.

A wizened astral mage stepped out of the back hallway. He wore a collar akin to Adi's, and she saw the blue streaks of astralium necrosis on his neck and hands. He carried a gnarled staff. When he entered the room, he thumped three times on the floorboards of the Red Wyrm.

"The Blood Queen," he barked.

Ajax, the Lord of Bones, shot to his feet to stand at attention. Adi rose, using the table as support because her knees wobbled. The mage shuffled to one side to allow Sasha Riven to enter the room. Adi gasped. The Blood Queen was more majestic than Adi remembered.

Sasha Riven stood before them in an ornate red and black gown. The bodice was black and high-waisted, with a square neckline and short, puffed sleeves. Deep red ribbon and black beads decorated the bust. The crimson satin skirts were tiered and trimmed in black lace and tulle. The exposed skin of her biceps and shoulder blades was white to the point of translucence, as if the woman had never been exposed to daylight. Blue veins under her skin looked like stellarium conduits. She wore elbow-length red gloves. On her fingers were polished metal claws, each connected to a bracelet by a delicate silver chain. The tips of her intricate rose gold crown featured tear-drop rubies the size of bird eggs and the band glinted with myriad diamonds and pearls. Those ornaments could cover Adi's debt a hundred times over.

The Blood Queen wore a circular porcelain mask that hid her face and shadowed her eyes so Adi could not see them. The sculpted mouth pouted, the lines of the lips extended up toward the cheeks. The immobile moue chilled Adi. A blood red rune glowed on each cheek below her eyes. These runes resembled astral runes Adi had picked up while deciphering her own magic, but with subtle differences.

Behind the Queen traipsed a masked creature clad in black from head to toe. From his size and general shape, Adi assumed he was human. He carried a quarterstaff, each end shod in iron. He moved with a lithe, muscular grace that implied his expertise with the weapon.

"Lord Ajax," the Blood Queen said. The mask made her feminine voice resonate. "You have snared my pirate. And a Talon, too. Welcome, Seneschal, to the Red Wyrm. Your visit is unexpected."

Even Devlin appeared nervous at the sight of the Blood Queen. He bowed. "I appreciate your hospitality."

Adi quivered when the Blood Queen stepped up to her and stroked a lustrous claw along her cheek. She felt a thin trickle of blood run down her chin, but she dared not wipe it away. Adi risked a glance at her face. Though they were hidden, she sensed Riven' eyes studying her. Adi tried to look down, but the Blood Queen's metal talons trapped Adi's chin. She did not struggle for fear of tearing her cheeks.

The Blood Queen tapped one claw on Adi's collar, scoffed, and released her as if disappointed.

"Lord Ajax, I understand Apyreon is lost to us and that Palestrina has betrayed us."

Ajax stood, his eyes downcast. "Yes, my Queen."

"It is a pity that Apyreon was not recovered."

"I am sorry, my Queen."

"That fault is not yours." The Blood Queen's impassive visage settled once more on Adi who flushed scarlet.

"Fedhani is dead," Devlin said. "I would ask that we suspend hostilities between us until I can consolidate Fedhani's power under my own. In exchange, I will hunt down and kill Palestrina for you. Are those terms acceptable to you?"

"Perhaps."

Devlin added, "I want the pirate as well."

"Do you?"

"She made a deal: my help in return for Palestrina's life. Her debt to me remains so long as Palestrina lives."

Riven backhanded Adi across the face. She yelped, flailing her arms to maintain her balance.

"Stupid girl," the Blood Queen hissed.

The force of the blow caused Adi to bite her tongue. Coppery blood filled her mouth and she spat it out onto the floor of the Red Wyrm. Sasha Riven adjusted her skirts and crouched in front of Adi.

"Did you know Palestrina intended to betray me?" There was no room for mercy in that monotone.

"N-n-no."

"Then you plotted to murder one of my generals?"

"I did what I had to do to retrieve Apyreon."

"Did you think it worth Palestrina's life?"

Adi mustered her courage and faced the mask. "Do you? I would murder a hundred Palestrinas to save my son."

The Blood Queen snickered. "I almost forgot your son Lucas, my hostage for your good behavior. I can understand, I am a mother too. Did you know that? Few people do. Security, you know? I couldn't have someone using my children as leverage against me." The Blood Queen rose. "Xander tells me you've been an absentee mother."

"You stay away from Xander," Adi hissed. The Blood Queen slapped her again. This time her head bounced off the floor and her vision swam. She shook her head to clear it and spit more blood. The Blood Queen turned to Devlin.

"Crestone owes me a prior debt and thus represents a significant investment. She belongs to me until such time as she pays those debts. My indenture was in no position to make such a deal with you. I offer a hundred spyres for your assistance at Alhambra's. I will add this to Adi's debt at the standard fourteen percent interest."

"Bah," Devlin scoffed, "you cheat me, Sasha. I want 'Trina dead. Besides, I lost good men tonight. One hundred spyres does not begin to make that whole."

"Greedy Devlin," the Blood Queen crooned menacingly. Ajax stepped back. "You will annex Fedhani's territory, including the revenue from her shipping operations. If you're half the businessman she was, you'll find yourself more than whole."

"Five hundred gold spyres," Devlin insisted. "And I want in on whatever this Apyreon thing is."

"It was unfortunate for you, Devlin, that Adi brought you into this."

"What do you mean?"

The Blood Queen's shoulders tensed and Adi caught a flicker of movement from Sasha's left hand. The man in black punched Devlin in the stomach with the iron-tipped quarterstaff faster than Adi's mind could register the spinning wood. The Seraph doubled over, clutching his abdomen. The Blood Queen drew one swift finger across his throat. Arterial blood sprayed across the floor from Devlin's open neck. The Talon slumped to his knees, gurgling. His yellow eyes met Adi's before he keeled over.

Adi scrambled away from the fallen gang lord whose heart emptied his body onto the Red Wyrm's floor. The Blood Queen watched her as she wiped the blood from her gleaming claw with a velvet handkerchief.

"His death is on you," the Blood Queen said. Ajax grabbed Devlin by the ankles and dragged him toward the back hall, leaving a wide red smear as he went. Adi swallowed hard against her nausea.

"Why did you do that?" Adi asked. "He would have taken your deal eventually."

The Blood Queen tossed aside the bloody cloth and inspected her hands to ensure not a trace of red remained. "Do you know why Devlin asked you to kill Palestrina?"

"To weaken you?"

The Blood Queen clucked her disappointment. "No. They were once lovers."

"Lovers?" Adi's voice cracked in surprise. She could not imagine either one of them sharing a tender moment. The Blood Queen leaned down so the bone-white mask was inches from her face. She smelled charcoal and bergamot, and oddly, fresh blood.

"Do you know what happened?"

Adi shook her head as a weight dropped into the pit of her stomach. *I do not want to know,* she realized.

But the Blood Queen continued speaking. "She murdered her own children. All four of them. She stabbed them to death and dumped them in a well."

Adi felt sick. An unbidden image of driving a knife into Lucas's body flashed in her mind. It mingled with the horror of Devlin's death. She turned her head and vomited. She was grateful it did not splash the Blood Queen's abundant skirts or she might have followed Devlin into death.

*And Lucas would join me soon enough.*

The Blood Queen backed away, laughing, as Adi heaved again.

"You are so hard on yourself, Adi," Sasha said. "But know this. You cannot trade motherhood for guilt. Guilt does not feed and care for a child, certainly not from across the World System." The Blood Queen stroked her chin. "Maybe I'll kill him as a favor to you. Then you will be free to focus on clearing your debts to me."

"No!" Adi shouted. She tried to stand, but her foot slipped in her vomit and she fell hard onto her rump. "Please don't. I'll do anything."

"I know, Adi. A mother fashions her chains in her own womb. You will never be free while your heart wanders outside your body."

"What do you want from me?"

"You know the answer to that."

Adi pushed herself up into a chair and leaned heavily against the table. "Apyreon."

The Blood Queen snapped her fingers, the metal claws clinking. "That's it."

"Why?"

"Excuse me?"

"What will you do with it?"

"You wouldn't believe me if I told you."

"My life and the life of my son hang in the balance. I have a right to know."

The Blood Queen clicked her tongue. "Adi, you have no lack of bravado. You're fortunate to be such an asset. I will tell you."

"You will?" Adi sat up. She had not expected this. She had been stalling, trying to pull herself together.

"But first, you are wrong about one thing."

"What?"

"Millions of lives depend upon my acquisition of Apyreon. If you fail me, the World System fails. Xys's destruction will just be the beginning."

"What are you talking about?"

"I am an unlikely savior, I know, but that is what I am, and you are my errant disciple."

Adi shook her head to clear it. *She's not making any sense.* "You can use Apyreon to save Xys?"

The Blood Queen chuckled. "I could, but I won't. Xys is a necessary sacrifice in a longer, more dangerous game."

"What kind of savior sacrifices an entire moon?"

"A greater threat arises; I will do what I must."

*She is insane,* Adi realized. "How will you save us?"

The Blood Queen hesitated a moment then said, "I will seize the Astral Throne. I will unite the World System behind a strong ruler to face the coming darkness. Justus Callire and that pompous wife of his are fools. They are not willing to do what is necessary."

The Blood Queen wore a choker of pressed roses in transparent glass. The center flower glowed with a soft, red light. Sasha followed Adi's gaze and placed a tinkling hand over her own throat.

"That's not a dragonstone," Adi said.

"Don't lose focus, Adi."

Adi's mind swirled with possibilities. "What darkness? What threat is terrible enough to sacrifice a moon?"

"Your incredulity is endearing. You act as though it is the first time someone has done so."

"What are you talking about?"

"You are a woman of action, not a woman of scholarship, I see. I am surprised your sister did not tell you."

"Beatrice? Wait, how did you know she is my sister? How do you know who I am?"

"How quickly endearing becomes tiresome." The Blood Queen let out a long breath behind her mask. "I do not like ignorance, Adison Faide. It is good business to know the business of the Imperial nobility. I knew Lord Faide's eldest surviving daughter ran away. I knew his second daughter passed the Crucible and accepted her prophetic gift. When she arrived here, I had suspicions about you. When she visited you at Stella's Echo, these were confirmed, and when Xander Marrion entered the Red Wyrm for the first time and offered—nay begged—to pay off your debts, I knew for certain."

"You've been spying on me? And the governor's guests?"

Riven tilted her head just enough to convey her exasperation.

"You're an asset, Adi. As for the governor, everyone has spies inside all the manors of the nobility. Their actions shape the World System, and I need to know what form their actions will take."

"You keep telling me how valuable I am. One ruby in that crown would more than pay my debts to you. If it's not the money, where is my worth? Why me? If Apyreon is so important to your plans, why isn't every loyal thug scouring the moons for Palestrina right now?"

The Blood Queen clapped her hands. "An excellent question, and one you must discover the answer to. As for Palestrina"—her voice dropped back into that dangerous monotone—"there is nowhere in the World System that Seraph can hide from me."

Adi shivered, knowing it to be true. A connection snicked into place in Adi's mind, and she stared at the Blood Queen, mouth agape.

"Pallantier," Adi said when her surprise had abated enough that she could speak.

"Very good, Adi. I might make a scholar of you yet."

"You said that Xys's destruction was part of your plan, part of your game. That means"—the words tumbled from Adi's mouth in a jumble,—"Xys's orbit began to fail when Pallantier disappeared. You did that. You killed one of the Children of Solo?" The rose at Sasha's neck glowed brighter. Adi made the sign of the Ring. "What are you?"

"You flatter me, Adison. I only incapacitated a god. I assure you, Pallantier is alive, though partially exsanguinated. The blood of a god is quite useful. I had help, too. One does not capture and contain a god without help. Even I require some assistance at times."

"Who could have possibly helped you in this besides... another god?" Adi paled. "Djinnar, Pallantier's brother." *Phoebe's Golden Light! What reception can Theo's delegation expect? Beatrice is with him.*

Adi forced those thoughts aside. She could not afford to be distracted.

"My Queen." Ajax's voice shattered Adi's stunned silence and she jumped. She had not noticed his return. "Time grows short."

The Blood Queen produced a pocket watch from the folds of her crimson dress and clicked it open. Adi saw an intricate tree with jeweled embellishments engraved on the watch cover.

"You are right," the Blood Queen said. "I am needed elsewhere, and Adi must catch a ship."

"Where am I going?" No emotion registered on the Queen's pale mask, but Adi imagined surprise.

"Why to Tyre, of course. Thail to be more specific. You might get there before the city watch and the Imperial Guard catch you."

"You'll let me go to Lucas?"

"Is that what you want?"

"It is. More than anything." Adi said before she could stop herself, and for the first time in years, she realized it was true. The fear of facing him had faded into the background of her thoughts and she felt only a fierce desire to hold her son.

"Then listen closely and do not interrupt. Go to Thail and collect your son. Ajax will accompany you."

Adi opened her mouth to protest, but the Blood Queen silenced her with a raised finger.

"This is not a negotiation." The Blood Queen continued, "Then you will speak with a scholar at the University of Tyre. He will tell you everything he knows about the workshop of Anaximander. You will use this information to locate the workshop and recover Apyreon's counterpart, Tethysteon. In the meantime, my agents will hunt down Palestrina. When I know where she took Apyreon, I will tell you.

"You have failed me twice. You failed to secure Apyreon on the *Sidereal* and you failed at Alhambra's. Do not fail me a third time. I am making an exception because I feel an affinity with you as a mother and we are entering unprecedented times."

Adi exhaled.

"I cannot allow your failures to go unpunished. For the *Sidereal,* I am increasing the interest on your debt from fourteen to twenty-two percent. If you die or attempt to run, this debt will pass to your loved ones, Xander, Rehka, and that new one, Iris."

"Not Lucas?"

"No, because Ajax will kill Lucas. His debt will be a blood debt from his mother."

Tears welled in Adi's eyes.

"For the second failure"—the Blood Queen gestured to the Lord of Bones. Ajax reached into his jacket pocket and withdrew Adi's dragonstone. Hope flared in Adi.

*Will she return it to me? What sort of twisted punishment is this?*

The Blood Queen took the jade cabochon in her claws and inspected it at a distance, as if it might bite. With her dragonstone so close, Adi felt the buzz of her astral potential. It called to her. She saw the familiar sparkle of astral dust in the air. The Blood Queen stood so close to Adi that she could have snatched it from the woman's fingertips.

*To have her son and her magic—*

The Blood Queen squeezed the stone in her fist.

*"Svino,"* she said and opened her palm to reveal a small pile of dull green dust.

"No!" Adi cried. The buzzing in her veins subsided. The ambient astral dust faded from view and she felt lightning pulse through her then subside. She slumped against the table. "Why did you do that? You cut me off from controlled power. I could have used that to help recover your artifacts."

"I have only closed one door to you. Besides, you are a woman of resources and luck. I have faith in you, Adison Faide of House Azure."

The Blood Queen dumped the remains of the dragonstone onto the table. Adi traced a finger through the dust, hoping for residual connection, but it was inert.

"You have suffered your punishments and are aware of the stakes. Now I will do you two favors. First, I give you this."

The Blood Queen produced a vial stoppered with a wax seal. She shook it before handing it to Adi. Inside swirled a dark crimson fluid, tinged with green. As Adi watched, the fluid sparkled then separated into crimson and emerald layers, the crimson floating on top like oil on water. Adi shook it and the two fluids recombined temporarily.

"What is it?" she asked.

"Celestial ichor."

Adi almost hurled the vial across the room. "This is Pallantier's blood!"

"Yes, celestial ichor is a combination of blood and aether."

Adi slipped the vial into a belt pouch. "What do I do with it?"

"Another answer you'll have to discover on your own."

"What is the second favor?"

The Blood Queen motioned Ajax, who withdrew a branding iron from the embers in the hearth. Adi rose to run, but Sasha grabbed her wrist, the claws digging into her forearm. Adi struggled, but the Blood Queen was powerful. Adi thrashed and the metal knives burrowed deeper into her skin. Tears blurred her vision so she could not see Ajax apply the hot iron to her forearm.

Adi screamed as the brand seared her flesh. The stink made her choke. Then the Blood Queen released her. Adi retched and flailed against vertigo, crashing against the edge of the table. She dashed the tears from her eyes so she could see the crisp brown mark surrounded by angry red skin. It was a drop, representing blood, tears, or water, about as long as the end of her thumb.

Ajax set the brand on the edge of the hearth before grabbing her wrist and smearing the burn with a rank green ointment that stung. Then he bound her forearm with gauze. Adi winced each time the delicate fabric crossed the wound.

"Isn't the collar enough?" Adi gasped when she could speak again.

"The collar is for your indenture; this is for your future."

"How is branding me a favor?"

"It is a foundation upon which you can build a powerful life."

Adi had no idea what the woman meant. She knew of no traditions, magical or otherwise, that relied on branding their adherents. The Blood Queen had no visible brands or tattoos. Adi squeezed her eyes shut and sobbed as Ajax tied off the bandage.

"We are done here," the Blood Queen said when he had finished. She pivoted and strode back to the staircase. She paused and regarded Adi. "I will grant you one more boon in anticipation of your success."

Adi wilted. "I cannot bear any more favors from you."

"I think you will like this one. It's a ship, the *Starforged*. You'll find it in quarantine on the sixteenth level of the aeroport. Spring it and it's yours."

"Quarantine?"

"For now, I am still a gang lord and the *Starforged* is a smuggler's vessel." The Blood Queen spun in a twirl of skirts and ascended the stairs.

Adi's arm throbbed. She glared at Ajax. He grinned at her, his white teeth brilliant.

"Captain Crestone, what's your plan?"

The way he used her title made Adi loath her rank.

She swept up her tricorn from the floor. She tidied it up and placed it on her head. Without a word, she left the Red Wyrm for the aeroport. Ajax followed close on her heels.

## CHAPTER FIFTY-NINE
# THEO VANGUARD
## MOON OF XYS, DJINNDAY, 2ND OF LUXOR

The *Penumbra* swayed as it pulled away from the pier. Theo held his bride's hand, feeling relief at the widening gap between them and his father. Beside them, Art waved enthusiastically to his children. They ran, fearless, to the end of the fourteen-story drop so they could see him for as long as possible. Father Heilig and Congressman Marrion watched the ship depart, both with dour looks on their faces, lost in their own thoughts. It was odd that his brother had made no appearance at either the wedding or their departure. He wondered when he might see Isaiah again, and the uncertainty of it made him suddenly sad.

When the pier had dwindled on the horizon, Theo turned to his bride and cleared his throat. The duty of consummation weighed on him.

"Shall we retire to the stateroom?" he asked.

Hannah's nod was curt. "Please, lead the way."

Theo excused himself from the company at the railing and led Hannah belowdecks.

The ship boasted a resplendent stateroom with a four-poster bed and a clawfoot tub. It even had a small balcony on the stern large enough for two deck chairs. Theo shifted from foot to foot while Hannah's handmaidens undertook the laborious chore of removing her dress. Lord Vanguard had not provided Theo with a valet.

*Fewer witnesses for the treason he's forcing me to commit.* Theo smiled. His father had outmaneuvered him once again. He had married Lady Valefyre. When they returned from Maxon, she was expected to be pregnant, and he would have to take over as master of the Balan Estates after resigning from the Imperial Navy. *Still, I got one thing I wanted—and Beatrice is here.*

The maids pulled free the ribbon holding Hannah's bodice closed. They set the upper garment aside and began untying the corset beneath. Theo set his valise on the bed and opened it. He had not brought much: a hastily tailored shirt and breeches, a paisley satin vest in the colors of House Vanguard, underclothes, a few toiletries, and the book of Valefyre genealogy from the Void Temple. He rooted through them, uncomfortable watching as Hannah disrobed.

She gasped as the corset came free to reveal the upper portion of the chemise. The maids then turned their attention to the petticoats. Theo glimpsed the fabric laying over the curve of her breast. Hannah caught his eye. Theo looked away, heat rising in his cheeks.

*Fool,* Theo berated himself, *she is your wife.* When he found the courage to glance at his bride again, her eyes were fixed on the floor and her face was flushed.

Theo remembered that his brother Paul had purchased a prostitute for Theo's fifteenth birthday.

"Welcome to manhood," Paul had laughed and clapped him on the back when Theo emerged pale and sweaty from the brothel. At the naval academy, he had been too worried that he might father a bastard, adding ammunition to his father's wrath at Theo's disappointing life choices. Then there was Beatrice.

Hannah cleared her throat. Theo looked up from his valise to where she stood at the foot of the bed in her chemise, the maids dismissed. Her red hair hung in loose curls down to her freckled shoulders, her green eyes were wide. She looked to Theo as if she might bolt.

*Does she feel as trapped as I do?* Theo wondered.

"Do you want me to help you undress?" Hannah asked him.

Theo shut the valise. "I—" he closed his mouth before he started stammering. Hannah came to him around the corner of the bed and began to undo the buttons of his uniform jacket.

A sharp knock on the door made the newlyweds jump.

"Who is it?" Theo called.

"Fincher, sir. Commander Vanguard, the captain and Mr. Dreggs request your presence in the captain's quarters."

Fincher was the first mate.

"Can it wait?" but Theo was already rebuttoning his jacket. Hannah's face was impassive as she draped a green satin robe over her chemise.

"Mr. Dreggs insists its urgent."

Theo opened the door two inches to protect his bride's modesty. Haverford Dreggs was the legal representative from Xander Marrion's office, given the unenviable task of the delegation's logistics and communication with the outside world.

Theo's voice rang with authority. "What is so urgent that he interrupts my wedding night?"

"I'm sorry sir, I don't know." The man's voice quavered.

As the ranking officer Theo commanded the delegation. He could refuse. He *should* refuse to see anyone until after breakfast. He had not spoken with Dreggs other than a frosty greeting when the man had come aboard, so he had no sense of the man's disposition.

*Is this a grab at authority? Is he simply nervous? Could something be wrong already?*

"Very well, lead me to him." Theo turned to Hannah. "My apologies, but I must see to whatever this is."

"I understand." She kissed him on the cheek. Fincher looked away, abashed.

"Pardon, ma'am," he mumbled.

Theo followed Fincher down the hallway toward the ship's prow where he knocked once more, this time on the captain's door.

"Enter," came a stern voice from within.

Fincher opened the door and Theo strode inside. The captain's quarters were small, but well-appointed. There was a large feather bed built against the port hull, and a wood-burning stove that vented out a porthole. The desk was stuffed with maps and charts and looked to be a Tyrian antique. Theo was not normally one for antiques, but the heavy wood of the Tyrian style was popular with Imperial military officers.

The quarters were not large enough to accommodate the group of people crammed around the central table. The captain was perusing a map of Maxon's eastern reach and consulting Lady Naima Lillian. Mr. Dreggs was rifling through a stack of paper. Lady Lillian's wings looked cramped against the bulkhead. The captain stood and snapped to attention when Theo entered.

"At ease," Theo said. "What seems to be the problem?"

"Problem, sir?" the captain asked.

"Something so important you requested my presence here on my wedding night." Theo raised an imperious brow at the man, who flushed.

Mr. Dreggs broke in. "Yes, take a look at this, Theo." He waved a parchment at Theo. The captain blanched at the lawyer's familiarity.

"Commander Vanguard will be sufficient until we are better acquainted," Theo said, taking the missive.

"My apologies, Commander," Dreggs said. His voice indicated that he was not at all sorry.

"What is this?"

"Your father—High Chancellor Vanguard, gifted me this stack of correspondence upon our departure. This one is from the garrison commander at Fort Jasper. I thought you would want to see it in case it required any immediate corrections to our course."

"Fort Jasper?"

"It is the border fort between the Imperial holdings on Maxon and the Veldt," Lady Lillian explained.

"That's where my brother died." Theo struggled to focus his exhausted mind on the topic. He had not known that the delegation would pass through his brother's final posting. With other pressing events, he had not reviewed the route or considered the delegation's mission other than his desire to be part of it. He studied the map spread out on the table.

"Where will the aerogate gate deposit us?" he asked.

"Just outside Planktown," the captain answered.

"How long before we reach the gate?"

The captain checked his watch. "Four hours."

Someone knocked on the captain's door.

"Who is it?" the captain called.

"Beatrice," came the voice.

"Enter."

Beatrice's usually impeccable hair was disheveled, and her dress rumpled. Theo wondered if she had a maid with her. She stood beside him, their arms touching in the crowded cabin. The hairs on Theo's neck rose. He cleared his throat and tried to ignore her.

*What was I talking about?*

"Our course, sir," Dreggs reminded him.

Theo scanned the parchment in his hand. A large band of Eldarian separatists had attacked Fort Jasper two days prior, damaging the eastern wall and causing the fort chamberlain to close the border.

"How long before we reach Fort Jasper?"

"We take on coal in Planktown, then two days to Fort Jasper," the captain said.

"And how far from there to our final destination."

"Unclear, sir," Dreggs said. "The chamberlain has the authority to prevent us from crossing the border. Given the recent fighting, he may also refuse to provide us with an escort. The Eldarians do not permit airships above the grasslands. Cedar Falls is running at record water levels, so the descent from the Jasper Plateau into the Veldt may be more treacherous on foot than usual. The frontier command at Fort Expedition will want to retaliate for the attack. That will complicate our journey."

"Has frontier command been informed of our delegation?"

"Yes, sir."

"And?"

Dreggs shifted from foot to foot.

Beatrice spoke up. "I suspect they will not change their plans for a doomed expedition."

Theo turned to the prophet. "Have you seen something?"

"No, but I did some reading. There has not been a successful pilgrimage to the God of Destruction since our emperor's grandfather sat the throne seven decades ago."

"Why not?"

"The Eldarians often deny foreigners access to the grasslands. Or the god rejects the embassy, or weather, disease, mutiny, and the dangers of the Forest of Bosque take their toll. The Society of Astrologia has chronicled sixteen attempts over the decades. They failed for one or more of these reasons."

"If we do not reach Djinnar," Art said, his voice solemn, "many people on Xys will die because we cannot evacuate them. Xander made it clear that the convergence of gates at Ourania is our last chance."

"If the destruction of Xys is as imminent as your prophecies would have us believe, why isn't the Empire evacuating people now? Why are people not migrating of their own volition?" Theo said.

"Solvigant is their home," Beatrice said. Theo sighed and rubbed his temples. "The Empire will not abandon Xys until the last possible minute,"

"Why not?" Theo asked.

Eyes darted around the table, each person hoping someone else would answer.

"Military High Command would see it as a defeat," the captain said at last.

"By whom?"

"If Xys is destroyed, the Empire gets smaller."

"The Empire is its people, not a broken moon. Save the people and the number of subjects remains the same."

"Solvigant is home to over four million people. Where will they go?" Beatrice asked.

"Saba. Isn't that why your husband, Lord Marrion, got himself appointed ambassador?"

Beatrice shrugged, "My husband's intentions are unknown to me."

Theo wanted to press her, but not in front of an audience. "What is High Command doing to save Xys then?"

The captain spread his hands wide as if to say, *"Your guess is as good as mine."*

*Because the emperor wants to destroy Xys,* Theo knew, but could not say.

"Resources," Art said. Theo looked at him, confused.

"It's another reason to delay evacuation. As Xys's orbit decays, the increased proximity to Solo attracts greater amounts of astral dust into the arrays. The emperor and his queen are stockpiling as much as possible."

"And the Society of Astrologia," Dreggs said.

Beatrice nodded, her smile grim. "And the Society, yes. Denial is another reason not to evacuate."

"You mean some people believe that Xys's descent will simply stop?" Theo's eyebrows rose.

"The powerful of Xys have difficulty reconciling their waning authority with what they feel they deserve." Beatrice said. "You come from one of the most powerful noble families in the Imperium. Is that so hard to believe?"

"It makes too much sense, unfortunately." Theo closed his eyes. An image of Hannah, pressed against him in her chemise, undoing the buttons of his uniform invaded his consciousness. He sighed and pushed the image aside. When he opened his eyes, Beatrice was staring at him. Theo held her gaze as long as he could but looked away first.

"The delegation is the only hope the people of Xys have to evacuate efficiently," Beatrice said.

"She's right," Art said. "Only the pilgrimage sight of Skob has reliable access to the requisite number of gates, including gates to Saba, to evacuate. If Beatrice's predictions are true—"

Beatrice's voice was even and cold. "They are."

"If they are true," Beatrice continued, "Djinnar's permission is the only way to circumvent the prescribed pilgrimage route before the gate behavior becomes erratic."

"What about Pallantier?" Theo asked, "Xys is their home moon. They are Djinnar's brother god."

"A question for Art, I believe," Dreggs said.

Theo turned his attention back to the map. "Is there another way into the Veldt besides Fort Jasper?"

"The Tholossian Rift is vast," the captain said. "Cedar Falls is the best entry point; it's why Fort Jasper was built. There is a secondary route east from Fort Expedition, but it traverses the Bernian jungle. We'd have to go on foot, or the Eldarians might mistake us for an invasion force or military scouts." The captain paused to clear his throat. "With the women and the superstitious nature of the crew, it could take weeks. No offense of course."

"Superstition?"

"Nefeshi," the captain replied.

"If they exist," Theo said, "they're harmless."

"Oh, they exist," Beatrice said, "and their harmlessness depends on which stories you believe."

"What shall we do, sir?" Dreggs asked Theo.

Theo sighed. "We will continue our current course. As soon as we dock in Planktown, Dreggs will send a letter to the chamberlain impressing upon him the seriousness of our delegation."

"And if Fort Expedition decides to retaliate against the Eldarians?" Dreggs pressed.

"A military incursion might make it easier for us to slip into the Veldt, and albeit more dangerous once across the border if the enemy is on high alert." Theo chaffed at Dreggs's questions. *Why does he think I would have further information on the local politics on a moon I have never visited? Is he trying to undermine my authority on this expedition?*

"Very good, sir." Dreggs said.

"Understood," the captain replied.

"We are done here. I am going to retire to my stateroom," Theo said. "Unless there is an Eldarian air assault on the Xyssian side of the aerogate and the *Penumbra* is set ablaze, I am not to be disturbed."

There was a general rumble of assent around the table and the captain winked at him. Theo turned and had to squeeze past Beatrice to open the door. He nodded to her. She did not acknowledge him but watched him go.

Theo strode back down the narrow corridor to his stateroom at the stern. He entered without knocking. The room appeared empty and a handful of hooded lanterns cast long shadows. He was about to call out when he heard voices on the balcony. He squinted across the dim room and through the frosted glass of the rear portholes. Theo made out two shapes.

*Who would visit our stateroom at this hour?* Theo wondered. *Everyone of import was in the captain's quarters.*

"You did well," he heard Hannah say.

"Thank you, milady." The other voice was soft and hoarse. Another woman.

*A maidservant?* Theo stifled the urge to call out. Something within him bristled. *Who would have known I was called away. What is Hannah hiding?* Theo crept closer to the balcony door, careful not to bang a knee on the clawfoot tub. He stood in the shadows beside the armoire and peered through the narrow opening of the balcony door. The other woman knelt before Hannah. Though her back was to Theo and she wore a dark robe, he recognized her. Her chiropteran wings were folded against her back and Theo caught the gleam of a shotel through a gap in the robe's fabric: Palestrina.

*What is she doing here?*

Theo suppressed the sudden urge to rush forward and defend his bride from the deadly Seraph, yet Palestrina crouched on one knee, her head lowered in obeisance.

*Obeisance? To Hannah?*

Theo listened.

"What about Crestone?" Hannah asked.

"An entire platoon of city watch and Imperial Guards arrived at the aeroport to apprehend her. She must be in custody by now," Palestrina said.

"And the Blood Queen?"

"She will know by morning that I have betrayed her if she does not already know. She will come for me."

"The newly armed White Rabbits will preoccupy her."

"Do not underestimate Sasha Riven."

Shadow obscured Hannah's face, but he could see her grimace in dissatisfaction.

"What of the device?" Palestrina asked. She took a leather pouch from within her robe and offered it to Hannah, who took it and peered within.

"It is beautiful." Hannah said, admiration clear in her voice. "Where is its box?"

"I believe Stuart Royal removed it from its box."

Hannah clenched her fists and Theo thought she might toss the bag over the rail.

*Why does Palestrina have Apyreon? What else could it be?* The hair rose on the nape of Theo's neck.

"You must take it to Hornblatt," Hannah said.

"What about Ilia?"

"Hornblatt will use it to help locate Tethysteon."

Palestrina nodded.

"Go to Thail," Hannah repeated. "Once Tethysteon's whereabouts are known, go to Caelia. Ilia journeys there in a fortnight."

"How will I know it is Ilia?"

"I will write the conclave in Caelia to expect you before Ilia's arrival." Hannah handed the bag back to Palestrina. "Rise and receive your blessing, Knight of Acadia."

Palestrina stood. She towered over Hannah, but the Seraph bent her head low to receive the blessing.

*They're done,* Theo realized. He crept back across the stateroom and out the door. He waited for the faint thump of the Seraph's powerful wingbeats. When he was sure Palestrina had departed, he tapped the door and opened it.

"Hannah," he called into the dim room. His wife strode in from the balcony and let the green satin robe fall open. She had removed the chemise and Theo stared at her nubile nakedness, her ample breasts, the pale flesh of her hips, and the thatch of hair between her legs.

All thoughts of conversation or interrogation vanished from Theo's mind along with his guilt at eavesdropping on his wife. As she crossed the dim room, Hannah's face shed the grim authority it had held while she was talking with Palestrina. Theo saw her eyes change as they focused on him and her posture softened. He saw the coy maiden she had been when her maidservants were present. The transition sent a twitch of unease through his growing arousal, but he banished his concerns for now.

"It's cold and lonely in this room without my husband on our wedding night."

Indeed, Theo could see goose prickles on her exposed skin. He took a tentative step towards her, then another. His mind skittered between the troubles at Fort Jasper, the visit from Palestrina, and the supple curves of his young wife revealed before him.

Hannah closed the gap between them, pressing her body against him and squirming in a way that seemed awkward at first, but he soon felt himself stiffen in anticipation. Blood rushed to his cheeks and his loins, and for a moment he felt betrayed by his body. Then

Hannah's mouth closed on his, her tongue playing against his lips. He relented, opening his mouth to accept hers, his shoulders sagging.

Hannah began the laborious task of removing his dress uniform while kissing his neck and the hollow in his collarbones. Theo shivered. She pushed him back onto the bed to remove his trousers.

"What worries you, my husband?" she asked him. "Am I not to your liking?"

"You are incredibly beautiful."

"Then why do you hesitate? I am your bride. My body is your right, a child our obligation."

Theo winced. Hannah noticed this, but she continued disrobing him.

He said, "It is only that, the obligation."

"Is making love to a beautiful woman such a terrible obligation?" She pushed Theo onto his back and straddled him. She shifted her hips against his and his breath hitched.

*How is this 'making love'?* Theo wondered. *Can't we take some time to learn one another first?* The rhythm of her hips intoxicated him, and Theo clenched, afraid he would finish before he was fully naked.

He opened his mouth to speak, but Hannah silenced him with a kiss.

"Do not look so conflicted, husband," she whispered in his ear. "I will help you with your obligation."

Theo abandoned his last sliver of resistance and brought his hands up to caress his bride, to celebrate the pliant skin beneath his fingers, the lithe body of this young woman, his wife.

*My father's machinations are not all so terrible,* Theo thought before all words slipped from his mind. There was a final flash of Beatrice, of those limitless blue, prophetic eyes, but the image disappeared as Hannah removed his final undergarment and they became well and truly married.

# CHAPTER SIXTY

# ADI CRESTONE

## MOON OF XYS, MILLSDAY, 3RD OF LUXOR

Adi and Ajax entered the aeroport lobby. Groggy passengers waited for access to their departure gates. An industrialist in a rumpled suit paced along an empty row of seats clutching a briefcase. A group of young Grym dozed, sprawled across the floor with their backpacks. A pair of Seraphs, garbed in the chestnut robes of Strolen the Smith, God of Order, sipped burnt coffee from paper cups. A Dragon clad in the regalia of the scholars of the Society of Astrologia scribbled away in a leather-bound tome. A mother slept on a bench under a pile of four children. Adi thought of Vista and the children he had left behind when he gave his life to help her. Grief threatened to overwhelm her. She swallowed hard. This was not the time to lose control. She resolved that Ajax would not see her pain.

Adi scanned the room for Iris. Gears pinged and the large clock in the middle of the room chimed half past midnight. The ruddy reflected light of Solo mingled with the oily gas lamps of the aeroport, casting long shadows across the space. Adi wasn't sure how much time she had. By now, the city watch was aware of the conflagration at Alhambra's. An attack on the cargo aeroport would result in the closure of shipping lanes and an increased security presence at major gates and the passenger aeroport. The sooner she could locate Iris and spring the *Starforged* from impound, the easier it would be to escape Xys for Tyre. With the notoriety of the Lord of Bones, the coal freighter was no longer an option.

Then Adi realized that before the day was over, she would see Lucas. The thought of holding her son caused her heart to ache and a weight of terror to drop into her stomach. She pushed it out of her mind. Right now, she needed to focus.

A lone ticket clerk sat behind an ornate wooden desk with a metal screen shuffling a deck of cards. On the wall behind him was a bulletin board. Adi recognized the likeness of her own wanted poster. The clerk looked up at the newcomers, and shock blossomed on his face at the sight of the Lord of Bones. A commotion at the entrance caught Adi's attention. A half dozen Imperial Guardsmen dismounted their armored steeds and clomped up the stairs toward the aeroport.

"We need to move," Adi hissed to Ajax and limped toward the twin curved staircases at the back of the main lobby. Her ribs still ached from the fight outside Bruto Station and her body was beginning to throb from the wounds sustained at Alhambra's. The thought of climbing sixteen flights of stairs to the impound level exhausted her. There was no time, however. If they didn't move now, Adi would spend the rest of her days before Xys's destruction in Duneharrow prison.

*If the Blood Queen allows it,* Adi thought.

She couldn't find Iris. *Maybe she changed her mind. I can hardly blame her.*

A few waiting passengers cast somnolent looks their way as they made their way across the lobby, but they averted their eyes when they took her in. She realized how battered she must look. Dried blood caked the left side of her face where the void mage's projectile had grazed her ear. Her jaw was bruised and swollen, and her arm oozed through the bandages where the Blood Queen had branded her. She was carrying a grenado in a bandolier and a pair of daggers on her belt.

The Imperial Guard entered the aeroport and began questioning the clerk. Adi did not wait to see where they went next. She took the steps two at a time, gasping as she turned on each landing. Her ankle throbbed and her ribs burned. Ajax's skeletal armor jangled behind her. He was whistling. She paused on the landing for the sixth floor to steady herself, panting. She resisted the urge to scratch the painful burn on her forearm.

"Do you have a plan?" Ajax asked from behind her. His breathing was calm, unlabored.

"I'm open to suggestions."

"The *Starforged* will be guarded."

"Those Imperial Guards will be looking for me. The ticket clerk recognized you. But first, we must make it to the impound level."

"Adi?"

Adi swiveled toward the voice.

It was Iris, wearing a light gray traveling cloak and carrying a leather valise. Adi smiled and relief flooded through her. She let out a breath she had not realized she was holding.

Wright was with her and, to Adi's surprise, so was Verdun. He was carrying a battered leather suitcase in one hand, his large tap mallet was slung over the other shoulder.

The color drained from Iris's face when she saw Adi's condition. She rushed to Adi's side.

"Are you all right?"

"Iris," Adi panted, "I didn't think you would come." She leaned her forehead against Iris's, tipping Adi's tricorn back at an awkward angle. For a moment, she said nothing, just basked in the sandalwood and cardamom of Iris's perfume.

"We have a problem," Verdun said, interrupting their moment. "The city watch is checking passports and papers on all the boarding levels, regardless of vessel."

Adi straightened and eyed the jungle Ankhim. "What are you doing here?"

He grinned. "I'm coming with you."

"You can't. What about Stella? What about the Echo?"

Verdun laughed. "Stella wanted to come herself. This was the only way I could talk her out of it. My apprentice can manage the taps while I'm gone."

Adi resisted the urge to hug him in front of Ajax and Wright. She didn't know Verdun well, but she was grateful for his aid.

"We can't take the freighter with the Lord of Bones anyway. It would draw too much attention."

"What is he doing here?" Wright asked, pointing at Ajax.

"His presence is a condition of our escape."

"I thought I made myself clear. I don't work for the Blood Queen."

Ajax flashed him a wicked grin. Iris blanched and Verdun shifted as if expecting a fight.

"I'm still your captain," Adi said. "This is still my last assignment for the Blood Queen."

Ajax chuckled. Adi ignored him.

"I want nothing to do with that creature," Wright spat.

Ajax's grin faded as his jaw tensed. Adi had no doubt he would kill Wright here and now, consequences be damned. She glanced back down the stairs. A group of stevedores was whispering and pointing toward them. One took off toward the lobby.

*Djinnar's blood, they've recognized us.*

"We don't have time for this. There is no ship without Ajax. I don't like it either, but the choices are work with Ajax or swing from the gallows." Adi's mind raced. "We need to get to the impound level. If you're coming with me, let's move." She brushed past them all and bounded up the stairs.

The clock chimed the three-quarter hour. Adi swore under her breath and redoubled her efforts, ignoring a nasty stitch in her side. She reached the fourteenth-floor gasping and trembling, her face flushed from the exertion. Her knees wobbled and she could not remember the last time she had eaten.

Several city watchmen stood in the doorway between a small lobby and the boarding area, checking passports. An alarm bell began to clang.

Level fourteen belonged to the freight section of the aeroport. Reinforced decking replaced polished wood flooring. Though it was late in the day, freight was a twenty-four-hour operation. Everywhere, porters, stewards, and dockhands hauled crates of all sizes and shapes back and forth between berths. Solvigant relied heavily on imports, and that meant working around the clock for the entire staff.

The alarm bell was louder here. Adi heard the rising whir of a klaxon warming up.

*Would the city watch really shut down the entire aeroport to find me? They might.*

Adi trotted toward the central staircase.

"What's your plan?" Iris asked.

"The ship is called the *Starforged*. It's an impounded smuggler's vessel."

"Sounds dangerous."

"It's our only option. Follow me." A troop of watchmen jogged toward them in formation, weapons ready. Adi turned to head further up the central staircase. In normal circumstances, she would have enjoyed leading them on a merry chase through the aeroport, but not with Iris and the rest of her crew, and not with how exhausted she was. The Imperial Guard would be marshaling their forces below. Adi had no time for pursuit games.

*I have a crew,* Adi thought, *albeit a strange one: a brewer, a sailor, a prostitute, and gang lord.* Still, the thought of it charmed her.

"Hurry!" Adi took Iris's hand and hustled her up the stairs. Verdun, Wright, and Ajax followed. Adi heard a watchmen's cry of recognition, and the troop broke into a sprint behind them.

When they emerged onto the next level, a Karisian freighter named *Cerul's Horn* was pulling away from the pier, signal flags flying. Grunting, Adi pushed herself up the final flight to the sixteenth floor.

"Where is this ship?" Iris asked.

The city watchmen reached the top of the stairs, and Adi had only her daggers and a grenado.

"Run"—Adi pointed around the corner—"that way."

Iris hefted her valise in one hand, her skirts in the other, and bolted.

"Verdun, keep her safe," Adi shouted. The emerald-skinned brewer took off after the fleeing woman. Adi parried the first watchman's blow and punched him in the belly. He doubled over and dropped his sword. Adi kicked it behind her, then swept her dagger across the man's chest. He dodged and avoided death, but the sharp blade opened a red gash across his torso. Adi kicked another watchman in the groin and he crumpled. She tossed her dagger at a third, catching him in the gut. He fumbled his blade as he clutched at the dark blood welling from his wound.

Wright was beside her, daggers whirling. He was in much better condition than she was and made quick work of the watchmen who challenged him. Ajax was a blur of fists and feet. He used his bone armor with practiced deftness, letting the ossified plates deflect blows while he snuck in under a watchman's defense and punched him in the face. The Lord of Bones was a mesmerizing clatter and whirl of death. Adi was so entranced watching him fight that a city watchman nearly ran her through, but she managed to jump aside at the last second. The man stumbled forward, expecting the resistance of Adi's torso and finding nothing but air. She kicked him hard in the side of the knee. Bones crunched and he screamed, dropped his blade, and fell away from the fray.

Adi ran, scooping up the first watchman's sword as she passed.

"On me!" she shouted to Wright and ran after Iris around the curve of the hallway. A door banged open as they ran past and Imperial Guardsmen emerged from the crewmen's stairs.

"Keep running!" Adi shouted when Verdun looked back.

An arrow whistled overhead and thumped into the ceiling twenty paces ahead of them. Another *thunked* overhead. Adi ducked.

*They're aiming high. Broc must want to speak with me before I hang.*

More arrows whistled past.

"Stop!" one of the soldiers shouted. "Halt in the name of the emperor." When she and her crew did not stop, the crossbowmen loosed their quarrels.

*Better to be dead than fail Lucas. Ajax and Wright are soldiers, but Iris and Verdun don't deserve this.* Adi hesitated, then stumbled. She caught herself and found her stride again. She concentrated on the swish of Iris's skirts ahead of her. *They've made their choices, I guess.*

The impound came into view.

"Iris! Turn right!"

Two city watchmen barred their way. Verdun dropped his suitcase and gripped his hammer in both hands. He dodged a watchman's blade and brought the hammer up in a sweeping arc into the man's ribs. The soldier grunted as the air was driven from his lungs and he crumpled. The second watchman scored a shallow cut on Verdun's bicep. The brewer roared and backhanded the soldier. His head snapped to the side, and he collapsed unconscious beside his partner. The Ankhim panted and reached down to retrieve his suitcase.

"Verdun," Adi shouted. "Are you all right? You're bleeding."

He inspected the wound. "It's nothing."

Arrows *thunked* into the wood beside him. The Imperial Guard was closing in and their shots were becoming more accurate.

"Let's move!" Adi dashed through the doorway into the impound. "Which berth?" she asked Ajax.

He shrugged. Not a bead of sweat showed on his brow. Adi swore. He was enjoying himself. She wanted to shake him.

The clerk's desk was empty. The alarm pounded in Adi's ears, drowning out everything else.

"Verdun, bar the doors. We need time to find and ready the ship."

Moments before the first wave of guardsmen crashed into the wood, the brewer slammed the doors shut and dropped the heavy metal bar into place. The doors heaved and splintered but held. The metal bar bent slightly but did not twist the brackets. Not yet. The barricade would buy them a few minutes at least.

Adi jogged the length of the curving hallway looking for the *Starforged*. Iris followed, her breathing rapid, her hair disheveled. Adi thought she looked beautiful but couldn't summon the breath to say so.

The first two berths were empty and the third held a dilapidated mining freighter. The *Starforged* was in berth number four.

"That's it?" Adi protested. "You told me it was a smuggling vessel."

She pointed toward the converted tug and glared at Ajax.

"It is," Ajax insisted. "No one inspects tugs."

Tugs were small airships used by freight companies to cut transit times. They were little more than glorified floating engines that quickened the pace of a freighter like horses added to a carriage team. Tugs required minimal crew and carried light armament as some cargo required armed escorts.

Adi touched Iris's arm to steer her toward the tug. Adi jumped over the railing and slid the gangplank toward the pier. Behind them, she could hear the shouts and efforts of the guardsmen as they hammered against the doors of the impound level. Iris sprinted aboard, followed by the rest of the crew. Adi pulled the gangway up and stowed it. She cut the stern mooring line with the sword, the blade notching the gunwale. There was a crash as the doors shuddered and finally gave way. Guardsmen poured into the hallway behind them.

"Cut the fore deck line," she yelled at Wright as an arrow struck the cabin wall. Its shaft quivered inches from Adi's face.

"Iris, cut the spar lines." She tossed the sword to Iris who fumbled the unfamiliar weapon. It clattered onto the deck and slid toward the bow. The soldiers were nearly upon them, but Adi had no time to grab it.

The ship looked more like a houseboat than an industrial tug. Its rigging consisted of a single spherical balloon behind a square-top mainsail. The helm manipulated a rudder as tall as the body of the ship, situated behind a steam-driven propeller. Adi checked the gauges.

"Verdun, go below and start the boiler."

*Praise to the Nine, the balloon's inflated.* Adi shouted with delight. They would not be able to get far before the boiler was hot enough to drive the propeller, but there was enough wind to get them off the pier.

She saw Ajax throw the bowline clear from the fore cleat.

"Hold on!" Adi called. She disengaged the propeller and helm locks and the ship lurched forward. Adi spun the wheel hard to starboard... and the ship banked hard to port. Adi narrowly avoided ramming the pier.

"Djinnar's blood. I hate reverse rigging."

She threw all her weight into the helm and spun it to port. The ship finally swung to starboard and the rudder skimmed the pier.

An Imperial Guardsman reached the tug and leapt onto the stern. He grabbed Adi's shoulder and yanked her around. She snatched at the control panel to maintain her balance and accidentally hit the toggle to vent the balloon. The wheel spun and the prow pitched downward as the ship lost buoyancy. Iris screamed and clung to the railing as everything that was not secured to the deck tumbled off the bow.

Adi blocked the soldier's wild swing and shoved him against the railing. They struggled. She tried to pry his sword from his fingers, but the soldier's grip was strong. He kneed Adi in the stomach. She stumbled backward and slammed her back against the helm. The soldier lunged, aiming for Adi's abdomen. She jumped aside but lost her footing on the pitching deck and fell hard. The soldier raised his blade. Adi shielded her face with her hands, knowing it would not stop the killing blow.

But it was the soldier's body and not his blade that fell on her. When Adi shoved the big man aside, she saw Wright clinging to the cabin with one hand and wielding the boat hook with the other. The gleam in his eyes matched her grin.

"Good to be back on a ship," he said.

Adi pulled herself to her feet and braced herself against the ship's dive. She took the boat hook from Wright and shoved the handle through the spinning helm. The handle smashed against the control panel and stopped the wheel's spin. Adi flipped the toggle to close and stabilize the balloon and grasped the wheel with both hands. Wright heaved the unconscious soldier off the deck.

"Pull the hook free," she said. Wright grasped the boat hook and heaved. Adi grimaced as the weight of the rudder shifted to her arms and shoulders. She grunted with the strain of righting the small tug, but she managed it. When they were level again, she rechecked the gauges.

"We need more coal in the firebox. Go below and relieve Verdun. I'll get us out of here."

Wright ducked inside the cabin and hurried down the ladder to the boiler room. Adi looked around. The impound pier was now several stories above them after their abrupt descent. By some miracle of the Nine, they had avoided colliding with any airships docked at the lower piers. A pair of small, swift vessels pulled away from an upper level. Adi saw a dozen city watchmen peering over the rail at her. Adi swore, but there was no avoiding it. She needed to gain altitude to clear the city. They were sailing north-northwest, and Adi could steer north-northeast as she rose, but she knew she would have to engage them at some point. The watchmen would not give up their pursuit unless she made it too dangerous for them to continue.

"Ajax," she shouted, "can you man the helm?"

"I know my way around a ship well enough."

"Hold her steady here and wait for my signal. We'll need to climb fast so hold on."

Ajax looked her up and down. Adi expected an argument, instead he stepped in and took the wheel. She climbed the ladder onto the cabin's roof and located the stellarium array. The thought of her crushed dragonstone made her momentarily fumble her hold on the balloon's rigging. She snatched it, catching herself, as tears stung her eyes.

The steam engine whirred and she felt their speed increase.

*Wright must be shoveling like mad.*

Adi lit the pilot light to the burner and said a prayer to the Nine.

"Ajax, get ready. The lift will put pressure on the rudder"

The aeroport klaxon shrilled across the warm night.

Adi opened the gas line all the way. There was a slight delay before she heard a hiss letting her know the gas was flowing. The orange kerosene flame roared to life above her. Moments later, the balloon began to rise. She hoped to come up fast behind the watchmen.

*Wright, slow down*, she thought. *We don't want to come up in front of them.* She quickly burned through an entire kerosene canister and popped the empty one free, tossing it into the box for spent cans. She threaded in the new canister with practiced ease. She counted six full canisters inside a storage box built for fifteen. That was a problem for later. She opened the burner full blast again. From her position beneath the sphere of the balloon, Adi could not see the other ship. She counted the floors of the aeroport as they rose.

*Thirteen. Fourteen. Fifteen.*

She heard shouting and she throttled back the burner. She jumped down from the top of the cabin. Once she was on the deck, she saw that they were rising directly underneath the watchmen.

"Ajax, hard to port."

Ajax spun the wheel.

The ship banked and they avoided a direct collision with the other craft. To her horror, the balloon and its rigging scraped against the hull of the watchmen's vessel. Adi heard ropes snap as some of the rigging rubbed clean through. She prayed the gas bag did not tear and that none of the city watchmen thought to puncture it as it slid past. The rapid out-gassing would take both vessels down, but an angry watchman unaccustomed to airships might not know this.

The gas bag held and soon they were level with the other ship. Arrows whizzed past so she dove behind the shelter of the cabin. Adi struck a match, adjusted the fuse on her final grenado, and lit it. She tucked the lit bomb back in her bandolier and hauled herself back onto the roof of the cabin. She opened the burner full bore. The *Starforged* rose and she chucked the grenado onto the deck of the other ship. Adi watched the terrible realization sweep through the city watchmen. One of them tried to kick the bomb over the side, but it clanked against a docking cleat and rolled back toward him. She felt a twinge of guilt right before the grenado exploded.

The injured ship lurched to starboard and dropped fast, shedding wounded watchmen who screamed and clutched at their comrades. Flames licked at the port side of the cabin and climbed toward the rigging. The watchmen's ship faltered, then fell when the dry fabric of their balloon ignited. The rising heat from the fire pummeled the *Starforged*. Ajax steered them away from the turbulence and the little tug righted itself.

Adi exhaled. Then she looked back toward the aeroport and cursed. Two Huxstable 135s, fast and well-armed, were bearing down on them. Their decks bristled with watchmen and Imperial soldiers.

The *Starforged* was not free yet.

# CHAPTER SIXTY-ONE

# ADI CRESTONE

## MOON OF XYS, MILLSDAY, 3RD OF LUXOR

Verdun emerged onto the stern, coal dust smeared on his face and clothes.

"What happened?" he asked Adi.

"I blew up the other tug. The heat of the fire rocked the ship."

"I thought we were going down for a minute."

"We still might." Adi pointed to where the two pursuing dirigibles were quickly closing the gap. As if in response to their conversation a small iron ball whined down the port side.

"They're shooting at us!" Iris exclaimed. Another ball whizzed past, nicking the starboard railing.

"It's a breech-loaded swivel gun," Adi said. Iris only looked at her. "That means the shots will come faster. You should go inside the cabin until we're clear."

"How will we get clear?" Iris watched their pursuers drawing ever closer. Adi knew the Huxstables were sleeker and more aerodynamic than the tug. They had better insulation on the fireboxes to retain heat, and they recycled their exhaust to warm the input water faster. Two more shots passed so close that Adi and Verdun ducked. Splinters of wood erupted from the starboard side of the cabin as the shot tore away pieces of the siding.

"I'll think of something," Adi said. "Go inside."

"We have another problem," Verdun said.

Adi looked around but saw no other ships in the vicinity. "What's that?"

"We're out of coal."

Wright emerged from the boiler room coated in a thin layer of black coal dust.

Adi looked down at the gauge on the control panel. Already the temperature was falling. "Nine bloody gods."

"They must not have loaded the ship since it was in impound," Wright said. "The water tank is only half full and there are no spinners."

"I saw the array," Adi said. "Hard to believe this tug has stellarium engines." Tugs were often local haulers, merely used to aid large freighters to and from aerogates, not entering the laneway through the void themselves. There was no speed advantage in the void.

"It was a retrofit," Ajax said. "We needed interlunar transport."

Another shot from the deck gun struck the tug starboard near where the upper rudder strut connected to the top of the cabin.

"If they damage the rudder, we're done," Adi said.

Her mind raced. The Huxstables were only a hundred yards behind them. Shots from the deck guns would soon become much more accurate. Neither of the ships in pursuit displayed the cerulean glow of stellarium engines under thrust.

*They don't have spinners or an astral mage either,* Adi realized. *If I could engage ours, it might be enough speed to get us away.*

Of course, there was always the possibility that the Huxstables did have the capability but were not using it because they were fast enough to catch the tug without expending the stellarium.

Adi flinched as another shot from the deck guns blew a handle off the wheel, perilously close to the starboard tiller rope.

*We won't survive this barrage much longer. There's no more time to dither.*

"Wright, take the helm," Adi said. "And keep your head down."

"Where are we headed?"

Adi pointed across the bow. "See those red rock bluffs in the distance?" Wright nodded. "Keep us pointed in that direction."

"Aye, Captain. What are you going to do?"

"I am going to engage the stellarium engines."

Iris gasped. "But you don't have your dragonstone. Won't that be painful?"

Adi glanced at Ajax and grimaced. She had risked channeling tiny amounts of stellarium since handing over her dragonstone and that had been painful enough. This would be excruciating.

Adi turned to Ajax. "You're not a mage."

"I am not," he replied.

"It's too dangerous, Adi," Iris complained. "It could kill you."

"I wish there was another way to outrun those Huxstables, but there isn't."

"Adi," Verdun said, "I've seen what astralium necrosis does to mages. Lucas can't lose his mother when you're so close to being reunited."

*You have?* Adi wanted to ask, but it was not the time. "We have no other choice." Without waiting for further objections, she ducked into the cabin.

Adi slid down the short ladder into the engine room. The engine and boiler, complete with its inputs, coal and water, filled the tug's hold. She saw the coal bins, balanced on either side, were completely empty. The water tank was in the prow, and it was low enough that Adi could hear it sloshing with the movement of the tug. The boiler would remain hot for a while at least. Adi surveyed the machinery and located the spinner input. The ship's focus was a large chunk of polished tiger's eye. Adi placed one hand on the stone and the other on the array terminal.

She said a prayer to Lillian of the Twins, the twin gods Mance and Lillian, who governed the flow of stellarium and thus the power of astral magic. Adi had not honored Lillian in some time and knew she could be a fickle goddess. She prayed anyway.

*At least it's still dark outside,* Adi thought. It was easier to channel stellarium at night when sunlight couldn't interfere with the flow of the astral dust. Without a focus she wouldn't be able to prevent the stellarium from burning her from the inside out.

*This is going to hurt.*

Verdun slid down the ladder.

"What are you doing?" Adi asked.

"I didn't want you burning to a crisp down here by yourself."

The Ankhim's tenderness surprised Adi. He was more like Stella than Adi realized, a harsh exterior over a bleeding heart.

"Thank you. Whatever happens, don't touch me. It could kill you too. Understood?"

Verdun grinned trying to lighten the mood. "Aye, Captain."

Adi checked the temperature of the boiler. It held steady, but for how long it would continue to do so, Adi didn't know. Iris shouted something incomprehensible as Adi steeled herself and a shot blasted through the rear hull. She ducked, her hand slipping off the array terminal. The bullet punched through the piping connecting the boiler to the engine before falling into the water tank. A thin gout of steam whistled from the hole in the pipe. The pressure dropped precipitously, and the ship lurched.

"Hurry, Adi!" This time she heard Iris's shout.

Adi grabbed ahold of the array terminal and opened herself to the flow of stellarium. She cried out, her hand nearly slipping from the ship's focus as the first burning wave passed through her. The stellarium flowed from the array, through her body, and into the ship. It felt as if her blood vessels were filled with crushed glass. Adi gasped and it was all she could do to not black out. There were more thumps, more shots from the deck guns, but they sounded as if they were miles away. Pain wracked her body. She felt the tug pick up speed.

Blue light pulsed from the tiger's eye and flashes licked across her skin, as if a thunderstorm raged inside her. The tug accelerated. Adi sagged, letting the entire weight of her body hang from the terminal array. Her visible skin turned splotchy and red. She gritted her teeth and held on. The stellarium burned in her blood. The edges of her vision blurred. When the ship rolled to starboard, she clung harder to the terminal.

She gripped the stone until she felt her fingernails bending backward. Her breath came in ragged gasps and the edges of her vision went gray. The engine room swam with brilliant bursts of blue and white light. Adi did not know how fast they were going, or how long she channeled the stellarium. She could no longer feel her legs and her teeth buzzed in her mouth until she feared they would drop out. Darkness closed in around her. The ship pitched to port and she lost her grip on the terminal. She skidded across the engine room floor and slammed against one of the coal bins. Pain exploded in her side right before she finally lost consciousness.

Adi awoke to Iris's worried face bent over her own. Her vision moved in and out of focus. She was lying on a cot, her head on a thin pillow, and a worn blanket pulled to her chin. The cabin was chilly and the tug was swaying a bit, as if in a calm breeze. Daylight filtered through greasy portholes. Verdun watched from the doorway, a pensive expression on his pinched face.

"You're awake!" Iris cried. She hugged Adi, who yelped. Iris released her. "Sorry." Iris's hands tweaked the blanket, but she did not touch Adi.

"S'okay." She tried to sit up, but the world spun. Iris gently pressed Adi's shoulders against the cot.

"Just relax."

"We made it?"

Iris smiled. "We did. I had no idea this little tug could go that fast."

"Where are we?"

"Floating somewhere above the desert northeast of Solvigant."

"The Huxstables?"

"They gave up when stellarium appeared in our exhaust."

Adi breathed a sigh of relief. Her gambit had paid off. The watchmen had not had time to load their vessels with spinners or didn't have an astral mage. Adi looked at her hands. A thick line of burned skin extended from the center of each palm down the inside of her arms before disappearing beneath the fabric of her shirt. She pulled her shirt away and inspected her chest. The line of burned flesh continued up both biceps and along her collarbones until it met on her sternum.

"Will that heal if we get medications at our destination? Where is our destination by the way?"

"Yes, it will." Adi looked up at Iris. "We're bound for Tyre."

"Lucas?"

"Yes, Lucas. Then the university."

Iris looked confused. "Why the university?"

"A Blood Queen contact is expecting us."

"To do what?"

"To learn about Anaximander's workshop. While the Blood Queen's contacts track down Palestrina, we're to recover the other half of the device. Tethysteon, it's called."

"Then the Blood Queen will release you from your indenture?"

Adi shrugged and immediately regretted it as pain lanced through her chest. "There should be maps, a sextant, and an astrolabe somewhere in the cabin."

"On the table."

"We need to chart a course for the nearest gate to Tyre."

"Do you think the city watch will be monitoring them?"

"I don't think Broc knows about Lucas. We'll have to rely on that. We don't have time to go jumping between moons to confuse any pursuers. Help me get up."

"I don't think that's a good idea," Iris protested, but Adi was already levering herself from the cot. Her arms trembled violently and she thought she might be sick. Iris helped her up and she sat, breathing hard. When the world stopped spinning, she settled a hand on Iris's shoulder and gripped the edge of the mess counter with the other. Adi pulled and Iris rose from her crouch, lifting Adi to her feet.

"Who's driving the ship?"

"Wright has the helm. We've been floating for three hours. Whenever we lose altitude, I fire up the burner. We're down to three canisters."

With Iris's help, Adi shuffled across the cabin. She took it one slow step at a time, inching out onto the deck. She slumped against the cabin wall to catch her breath and waited for her vision to adjust to the fierce sunlight over the desert. Sand stretched out behind them in all directions. There was no sign of Solvigant on the horizon.

"Several sections of the stellarium array looked burned out or broken," Iris said from behind her. They could not use the stellarium engines again until it was repaired. Not that Adi had any desire to do so.

"Some of that happened when we came up underneath the other tug, but the uncontrolled flow must have scorched it.

"Yet here we are, sailing along, not a watchman in sight," Wright said from the helm, "Good to see you up, Captain."

"It doesn't feel great."

"You look terrible," Ajax said. Adi looked up. He was sitting beside the burner apparatus, legs dangling.

*How can he wear that suit in this climate?* Adi wondered.

"No thanks to you and the Blood Queen. If you hadn't destroyed my dragonstone—"

"Further incentive not to fail again."

Adi grimaced. Staring up at the Lord of Bones, framed by the sun, was giving her a headache. "Do you even want to find these artifacts?"

"My Queen will never sacrifice the discipline of her organization for a single mission. Failure will always be punished. Best you don't forget that, *Captain.*" He spat her title and filled it sarcasm and bile.

Adi scoffed and shambled back into the cabin.

They spent the next hour poring over the vessel's charts looking for the closest gate to Tyre. Then Adi calculated their trajectory relative to the cycle of the gate. There was a hydrogate skimming along the surface of the Boiled Sea a day's flight away if the winds favored them. They were short on kerosene canisters, but she knew a trick or two that might help them squeeze a little extra time from the burner and they could catch the updrafts from the desert below.

"The hydrogate will work, but we need to inspect the hull and patch any holes. There's one in the engine room. I don't know if there are more," Adi said.

The gate would deposit them on the Heartspring Ocean near Thail. Adi rejoiced when she realized this. Lucas's school was in Thail so they could pick him up on their way to find the delegation.

Without coal, they had to rely on the winds and the tug's square-rigged mainsail. Adi prayed to Phoebe and the rest of the Nine that they would not be becalmed.

The sun was at its zenith and the rings of Solo were peeking above the horizon when Adi relieved Wright at the helm. She adjusted the wheel to their new course and listened to the creak of the ropes, felt the gentle sway of the gas bag, and smiled at the crack of the mainsail as it filled with wind. It felt right to be back at the helm of a ship.

Adi tacked southeast toward the Boiled Sea.

*Lucas, here I come.*

# CHAPTER SIXTY-TWO

# ION RUCINARE

## MOON OF XYS, MILLSDAY, 3RD OF LUXOR

Ion awoke with a start. The details of his unsettling dream evaporated. His fingers clutched at the carpet for reasons he could not remember. Sunlight filtered through the gauzy curtain over the porthole. Combined with the exhaust from the nearby engines, the heat in the room felt oppressive. His throat was dry. He licked his lips and sat up and gasped when he saw Rehka watching him. She was propped upright with thin pillows and sweat beaded on her brow.

"You were glowing." Rehka's voice cracked.

"I was?"

"Blue and green." Rehka gestured to a scorched black mark on the far wall. "And there was lightning."

"From me?" Ion looked around for other burn marks.

"You're a mage."

"I am not," Ion snapped, as if she had insulted him.

"You have the potential then, both astral and aetherial potential."

"How do you know?"

"I'm a Dragon. We have an affinity with magic, especially astral magic." Rehka winced as a spasm of pain wracked her body. "What happened to me?"

"You don't remember?'

"I remember fighting city watchmen in the street."

Ion flushed and traced patterns in the carpet with an index finger. "Some of the bruises are from me."

"What do you mean?"

"I tried to stop the fighting. I don't remember much, but I was floating and there were waves of red light. Captain Crestone said it was magic. She said I had to see some lady from the Society. I didn't want to. I wanted to go with the captain, but she said it was too dangerous. She said—"

"Captain Crestone," Rehka cut him off, then had to wait as a fit of coughing seized her. "Where is Adi?"

Ion shrugged. "I dunno. She fled the Echo to go to a place called Alhambra's. Do you think she's all right?"

"How would I know?" Rehka snapped. Ion flinched and Rehka relented. "I'm sure she had a plan. She was always good at conjuring plans from thin air. If there was a fourth type of magic, it'd be Adi's ability to conjure escape plans."

Ion forced a smile, unconvinced by the Dragon's reassurance.

"Where are we?" Rehka asked. "What day is it?"

"On a ship." Ion rose from the floor and began to put on his clothes. Rehka watched him and he avoided meeting her gaze.

"I figured as much. Where are we going?"

"The ship is *Cerul's Horn*; we're headed to Caelia. Today is Millsday."

"What? Why Caelia?"

"Captain Crestone said I had to go there, I already told you." Ion pulled his shirt over his head.

"Why am *I* here?"

"Bale said your injuries were severe enough that you needed to return to Flynt."

"My father is here? Where is he?"

"He didn't make it."

"He *what*?" Rehka sat up straight in bed. Ion held both hands before him as if fending off an attack.

"I didn't mean it like that. He put us on the ship. He was going to go back to the apothecary for his things and return, but the ship left early."

"I must speak with the captain. I need to get word to my men." Rehka swung her legs over the side of the bed and grasped the small table mounted on the wall to steady herself. She rose a few inches off the bed before slumping back. "My head feels like someone smashed it with a hammer. Your magic did this?"

Ion shrank back from the venom in her voice. "I-I don't think so. You were injured outside Bruto Station. The doctors had to take your arm."

"Broc," Rehka growled the inspector's name, then stared at the stump of her arm where it ended below her elbow.

"I don't think you should get up. I can fetch the captain." Ion wanted to leave the room. Rehka's anger made the small space hotter. The mercenary tried again to rise but could not.

"Very well." Rehka lowered herself onto the pillows. "Find me the captain." Ion turned to go. "And some water."

"Anything else?"

"Open the cursed window, it's sweltering in here."

Ion climbed up on the shelf, undid the latch on the porthole, and the window swung inward. Ion secured it to the wall with a small metal hook. He gazed beyond the walkway to an endless stretch of dunes like those around Castes. However, he saw no evidence of life below, only endless Xyssian desert. Hot wind laden with grit caressed his cheeks.

He fled the room before Rehka asked any more of him.

The dirigible's motion pitched Ion forward on the deck. Frantic, he snatched the guide rope before looking at the desert far below. Vertigo washed over him and he leaned away from the precipitous drop. He had not felt seasick like this since he was a child of four when his father had first taken him out to fish. Except they had not fished, instead his father had lectured him about the virtues of being a good man. The wind had picked up, raising waves on the Boiled Sea, and Ion had suffered an intense bout of seasickness. Years later, long after his parents had left, Ion realized his father had been saying his farewells.

Ion took several breaths to steady himself, then turned toward the ship's prow. The woman in the fancy purple dress was standing on the gangway. She eyed him until he stared back at her. She sniffed into a handkerchief and disappeared into her cabin. Ion held onto the guide ropes and staggered along. He gained confidence in his footing and by the time he reached the doorway that led to the upper decks, he was able to let go of the ropes. He surveyed the desert again, feeling a surge of pride when the vertigo did not return. In the distance, he spotted another airship sailing in the opposite direction, toward Solvigant, its shimmering tail of aether visible as it emerged from an aerogate.

"A wasteland if I ever seen one," a gruff voice startled Ion. He whirled to face the newcomer. One of the crew was gazing out over the sandy expanse. He had a thick pink scar across his chin. The sailor placed a gleaming metal hand on the rope and Ion blinked.

"You're a clunker," he said. The sailor snatched his hand away and shoved it into his trouser pocket.

"Sorry, lad, don't mean to offend." The sailor turned to go.

"No!" Ion protested, "I mean, I'm sorry, I meant no offense, sir. I've never talked to a clunker." The sailor faced him and studied Ion to see if the boy was teasing him.

"Lots of clunkers are sailors. The cargo captains need strong crew and we're never in port long enough to rile the locals."

"But you are people," Ion insisted.

"People with metal parts, magic parts. It makes many folk uncomfortable."

"Not me." To Ion's surprise, the sailor relaxed.

"Good lad, then. Where are you off to this morning?"

"I need to find the captain."

"Why?"

Ion hesitated, unsure how to explain Rehka's request. "My cabin mate is injured. Her father was supposed to travel with us and tend to her, but he missed the ship."

"The Dragon lady they brought on the stretcher?"

Ion nodded. "She wants to send a message back to Solvigant."

"Captain won't spare a carrier pigeon for an irritated passenger. Does she need a doctor?"

"Do you have one aboard?"

"We're a cargo ship, primarily. Not much call for a doctor, I'm afraid. Jenkins is our medic, more of a veterinarian and a butcher, but he'll have to do 'til we reach Caelia."

Excitement surged in Ion. "When do we reach the aerogate?"

The sailor checked his pocket watch. "This evening, half past eight. Course it won't be evening on Karis."

"It won't?"

The sailor produced a second watch. "Only a bit before noon when we cross over."

"I've never left Xys," said Ion, embarrassed.

The sailor grinned. "Come up to the spar deck at the base of the shrouds at eight sharp. I'll show you the best way to witness it."

"Really?"

The sailor ruffled Ion's hair. "It's a right proper sight."

"Thank you, sir,"

"M'name's Farris. You're about the same age as my own boy. It does me good to be reminded of him."

Ion heard sadness in Farris's voice. Ion's stomach growled.

"Which way to the mess, sir?"

"Growing boy." Farris laughed. "Take the second door ahead, down the stairs, then right."

"Thank you," Ion said over his shoulder as he scampered away.

As a cargo freighter, *Cerul's Horn* had no gun deck. Instead, it had a mezzanine, a deck that held the mess hall, crew quarters, sick bay, and the engineering room. Everything was crowded together to make as much room for cargo as possible.

The cook apologized for the meager offerings as he slopped a thick, brown stew into a clay bowl, but Ion thought it a feast. He could not remember if he had eaten since the incident at the city watch station. He wolfed down his initial helping then requested another, mopping up the remains with crusty brown bread. When he was finished, he leaned back against the bulkhead and sighed in satisfaction.

"You're the first passenger to appreciate my food," the cook said from where he was scrubbing pots in the galley.

"It was delicious. When's lunch?"

"Only two meals a day, lad. That's all we have the stores for. Dinner starts at six sharp. But come around in the early afternoon, I might have something for you."

Ion crunched the last of his bread. "Can I get some stew for my cabin mate?"

The cook raised an eyebrow. "We don't have enough for thirds."

"It's for my cabin mate, honest," Ion said. "She's injured and can't make it up here herself."

The cook ladled out another bowl and handed it over.

"Thank you." Ion headed back to his cabin. When he arrived, the cabin door was open, and four crew members jostled and swore inside. Rehka thrashed on the bed.

"Hold her still," said a man with a syringe, presumably Jenkins. The crewmen struggled to restrain the thrashing Dragon.

"Let go of me!" Rehka shouted.

"What are you doing to my friend Rehka?" Ion said.

Everyone paused to stare at him.

"It's a sedative, lad," Jenkins said. "I need to change her bandages and check the wounds for infection."

"Don't touch me!" Rehka snarled.

Ion looked at her. Blood oozed from the bandage covering her stump and her shirt clung to her with sweat and spots of blood. She had torn several of the stitches in her face.

"Bale's not here and your wounds need care." Ion set the stew on the writing desk. "Let them help, Rehka."

"It's Captain Balefire!" she snarled at him. "I'll be fine. I don't need this hack's ministrations. There will be Dragon healers on Flynt. I need to find my father and get word to my men." Ion shrank into the corner. Jenkins took advantage of the distraction and jabbed her thigh with the syringe. Rehka tried to pull away, but firm hands held her down as Jenkins depressed the plunger. The Dragon fumed and swore, threatening them all with elaborate painful deaths. The sailors held on. A few minutes passed and her words slowed, then slurred, and her eyelids drooped. A few minutes later she lay snoring. Jenkins dismissed the other crewmen and began removing Rehka's dirty bandages.

The sight of her lacerated face turned Ion's stomach. He swallowed hard, refusing to surrender his recent breakfast. Satisfied that Rehka was in capable hands, Ion left the cabin again. He spent the day wandering the ship, exploring every hold and room. The sailors accommodated the inquiries of the cheerful twelve-year-old. With clear weather and light wind, they had little else to occupy the hours before they crossed over to Karis.

At the appointed hour, Ion met Farris on the spar deck. Long twilight shadows bathed *Cerul's Horn*. Below the ship, the terrain had changed from dunes to rocky outcroppings and scrubland. Solo's light glinted orange and red over distant lakes. The air was still hot and dry and carried enough sand that many of the crewmen spent the day sweeping the exposed decks. Off the port bow, Ion saw the iridescent form of the aerogate.

He had been watching it grow larger for some time with a mix of excitement and fear. Until he had snuck aboard the terrane to Solvigant, he had never left Castes. Now, a week later, he was about to leave Xys itself.

"Where are we?" Ion asked Farris. The sailor was adjusting buckles on a safety harness.

"The western boundary of Skob." He held out the harness so Ion could put it on. "Sail due east for two more days and you'd arrive at the pilgrimage site. Not much there now, though, besides the Caretakers." The emphasis he put on the last word made it sound to Ion like a title.

"Caretakers?"

"The folks who tend the pilgrimage sites while Solvigant is elsewhere."

"I thought the sites were empty."

"Mostly, but someone has to tend the infrastructure and maintain the wealthy estates." Farris cinched the straps around Ion's waist and shoulders.

"What is this for?" Ion asked.

"We got to hurry up to the lookout."

"The lookout?"

Farris gestured up the shroud toward the gas bag. "It's atop there. A helluva view."

Ion gazed up at the slick curvature of the massive balloon. "Up there?"

"Don't fret," Farris reassured him, "the harness'll hold ya should anything happen."

"The captain approved this?"

Farris winked and held a finger to his lips. "Best we don't notify the captain. All right, you're ready. See here, ya have two clips. One should always be on the rigging, two is better. When ya must cross to a different line, undo one, clip it, then do t'other. Got it?"

Ion swallowed hard but nodded.

"Follow me then, lad."

Farris climbed up the rigging like a spider at home in its web and soon reached the top of the shroud. Ion followed, eyes locked on the ropes and knots, careful with his clipping and unclipping. When he reached the intersection between shrouds and the bag, he found the bag steadier than the ship dangling below it. The ship, suspended by the rigging, swayed with the wind as if it held waves like the sea. The gas bag plowed straight ahead through the light breeze.

Ion followed Farris as the sailor edged out along the rigging toward a rope ladder that curved around the swollen body of the gas bag. Ion followed, careful to follow Farris's instructions about keeping one clip always attached when he crossed intersections in the rigging. His arms ached with the effort of clinging to the ladder as it crossed the underside of the bag. He was grateful when they reached the midline, and the angle changed to follow the upper curve of the bag.

Ion glanced down once before the ground disappeared behind the curvature. He could not see the ship suspended below, so his view fell straight to the scrublands. He shut his eyes and swallowed hard against the vertigo. The rocky green landscape wavered as if Ion were viewing it through clear water. Behind the ship he could see faint stars, ahead of the ship the sun was setting. Near the prow, the iridescent blue and red shimmer of the aerogate loomed large and cast awkward shadows across the gas bag, making it appear as if the whole thing were made of stained glass. The beauty of it overcame the vertigo caused by their altitude and the angle of his climb. His hands were sweaty and slipped on the clips of his harness.

"Hurry, lad," Farris's voice from above, "we're nearly at the gate, and we don't want to be caught on the rigging in the void."

"Why not?" Ion asked, but Farris did not answer. He climbed faster, wiping each hand on his trousers before continuing. The climb became easier, and soon they reached the belvedere. It looked like a cottage, about the size of the one he and his grandfather had occupied in Castes, but it was open to the elements. A large astral dust array sprouted from the roof like the dorsal fin of a great fish. Two men worked inside the lookout. One alternated between monitoring the aerogate through a spyglass and making notations on a piece of parchment. The other wore the blue robes of an astral mage and stood by, awaiting a signal.

Farris led Ion the last few meters across the spongy skin of the gas bag and ushered him into the lookout.

"What the hell, Farris?" protested the man with the spyglass when they entered.

"Lad's never been off moon," Farris said. The two men nodded at Ion.

He watched, fascinated, as the aerogate loomed closer, now larger than *Cerul's Horn*. *I had no idea they were so huge!* Ion thought and fought down another wave of fear.

"Maybe we shouldn't go through it," he said.

Farris chuckled, "That's a normal reaction the first few times you pass through a gate."

"A fear of the void," the astral mage said. "It's natural."

A fist-sized chunk of amethyst began glowing on a panel beside the mage.

"What's that?" Ion asked.

"A focus. I use it to channel astral dust through *Cerul's Horn*. It protects the ship during interlunar transport."

Ion glanced around. Solo's rings were breaking above the horizon behind them and he whispered a farewell.

"She'll still watch over us from Karis, lad," Farris said, overhearing his whispers, "She's loyal, that one. The one constant in this whole World System."

Ion felt a bit better at the sailor's words. The oscillating colors of the aerogate drew his attention and he beheld the most incredible night sky he had ever seen.

The sailor with the spyglass checked his bearings on a compass. On closer inspection, Ion realized it was unlike any compass he had ever seen.

"What's that?"

"It's a void barometer."

"What's it do?" He had to shout over the rising wind.

"Hush, lad," Farris said. "Enjoy the ride and let these men do their jobs."

The astral mage grasped the focus with one hand and laid the other on the terminal array. Blue light seeped into the mage, then out into the floor before flowing down the rigging and over the curve of the bag.

"Ship is secured," the mage shouted after a few moments.

The sailor scribbled hasty records in his log. The blue and red of the gate had slipped to its edges and the middle was now a black so intense it swallowed the light of Xys's twilight. Millions of stars filled the circular expanse.

"You should hold on," Farris shouted.

Ion gripped the windowsill, knuckles white. He fought against the sudden urge to flee the belvedere and run pell-mell down the gas bag toward the stern. Farris's reassuring hand on his shoulder kept him focused on their progress.

"Contact," the sailor yelled.

"Contact with what?" Ion shouted.

The aerogate swallowed them.

The wind stopped. All the sound vanished.

The silent ship pulsed with astral magic as all around them the void stretched out to infinity. Ion had never known so many stars existed. All around him, millions of them shone in the blackness. He had spent nights in his small boat on the Boiled Sea, far from any interfering light, but he had never seen anything like this. Xys's proximity to Solo meant that even at night, the natural light of the celestial bodies washed out much of the sky.

Ion gazed around, his mouth open in wonder, tears on his cheeks. The grizzled sailor Farris also seemed transfixed by the beauty of the void. Ion thought about the terrible fury of the void mage, and wondered how such monstrous magic might draw its power from this wonder.

"Where's Solo?" Ion asked, breaking the silence.

Farris made the sign of the Ring before answering. "Her light doesn't shine in the void, lad. This is Kade's realm."

The thought unnerved Ion and drained the luster from the wide expanse around him. The ringed goddess had watched over him his entire life. Her absence here made him shiver.

"What is that?" Ion pointed to the starboard, toward a place where several stars and the space around them bulged, distorted as if he were viewing them through a glass ball. The phenomenon rolled across the horizon created by the void and the curve of the gas bag.

Farris looked and his face paled. He leaned forward and whispered something to the astral mage, who still stood with his hands on the focus and the terminal, his face strained.

"Balechtoplasm," Farris shouted.

"What?"

"An astral whale."

"Is it dangerous?"

Farris did not respond, which Ion took to be a bad sign. The creature was getting closer, or rather the distortion created in front of the star field was bigger.

"Hold course," the lookout said to the astral mage.

"You see that?" Farris directed Ion's gaze toward a sphere of swirling green light off the prow of the gas bag. "That's Karis; we're nearly there."

Ion watched as the astral whale and the other side of the gate grew closer. A horn sounded from below, on the deck of the ship.

"They must've spotted it," Farris said. There was another blast and Farris swore under his breath.

"What does that mean?" Ion asked, frightened.

"A second balechtoplasm. A second whale." They heard a third blast.

"Djinnar's blood," the lookout swore, "it's a whole pod."

Ion studied the distortion and realized that there were now half a dozen distended areas of the starfield, moving back and forth and amongst each other like dancers.

"What are they doing?"

"Using the same laneway that we are," the lookout growled. "Hold on tight."

There was a rush of turbulence, and the whole ship shuddered. The sudden lurch dropped Ion dropped to one knee. The astral mage fought to keep his footing. The blue web of light surrounding the ship flickered before returning to its previous brightness.

"He rammed us," Farris shouted. "What are they doing?"

Ion whined, "Farris, what's happening?"

"Hush and hold on, lad," Farris said and gave Ion's shoulder another reassuring squeeze.

*Cerul's Horn* lurched hard to port as another astral whale knocked against the ship, then a third. There were more horn blasts from below. Ion realized the ship was rotating to port.

"By the Nine," the lookout swore, "they've punctured the gas bag. We're venting!"

"Farris, what's happening?"

"Don't worry, Ion. Wait here. I've got to patch the leak."

The lookout wound a klaxon and Ion covered his ears. Farris opened the door to the belvedere and bolted down the bag, his anchor line skimming along the rigging's safety rope. Ion watched him go. The astral whale rammed them again. This time Ion lost his balance. He heard a sharp crack as the impact tossed the astral mage against the far wall of the belvedere. He slumped to the floor, unconscious. The blue light which had flowed from the terminal array through the mage and around the ship flickered and went out, casting *Cerul's Horn* into darkness.

# CHAPTER SIXTY-THREE

# ADI CRESTONE

## MOON OF XYS, TYRSDAY, 4TH OF LUXOR

The Boiled Sea appeared as an oily orange and black smear on the horizon. Adi yawned and took one hand off the helm to slap herself awake. The state of their beleaguered ship required constant attention to wind speed and dirigible elevation. The wind from the sea had blown all day at a constant four to six knots, which forced Adi to tack to compensate for the resistance on the balloon. Adi had piloted sea-going vessels, not wind-going ones. While there were similarities, the differences were stark enough that Adi worried she was missing crucial details that would help them squeeze greater speed from the ship or distance from the fuel canisters.

"Wright," Adi called, "get ready to fire the burner."

"We're on our last canister," Wright said from his position on the roof of the cabin.

"The Sea is close; it will be enough. Fire the burner on my mark. Verdun, prepare to trim the sail." *Phoebe's Light, let it be enough.*

She turned the helm to tack to starboard. The wind stiffened and the rigging groaned at the course correction. The tug drifted along, losing altitude bit by bit. Adi squinted against the wind to get a better look at the coastline. The sulfurous mineral scent of the russet-hued sea stung her nose as they approached the border between the dunes and the rank water. The wind whipped up sprays of yellowish foam as the waves crested close to shore.

To the west, a thin line of smoke drifted upward in the direction of Castes. Adi had the fanciful notion that the astral engines of the *Sidereal* might still be smoldering atop a distant dune crest. Barely a week had passed since her flight from Thail. Despite the battle with HMS *Dragonhammer*, she had returned to Xys optimistic that her days of subjugation to the Blood Queen were over.

*So much has changed in a week,* she thought as she tacked to port. The foresail slackened as the tug came around, then filled once more. *I leave a wanted criminal still beholden to Sasha Riven.* The sudden thought of the Blood Queen's vengeance filled Adi with a deep sense of foreboding.

*I do not envy Palestrina.*

"Adi, we're getting too low."

Adi banished her thoughts of failure and vengeance as Iris's face peered from the cabin. The tug was falling toward the dunes.

"Fire the burner!" she yelled to Wright.

Adi heard the roar of the flame as the pilot light ignited the fuel. The tug jerked upward and she felt the rise in her stomach. Wright's concern that they would collide with the dune crests just below the tug had caused him to open the burner full bore for too long. Her view of the dunes shifted from a few nearby slopes to a broad tapestry of wind-carved ridges stretching for miles on either side of them.

"That's enough," Adi called. The roar of the burner continued. "Shut it off! We're going to need at least two charges between here and the coastline."

The gout of flame subsided. The tug leveled off and Adi's stomach settled. Wright's face appeared once more from the roof of the cabin.

"Sorry," he said, "I got a little carried away."

Adi offered him a reassuring smile. "Verdun, come down and take the helm."

"Are you sure?"

"Just hold her steady. I need to check the charts to make sure we're still on course for the hydrogate."

"I'm not much of a sailor, I'm afraid."

"You must have been on airships before." Adi said.

"I didn't like them then, either," Verdun said. Adi directed him to stand at the wheel.

"Hold on here and here," Adi said, indicating he should grasp the spokes two felloes apart for a wide, strong grip and not releasing her own grip until Verdun's hands engaged the wheel.

"Like this?" he asked.

"Perfect."

She retreated into the cabin where Iris was puttering in the mess. Adi inhaled and caught a whiff of citrus and cedar in Iris's dark curls.

*How had the woman kept her coiffure so perfect through that chase?* Adi wondered. She reeked of blood and sweat. Her clothes were torn and she still had a hundred tiny cuts from the battle at Alhambra's and her subsequent flight through the aeroport. Her first order of business when they arrived in Thail was to find an inn and clean up.

*Then I must find Lucas.*

The thought of seeing her son after so long chilled her blood.

"Are you all right? You look pale." Iris said.

"I'll feel better after a warm meal and a hot bath, but I'll make do until then."

Adi picked up the quill pen and compass and figured their distance from the hydrogate for the fourth or fifth time. She wanted to spend as little time on the Boiled Sea as possible because she had none of the instruments normally required for transit through the void. A void hygrometer would have allowed her to track the gate's location instead of relying on charts and tables. A void barometer measured void activity to prepare for any exigencies that might occur during transit. She had neither.

Nor did she possess any reports about weather or traffic patterns on the other side of the gate. A storm could be raging or they could ram into a ship traveling the other way. Adi doubted the latter possibility since few ships transited the Boiled Sea gates anymore. Most ships in and out of Solvigant these days were airships, more suited to the city's position in Veria.

But they were sailing blind. Adi had made a handful of blind void crossings in her years with Rehka on the *Snowcrest.* Each one had been harrowing in a unique way and she had no desire to relive any of them. Then there was the matter of the tug's fried astral array.

"Adi, we're getting low," Verdun called from the helm.

Adi checked her math once more. They were too low, too soon. She had hoped they would have enough fuel to float over the Boiled Sea, but now they would have to land on the choppy waters and sail the last distance to the gate.

*The wind is stronger than I realized,* Adi thought. *There's too much resistance on the balloon.*

"Adi!" Verdun called again, and she heard the anxiety in his voice.

"Wright, fire the burner," Adi said stepping from the cabin. The wind had indeed strengthened. "Verdun, see those marks between the handles where your hands are?"

He nodded.

"That's a felloe. Turn the wheel seven felloes to port, counting from the top as if it were twelve on the clock. That will tack us to starboard. Turn it slowly; count three seconds between each felloe or the wind will push us around too fast. I'll be right back."

Adi glanced toward the prow, where Ajax sat, his feet dangling off the foredeck. Since they'd escaped, he had not offered any assistance.

"Aye, Captain," came Verdun's report. Despite his airsickness, he was enjoying the adventure.

"We should clear the dune." She tried to sound confident.

Verdun turned the wheel and counted aloud. She risked a peek over the starboard railing. The sprawling dunes were only three fathoms below the keel. Adi clambered up the ladder and sat beside Wright. She thumbed the manual ignition and fired the burner. There was a hiss of gas and then a rush of heat as the pilot light ignited the fuel and flames roared up into the balloon. The tug rose once more, and she breathed easier.

The Boiled Sea loomed before them, amber and black as if stuck in perpetual twilight. She guessed the amplitude of the waves at three to four feet. Not terrible, but not ideal given the small size of their craft. The shoreline was empty of any sign of civilization except for a single rotting hulk. The decking was gone, and the hull planking on the port side was missing. The ribs below the port gunwales poked through the gap, reminding Adi of a dead animal. Birds had built messy nests in the remaining rigging and yardarms.

She cranked the valve to close the burner but the flame continued to burn. She opened and closed the valve once more, to no effect.

"Djinnar's blood," Adi swore.

"That's seven felloes." Verdun called. Adi looked up and saw the tug was once again tacking southwest.

"Great work," Adi yelled down.

"We're higher than we have been."

"Feed valve is busted." Adi stood beside the roaring flame of the burner and fought the urge to kick and yell and punch the valve. *For all the good that'd do,* she thought. She descended the ladder instead and took the helm.

"That's all the fuel. We'll have to ride it down to the sea. If we can clear that last row of dunes, we should be safe down to the water." *That's a big "if,"* Adi thought, wincing.

"You're going to sail this thing? On the Boiled Sea?" Iris pointed to the choppy water in the distance. "I thought it was an airship."

"Same principle," Adi said with more enthusiasm than she felt.

"Will it float?"

"Definitely." Adi grinned. When Iris's brows rose, she changed it to, "Probably. We patched the holes below. If we can get through to the gate, we'll be fine."

Iris started to speak but stopped. She cocked her head to one side, listening.

"What is it?" Adi asked.

"Do you hear that?" Ajax said from his perch.

"Hear what?" Then she caught the sound. A high-pitched whine, rising and falling in volume at regular intervals.

"It's a klaxon," he said. Adi let go of the helm so she could look behind them. She scanned the darkening evening sky between fast-moving clouds.

"There!" Adi pointed, squinting into the looking glass. Sailing directly toward them, backlit by the rings of Solo, a Huxstable 135 flying the flags of Solvigant and the city watch was pursuing them at speed.

"How did they find us?" Iris asked.

Adi swore. "Broc. He must have expected me to use gates near Castes after the *Sidereal* and sent watchmen." *He's too clever.*

"What can we do?" Iris asked.

"We only need to make it to the gate. Those are city watchmen, not Imperial soldiers. If we can make it to the gate, we'll pass out of the watch's jurisdiction."

"They're gaining fast."

Adi's mind raced. They had no fuel and no way to go faster. They were at the mercy of the wind. If they tacked too quickly or tried to evade, the wind resistance would force them down before they could clear the last row of dunes. Adi glanced behind them again. The Huxstable, sleek and glowing blue from its astral engines, devoured the sky between them.

"What's the plan?" Iris said.

"Check for ranged armaments in the cabin or the hold."

"I don't think there are any."

"Just check!"

Iris flinched at the whip of command in Adi's voice. She watched Iris duck into the cabin. She knew there were no weapons. She had searched the whole tug from prow to stern, balloon to keel. But looking would give Iris something to do other than watch their pursuers close the gap. When the shots started flying, Iris would be safer inside the cabin.

Adi wished for something else to do. Without steam or astral dust, none of the switches or levers on the control panel would produce results. She could only wait and hope that they reached the gate before the Huxstable reached them.

*And if we don't?* Adi asked herself. She gritted her teeth. *We must.*

She checked her watch, then glanced over the railing at the dunes below. They were twenty fathoms away, but the tug's glide path was steep. Adi flinched when the Huxstable's deck gun barked. She braced for the impact, but none came. *They're still out of range.*

"Verdun!" Adi shouted. "Throw everything overboard."

"What do you mean?"

"Everything that isn't nailed down, chuck it. Wright help him." Adi grabbed a thick coil of rope and tossed it over the side. Iris emerged from the cabin with an armload of pans and utensils from the galley. Adi's crew heaved anything not completely essential over the rails. More reports from the deck gun from the Huxstable punctuated their work, but nothing struck them. Wright heaved the table over the gunwale and looked back at their pursuers.

"They'll be in range soon," he reported

Adi moved to the prow of the ship and gazed through her spyglass at the fitful waves of the Boiled Sea. She scanned the wind-whipped surface for any sign of the hydrogate. The ship's charts insisted it would be there. Adi had triple-checked her math. Everything matched. She stared at the spot just offshore where the gate should be and saw nothing, only dark, tempestuous water.

"The gate!" Iris cried. Adi put down her glass.

Iris was pointing at a spot twelve degrees port of the bow. Adi followed the line of the woman's finger and there it was. It was seven hundred meters northwest of where it was supposed to be, but it was there.

"Hail Solo!" Adi shouted and hugged Iris. The two women laughed and shouted their relief into the wind. Then the prow dipped abruptly and the small ship lurched. A loud tearing sound emanated from the keel. The suddenness of it almost pitched everyone over the side. Iris tumbled backward and Adi groped for anything to hold her weight. Her probing hand found the port side balloon rigging. She reached for Iris who flailed, eyes wide and panicked until Adi caught hold of the woman's wrist and yanked her back.

For a split second they hung there, the tug tilted forward, nothing but Adi's grip on the rigging preventing them from plunging toward the precipitous slope of the dune below.

Ajax held onto the fore rigging, his feet on the deck railing. Wright tumbled toward the cabin and managed to catch one of the docking cleats. Verdun cried out and slid toward Ajax, threatening to dislodge the Lord of Bones.

Then the balloon's buoyancy righted the tug. Everyone collapsed onto the deck.

"What happened?" Iris asked getting to her knees. Adi looked behind them and saw a massive dune with a V-shaped notch in its sandy ridge.

"We skimmed the top of the dune," Adi said. They had been so busy lightening the ship, she hadn't been paying attention to their dwindling altitude.

"Skimmed, my ass! Are we all right?"

Adi stood and looked around. Everything was intact.

"As long as the hull didn't crack we'll make it."

"How will we know?"

"We'll know when we hit the sea."

"What?"

The Huxstable cruised over the dune and the fore deck gun barked again.

Adi grabbed the wheel. They were approaching the coastline too fast. Slowing the tug so it would land safely on the water was one of the few things Adi could do in these circumstances. She turned the small airship directly into the wind and the tug shuddered as a sudden down draft dropped them a half-fathom.

"Find some rope," Adi shouted.

"We tossed it all!"

Adi handed Wright her boot knife. "Cut two lengths out of the excess rigging somewhere."

"What excess?"

"Just cut some. We don't have time."

Adi pointed the prow of the tug at the gate. It was larger than she had expected, big enough for a freighter. Water swirled around its edges like the periphery of a great vertical whirlpool. Inside, the vast, familiar star field flickered.

*Flickered? That's strange. Gates don't flicker.* The prophetic words of Adi's stepsister Beatrice floated into Adi's mind. *The proximity of Solo will wreak havoc on the gates.*

"Djinnar's blood."

The gate flickered and disappeared. Adi held her breath and counted seconds. Four seconds elapsed and the large hydrogate popped back into existence. She exhaled.

Wright thrust a coil of rope toward Adi. "Here."

"Tie it around my waste, then loop it around the pedestal and tie it off to that anchor cleat over there."

"What? Why?"

The Boiled Sea was close now. The roiling water filled the horizon in front of the tug. The gate flickered out and came back into existence once more.

"We have no astral array."

"I wouldn't let you use it again anyway."

"We have nothing to protect us against the void when we enter the gate. It will be like free falling. Tie me off then go secure yourself in the cabin."

The Huxstable was upon them. Adi could make out a man on the prow shouting into a bullhorn, but the wind carried his words away. She did not think the watchmen would do anything so stupid as land their airship on the sea, but she did not want to take that chance. If they closed the gap before the tug landed, they could board her and haul the ship back up with the power of the Huxstable's engines.

"Hurry," Adi said as Wright snugged the rope at Adi's waist and looped it around the pedestal.

"Watch the tiller ropes," Adi said.

"Why not come in the cabin?"

"I have to steer."

"Won't we stay in the laneway between the gates?" Wright tied the rope to the cleat. "I didn't think it was possible to fall out of it."

"I must steer us into the gate, and I don't know if you can fall out of a laneway," Adi admitted. "But I don't want to find out."

"You're secure."

Iris stepped forward and kissed Adi full on the lips. "Be careful."

Adi grinned. "Get inside."

At that moment, the Huxstable reached them. Watchmen braced against the railing, twirled, and threw grappling hooks. Two spiked lines fell short, but three sunk their teeth into the tug's starboard railing.

"Wright, cut the lines," Adi shouted. She could hear the waves now and felt warm, sticky spray in the air. The tug would slam down into the water at any moment. She wanted to shed speed to reduce the shock of their impact but couldn't risk the Huxstable getting in front of them. The top of the gate rose in Adi's vision, flickered, then became substantial once more.

"Phoebe, Goddess of Light protect me," Adi whispered, then she recited the pirate's prayer to Darak, Goddess of Nature. The watchmen pulled their grapples tight, and the tug lurched to starboard. She barely managed to maintain her grip on the spokes as she fought to right the tug against the weight of their pursuers. An audible *twang* reverberated through the ship as Wright cut the first grapple, Ajax the second, then a third. A watchman had begun to climb down and he screamed as he plunged into the roiling waters below.

"Hold on," Adi shouted as she turned the tug into the wind, shedding as much speed as possible. The foresail filled with the wind's resistance and snapped backward. The front of the balloon went concave, the rigging stretched as the balloon rocked back. Adi's gambit had worked, however. The *Starforged* shed all its speed and the force of the wind in the sails and on the balloon lifted the prow. Adi bent her knees and let go of the wheel to brace for impact.

"Grab onto something!"

There was no reply, and a moment later the hull of the ship smacked against the surface of the Boiled Sea and skipped back into the air before smacking down again. The *Starforged* bounced half a dozen times like a stone skipping along the surface of a pond. On the fourth bounce a resounding crack emanated from beneath the stern and Adi was sure that either the propeller or the rudder had broken.

When the tug settled onto the water for the final time, the churning current caught the small vessel and spun it violently. The wheel whirled, and the whole tug rolled hard to port. Adi heard Iris cry out but could not look around for her. Adi waited, braced against the wall of the cabin until the crosscurrent spat them out and the ship calmed enough that she could safely grab the wheel. Even so, Wright had to help to keep her from being bowled over.

She gazed at the hull of Huxstable above them. The sleek ship had no keel. Any attempt to land the top-heavy gun ship in choppy water would flip it. The *Starforged* did not have a sea-going keel, but it had tall aerodynamic fins on the hull to help with stability under a heavy load. Even with those fins the tug rocked dangerously over each rolling wave.

"Everyone all right?"

"I'm okay," Iris said.

A chorus of other voices followed.

Adi glanced over her shoulder. Iris was clinging to the starboard railing for dear life. She was soaking wet, but alive and still aboard. Verdun was working to pull her back onto the deck.

"Get in the cabin!"

Iris looked as though she might vomit, but she released the railing and fell into the Ankhim's arms. Adi oriented herself and sought the gate. Off the bow she saw the distant hulk rotting on the shoreline.

*We're backward,* Adi realized. *I have to bring the ship around before we run aground.*

Adi worked the wheel to turn the ship around to its starboard side. The rudder was as tall as the tug and designed to manipulate air currents off the fan, not to encounter the heavy resistance of water. The tug turned, but it took all of Adi's strength. She braced her feet against the pedestal and used her entire bodyweight to turn the wheel felloe by felloe until the tug's nose pointed back toward the flickering gate.

*Pallantier, God of Creation, wherever you are, don't shut the door in my face,* Adi prayed.

A new rope dangled before Adi, then a second dropped into view. She looked up at the Huxstable keeping pace above them. City watchmen peered over the railing at her. Then one hoisted himself over the edge and started down the rope.

*They're rappelling onto the ship,* Adi realized.

"Wright, climb up and trim the sail. Careful in the rigging."

The first watchman slid down onto the roiling deck. Ajax was ready for him. He stabbed the watchman in the stomach with a bone knife and pushed him over the gunwale. The tug rocked hard back to starboard and the second watchman missed the deck completely. Adi heard him splash into the water near the port bow. She grabbed the wheel once more and forced the prow toward the hydrogate. The tug groaned as it slowly turned. Adi prayed the rudder would hold long enough to get them through the gate.

The starfield flickered out of existence. When it reappeared, it was twenty meters to starboard. Adi corrected course. The failure of the two men to rappel onto the tug had bought her time. She imagined the city watch commander fuming on the deck of his gunship and she grinned.

Closer to the gate, the wind picked up and drowned out all sound. Ahead of them the water churned, the currents swirling in unpredictable directions. Adi released the wheel and let the attraction of the hydrogate reel them in. She looked again toward the Huxstable, then dove out of the way as a musket ball ricocheted off the wall of the cabin. Half a dozen watchmen were loading muskets along the airship's railing, their captain gesticulating at Adi. Tied to the pedestal, she could not go far, but she took what cover she could, putting the wheel between herself and the armed watchmen. Four more shots cracked off and splinters of wood shot up around her feet.

The gate had flickered out again.

She glanced around. *Where, by Djinnar's blood, is that gate?*

"Curse the Nine!" Adi shouted her frustration into the wind. She felt guilty about cursing the gods the moment she needed their help the most, so she whispered an apology to Solo and her daughter Phoebe, Goddess of Light. The watchmen were reloading. She prayed to Pallantier who made Xys his home and held dominion over the gates. She leaned against the pedestal and squeezed her eyes shut, praying with her whole heart.

She felt the gate reappear in a *pop!* of aetherial magic that made the hair on her neck and arms rise. She opened her eyes in time to see the hydrogate looming above the tug. The musketeers on the Huxstable were gone. The ship was attempting a frantic turn to avoid entering the gate. Adi stood and took the wheel once more. The tug sailed over the edge of the hydrogate and plummeted into the void.

# CHAPTER SIXTY-FOUR

# THEO VANGUARD

## MOON OF MAXON, TYRSDAY, 4TH OF LUXOR

Theo awoke naked, sweaty, and alone, tangled in the sheets of the four-poster bed. Harsh sunlight streamed through the portholes casting hot bars of light over his face and torso. He threw aside the sheets, stood, and stretched to his full height, shoulders and knees popping. He had to search through the tangled sheets for his underclothes before he could pull on his trousers. He wanted a cup of coffee, but not enough to disturb the peace of the morning. He gulped water from an ewer on the nightstand and stumbled onto the balcony, blinking against the brilliant light of the morning sun. He was surprised Hannah was not asleep beside him, but she could not have gone far.

The luminous waters of Crystal Bay winked up at him from twenty fathoms below. He could see fishing vessels and sea-going freighters cutting paths of white wakes upon the turquoise surface of the bay. Theo's naval career had never brought him to Maxon, though as a young child he had traveled with his father to Somerset, the capital of the Imperial holdings on Maxon. He had only vague memories of those whirlwind diplomatic trips. Somerset was far north of Planktown and Theo doubted he would have occasion to travel there.

He sat back in one of the deck chairs and put his feet up on the balcony railing. Another airship passed along the port side, heading south toward the aerogate. He was reticent to leave the stateroom. He was certain the *Penumbra* would make port in Planktown within the hour, then his responsibilities as leader of the delegation would demand his attention. For now, Hannah was elsewhere on the ship and Theo relished this time to himself.

His right hand throbbed dully. He pulled back the bandage to get a better look at the wound. The edges were still red and inflamed. He would need to see a physicker in Planktown to get additional sanitary salve. Theo flexed his fingers. Tiny spasms of pain blossomed in his knuckles. A week had passed since he had killed Joshua Mung to escape captivity under Crestone, but Theo was impatient for the wound to heal. He was concerned that the injury diminished his ability to wield a sword. The location of the bite would also make healing long and difficult. He had to keep the hand quiet, anything more vigorous than holding a fork would break the wound open.

*No more jailbreaks or brawls,* he thought. *No more murders.*

Theo settled the bandage and leaned back in his seat, warmed by the sun. He was a man who had consummated his marriage. His toes tingled at the thought of Hannah's naked body atop him. She had transformed a legal necessity imposed by his father into a pleasant, even ecstatic, experience. Theo had noticed her confidence in the act, which suggested that she was not, despite formal conventions, a virgin. Given that neither of them had had any control over their respective futures, he did not blame her. As far as they both knew, she had not been pregnant prior to the wedding, and that was all that mattered to him. Theo hoped that conceiving an heir would involve more such nights.

The thought of his new wife and her experiences prior to their marriage reminded him of Palestrina and the clandestine rendezvous on this very balcony. Once he recalled the image of the Seraph kneeling before Hannah he could not push it away. He had never heard of the Knights of Acadia and did not know who they might be.

*What sort of secret organization promotes a sixteen-year-old to such apparent authority? Was that status earned or inherited?* Theo wondered.

He had every right as her husband to confront her about it and demand answers, but something told him that such a conversation would not be productive. He did not know Hannah well, but from the limited interactions he had had with her at the governor's mansion, at Stella's Echo, and last night, she was not a fawning young noblewoman giddy with her fortunate marriage and ready to curtail her life to suit his preferences. He sensed her determination and perspicacity and suspected that she would stand her ground if he confronted her. He had no desire to press his concerns until he knew her better.

*I do know her better than I did yesterday.* Theo grinned. *What am I accusing her of, after all?*

*What about Apyreon? Why is she, or these Knights of Acadia, interested in the device? Did Father choose her because of this affiliation?* Theo sighed and slumped forward on the chair, his elbows on his knees.

*At least Crestone is no longer my problem.* He shoved away a pang of guilt at the thought. Crestone was a pirate and a thief, a criminal who had wanted to ransom him.

*She's also a wanted criminal because I murdered a man.*

Theo believed that, as a pirate, Crestone must have murdered before. He was sure the woman had a lengthy list of crimes to her name on several moons. One false accusation did not drown out a lifetime of criminality.

There was a light knock on the balcony door. Theo started and opened his eyes to see Hannah standing there. One of her maidservants held two steaming mugs of coffee. Theo would have to learn their names. He smiled at Hannah and rose from his seat to accept the proffered cup. When he leaned in to kiss her, she tilted her chin so that his lips grazed her cheek instead.

*She's back to the coy maiden in daylight,* Theo thought.

"Thank you for the coffee. You're up early this morning," Theo said, stepping back to the balcony railing to admire his wife. She wore a pastel pink riding habit with double-breasted silver buttons. Theo wondered how she was not sweltering. Her red hair was impeccably styled and he could see no moisture on her face.

"Good morning, husband."

Theo looked out over the water and sipped his coffee. "Have you been to Maxon before?"

"My mother is from Thalib."

Surprised, Theo looked at her. "The jungle islands to the south? I had no idea."

"You know of them?"

"Only from maps. You don't look Thalibian."

"How many people do you know from there?"

Theo gazed into his coffee mug, chastened. "Only one." When he looked up again Hannah grinned at him.

*She's teasing me,* he realized.

"You're correct," she said. "I look nothing like the people from the southern islands. My father is from Eginheim in the far north of Highgaard. I inherited all my looks from him, I'm afraid."

"Afraid? You are a beautiful woman."

It was Hannah's turn to blush and look away. "Thank you, husband."

"Theo, please. We cannot spend our lives referring to one another as 'husband' and 'wife.'"

"As you wish, Theo."

"You are well-traveled on Maxon then?"

"No. My father was a marine commander here at the time he met my mother. He was stationed there. The Empire annexed Thalib at the end of the Marauder's War when I was two years old. My father was recalled to Thail and promoted to colonel."

"Your father is Maxwell Valefyre."

Hannah nodded.

"I've heard of him." Theo knew the man by reputation only. He was a general now, a member of the Imperial Directorate, a collection of high-ranking officials who advised the emperor on military strategy. "I didn't know he had risen through the marines." Theo had had little direct interaction with the naval commando forces. He knew they often referred to themselves as the Sunken because they believed the highest honor was dying in naval combat for the emperor. They were a wild and lethal group of soldiers.

"My mother has family in Somerset and Xern and my brother just rotated out of Fort Expedition, but I haven't visited Maxon since my maternal grandmother passed away six years ago."

"You have a brother?"

"I do, and a sister."

Shame warmed Theo's face. "I know so little about you."

Hannah stepped forward and placed a gloved hand on his arm. "We will have our whole lives to get to know one another, Theo. It's only been three days."

"You're right, of course."

"Now, however, we must prepare for our arrival in Planktown. The captain asked me to rouse you. We arrive in thirty minutes."

On cue, the ship's steam whistle shrieked.

"Planktown!" shouted the bosun from the deck above.

Theo drained the rest of his coffee and hurried into the stateroom to finish dressing. It was an odd sensation to have Hannah help him dress, but not an unpleasant one. She buttoned his uppermost button and kissed him.

"You look every bit the naval commander," she said.

Theo grimaced. "This will be my last command."

"I am sure you are worthy of it."

Half an hour later, Theo was standing on deck beside Hannah while the dockhands secured the *Penumbra* to the aeroport pier. The humidity and intensity of the sun had him sweating in his uniform. He wished he looked half as composed and serene as his lady wife. He would have to acquire clothing better suited to the equatorial climate of Planktown and their expedition's destination to the east. After a week in the skin-cracking dryness of Solvigant, Planktown's humidity felt oppressive. It helped that the gravitational force of Maxon was slightly less than that of Xys so he had a little extra spring in his step.

Haverford Dreggs paced the deck nearby, checking his watch often as if he were late for an important meeting.

"You've drafted the correspondence to the chamberlain at Fort Jasper?" Theo asked him.

"Yes, Commander." Dreggs used Theo's formal title, as he had insisted, but Theo could discern the faintest hint of sarcasm in the man's tone.

"You look uncomfortable, husband," Hannah whispered to him as the ship's crew secured the gangplank to the gunwale.

"The humidity does not agree with my formal navy blacks, I'm afraid."

"It does make you look quite distinguished."

Theo let out a surprised laugh. It was the first public compliment she had paid him in their limited acquaintance.

*Is she flirting with me?*

Art approached them looking enthusiastic, rested, and ready to begin their journey. His tail twitched erratically as he gazed out toward the sprawling timbers of Planktown. Theo realized that he, too, was excited. On Xys, the delegation had seemed a distant idea, an adventure that would put more distance between himself and his father while doing some good for the people of Solvigant. Now that they were about to set foot in a foreign town on a different moon, their mission felt more real. This was the true beginning of their pilgrimage.

Art bowed. "Good morning, Commander."

"A good morning to you, Acolyte." Theo smiled and they shook hands, chuckling. Dreggs snorted, but Theo ignored him.

"Have you been to Maxon before?" Theo asked.

"Never before, no." Art's words were short and clipped. "Born on Aleph, joined the Sons of Destruction on Tyre, and was posted to Solvigant on Xys. That is the full record of my travels. The governor did occasionally send me to Highgaard, but I saw few of the sights."

"Well, we'll discover it together, then." Theo turned to the captain. "How long before we sail?"

"The coal barge will be here in two hours, another couple of hours to load fuel and provisions. Mid-afternoon sir." The captain punctuated his speech with a crisp salute.

"Very good, Captain."

"I do recommend, sir, that we make haste. The reports from the local haruspex indicate foul weather." Theo looked around at the pristine blue sky. He could not see a single cloud.

"Are you sure?"

"I have ignored the reports enough times to know it is a mistake to do so, sir."

"Very well, Captain, I will instruct our people to make quick work of their port tasks." Theo turned to the bureaucrat. "Did you hear that, Dreggs?"

"Yes, sir."

Theo offered Hannah his arm. "Lady Vanguard, will you accompany me to the mayor's estate?"

Hannah stepped up to him and brushed lint from his epaulets. "You will have to make do with Art. I have other business."

Theo was taken aback. "What other business?" The words came out harsher than he meant, but Hannah just laughed. Theo enjoyed her laughter. It was light and clear, the naïve laughter of an untroubled young noblewoman. He found he wanted to elicit that response from her more often.

"What business does any young noble bride have?" Hannah inquired.

Theo shook his head.

"Shopping! It may be a while before we are in a place with the luxuries of Planktown."

*What about money?* Theo wondered. *Am I required to offer her some? Does she have her own?* Theo's father had given him some cash before departing, but it was not an amount that would impress a well-born aristocratic woman. There were so many parts of marriage that baffled Theo, but Hannah did not seem concerned, so he did not bring it up.

"Will you be safe?"

"I have my maids."

"I can spare a few sailors, sir," the captain offered.

"That won't be necessary," Hannah insisted, and Theo heard the steel edge in her voice. It was the same honed authority she had displayed the night before with Palestrina.

"Very well, then," Theo said. "At least let me call you a litter."

Hannah nodded her acceptance of this compromise, then leaned in and kissed him. Theo flushed in front of the entire delegation. When she drew back, he studied her face, appreciating her smile.

Art paced near the gangplank.

"To the mayor's manor then?" he asked Theo.

"Where is Beatrice?"

Hannah stiffened beside him.

"In her cabin, sir," said Fincher, the first mate. "She says she is feeling ill."

"Does she require a physicker?"

"She says it is not that kind of illness, sir."

Theo did not know what that might mean, but he did not want to seem overly concerned about Beatrice's welfare in front of Hannah.

"Send for one anyway. If Lady Marrion does not require it, the doctor can still see to my hand before we sail."

"Of course, sir." Fincher bowed and hustled away.

Dreggs, Hannah, Theo, and Art descended the gangway. A lift lowered them to ground level. At the exit, Dreggs headed in the direction of the post and Theo helped Hannah into an ornate green litter carried by four sturdy Ankhim; their broad feet did not sink as deeply into the mud of the street as those of other species.

Theo regretted that he only had dress shoes. He must make time before their departure to visit an outfitter. He had nothing appropriate for traveling through wild country on foot.

Planktown's aeroport stood on the shore of Crystal Bay. It reached only half as high as the aeroport tower in Solvigant. Theo, eyeing the structure, thought it leaned toward the water.

"The mayor is expecting us," Art said. "Should we find our own litter? The mud prevents the use of horse-drawn carriages."

Theo stepped onto the boardwalk and scraped the clinging mud off his shoes.

"I want to see Planktown. We can summon a litter for the return trip. It will be easier to do from the mayor's mansion anyway."

Art checked his watch and clicked his tongue. "You want to keep him waiting?"

"There was no emissary at the pier," Theo said. "It would seem the mayor is not interested in propriety or expediency."

Art laughed. "Theo the diplomat is a tad vindictive."

"Just a curious tourist. Do you know where the manor is?"

"I saw it from the ship on the way in. I think I can get us there."

"Lead the way, then."

The two companions tromped down the boardwalk in single file, the Faelani squirrel alert and interested in the city's particular features.

Due to the size and weight of the aeroport, the structure was one of the few in Planktown built on the coast. The rest of the city was an assortment of floating piers, boardwalks, and sunken pilings that stretched far out into the bay. Theo surveyed the local architecture, shops, and the small watercraft that glided between the floating platforms. The clear blue water beneath the city captivated him.

While Art asked a local fishmonger for directions, Theo crouched and dipped his fingers in the sea. It was warm as bathwater, but salty on the tongue. Theo's experience with oceans on Tyre and Highgaard were of the cold, gray variety.

Even more than the wooden structures built above the water's surface and the busy denizens of Planktown, Theo enjoyed the schools of bright fish that darted back and forth beneath the boardwalks. Puffer fish, lionfish, sea turtles, and other aquatic creatures Theo had only read about or seen in Thail's aquariums, glided lazily through the clear waters. Twice Theo was so enamored with the sea life beneath his feet that he bumped into someone. He managed not to knock them off the boardwalk, but it was a close call both times.

Theo undid his collar as they walked. Sweat soaked his dress uniform. There were more soldiers than Theo had expected. Several of them recognized Theo's rank by the epaulets and saluted him, which he returned. Though he did not recognize any of the men, it made him long for simpler days, when he was only the XO on the *Dragonhammer*.

*Where is my ship now?* Theo wondered. *Does the crew even notice my absence? Have they replaced me?*

With firm resolve, Theo pushed his nostalgia aside. His days as an Imperial Naval officer were over. He needed to focus on the task at hand.

He returned his attention to Planktown. Art had outdistanced Theo by two hundred yards and Theo hustled to catch up.

"What do you know about the mayor?" Theo asked, a little breathless, when he reached Art.

"His name is Feldspar Grimbaldark."

"That's a Grym name."

"Indeed."

"You don't see many of them in Imperial bureaucracy."

"He made his fortune in the Behlian sapphire mines before being elected mayor of Planktown."

"You mean he purchased his position."

Art shrugged. "I asked my brothers who have been to Maxon before. Grimbaldark is an ambitious man. He wants to be governor of Maxon, but Governor Blumenthal is second cousin to the Empress, so he's unlikely to get satisfaction. What do we need from him anyway?"

"It would be rude as an Imperial delegation from Xys to not speak with the mayor."

"We're doing this for propriety?"

It was the first time Theo had heard irritation in Art's voice.

"We also need a Writ of Supply to commandeer supplies for the delegation in Fort Jasper. A Writ of Authority would override any reticence on the part of Fort Jasper's chamberlain to let us cross the border into Eldarian territory. A Writ of Passage would let us bypass any military checkpoints because of increased hostility between the two groups."

"Who knew visiting the God of Destruction required so much paperwork."

"Paperwork is the lifeblood of bureaucracy and Empire." Theo said, then winced, realizing he had just quoted his father.

Art stopped to let a procession of Priests of Darak cross the intersecting boardwalk before them. The whole city smelled of fish, overripe fruit, and something Theo could not put his finger on.

"What is that smell?"

"Fish?"

"No, the other one."

"Palm oil." Art pointed behind them toward the shore where two massive brick smokestacks rose next to the aeroport. "Planktown is the largest exporter of palm oil in the Empire. They also rub it into the wood to protect against damage from salt water."

"There's more than one exporter of palm oil? What do we use it for?"

"You know, Theo, I'm beginning to think you didn't read any of the provided material," Art teased.

"I wanted you to feel useful."

They rounded a corner and came to a halt. A wide floating plaza full of market stalls stretched out before them. Beyond the bustling bazaar was a squat wooden building flying the Imperial flag.

Art gestured past the crowd. "The mayor's house."

Theo buttoned up his jacket and ran his fingers through his damp hair.

"I'm impressed by how well you navigated us through that labyrinth of boardwalks."

"I've lived in a peripatetic city most of my life. You develop a keen sense of direction." Art's nose twitched, his whiskers quivering at the compliment.

It took them almost half an hour to squeeze through the crowded bazaar. Theo stopped on several occasions to admire the quality of the produce or run his fingers over a fine-looking tapestry.

"Somerset makes fine silks," Art said.

"You're a veritable compendium of useless knowledge."

Art feigned hurt, bringing one paw to his chest as if Theo had struck him. "That knowledge may save your ass from an Eldarian spear."

"If it does, I'll be sure to thank you."

"Perhaps a gift for your new bride?"

The silk suddenly felt scratchy and rough under Theo's fingers. "I don't know what she likes."

"I'm sure she'd just appreciate the sentiment." Art smiled. "Plus, it gives you an opportunity to learn what she likes."

"You're a wise man, Arthur Volaticus."

Theo purchased a long silk scarf of deep blues and greens, a seascape like the one beneath their feet. His bundle secured under one arm, the two exited the far end of the bazaar near the gatehouse in front of the mayor's residence.

Theo showed the guard his credentials and waited while the soldier strode off to announce their visit.

Art rubbed his paws together in excitement. "*Now* it feels like we're on an adventure."

Theo laughed and clapped Art on the back. He was grateful that he had found someone with whom he could be candid.

"Indeed, it does, my friend. It truly does."

# CHAPTER SIXTY-FIVE

# ION RUCINARE

## MOON OF KARIS, TYRSDAY, 4TH OF LUXOR

Ion stared into the void. The open belvedere admitted the steady light of countless stars. Despite the dire circumstances on *Cerul's Horn*, the void was silent. Ion looked toward the navigator but could make out only a dim shape hunched over the dark outline of the Astral Mage.

*I hope Farris is all right,* Ion thought.

He looked to starboard, in the direction the sailor had run, but saw nothing but the distant pinpricks of more stars. Pressure stoppered his ears and Ion shivered. He suddenly realized how cold he was. His teeth chattered and he wrapped his arms around himself for warmth. The ship shuddered and he dropped hard onto his knees. He opened his mouth to cry out in pain, but no sound emanated from him. Tears gathered in the corner of his eyes. He put his hands out in the darkness, found the astral array terminal, and used it to haul himself back to standing.

As his eyes adjusted to the blackness, he realized he could see a thin blue film in the void beyond the ship. It curved over the belvedere to form a tunnel that encased the freighter.

*It must be the laneway,* Ion realized. The gloom before him wavered and took on a sparkling quality. *An astral whale!*

Ion watched the void beyond the laneway as the sparkling, amorphous mass coalesced and became solid. A great blue orb slid open to reveal a massive eye. A crescent of white sclera gleamed around the wide gray pupil. Ion fell back in surprise, his left arm flailing for purchase to keep him upright. His fingers closed on the amethyst the astral mage had used as his focus and the serrated edges of the unpolished stone bit into his hands. He hissed, feeling blood trickle through his fingers. He inhaled, short and ragged, and tried to take another breath.

Two smaller eyes opened along the whale's rostrum, one green, one black. The creature was watching him, waiting for something to happen.

The amethyst pulsed with violet light beneath Ion's fingers. The massive balechtoplasm rolled, revealing a pale white belly. Then it shrieked and Ion covered his ears. The violet light of the focus went out. In the darkness, he saw that the creature's stomach reflected the starlight and translucent blue glow of the laneway. The whale flexed its ponderous tail, arching it away from the dirigible.

*It's going to strike the ship!*

Ion grasped the array and focus again. The violet light flared, nearly blinding him. The whale slapped its tail hard against the frigate. Ion heard the great *thump* followed by cracking wood and a terrific shudder that reverberated through the belvedere. Shimmery opalescence started at the whale's head and spread down its body as it faded to translucence. The tail arched away again and Ion braced himself for another blow. The impact came just before the astral creature disappeared, once more merely a warping of the star field beyond the laneway.

Fear pulsed through Ion and a surge of delicate violet lightning raced up his left arm. Panicked, Ion released the amethyst and the lightning faded.

*It's a focus,* he reminded himself. *A channel for Astral magic. Captain Crestone said I could use magic.*

Ion placed his hand on the gemstone, mindful of the cuts on his palm. The light flared once more. He looked at his right hand on the terminal array and willed the light to appear there, too. He gazed out the front of the belvedere and realized he could see the distant green circle that was the other side of the gate. There was enough light flowing through him into the focus that he could make out the slack-jawed expression on the navigator's face. Fear glinted in the man's eyes.

Blue light crept along the edges of the gas bag away from the belvedere. A strong wind pressed into Ion's body, threatening to dislodge him. He let go of the terminal array to brace himself against that force and the light winked out. When he grabbed the array again, blue light flared, followed by a green pulse. The blue-green pulses flowed outward along the gas bag. The alternating colors beat a steady rhythm, like a heartbeat.

The ship rocked as another astral whale brushed against the port side. Ion lurched into the panel. He tightened his grip on the focus and the array. Blood squelched between the fingers of his left hand. The wind intensified as the light spread over the curved sides of the gas bag, the rhythm of the colors matching his pulse. He felt as if he was standing inside a terrible sandstorm. Gale-force wind roared in his ears. His muscles ached with the strain of holding on.

His feet lifted from the floor as they had on the street in Solvigant in front of the city watch station. The pulsing light quickened until he could not tell green from blue, there was only brilliant yellow. Ion gritted his teeth against the swirling wind and risked a glance toward the gate. The pale green orb of Karis beyond the aerogate was growing larger.

*It's working! The ship is moving forward.*

Excited, Ion pumped his fist in the air. The wind subsided and the light flickered. Realizing his mistake, he gripped the terminal array again. The light flared bright in the void and the howling wind redoubled. He was forced to squint against the gusts, so he could no longer track the motions of the whales. His feet dangled above his head, the force of the magic suspending him inside the belvedere. His hair whipped against his face and stung his eyes. His muscles ached. His fingers were white and he could no longer feel them. He willed his grip on the array to hold.

The gate's terminus drew closer.

Ion cried out against the strain, and just when he thought the force of the gale would suck him out of the belvedere, he felt firm hands grab his ankles and push him down toward the floor. He glanced down and saw the Astral Mage, his face flushed from the blow to his head. The man had wrapped his feet around the legs of the navigator's table and forced Ion's ankles under his own arm pits.

Feeling more secure, Ion redoubled his efforts. He could not say how he was doing this, but he felt the magic flowing through him intensify. The gate's exit, closer now, scintillated with opalescent light. A translucent shape drifted between *Cerul's Horn* and the gate.

*Another whale.* Ion moaned.

The blob turned toward them, growing larger.

*Not larger,* Ion realized, *closer. It's charging the ship.*

Ion steeled himself for a head-on collision. but the impact never came. The balechto-plasm pulled up at the last moment, rolling away from the ship, flashing opaque and then translucent again. The huge animal's speed fascinated Ion.

The fierce wind yanked Ion off the terminal. He flailed trying to reach the array as the yellow light blinked out across the gas bag. He strained to regain his grip, pushing against the mage's hold on his ankles. His fingers brushed the terminal, but he could not clasp it. The ship slowed and they fell away from the distant gate.

Then strong fingers gripped his wrist. Startled, Ion blinked at the navigator, who grasped the boy's hands and pressed them toward the terminal. Their combined strength was enough. Ion clung to it, yelling profanities into the void that would have made his grandfather blush. Golden light shot out of the belvedere and encapsulated the ship. Once again, they drew closer to the gate.

The three men in the belvedere clutched one another for dear life as the magic raged around them. Ion watched in horror as the navigator shrank beside him. Deep hollows formed under the man's eyes. His hair grew longer, then turned white. His skin cracked and bled. Ion screamed as the man rotted away before his eyes. The approaching gate cast the whole affair in a sickly green light. The navigator's skin flaked, then his muscles, then his bones. He blew away as a fine dust in the howling wind.

Ion screamed.

*Cerul's Horn* shuddered. The wind stopped and Ion's body sagged between the mage's grip and the terminal. Ion's screams of terror became screams of anguish as paroxysms of agony contorted his body. Some part of him not lost to the pain realized this was important. He could hear himself. He could hear his screams.

Another voice cut through his pain. "Let go, lad. Let go."

Ion looked toward the voice. He saw Farris's kind face contorted with worry as he tried to catch Ion's attention.

"Let go. That's enough. Let go."

Ion looked past the array and saw miles of deciduous forest and snow-capped mountains. Airships dotted the sky, and something indiscernible and enormous sailed between them.

"Let go, lad!" Farris shouted.

Ion willed his fingers to open. His feet slammed to the ground. For a moment, Ion stood, pale and shaking. Then he tumbled backward into the waiting arms of the Astral Mage. The mage lowered Ion to the ground and propped him against the half wall of the belvedere. Ion's limbs twisted and cramped as his muscles shook off the pain. The concern on Farris's face convinced Ion that he might be dying.

He studied his trembling hands. His skin was a bloodless white, but the tips of his fingers were black. He saw red, inflamed handprints on his wrist and forearm.

*The navigator,* Ion knew.

"What happened?" His voice sounded distant and echoed as if he were speaking from the bottom of a well.

Farris knelt beside him. "You saved us, lad. You saved *Cerul's Horn*."

"The navigator—"

Farris made the sign of the Ring and looked at the astral mage. The mage was bleeding from a shallow cut on his temple where his temple had struck the belvedere's railing. He stared at Ion as if the boy had grown a second head. Farris snapped his fingers in front of the man's face to get his attention.

"Wim," Farris said, his voice stern, "what, by Solo and all her children, was that?"

"Aetherial magic," Wim said. "Blood magic. Illicit magic."

Farris's expression turned grim. "Isn't that what powers the gates?"

"Part of it." Wim said.

"Can't be so bad then," Farris said.

"That boy is an abomination, one of the double-sentient," Wim hissed, taking a blade from his belt. Color rose in his cheeks.

"Now, now," Farris said, moving between Wim and the boy.

Ion was too weak to defend himself.

"I don't care what he is," Farris said taking a step toward the mage, "he just saved our lives."

"That was aetherial magic," Wim insisted. "The Imperial Court forbids it. We should kill him."

Ion knew he ought to care about Wim's intention, but after the ordeal in the void, he found it difficult to care about anything. He felt as if the huge gray eye of the balechto-plasm still gazed at him from the laneway boundary, as if *Cerul's Horn* were still careening through the black void. Ion wanted to scream and cry. He wanted to dance and laugh. He was a grain of sand, Solvigant a mote of dust, Xys, Solo, the entire World System nothing in the infinity of the void.

It did not matter if Wim killed him. Nothing, not Apyreon, his grandfather's death, Farris, *Cerul's Horn*, Caelia, Captain Crestone, none of it meant anything compared to the might of the boundless nothing.

Pressure built up in Ion's gut, a wriggling, bubbling laughter that threatened to overwhelm him. He tried to swallow it down, to keep it in, but it was no use. He laughed. It was a barking cackle that brought both sailors up short. Once he surrendered to the laugh, he could not stop it rolling out of him. His face turned red and his lungs burned. Still, the laughter came.

"He has the madness," Farris said.

"Void sickness," Wim confirmed.

"We need to take him below to the ship," Farris said.

Wim lunged, knife blade glistening in the noonday sun. In his hysteria, Ion witnessed the attack in slow motion. The blade moved toward him through the air as if through water. Farris moved to intercept it. The whole dance was hilarious, pointless, and terrifying.

Farris's metal hand closed around Wim's outstretched wrist.

Ion's laughter had degraded into a choking wheeze. He was going to suffocate before Wim could stab him. Even in his madness, Ion heard the bones in Wim's wrist break. The mage's face contorted in pain and rage. The knife clattered to the floor of the belvedere. Wim tried to grab at Ion, but Farris was in the way. The crewman pivoted and drove his knee into Wim's stomach. The mage doubled over, his face going as purple as Ion's.

*I need to breathe!* Ion thought through spasms of exhausted laughter.

Wim recovered himself enough to grab the knife. Farris drove his hip into the man. The mage stumbled, hit the half wall of the belvedere, and flipped over it. Ion heard his shouts as the man scrabbled for purchase on the gas bag. Farris vaulted over the half wall. Ion was not sure if Farris meant to save Wim or finish the job. Blackness frayed the edges of his vision.

*The void is breaking in! It's coming for me!* Ion curled into a miserable ball and rocked back and forth, his head swimming and lungs burning.

Moments later, Farris returned. He put his hands on Ion's shoulders.

"Breathe, lad," the sailor commanded. "Breathe."

Ion was too far gone to comply. Farris slapped him across the face once, then again. Ion's head rocked one way, then the other. It had no effect. The world was turning gray, the color bleeding away into nothing.

*Nothing. It's all nothing.*

Farris picked up the knife and held it near Ion's face.

*He's going to cut my throat,* Ion thought. *Just as well.* Ion did not want to live in a world that did not matter, did not want to think about the vast void pressing in all around him. He did not want to live in a world where he could not breathe.

Farris brought the knife to Ion's cheek and made a shallow cut. There was a flash of pain and he sucked in a breath. Farris pressed the blade into the wound on Ion's fingers. Ion gasped and color rushed back into the world. He rocked forward onto all fours and vomited watery bile. Farris's fleshy hand rubbed Ion's back in smooth circles.

"There, there, lad. You're going to be all right. Get it out. That's it."

Ion wiped his mouth with a red-smeared hand. Blood dripped from his cheek onto the floorboards. He inhaled a shaky breath and reveled in the delicious cool air that filled his lungs.

"Can you stand? We don't have much time, lad."

With Farris's help Ion got to his feet. The sailor handed him a handkerchief. Ion could only gaze at it, uncertain what to do with it.

"For your face."

Ion half-heartedly dabbed his face. The handkerchief came away stained with blood. Farris must have seen the panic in his eyes.

"You're going to be all right, lad. It's a superficial cut. It'll bleed for a while, but it'll heal up fine."

"Why did you do that?"

Farris, the grizzled clunker sailor who had just thrown an Astral Mage off the belvedere to save Ion's life flushed at the harsh words of a twelve-year-old boy.

"I needed to get your attention away from the void."

"What happened?"

"In the void or afterward?"

"Both."

"In the void, I have no idea. I've never seen whales so aggressive. Afterward, void sickness. We sailors just call it the madness, but it happens to a lot of first-time travelers. I apologize, lad. I should've warned you."

Ion gazed out at the distant snow-capped peaks. "Thank you."

"Don't mention it."

"This is Karis?"

"Aye." Farris pointed toward a small hamlet nestled near the base of one of the high mountains. "That's Caelia."

Ion stepped to the front of the belvedere to get a better view. Caelia was laid out like a pie. A squat aeroport tower stood at the center of several roads that radiated outward like the spokes of a wheel. Each slice of the town was packed with cottages whose peaked roofs mirrored the mountains.

"Where's the Society temple?"

Farris pointed to a distant peak. "That's Mount Fen. Below it is Fenzer Pass. The temple is through there in the Vale of the Twins. It's a three- or four-day journey from Caelia depending on the weather."

An enormous shadow passed over the gas bag, startling Ion. He leaned over the half wall and gazed upward, shielding his eyes with his clean hand.

"What was that?"

Farris chuckled and pointed three points off starboard. "Watch there."

Ion looked where the sailor indicated and saw nothing. Then another shadow danced across the gas bag and a moment later Ion saw it and shouted with glee.

"A Dragon!"

"Aye, lad, and a special one it is."

Ion gaped at the flying reptile. From nose to tail, it was the same length as *Cerul's Horn*. The whales in the void had been ponderous and slow, the Dragon was graceful and swift. Its golden scales glimmered in the light of early afternoon and a crest of golden horn and leather spandrels stretched down its spine. Its leathery wings were open in a smooth glide that appeared effortless.

"Amazing," Ion said and smiled at Farris. As if the majestic creature had heard, the gold reptilian head turned toward them. Two white horns jutted upward above intelligent green eyes. Dragons were not allowed to take this form in Solvigant, so Ion had never beheld one. A peripatetic city of canvas and desiccated wood was too vulnerable to the downdraft of air from powerful wings or the volatile fire of their breath.

The Dragon roared. Ion covered his ears in delight. He laughed, and this time it was the innocent laughter of a carefree boy. The Dragon turned toward them. With a casual flap of its wings, it was beside them, then past them. The Dragon buzzed the belvedere and Ion ducked instinctively. There was a rumble like a cascade of large stones.

"What was that sound?" Ion asked.

Farris was smiling. "The Dragon, lad. The Dragon."

"You said he was special."

"That I did. Gold Dragons are rare. He's from an aristocratic family on Flynt."

The Dragon roared again and executed a perfect barrel roll over the top of *Cerul's Horn*.

"He's amazing!" Ion exclaimed but stopped short when he saw tears in Farris's eyes. "You said we don't have much time. You weren't talking about Caelia."

Farris shook his head. "No, lad. That I wasn't."

"You're going to be in trouble for the mage."

"Aye, I am."

"But you fixed the leak. You saved us as much as I did."

"No. When the lights went out, I ran back to the belvedere. They'll be running the burners full bore until we make port to keep us aloft."

"You came back to see if I was okay?"

"Good thing I did, too. Wim's a stodgy old bastard. Was, anyway."

"You killed him."

Farris nodded, his gaze distant.

"Am I going to be in trouble?"

Farris placed a gentle metal hand on Ion's shoulder. "No. You saved our lives, and you saved our ship. Plus, I suspect the Society will want to speak with you about all that back there." He gestured to where the aerogate was dwindling behind them.

"I don't know what happened. I just—I didn't want—It just happened."

"Aye, lad. I know. You're going to be all right."

The Dragon, now far to port, flapped its wings and roared. To Ion, it seemed like a roar of delight. He guessed the impressive creature loved flying. It was a beautiful day, despite a chill that clung to him from the void. He heard his own manic laughter echo in his mind and pushed it aside. The Dragon roared a third time, and brilliant red flame shot from his open maw in a blazing arc across the sky. Ion applauded.

*Can Rehka do that?* Ion experienced a pang of jealousy. *What a wonder flying must be. And to have such power.*

Farris must have taken the pensive look on Ion's face for fear.

"You're going to be all right, lad."

"I know," Ion said, but he did not mean it.

The Dragon flapped its vast wings and sped ahead of *Cerul's Horn*. In moments it shrank to a golden speck, like a daylight star above the distant mountains.

Ion took Farris's metal hand and held it. Together they watched the legendary creature until its golden light disappeared.

# Chapter Sixty-Six

# ADI CRESTONE

## The Void, Outside Time

The *Starforged* fell through the void. Adi clung to the wheel. The small dirigible bounced along the surface of the laneway with a muted *thud*. If Wright had not secured Adi to the deck, the impact would have thrown her from the ship. As it was, she was tossed wide of the pedestal. She slid on her stomach across the foredeck until she slammed against the port gunwale. The tug careened onward like a stone skipping off the surface of a lake. Adi's right arm was tangled in the rope. She worked to free it but could not do so before the ship listed hard to starboard and ricocheted once more off the laneway.

The force of the impact propelled Adi forward toward the port wall of the cabin, now below her. Her tangled arm broke and she screamed into the void. Her limp arm slipped free, and she fell toward the cabin. The rope around her waist caught her before she hit the wall. She hung, suspended in midair, while the tug rolled further to starboard. It skipped off the laneway again, swinging Adi into the balloon's rigging. She heard shouts from Wright and Verdun but could not identify their location.

*We're going to capsize!* Adi realized. *We don't have enough speed to reach the other side of the gate.*

Adi held onto the rigging with her good arm. The drag on the ship from hitting the laneway slowed them. Behind them, Adi could see broken pieces of the rudder, propeller, the aerofins... and something worse.

*The laneway is cracking!*

Adi had never heard of a broken laneway, but she had never ridden a ship careening through one like a billiard ball. Not that it would matter. The ship would roll over and the suspended wooden hull would crash down onto the gas bag, crushing Adi and her crew in a tangle of planks and canvas. The swaying tug descended toward the laneway once more. Adi reached for her magic. She strained, imagining the focus stone on the tug's navigation array. She clutched at the collar of her shirt, willing her fingers to remember the worry-worn smoothness of her dragonstone. Nothing happened.

The ship rolled upside down and tipped forward. The prow scraped across the laneway, screeching like a jammed iron cog. The laneway bulged outward, then shattered with the hiss and pops of thousands of crystalline fractures. Countless pieces refracted the light of infinite stars.

Adi flew from the rigging. The rope around her waist stretched taught, then snapped as the pedestal came free of the deck. The *Starforged* broke up around her.

"Iris!" she screamed, but there was no sound in the sudden vacuum. A ferocious cold seized her body. She could not suck in a breath. Her momentum propelled her away from the battered tug at an alarming rate. Tears froze in the corners of her eyes. The myriad stars in her vision began to wink out.

Adi crashed into the meadow so hard the force of it drove the remaining breath from her lungs. She lay beneath an azure sky and struggled to inhale. Her broken arm throbbed. She suspected the fall had broken other bones as well. Darkness played at the edges of her vision, but she refused to lose consciousness. When she could breathe once more, her exhalations had a gurgling, watery quality to them. She tried to sit up, but intense pain in her chest forced her back down. She rolled onto one side, then pushed herself into a sitting position. This made breathing harder.

"Iris!" she called. The cry made her wince. Her ear drum had ruptured. She checked her face with her good hand. Blood trickled from her ears and nose. "Verdun," she called. There was no response. "Wright." Silence.

She sat on a hillside covered in tall grass that swayed in a light breeze. The slope ended at the shore of a large lake. Lateen-sailed fishing sloops tacked across the surface of the water. A herd of longhorn cattle grazed along the distant shore below an idyllic hamlet. Near where Adi sat, sheep with their lambs frolicked near a copse of trees. Fair-weather clouds floated above her. A bright, hot sun shone near the apex of the sky. A familiar moon hung low on the horizon, but Adi could not name it. She could not see Solo. She had never imagined what a sky without the gas giant might look like.

*Where am I?* Adi wondered. *Where's Iris? Where's my crew?* She coughed, flecking her pants with blood. *It's a beautiful place to die. If only I could say goodbye to Lucas.*

"Hello, Grandmother," said a husky woman's voice from behind Adi. She tried to turn but found it took too much effort. There was an animal quality to the voice in how the speaker rolled the *R* at the end of "grandmother."

"Who are you?" Adi demanded "Where am I?"

"I have named you and you are in a place that no longer exists."

"That doesn't make sense."

Speaking was difficult. Adi spat a glob of blood and phlegm onto the grass beside her. The grass rustled and the speaker moved into view. Adi expelled another wad of bloody mucus. The woman was like no Faelani Adi had ever seen. The creature walked on all fours and had the sleek body of a panther. Above her feline shoulders rose the torso of a human woman. Polished plate mail covered her breasts, and an ornate circular collar protruded from around neck. Beneath blue hair was a woman's face with a sharp nose and pointed ears. Wide, feathery wings lay folded along the creature's back, the long feathers glinting with silver highlights. But it was her eyes that transfixed Adi. Instead of sclera, iris, and pupil, Adi could see only the roiling gaseous layers of Solo, as if this being contained the Mother goddess herself.

"Solo?" Adi ventured.

The creature laughed, a warm rumbling sound. "No."

"Who are you?"

"Your time is too precious for me to repeat myself."

"Am I dying?"

"All mortals die."

"Have you come to watch me die?"

"I have come to warn you."

"Any threat won't matter to me in a few moments."

The creature stepped close and sat in front of Adi. Like an over-eager dog, she placed one paw on each of Adi's shoulders. Adi smelled something sweet and strange, and noticed the paws felt light on her broken body. She wanted to pull away but could not take her gaze from the swirling orange eyes.

"You will not die *now*, Adison Crestone."

A warming glow suffused Adi's body, like sunlight on a spring afternoon. Memories cascaded through her. Her father grieved over the corpse of her dead mother. Adi raced astral yachts on the Azure Sea. Hubert pulled her into his room, his grin evil. Adi fled Saba, gave birth to Lucas in a Solvigant alley, and Stella took her in. Adi found her magic, worked as a prostitute, and met Rehka. Adi abandoned Lucas. A decade of adventures with Rehka filled her vision, their nights together, their close calls. Then Rehka abandoned her, and Adi scuttled the *Snowcrest*. She met the Blood Queen, felt the cold iron collar close around her neck. She saw all the crimes she had committed in the hope of clearing her debts. She met Captain Torrance and watched a cannonball tear him in half. The events of the past week flitted past in rapid succession.

The creature removed her forepaws from Adi's shoulders and she slumped sideways onto the soft grass. She realized she was weeping and tried to stem the flow of tears. She sniffled and wiped snot from her face on her left sleeve, her broken arm. It didn't hurt. Her arm bent in all the right places. Adi flexed her fingers, checked the bruising on her jaw and her fractured ribs, but there was no pain. Only the brand on her arm remained, bloody and oozing, and there was a burn on her chest that vaguely resembled a six-pointed star. Otherwise, she felt whole and complete, better than she had in a long time. Adi looked up at the feline creature.

"How did you do that?"

The creature's mouth wore a sardonic smile, but she did not respond.

"You healed me. That magic, that amount of magic, it's incredible. It's impossible. Not even a skilled wayfaring Passerine could heal all my injuries at once."

"You are far from healed, Grandmother."

Adi stood and flexed her knees. She felt ten years younger. She wanted to run through the grass, climb a tree, swim in the lake, but the creature's words brought her up short.

"Why do you call me that?" Adi said.

"Because it is true."

"My son is only fifteen and he is a man, not whatever you are."

"Nevertheless, it is true. I cannot lie to you."

It was impossible to read anything in those cloud-filled eyes, but remnants of the warmth that had suffused Adi moments before remained and she knew the creature's words to be true. Somehow, she knew they could be nothing else.

"What are you?"

"I am your granddaughter."

Adi's fists balled in frustration, then she had an idea. "What else are you?"

The creature displayed that sardonic smile again. "Very good. I am an acolyte. I am a granddaughter. I am a Vixhallian Agramin. I am a cleric. I am a sphynx."

"What's a Vish-alien Agro-men?" Adi stumbled over the unfamiliar words. She had never heard of such a creature, but her time adventuring on the *Snowcrest* had taught her that the World System was vast and full of surprises.

"A creature of the void."

"We are in the void?"

"Everything is in the void."

"Where is Iris? Where's my crew?"

"Your crew is salvaging the *Starforged*. Iris is drowning, I believe."

"*What?* How can I save her?"

"Do you want to save her?"

"Of course."

The creature studied Adi as if she had said something profound. Adi shivered and looked away from the sphynx. It was snowing now. The lake had frozen over and fresh snow blanketed the grass.

"I have to save Iris." Adi said.

"That may happen later."

"What do you mean 'may'?"

The same sardonic smile. Adi wanted to scream.

"What do I call you?"

"Quezzibantabulifaniquorum. It is Yaziri for 'one who quests and questions.'"

"I can't say that." Adi had never heard of the language.

"Esme will suffice for the time we are together."

"What did you want to warn me about, Esme?"

"My mistress has named you Uralia-Graine."

"Is Solo your mistress?"

"You are missing the point. You're asking the wrong question."

"That name, Ur-whatever you said, what does it mean? It is Naupaxi, too?"

"It is. Walk with me."

Esme turned, her elegant tail swishing through the tall brown grass. Adi saw that it was autumn now. Red and yellow leaves floated from the trees to land on the calm surface of the lake. The sheep returned over a hill, their summer wool thick and full of brambles. Adi opened her mouth to protest but thought better of it. She walked beside the sphynx toward the water's edge. When they reached the lakeshore, Esme sat on her haunches and spoke once more.

"Uralia-graine. It means 'one who protects and watches over the first seed.'"

"I don't understand."

"It is a difficult word to translate into your tongue, I admit. It can also mean 'the first gardener of the divine light' and 'the warrior who protects the blooming flower.'"

"What does that have to do with me? I'm no gardener, nor do flowers flourish on Xys."

"You are wrong." Esme's voice took on a hard edge. "My mistress has named you and her illuminated knowledge is never wrong."

"Your mistress is one of the gods? A child of Solo?"

"That does not matter to what you must do."

"What? What must I do? I must save Iris who is drowning somewhere. I must return to my crew."

Esme placed one paw gingerly in the water of the lake as if evaluating the temperature before deciding whether to dive in.

"Is Iris drowning in that lake?" Adi began to strip off her shirt.

Esme looked at Adi with those enigmatic eyes, one eyebrow raised with an opinion of that question.

"What?" Adi paused, her shirt half off.

"That is not a lake."

Adi lowered her shirt. "What is it?"

"It is nothing. It *was* a lake. I told you it no longer exists. Now it is only a shadow, and a mirror."

Adi's head hurt. *I need to save Iris.* "Tell me what I must do, then. What is this name your mistress has given me?"

Esme stirred the water, sending ripples onto the glass surface and startling minnows in the shallows. Adi knelt and dipped her fingers in the cool water.

*It certainly feels like a lake.*

Adi saw spring thunderclouds on the horizon. Then the wind intensified and hail pelted the surface of the lake. Adi drew her tricorn down to protect her face from the weather and discovered that she was not wet. Esme watched her with that same sardonic smile.

"I cannot tell you everything you need to know."

"Why not?"

"My mistress's brother is close by. If he finds you here, dying will be the least of your troubles."

Wary, Adi glanced around but saw no one. "Tell me what you can, then, and let me go before we run out of time."

"We cannot run out of time here," Esme said.

Adi sighed. "Why not?"

"You stand in the void in a place made of pieces of time. You stand beside a lake on a moon which no longer exists, with your granddaughter who does not yet exist, while you live in the present hunted and honored by beings who have always existed."

Adi rubbed her temples. "You're not making sense."

"Uralia-graine, Adison Faide, Adi Crestone, Grandmother, here is what you must do." Adi leaned in. "You must save Xys. You must protect the seed."

Adi rocked back on her heels. "I just want to save my son."

"They may be one and the same." Esme shrugged, "They may not."

"Theo Vanguard is on a mission now to save the people of Xys. Let him be the Uralia-Graine."

Esme placed a paw on her chin as if considering this. After a long silence, she shook her head and said, "No, it must be you."

"Why me?"

"Because you are the Uralia-Graine, and Vanguard is from the line of Chaos."

*The line of Chaos?* Adi knew so little history of House Vanguard.

Adi said, "Your mistress is Solo. You are Pallantier, one of the gods, one of the Children of Solo. Can you not save Xys yourself? Return to your home on the moon and stop its decaying orbit?"

"You are half-right, Grandmother. I am not Pallantier of Xys. We are all children of Solo in one way or another, are we not? Besides, my mistress has a brother. Solo is singular among the gods. She has no kin. That is two incorrect guesses."

"How many guesses do I get?"

"There are many riddles around the Uralia-Graine. Do not be distracted by solving those not set out for you. The identity of my mistress is not your riddle."

Adi groaned. "No."

"No, what?"

"No, I do not want to be this 'Grain' person. I am no one's avatar. I am many things: a pirate and a gangster, a thug who wants to be a mother instead. Besides, I have no idea how to save an entire moon or whatever this seed is. Tell Solo to release Xys from her clutching grasp. I want my own life with my son."

"You lie." Esme was angry. "You want nothing of the sort."

"Excuse me?"

"You are a petulant child grasping at shiny baubles hoping they have meaning inside, hoping that you can run away from your life and hide behind adventure. You pretend that dreadful things happen to you. You are not a hero, Adison Crestone. You are barely a mother, and you are not a particularly good pirate."

Adi slapped the sphinx.

"Djinnar's blood," Adi swore. The creature's flesh felt like supple leather with the sharp barbs of shark skin.

"Do not take the name of the Lord of Farewells in vain here."

Adi had never heard the God of Destruction referred to in such a way.

"Well," she spluttered, "do not speak to your grandmother that way."

Esme laughed and grinned, revealing feline teeth. "You are learning."

Adi rubbed her hand on her thigh to take the sting out of it.

*What kind of fool slaps a creature of the void? I'm lucky I don't have to ask her to heal the hand that struck her.*

Adi changed the subject. "Balthasar said Apyreon has great powers. Can it be used to save Xys?"

"Bale said that? Interesting." Esme stroked her chin once more. "Apyreon is the soil in which the divine seed can grow. You must destroy it."

"Absolutely not." Adi was so stunned by the idea that she glossed over Esme's familiarity with Balthasar. "Handing Apyreon over to the Blood Queen is the only way to save my son. I must find it."

Adi saw that it was summer once again.

"The seasons have come full circle," Esme said. "It is time for you to go. Find Apyreon and destroy it. Any other ideas or ambitions you may have are grains of sand in an hourglass. The coming storm will shatter your glass and fling that sand to the farthest reaches of the World System if you do not heed the will of my mistress—if you do not accept your name. There is a power greater than any of the magics in a name."

Esme rose to her feet and began to walk away from the lake. Adi turned to watch her go when a thought struck her.

"How do I get out of here?"

Esme turned around, that familiar smile on her lips. "Swim."

With that, the sphynx bounded straight for Adi, striking her in the midsection. Adi flew backward over the water. She flailed her arms to keep herself upright, but it was no use. The last thing she saw before she crashed into the lake was Esme leaping skyward and exploding into a thousand stars.

Adi smacked into the water on her back. It was cold and murky. She exhaled bubbles to get her bearings in the turbid lake water, but before she could take one stroke, the watery world spun. She watched the bubbles drift upward, lurch, then change direction and drift past her face in the opposite way. Adi followed them through three fathoms of clear blue water, sunlight refracting in its crystalline depths. She kicked hard toward the surface. A grouper flashed past her just as the water became cold seawater.

Adi broke the surface and inhaled deeply. Early morning sunlight sparkled on the ocean around her. Solo was setting on the western horizon. Near it was Aleph, the green home moon of the Faelani. She was back in the World System. Something bumped her shoulder. Adi treaded water and twisted around to examine the piece of wooden flotsam. Debris, fabric, rope, and shattered planks floated around her.

The Starforged. *Iris!*

"Iris!" Adi called. "Iris, where are you?"

There was no answer. *Esme said Iris was drowning.*

"Captain Crestone!" *Wright!*

Adi looked toward the sound and saw Verdun, Ajax, and her first mate floating on the remains of the *Starforged*. It listed precipitously to starboard. The rudder was gone, the propeller smashed. She wondered that it still floated at all.

"Where is Iris?" she called.

"She was thrown from the ship when we emerged from the laneway," Verdun called.

"Swim aboard," Ajax said.

"Not without Iris."

Adi took a deep breath and plunged under the water. To her relief, she was above a sandbar. The water was clear and shallow enough that she could see all the way to the bottom. A tangle of fabric and rope covered much of the sea floor.

*The balloon. Where's Iris?*

Adi scanned the water all around. On one side brightly colored fish flitted among coral. Adi surfaced for another breath and dove again.

*There!*

Off to her right, the sea floor dropped off a precipice into darkness. Adi saw Iris's splayed form sinking toward the edge, her curls floating in a wide circle around her face. Adi surfaced for another breath, then swam until she was above Iris then dove, stroking hard. She grabbed Iris under her armpits and kicked, straining toward the surface. Adi's lungs burned, her arms cramped with the effort of holding Iris and her heavy clothing.

Finally, they broke the surface, Adi spluttering and Iris limp. Using one arm, Adi towed the unresponsive woman toward the *Starforged*. Verdun held the gangplank, while Ajax extended the boat hook. Adi grabbed it to steady herself. The Ankhim strained to hold the boarding plank while Wright crawled along it and took hold of Iris. He secured rope from the destroyed rigging under her armpits and scampered back aboard before Verdun lost his endurance.

The three men heaved and hauled the unconscious Iris onto the deck. The *Starforged* rocked to port, and Adi worried it would capsize. The ship slowly righted itself and Verdun lowered the rope again so Adi could climb aboard. She hoisted herself onto the damaged vessel. It tilted but did not tip them off. Adi placed her fingers against Iris's throat and found a faint, slow pulse. She wasn't breathing.

"Djinnar's boiled blood and phlegm," Adi swore when her hand encountered stiff resistance over Iris's chest. *Who flees a moon in a Solo-forsaken corset?*

Adi grabbed the bodice with both hands and tore the dress away. She had nothing sharp to cut open the corset. She placed her lips over Iris's mouth and exhaled twice while holding the woman's nose. Then she heaved the woman onto her side. Adi's fingers trembled as she fought the intricate knots. She recognized Stella's handiwork in the elaborate ties.

"Breathe, damn you, breathe." Adi repeated the mantra and willed Iris's chest to move. The knot came loose and she yanked the laces from the loops. Halfway down the row she rolled Iris onto her back and breathed twice into her lungs.

"If you die, Solo help me, I will find Esme and kill her myself, granddaughter or no."

Adi pumped the woman's lungs, breathed, pumped, breathed, and pumped. It was much easier with the corset loosened.

Her arms ached. Iris's lips were a bluish-purple. Adi was about to give up when Iris coughed and arched her back. Adi was so excited that she almost tipped them both off the deck. She rolled Iris onto her side so she could cough out the water. Joyful tears ran down Adi's cheeks, and she said a prayer to Phoebe, Goddess of Light. Iris coughed and spluttered while Adi patted her firmly on the back.

"What happened?" Iris said at last.

"We made it," Adi said, laughing.

"Why are you crying? Was I dead?" Iris touched Adi's jawline. "Your face!"

"What?"

"The cuts and bruises are gone."

"It's a strange story. First, we need to get off the water."

"We have no oars," Wright said, "and no means of propulsion. We're floating."

Iris tried to sit up.

"Stay low. We'll be more stable if you don't sit up."

Adi surveyed the horizon and saw nothing but calm sea and open sky. She felt the pouches and loops around her belt and found her spyglass. She withdrew it and extended it to its full length. Giddy with the excitement of Iris's survival, she scanned right past the ship before the bright sail registered. She swept that area of the sea again and a fine vessel under full sail blossomed in the spyglass.

"There's a ship!" She passed the spyglass to Wright. "Hold that." She withdrew a signal mirror and directed flashes of brilliant sunlight toward the distant vessel. She held the mirror aloft until her arm began to go numb from the effort. She peered through the spyglass again and saw the ship had turned to face them and it was moving closer. The distant sails now filled the glass.

"Hail Solo!" Adi cried and kissed a startled Iris. "They've seen us."

Verdun whooped behind her. Even Ajax appeared relieved.

Soon they could see the sails on the horizon without the aid of the spyglass. There was nothing to protect them from the sun and by the time they could read *Heathwood* on the prow of the ship, Adi was well and truly burned. Despite her olive complexion, Iris's face was also reddening. Adi did not know if Ankhim could burn, and the heat seemed not to affect the Lord of Bones.

"It looks like a merchant vessel," Adi said.

"I don't care what it is as long as there's shade and fresh water," Iris said.

The sun had reached its zenith by the time the merchant ship pulled up alongside them. Sailors looked over the railing. One of them, a dark blue Ankhim, called out to them.

"Ahoy there. Hail Solo."

"Hail Solo," Adi called. "Good to see you."

"What's the trouble?"

"Pirates. Who are you?"

"This is the *Heathwood*. You won't find a finer, faster, fitter merchant vessel on the Heartspring. Name's Sham, and I'm the XO of this beautiful vessel."

Adi breathed a sigh of relief. His welcome seemed genuine enough.

"Where are you headed?" she asked.

"Thail," he motioned to the northwest. "And where be ye coming from might I ask? There's been no storms and the closest hydrogate is forty leagues southeast."

Adi pictured the charts from the *Starforged*'s cabin. "Highgaard, we came through the hydrogate five days ago. It's a long story, and not one I'm sure you'd believe. Can you give us a tow?"

Sham smiled. "I'm a sailor, ma'am, the stranger the yarn, the more truth innit, I say."

Adi returned the smile. She could learn to like Sham.

"Aye, we're nearly there, we can tow you in."

For the next hour, the crew of the *Heathwood* passed back and forth between the two ships securing lines to the *Starforged*. Adi instructed Ajax to keep a low profile. She didn't want to take the chance that someone might recognize him.

"Come aboard" Sham said when the *Starforged* was secure. "I'll let the captain know when you're safely aboard. It's lucky we saw your mirror. From Fleecedeep, we are."

Adi wracked her brain, trying to remember her geography. "That's on Maxon, is it not? South of Crystal Bay."

"Aye, that it is, ma'am. Have you been there?"

"I haven't, but I'm glad it's home to such amiable merchant sailors as this lot."

Sham pounded his chest in pleasure. "It truly is ma'am. We're happy to help." He stepped forward and lowered his voice, "Unless of course, you be pirates yourselves, then it's off the plank with ye, I'm afraid."

Adi paled. Iris let out a nervous laugh.

"Of course not," he said. "Whoever heard of lady pirates anyway."

The crew around them laughed, but Adi felt a real tension dissipate.

Ajax stayed behind to monitor their ship, while Adi and the rest of her rag tag crew transferred to the *Heathwood*.

"What takes you to Thail, ma'am?" Sham asked when they were aboard.

"A family reunion." Adi said.

"That's nice. Right and proper, innit? Well, let's get you cleaned up then. We don't have ladies' clothes aboard, but we do have an empty cabin. I'll have the crew scrounge around and see what'n we can find. Let's get you out of the sun. Follow me. Barnard, bring water for these famished folk."

Adi took Iris's hand, and they followed Sham below deck. When they emerged an hour later, clean and dry, they saw the city of Thail nestled against Mount Baldwin. Adi could even make out the stone octagonal tower belonging to the Thail School of Engineering. Somewhere in that huge structure she would find Lucas.

"Is that Gaash?" Adi asked pointing to the orb rising over the stark mountains.

"Aye," Sham said. "Phoebe's moon."

*Phoebe, the Goddess of Light.* A sudden realization struck Adi. *Esme, you devil.*

She had not recognized it on the lakeshore with Esme, but Tyre was much closer to Gaash than Xys. The riddle of Esme's mistress had been staring her in the face throughout her entire interaction with the strange creature.

"Phoebe," Adi whispered. "Phoebe is your mistress. The one goddess I've honored my whole life."

"What did you say?" Iris asked from beside her.

"It's nothing." But Adi felt she had discovered an answer that only created more questions.

*What if I have to choose between the Goddess of Light and my son?*

She watched Thail grow larger on the horizon. Evening stars began to appear in the twilight and Solo rose behind them. Adi said another prayer to Phoebe when the *Heathwood* put into the pier. As they disembarked, she could have sworn she heard Esme's husky voice echoing in her mind.

*"Congratulations, Adison, you have solved the wrong riddle."*

The End of Book 1

# APPENDIX I

## WORLD SYSTEM CHARACTERS

## Storytellers

- *Adison "Adi" Faide/Crestone, Captain* – Daughter of Lord Daniel Faide of Saba, she ran away to Xys at 15 to make a life for herself, changing her name to Crestone. She worked as a prostitute, a pirate, and a Blood Queen indenture.

- *Ion Rucinare* – A twelve-year-old boy living as a fisherman in the seaside village of Castes on Xys with his grandfather.

- *Theodore "Theo" Vanguard* – Youngest son of Lord Simon Vanguard and a commander in the imperial navy.

## The People of Xys

- *Ajax Hawthorne, Lord of Bones* – One of three Blood Queen generals.

- *Arthur Volaticus* – Neophyte from the Sons of Destruction assigned to accompany Theo on his pilgrimage to visit the God of Destruction. A Faelani who appears as a flying squirrel. Violet Volaticus is his wife. Their three children are Arthur Volaticus III, Bella, and Mary.

- *Balthasar "Bale" Drake* – A blue dragon, Rehka's father, and owner of Drake's Apothecary on Goldwynd Alley in Solvigant on Xys.

- *Beatrice Marrion* – Daughter of Lord Daniel Faide and half-sister to Adi Crestone. Her mother was a wayfaring Passerine. Beatrice is married to Lord Hubert Marrion and survived the crucible which forged her into a prophet.

- *Becca Henge* – A junior inspector in the city watch, her father is the minor Xyssian politician Victor Henge.

- *Chris Lynton, Commander* - Leader of the Solvigant city watch.

- *Deborah Vake* – A wayfaring Passerine and a doctor. Married to Roald Vake.

- *Devlin Seneschal, Talon* – One of four Talons who lead a notorious criminal enterprise in Solvigant. Devlin is a blue Seraph and an accomplished engineer. He has a history with Palestrina.

- *Duncan Harrow* – A Water Knife mercenary and one of Rehka's lieutenants.

- *Eliot Gambol, Governor* – As Imperial Governor of Xys, he answers directly to the chancellors and the emperor.

- *Hayden Farris* – Clunker and sailor on *Cerul's Horn*, who befriends Ion.

- *Hubert Marrion* – Youngest son of House Marrion and brother to Xander. Hubert raped Adi and impregnated her when she was fourteen. He is now married to her half-sister Beatrice and has been appointed Sabaian Ambassador to Xys.

- *Iris Korriga* – A prostitute from Highgaard working at Stella's Echo in Solvigant.

- *Joe Damgaard* – Broc's former partner. Murdered by White Rabbit thugs.

- *Leyala Fedhani, Alhambra* – One of four Talons who lead a notorious criminal enterprise in Solvigant known as the Order of the Talon.

- *Limon Heilig* – Archdeacon of the Temple of the Nine in Solvigant

- *Melanie Krimpet* – Xander's chief secretary and eldest daughter of Viscount Toller Krimpet.

- *Melinda the Ancient* – A fixture at Stella's Echo, she is an old, blind scholar.

- *Oto the Anvil* – Devlin Seneschal's right hand man and confidant.

- *Palestrina, Lady of Spiders* – One of three Blood Queen generals, she is a gray Seraph with a checkered past that includes a liaison with Devlin Seneschal.

- *Peter Wright* – A Grym sailor and Adi's first mate.

- *Petry Dogollon, Lord of Pain* – One of three Blood Queen generals, he is an albino Ankhim and a clunker.

- *Rehka Drake* – Daughter of Balthasar Drake and former lover to Adi Crestone. Rehka is a polychrome dragon unable to reconcile her human and dragon form and a Water Knife mercenary.

- *Rictor Grange* – A member of the White Rabbit gang, and a lieutenant to Stuart Royal. He is one of four thugs who jump Adi and steal Apyreon.

- *Roald Vake* – A wayfaring Passerine and a doctor. Married to Deborah Vake.

- *Sasha Riven, The Blood Queen* – Leader of the largest criminal enterprise in Solvigant.

- *Solomon Broc, Senior Inspector* – A Faelani badger, Broc is a senior inspector in the Solvigant city watch. His former partner is killed by gang violence and vows to catch those responsible.

- *Stella Volpes* – A Faelani fox, she runs the brothel Stella's Echo where Adi used to work and that she currently uses as her headquarters in Solvigant.

- *Stuart Royal* – A Faelani rabbit, he leads the White Rabbits and is a powerful astral mage.

- *Tabitha Gambol* – Theo's cousin and wife to Lord Gambol. Tabi contracted Feverfire sickness on Xys and is confined to a wheeled chair. Her maiden name is Loire.

- *Tabrin Wik* – A Grym clunker, antiquities dealer, and proprietor of the Iron Dirigible.

- *Verdun Veikau* – A forest Ankhim and brewer, he keeps the bar at Stella's Echo stocked and is Stella's lover.

- *Victor Henge* – Becca's father and a minor politician in the Xyssian congress.

- *Vista Sommers* – A mountain Ankhim, sailor, and engineer who joins Adi's crew after Torrance is killed.

- *Vivian Cosse* – A working girl at Stella's Echo.

- *Wim Mance* – The astral mage posted on *Cerul's Horn*.

- *Xander Marrion* – Oldest son of House Marrion in Viridia on Saba, he was betrothed to Adi before she ran away. He is now a respected member of the Xyssian congress, though he has been disinherited by his father for disobedience.

- *Xevon Topstay* – Chancellor of the Treasury and Blood Queen loyalist

## The People of Tyre

- *Aretha Castleton* – Betrothed to Joshua Vanguard, third son of High Chancellor Simon Vanguard.

- *Hannah Valefyre* – Youngest daughter of House Valefyre, member of the Knights of Acadia, and betrothed to Theo Vanguard.

- *Justus Solaric Callire, IV, Emperor* – Emperor of the Solan Empire comprising parts of 7 of the 10 moons.

- *Lucas Crestone* – Adi's fifteen-year-old son, currently enrolled in the Thail Academy of Engineering.

- *Lucius Torrance, Captain* – Mercenary ship captain on the Blood Queen's payroll.

- *Isaiah Vanguard, First Tier Void Mage* – Fourth son of Simon Vanguard and older brother to Theo, he is proficient in void magic.

- *Simon Vanguard, High Chancellor* – Father of Theo and Isaiah, he is High Chancellor to Emperor Justus Callire. Simon has five sons: Paul, Dante, Joshua, Isaiah, and Theodore.

## Legends of the World System

- *The Sojourners* – Arthur Phaeton, Kade Vanguard, Penelope Laird, and Selene Faide were ancient travelers from another World System. They are credited with creating the gates between moons, and introducing aetherial magic.

- *Maxon Laird* – The son of Sojourner's Arthur and Penelope, he was a legendary adventurer who fell in love with Selene. Their union birthed the Faide bloodline.

- *Marya Ghent* – Daughter of Celeste Phaeton, a descendant of the Kratoi. An anthropologist and explorer. Her sister, Phaedra founded House Valefyre.

### Solo and her Children

- *Corendar* – Father of the Gods and Solo's former lover. He was the God of Chaos until Kade overthrew him and confined him to dark Basalt.

- *Darach* – Youngest daughter of Solo, she is the Goddess of Nature and resides on the moon Saba.

- *Djinnar* – Twin brother to Pallantier, he is the God of Destruction and resides on the moon Maxon.

- *Kade* – A Sojourner who overthrew Corendar during the fall of Acadia and became the God of Chaos. He resides on the moon Behl.

- *Lillian* – Goddess of astral magic, she resides on the moon Aleph.

- *Mance* – God of astral magic, he resides on the moon Karis

- *Pallantier* – Twin brother to Djinnar, he is an androgyne and the God of Creation. He resides on the moon Xys.

- *Phoebe* – Eldest daughter of Solo, the Goddess of Light resides on the moon Gaash.

- *Solo* – Mother of the gods and Corendar's former lover. The ringed gas giant around which the moons orbit is her embodiment.

- *Strolen* – The God of Order resides on the moon Highgaard

- *Yeom* – The God of Civilization resides on the moon Tyre.

# APPENDIX 2

## CHILDREN OF SOLO

Solo and Corendar, the mother and father of the gods respectively, gave a moon to each of their children. The moons and their gods are listed below radiating outward from Solo, the ringed gas giant and embodiment of the Mother.

Xys:

- Capital: Solvigant, the City Peripatetic

- Governor: Eliot Gambol

- Topography: Desert, Scrub

- God: Pallantier, God of Creation

Highgaard

- Capital: Oringrad

- Governor: Luthor Torsson

- Topography: Mountainous

- God: Strolen, God of Order

Aleph:

- Capital: Belhaven

- Ruler: Forest Council. Aleph does not fall under Imperial rule, but is ruled by a council of Faelani elders representing each of the major and minor houses.

- Topography: Dense Forest, Taiga

- God: Lillian, Goddess of Astral Magic

Tyre:
- Capital: Thail

- Governor: Derrick Thornwood. Though the emperor resides in Thail, Lord Thornwood is responsible for overseeing activity on the moon Tyre, while the emperor oversees the entirety of his holdings.

- Topography: Woodland, Mountainous

- God: Yeom, God of Civilization

Saba
- Capital: Azurielle

- Governor: Sybil Faide

- Topography: Oceanic, Verdant Islands

- God: Darak, Goddess of Nature

Maxon/Seniphet – The Maxon half is ruled by the Empire, the Seniphet half by the Eldarians
- Capital: Somerset/Yazan

- Rulers: Governor Oswald Blumenthal/Prince Amir qat-Eldar

- Topography: Plains, Forests, Seas, Active Tectonics

- God: Djinnar, God of Destruction

Karis
- Capital: Caelia

- Governor: Anthar Preeves

- Topography: Wild landscapes, the largest and least populated of the moons

- God: Mance, God of Astral Magic

Flynt

- Capital: Fyrehaven

- Ruler: Airene, elected from Draconian Parliament to serve a six-year term.

- Notable Topography: Volcanic

- God: Zalivex the winged lizard of the void, not one of Solo's Children

Gaash

- Capital:

- Ruler: King Cliven Aarondell. Does not fall under Imperial Rule.

- Topography: Steppe

- God: Phoebe, Goddess of Light

Behl

- Capital: Kahvit

- Governor: Dane Rhystar

- Topography: Rocky, inhospitable

- God: Kade, God of Chaos

# GRATITUDE

It took me too long to develop the confidence to dive off the deep end and commit myself to writing fantasy, science fiction, and steampunk. I owe thanks to many people for helping me build that confidence and for shaping this work. Good literature requires an incredible team to produce, and I am fortunate to have many people to thank. Thank you to my incredible wife, LeAnna, for making this crazy world a better place and for allaying so many of my doubts. Thank you to my mother for instilling in me a love of all things literary. Thank you to my father, who instilled in me an entrepreneurial spirit. Thank you Anne Larsen at Learn to Fix Your Fiction for being a mentor, editor, coach, and friend. Thank you to Dan Manzanares for introducing me to Superstars Writing Seminars. Our monthly beers help keep me sane. Thank you to Mia Kleve at Mrk'd Up Editing. Your insight and dedication to your craft have gone a long way to improving this work. Thank you to my beta readers Aaron, Chris, Clara, Clay, Emily, and Martha. Thank you to my incredible writing group: Anastasia, Garrett, Julie, Michael, Reina, and Shelley. Six years strong we've been writing together! It is wonderful to see everyone's work coming to fruition. Thank you to my D&D group Aaron, Chris, Colleen, Craig, Garrett, LeAnna, and Mackenzie. Your shenanigans always spark my creativity, and I am grateful to call you all friends. Thank you to my friend, neighbor, and former boss Jeff. Thank you for supporting and encouraging me as I made the transition from one art medium to another. Thank you to my friend and former business partner, Ben. Your tireless dedication inspired me to always pursue my dreams and helped me develop the confidence necessary to do so. Thank you to Justin Scott. Your artwork made this book come alive. Thank you to the many incredible instructors at Lighthouse Writers Workshop in Denver including Alex, Courtney, Doug, Richard, and Sarah. Your dedication to and enthusiasm for your craft has inspired countless writers. Thank you, dear reader, for taking time from your epic and fascinating lives to read this book. It is you who bring this book to life. Without you, I would be shouting alone into the void. Hail Solo!

# ABOUT THE AUTHOR

Andrew Moore grew up in Indiana and now lives in the suburbs of Denver, Colorado with his wife, two dogs, and two cats. He is an avid writer of stories and rider of bikes. Andrew's love of fantasy blossomed early when he fell in love with such books as Redwall by Brian Jacques and the Dragonlance Chronicles by Margaret Weiss and Tracy Hickman. Dungeons and Dragons, with its polyhedral dice and rich worldbuilding, ignited the boosters that would rocket him towards writing.

Andrew graduated with honors from Indiana University with undergraduate degrees in Philosophy and Classical Literature. He completed a post-baccalaureate at the University of Pennsylvania before obtaining his Master's in Classical Archaeology from CU Boulder. He worked as an archaeologist and scholar in Germany, Greece, Turkey, and Jordan. In Colorado, Andrew taught philosophy, history, and literature at Rocky Mountain College of Art and Design, before leaving formal academia to pursue a passion in brewing beer. His brewery brainchild, The Intrepid Sojourner Beer Project, closed during the Covid-19 pandemic, but not before winning many awards both domestic and international.

Now, with the incredible support of his wife and family, Andrew writes full time. When he isn't inventing stories in front of the computer screen, you can find him on his bicycle training for ultra endurance bikepacking races. He'll be racing in the Hellenic Mountain Race in May 2025 and has qualified for the 2026 Iditarod Trail Invitational. You can follow his writing and adventures at www.adhmoore.com. Sign up for the newsletter to stay abreast of new material, events, and special releases.

www.adhmoore.com

facebook.com/steamandstars/

@adhmoore

If you enjoyed *Children of Solo*, try the fantasy of Jacqueline Fellows:

The tale of a primitive civilization forced to confront its own imminent demise, searching for a savior in a harsh world.

### The Devils' Crucible:

Book One of

*The Days of the Bluestar*

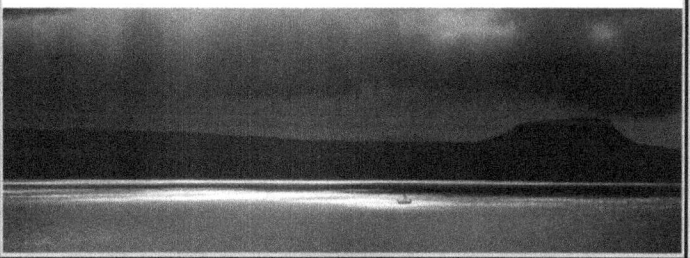

"Fellows has created an exciting low-magic fantasy with thrilling action and epic, large-scale battles. Few fantasy books can capture city sieges as well as this author."

- Mark Heisey,
*US Review of Books*

### The Sherangivan

As his country battles for survival, a young man's inner demons take on a life of their own.

Ordering information and opening pages at mathiaskeyfantasy.com

Mathias Key
Fantasy

www.ingramcontent.com/pod-product-compliance
Lightning Source LLC
Chambersburg PA
CBHW060810120726
47909CB00006B/1852